PENGUIN BOOKS

THREAT VECTOR

Thirty years ago Tom Clancy was a Maryland insurance broker with a passion for naval history. Years before, he had been an English major at Baltimore's Loyola College and had always dreamed of writing a novel. His first effort, *The Hunt for Red October*, sold briskly as a result of rave reviews, then catapulted on to the *New York Times* bestseller list after President Reagan pronounced it 'the perfect yarn'. From that day forward, Clancy established himself as an undisputed master at blending exceptional realism and authenticity, intricate plotting, and razor-sharp suspense. He passed away in October 2013.

D0724870

Threat Vector

TOM CLANCY
with MARK GREANEY

PENGUIN BOOKS

PENGUIN BOOKS

Published by the Penguin Group
Penguin Books Ltd, 80 Strand, London WC2R ORL, England
Penguin Group (USA) Inc., 375 Hudson Street, New York, New York 10014, USA
Penguin Group (Canada), 90 Eglinton Avenue East, Suite 700, Toronto, Ontario, Canada M4P 2Y3
(a division of Pearson Penguin Canada Inc.)
Penguin Ireland, 25 St Stephen's Green, Dublin 2, Ireland (a division of Penguin Books Ltd)
Penguin Group (Australia), 707 Collins Street, Melbourne, Victoria 3008, Australia
(a division of Pearson Australia Group Pty Ltd)
Penguin Books India Pvt Ltd, 11 Community Centre, Panchsheel Park, New Delhi – 110 017, India
Penguin Group (NZ), 67 Apollo Drive, Rosedale, Auckland 0632, New Zealand
(a division of Pearson New Zealand Ltd)
Penguin Books (South Africa) (Pty) Ltd, Block D, Rosebank Office Park,
181 Jan Smuts Avenue, Parktown North, Gauteng, Johannesburg 2193, South Africa

Penguin Books Ltd, Registered Offices: 80 Strand, London WC2R ORL, England

www.penguin.com

First published in the United States of America by G. P. Putnam's Sons 2012
First published in Great Britain by Michael Joseph, 2012
First published in Penguin Books 2013

002

Typeset by Palimpsest Book Production Limited, Falkirk, Stirlingshire
Printed in Great Britain by Clays Ltd, St Ives plc

PAPERBACK ISBN: 978–0–718–19812–1
OPEN MARKET ISBN: 978–0–718–19813–8

www.greenpenguin.co.uk

MIX
Paper from
responsible sources
FSC® C018179

Penguin Books is committed to a sustainable
future for our business, our readers and our planet.
This book is made from Forest Stewardship
Council™ certified paper.

Principal Characters

United States Government

- John Patrick 'Jack' Ryan: President of the United States
- Arnold van Damm: the President's chief of staff
- Robert Burgess: secretary of defense
- Scott Adler: secretary of state
- Mary Patricia Foley: director of national intelligence
- Colleen Hurst: national security adviser
- Jay Canfield: director of the Central Intelligence Agency
- Kenneth Li: U.S. ambassador to China
- Adam Yao: operations officer, National Clandestine Service, Central Intelligence Agency
- Melanie Kraft: reports officer, Central Intelligence Agency (on loan to Office of the Director of National Intelligence)
- Darren Lipton: senior special agent, Federal Bureau of Investigation, National Security Branch, Counterintelligence Division

United States Military

- Admiral Mark Jorgensen: United States Navy, commander Pacific Fleet
- General Henry Bloom: United States Air Force, commander United States Cyber Command

- Captain Brandon 'Trash' White: United States Marine Corps, F/A-18C Hornet pilot
- Major Scott 'Cheese' Stilton: United States Marine Corps, F/A-18C Hornet pilot
- Chief Petty Officer Michael Meyer: United States Navy, SEAL Team Six element leader

The Campus

- Gerry Hendley: director of Hendley Associates/ director of The Campus
- Sam Granger: director of operations
- John Clark: operations officer
- Domingo 'Ding' Chavez: operations officer
- Dominic Caruso: operations officer
- Sam Driscoll: operations officer
- Jack Ryan, Jr: operations officer/analyst
- Rick Bell: director of analysis
- Tony Wills: analyst
- Gavin Biery: director of information technology

The Chinese

- Wei Zhen Lin: president of the People's Republic of China/general secretary of the Communist Party of China
- Su Ke Qiang: chairman of the Central Military Commission of China
- Wu Fan Jun: intelligence officer, Ministry of State Security, Shanghai

- Dr Tong Kwok Kwan, aka 'Center': computer network operations director of Ghost Ship
- Zha Shu Hai, aka 'FastByte22': Interpol-wanted cybercriminal
- Crane: Leader of 'Vancouver Cell'
- Han: factory owner and high-tech counterfeiter

Additional Characters

- Valentin Olegovich Kovalenko: Ex-SVR (Russian foreign intelligence), assistant *rezident* of London Station
- Todd Wicks: territory sales manager of Advantage Technology Solutions
- Charlie 'DarkGod' Levy: amateur hacker
- Dr Cathy Ryan: wife of President Jack Ryan
- Sandy Clark: wife of John Clark
- Dr Patsy Clark: wife of Domingo Chavez/daughter of John Clark
- Emad Kartal: ex-Libyan intelligence officer, communications specialist

Prologue

These were grim days for former operatives of the Jama-hiriya Security Organization, the dreaded national intelligence service of Libya under Moammar Gaddafi. Those members of the JSO who had managed to survive the revolution in their home nation were now scattered and in hiding, fearing the day when their cruel and brutal past would catch up with them in a cruel and brutal way.

After the fall of Tripoli to Western-backed rebels the year before, some JSO operatives had remained in Libya, hoping that by changing their identities they would save themselves from reprisal. This rarely worked, as others knew their secrets and were all too happy to finger them to revolutionist head-hunters, either to settle old scores or to win new favors. Gaddafi's spies in Libya were rounded up wherever they hid, tortured, and then killed; in other words, they were treated no worse than they deserved, though the West had held out some naive hope that fair trials for past crimes would be the order of the day when the rebels took power.

But no, mercy did not follow Gaddafi's death any more than mercy had preceded it.

Meet the new boss, same as the old.

The smarter JSO spies made it out of Libya before capture, and some went to other African nations. Tunisia was close, but it was hostile to former spies of the Mad Dog of the Middle East, a fitting nickname bestowed on Gaddafi by Ronald Reagan. Chad was desolate and similarly unwelcoming to the Libyans. A few made it into Algeria and a few more into Niger, and in both places they found some measure of security, but as guests of these dirt-poor regimes their future prospects were severely limited.

One group of former Jamahiriya Security Organization operators, however, fared better than the rest of their hunted colleagues because they possessed a marked advantage. For years this small cell of spies had been working not just in the interests of the Gaddafi regime, but also for their own personal enrichment. They accepted after-hours work for hire, both in Libya and abroad, doing odd jobs for organized criminal elements, for Al-Qaeda, for the Umayyad Revolutionary Council, even for the intelligence organizations of some other Middle Eastern nations.

In this work the group had suffered losses even before the fall of their government. Several had been killed by American operators a year before Gaddafi's death, and during the revolution several more died at the port of Tobruk in a NATO airstrike. Two others were captured boarding a flight out of Misrata and burned with electric shocks before being hung naked from meat hooks at the market. But the cell's seven surviving members did make it out of the country, and even though their years of extracurricular assignments had failed to make them rich men, when it came time to jump like rats from the ship called the Great Socialist People's Libyan Arab Jamahiriya, their international connections helped keep them safe from the rebels back home.

The seven made their way to Istanbul, Turkey, where they were sponsored by elements in the local underworld who owed them a favor. Soon two of their number left the cell and went into honest work. One became a jewelry store security guard and the other found a job in a local plastics factory.

The other five remained in the spy game, and they farmed

themselves out as a highly experienced unit of intelligence professionals. They also attempted to focus on both their personal security and their operational security, knowing that only by maintaining strict PERSEC *and* OPSEC could they be safe from the threat of reprisals from agents of the new government of Libya, just across the Mediterranean Sea.

This attention to security kept them safe for a few months, but complacency returned, one of their number grew overconfident, and he did not do as he was told. In a breach of PERSEC, he contacted an old friend in Tripoli, and the friend, a man who had switched allegiance to the new government to keep his head attached to his neck, reported the contact to Libya's new and fledgling intelligence service.

Though Tripoli's new crop of spies was excited by the news that a collection of their old enemies had been tracked to Istanbul, they were in no position to act on the intel. Infiltrating a team into a foreign capital with a kill/capture objective was no move for a rookie agency just finding its way around its new building.

But another entity intercepted the information, and it had both the means and the motive to act.

Soon the Istanbul cell members of former JSO operatives became targets. Not targets of the Libyan revolutionaries looking to eradicate the last vestiges of the Gaddafi regime. Not targets of a Western intelligence agency looking to settle scores with members of a former enemy spy shop.

No, the five Libyans became targets of an off-the-books assassination team from the United States of America.

More than a year earlier, a member of the JSO cell had shot and killed a man named Brian Caruso, the brother of one of the Americans, and a friend of the rest. The shooter had died soon after, but his cell lived on, surviving the revolution, and now they flourished in their new lives in Turkey.

But Brian's brother and Brian's friends did not forget.

Nor did they forgive.

I

The five Americans had been lying low in the decrepit hotel room for hours, waiting for nightfall.

Sheets of warm rain rapped on the window, generating the majority of the sound in the dim room, as there was little talk among the men. This room had served as the base of operations for the team, though four of the five had stayed at other hotels throughout the city during their weeklong stay. Now that preparations were complete, those four had checked out of their quarters and consolidated their gear and themselves here with the fifth man in their group.

Though they all were still as stones now, they had been a blur of activity over the past week. They had surveilled targets; developed op plans; established covers; memorized their primary, secondary, and tertiary exfiltration routes; and coordinated the logistics of the mission to come.

But preparations were now complete, and there was nothing left to do but sit and wait for darkness.

A rumble of thunder rolled in from the south, a lightning strike far out in the Sea of Marmara illuminated the five statues in the room for an instant, and then the darkness covered them once again.

This hotel was situated in the Sultanahmet district of Istanbul, and it was chosen as the team safe house due to the courtyard parking for their vehicles and the fact that it was more or less equidistant to where the operations would be carried out later in the evening. The hotel was not, however, chosen for the vinyl bedspreads or the grimy hallways or the surly staff or the stench of pot smoke that wafted up from the youth hostel on the ground floor.

But the Americans did not complain about their accommodations; they thought only of their tasks ahead.

At seven p.m. the leader of the cell looked down to the chronograph on his wrist; it was fastened over bandaging that covered his entire hand and a portion of his forearm. As he stood up from a wooden chair, he said, 'We'll head out one at a time. Five-minute separation.'

The others – two seated on a bed speckled with rat shit, one leaning against the wall by the door, and one more standing by the window – all nodded.

The leader continued. 'I sure as hell do *not* like splitting up the op like this. This is not how we do business. But frankly . . . circumstances dictate our actions. If we don't do these mutts damn near simultaneously, word will get out and the roaches will scatter in the light.'

The others listened without responding. They'd been over this a dozen times in the past week. They knew the difficulties, they knew the risks, and they knew their leader's reservations.

Their leader's name was John Clark; he'd been doing this sort of thing since before the youngest of the men on his team had been born, so his words carried weight.

'I've said it before, gentlemen, but indulge me one more time. No points for style on this one.' He paused. 'In and out. Quick and cold. No hesitation. No mercy.'

They all nodded again.

Clark finished his speech and then slipped a blue raincoat over his three-piece pinstripe suit. He stepped over to the window and reached out with his left hand, shaking the offered left hand of Domingo 'Ding' Chavez. Ding was dressed in a three-quarter-length leather coat and a heavy watch cap. A canvas bag lay at his feet.

6

Ding saw perspiration on his mentor's face. He knew Clark had to be in pain, but he'd not complained all week. Chavez asked, 'You up for this, John?'

Clark nodded. 'I'll get it done.'

John then reached a hand out to Sam Driscoll, who stood up from the bed. Sam was dressed in a denim jacket and jeans, but he also wore knee and elbow pads and, on the bed next to where he'd been sitting, a black motorcycle crash helmet lay on its side.

'Mr C.,' Sam said.

John asked, 'You ready for the fly swat?'

''Bout as ready as I'm gonna get.'

'It's all about the angle. Get the angle right, commit to it, and let momentum do the rest.'

Sam just nodded as another flash of lightning lit up the room.

John stepped over to Jack Ryan, Jr. Jack was in head-to-toe black; cotton pants, a pullover knit sweater, and a knit mask rolled up above his face so it looked like a watch cap, similar to the one worn by Chavez. He also wore soft-soled shoes that looked like black slippers. With a handshake Clark said, 'Good luck, Junior,' to the twenty-seven-year-old Ryan.

'I'll be fine.'

'I know you will.'

Last, John walked around the bed, and here he shook the left hand of Dominic Caruso. Dom wore a red-and-gold soccer jersey and a bright gold scarf, upon which the word *Galatasaray* was emblazoned in red. His attire stood out from the muted colors around the room, but his countenance was much less bright than his dress.

With a severe expression Dom said, 'Brian was *my* brother, John. I don't need –'

Clark interrupted. 'Have we talked about this?'

'Yes, but –'

'Son, whatever our five targets are up to here in Turkey, this op has gone way past simple revenge for your brother. Still . . . we are all Brian's brothers today. We are all in this together.'

'Right. But –'

'I want your mind on your job. Nothing else. Every one of us knows what we are doing. These JSO assholes have committed other crimes against their own people and against the U.S. And it's clear from their present movements that they are up to no good. Nobody else is going to stop them. It's up to us to shut them down.'

Dom nodded distractedly.

Clark added, 'These fuckers have it coming.'

'I know.'

'Are you good to go?'

Now the young man's bearded chin rose. He looked into Clark's eyes. With a resolute tone he said, 'Absolutely.'

And with that John Clark picked up his briefcase with his non-bandaged hand and left the room without another word.

The four remaining Americans checked their watches and then stood or sat quietly, listening to the rain pelt the window.

The man the Americans had dubbed Target One sat at his regular bistro table at the sidewalk café in front of the May Hotel on Mimar Hayrettin. Most nights, when the weather was nice, he stopped here for a shot or two of raki in chilled sparkling water. The weather this evening was awful, but the long canopy hung over the sidewalk tables by the staff of the May kept him dry.

There were just a few other patrons seated under the canopy, couples smoking and drinking together before either heading back up to their rooms in the hotel or out to other Old Town nightlife destinations.

Target One had grown to live for his evening glass of raki. The anise-flavored milky white drink made from grape pomace was alcoholic, and forbidden in his home country of Libya and other nations where the more liberal Hanafi school of Islam is not de rigueur, but the ex-JSO spy had been forced into the occasional use of alcohol for tradecraft purposes during his service abroad. Now that he had become a wanted man, he'd grown to rely on the slight buzz from the liquor to help relax him and aid in his sleep, though even the liberal Hanafi school does not permit intoxication.

There were just a few vehicles rolling by on the cobblestone street ten feet from his table. This road was hardly a busy thoroughfare, even on weekend nights with clear skies. There was some foot traffic on the pavement around him, however, and Target One was enjoying himself watching the attractive women of Istanbul pass by under their umbrellas.

The occasional view of the legs of a sexy woman, coupled with the warming buzz of the raki, made this rainy night especially pleasant for the man seated at the sidewalk café.

At nine p.m., Sam Driscoll drove his silver Fiat Linea calmly and carefully through the evening traffic that flowed into Istanbul's Old Town from the outlying neighborhoods.

The city lights sparkled on his wet windshield. Traffic had thinned out more and more the deeper he got into Old Town, and as the American stopped for a red light, he glanced quickly at a GPS locator Velcroed onto the dashboard. Once he reconfirmed the distance to his target, he reached over to the passenger seat and wrapped his hand around his motor-cycle helmet. As the light changed he did a long neck roll to relax himself, slipped the crash helmet over his head, and then lowered the visor over his eyes.

He winced at what was to come, he could not help it. Even though his heart was pounding and nearly every synapse of his brain was firing in the focus of his operation, he still found the perspective to shake his head and talk to himself.

He'd done a lot of nasty things in his days as a soldier and an operator, but he had never done this.

'A goddamned fly swat.'

The Libyan took his first sip from his second glass of raki of the evening as a silver Fiat headed quickly up the street, some eighty yards to his north. Target One was looking in the opposite direction; a beautiful Turkish girl with a red umbrella in her left hand and a leash to her miniature schnauzer in her right passed by on the sidewalk, and the seated man had a great view of her long and toned legs.

But a shout to his left caused him to shift his attention toward the intersection in front of him, and there he saw the silver Fiat, a blur, racing through the light. He watched the four-door shoot up the quiet street.

He expected it to shoot on by.

He brought his drink to his lips; he was not worried.

Not until the car veered hard to the left with a squeal of its wet tires, and the Libyan found himself staring down the approaching front grille of the car.

With the little glass still in his hand, Target One stood quickly, but his feet were fixed to the pavement. He had nowhere to run.

The woman walking the miniature schnauzer screamed.

The silver Fiat slammed into the man at the bistro table, striking him square, running him down, and sending him hard into the brick wall of the May Hotel, pinning him there, half under and half in front of the vehicle. The Libyan's rib cage shattered and splintered, sending shards of bone through his vital organs like shot from a riot gun.

Witnesses at the café and on the street around it reported later that the man in the black crash helmet behind the wheel took a calm moment to put his vehicle into reverse, even checking the rearview mirror, before backing into the intersection and driving off toward the north. His actions seemed no different than those of a man on a Sunday drive who had just pulled into a parking space at the market, realized he had left his wallet at home, and then backed out to return for it.

One kilometer southeast of the incident, Driscoll parked the four-door Fiat in a private drive. The little car's hood was bent and its front grille and bumper were torn and dented, but Sam positioned the car nose in so the damage would not be evident from the street. He stepped out of the vehicle and walked to a scooter locked on a chain nearby. Before unlocking it with a key and motoring away into the rainy night, he transmitted a brief message into the radio feature of his encrypted mobile phone.

'Target One is down. Sam is clear.'

The Çirağan Palace is an opulent mansion that was built in the 1860s for Abdülaziz I, a sultan who reigned in the midst of the Ottoman Empire's long decline. After his lavish spending put his nation into debt he was deposed and 'encouraged' to commit suicide with, of all things, a pair of scissors.

Nowhere was the extravagance that led to the downfall of Abdülaziz more on display than the Çirağan. It was now a five-star hotel, its manicured lawns and crystal clear pools running from the façade of the palace buildings to the western shoreline of the Bosphorus Strait, the water line that separates Europe from Asia.

The Tuğra restaurant on the first floor of the Çirağan Palace has magnificent high-ceilinged rooms with windows affording wide views of the hotel grounds and the strait beyond, and even during the rain shower that persisted this Tuesday evening, the bright lights of passing yachts could be seen and enjoyed by the diners at their tables.

Along with the many wealthy tourists enjoying their exquisite meals, there were also quite a few businessmen and women from all over the world, alone and in groups of varying number, dining in the restaurant.

John Clark fit in nicely, dining by himself at a table adorned with crystal, fine bone china, and gold-plated flatware. He'd been seated at a small table near the entrance, far away from the grand windows overlooking the water. His waiter was a handsome middle-aged man in a black tuxedo, and he brought Clark a sumptuous meal, and while the American could not say he did not enjoy the food, his focus was on a table far across the room.

Moments after John bit into his first tender bite of monk-fish, the maître d' seated three Arab men in expensive suits at the table by the window, and a waiter took their order for cocktails.

Two of the men were guests of the hotel; Clark knew this from his team's surveillance and the hard work of the intel-ligence analysts employed by his organization. They were Omani bankers, and they were of no interest to him. But the third man, a fifty-year-old Libyan with gray hair and a trim beard, *was* John's concern.

He was Target Two.

As Clark ate with his fork in his left hand, a maneuver the right-handed American had been forced to learn since his injury, he used a tiny flesh-colored hearing amplifier in his right ear to focus on the men's voices. It was difficult to sep-arate them from others speaking in the restaurant, but after a few minutes he was able to pick out the words of Target Two.

Clark returned his attention to his monkfish and waited.

A few minutes later a waiter took the dinner order at the table of Arabs by the window. Clark heard his target order the Kulbasti veal, and the other men ordered different dishes.

This was good. Had the Omanis ordered the same as their Libyan dining companion, then Clark would have switched to plan B. Plan B would go down out in the street, and in the street John had a hell of a lot more unknowns to deal with than he did here in the Tuğra.

But each man had ordered a unique entrée, and Clark silently thanked his luck, then he popped the earpiece out of his ear and slipped it back into his pocket.

John sipped an after-dinner port while his target's table was served cold soups and white wine. The American avoided looking down at his watch; he was on a precise timetable but

13

knew better than to give any outward appearance of anxiety or fretfulness. Instead he enjoyed his port and counted off the minutes in his head.

Shortly before the soup bowls were cleared from the table of Arab men, Clark asked his waiter to point the way to the men's room, and he was directed past the kitchen. In the bathroom John slipped into a stall and sat down, and quickly began unwrapping the bandaging around his forearm.

The bandage was not a ruse; his wounded hand was real and it hurt like hell. A few months earlier it had been smashed with a hammer, and he'd undergone three surgeries to repair bones and joints in the intervening months, but he'd not enjoyed a decent night's sleep since the day of his injury.

But even though the bandaging was real, it did serve an additional purpose. Under the heavy wrapping, between the two splints that held his index and middle fingers in fixed positions, he had secreted a small injector. It was positioned so that with his thumb he could push the narrow tip out of the wrapping, pop off the cap that covered the needle, and plunge it into his target.

But that was plan B, the less desirable action, and John had decided to go for plan A.

He removed the injector and placed it in his pocket, and then slowly and gingerly rewrapped his hand.

The injector contained two hundred milligrams of a special form of succinylcholine poison. The dose in the plastic device could be either injected into a target or ingested. Both methods of transfer to the victim would be lethal, though injection was, not surprisingly, the far more efficient delivery method for the poison.

John left the bathroom with the device hidden in his left hand.

Clark's timing was less than perfect. As he came out of the

bathroom and passed by the entrance to the kitchen, he had hoped to see his target's waiter exiting with the entrées, but the hallway was empty. John pretended to regard the paintings on the walls, and then the ornate gilded molding in the hallway. Finally the waiter appeared with a tray full of covered dishes on his shoulder. John stood between the man and the dining room, and he demanded the server put down the tray on a tray jack right there and fetch him the chef. The waiter, hiding his frustration behind a veneer of politeness, did as he was told.

As the man disappeared behind the swinging door, Clark quickly checked the covered dishes, found the veal, and then dispensed the poison from the injector directly into the center of the thin piece of meat. A few clear bubbles appeared in the sauce, but the vast majority of the poison was now infused in the veal itself.

When the head chef appeared a moment later, Clark had already re-covered the dish and pocketed the injector. He thanked the man effusively for a splendid dinner, and the waiter delivered the food quickly to his table so that the dishes were not refused by the guests for being served cold.

Minutes later John paid his bill, and he stood to leave his table. His waiter brought him his raincoat, and as he put it on he glanced over quickly at Target Two. The Libyan was just finishing the last bite of the Kulbasti veal; he was deep in conversation with his Omani companions.

As Clark headed out into the lobby of the hotel, behind him Target Two loosened his tie.

Twenty minutes later the sixty-five-year-old American stood under his umbrella in Büyükşehir Belediyesi Park, just across the street from the hotel and restaurant, and he watched as an ambulance raced to the entrance.

The poison was deadly; there was no antidote that any

ambulance on earth would carry in its onboard narcotic box.

Either Target Two was already dead or he would be so shortly. It would look to doctors as if the man had suffered a cardiac arrest, so there would likely be no investigation into the other patrons of the Tuğra who just happened to be dining around the time of the unfortunate, but perfectly natural, event.

Clark turned away and headed toward Muvezzi Street, fifty yards to the west. There he caught a taxi, telling the driver to take him to the airport. He had no luggage, only his umbrella and a mobile phone. He pressed the push-to-talk button on his phone as the cab rolled off into the night. 'Two is down. I am clear,' he said, softly, before disconnecting the call and slipping the phone under his raincoat and into the breast pocket of his suit coat with his left hand.

Domingo Chavez took the calls from Driscoll and then Clark, and now he focused on his own portion of the operation. He sat alone on the old state-owned passenger ferry between Karaköy, on the European bank of the Bosphorus, and Üsküdar, on the Asian bank. On both sides of him in the cabin of the huge boat, red wooden benches were full of men and women traveling slowly but surely to their destinations, rocking along with the swells of the strait.

Ding's target was alone, just as his surveillance indicated he would be. The short forty-minute crossing meant Chavez would need to take his man here on the ferry, lest the target receive word that one of his colleagues had been killed and adopt defensive measures to protect himself.

Target Three was a thickly built thirty-five-year-old. He sat on the bench by the window reading a book for a while, but after fifteen minutes he went out on the deck to smoke.

After taking a few moments to make certain no one else in

the large passenger cabin paid any attention to the Libyan as he stepped outside, Chavez left his seat and headed out another door.

The rain was steady and the low cloud cover blocked off even the faintest light from the moon, and Chavez did his best to move in the long shadows cast from the lights along the narrow lower deck. He headed to a position on the railing some fifty feet aft of his target, and he stood there in the dim, looking out at the twinkling lights of the shoreline and the moving blackness as a catamaran crossed under the Galata Bridge in front of the lights.

Out of the corner of his eye he watched his target smoking near the rail. The upper deck shielded him from the rain. Two other men stood at the rails, but Ding had been following his man for days, and he knew the Libyan would linger out here for a while.

Chavez waited in the shadows, and finally the others went back inside.

Ding slowly began approaching the man from behind.

Target Three had gotten lazy in his PERSEC, but he could not have made it as long as he did as both an operative of his state security service and a freelance spy by being a fool. He was on guard. When Ding was forced to cross in front of a deck light to close in on his target, the man saw the moving shadow, and he flicked away his cigarette and spun around. His hand slid down into his coat pocket.

Chavez launched himself at his target. With three lightning-fast steps he arrived at the edge of the railing and shoved his left hand down to secure whatever weapon the big Libyan was reaching for. In Ding's right hand he swung a black leather sap down hard against the left temple of the man, and with a loud crack Target Three went out cold, slumping down between the railing and Chavez.

The American slipped the sap back into his pocket and then hefted the unconscious man by his head. He looked around quickly to make sure no one was around, and then with a short, brutal twist he snapped his target's neck. After a final glance up and down the lower deck to make sure he remained in the clear, Ding rolled the Libyan up onto the railing and let him tip over the side. The body disappeared into the night. Only the faintest splash could be heard above the sounds of the ocean and the rumbling engines of the ferry.

Chavez returned to a different seat on the red bench in the passenger cabin a few minutes later. Here he made a quick transmission on his mobile device.

'Three is down. Ding is clear.'

The new Türk Telecom Arena seats more than fifty-two thousand spectators and fills to capacity when local Istanbul soccer team Galatasaray takes the pitch. Though it was a rainy night, the huge crowd remained dry, as they were protected under a roof that was open only above the playing field itself.

The match tonight against crosstown rival Beşiktaş had the stands overflowing with locals, but one foreigner in attendance did not watch much of the play on the field. Dominic Caruso, who knew precious little about the game of soccer, instead focused his attention on Target Four, a thirty-one-year-old bearded Libyan who'd come to the match with a group of Turkish acquaintances. Dom had paid a man sitting alone just a few rows above his target to trade seats with him, so now the American had a good view of his target, as well as a quick outlet to the exit above.

For the first half of the match there was little for Caruso to do but cheer when those around him cheered, and stand when they stood, which was virtually all of the time. At half-time the seats all but emptied as fans headed for concession stands and restrooms, but Target Four and most of his mates remained in their seats, so Caruso did the same.

A goal by Galatasaray against the run of play livened the crowd just after halftime. Shortly after this, with thirty-five minutes remaining in the match, the Libyan looked down at his mobile phone, then turned and headed for the stairs.

Caruso shot up the stairs ahead of his target, and he rushed to the closest bathroom. He stood outside the exit and waited for his target.

Within thirty seconds Target Four entered the bathroom. Quickly Dominic pulled from his jacket a white paper sign that read *Kapalı*, or 'Closed,' and taped it onto the exit door of the restroom. He pulled an identical sign out and taped it to the entrance. He entered the bathroom and shut the door behind him.

He found Target Four at a bank of urinals, alongside two men. The other pair was together, and soon they washed up and headed back out the door. Dom had stepped up to a urinal four down from his target, and while he stood there he reached into the front of his pants under his jacket and retrieved his stiletto.

Target Four zipped up, stepped back from the urinal, and walked toward the sink. As he passed the man wearing the Galatasaray jersey and scarf, the man suddenly spun toward him. The Libyan felt the impact of something on his stomach, and then found himself being pushed back by the stranger, all the way into one of the stalls on the far side of the bathroom. He tried to reach for the knife that he kept in his pocket, but his attacker's force against him was so relentless he could only stumble back on his heels.

Both men fell into the stall and onto the toilet.

Only then did the young Libyan look down at where he had felt the punch to his gut. The hilt of a knife protruded from his stomach.

Panic and then weakness overtook him.

His attacker shoved him down onto the floor next to the toilet. He leaned forward, into the Libyan's ear. 'This is for my brother, Brian Caruso. Your people killed him in Libya, and tonight, every last one of you is going to pay with your lives.'

Target Four's eyes narrowed in confusion. He spoke English, so he understood what the man said, but he did not know anyone named Brian. He'd killed many men, some in Libya, but they were Libyans, Jews, rebels. Enemies of Colonel Gaddafi.

He'd never killed an American. He had no idea what this Galatasaray fan was talking about.

Target Four died, slumped on the floor by the toilet in the bathroom of the sports stadium, certain that this all must have been some terrible mistake.

Caruso pulled off his blood-covered soccer jersey, revealing a white T-shirt. This he ripped off as well, and under it was another jersey, this one for the rival team. The black and white colors of Beşiktaş would help him blend in with the crowd just as he had in the red and gold of Galatasaray.

He jammed the T-shirt and the Galatasaray jersey into the waistband of his pants, pulled a black cap out of his pocket, and put it on his head.

He stood over the dead man a moment more. In the blind fury of revenge he wanted to spit on the dead body, but he fought the urge, as he knew it would be foolish for him to leave his DNA at the scene. So instead he just turned away, walked out of the bathroom, pulling both *Kapalı* signs off the doors as he headed toward the exit of the stadium.

As he passed through the turnstiles at the exit, leaving the cover of the stadium and walking into the heavy rain, he pulled his mobile from the side pocket of his cargo pants.

'Target Four eliminated. Dom's clear. Easy money.'

3

Jack Ryan, Jr, had been tasked with eliminating the target with the fewest question marks surrounding him. A lone man sitting at his desk in his apartment, or so said all their surveillance.

It was supposed to be the easiest op of the night, and Jack understood this, just like he understood he was getting the mission for the simple fact that he was still the low man on the operational totem pole. He had worked high-risk clandestine ops all over the world, but still fewer than the four other operators in his unit.

Initially he was going to be sent on the op at the Çirağan Palace to go after Target Two. It was decided that dousing a piece of meat with poison would be the easiest hit of the night. But Clark ended up getting that op because a sixty-five-year-old man dining alone would not be a queer occurrence in a five-star restaurant, where a young Westerner, just a couple of years out of college, eating such a meal in such a place all by himself would pique the interest of the restaurant staff to the degree that someone might remember the lone diner after the fact in the unlikely event authorities came with questions when another patron dropped dead a few tables over.

So Jack Junior was tasked with taking down Target Five, a communications specialist for the ex-JSO cell, named Emad Kartal. Certainly not a walk in the park, but, the men of The Campus decided, Jack had it covered.

Kartal spent virtually every evening on his computer, and it was ultimately this habit that brought about the eventual compromise of the JSO cell. Six weeks earlier he'd sent a message to a friend in Libya, and this message had been picked up and decoded, and Ryan and his fellow analysts back in the States had subsequently intercepted the intelligence.

They'd further compromised both the man and his cell by hacking into his mobile phone's voice mail; from this, they'd listened to correspondence among the cell members that indicated they were working together.

At eleven p.m., Ryan found himself entering the apartment building of his target via a counterfeit keycard created by the technical gurus of his organization. The building was in the Taksim neighborhood and within sight of the five-hundred-year-old Cihangir Mosque. It was a slightly upscale property in an upscale neighborhood, but the flats themselves were tightly packed-together studio units, eight to a floor. Jack's objective was on the third floor, smack in the middle of the five-story building.

Ryan's orders for the hit had been succinct. Make entry on Target Five's flat, confirm the target visually, and then shoot him three times in the chest or head with subsonic rounds fired from his .22-caliber suppressed pistol.

Ryan climbed the wooden staircase in his soft-soled shoes. While doing so, he pulled his black cotton ski mask down over his face. He was the only man operating with a mask tonight, simply because he was the one member of the team not working in public, where a masked man would draw more attention.

He made his way to the third floor, and then entered the brightly lit hallway. His target was three doors down on the left, and as the young American passed the other units he heard people talking, the sounds of televisions and radios and phone conversations. The walls were thin, which was not good news, but at least the other residents of the floor were making some noise themselves. Jack hoped his silencer and his quieter-than-normal subsonic ammo would work as advertised.

At his target's door he heard the sounds of rap music coming from inside the flat. This *was* good news, as it would aid in masking Ryan's approach.

His target's door was locked, but Ryan had instructions on how to get in. Clark had been in the building four times in the past week during his target reconnaissance before he'd switched ops with the youngest member of the team, and Clark had managed to pick several of the locks of unoccupied flats. The locks were old and not terribly difficult, so he bought a similar model at a local hardware store, then spent an evening tutoring Jack on how to quickly and quietly defeat the device.

Clark's instruction proved effective. With only the faint sounds of the soft scratching of metal on metal, Jack picked the door lock in less than twenty seconds. He drew his pistol and stood back up, then opened the door.

In the studio flat he found what he expected. Across a small kitchen was a living area, and then, at the far wall, a desk facing away from the entrance. At the desk a man sat with his back to Ryan in front of a bank of three large flatscreen computer monitors as well as various peripherals, books, magazines, and other items within reach. Foam containers of half-eaten Chinese takeout sat in a plastic bag. Next to this, Ryan confirmed the presence of a weapon. Jack knew handguns, but he could not immediately identify the semiautomatic pistol just a foot from Emad Kartal's right hand.

Jack stepped into the kitchen and quietly pulled the door closed behind him.

The kitchen was bathed in light, but the living area where his target sat was dark, other than the light coming from the computer monitors. Ryan checked the windows to his left to make sure no one could see in from the apartments across the street. Confident his act would go undetected, he took a few steps forward, closer to his target, so that the gunfire would be centered in the room and no closer to the hallway than necessary.

The rap music thumped throughout the room.

Perhaps Jack made a noise. Maybe he threw a shadow across the shiny surfaces in front of his victim, or cast his reflection on the glass of the monitors. For whatever reason, the JSO man suddenly kicked back his chair and spun around, reaching desperately for his Turkish-made Zigana 9-millimeter semiautomatic. He took the weapon in his fingertips and raised it at the intruder while he was still in the process of obtaining a firing grip on the gun.

Jack identified the target from his surveillance photos and then he fired once, sending a tiny .22-caliber bullet into the man's stomach, right where the back of his head would have been had the man not startled. The Libyan dropped his pistol and lurched back onto his desk, not from the force of the impact but rather from the natural urge to escape the searing pain of the bullet wound.

Jack fired again, hitting the man in the chest this time, and then again, this bullet striking dead-center mass, between the pectoral muscles. The middle of the man's white undershirt bloomed dark red.

The Libyan clutched his chest, grunted as he spun around, and then slumped over on his desk. His legs gave out totally and gravity took over. The ex-JSO operative slid down onto the floor and rolled onto his back.

Quickly Ryan walked up to the man and raised his weapon

for a final shot to the head. But then he thought better of it; he knew the report of the gun, though quiet, was in no way silent, and he also knew this apartment was surrounded by other units that were occupied. Instead of creating another noise that could be heard by a dozen or so potential witnesses, he knelt down, felt for the man's carotid artery, and determined him to be dead.

Ryan stood to leave, but his eyes flicked up to the desktop computer and the three monitors on the desk. The hard drive of the machine would contain a treasure trove of intelligence, Jack knew, and as an analyst, he found nothing on this earth more enticing than an intel dump at his fingertips.

Too bad his orders were to leave everything behind and bolt the instant he neutralized his target.

Jack stood quietly for a few seconds, listening to the ambient noises around him.

No screams, no shouts, no sirens.

He felt confident no one heard the gunfire. Maybe he could find out what the Libyans were working on. They'd picked up only bits and pieces during their surveillance, just enough to know the JSO men were operational, likely doing work for some syndicate based outside of Istanbul. Jack wondered if he could find enough pieces here on Emad Kartal's computer to put the puzzle together.

Shit, thought Jack. Could be drugs, forced prostitution, kidnapping. Ninety seconds' work right now might well save lives.

Jack Ryan quickly dropped to his knees in front of the desk, pulled the keyboard closer, and grabbed the mouse.

Though he was not wearing gloves, he wasn't worried at all about leaving prints. He'd painted New-Skin onto the tips of his fingers; it was a clear, tacky substance that dried clean and clear and was used as a liquid bandage. All the operators were using it in situations where gloves were either not practical or would look out of place.

Jack pulled up a list of files on the machine and slid the folders over to the monitor closest to him. There was a splatter of blood from Kartal's chest wound diagonally across the monitor, so Jack grabbed a dirty napkin out of the bag of half-eaten Chinese take-out food and wiped the screen clean.

Many of the files were encrypted, and Ryan knew he did not have the time to try and decrypt them here. Instead he looked around the desk and found a plastic baggie with a dozen or so portable flash drives in it. He pulled out one of the drives and slid it into a USB port on the front side of the computer, then copied the files to the drive.

He saw Target Five's e-mail client open, and he began pulling up e-mails. Many were in Arabic, one looked like it might have been in Turkish, and a few were just files without any subject headings or text. One after another he opened these e-mails and clicked on attachments.

His earpiece chirped. Jack tapped it with his fingertip. 'Go for Jack.'

'Ryan?' It was Chavez. 'You're late reporting in. What's your status?'

'Sorry. Just a slight delay. Target Five is down.'

'There a problem?'

'Negative.'

'You clear?'

'Not yet. Getting a sweet intel dump off the subject's PC. Another thirty seconds and I'm done.'

'Negative, Ryan. Leave whatever you find. Get out of there. You've got no support.'

'Roger that.'

Ryan stopped clicking through the e-mails, but a new

message appeared in Kartal's inbox. Instinctively he double-clicked on the attached folder and JPEG photos opened in a grid across one of the monitors in front of him. 'What if we can use this stuff?' he asked, distraction in his voice as he expanded the first photo in the grid.

'Quick and clean, kid.'

But Jack was not listening to Chavez now. He scrolled through the images hurriedly at first, but then he slowed and looked at them carefully.

And then he stopped.

'Ryan? You there?'

'Oh my God,' he said, softly.

'What is it?'

'It's . . . it's *us*. We're burned, Ding.'

'What are you talking about?'

The images on the screen in front of Jack seemed to be taken from security cameras, and the quality of the shots varied, but they were all good enough for Jack to ID his team. John Clark standing in the doorway of a luxurious restaurant. Sam Driscoll driving a scooter up a rainswept street. Dom Caruso walking through a turnstile in a cavernous passage, like that of a sports stadium. Domingo Chavez talking into his mobile phone on a bench inside a ferryboat.

Jack came to the realization quickly that these pictures had been taken this evening. All within the last hour or so.

As Ryan rose from his knees, his legs felt weak from the near panic of knowing his team's actions tonight in Istanbul were under surveillance. Another message popped up at the top of the inbox. Jack all but dove at the mouse to open it.

The e-mail contained one image; he double-clicked to open it.

Jack saw a masked man kneeling at a keyboard, his intense eyes peering at a point just below the camera that captured the image. Behind the masked man, on the floor, Ryan could just make out the foot and leg of a man lying on his back.

Ryan turned his head away from the monitor, looked back over his left shoulder, and saw Target Five's foot sticking up.

Jack looked on the top of the center monitor and saw the small camera built into the display's bezel.

This image had been taken sometime in the last sixty seconds, while Ryan downloaded data off the hard drive.

He was being watched this very second.

Before Jack could say anything else, Chavez's voice blasted his right ear. 'Fucking split *now*, Jack! That's a *goddamned* order!'

'I'm gone,' he said, his voice a whisper. His eyes locked onto the lens of the tiny webcam, and his thoughts on whoever was behind it, looking at him right now.

He started to reach for the USB drive in the computer, but it occurred to him this machine would retain all the pictures of his team on it, which could easily be seen by whoever came to investigate Target Five's death.

In a flurry of movement Jack dropped to the floor, unplugged the computer, and frantically ripped cables and cords out of the back of the machine. He hefted the entire thirty-pound device and carried it with him out the door of the flat, down the stairs, and out into the street. He ran through the rain, which was prudent as well as good tradecraft. It seemed a fitting thing for a man with a computer clutched in his arms to do in the rain. His car was a block away; he dumped the machine in the backseat and then drove out of Taksim toward the airport.

As he drove he called Chavez back.

'Go for Ding.'

'It's Ryan. I'm clear, but . . . shit. *None* of us are clear. All five of us have been under surveillance tonight.'

'By *who*?'

'No idea, but *somebody* is watching us. They sent images of the entire team to Target Five. I took the hard drive with the pictures on it. I'll be at the airport in twenty minutes, and we can –'

'Negative. If somebody is playing us you don't know that that box of wires in your car is not bugged or fitted with a beacon. Don't bring that shit anywhere near our exfil.'

Jack realized Ding was right. He thought it over for a second.

'I've got a screwdriver on my utility knife. I'm going to pull over in a public place and remove the drive from the tower. I'll inspect it and leave the rest right there. Dump the car, too, in case anyone planted something while I was in Five's flat. I'll find another way to the airport.'

'Haul ass, kid.'

'Yeah. Ryan out.'

Jack drove through the rain, passing intersections with mounted traffic cameras high above, and he had the sick feeling that his every move was being watched by an unblinking eye.

4

Wei Zhen Lin was an economist by trade, he had never served in his nation's military, and consequently he had never even touched a firearm. This fact weighed heavily on him as he looked over the large black pistol on his desk blotter as if it was some rare artifact.

He wondered if he would be able to fire the weapon accurately, though he suspected he would not need much skill to shoot himself in the head.

He'd been given a thirty-second primer on the gun's operation by Fung, his principal close protection agent, the same man who'd loaned him the weapon. Fung had chambered a round and flipped off the safety for his protectee's benefit, and then, in a grave yet still somewhat patronizing tone, the ex-police officer had explained to Wei how to hold the weapon, and how to press the trigger.

Wei had asked his bodyguard where, exactly, he should point the gun for maximum effect, and the response Wei received was not as precise as the former economist would have liked.

Fung explained with a shrug that placing the muzzle against most any part of the skull around the brain should do the trick as long as medical attention was delayed, and then Fung promised that he would see to it that medical attention was, in fact, delayed.

And then, with a curt nod, the bodyguard had left Wei Zhen Lin alone in his office, sitting behind his desk with the pistol in front of him.

Wei snorted. 'A fine bodyguard Fung turned out to be.'

He hefted the pistol in his hands. It was heavier than he expected, but the weight was balanced. Its grip was surprisingly thick, it felt fatter in his hand than he'd imagined a gun would be, but that was not to say he'd spent much time at all thinking about firearms.

And then, after looking the weapon over closely for a moment, reading the serial number and the manufacturing stamp just out of curiosity, Wei Zhen Lin, the president of the People's Republic of China and the general secretary of the Communist Party of China, placed the muzzle of the weapon against his right temple and pressed his fingertip against the trigger.

Wei was an unlikely man to lead his country, and that was, to a large degree, why he decided to kill himself.

At the time of Wei Zhen Lin's birth in 1958, Wei's father, then already sixty years old, was one of thirteen members of the Seventh Politburo of the Communist Party of China. The older Wei had been a journalist by trade, a writer and newspaper editor, but in the 1930s he left his job and joined the Propaganda Department of the CPC. He was with Mao Zedong during the Long March, an eight-thousand-mile circling retreat that solidified Mao as a national hero and the leader of Communist China, and which also secured a comfortable future for many of the men around him.

Men like Wei's father, through the happenstance of history that put them alongside Mao during the revolution, were considered heroes themselves, and they filled leadership positions in Beijing for the next fifty years.

Zhen Lin was born into this privilege, raised in Beijing, and then sent to an exclusive boarding school in Switzerland. At the Collège Alpin International Beau Soleil near Lake

Geneva he developed friendships with other children of the party, sons of party officials and marshals and generals, and by the time he returned to Beijing University to study economics, it was all but preordained that he and many of his Chinese friends from boarding school would go into government service in one form or another.

Wei was a member of a group that became known as the Princelings. They were the rising stars in politics, the military, or in business in China who were the sons or daughters of former top party officials, most of them high-ranking Maoists who had fought in the revolution. In a society that denied the existence of an upper class, the Princelings were unquestionably the elite, and they alone were in possession of the money, power, *and* political connections that gave them the authority to rule the next generation.

After he graduated from college Wei became a municipal official in Chongqing, rising to the role of assistant deputy mayor. He left public service a few years later to go to Nanjing University Business School for his master's in economics and a doctorate in administration, and then he spent the latter half of the 1980s and all of the 1990s in the international finance sector in Shanghai, one of China's new Special Economic Zones. The SEZs were areas established by the Communist central government where many national laws were suspended to allow more free-market practices in order to encourage foreign investment. This experiment with pockets of quasi-capitalism had been an unmitigated success, and Wei's education in economics, and to a greater extent his business and party connections, put him at the center of China's financial growth and positioned him for even greater things to come.

He was elected mayor of Shanghai, China's largest city, at the turn of the millennium. Here he pressed for further investment from abroad and further expansion of free-market principles.

Wei was handsome and charismatic, and popular with Western business interests, and his star rose at home and around the world as the face of the New China. But he was also a proponent of strict social order. He supported only economic freedom; the residents of his city saw no liberalization whatsoever in their personal freedoms.

With China's humiliating loss to Russia and the USA in the war over Siberia's gold mines and oil fields, the majority of the government in Beijing was sacked, and Wei, the young, vibrant symbol of the New China, was called to national service. He became the Shanghai party chief of the Communist Party and a member of the Sixteenth Politburo.

For the next few years Wei split his time between Beijing and Shanghai. He was a rarity in government, a pro-business communist who worked to expand the SEZs and other free-market areas across China while, at the same time, supporting hard-line stances in the Politburo against liberal political thought and individual liberty.

He was a child of Mao and the party, *and* he was a student of international finance. Economic liberalism was a means to an end for Wei, a way to bring foreign money into the country to *strengthen* the Communist Party, not a way to subvert it.

After China's brief war with Russia and the United States, it was thought by many that China's economic hardships would destroy the country. Famine, a complete breakdown of national and provincial infrastructure, and ultimately anarchy were on the horizon. Only through the work of Wei and others like him was China able to stave off a collapse. Wei pressed for the expansion of the Special Economic Zones and the establishment of dozens of smaller free-market and free-trade areas.

A desperate Politburo conceded, Wei's plan was implemented in its entirety, and China's quasi-capitalism grew by leaps and bounds.

The gambit paid off. Wei, the chief architect of the financial reform plan, was rewarded for his work. His successes, along with his Princeling status and political pedigree, made him a natural to take over the role of China's minister of commerce in the Seventeenth Politburo. As he stepped into the role of director of national financial policy, China's economy was blessed with double-digit growth rates that seemed like they would last forever.

But then the bubble burst.

The world economy entered a protracted downturn shortly after Wei became commerce minister. Both foreign investment into China and exports out of China were hit hard. These two components of the economy, both of which Wei deserved credit for revolutionizing, were the major driving factors of the nation's double-digit growth rate. They were wellsprings of money that all but dried up when the world stopped buying.

A further expansion of SEZs orchestrated by Wei failed to stop the downward spiral toward catastrophe. Chinese purchases of real estate and currency futures around the world turned into money pits as the European financial crisis and the American real estate downturn broke.

Wei knew how the winds blew in Beijing. His earlier success in free-market reforms to save his country would now be used against him. His political enemies would hold up his economic model as a failure and claim that increasing China's business relationships with the rest of the world had only exposed China to the infectious disease of capitalism.

So Minister Wei hid the truth of China's failing economic model by shifting his focus to gargantuan state projects, and by encouraging loans to regional governments to build or upgrade roads and buildings and ports and telecommunication infrastructure. These were the types of investments seen in the old communist economic model, a central government policy to foster economic expansion via massive central planning schemes.

This looked good on paper, and Wei presented growth rates in meetings for three consecutive years that, while not as good as in those first years of expansion after the war, still hovered at a respectable eight or nine percent. He dazzled the Politburo and the lesser houses of government in China, as well as the world's press, with facts and figures that painted the picture that he wanted them to see.

But it was smoke and mirrors, Wei knew, because the borrowing would never be repaid. Demand for Chinese exports had weakened to a relative trickle, regional government debt had reached seventy percent of GDP, twenty-five percent of all loans were nonperforming in Chinese banks, and still Wei and his ministry encouraged more borrowing, more spending, more building.

It was a house of cards.

And coinciding with Wei's desperate attempt to hide his nation's economic problems, a new troubling phenomenon swept across his country like a typhoon.

It was called the Tuidang movement.

After the central government's woeful response to a calamitous earthquake, protests filled the streets all over the nation. The government pushed back against the protesters, certainly not as forcefully as they could have, but with each arrest or discharge of tear gas the situation grew more unstable.

As the leadership of the crowds was dragged off and imprisoned, the demonstrations moved off the streets for a time, and the Ministry of Public Security felt they had the situation well in control. But the protests moved online in the new social networking and chat board sites available in China and abroad, via well-known workarounds to get past Chinese government Internet filters.

Here, on hundreds of millions of computers and smart phones, the spontaneous protests turned into a well-organized and powerful movement. The CPC was slow to react, while the Ministry of Public Security had batons and pepper spray and paddy wagons but no effective weapons with which to counterpunch the electronic 1's and 0's of a viral uprising in cyberspace. The online manifestation of the protests morphed into a revolt over the span of many months, culminating in Tuidang.

Tuidang, or 'renounce the party,' was a movement whereby first hundreds, then thousands, and then millions of Chinese citizens publicly left the Communist Party of China. They could do it online, anonymously, or they could make a public announcement outside the country.

In four years the Tuidang movement boasted more than two hundred million renunciations.

It was not the raw number of people who had left the party in the past four years that had the party concerned. In truth, it was difficult to determine the true number of renunciations, because many of the names on the list distributed by the leadership of the Tuidang movement contained pseudonyms and common names that could not be independently verified. Two hundred million dissenters may have been, in truth, only fifty million dissenters. But it was the negative publicity created for the party by those who publicly renounced their membership abroad, and the attention that the success of the uprising was getting in the rest of the world, that scared the Politburo.

Commerce Minister Wei watched the growing Tuidang

movement and the anger, confusion, and fear that it created within the Politburo, and he considered the hidden economic problems of his nation. He knew that now was not the time to reveal the looming crisis. Any major austerity reforms would have to wait.

Now was no time to show the central government's weakness in dealing with *anything*. It would only inflame the masses and bolster the revolt.

At the Eighteenth Party Congress something incredible happened that was completely unforeseen by Wei Zhen Lin. He was named president of China and general secretary of the Communist Party, making him the ruler of his house of cards.

The election had been, in Chinese Politburo terms, a raucous affair. The two standing members deemed the most likely to take over had both fallen from grace within weeks of the congress, one for a corruption scandal in his home city of Tianjin, and the other due to an arrest of a subordinate and a charge of espionage. Of the remaining Standing Committee members eligible in the election, all but one were members of alliances with one or the other of the disgraced men.

Wei was the odd man out. He was considered an outsider still, unaligned with either faction, so at the relatively tender age of fifty-four he was elected as the compromise candidate.

The three highest offices in China are the president, the general secretary of the Communist Party of China, and the chairmanship of the Central Military Commission, the chief of the military. At times the same person holds all three roles simultaneously, but in Wei's case, the CMC chairmanship went to another man, Su Ke Qiang, a four-star general in the People's Liberation Army. Su, the son of one of Mao's most trusted marshals, had been a childhood friend of Wei's, together in Beijing and together in Switzerland. Their simultaneous ascendance to the highest levels of power in the nation proved that the Princelings' time to rule had come.

But from the beginning Wei knew the co-leadership would not mean partnership. Su had been a vocal proponent of military expansionism; he'd given hawkish speeches for domestic consumption about the might of the People's Liberation Army and China's destiny as the regional leader and a world power. He and his general staff had been expanding the military over the past decade, thanks to twenty percent annual increases in spending, and Wei knew that Su was not the type of general to build his army only so that they would impress on the parade ground.

Wei knew Su wanted war, and as far as Wei was concerned, a war was the last thing China needed.

Three months after taking two of the three reins of power, at a Standing Committee meeting at Zhongnanhai, the walled government compound in Beijing west of the Forbidden City and Tiananmen Square, Wei made a tactical decision that would result in his placing a pistol against his temple just a month later. He saw it as inevitable that the truth about the nation's finances would come out, at the very least to those on the Standing Committee. Already rumors of problems were filtering out of the Ministry of Commerce and up from the provinces. So Wei decided to head off the rumors by informing the committee about the coming crisis in 'his' economy. To a room of expressionless faces, he announced that he would propose a curtailing of regional borrowing and a number of other austerity measures. This, he explained, would strengthen the nation's economy over time, but it would also have the unfortunate effect of a short-term downturn of the economy.

'How short-term?' he was asked by the party secretary of the State Council.

Wei lied. 'Two to three years.' His number crunchers told him his austerity reforms would need to be in place for closer to five years in order to have the desired effect.

'How much will the growth rate drop?' This was asked by the secretary of the Central Commission of Discipline Inspection.

Wei hesitated briefly, and then spoke in a calm but pleasant voice. 'If our plan is enacted, growth will necessarily contract by, we estimate, ten basis points during the first year of implementation.'

There were gasps throughout the room.

The secretary said, 'Growth is currently at eight percent. You are telling us we will experience *contraction*?'

'Yes.'

The chairman of the Central Guidance Commission for Building Spiritual Civilization shouted to the room, 'We have had thirty-five years of growth! Even the year after the war, we did not contract!'

Wei shook his head and replied in a calm manner, striking a stark contrast with most of the rest of the men in the room, who had grown animated. 'We were deceived. I have looked at the ledgers for those years. Growth came, mostly as a result of foreign trade expansion that I initiated, but it did not happen in the first year after the war.'

Wei saw, rather quickly, that most in the room did not believe him. As far as he was concerned, he was merely a messenger informing others of this crisis, he was not responsible for it, but the other Standing Committee members began leveling accusations. Wei responded forcefully, demanding that they listen to his plan to right the economy, but instead the others spoke of the growing dissent in the streets, and fretted among themselves about how the new problems would affect their standing in the Politburo at large.

The meeting only deteriorated from there. Wei went on the defensive, and by the end of the afternoon he had retreated to his quarters in the compound of Zhongnanhai, knowing that he had overestimated the ability of his fellow Standing Committee members to understand the grave nature of the threat. The men were not listening to his plan; there *would be* no more discussion of his plan.

He had become secretary and president because he had not joined an alliance, but in those hours of discussions about the grim future of the Chinese economy, he realized he could have done with some friends on the Standing Committee.

As an experienced politician with a strong sense of real-politik, he knew his chances for saving his own skin in the current political climate were small unless he announced that the growth and prosperity proclaimed by thirty-five years of previous leadership would continue under his leadership. And as a brilliant economist with complete access to the ultra-secret financial ledgers of his country, he knew that prosperity in China was about to grind to a halt, and a reversal of fortune was the only future.

And it was not just the economy. A totalitarian regime could – theoretically, at least – paper over many fiscal problems. To one degree or another this is what he had been doing for years, using massive public-sector projects to stimulate the economy and give an unrealistic impression of its viability.

But Wei knew his nation was sitting on a powder keg of dissent that was growing by the day.

Three weeks after the disastrous meeting in Zhongnanhai compound, Wei realized his hold on power was under threat.

While on a diplomatic trip to Hungary, one of the Standing Committee members, the director of the Propaganda Department of the Communist Party, ordered all the state-run media outlets in the nation, as well as CPC-controlled news services abroad, to begin airing reports critical of Wei's economic leadership. This was unheard of, and Wei was furious. He raced back to Beijing and demanded a meeting with the propaganda director but was told the man was in Singapore until the end of the week. Wei then convened an emergency meeting at Zhongnanhai for the entire twenty-five-member Politburo, but only sixteen members appeared as requested.

Within days, charges of corruption appeared in the media, claims that Wei had abused his power for personal gain while mayor of Shanghai. The charges were corroborated with signed statements by dozens of Wei's former aides and business associates in China and abroad.

Wei was not corrupt. As the mayor of Shanghai he'd fought corruption wherever he found it, in local business, in the police force, in the party apparatus. In this endeavor he made enemies, and these enemies were only too willing to give false witness against him, especially in cases where the high-ranking coup organizers made offers of political access in return for their statements.

An arrest warrant was issued for the Princeling leader by the Ministry of Public Security, China's equivalent of the U.S. Department of Justice.

Wei knew exactly what was going on. This was an attempted coup.

The coup came to a head on the morning of the sixth day of the crisis, when the vice president stepped in front of cameras in Zhongnanhai and announced to a stunned international media that until the unfortunate affair involving President Wei was resolved, he would be taking charge of the government. The vice president then announced that the president was, officially, a fugitive from justice.

At the time Wei himself was only four hundred meters away in his living quarters at Zhongnanhai. A few loyalists had rallied at his side, but it seemed as though the tide had turned against him. He was informed by the office of the vice president that he had until ten a.m. the next morning to allow representatives from the Ministry of Public Security into his compound to effect his arrest. If he did not go quietly, he would be taken by force.

Late in the evening on the sixth day Wei finally went on the offensive. He identified those in his party who were conspiring against him, and he convened a secret meeting with the rest of the Politburo Standing Committee. He stressed to the five men who were not conspirators that he considered himself a 'first among equals' and, should he remain president and general secretary, he would rule with an eye toward collective leadership. In short, he promised that each and every one of them would have more power than they would have if they put someone else in his place.

His reception from the Standing Committee was cold. It was as if they were looking at a doomed man, and they showed little interest in aligning themselves with him. The second-most-powerful man in China, the chairman of the Central Military Commission, Su Ke Qiang, did not say a single word during the meeting.

Throughout the night Wei had no idea if he would be overthrown in the morning – arrested and imprisoned, forced to sign a false confession, and executed. In the predawn hours his future looked even darker. Three of the five PSC members who had yet to commit to the coup sent word that, though they would not encourage his deposal, they did not have the political clout to help him.

At five a.m. Wei met with his staff and told them he would step down for the good of the nation. The Ministry of Public Security was notified that Wei would surrender, and an arrest team was dispatched to Zhongnanhai from the MPS building on East Chang'an Avenue, on the other side of Tiananmen Square.

Wei told them he would go quietly.

But Wei had decided that he would *not* go quietly.

He would not go at all.

The fifty-four-year-old Princeling had no desire to play the role of a prop in a political theater, used by his enemies as the scapegoat for the country's downfall.

They could have him in death, they could do with his legacy what they wished, but he would not be around to watch it.

As the police contingent from the Ministry of Public Security drove toward the government compound, Wei spoke to the director of his personal security, and Fung agreed to supply him with a pistol and a tutorial on its use.

Wei held the big black QSZ-92 pistol to his head; his hand trembled slightly, but he found himself to be rather composed, considering the situation. As he closed his eyes and began pressing the trigger harder, he felt his tremors increase; the quivering grew in his body, beginning in his feet and traveling upward.

Wei worried he would shake the muzzle off target and miss his brain, so he pressed the gun harder into his temple.

A shout came from the hallway outside his office. It was Fung's voice, excited.

Curious, Wei opened his eyes.

The office door flew open now, Fung ran in, and Wei's body shook to the point he worried Fung would see his weakness.

He lowered the gun quickly.

'What is it?' Wei demanded.

Fung's eyes were wide; he wore an incongruous smile on his face. He said, 'General Secretary! Tanks! Tanks in the street!'

Wei lowered the gun carefully. *What did this mean?* 'It's just MPS. MPS has armored vehicles,' he responded.

'No, sir! Not armored personnel carriers. *Tanks!* Long lines of tanks coming from the direction of Tiananmen Square!'

'Tanks? *Whose* tanks?'

'Su! It must be General . . . excuse me, I mean Chairman Su! He is sending heavy armor to protect you. The MPS won't dare arrest you in defiance of the PLA. How can they?'

Wei could not believe this turn of events. Su Ke Qiang, the Princeling four-star PLA general and the chairman of the Central Military Commission, and one of the men he had made a direct appeal to the evening before, had come to his aid at the last possible moment.

The president of China and the general secretary of the CPC slid the pistol across the desk to his principal protection agent. 'Major Fung . . . It appears I will not be needing this today. Take it from me before I hurt myself.'

Fung took the pistol, engaged the safety, and slid it into the holster on his hip. 'I am very relieved, Mr President.'

Wei did not think that Fung really cared whether he lived or died, but in this heady moment the president stood and shook his bodyguard's hand anyway.

Any allies, even conditional allies, were worth having on a day like this.

Wei looked out the window of his office now, across the compound and to a point in the distance beyond the walls of Zhongnanhai. Tanks filled the streets, armed People's

Liberation Army troops walked in neat rows alongside the armor, their rifles in the crooks of their arms.

As the rumbling of the approaching tanks shook the floor and rattled books, fixtures, and furniture in the office, Wei smiled, but his smile soon wavered.

'Su?' he said to himself in bewilderment. 'Of all people to save me . . . why Su?'

But he knew the answer. Though Wei was happy and thankful for the intervention of the military, he realized, even in those first moments, that his survival made him weaker, not stronger. There would be a quid pro quo.

For the rest of his rule, Wei Zhen Lin knew, he would be beholden to Su and his generals, and he knew exactly what they wanted from him.

5

John Clark stood at his kitchen sink; he looked out the window and watched mist form in his back pasture as a gray afternoon turned into a grayer evening. He was alone, for a few minutes more anyway, and he decided he could put off no longer what he'd been dreading all day.

Clark and his wife, Sandy, lived in this farmhouse on fifty acres of rolling fields and forestland in Frederick County, Maryland, close to the Pennsylvania state line. Farm life was still new to John; just a few years ago the thought of himself as a country gentleman sipping iced tea on his back porch would have made him either chuckle or cringe.

But he loved his new place, Sandy loved it even more, and John Patrick, his grandson, absolutely adored his visits out to the country to see Grandpa and Grandma.

Clark wasn't one for lengthy reflection; he preferred to live in the moment. But as he surveyed his property and thought about the task at hand, he did have to admit that he had managed to put together a good personal life for himself.

But now it was time to see if his professional life was over.

It was time to remove his bandages and test the function of his wounded hand.

Again.

Eight months earlier his hand had been broken – no, his hand had been *shattered* – by unskilled but energetic torturers in a seedy warehouse in the Mitino district of northwest Moscow. He'd suffered nine fractures to bones in his fingers, palm, and wrist, and had spent much of his time since the injury either preparing for or recovering from three surgeries.

He was two weeks post his fourth time under the knife, and today was the first day his surgeon would allow him to test the strength and mobility of the appendage.

A quick look at the clock on the wall told him that Sandy and Patsy would be home in a few minutes. His wife and his daughter had driven together to Westminster for groceries. They told him to wait on the function test of his hand until they returned, so they could be present. They claimed they wanted to be there to celebrate his recovery with dinner and wine, but John knew the real reason: They did not want him going through this alone. They were worried about a poor outcome, and they wanted to be close for moral support if he was not able to move his fingers any better than he could before surgery.

He agreed to their request at the time, but now he realized he needed to do this by himself. He was too anxious to wait, he was too proud to strain and struggle in front of his wife and daughter, but more than this, he knew he would need to push himself much further than his daughter, the doctor, or his wife, the nurse, would allow.

They were worried he might hurt himself, but John wasn't worried about pain. He'd learned to process pain better than almost anyone in the world. No, John worried he might fail. He'd do whatever he physically could to avoid it, and he had a feeling it would not be pretty to watch. He'd test his strength and mobility by pushing himself as far as humanly possible.

Standing at the kitchen counter, he unwrapped his bandages and removed the small metal splints from between his fingers. Turning away from the window, he left the dressings on the counter and moved to the living room. There he sat on his leather chair and raised his hand to examine it. The surgical scars, both new and old, were small and not particularly dramatic, but he knew they belied the incredible damage done to his hand. His orthopedic surgeon at Johns Hopkins was regarded as one of the best in the world, and he had performed the surgery through tiny incisions, using laparoscopic cameras and fluoroscopic images to help him find his way to the damaged bones and scar tissue.

John knew that even though his hand did not look too bad, his chances for a complete recovery were less than fifty percent.

Perhaps if the blunt trauma had been just a little higher on the hand, then the joints of the fingers would have less scar tissue, the doctors had said. Perhaps if he had been a little younger, his ability to heal would be enough to ensure a complete recovery, they hinted without saying.

John Clark knew there wasn't a damn thing he could do about either issue.

He pushed the poor prognosis out of his mind and steeled himself for success.

He picked a racquetball off the coffee table in front of him and he looked it over – his eyes fixed with resolve.

'Here we go.'

Clark slowly began closing his fingers around the ball.

Almost immediately he realized he was still unable to completely mobilize his index finger.

His trigger finger.

Shit.

Both the proximal and middle phalanx bones had been virtually crushed by the torturer's hammer, and the interphalangeal joint, already slightly arthritic from a lifetime of trigger pulling, was now severely damaged.

As his other fingertips pressed into the little blue ball, his trigger finger merely twitched.

He pushed this setback, and the sharp burning sensation that came with it, out of his mind and squeezed harder.

It hurt more. He grunted with the pain but kept trying to crush the little racquetball in his fist.

His thumb seemed as good as new, his last two fingers compressed the ball nicely, and his middle finger formed around it, its mobility restored by the surgery, though it did not seem to retain much strength.

He squeezed tighter on the ball, and a sharp ache in the back of his hand grew. Clark winced, but squeezed harder. The index finger had stopped twitching and relaxed, the frail muscles exhausted, and it went almost ramrod straight.

His hand hurt from the wrist all the way to his fingertips while he squeezed now.

He could live with the pain, and he could live with a slight lack of grip strength.

But the trigger finger was all but nonfunctional.

John relaxed his hand and the pain lessened. Sweat had formed on his forehead and around his collar.

The ball dropped to the hardwood floor and bounced across the room.

Yes, this was just his first test after the surgery, but he knew. He knew without a doubt that his hand would never be the same.

John's right hand was damaged now, but he knew he could shoot a gun left-handed. Every Navy SEAL, and every CIA Special Activities Division paramilitary operations officer, spends more time on weak-hand shooting than most law enforcement officers do on strong-hand shooting, and John had spent nearly forty years as either a SEAL or a CIA operator. Weak-hand fire was necessary training for every shooter, because every shooter ran a real risk of getting wounded on or near his gun hand.

There is a widely held theory behind this phenomenon. When faced with the imminent danger of a gunfight, a potential victim tends to focus acutely on that which is threatening him. Not just the threat of the attacker, but the threat of the weapon itself. The little fire-breathing, lead-spitting tool that is trying to reach out and rip the intended victim apart. For this reason it is disproportionately common for people involved in gunfights to take damage to their dominant firing hand or arm. The other gunfighter is looking at and focusing on the gun as he fires back, so it only stands to reason that much of his fire is directed right at the gun itself.

Weak-hand shooting is, therefore, an absolutely crucial skill to develop by anyone who might find him- or herself up against an armed opponent.

Clark knew he could fire a gun accurately again with his left hand if he stepped up his practice.

But it wasn't just the hand. It was the rest of him, too.

'You're old, John,' he said to himself as he stood up and walked out to the back porch. He looked out on the pasture again, watched the mist roll across the dewy grass, saw a red fox dart out of the trees and race across open ground. Pooled rainwater splashed into the air behind it as it skittered back into the forest.

Yeah, Clark told himself. He *was* old for operational work.

But not *that* old. John was roughly the same age as both Bruce Springsteen and Sylvester Stallone, and they were still going strong in careers that required no small amount of physicality, even if there was no danger involved. And he'd recently read an article in the paper about a sixty-year-old Marine staff sergeant fighting in Afghanistan, walking daily mountain patrols in enemy territory with men young enough to be his grandchildren.

John thought he'd love to drink a beer with that guy, two

tough sons of bitches sharing stories about the old days.

Age is just a number, John had always said.

But the body? The body was real, and as the number of years ticked ever higher, the mileage put on a man in John Clark's profession wore the body down as certainly as a swiftly moving stream cuts a depression through a valley. Springsteen and Stallone and the other geezers out there jumping around for a living had jobs that did not require one-fiftieth the hardship that Clark had endured, and no amount of rationalizing could change that.

Clark heard his wife's SUV pull up in the gravel drive. He sat down on a rocker on the back porch and waited for them to come in.

A man in his mid-sixties sitting on the porch of a quiet farmhouse created a vision of peace and tranquility. But the image was deceptive. Inside the mind of John Clark, his prevailing thought was that he would like to get his good hand around the throat of that son of a bitch Valentin Kovalenko, the opportunistic Russian snake who did this to him, and then he'd like to test the strength and mobility of that hand on that bastard's windpipe.

But that would never happen.

'John?' Sandy called from the kitchen.

The girls came in through the kitchen door behind him. John wiped the last vestiges of his sweat from his forehead, and he called, 'I'm out here.'

A moment later Patsy and Sandy sat outside on the porch with him, waiting for him to speak. They'd each spent a minute chastising him for not waiting on their return. But any frustration melted away quickly when they read his mood. He was somber. Mother and daughter leaned forward anxiously, worried looks on both their faces.

'It moves. It grips . . . a bit. Maybe after some PT it will improve a little more.'

Patsy said, 'But?'

Clark shook his head. 'Not the outcome we'd hoped for.'

Sandy moved to him, sat in his lap, and hugged him tightly.

'It's okay,' he said, comforting her. 'Could have been a hell of a lot worse.' Clark thought for a moment. His torturers had been about a second away from driving a scalpel through his eye. He had not told Sandy or Patsy about this, of course, but it did pop into his head every now and then when he was dealing with his battered hand. He had a damn lot to be thankful for, and he knew it.

He continued. 'I'm going to concentrate on PT for a while. The docs have done their part to fix me up; time for me to do mine.'

Sandy released the hug, sat up, and looked John in the eye.

'What are you saying?'

'I'm saying it's time for me to pack it in. I'll talk to Ding first, but I'm going to go in and see Gerry on Monday.' He hesitated a long time before saying, 'I'm done.'

'Done?'

'I'm going to retire. Really retire.'

Though she clearly tried to hide it, John saw a relief in Sandy's face that he had not seen in years. In decades. It was virtually the same as joy.

She had never complained about his work. She'd spent decades enduring his late-night dashes out of the house with no information as to where he was headed, his spending weeks away at a time, sometimes coming home bloodied and bruised and, more distressing to her, silent for days before he lightened up, his mind left the mission that he'd just returned from, and he could once again smile and relax and sleep through the night.

Their years in the UK with NATO's counterterror unit Rainbow had been some of the best times of her life. His hours were almost normal and their time together had been well spent. But still, even during their time in the UK, she knew that the fate of dozens of young men rested on his shoulders, and she knew this weighed heavily on him.

With their return to the States and his employment at Hendley Associates, once again Sandy saw the stress and strain on his body and mind. He was an operator in the field again – she knew this without a doubt, though he rarely went into details about his activities away from home.

The previous year her husband had been dubbed an international outlaw by the American press, he'd gone on the run, and she'd worried day and night while he was away. The matter had been put to bed in the press quickly and cleanly with a public apology by the outgoing U.S. President and John's life had been given back to him, but when he'd come back from wherever he'd been off to, it was not to come home. It was, instead, to go into the hospital. He'd been beaten badly, to within an inch of his life, one of his surgeons had told Sandy quietly in a waiting room while John was under anesthesia, and though he'd come out of his ordeal with a damaged right hand, she thanked God every day that he'd come out of it at all.

John talked it over with the two women in his life for a few minutes more, but any doubts he had about his decision were put to rest the instant he saw the relief in Sandy's eyes.

Sandy deserved this. Patsy deserved this, too. And his grandchild deserved a grandfather who would be around for a while. Long enough to cheer him on at baseball games, long enough to stand proudly at his graduation, long enough, just maybe, to watch him walk down the aisle.

John knew that, considering the line of work he'd been in since Vietnam, he'd lived most of his life on borrowed time.

That was over now. He was out.

Clark was surprised to find himself at peace with his decision to retire, though he imagined he *would* harbor one regret – that he never got a chance to wrap his hand around the throat of Valentin Kovalenko.

Oh, well, he thought as he gave a gentle hug to his daughter and headed into the kitchen to help with dinner. Wherever Kovalenko was right now, John was near certain he wasn't exactly enjoying himself.

6

Matrosskaya Tishina is a street in northern Moscow, but it also serves as shorthand for a facility with a much longer name. Federal Budget Institution IZ-77/1 of the Office of the Federal Penitentiary Service of Russia in the City of Moscow does not roll so trippingly off the tongue, so those referring to the massive detention facility on Matrosskaya Tishina normally just refer to the street itself.

It is one of Russia's largest and oldest pretrial lockups, built in the eighteenth century, and it shows its age. Though the seven-story façade that faces the street is well maintained and almost regal in appearance, the cells inside are small and decrepit, the beds and bedding are infested with lice, and the plumbing is unable to keep up with the building's current population, which is more than three times the capacity for which it was built.

Just before four in the morning, a narrow gurney with squeaky wheels rolled down a green-and-white painted hallway inside the old main building of Matrosskaya Tishina. Four guards pushed and pulled it along while the prisoner on the bed fought against his bindings.

His shouts echoed off the poured concrete floors and the cinder-block walls, a sound just louder and no less shrill than the squeaky wheels.

'Answer me, damn you! What's going on? I am not ill! Who ordered me transported?'

The guards did not answer; obeying the profane commands of prisoners in their charge was precisely the opposite of their job description. They just kept rolling the gurney down the hall. They stopped at a partition of iron grating and waited for the gate in the center to be unlocked. With a loud click the gate opened, and they pushed their prisoner through and rolled him on.

The man on the gurney had not told the truth. He *was* ill. Everyone who had spent any time behind bars in this hell-hole was ill, and this man suffered from bronchitis as well as ringworm.

Though his physical condition would be appalling to a citizen on the outside, the prisoner was no worse than most of his cellmates, and he was correct in his fear that he had not been hauled from his cell in the middle of the night in order to receive treatment for maladies shared by virtually every other prisoner in the building.

He yelled again at the four men, and again they took no notice of him.

After more than eight months here at Matrosskaya Tishina, thirty-six-year-old Valentin Kovalenko still had not gotten used to being ignored. As a former assistant *rezident* of Russia's foreign intelligence arm, the Sluzhba Vneshney Razvedki, he had grown accustomed to having his questions answered and his orders obeyed. He'd been a rising star in the SVR from his early twenties until his mid-thirties, achieving the plum assignment of number-two man in their London Station. Then, some months ago, a personal and professional gamble had failed, and he'd gone from meteoric rise to free-fall drop.

Since his arrest by internal security officers in a warehouse in Moscow's Mitino district in January he'd been held at the pretrial facility under an executive order of the office of the president, and he'd been told by those few prison officials that he'd met that his case would be delayed and delayed again, and he should mentally prepare himself to spend years in his cell. Then, if he was lucky, all would be forgotten and he'd be sent home. On the other hand, they warned, he could be shipped east and ordered to serve time in Russia's gulag system.

This, Kovalenko knew, would be a virtual death sentence.

For now he spent his days fighting for a corner of a cell shared by one hundred prisoners and his nights sleeping in shifts on a bug-ridden cot. Disease and disputes and despair encompassed every hour of every day.

From other inmates he learned that the average wait to see a judge for someone whose case had not been sped up by bribes or political corruption was between two and four years. Valentin Kovalenko knew he did not have two to four years. When the other inmates in his cell learned who he was, a former high-ranking member of Russian intelligence, he would likely be beaten to death within two to four minutes.

Most residents of Matrosskaya Tishina were no great fans of the government.

This threat of exposure and then reprisal had been used effectively by Kovalenko's enemies outside the prison, mostly at the Federal'naya Sluzhba Besopasnosti, Russian internal security, because it ensured that their inconvenient prisoner would keep his mouth shut while on the inside.

In the first month or two of incarceration Kovalenko had had sporadic contact with his frantic and confused wife, and in their brief phone conversations he'd only assured her that everything would be straightened out and that she had nothing to worry about.

But his wife stopped coming to the prison, and then she stopped calling. And then, he had been told by the assistant warden, his wife had filed for dissolution of the marriage and full custody of his children.

But this was not the worst news. Rumors began filtering down to Kovalenko that no one was working on his case. It was frustrating no one was on his defense, but the fact no one was working on his prosecution was even more ominous. He was just sitting here, in a cage, rotting away.

He worried he would be dead of disease inside of six months.

As the gurney turned to the right and rolled under a recessed light in the ceiling, Kovalenko looked at the guards. He did not recognize any of them, but to him they appeared to be just as robotic as the rest of the staff here. He knew he would get no useful information from them, but out of growing panic he shouted again as they took him through another gate that led out of his cell block and into an administrative portion of the facility.

In another moment he was wheeled into the prison infirmary.

Valentin Kovalenko knew what was happening. He'd imagined this. He expected this. He could have penned the script for this event himself. The late-night rousing. The leather bindings on the gurney with the squeaky wheels. The silent guards and the trip into the bowels of the prison.

He was about to be executed. In secret and in defiance of the law, his enemies were going to remove him from their list of worries.

The massive infirmary was empty of doctors, nurses, or any prison employees except for the men who rolled his gurney, and this reconfirmed Kovalenko's fears. He'd been taken here once before, when a guard's rubber club had opened a wound on his face that needed stitches, and even though that had happened late at night, the medical facility had been well staffed.

Tonight, however, it appeared as though someone had cleared out any witnesses.

Valentin fought against his wrist and ankle straps in vain.

The four guards rolled him into an exam room that appeared to be empty, and then they backed out of the doorway, shutting the door behind them and leaving him in the dark, bound and helpless. Kovalenko shouted as they left, but when the door closed, he looked around in the low light. To his right was a rolling curtain partition, and behind this he could hear movement.

He was *not* alone.

Kovalenko asked, 'Who's there?'

'Who are *you*? What is this place?' replied a gruff male voice. The man sounded like he was just on the other side of the partition, also on a gurney, perhaps.

'Look around, fool! This is the infirmary. I asked who you are?'

Before the man behind the curtain answered, the door opened again, and two men entered. Both wore lab coats, and both were older than Kovalenko. He put them in their fifties. Valentin had never seen them before but assumed them to be doctors.

Both men looked nervous.

Neither doctor regarded Kovalenko on his gurney by the door as they passed by. They then removed the curtain partition, rolling it out of the way up against the wall, giving Kovalenko a view of the rest of the space. In the faint light he saw another man on a gurney; the second prisoner's body below the shoulders was covered by a sheet, but he was clearly bound by his hands and feet much the same as was Kovalenko.

The other prisoner looked at the doctors now. 'What is this? Who are you?'

Valentin wondered what was wrong with the man. *Who are*

you? Was it not clear where he was and who they were? The better question would have been *'What the hell is going on?'*

'What the hell is going on?' Kovalenko shouted at the two older men, but they ignored him and walked now to the foot of the other prisoner's bed.

One of the doctors had a black canvas bag on his shoulder, and he reached into the bag and took out a syringe. With a quiver in his hands and a tightness in his jaw that Valentin could register even in the dim, the man popped the cap off the syringe, and then he lifted the sheet off the bare feet of the other prisoner.

'What the fuck are you doing? Don't touch me with –'

The doctor took hold of the man's big toe while Kovalenko watched in horror and utter confusion. Valentin quickly looked up at the prisoner and saw similar bewilderment on the man's face.

It took the doctor with the syringe a moment to separate the skin from the nail at the tip of the man's toe, but as soon as he accomplished this he jabbed the needle deep under the nail and pressed the plunger.

The man screamed in terror and pain as Kovalenko looked on.

'What is that?' Valentin demanded. 'What are you doing to this man?'

The needle came out of the toe, and the doctor tossed the syringe into the bag. He wiped the site with an alcohol prep pad, and then he and his colleague just stood at the foot of both gurneys, their eyes fixed on the man to Valentin's right.

Kovalenko realized the other man had fallen silent. He looked over at his face again and saw confusion, but before Valentin's eyes the face contorted in sudden and sharp pain.

Through clenched teeth the prisoner growled, 'What did you do to me?'

The two doctors just stood there, watching, tension in their own faces.

After a moment more the man on the gurney began thrashing against his bindings; his hips rose high in the air and his head jerked from side to side.

Valentin Kovalenko shouted for help at the top of his lungs.

Foam and spit came out of the agonized man's mouth, followed by a guttural moan. He kept convulsing at the limit of his straps, as if he was trying in vain to expel whatever toxin had been injected into him.

It took the prisoner a slow, torturous minute to die. When he stilled, when his body came to rest contorted but restrained by the straps, the man's wide eyes seemed to stare right at Kovalenko.

The ex-SVR assistant *rezident* looked toward the doctors. His voice was hoarse from his shouting. 'What did you do?'

The man with the bag on his shoulder stepped over to the foot of Kovalenko's gurney and reached inside his bag.

As he did this, the other man pulled the bedsheet off Kovalenko's legs and feet.

Valentin screamed again, his voice cracking and faltering. 'Listen to me! Just listen! Don't touch me! I have associates who will pay you . . . pay you or kill you if you –'

Valentin Kovalenko shut up when he saw the pistol.

From out of the bag the doctor had retrieved not a syringe, but instead a small stainless-steel automatic, and he leveled it at Kovalenko. The other man stepped up to the gurney and began unfastening the bindings around the younger Russian's arms and legs. Kovalenko lay there quietly, sweat alternately stinging his eyes and chilling him where it had dampened the sheets.

He blinked out the sweat and kept his eyes fixed on the pistol.

When the unarmed doctor finished releasing Valentin from the leather straps, he stepped back to his colleague. Valentin sat up slowly on the gurney, keeping his hands slightly raised and his eyes locked onto the pistol in the quivering hand of the man who had just murdered the other patient.

'What do you want?' Valentin asked.

Neither of the two men spoke, but the one with the pistol – Kovalenko identified it now as a Walther PPK/S – used the barrel of his tiny weapon as a pointer. He twitched it toward a canvas duffel on the floor.

The Russian prisoner slid off the gurney and knelt down to the bag. He had a hard time taking his eyes off the gun, but when he finally did he found a full change of clothes and a pair of tennis shoes. He looked up to the two older men, and they just nodded at him.

Valentin changed out of his prison garb and into worn blue jeans and a brown pullover that smelled like body odor. The two men just watched him. 'What's happening?' he asked while he dressed, but they did not speak. 'Okay. Never mind,' he said. He'd given up getting answers, and it certainly did not look as though they were about to kill him, so he allowed them their silence.

Were these murderers actually helping him escape?

They left the infirmary with Kovalenko in the lead and the doctors walking three meters behind him with the Walther leveled at his back. One of the men said, 'To the right,' and his nervous voice echoed in the long and dark hallway. Valentin did as he was instructed. They led him up another quiet corridor, down a staircase, through two iron gates that were unlocked and propped open with waste bins, and then to a large iron door.

Kovalenko had not seen another soul during the entire walk through this part of the detention center.

'Knock,' instructed one of the men.

Valentin rapped on the iron door lightly with his knuckles.

He stood there for a moment, silence around him except for the thumping in his chest and a wheezing in his lungs from where the bronchitis affected his breathing. He felt dizzy and his body was weak; he hoped like hell this jailbreak, or whatever was going on right now, would not require him to run, jump, or climb any distance.

After waiting several more seconds, he turned back around to the men behind him.

The hallway was empty.

Bolts in the iron door were disengaged, the door creaked open on old hinges, and the Russian prisoner faced the outside.

Valentin Kovalenko had experienced a few hours of semi-fresh air in the past eight months; he'd been taken to the exercise court on the roof once a week and it was open to the sky save for a rusted wire grille, but the warm predawn breeze that brushed his face now as he stood at the edge of freedom was the freshest, most beautiful feeling he'd ever experienced.

There were no wires or moats or towers or dogs. Just a small parking lot in front of him, a few two-door civilian cars parked along a wall on the other side. And off to his right lay a dusty street stretching as far as he could see under weak streetlamps.

A street sign read *Ulitsa Matrosskaya Tishina*.

He was no longer alone. A young guard had opened the door from the outside. Valentin could barely see him as the lightbulb in the fixture above the door had been removed from its socket. The guard stepped past Valentin, inside the prison, and he pushed Valentin outside, and then he pulled the door.

It clanged as it shut, and then a pair of bolt locks were engaged.

And just like that, Valentin Kovalenko was free.

For about five seconds.

Then he saw the black BMW 7 Series sedan idling across the street. Its lights were off, but the heat from the exhaust rose to diffuse the glow of the streetlamp above it. This was the only sign of life he could see, so Kovalenko walked slowly in that direction.

The back door of the vehicle opened, as if beckoning him forward.

Valentin cocked his head. Someone had a sense for melodrama. Hardly necessary after what he'd been through.

The ex-spy picked up the pace and crossed the street to the BMW, and then he tucked himself inside.

'Shut the door,' came a voice from the dark. The interior lights of the backseat were off, and a smoked-glass partition separated the rear from the front seat. Kovalenko saw a figure against the far door, almost facing him. The man was big and broad, but otherwise Valentin could not make out any of the man's features. He had been hoping to find a friendly face, but he felt certain almost immediately that he did not know this person.

Kovalenko closed the door, and the sedan rolled forward slowly.

A faint red light came on now, its origins difficult to determine, and Kovalenko saw the man back here with him a little better. He was much older than Valentin; he had a thick, almost square head and sunken eyes. He also had the look of toughness and importance that was common among the upper levels of Russian organized crime.

Kovalenko was disappointed. He'd hoped a former colleague or a government official sympathetic to his plight had sprung him from the prison, but instead, all indications now were that his savior was the mafia.

The two men just looked at each other.

Kovalenko got tired of the staring contest. 'I don't recognize you, so I do not know what I should say. Should I say "Thank you," or should I say "Oh, God, not *you*"?'

'I am no one important, Valentin Olegovich.'

Kovalenko picked up the accent as being from Saint Petersburg. He felt even more certain this man was organized crime, as Saint Petersburg was a hotbed of criminal activity.

The man continued, 'I represent interests that have just spent a great deal of treasure, both financial and otherwise, to have you removed from your obligations to the state.'

The BMW 7 Series headed south, this Valentin could tell from the street signs that passed. He said, 'Thank you. And thank your associates. Am I free to go?' He presumed he was not, but he wanted to get the dialogue moving a little faster so that he could get answers.

'You are only free to go back to prison.' The man shrugged. 'Or to go to work for your new benefactor. You were not released from jail, you just escaped.'

'I gathered that when you killed the other prisoner.'

'He was not a prisoner. He was some drunk picked up at the rail yard. There will be no autopsy. It will be registered as you who died in the infirmary, from a heart attack, but you can't very well return to your previous life.'

'So . . . I am implicated in this crime?'

'Yes. But don't feel like this will affect your criminal case. There *was* no case. You had two possible futures. You were either going to be sent to the gulag, or you were going to be killed right there in the infirmary. Trust me, you would not be the first man to be executed in secret at Matrosskaya Tishina.'

'What about my family?'

'Your family?'

Kovalenko cocked his head. 'Yes. Lyudmila and my boys.'

The man with the square head said, 'Ah, you are speaking of the family of Valentin Olegovich Kovalenko. He was a prisoner who died of a heart attack in Matrosskaya Tishina prison. You, sir, have no family. No friends. Nothing but your new benefactor. Your allegiance to him for saving your life is your only reason to exist now.'

So his family was gone, and the mob was his new family? No. Kovalenko brought his chin up and his shoulders back. *'Ida na hui,'* he said. It was a Russian vulgarity, untranslatable into English but akin to 'Fuck you.'

The mobster rapped his knuckles on the partition to the front seat, then he asked, 'Do you think that somehow the bitch that left you and took your kids would react pleasantly to you showing up at her door, a man on the run from the police for murder, a man who had been targeted for termination by the Kremlin? She will be happy to learn of your death tomorrow. She won't have the continued embarrassment of a husband in prison.'

The BMW came to a slow halt. Valentin looked out the window, wondering where they were, and he saw the long yellow-and-white walls of Matrosskaya Tishina prison once again.

'This is where you can get out. I know who you used to be, a bright young star of Russian intelligence, but that is no more. You are no longer someone who can say *"Ida na hui"* to me. You are a local criminal and an international outlaw. I'll tell my employer that you said *"Ida na hui,"* and he will leave you to fend for yourself. Or, if you prefer, I will deliver you to the train station; you can go home to your whore wife, and she will turn you in.'

The door to the BMW opened and the driver stood by it.

With the thought of returning to prison, Kovalenko felt a new cold sweat on his neck and back. After several seconds of silence, Valentin shrugged. 'You make a compelling argument. Let's get out of here.'

The man with the square head just stared at him. His face perfectly impassive. Finally he looked out to the driver. 'Let's go.'

The back door closed, the driver's door opened and shut, and then, for the second time in the past five minutes, Valentin Kovalenko was driven away from the detention facility.

He looked out the window for a moment, trying to get hold of himself so that he could take control of this conversation and positively affect his destiny.

'I will need to leave Russia.'

'Yes. That has been arranged. Your employer is abroad, and you will serve outside of Russia as well. You will see a doctor about your health, and then you will continue your career in the intelligence work, after a fashion, but not in the same location as your employer. You will be recruiting and running agents, executing your benefactor's directives. You will be remunerated much better than you had been while working for the Russian intelligence service, but you will, essentially, work alone.'

'Are you saying I will not meet my employer?'

The burly man said, 'I have worked for him for almost two years, and I have never met him. I do not even know if he is a he.'

Kovalenko raised his eyebrows. 'You are not speaking of a national actor. So this is not a foreign state. This is . . . some sort of illegal enterprise?' He knew that it was; he was only feigning surprise to show his distaste.

His answer came in the form of a short nod.

Valentin's shoulders slumped a little. He was tired from his sickness and the adrenaline waning in his blood after the murder of the man and his own thoughts of death. After several seconds he said, 'I suppose I have no choice but to join your band of merry criminals.'

'It's not my band, and they are not merry. That is not how this operation is run. We . . . you, me, others . . . we get orders via Cryptogram.'

'What is Cryptogram?'

'Secure instant messaging. A system of communication that can't be read, can't be hacked, and immediately erases itself.'

'On the computer?'

'Yes.'

Valentin realized he'd have to get a computer. 'So you are not my handler?'

The Russian just shook his head. 'My job is done. *We're* done. I suppose you will never see me again as long as you live.'

'Okay.'

'You will be taken to a house where documents and instructions will be delivered to you by courier. Maybe tomorrow. Maybe later. Then my people will get you out of the city. Out of the country.'

Kovalenko looked back out the window, and he saw they were heading into central Moscow.

'I will give a warning, Valentin Olegovich. Your employer – I should say our mutual employer – has people everywhere.'

'Everywhere?'

'If you attempt to flee your duties, to renege on your compact, his people will find you, and they will not hesitate to hold you to account. They know everything, and they see everything.'

'I get it.'

For the first time, the square-headed man chuckled. 'No. You do not get it. You cannot possibly get it at this point. But trust me. Cross them in *any* way at *any* time, and you will instantly come to know their omniscience. They are like gods.'

It was obvious to the urbane and educated Valentin Kovalenko that he was far worldlier than this criminal scumbag sitting next to him. It was likely this man had no experience working with a well-run outfit before going to work for this foreign employer, but Valentin was hardly stressed about the scope and reach of his new boss. He'd worked in Russian intelligence, and it was, after all, a tier-one spy agency.

'One more warning.'

'I'm listening.'

'This is not an organization from which you will someday resign or retire. You will work at their bidding as long as they want you to.'

'I see.'

The square-headed Russian shrugged. 'It was this or die in prison. You'll be doing yourself a favor by keeping that in your head. Every day of life is a gift given to you. You should enjoy your life, and make the most of it.'

Kovalenko looked out the window, watching predawn Moscow pass by. *A motivational speech from a blockheaded mobster.*

Valentin sighed.

He was going to miss his old life.

7

Jack Ryan woke at 5:14 a.m., a minute before his iPhone was set to rouse him. He turned off the alarm before it disturbed the naked girl sleeping tangled in the sheets next to him, and he used the light from the screen to look her over. He did this most mornings, but he never told her.

Melanie Kraft lay on her side, facing him, but her long dark hair covered her face. Her left shoulder, soft yet toned, glowed in the light.

Jack smiled, then reached over after a moment, and stroked her hair out of her eyes.

Her eyes opened. It took her a few seconds to waken and form a sentient thought into a word. 'Hi.' Her voice was a whisper.

'Hi,' Jack said.

'Is it Saturday?' she asked, her tone both hopeful and playful, though she was still wiping the cobwebs from her brain.

'Monday,' Jack replied.

She rolled onto her back, exposing her breasts. 'Damn. How did that happen?'

Jack kept his eyes on her as he shrugged. 'Earth's revolution. Distance from the sun. Stuff like that. I probably learned it in fourth grade, but I've forgotten.'

Melanie started to fall back to sleep.

'I'll make coffee,' he said, and he rolled off the bed.

She nodded distantly, and the hair that Ryan had lifted off her face fell back over her eyes.

*

Five minutes later they sipped steaming mugs of coffee together on the sofa in the living room of Jack's Columbia, Maryland, apartment. Jack wore tracksuit pants and a Georgetown T-shirt. Melanie was in her bathrobe. She kept a lot of clothes and personal items here at Jack's place. More and more as the weeks went by, and Jack did not mind at all.

After all, she was beautiful, and he was in love.

They had been dating exclusively for a few months now, and already this was the longest exclusive relationship of Jack's life. He had even taken her to the White House to meet his parents a few weeks back; by design, he and Melanie were ushered into the living quarters away from the press, and Jack had introduced his girlfriend to his mother in the West Sitting Hall just off the President's Dining Room. The two women sat on the sofa under the beautiful half-moon window and chatted about Alexandria, her job, and their mutual respect for Melanie's boss, Mary Pat Foley. Ryan spent the time looking at Melanie; he was captivated by her poise and calm. He'd brought girls home to Mom before, of course, but they'd usually just managed to survive the experience. Melanie, on the other hand, seemed to genuinely enjoy spending time with his mother.

Jack's father, the President of the United States, slipped in while the women were chatting. Junior saw his allegedly tough father turn to jelly within moments of meeting his son's brilliant and beautiful girlfriend. He was all smiles and bright banter; Junior chuckled to himself watching his dad trying to lay on some extra charm.

They had dinner in the dining room and the conversation was fun and flowing, Jack Junior spoke the least, but once in a while he caught Melanie's eyes and they smiled at each other.

Jack was not surprised at all that Melanie asked the vast majority of the questions, and she spent as little time as possible talking about herself. Her mom had passed away, her father had been an Air Force colonel, and she'd spent much of her childhood abroad. This she told the President and First Lady when they asked, and it was just about all Ryan, Jr, knew about her childhood himself.

Jack was certain the Secret Service detail that approved her visit to the White House knew more about his girlfriend's past than he did.

After dinner, after they slipped out of the White House just as covertly as they'd slipped in, Melanie confessed to Jack that she'd been nervous at first, but his parents had been so down to earth that she'd forgotten for large parts of the evening that she was in the presence of the commander-in-chief and the chief of surgery at Johns Hopkins's Wilmer Eye Institute.

Jack thought back on that evening while he eyed Melanie's curves through her bathrobe.

She saw him looking at her, and she asked, 'Gym or run?' They did one or the other most every morning, whether or not they had spent the night in the same bed. When she stayed at his place, they worked out in the gym here in Jack's building, or else they ran a three-mile course that took them around nearby Wilde Lake and through Fairway Hills golf course.

Jack Ryan, on the other hand, never stayed at Melanie's apartment in Alexandria. He thought it odd that she'd never invited him to sleep over, but she always explained it away, saying she felt self-conscious about her tiny carriage-house digs, an apartment that wasn't even as big as the living room in Jack's place.

He did not push the issue. Melanie was the love of his life, of this he was certain, but she was also a little mysterious and guarded. At times even evasive.

It came from her training at CIA, he was sure, and it only added to her allure.

When he just kept looking at her, not answering her question, she smiled behind her mug of coffee. 'Gym or run, Jack?'

He shrugged. 'Sixty degrees. No rain.'

Melanie nodded. 'Run it is.' She put her mug down and stood to go back to the bedroom to change.

Jack watched her walk away, and then he called out from behind, 'Actually, there *is* a third option for exercise this morning.'

Melanie stopped, turned back to him. Now her lips formed a sly smile. 'What might that be, Mr Ryan?'

'Scientists say sex burns more calories than jogging. It's better for the heart, too.'

Her eyebrows rose. 'Scientists say this?'

He nodded. 'They do.'

'There is always the risk of overtraining. Burning out.'

Ryan laughed. 'No chance at all.'

'Well, then,' she said. Melanie opened her robe and let it fall to the hardwood floor, then turned and walked naked into the bedroom.

Jack took one last swig of coffee and rose to follow.

It was going to be a good day.

At seven-thirty Melanie was showered, dressed, and standing in the doorway of Jack's apartment with her purse on her shoulder. Her long hair was back in a ponytail, and her sunglasses were high on her head. She kissed Jack good-bye, a long kiss that let him know that she did not want to leave and she could not wait to see him again, and then she headed up the hall to the elevator. Melanie had a long morning commute to McLean, Virginia. She was an analyst for the CIA, but had recently moved from the National Counterterrorism Center, across the parking lot at Liberty Crossing, to the Office of the Director of National Intelligence, following her boss Mary Pat Foley's move from deputy director of NCTC to her new cabinet-level position as director of national intelligence.

Jack was only half dressed, but he did not have to worry about a long commute. He worked much closer, just down the road in West Odenton, so he finished putting on his suit and tie, then lingered over another cup of coffee while he watched CNN on the sixty-inch plasma TV in the living room. A little after eight he headed downstairs to the parking lot of his building and successfully fought the urge to look for his huge canary-yellow truck. Instead he climbed into the black BMW 3 Series that he'd been driving for the past six months, and he headed out of the parking lot.

The Hummer had been fun, his own way to show his individuality and spirit, but from a personal-security perspective, he might as well have been driving a three-ton homing beacon. Anyone attempting to follow him through beltway traffic could do so with ease from triple the distance normally needed for a vehicle follow.

This allowance for his own security should have been made by Jack himself, as his profession necessitated watching his back 24/7, but in truth, losing the canary-yellow bull's-eye was not his idea.

It came in the form of a polite but strongly worded suggestion from the U.S. Secret Service.

Although Jack had refused the Secret Service protection that came standard for an adult child of a current inhabitant of the Oval Office, Jack had been nearly compelled by his father's protection detail to go to a series of private meetings with agents who gave him pointers on staying safe.

Even though his mother and father did not like him going without protection, they both understood why he had to refuse. It would have been, to say the least, *problematic* to do what Jack Ryan, Jr, did for a living with a government agent shouldering up on either side of him. The Secret Service was not happy about his decision to go it alone – but they, of course, would have been exponentially more unhappy had they any idea how often he put himself in harm's way.

During the meetings they peppered him with tips and suggestions on how to maintain a low profile, and on the subject of maintaining a low profile, the first topic had been the Hummer.

And the Hummer was the first to go.

Jack understood the logic, of course. There were tens of thousands of black Beamers on the road, and his new car's tinted windows made him even more invisible. Plus, Jack recognized, he could switch out his ride a lot easier than he could change his face. He still looked remarkably like the son of the President of the United States; there wasn't much he could do about that, short of cosmetic surgery.

He was known, there was no getting around that, but he was hardly a celebrity.

His mom and dad had done their best to keep him and his brothers and sisters away from cameras since his father went into politics, and Jack himself had refrained from doing anything that would put him in the limelight other than the semi-official duties required of a child of a presidential candidate and president. Unlike seemingly tens of thousands of B-list celebrities and wannabe reality stars in America, even before Jack went into covert work at The Campus, he saw fame as nothing more than a pain in the ass.

He had his friends, he had his family; why did he give a damn if a bunch of people he didn't know knew who he was?

Other than the night of his father's win and his inauguration day some two months later, Jack had not been on television in years. And although the average American knew Jack Ryan had a son everybody called 'Junior,' they would not necessarily be able to pick him out of a lineup of tall, dark-haired, good-looking American men in their middle to late twenties.

Jack wanted to keep it that way, because it was convenient to do so, and it just might help him stay alive.

8

The sign outside the nine-story office building where Jack worked read *Hendley Associates*, which said nothing about what went on inside. The innocuous design of the signage fit the mild-mannered appearance of the structure itself. The building looked exactly like thousands of simple offices across America. Anyone driving by who gave it a passing glance might take it for a credit union bureau, an administrative center for a telecommunications firm, a human resources agency, or a PR company. There was a large array of satellite dishes on the roof, and a fenced-in antenna farm next to the building, but these were hardly noticeable from the street, and even if they were noticed, they would not strike the average commuter as something out of the ordinary.

The one-in-a-million passerby who might do any further research into the company would see that it was an international finance concern, one of many around the greater D.C. metro area, and the one novel feature of the company was that it was owned and directed by a former U.S. senator.

Of course, there were more unique features to the organization inside the brick-and-glass structure along the road. Though there was little physical security outside other than a low fence and a few closed-circuit cameras, inside, hidden behind the 'white side' financial trading firm, was a 'black side' intelligence operation unknown to all but an incredibly small minority in the U.S. intelligence community. The Campus, the unofficial name given to the off-the-books spy shop, had been envisioned years earlier by President Jack Ryan during his first administration. He'd set up the operation with a few close allies in the intelligence community, and helmed it with former senator Gerry Hendley.

The Campus possessed some of the brightest analysts in the community, some of the best technological minds, and, thanks to the satellites on the roof and the code breakers in the IT department, a direct line of access into the computer networks of the Central Intelligence Agency and the National Security Agency.

The entire operation was also completely self-funded, as the cover firm, Hendley Associates, was a successful but low-profile financial management firm. The company's success in picking stocks, bonds, and currencies was helped greatly by the gigabytes of raw intelligence data that streamed into the building each day.

Ryan rolled past the sign, parked in the lot, and then entered the lobby with his leather messenger bag over his shoulder. Behind the security desk, a guard with a nameplate on his jacket that read *Chambers* stood with a smile.

'Morning, Jack. How's the wife?'

'Morning, Ernie. I'm not married.'

'I'll check back tomorrow.'

'Right.'

It was a daily joke between the two, although Ryan didn't really get it.

Jack headed to the elevator.

Jack Ryan, Jr, the eldest child of the President of the United States, had worked here at Hendley Associates for nearly four years. Though he was officially an associate financial manager, the vast majority of his work involved intelligence analysis. He had also expanded his responsibilities to become one of The Campus's five operations officers.

In his operational role he'd seen action – a lot of action – over the past three years, although since returning from Istanbul the only action he'd seen had been a few training evolutions with Domingo Chavez, Sam Driscoll, and Dominic Caruso.

They'd spent time in dojos working on hand-to-hand skills, at indoor and outdoor firing ranges around Maryland and Virginia keeping their perishable gunfighting skills as sharp as possible, and they'd practiced surveillance and countersurveillance measures by driving up to Baltimore or down to D.C., immersing themselves in the bustle of the crowded cities and then either tailing Campus trainers or attempting to shake trainers who'd been tasked with sticking on their tails.

It was fascinating work, and extremely practical for men who, from time to time, had to put their life on the line in offensive operations around the globe. But it wasn't real fieldwork, and Jack Junior did not join Hendley Associates' black side in order to train at a shooting range or in a dojo or to chase or run from some guy who he'd be having a beer with later that afternoon.

No, he wanted fieldwork, the adrenaline-pumping action that he had experienced numerous times over the past few years. It was addictive – to a man in his twenties, anyway – and Ryan was suffering from withdrawal.

But now all the action was on hold, and The Campus's future was in doubt, all because of something everyone now referred to as the Istanbul Drive.

It was just a few gigabytes of digital images, e-mail traffic, software applications, and other electronic miscellany retrieved from Emad Kartal's desktop computer the night Jack shot him dead in a flat in the Taksim neighborhood of Istanbul.

The night of the hit Gerry Hendley, the head of The Campus, had ordered his men to cease all offensive operations until they dealt with whoever had them under surveillance. The five operators who had become well accustomed to globetrotting in the company Gulfstream now found themselves all but chained to their desks. Along with the analysts of the organization, they spent their days desperately trying to find out who had been so effectively monitoring their actions during the five assassinations in Turkey.

Somebody had seen them and recorded them in flagrante delicto, any and all evidence relating to the surveillance had been preserved by Ryan's taking of the drive, and for weeks The Campus had been scrambling to find out just how much trouble they were in.

As Jack dropped down into his desk chair and lit up his computer, he thought back to the night of the hit. When he pulled the drive out of Emad's desktop, he'd first planned on just returning to The Campus with the device so he could rush it to Gavin Biery, the shop's director of technology and an expert hacker with a doctorate in mathematics from Harvard and work stints at IBM and NSA.

But Biery nixed that idea immediately. Instead, Gavin met the airplane and the returning operatives at Baltimore Washington Airport, and then rushed them, and their drive, to a nearby hotel. In a two-and-a-half-star suite he disassembled the drive and inspected it for any physical tracking device while the five exhausted operators set up perimeter security, guarding the windows, doors, and parking lot in case a hidden beacon had already alerted an enemy to the drive's location. After two hours' work Biery was satisfied that the drive was clean, so he returned to Hendley Associates with the rest of the team and the one potential clue about who had been watching them in Istanbul.

Even though the rest of The Campus was spooked by the compromisation of their actions in Turkey, most still thought Biery was operating with an unreasonable amount of caution, bordering on paranoia. This surprised no one, however, because Gavin's network security measures around Hendley Associates were legendary. Behind his back he was called the Digital Nazi for demanding weekly security meetings and frequent password-changing schedules in order for employees to 'earn' access to his network.

Biery had promised his colleagues many times over the years that no computer virus would ever get into his network, and to keep his promise, he remained ever vigilant, if, at times, a thorn in the side of the rest of the employees in the building.

The Campus's computer network was his baby, he proclaimed proudly, and he protected it from any potential harm.

When Biery returned with the drive to the technology shop at The Campus, he took the paperback book-size device and placed it in a safe with a combination lock. Ryan and Operations Director Sam Granger, who happened to be standing close by at the time, looked on in bewilderment at this, but Biery explained that he would be the only person in the building with access to the drive. Even though he'd established to his satisfaction that there was no locator on the device, Biery had no idea if there was a virus or other corrupt malware hidden on the drive. He'd rather not have the untested piece of equipment anywhere on the physical property, but barring that, he would personally maintain security of the drive and control all access to it.

Gavin then set up a desktop computer in a second-floor conference room with keycard access. This computer was not part of any network in the building, and it had neither wired nor wireless modem nor Bluetooth capability. It was completely isolated in both the real world and the cyber-world.

Jack Ryan sarcastically asked Biery if he was worried that the drive might grow legs and try to break out of the room. Biery had replied at the time, 'No, Jack, but I *am* worried that one of you guys might be working late one night and try to slip a USB thumb drive into the room or a laptop with a sync cable because you are too rushed or lazy to do things my way.'

At first Biery demanded that he be the only person in the room with the computer while the computer was on, but Rick Bell, director of analysis for The Campus, had immediately protested on the quite reasonable grounds that Biery was not an analyst, and he did not know what to look for or even how to recognize and interpret much in the way of intelligence data.

It was finally agreed to by all that for the first session with the drive, only one analyst, Jack Junior, should be with Biery in the conference room, and Jack would be armed with nothing more than a legal pad and a pen, and a wired phone connection to his coworkers at their desks in case network computing power was needed for research during the investigation.

Before entering the room, Gavin hesitated. He turned to Jack. 'Any chance you would voluntarily submit to a pat-down?'

'No problem.'

Biery was pleasantly surprised. 'Really?'

Jack looked at him. 'Of course. And just to be doubly sure, how 'bout I undergo a body-cavity search? You want me to assume the position against the wall here?'

'Okay, Jack. No need to be a smart ass. I need to know that

you don't have a USB drive, a smart phone, anything that might get infected by whatever we find on this drive.'

'I don't, Gav. I *told* you that I don't. Why can't you just allow for the possibility that there are other people around here who don't want to screw up our network? You don't have the corner on the market on operational security. We've done everything you requested, but I'm not about to let you pat me down.'

Biery thought it over for a second. 'If the network is compromised at all . . .'

'I get it,' Jack assured him.

Biery and Ryan entered the conference room. Biery removed the Istanbul Drive from its strongbox, then wired it to the PC. He turned the machine back on and waited for it to boot up.

Their first sweep of the drive's contents showed them that the operating system was the latest version of Windows, and there were quite a few programs, e-mails, documents, and spreadsheets that they would need to go through.

The e-mail program and the documents were password-protected, but Gavin Biery knew this particular encryption program backward and forward, and he finessed his way through in minutes via a back door that he and his team knew about.

Together Biery and Ryan looked through the e-mails first. They were prepared to pull in Arabic- and Turkish-speaking analysts from Rick Bell's team on the third floor, and they did find dozens of documents in both languages on the drive, but it quickly became apparent that much of the data, and likely the data most relevant to the investigation, was in English.

They found nearly three dozen English e-mails going back about six months from the same address. As they read through them in chronological order, Jack spoke into the phone to the other analysts. 'From his e-mails, it looks like our man in Istanbul was working directly with an English speaker. This guy communicated under the code name of Center. Doesn't ring a bell from any data mining we've done on known personality aliases, but that's no surprise. We've been focusing on terrorists, and this is looking like it's a different animal.'

Jack read through e-mails and relayed what he found. 'The Libyan negotiated payment for a retainer-like relationship with Center, was told that he and his cell would be needed for odd jobs around town . . .' Jack paused while he dug into the next e-mail. 'Here they were sent out to rent some warehouse space' – another e-mail opened – 'here they were ordered to pick up a package and deliver it to a man on a freighter docked at Istanbul Port. Another e-mail has them picking up a case from a guy at Cengiz Topel Airport. No mention of the contents, but that's not surprising. They also did some reconnaissance work at the offices of Turkcell, the mobile phone provider.'

Jack summarized after looking through a few more e-mails: 'Just low-rent gofer stuff. Nothing too interesting.'

Except, Jack thought to himself, all the pictures of himself and his colleagues.

Further digging into the e-mails revealed another secret. Just eleven days before the Campus hit, Center had stopped all e-mail communications with the Libyan. The last e-mail from Center said, simply, 'Switch communication protocol immediately and delete all existing correspondence.'

Jack thought this was interesting. 'I wonder what the new communication protocol was.'

Biery answered after looking through the system for a few seconds. 'I can answer that. He installed Cryptogram the same day that e-mail came.'

'What's Cryptogram?'

'It's like instant messaging for spies and crooks. Center

and Kartal could chat back and forth over the Internet and even send each other files, all on an encrypted forum, knowing that no one was looking in at the conversation and all traces of the conversation would be immediately and permanently scrubbed from both machines, and not hosted on any server in between.'

'It's unbreakable?'

'Nothing is unbreakable. You can be sure that somewhere some hacker is doing his best to pick apart Cryptogram and others like it, trying to find a way to defeat its security. But so far no exploits have been discovered. We use something like it here at The Campus, but Cryptogram is actually a generation improved from what we have. I'll be switching us soon. CIA has something about four gens older.'

'But . . .' Jack read back over the brief e-mail. 'He ordered Kartal to erase the old e-mails.'

'That's right.'

'Clearly he didn't do what he was told.'

'Nope,' Gavin said. 'I guess Center didn't know his man in Turkey didn't remove them. Or else he didn't really care.'

Jack answered back: 'I think it's safe to assume he *did* know and he *did* care.'

'Why do you say that?'

'Because Center sat there and watched us kill Kartal's buddies and he did not warn Kartal that his cell was under attack.'

'That's a good point.'

'Jesus,' muttered Jack, thinking about the implications. 'This bastard Center takes his computer security seriously.'

'A man after my own heart,' Gavin Biery said, with no indication of sarcasm.

After the English-language e-mails had been checked, they went to work with the translators on the other electronic correspondence, but there was nothing of interest save for some communication between the members of the Libyan ex-JSO cell and some back-and-forth chitchat between Kartal and an old colleague in Tripoli.

Next Biery tried to trace the e-mail address from Center, but very quickly it became clear that the mysterious benefactor of the Libyan cell was using a complicated spoofing system that bounced his connection from one proxy server to another around the world. Biery tracked the source of the e-mails back through four locations, finally making his way to a node at the South Valley branch of the Albuquerque/Bernalillo County Library system in New Mexico.

When he announced this fact to Jack, Ryan said, 'Nice work. I'll talk to Granger about sending a couple of operators there to check it out.'

Biery just looked at the younger man for a moment before saying, 'Don't be naive, Ryan. The only thing I *have* managed to do is rule out Albuquerque's South Valley branch library as Center's base of operations. He's not there. There are probably another dozen relay stations between him and us.'

When that did not pan out as they hoped, Jack and Gavin began going through Kartal's financial software, tracking the wire transfers Center sent to the Libyans as payment for their footwork in Istanbul. The transfers came from the Abu Dhabi Commercial Bank Ltd. in Dubai, and at first they looked like they would be a solid lead as to the identity of Center. But one of Biery's computer geeks hacked into the bank's account-holder data. A trace of the owner of the account revealed that the money had been illegally transferred out – electronically stolen – from a Dubai-based hotel group's employee payroll fund.

While this was a dead end as far as identifying Center, it did provide a clue. To Biery, the computer network expert, this was evidence that Center was himself a skilled hacker.

Scanning through the systems file folder, Gavin found something interesting. 'Well, hello there,' he said as he began clicking open files, moving around windows, and firing his cursor all over areas to highlight lines of text at a speed that Ryan found impossible to track with his eyes.

'What is all that stuff?' Jack asked.

'It's a pretty nice attack tool kit.'

'What does it do?'

Gavin did not slow his manipulation of the windows and files on the screen. Jack guessed he'd looked at about twenty different files in the past forty-five seconds or so. As he clicked and, Jack assumed, absorbed all the data on the screen in front of him, he answered, 'The Libyan could have used this stuff to break into computers and computer networks, steal passwords, get hold of personal information, change data around, clean out bank accounts. You know, the usual bad stuff.'

'So . . . Kartal was a hacker?'

Gavin closed all the windows and turned around in his chair to face Jack. 'Nah. This isn't real hacking.'

'What do you mean?'

'This is a tool kit for a script kiddie.'

'A what?'

'It's the term for someone who can't write malicious code themselves, so instead they use a ready-made package like this, created by someone else. This attack tool kit is like a Swiss Army Knife of cybercrime gadgets. User-friendly hacking materials – malware, viruses, key loggers, password-breaking code, stuff like that. The script kiddie just sends this out to a target computer, and it does all the work for him.'

Biery's attention returned to the monitor, and he began looking at some more files. 'There's even an instruction manual for him here, and special tips on how to gain access to computers run by network administrators.'

'If he gains access to a single computer run by an administrator, he can see other things on whatever network the computer is part of?'

'Right-o, Jack. Just think of yourself. You come into work, light up your node, put in your password –'

'And then do whatever the hell I want.'

Biery shook his head. 'Well, you have user-level access, so you do whatever the hell I let you. I have administrator access. You can see a lot of data on our network, but I have a lot more access and control at my fingertips.'

'So this Libyan had the tools to slip into certain networks as an administrator. What kind of networks? I mean, what type of companies, industries? What could he get into with these scripts?'

'The type of industry doesn't have anything to do with it. He could target any industry. If he wanted to steal credit card numbers, for example, he might attack restaurants or retail point-of-sale or something like that. But if he wanted to get into a university system, an airline, a government agency, a federal reserve bank, he could do all that just as easily. The tools to break into networks don't discriminate by industry. The tools will do whatever they can to find a way to root into the network via different attack vectors and vulnerabilities.'

'Like?'

'Like passwords called "password" or "admin" or "1234" or "Letmein" or something else easy to guess, or ports left open that would allow access, or information that is not behind the firewall that might reveal information about who has access to what info, so then the attacker can target those people via social media and the meat space, so that he can make an educated guess about what their password might be. A lot of it is the exact same social-engineering stuff you spies do.'

'Back up a second. What the hell is the "meat space"?'

'The real world, Jack. You and me. Physical stuff. Not cyberspace.'

Jack shrugged his shoulders. 'Okay.'

'Haven't you read any William Gibson?'

Ryan confessed that he had not, and Biery gave him a look of utter bewilderment.

Jack did his best to get Biery back on the task at hand. 'Can you tell who he used the attack tool kit on?'

Biery looked it over for a moment more. 'Actually, nobody.'

'Why not?'

'I don't know, but he never launched any of this stuff. He downloaded it one week to the day before you whacked him, but he never used it.'

'Where did he get it?'

Biery considered this for a moment, and then he opened the drive's Web browser. Quickly he scanned through the history of the webpages Kartal visited, going back several weeks. Finally he said, 'Script kiddies can buy these tool kits on the Internet on special underground economy sites. But I don't think that's where he got it. I'd bet money that this Center character sent it to him via Cryptogram. He got it after the e-mails between them ceased and Cryptogram was launched, and the Libyan didn't go anywhere on the Internet that would have these tools for sale.'

'Interesting,' Jack said, but he wasn't sure what that meant. 'If Center sent it to him, maybe it was part of a bigger plan. Something that never got off the ground.'

'Maybe. Even though this stuff isn't the highest-level hacking known to man, it can still be pretty damaging. Last year the computer network of the Federal Reserve Bank of Cleveland was hacked. The FBI spent months and millions on the investigation, only to find out that their culprit was a seventeen-year-old operating out of a karaoke bar and cyber-café in Malaysia.'

'Damn. And he used a tool kit like this?'

'Yep. The vast majority of hacks are done by some flunky who only knows how to click his mouse. The real malicious code is written by what are called black-hat hackers. They are the bad guys. Kartal may have the attack tool kit on his machine, but I have a feeling Center is the black-hat who sent it to him.'

After all the documents were mined by Jack for intelligence value, Gavin Biery began hunting through the device's software, looking for any clues as to how Center had been able to remotely operate the camera. There was no obvious application to do this present on the drive, and no e-mails between Kartal and Center discussing Center's access, so Biery concluded that the mysterious Center had probably hacked the Libyan's computer without his knowledge. Biery decided he would take as long as required to ferret out the hacking tools Center used in order to learn more about Center's identity.

In this endeavor Jack Junior was out of his element; he could no more pull intel out of raw software code than he could read Sanskrit.

Ryan rejoined his fellow analysts and went to work looking into the Libyan cell and their mysterious benefactor via other means, while Biery spent virtually every waking minute when he was not working on other Hendley/Campus IT duties huddled in his lonely but secure conference room with the Istanbul Drive.

It took Gavin weeks to open and test and retest every one

of the hundreds of executable files on the drive in order to see what it did and how it affected the rest of the machine, and when this task yielded nothing of value he then drilled down into the source code, the text-based instructions of each program, tens of thousands of lines of data that, ultimately, revealed nothing more than the executables.

Then, after he'd expended weeks of effort, he began digging into the machine code. This was the computer language sequence, long strings of 1's and 0's that *really* told the processor what to do.

While the source code was high-tech and arcane, the machine code was nigh on indecipherable to anyone but an expert in computer programming.

It was mind-numbingly boring, even for a guy who lived for computer code, but despite suggestions from his fellow computer geeks that he was chasing ghosts in the machine, and nudges from the top brass at Hendley to hurry up or declare the exercise fruitless, Gavin kept working at his slow, methodical pace.

Jack had been thinking about the night in Istanbul and the subsequent monthlong investigation while he waited for his computer to boot up. He realized he'd lost track of time for a moment, snapping out of it to find himself staring at the camera above his computer monitor. It was a built-in device that was sometimes used for Web chat communications with other departments around the building. Even though Gavin had pronounced the company network impregnable, Jack still spent a lot of time with that twitchy feeling that he was being watched.

He looked deeply into the camera, still thinking of that night in Istanbul.

With a shake of his head he said, 'You're too young to be paranoid.'

He stood to head over to the break room for a cup of coffee, but before he walked off he grabbed a Post-it note from a pad next to his keyboard, then stuck the gummed portion of the paper over the camera lens.

A low-tech solution to a high-tech problem, more for his own peace of mind than anything else.

As Jack turned he took one step toward the hallway before he stopped suddenly, heaving in surprise.

In front of him stood Gavin Biery.

Jack saw Biery virtually every workday, and the guy never exactly appeared to be the epitome of good health, but today he looked like death warmed over. Here at eight-thirty a.m. his clothes were wrinkled, his thinning gray-brown hair was askew, and dark baggy circles hung pronounced above his fleshy cheeks.

On the best of days Gavin was a guy whose face looked like the only light it ever saw was the glow of his LCD monitor, but today he looked like a vampire in his coffin.

'Holy shit, Gav. Did you spend the night here?'

'The weekend, actually,' answered Biery in a tired but excited voice.

'You need some coffee?'

'Ryan . . . at this point, I *bleed* coffee.'

Jack chuckled at this. 'Well, at least tell me your shitty weekend was worth it.'

Now Biery's soft face tightened into a smile. 'I found it. I freaking found it!'

'You found what?'

'I found remnants of the malware on the Istanbul Drive. It's not much, but it's a clue.'

Jack pumped his fist into the air. 'Awesome!' he said, but internally he could not help but think, *It's about damn time.*

9

While Ryan and Biery headed together down to the technology department, John Clark sat in his office, drumming the fingers of his good hand on his desk. It was just past eight-thirty; the director of operations of The Campus, Sam Granger, would have been in his office and working for more than an hour already, and the director of The Campus and the 'white side' operation, Hendley Associates, Gerry Hendley, would just now be settling into his office.

No reason to put this off any longer. Clark picked up the phone and pushed a number.

'Granger.'

'Hey, Sam, it's John.'

'Morning. Good weekend?'

No. Not really, he thought. 'It was fine. Hey, can I come talk to you and Gerry when you guys get a moment?'

'You bet. Gerry just walked in the door. We're free right now. Come on.'

'Roger.'

Five minutes later Clark stepped into the office of Gerry Hendley on the ninth floor of the building. Gerry stepped around his desk and executed the left-handed handshake that most everyone in the building had been offering Clark since January. Sam stood from a chair in front of Gerry's desk and led John to the chair next to his.

Out the window behind Hendley's desk, rolling Maryland cornfields and horse farms ran north toward Baltimore.

Gerry said, 'What's up, John?'

'Gentlemen, I've decided it's time to face facts. The right hand is not coming back. Not one hundred percent. Say seventy-five percent, tops, and that's only after a hell of a lot more therapy. May be another surgery or two in my future.'

Hendley winced. 'Damn it, John. I'm sorry to hear that. We were all hoping this time under the knife would be the one that made you one hundred percent again.'

'Yeah. Me, too.'

Sam said, 'You take as much time as you need. With the ongoing investigation into the Istanbul Drive, the stand-down could last several more weeks, and if analysis doesn't –'

'No,' John said flatly with a shake of his head. 'It's time for me to pack it in. To retire.'

Sam and Gerry just stared at him. Finally Sam said, 'You are a crucial part of this operation, John.'

Clark sighed. 'I *was*. That son of a bitch Valentin Kovalenko and his henchmen ended it.'

'Bullshit. You've got more capabilities than most of the National Clandestine Service at Langley.'

'Thanks, Gerry, but I've got to hope the CIA is sticking to paramilitary operations officers who can hold a firearm with their dominant hand if required to do so. That skill is beyond my capabilities at the moment.'

Neither Gerry nor Sam had a response to this.

Clark continued, 'It's not just the hand. My clandestine fieldwork potential was damaged by all the press about me last year. Yeah, the heat is off at the moment, most of the media ran off with their tails between their legs when it came out that they were spreading propaganda for Russian intelligence, but think about it, Gerry. It will just take one intrepid reporter on a slow news day to do one of those "Where are they now?" stories. He'll tail me here, they'll dig a little deeper, and then next thing you know *60 Minutes* will be down at reception with a camera, asking for a moment of your time.'

Hendley's eyes narrowed. 'I'll tell them to get the hell off my property.'

Clark smiled. 'If it was only that easy. Seriously. I don't want to see another convoy of black SUVs with FBI tactical guys pulling up on my farm. Once was more than enough.'

Sam said, 'The kind of expertise you possess is invaluable. How 'bout you hang it up, operationally speaking, and transition to more of a behind-the-scenes role?'

Clark had thought about this, of course, but in the end he realized that The Campus was set up as efficiently as possible.

'I'm not going to just roam the halls here, Sam.'

'What are you talking about? You keep the same office. You continue to do –'

'Guys, we've been in stand-down mode since Istanbul. The entire team is working their computers eight hours a day. It's a sad fact that my grandson is better with a computer than I am. There is absolutely nothing here for me to do now, and, should the Istanbul Drive get resolved and the operators get the green light to go back into the field, in my diminished capacity, I won't be taking part.'

Gerry asked, 'What does Sandy say about you roaming the halls at home?'

Clark laughed at this. 'Yeah, it's going to be a transition for both of us. I've got lots to do around the farm, and God knows why, but she seems to want me around. She may get sick of me, but I owe her the opportunity to find out.'

Gerry understood. He wondered what he would be doing now if his wife and kids were still alive. He'd lost them in a car crash several years ago, and he'd been alone ever since. His work was his life, and he would not wish that life on a man who clearly had someone at home who wanted him there.

Where would Gerry be if his family were still alive? Gerry knew he would not be working sixty to seventy hours a week at Hendley Associates and The Campus. He would damn well find a way to enjoy his family.

He could hardly begrudge John Clark one second of a life that Gerry would give anything to have for himself.

Still, Hendley ran The Campus, and Clark was one hell of an asset. He had to do what he could to keep him. 'Are you sure about this, John? Why don't you take some more time to think it over?'

John shook his head. 'I've thought about nothing else. I'm sure. I'll be at my place. Twenty-four hours a day, seven days a week, I'm available for you or anyone on the team. But not in an official capacity.'

'Have you talked to Ding?'

'Yeah. We spent all day yesterday at the farm. He tried to talk me out of it, but he understands.'

Gerry stood from his desk and extended his left hand. 'I understand and accept your resignation. But please don't ever forget. You always have a place here, John.'

Sam echoed the sentiment.

'Thanks, guys.'

While Clark was upstairs in Hendley's office, Jack Ryan, Jr, and Gavin Biery sat in the locked conference room just off Biery's second-floor office. In front of them was a small table, upon which the desktop computer sat with the cover removed, exposing all the components, wires, and boards of the device. Additional peripheral components were attached to the system via cables of different thickness, color, and type, and these pieces were strewn across the table haphazardly.

Other than the computer hardware, a telephone, a single coffee mug that had left dozens of small brown rings on the white table, and a yellow legal pad, there was nothing else in sight.

Ryan had spent many hours in this place over the past two months, but that was nothing compared to the time Biery had spent here.

On the monitor in front of Ryan was a screen full of numbers and dashes and other characters.

Gavin said, 'First, you've got to understand one thing.'

'What's that?'

'This guy, if Center *is* a guy, is good. He's a first-rate black-hat hacker.' Biery shook his head in amazement. 'The code obfuscation is like nothing I've ever seen.

'He's using a totally new species of malware, something I couldn't find without a long, exhaustive manual search of the machine code.'

Jack nodded. He motioned to a string of numbers on the monitor. 'So, is this the virus?'

'A portion of it. A virus has two stages to it. The delivery method and the payload. The payload is still hidden on the drive. It's a RAT, a remote-access tool. It's some sort of a peer-to-peer protocol, but I haven't been able to ferret it out yet. It's that well hidden inside another application. What you are looking at right here is a portion of the delivery method. Center removed most of it after he got in, but he missed this little string.'

'Why was it removed?'

'He's covering his tracks. A good hacker – like me, for instance – always goes behind himself to clean up. Think about a thief breaking into a house. Once he makes entry through a window, the first thing he does is close the window behind him so no one knows anybody is inside. He did not need the delivery system any longer once he was inside the computer, so he erased it.'

'Except he did not erase it all.'

'Exactly. And that is important.'

'Why?'

'Because this is a digital fingerprint. This could be something in his own malware that he does not know about, doesn't know he's leaving behind.'

Jack understood. 'You mean he might leave it on other machines, so if you see this again, then you will know that Center is involved.'

'Yes. You would know that this extremely rare malware was involved, and the attacker, just like Center, did not clean this one part off the machine. You can infer, I think, that it *could* be the same guy.'

'Any idea how he managed to get his virus on Kartal's computer?'

'For a guy with skills like Center's, it would have been child's play. The tough part about installing a virus is the social engineering – that is, getting human beings to do what you want them to do. Click a program, go to a website, give up your password, plug in a USB drive, stuff like that. Center and the Libyan knew one another, they had communication between one another, and, from the e-mails, it's clear the Libyan did not suspect Center was spying on his machine, operating his webcam, going through back doors in the software to install files and delete the footprints he left. He had Kartal hook, line, and sinker.'

'Very cool,' said Jack. The world of computer hacking was arcane to him, but he recognized that in many respects, espionage was espionage, and many of the principles were similar.

Gavin sighed now. 'I'm not finished looking through this

drive. It might take another month or more. For now all we really have is an electronic fingerprint that we can tie to Center if we see it again. It's not much, but it's something.'

Jack said, 'I need to have a meeting with Gerry and the other operators and let them know your findings. Do you want me to do it alone so you can go home and get some sleep?'

Gavin shook his head. 'No. I'll be okay. I want to be there.'

10

Todd Wicks had never done anything like this, but, then again, Todd Wicks had never been to Shanghai.

He was here in town for the Shanghai Hi-Tech Expo, and though this wasn't his first international trade show, this was, without question, the first time he'd met a beautiful girl in the lobby bar of his hotel who made it abundantly clear that she wanted him to come up to her room.

She was a prostitute. Todd wasn't the worldliest guy around, but he managed to figure this out pretty quickly. Her name was Bao, and this meant, she told him in her heavy but alluring accent, 'precious treasure.' She was gorgeous, maybe twenty-three years old, with long, straight black hair the color and luster of Shanxi black granite and a tight red dress that was at once both glamorous and sexy. Her body was long and lean; when he first saw her, he thought she might be a movie star or a dancer, but when he caught her eye, she lifted her glass of chardonnay off the marble bar with delicate fingers and floated over to him with a gentle but confident smile.

It was at this point Todd realized she was a 'working girl,' and she was working.

He asked her if he could buy her a drink, and the bartender refilled her wineglass.

Again, Todd Wicks did not do things like this, but she was so far beyond stunning that, he told himself, he would have to make an exception, just this once.

Before Shanghai, Todd was a nice guy with a nice life. At thirty-four years old, he was the Virginia/Maryland/D.C.

territory sales manager for Advantage Technology Solutions LLC, a California-based IT company. He owned a nice-sized home in Richmond's desirable West End, where he was dad to two good-looking children and husband to a wife smarter, better looking, and more successful in her field, pharmaceutical sales, than he was in his.

He had it all, he bore no complaints, and he had no enemies.

Not until that night.

Later, when he thought back on the evening, he blamed the vodka tonics he had been drinking since dinner with colleagues, and he blamed a slight light-headedness from cold medicine he had been taking since coming down with a sinus infection on the twenty-hour flight from Dulles.

And he blamed the damn girl. Bao, the precious treasure who fucked up his life.

Just before midnight Todd and Bao stepped out of the elevator on the eleventh floor of the Sheraton Shanghai Hongkou Hotel. They were arm in arm, Todd reeling a bit from drink and his heart pounding with excitement. As they walked to the end of the hallway, Todd felt neither guilt nor remorse for what he was about to do, only some concern about how he was going to hide the ATM withdrawal of 3,500 Chinese yuan – more than $500 – from his wife. But he told himself he'd worry about that in the morning.

Now was not the time to stress.

Her suite was the same as his, a king-size bed in a room off a sitting area with a sofa and a large-screen TV, but hers was illuminated with candles and scented with incense. They sat on the sofa and she offered him another drink from the bar, but now he was worried about his ability to perform while intoxicated, so he declined.

The small talk reeled Todd Wicks in every bit as much as the young woman's beauty. A story about her childhood was disarming; her questions about him and where he grew up, about his brothers and sisters, and her asking him about whatever sport it was that he played that kept him in such peak physical condition – all served to further mesmerize a man who was already more than willing to throw caution to the wind.

He loved her voice; it was small and halting but intelligent and confident. He wanted to ask her what a nice girl like her was doing in a place like this, but it didn't seem to fit. This was a nice place, and his lowered inhibitions made it hard for Todd to see anything wrong with what was going on. He couldn't see anything, for that matter, past her sparkling eyes and her plunging neckline.

She leaned forward to kiss him. He hadn't even handed over the 3,500 yuan, but he had the strong impression that she wasn't thinking about the money right now.

Todd knew he was a catch, surely ten times better than any other john she'd been with. Bao was into him, falling as hard as he, Todd had no doubt in his mind.

He kissed her deeply, put his hands on either side of her little face, and held her for more.

In minutes they slid off the couch onto the floor, and in minutes more her dress and heels were still there on the floor of the sitting room, but the two of them had moved to the bedroom. She lay on the bed; he stood naked above her.

He knelt down, his moist hands slid up the outsides of her legs, made their way to her underwear, and he tugged on them slightly. She was compliant, and he saw it as more evidence of her lust matching his. She lifted up to allow him to remove her silk panties from her narrow hips.

Her stomach was flat and toned, her alabaster skin radiant in the soft candlelight of the room.

Though Todd was on his knees he felt them shake under him. He rose slowly and unsteadily, and then he lay down on the bed.

In moments they were one. He was on top of her, he was seven thousand miles from home, and no one would ever know.

He moved slowly at first, but only for an instant, and then he moved faster and faster. Sweat dripped from his forehead onto her clenched face, her eyes tight with what he took as ecstasy.

He picked up the pace even more, and soon his eyes locked on her beautiful face as her head rolled from side to side in orgasm.

Yes, this was a transaction to her, it was her job, but he felt her feel *him*, and he could tell with absolute certainty that her orgasm was real and her flushed skin was hot from a feeling inside her unlike the other men that she'd been with in the past.

She was awash with emotion just the same as he.

He kept up his movements for a short time more, but in truth his stamina was not what he had hoped, and he came quickly.

As he gasped and panted on top of her, their bodies now still except for the movement of his lungs and the pounding of her heart, her eyes opened slowly.

He gazed deeply into them; golden sparkles flickered in the candlelight.

Just as he was about to tell her that she was perfect, her eyes blinked and then refocused on a point over his right shoulder.

Todd smiled, turned his head slowly to follow her gaze.

Standing at the edge of the bed, looming over Todd's naked body, was a severe-looking middle-aged Chinese woman in a matte gray pantsuit. In a voice like a knife being sharpened on a whetstone she said, 'Are you *quite* finished, Mr Wicks?'

'What the fuck?'

As he leapt off the girl and spun from the bed, Todd saw other men and women in the suite. There had to have been half a dozen strangers who had somehow slipped in while Todd was lost in the throes of ecstasy.

He fell on the floor, naked, and he scrambled on his hands and knees, looking for his pants.

His clothes were gone.

Ten minutes later Todd Wicks was still naked, though the woman in the gray pantsuit had brought him a towel from the bathroom. He sat on the edge of the bed with the towel pinched around his waist; he had to hold it tight because it was not large enough to cover him properly. The overhead lights were on and the candles had been blown out, and it was as if all the strangers around him had forgotten him. He sat there seminude as men and women in black and gray suits and raincoats milled about in the suite.

He had not seen Bao since she'd been hustled out the door in a robe, seconds after the intrusion.

On the fifty-two-inch flat-screen TV in the sitting area, well within Todd's view at the edge of the bed, a pair of men watched the playback of a recording they had obviously made from a surveillance camera. Todd glanced up at it when they turned it on, and he saw himself sitting on the sofa, making nervous small talk with Bao. They advanced the recording a few minutes and the angle changed; a second camera had apparently been secreted in the bedroom high in the corner by the bed.

Todd watched himself take his clothes off, stand there

naked and hard, and then kneel down between Bao's legs.

The men advanced the recording again. Todd grimaced as his very naked and white backside began gyrating at cartoonish speed.

'Jesus,' he muttered. He turned away. Watching this in a room full of men and women, a room full of strangers, was killing him. He wouldn't have had the stomach to watch himself having sex even if he was alone. His heart felt like it had been tied in a knot and the muscles in his lower back had cinched tight at the midline of his spine.

Todd felt like he was about to puke.

One of the two men standing at the television turned to him. He was older than Todd, maybe forty-five, and he had sad hangdog eyes and narrow shoulders. He took off his raincoat as he walked closer, hung it over his forearm, and he pulled a chair from the desk up to the edge of the bed before sitting down directly in front of Wicks.

The sad eyes stayed locked on Todd as the man's right hand came out and patted him on the shoulder gently. 'I am sorry about all this, Mr Wicks. This is very intrusive of us. I can't imagine how you must feel.'

Todd looked down at the floor.

The man's English was good; he spoke with British English inflections slightly clipped in the Asian style.

'I am Wu Fan Jun, detective with the Shanghai Municipal Police.'

Todd kept his eyes lowered to the floor, the embarrassment and humiliation unbearable. 'For the love of God, can I *please* put my pants back on?'

'I'm sorry, we have to log them into evidence. We will have something brought down from your room: 1844, is it?'

Wicks nodded.

To his right in the sitting room, the fifty-two-inch plasma

kept going. Todd glanced at it and saw himself from another angle.

It was no more flattering than the previous one had been. *What the hell? Did these guys edit this in real time?*

Todd heard the sounds of his own grunting and groaning.

'Can they turn that off? *Please?*'

Wu clapped his hands as if he himself had forgotten, then called out in Mandarin across the suite. Quickly a man rushed to the television and fiddled with the remote for several seconds.

Finally, mercifully, the screen went blank and Todd's own moans of lust left the otherwise silent room.

Wu said, 'There we are. Okay. I don't need to tell you, sir, that we have a delicate situation here.'

Todd just nodded, eyes on the floor.

'We have been investigating certain . . . untoward activities here in the hotel for some time. Prostitution is not legal in China, as it is unhealthy toward women.'

Todd said nothing.

'Do you have a family?'

Wicks started to say 'No,' a reflexive response to keep his family out of this, but he stopped himself. *I have fucking pictures of me and Sherry and the kids in my wallet, all over my fucking laptop.* He knew he could not deny they existed.

He nodded. 'A wife and two kids.'

'Boys? Girls?'

'One of each.'

'A lucky man. I myself have a wife and one son.'

Todd looked up at Wu now, into the hangdog eyes. 'What's going to happen, sir?'

'Mr Wicks, I am sorry about the situation you find yourself in, but I did not put you here. You provide us with evidence that we need in our case against the hotel. Their promotion of prostitution is a cause of great concern here in the city. Just imagine if it was your young daughter who had turned to a life of –'

'I'm really, *really* sorry. I don't *ever* do this sort of thing. I have no idea what came over me.'

'I see that you are not a bad man. If it were my decision to make, we would just record this as unfortunate, a tourist who got caught up in something unpleasant, and leave it at that. But . . . you must understand, I will have to arrest you and charge you with engaging a prostitute.' Wu smiled. 'How can I charge the hotel and the woman if I have no one else, no one to provide the third corner of the triangle that is this sad, sad crime?'

Todd Wicks nodded distantly, still not believing this was happening to him. But then he had a thought, and he jolted with excitement as he looked up. 'I could provide a statement. I could pay a fine. I could promise to –'

Wu shook his head, and the low bags under his eyes seemed to droop even farther. 'Todd, Todd, Todd. That sounded like you were trying to offer some sort of bribe.'

'No. Of course not. I would never consider –'

'No, Todd. *I* would never consider it. Here in China there is some corruption, I can acknowledge that. But not as much as the rest of the world insinuates, and, if I may be so intemperate to say, much of the corruption comes from Western influences.' Wu waved a small hand around the room, indicating that Todd himself had brought corruption on his poor nation, but he did not say it out loud. Instead he just shook his head and said, 'I don't know if there is anything I can do to help you.'

Todd said, 'I want to talk to the embassy.'

'There is a United States consulate here in Shanghai. The United States embassy is in Beijing.'

'Then I would like to speak with someone at the consulate.'

'Of course, that can be arranged. I will mention, however, as a family man myself, that notifying American consular officials of this situation will make it necessary for my office to provide our evidence to the consulate. It is important for us to show them that this is not some sort of unfair charge against you, you understand.'

Todd felt a glimmer of hope. Having the U.S. consulate know that he had cheated on his wife with a Chinese hooker would be even more humiliating, but maybe they could get him out of this.

'And please don't think the consulate can sweep this matter under the rug. Their involvement in this will be chiefly to notify your loved ones back in the United States about your situation, and to help you find a local attorney.'

Fuck that, thought Todd, and his glimmer of hope faded in an instant.

'What if I just plead guilty?'

'Then you will be here for some time. You will go to jail. Of course, if you fight the charge against you' – Wu scratched the back of his head – 'although I don't know how you would make that claim, as we have video and audio recordings of the entire . . . the entire act, but if you do, there will be a trial, and that will receive some publicity, certainly back in the States.'

Todd Wicks felt like he was going to be sick.

Just then, Wu raised a finger into the air as if he just had a thought. 'You know, Mr Wicks, I like you. I see you are a man who has made a serious mistake by listening to his prurient desires and not the wisdom of his brain, yes?'

Todd nodded vigorously. Was some sort of a lifeline coming?

'I can talk to my superiors to see if there is another way out of this for you.'

'Look . . . whatever you need me to do . . . I'll do it.'

Wu nodded thoughtfully. 'I think, for the benefit of your wife and your two small children, that would be best. I will make a phone call.'

Wu stepped out of the room, but he did not make a phone call because, in truth, he did not need to talk to anyone. He was not Shanghai police, he was not a family man, and he was not here investigating the hotel. No, these were all lies, and lying was an integral part of Wu's job. He was MSS, the Ministry of State Security, and Todd Wicks had just been caught in his honey trap.

Normally Wu attempted to lure targets of opportunity into his traps, but Todd Wicks of Richmond, Virginia, was different. Wu received an order from his superiors with a list of names of technology employees. The Shanghai Hi-Tech Expo was one of the largest in the world, and it was no great surprise that three of the men on his superior's wish list were in attendance. Wu had struck out with the first man, but he'd hit a home run with the second. As Wu stood in the hallway, he knew that in the suite on the other side of the wall he leaned on was an American man who would jump at the chance to spy for China.

He did not know what his leaders needed this Todd Wicks for, it was not his job to know, and it was not his way to care. Wu lived like a spider lives; his entire life, his complete being, was tuned to feel the twitches in his web that told him a new victim was approaching. He had wrapped Todd Wicks up in his web as he had done so many others, but already he was thinking about a Japanese salaryman in the same hotel, a target of opportunity Wu already had on the edge of his web, and a man Wu expected to wrap up before dawn.

Wu so loved the Shanghai Hi-Tech Expo.

Todd was still naked, though through the use of persistent hand gestures he'd persuaded one of the cops to bring him a towel that he could actually wear without pinching it together with one of his hands.

Wu entered the room and Todd looked to him hopefully, but Wu just shook his head sorrowfully and then said something to one of the younger officers.

Handcuffs appeared, and Todd was lifted off the bed.

'I have spoken to my superiors, and they would like me to bring you in.'

'Oh, Christ. Look, I can't –'

'The local jail is awful, Todd. I am personally and professionally humiliated to take an educated foreigner there. It is not up to the standards of your country, I can assure you.'

'I'm begging you, Mr Wu. Don't take me to jail. My family can't know about this. I'll lose everything. I fucked up. I *know* I fucked up, but I am begging you to let me go.'

Wu seemed to hesitate for a moment. After a tired shrug that conveyed noncommitment, he spoke softly to the five others in the room, and they quickly filed out, leaving Wu and Todd alone.

'Todd, I see by your travel papers that you are to leave China in three days' time.'

'That's right.'

'I may be able to prevent you spending time in jail, but it will require some help on your part.'

'I swear to you! Anything at all and I will do it.'

Wu still seemed to be vacillating, as if he could not decide.

Finally he stepped closer, then said softly, 'Go back to your room. Tomorrow, return to your normal routine here at the trade fair. Speak to no one about this.'

'Of course! Of course. Oh my God, I can't thank you enough!'

'You will be contacted, but perhaps not until you return to your country.'

Todd stopped his proclamations of thanks. 'Oh. Okay. That's . . . whatever you say.'

'Let me give you a warning as a friend, Todd. The people that will ask a favor of you will expect you to repay them. They will retain all the evidence against you about what happened here.'

'I understand,' he said, and it was true, he *did* understand. No, Todd Wicks was not particularly worldly, but at this point he had the distinct impression that he'd been set up.

Damn it! So fucking stupid.

But set up or not, they had him. He would do anything to keep that video from getting to his family.

He would do whatever Chinese intelligence asked him to do.

11

Jack Ryan, Jr, got the senior staff meeting scheduled for eleven a.m., and now he was back at his desk, looking over some more analysis that he would present today. His co-workers were focusing on material they had intercepted from CIA discussing the death of the five Libyans in Turkey two months ago. It was no surprise that CIA was more than a little curious about who the killers were, and Jack found it at once creepy and exciting to read the Langley spooks' theories about the well-orchestrated hit.

The smart ones knew good and well the new Libyan government's spies had not orchestrated this as a revenge operation against the Turkish cell, but beyond that there was little consensus.

The Office of the Director of National Intelligence had worked the equation for a few days, and even Jack's girlfriend, Melanie Kraft, had been tasked with going over the evidence about the assassinations. Five different killings in the same night, all in different manners and all against a cell with a decent level of communication between its members. Melanie was impressed, and in the report she had written for her boss, Mary Pat Foley, director of national intelligence, she had raved about the skill of the perpetrators.

Jack would love to tell her some night over a bottle of wine that he was one of the hit men.

No. Never. Jack pushed that out of his mind immediately.

Melanie had concluded that whoever the actors were in the assassinations, there was nothing to indicate they were any threat to the United States. The targets were enemies of the United States, after a fashion, and the perpetrators were talented killers who took some serious chances but managed to pull it off with skill and guile, so the ODNI did not linger over the event for long.

Even though the U.S. government's understanding of the events of the night in question was limited, its knowledge of the Libyan cell itself was interesting to Jack. NSA had managed to pull text messages off the five men's mobile devices. Jack read the translated transcripts from NSA – short, cryptic dialogue that made it clear that these men did not know any more about the identity or overall mission of this Center character than did Ryan himself.

Odd, Jack thought. *Who works for someone so shadowy they do not have a clue who they are working for?*

Either the Libyans were utter fools or their new employer was incredibly competent at his own security.

Jack did not think the Libyans were fools. Lazy in their PERSEC, perhaps, but that was a result of the fact that they felt the only group after them was the new Libyan intelligence agency, and the JSO men did not think much of their successors' capabilities.

Jack almost smiled at this as he scanned files on his monitor, looking for anything else from CIA with which to update the senior staff in his meeting.

Just then Jack felt a presence behind him. He looked over his shoulder to see his cousin, Dom Caruso, sitting down on the edge of Jack's wraparound desk. Standing behind Dom were Sam Driscoll and Domingo Chavez.

'Hey guys,' he said. 'I'll be ready to head up in about five minutes.'

They all had serious looks on their faces.

'What's wrong?' Jack asked.

Chavez answered, 'Clark quit.'

'Quit what?'

'He turned his resignation in to Gerry and Sam. He'll spend a day or two getting his stuff cleaned up, but he'll be out of here by midweek.'

'Oh, shit.' Ryan felt an immediate sense of foreboding. They needed Clark. 'Why?'

Dom said, 'His hand is still messed up. And he's worried all his shine time on TV last year might compromise The Campus. He's made his mind up. He's done.'

'Can he really stay away?'

Chavez nodded. 'John doesn't do things in half-measures. He's going to work on being a granddad and a husband.'

'And a country gentleman.' Dom said it with a smile.

Ding chuckled. 'Something like that, I guess. Jeez, who'd'a thunk it?'

The meeting started a few minutes late. John was not in attendance. He had an appointment with his orthopedic surgeon in Baltimore, and he was not one for dramatic good-byes, so he slipped out quietly as everyone was heading up to the ninth-floor conference room.

The early conversation was about John and John's decision to leave, but Hendley very quickly brought everyone's attention back to the problem at hand.

'Okay. We've spent a lot of time scratching our heads and looking over our shoulders. Jack warns me he doesn't have much in the way of answers for us today, but we're going to get an update from him and Gavin about the forensic investigation of the drive.'

Both Ryan and Gavin spoke to the others for fifteen minutes about everything they had learned from the hard drive as well as from CIA sources. They discussed the hacking of

Emad Kartal's computer by Center, the work Center gave the Libyans in Istanbul, and the fact that Center seemed to be setting the Libyans up to penetrate a network in the future, though he apparently changed his mind.

Gerry Hendley finally asked the question that everyone in the room wanted answered. 'But why? Why did this Center guy just sit there and watch you guys kill his entire cell of assets in Istanbul? What possible reason did he have?'

Ryan looked around the conference room for a moment. He drummed his fingers on the table. 'I don't know for sure.'

'But you have a suspicion?' asked Hendley.

Jack nodded. 'I suspect Center knew for some time that we were on our way to kill the Libyan cell.'

Hendley was gobsmacked. 'They knew about us before that night? How?'

'I have no idea. And I could be wrong.'

Chavez asked, 'If you are right, if he knew we were coming to Turkey to kill the Libyans who were working for him, why the hell didn't he warn the Libyans?'

Jack said, 'Again, just speculation. But . . . maybe they were bait. Maybe he wanted to watch us in action. Maybe he wanted to see if we could do it.'

Rick Bell, Jack's boss on the analytical side, leaned in to the table. 'You are taking some massive subjective leaps in your analysis, Jack.'

Ryan's hands came up in surrender. 'Yes. You are one hundred percent right about that. Maybe it's just a feeling I have at this point.'

'Go where the data leads. Not where your heart leads. No offense, but you might just be freaked out by finding yourself on candid camera,' Bell cautioned.

Jack agreed, but he wasn't crazy about the comment from the head of analysis. Ryan had an ego, and did not like admitting that he was letting his own personal prejudices into the equation. But deep inside he knew Rick was right. 'Understood. We're still trying to put this puzzle together. I'll keep at it.'

Chavez said, 'There is something I don't get, Gavin.'

'What's that?'

'Center ... this guy who obviously had control of the machine. He wanted Ryan to know he was watching.'

'Yeah, obviously.'

'If he was able to delete all but the faintest trace of his malware, why did he not delete every e-mail related to him and his operation?'

Gavin said, 'I've spent weeks racking my brain on that one, Domingo, and I think I've got it figured out. Center would have deleted the delivery malware as soon as he made a successful penetration on the computer, but he didn't scrub the rest of the drive, the e-mails and stuff, because he did not want to tip off Kartal that he had hacked his machine. Then, when Ryan got there and whacked Kartal, Center pushed those photos of the rest of the team to the computer so that Ryan would see them and e-mail them to his own address or grab a thumb drive or a DVD off the desk and load them on there.'

Jack interrupted, 'And then take them back here to The Campus and put them on my machine.'

'Exactly. His idea was cunning, but he messed up. He thought of every way Jack could have moved that data back to The Campus except for one.'

Hendley said, 'Stealing the whole damned computer.'

'That's right. Center sure as hell did not plan on Jack running out the front door with the computer under his arm. That was so dumb it was brilliant.'

Jack's eyes narrowed. 'Maybe it was just brilliant.'

'Whatever. The important thing is you didn't just bring a disk back home to check it out.'

Ryan explained for the benefit of anyone in the room who wasn't following. 'He was trying to use me to plant a virus on our system.'

Biery said, 'Damn right. He dangled those e-mails so you would bite, which you did, but he figured you'd leave with the digital data but not the entire device. I'm sure his plan was to completely sanitize the computer before the cops arrived.'

Hendley asked Biery, 'Could Center have infected our network that way?'

'If his malware was good enough, yes. My network has anti-intrusion measures that are better than any government network. Still . . . all it takes is one asshole with a thumb drive or a USB cable to bring all this down.'

Gerry Hendley looked off into space for a moment before saying, 'Guys . . . everything you have told us today makes me more certain that someone knows a lot more about us than we want them to. I don't know who this potential bad actor is, but until we get more information, our operational stand-down will continue. Rick, Jack, and the rest of the analytical team will keep up the hard work of finding out Center's identity through all the traffic we have access to from Fort Meade and Langley.'

Hendley turned to Gavin Biery. 'Gavin? Who is Center? Who does he work for? Why did he focus so hard on compromising us?'

'Beats me. I'm not an analyst.'

Gerry Hendley shook his head, unsatisfied with the non-answer. 'I'm asking for your best guess.'

Gavin Biery took off his glasses and rubbed them with his handkerchief. 'If I *had* to guess? I'd say it was the best, most organized, and most ruthless cyberespionage and cyberwarfare folks on the planet.

'I'd say it was the Chinese.'

The conference room erupted in low groans.

12

Wei Zhen Lin drank yellow peach juice from a tall glass as he stood in the sun. His toes were sunk into wet pebbled sand, and water licked his bare feet and rose to his ankles, nearly touching the fabric of his slacks, which he'd pulled up to his shins to keep dry.

Wei did not look like a beachgoer. He wore a white pinpoint oxford shirt and a regimental tie, and he held his sport coat over his shoulder with a crooked finger while he gazed out to sea, across blue-green water that shone under the noon sun.

It was a beautiful day. Wei caught himself wishing he came here more than once a year.

A voice called from behind. 'Zongshuji?' It was one of his titles, general secretary, and though Wei was president as well, his staff put his role as general secretary of the Communist Party well above his role as president of the country.

The party was more important than the nation.

Wei ignored the voice, and now he regarded two gray vessels in the water just a mile or so offshore. A pair of Type 062C coastal patrol boats sat motionless on the still water, their cannons and antiaircraft guns pointed skyward. They looked powerful, impressive, and ominous.

But to Wei they looked inadequate. It was a big ocean, a big sky, both were full of threats, and Wei knew that he had powerful enemies.

And he feared that after the meeting he was about to have

with his nation's top military official, his list of enemies would soon grow even larger.

The pinnacle of power in China is the nine-member Politburo Standing Committee, the tiny body that sets policy for the nation's 1.4 billion citizens. Each year in July the members of the PSC, as well as dozens if not hundreds of adjuncts and assistants, leave their offices in Beijing and travel one hundred seventy miles to the east to the secluded coastal resort of Beidaihe.

It is suggested that more strategic decisions affecting China and its people are decided in the small meeting rooms in the buildings in the forests and along the beaches of Beidaihe than in Beijing itself.

Security had been tight at this year's Standing Committee retreat, even more so than in recent times. And there was good reason for the extra protection. President and General Secretary Wei Zhen Lin had retained his hold on power, thanks to the backing of his nation's military, but popular dissent in the nation was growing against the Communist Party of China and protest rallies and civil disobedience, something not seen in large scale in China since the Tiananmen Square massacre of 1989, had sparked in several of the provinces. In addition to this, though the coup plotters had been arrested and imprisoned, many associates of the leadership of the plot still remained in positions of high authority, and Wei feared a second coup attempt more than anything else in this world.

In the more than ninety years the CPC had been in existence, it had never been as fractured as it was at this moment.

Several months ago Wei had been one second away from putting a bullet into his own brain. He woke most nights covered in sweat from the nightmares of reliving those moments, and these nightmares had created paranoia.

Despite his fears, Wei was well protected now. He remained under heightened guard by members of China's security and military forces, because China's security and military forces had a stake in the man now, they *owned* him, and they wanted him safe from harm.

But this provided little comfort for Wei, because he knew that, at any moment, the People's Liberation Army could turn against him, and his protectors would become his executioners.

The Beidaihe conference had closed the day before, the majority of the attendees had returned to the bustle and smog of Beijing, but President Wei had delayed his trip west for a day to meet with his closest ally in the Politburo. He had things to discuss with General Su, the chairman of the Central Military Commission and, he explained when he asked for the meeting, the government offices in Beijing were not a secure enough venue for this matter to be addressed.

Wei had high hopes for this informal meeting because the conference itself had been a failure.

He'd opened the week of talks with a frank and bleak update on the economy.

The news of the attempted coup had only scared more investors away from the nation, weakening the economy further. Wei's enemies had waved this fact around as even more evidence that his opening of China's markets to the world had made China beholden to the whims and whimsy of the capitalist whore nations. Had China remained closed, and traded exclusively with like-minded nations, then the economy would not have been so vulnerable.

Wei had listened to these statements from his political foes, and he had done so without any outward expression. But he found the assertions idiotic, and those making the assertions to be fools. China had benefited greatly from world trade, and had China remained closed off for the past thirty years, while the rest of the planet underwent mind-boggling economic development, either the Chinese would now be eating dirt like the North Koreans or, more likely, the proletariat would have stormed Zhongnanhai and killed every last man and woman in government office.

Ever since the coup attempt he had worked tirelessly, mostly in secret, on a new plan to right his nation's economic ship without destroying his government. He presented it at the retreat to the Standing Committee, and the Standing Committee had rejected it out of hand.

They made it plain enough to Wei; they held *him* responsible for the economic crisis, and they would not attach their support to any portion of his domestic plan to cut spending, wages, benefits, and economic development.

So Wei knew at yesterday's close of the Beidaihe conference that his preferred course of action was dead in the water.

Today he would lay the foundation for his secondary course of action. He felt it would work, but it would not be without hurdles as great or greater than some short-term domestic pain.

As he stood at the water's edge the voice from behind called again. 'General Secretary?'

Wei turned to the voice, found the man calling out among the phalanx of security guards surrounding him. It was Cha, his secretary.

'It's time?'

'I just received word. Chairman Su has arrived. We should get back.'

Wei nodded. He would have liked to stay out here all day

in his slacks and sleeves. But he had work to do, and this work would not keep.

He began walking up the beach, back to his obligations.

Wei Zhen Lin entered a small conference room adjacent to his quarters at the resort, and he found Chairman Su Ke Qiang waiting for him.

The two men embraced perfunctorily. Wei felt the collection of medals on General Su's left breast against his own chest.

Wei did not like Su, but he would not be in power without Su. He would likely not be alive without Su.

After their perfunctory embrace, Su smiled and took his seat at a small table adorned with an ornate traditional Chinese tea service. The big general – Su stood over six feet tall – poured tea for both men while their two secretaries took seats against the wall.

'Thank you for staying behind to speak with me,' Wei said.

'Not at all, *tongzhi*.' Comrade.

It was small talk at first, gossip about the other Standing Committee members and light discussion about the events of the retreat, but soon Wei's eyes hardened in seriousness. 'Comrade, I have tried to make our colleagues see the calamity that is about to transpire if we do not take desperate measures.'

'It has been a difficult week for you. You know that you have the full support of the PLA, and my own personal support, as well.'

Wei smiled. He knew that Su's support was hardly unconditional. It depended on Wei falling into line.

And Wei was about to do just that. 'Tell me about the readiness of your forces.'

'The readiness?'

'Yes. Are we strong? Are we prepared?'

Su's eyebrows rose. 'Prepared for *what*?'

Wei sighed for a moment. 'I tried to set in place difficult but necessary domestic austerity measures. I failed in this endeavor. But if we do nothing at all, by the end of the current five-year plan, China will find itself pushed back a generation or more in its development, we will be thrown from power, and the new leaders will drive us further into the past.'

Su said nothing.

Wei said, 'I now must accept my responsibility in adopting a new direction in improving China's strength.'

Wei looked into Su's eyes, and he saw the growing pleasure there as the realization came slowly.

Su asked, 'This new direction will require our military forces?'

With a nod, Wei answered, 'At the outset, there may be . . . *resistance* to my plan.'

'Resistance from within, or resistance from without?' Su asked before taking a sip of tea.

'I am speaking, Chairman, of foreign resistance.'

'I see,' said Su flatly. Wei knew that he was giving the man exactly what he wanted.

Su put down his cup and asked, 'What are you proposing?'

'I am proposing we project our military power to reassert ourselves in the region.'

'What will we gain from this?'

'Survival.'

'Survival?'

'An economic disaster can only be avoided by expanding territory, creating new sources of raw materials, new products and markets.'

'What territory are you talking about?'

'We need to project our interests more aggressively in the South China Sea.'

Su dropped the veil of detached interest and nodded vigorously. 'I absolutely agree. Recent events involving our neighbors have been troublesome. The South China Sea, territory that we have every right to control, is slipping away from us. The Philippine congress passed a Territorial Sea Baseline Bill, staking their claim to Huangyan Island, territory that belongs to our nation. India has entered into a partnership with Vietnam to drill for oil off Vietnam's coast, and they threaten to move their new aircraft carrier into the theater, provocatively challenging us and testing our resolve.

'Malaysia and Indonesia are actively interfering with our economic zones in the South China Sea, seriously affecting our fishery operations there.'

'Indeed,' Wei said, agreeing to all of Su's points.

The chairman was smiling as he said, 'With some carefully calculated advances into the South China Sea, we will bolster our nation's finances.'

Wei shook his head like a professor disappointed with his student's lack of comprehension of a fundamental principle. He said, 'No, Chairman Su. *That* will not save us. Perhaps I did not make the gravity of our economic problems clear. We are not going to *fish* our way back to prosperity.'

Su made no reaction to the condescension. 'Then there is more?'

'Total dominance in the South China Sea is step one, and it is necessary for us to enact steps two and three.' Wei paused, knowing that Su would not expect what he was about to say.

Wei also knew that this was his last jumping-off point. Once the next words left his lips there would be no going back.

After another moment's hesitation he said, 'Step two is returning Hong Kong to the mainland, abolishing the Hong Kong Basic Law, and keeping the territory as a Special Economic Zone. Our long-standing policy of "One country, two systems" will remain in effect, of course, but I want us to really *be* one country. Beijing should be receiving revenue streams from Hong Kong capitalists. We do provide them security, after all. My advisers tell me that if we can take Hong Kong, and its dirty little cousin Macau, and fold them as a single unit into the SEZ of Shenzhen, we will quadruple our gains over what we now receive from the territory. The money will support the CPC as well as the capitalists, who have been doing quite well for themselves there.

'I also want to push moral national education curriculums in schools and increased membership in the Communist Party among government employees in Hong Kong. "Nationalism" has become a dirty word to them, and I will put an end to that.'

Su nodded, but Wei saw the wheels spinning in his head. Right now the general would be thinking about resistance from the semi-autonomous state of Hong Kong, as well as resistance from the UK, the EU, America, Australia, and any other nation that had massive amounts of capital investment there.

Hong Kong and Macau were Special Administrative Regions of China, which meant they had enjoyed capitalism and nearly autonomous rule since the British handed them over in 1997. This was to last for fifty years, according to China's agreement. No one in China, certainly no *leader* of China, had ever proposed dissolving the autonomy of the two city-states and returning them to the mainland.

Su said, 'I see why we would need to control the South China Sea first. Many nations would find it in their national interests to fight to retain Hong Kong's current status.'

Wei all but waved this comment away. 'Yes, but I plan on making it very clear to the international community that I am a businessman, I am pro-free-market capitalism, and any change with how Hong Kong and Macau operate will be very minor and almost imperceptible to the outside world.'

Before Su could comment, Wei added, 'And step three will be the long-standing stated goal of our nation, the absorption of Taiwan. Doing this in the right way, turning it into the largest Special Economic Zone, will assure, my advisers project, a retention of the vast majority of its economic viability. Obviously there will be resistance from the Republic of China and its allies, but I am not talking about invading Taiwan. I am talking about reabsorbing through diplomacy and economic pressure, controlling access to waterways, and through this showing them, over time, that the only viable option for their people is for them to accept their future as a proud member of our New China.

'Remember, Chairman Su, that China's SEZs, an economic model I refined and promoted throughout my career, are looked on around the world as a success, a show of détente with capitalism. I personally am looked at by the West as a force for positive change. I am not naive, I recognize that my personal reputation will suffer after it becomes clear what our objectives are, but that is of no importance to me. Once we have what we need, we will grow beyond any prognostications we could make at this time. I will make it my responsibility to repair any relationships damaged by these actions.'

Su did not hide his surprise at the audacity of the plan put forth by the mild-mannered president, a man who was, after all, a mathematician and economist, and no military leader.

Wei saw this near shock on the general's face, and he smiled. 'I have studied the Americans. I understand them.

Their economy, to be sure, but also their culture and their politics. They have a saying. "Only Nixon could go to China." Do you know this saying?'

Su nodded. 'Of course.'

'Well, Chairman Su, I will see that they have a new saying: "Only Wei could retake Taiwan."'

Su recovered somewhat. 'The Politburo, even with the new membership after the . . . unpleasantness, will be difficult to convince. I say this with some expertise, having spent the better part of a decade encouraging a more hawkish stance with regard to our neighbors and our rightful ocean territory.'

Wei nodded thoughtfully. 'After the events that transpired recently, I no longer expect to persuade my comrades through reason alone. I won't make that mistake again. I would like, instead, to slowly begin maneuvers, politically and with your force projection, that will make step one of my vision a reality before proceeding with steps two and three. Once we have all the ocean territory around our two prizes, the Politburo will see that our goals are within our grasp.'

Su took this to mean that Wei would adopt small measures at first that would cascade into larger measures as success came closer.

'What is your time frame, *tongzhi*?'

'I want your help in determining that, of course. But speaking from the perspective of someone with an eye toward our economy, I think within two years the South China Sea, territorial waters five hundred miles to the south of our shores, should be under our control. Some three and a half million square kilometers of ocean. We will void our agreement with Hong Kong twelve months after this. Then Taiwan should be under our control by the end of the five-year cycle.'

Su thought carefully before speaking. Finally, he said, 'These are bold steps. But I agree they are necessary.'

Wei knew Su knew little about the economy past that portion of it that involved China's military-industrial complex. He surely did not know what was necessary to revive it. Su wanted military power projection, and that was all.

But Wei did not say this. He instead said, 'I am glad that you agree with me, Chairman. I will need your help through every step.'

Su nodded. 'You started our conversation by asking me about the readiness of our forces. Sea denial operations, which is what you are asking for here, are among the capabilities of our Navy, but I would like to discuss this further with my admirals and intelligence staff. I would ask that you give me a few days to speak to my leadership and prepare a plan, based on what you have just told me lies before us. My intelligence staff can pinpoint our exact needs.'

Wei nodded. 'Thank you. Please prepare a preliminary report to hand-deliver to me in one week's time. We will speak of this in my personal quarters back in Beijing, and nowhere else.'

Su stood to leave and the men shook hands. President Wei knew that Chairman Su already had detailed plans to take every island, shoal, sandbar, and reef in the South China Sea. He also had plans to deny all access to Taiwan and to shell and rocket it back to the Stone Age. He might not, however, have much contingency drawn up regarding Hong Kong. A week's time should be adequate for this.

Wei knew that Su would be ecstatic to return to his offices and to brief his senior staff about the activities to come.

Ten minutes later Chairman Su Ke Qiang arrived at the eight-vehicle convoy that would whisk him 175 miles back to the capital. With him was his adjunct Xia, a two-star who had served alongside Su through all of his senior commands. Xia had been in the room during the meeting with Wei, silently listening and taking notes.

Once in the back of an armored Roewe 950 sedan, the two men looked at each other for a long moment.

'Your thoughts?' the two-star asked his boss.

Su lit a cigarette as he said, 'Wei thinks we will fire a few warning shots into the South China Sea and the world community will step back and allow us to proceed unmolested.'

'And *you* think?'

Su smiled a sly but genuine smile as he slipped his lighter back into his coat pocket. '*I* think we are going to war.'

'War with who, sir?'

Su shrugged. 'America. Who else?'

'Excuse me for saying so, sir. But you do not sound displeased.'

Su laughed aloud behind a cloud of smoke. 'I welcome the endeavor. We are ready, and only by bloodying the nose of the foreign devils in a quick and decisive action will we be able to pursue all of our goals in the region.' He paused, then darkened a little before saying, 'We are ready . . . only if we act now. Wei's five-year plan is foolish. All his objectives need to be met within a year or the opportunity will be lost. Lightning war, attack quickly on all fronts, create a new reality on the ground that the world at large will have no choice but to accept. *That* is the only way to succeed.'

'Will Wei agree to this?'

The general shifted his large frame in his seat to look out the window as the eight-vehicle motorcade headed west toward Beijing.

With determination he replied, 'No. Therefore, I will have to create a reality that *he* will have no choice but to accept.'

13

Valentin Kovalenko awoke shortly before five a.m. in his room at the Blue Orange, a health club, vacation spa, and hotel in the northeastern Letňany district of Prague, Czech Republic. He'd spent three days here already, and he'd taken saunas and received massages and eaten excellent food, but apart from these luxuries he had prepared diligently for an operation he would undertake before dawn this morning.

His orders had come, as the mafia man who'd helped break him out of prison had promised, via a secure instant-messaging program called Cryptogram. Shortly after arriving at the safe house set up by the Saint Petersburg mafia, he'd been given a computer with the software, along with documents and money and instructions to locate himself in Western Europe. He had done as he was told, settling in the south of France and logging in to his machine once a day to check for further orders.

For two weeks there was no contact. He went to a local physician and received treatment and medicines for maladies lingering from his time in the Moscow prison, and he recovered his strength. Then one morning he opened Cryptogram and began his daily password and authentication process. Once that was completed, a single line of text appeared in the window of the instant messenger.

'Good morning.'

'Who are you?' Kovalenko typed.

'I am your handler, Mr Kovalenko.'

'What do I call you?'

'Call me Center.'

With a half-smile Valentin typed, 'May I know if that is Mr Center, or Ms Center, or are you perhaps a construct of the Internet itself?'

This pause was longer than the others.

'I think the latter is fair to say.' After a short pause the words on Kovalenko's screen came faster still. 'Are you prepared to get started?'

Valentin fired back a quick response. 'I want to know who I am working for.' It seemed reasonable, although he had been warned by the mobster that his new employer was not reasonable.

'I acknowledge your concern about your situation, but I do not have the time to assuage these concerns.'

Valentin Kovalenko imagined he was carrying on a conversation with the computer itself. The responses were stiff, wooden, and logical.

He is a native English speaker, Kovalenko thought to himself. But then he checked that. Even though Valentin was fluent in English, he could not be sure someone else was a native speaker. Perhaps if he heard him talk he would know for certain, but for now he just told himself his master was comfortable with the language.

Kovalenko asked, 'If you are an entity that serves to commit espionage via computer, what is my role?'

The reply appeared quickly: 'In-field human asset management. Your specialty.'

'The man who picked me up outside the prison said you were everywhere. All-knowing, all-seeing.'

'Is that a question?'

'If I refuse to follow instructions?'

'Use your imagination.'

Kovalenko's eyebrows rose. He was not sure if that

showed a sense of humor on the part of Center, or just a flat threat. He sighed. He'd already begun working for the entity by coming here and setting up his apartment and computer. It was clear he had no leverage to argue.

He typed, 'What are my instructions?'

Center answered this, which led Valentin to the job in Prague.

His physical recovery from the ravages of bronchitis and ringworm and a diet that consisted primarily of barley soup and moldy bread was an ongoing process. He had been healthy and fit before going into the Matrosskaya Tishina pretrial detention facility, and he retained the discipline to recover faster than most men.

The gym here at the Blue Orange had helped him along. He'd worked out for hours each of the past three days, and this, along with his early-morning jogs, had filled him with energy and vigor.

He dressed in his running gear, a black tracksuit with just a thin gray racing stripe on one side, and he pushed his black knit cap over his dirty-blond hair. He slipped a black-bladed folding knife, a set of lock picks, and small felt bag the size of his fist into his jacket pocket, and he zipped the pocket closed.

After this came dark gray socks and his black Brooks running shoes, and he put thin Under Armour gloves over his hands before heading out of his room.

In moments he was outside the hotel, jogging to the south in a cool light rain.

For the first kilometer of his run he jogged in the grass along Tupolevova, and he saw not a soul in the dark around him other than a couple of delivery vehicles that rumbled past on the street.

He turned west on Křivoklátská and kept his pace leisurely. He noticed that his heart was beating harder than usual this early in the run, and that surprised him somewhat. When he worked in London he would run ten kilometers through Hyde Park most mornings, and he barely broke a sweat except during the warmest months of the year.

He knew he wasn't as fit as he'd been in the UK, but, he suspected, his marginal health was not the reason for his thumping chest.

No, he was nervous this morning because he was back in the field.

Even though Valentin Kovalenko had risen to the rank of deputy *rezident* of the United Kingdom in Russia's foreign intelligence agency, the SVR, a person in that position does not customarily undertake actual field operations; brush passes and dead drops and black-bag jobs are the work of men lower on the espionage food chain. No, Valentin Kovalenko did most of his work as a spymaster from the comforts of his office in the Russian embassy or over beef Wellington at Hereford Road or perhaps ox cheek with watercress, bone marrow, and salsa cooked in a Josper oven at Les Deux Salons.

Those were the good old days, he thought to himself as he slowed his jog a bit to try to control the heavy thump in his chest. Today his work would not be particularly dangerous, though it would be considerably less highbrow than his life and work in London had been.

He had done his share of grunt work for Russia, of course; no one could make deputy *rezident* without coming up the ranks. He'd been an illegal, an operative working without official cover status for Russia, in many postings across Europe, as well as a brief stint in Australia. He'd been younger then, of course, just twenty-four when he worked in Sydney and still under thirty by the time he left operations for desk work. But he enjoyed the duty.

He turned on to Beranových, heading north, following a route he'd been running for the past two mornings, though today he would divert from the route, but for only a few minutes.

The rain picked up a bit, soaking him but giving him better cover than the darkness alone could provide.

Kovalenko smiled. Spies loved the dark. And spies loved the rain.

He felt good to be performing this task, though as far as he was concerned this was a weird little op, and whatever his minders hoped to achieve with it, Valentin thought the probability for success was rather low.

Just a few dozen meters after turning onto Beranových he looked both left and right, and then back over his shoulder. The street was clear, so he darted quickly to the right. He knelt down at a small iron gate in a whitewashed wall and quickly picked the simple lock. It was a residential gate, and the lock was a cinch, but it had been so long since he'd tested his lock-picking skills he allowed himself a brief smile as he put the picks back in his jacket.

In seconds he was in the front garden of a two-story home, and he ran forward, black clothing on a black morning, moving to the right of the house and then passing through a wooden gate that separated front yard from backyard. He ran past an aboveground swimming pool that was closed for the year, and he made his way between a potting shed and a storage shed to a back wall that ran along the eastern property line of the private home. In seconds Valentin Kovalenko was over this wall, dropping down into wet grass, where he found himself exactly where his research on Google Maps told him he would be.

He was now past the walls, exterior lights, and guard shacks surrounding the Science and Technology Park VZLÚ.

Kovalenko's new minder, the English speaker named Center who communicated via secure instant messaging, had not told him the point of today's exercise, or even much about the target itself other than the address and the marching orders of his mission there. But the Russian did his own research, and from it he learned that VZLÚ was an aerospace research and test facility, and the work here focused on aerodynamics, aircraft engines, and helicopter rotors.

It was a large campus comprising many buildings and different test sites.

Whatever Valentin's employer wanted here, it would not be up to Valentin himself to get it. Instead he'd been ordered to simply breach the physical security, and to leave some items behind.

Under cover of darkness and rain he knelt down in the first small parking lot he came to, and he took the bag out of his jacket pocket. From it he pulled a matte gray computer thumb drive and, against his better judgment, he simply laid it down in a parking space. The device was labeled 'Test results,' but he was careful to leave it facedown.

Kovalenko was no fool. He was certain this thumb drive did not contain any test results, or no real test results, anyway. It would contain a computer virus, and if Valentin's employer was any damn good, the virus would be disguised and built to execute as soon as it was attached via a USB port to any computer in the network here. The plan was, it was clear to Kovalenko, that someone would find the drive and put it into their computer to see what files it contained. As soon as anything was opened on the drive, some sort of a virus would infect the computer, and then the network itself.

Valentin had been instructed to place only one drive outside each building in the facility so that the ruse would have a better chance of success. If a half-dozen techies all walked into the same building having just found a mysterious device in the parking lot, it would be more likely that two or more of them would bump into each other and red flags would go up. It was still likely that most people who found the drive would have suspicions but, Kovalenko knew through his own research about the facility, the network connected the different divisions together, so only one successful infection of a client machine, anywhere inside the VZLÚ, would affect the work of them all.

Just like a phishing e-mail, Valentin Kovalenko himself was an attack vector.

It wasn't a bad plan, Valentin admitted, but he did not know the details of the mission that would convince him it would be a success. He wondered what would happen once it became clear to the IT department of the science and technology concern that two dozen similar or identical thumb drives had just appeared on their property. That would tip them off that a client-based hacking attempt was under way, and that would probably cause them to shut their network down to search for the virus. Valentin did not know much about computer espionage, but he found it hard to believe that the virus would not then be detected and wiped clean before any major compromise of the system had taken place.

But again, Center had not seen fit to include him in the planning of the operation. It was somewhat insulting, really. Kovalenko assumed he was working for a corporate espionage outfit; this guy and his goons would know Kovalenko had been a high-ranking intelligence operative, trusted to a crucial posting, in one of the greatest espionage concerns in the world, the SVR.

As he crawled on his hands and knees between two small utility trucks parked in the lot near the property's small grass-field airport, on his way to drop another thumb drive onto the wet concrete, he wondered just who the fuck these industrial spies thought they were, using him as their errand boy.

He did have to admit, though, that this beat prison, the risk was low, and the pay was good.

14

The second meeting between President and General Secretary Wei Zhen Lin and Chairman Su Ke Qiang took place in Zhongnanhai, the government compound in central Beijing. Both Su's and Wei's offices were here, as well as Wei's living quarters, so an evening private meeting was arranged between the two in the study off Wei's private bedroom.

Wei's secretary was present, as was Su's second-in-command, much as they had been a week before at the Beidaihe resort on the coast. This evening would be different, however, because this time Chairman Su would be the one making the presentation.

A valet served tea for both men, offered nothing to the two secretaries, and then left them alone.

Wei had given Su a week to work with his intelligence staff to adopt a plan to project their power further into the South China Sea as the opening move of Wei's gambit to absorb Hong Kong and Taiwan. He knew that Su would have slept little, eaten little, and thought about nothing else in the interim.

Su had been thinking about sending men, ships, and planes into the South China Sea for more than a decade, after all.

As they sat down for their meeting, Chairman Su held his report in his hand. A second copy was carried by Xia, Su's second-in-command, and Wei thought he would be given one of the reports to look over while they discussed it.

But before he handed over the document, Chairman Su said, '*Tongzhi*, recently you were almost thrown from power because you spoke the truth to those around you, the truth was difficult to hear, and those around you would not listen to it.'

Wei agreed with a nod.

'I now find myself in a position similar to the one you found yourself in. You have laid out a five-year plan to bring the nation back to a strength and glory not enjoyed in generations. Reluctantly, however, I have to tell you about some aspects of our current military situation that will make your five-year plan difficult, if not impossible.'

Wei cocked his head in surprise. 'The objectives I seek are not going to be won through military power alone. I only need military support in controlling the area. Are we not as strong as the annual reports have led us to believe?'

Su waved this away with his hand. 'We are strong, militarily. The strongest we have ever been, overall. Twenty percent growth in expenditures over the past two decades have built our land, sea, air, and space capabilities greatly.'

After this, Su heaved a sigh.

'Then tell me what troubles you.'

'I fear our strength is at its greatest point right now, right this moment, but our strength will soon wane relative to our adversaries'.'

Wei did not understand. He was on shaky ground with matters of a military nature. 'Why will it wane?'

Su paused long enough for Wei to understand that he would not answer the question immediately or directly. The explanation he would deliver would involve some background. 'We can, beginning tomorrow morning, eliminate any opposition in our region. But that is not what we need. We must prepare to combat one adversary, and one adversary only. Once we neutralize this foe, the rest of our potential conflicts will be won before they are even fought.'

Wei said, 'You think the United States will involve itself in our forays into the South China Sea?'

'I am certain of it, comrade.'

'And our military capability –'

'I will be frank with you. Our conventional capability is, overall, a shadow of that of the United States. In virtually every category, number of weapons, quality of equipment, training of forces, down to the last ship, aircraft, tank, truck, and sleeping bag, the Americans have superior equipment. They have also spent the last ten years fighting, while we have spent it training.'

Wei's face hardened. 'It sounds like our nation has been poorly served by our military during the two-decade-long modernization.'

Su was not angered by this comment. Instead he nodded. 'That is the other side of the coin. This is the good news. Many aspects of our strategic modernization have been successful.

'We have a great advantage in one war-fighting discipline. In any conflict with any adversary, it is a given fact that we will possess complete and utter information dominance.

'Chairman Mao's army, the army that your father and my father served in, has been replaced by something greater. Mechanized C4ISR. Command, Control, Computers, Communications, Intelligence, Surveillance, and Reconnaissance. We are well resourced, well connected, well organized. And our forces are in place for an immediate attack.'

'Attack? You are speaking of cyberwarfare?'

'Cyberwarfare and cyberespionage, communications between systems and forces to optimize their effect. The complete informationization of the battle space. We are the betters of the Americans by a wide margin.'

Wei said, 'You told me you had bad news. This sounds like good news.'

'The bad news, General Secretary, is that the timetable you asked me to support with my military is unrealistic.'

'But we must do this within the close of the party conference, within five years. Any longer and our leadership roles will diminish, and we cannot be certain that –'

'You misunderstand me,' said the chairman. 'I am saying there is no way we can take *more* than one year to achieve our objectives. You see, this new capability is our only real, true, tactical advantage over the Americans. And it is an incredible advantage. But it will wane. The Americans are building their cyberdefenses quickly, and their country and their forces are quick to adapt in the face of adversity. The U.S. network defense, at this moment, is based primarily on reactive controls. But America's Cyber Command is quickly changing that, and they are changing the landscape for the future of warfare. President Ryan has increased all resources for Cyber Command, and it will soon have an effect on our capabilities.'

Wei understood. 'You are saying the time to use this is now?'

'The window will close, and I fear it will not reopen. Ever again. America is catching up. Bills are moving along in their Congress that will modernize their domestic computer infrastructure. President Ryan's administration is taking the matter seriously. If we slowly trickle out our . . . *your* program for expansion, we will disadvantage ourselves greatly.'

'You want to begin immediately.'

'We *must* begin immediately. We must reassert our belief that the South China Sea territory is a core interest of China, and we must push for control of the sea now. Within days, not weeks, we must strengthen our patrols down to the Strait of Malacca and begin moving naval and marine forces to the Spratlys and Huangyan Island. I can land forces on some of the uninhabited islands within the week. It is all in the report. Then we must announce our new relationship with Hong Kong, and begin the blockade with Taiwan, all in the next six months. In a year, with our aggressive and forward-thinking attitude apparent to all, we will have met all our goals and the Americans will be too busy licking their own wounds to stop us.'

Wei thought it over for a moment. 'America is the only strategic threat?'

'Yes. Especially with Jack Ryan in the White House. Just as in our war with Russia, he is a problem once again. Not only from the direct threat of his military, but also in the bluster we are seeing from our neighbors. They tell themselves that China will do nothing against any ally of America as long as Ryan is in power.'

Wei said, 'Because he defeated us so soundly during the last war.'

Su took issue with this. 'It is debatable that he defeated us. The Russians were involved as well, you might remember.'

Wei put up a hand in apology. 'True, although I also remember that *we* attacked Russia.'

Su said flatly, 'We did not attack the United States. Even so, that was seven years ago, and still the American Navy routinely patrols the East China Sea, close to our waters. They have just sold another nine billion dollars' worth of military hardware to Taiwan. They threaten us with their access to the region. I do not have to tell you that eighty percent of the oil we use to fuel our nation comes through the Strait of Malacca, and the United States could threaten that flow with a carrier battle group. We must go on the offensive against them in order for your plan to succeed.'

Wei did not know much about military matters, but this fact was well known to everyone in the Politburo.

'But if we initiate hostilities, Ryan will –'

Su said, 'Comrade. We will initiate hostilities without Ryan knowing we are initiating hostilities. We can do this without revealing ourselves as the aggressors.'

Wei sipped tea. 'Some sort of computer attack?'

'Mr President, there is a secret operation of which you are not aware.'

Wei raised a narrow eyebrow behind his teacup. 'I should hope there are many secret operations of which I am not aware.'

Su smiled. 'Indeed. But this one, in particular, will be crucial to the realization of your goals. I only need to give one order and we will begin, slowly at first, and with great care that no positive attribution will be made to China, to damage the United States' ability to defeat us. We will send them off against other enemies, have them concentrate on issues at home that will require their focus and resources, and we can push our endeavors here in our region to the back of their consciousness.'

Wei said, 'That is a remarkable boast, Chairman Su.'

Su considered Wei's comment before saying, 'I don't make it lightly. We will strike many small cuts against the body, barely scratches to a giant like America. But the scratches will bleed, I promise you that. And the giant will weaken.'

'And they will not know it is we who are weakening them?'

'We will be an invisible army. America will not know they have been taken out at the knees by the PLA.'

'It sounds too good to be true.'

Su nodded slowly. 'There will be setbacks, failures of a tactical nature. No battle plan goes off without problems. But strategically we will succeed. I stake my reputation on this.'

Wei straightened in his chair. 'As the leader of our military forces, comrade, you will have to.'

Su smiled. 'I understand. But the infrastructure is in place, and we should exploit our advantage while we have it. The need is great. Our capability is great.'

Wei was taken aback that Su was, clearly, asking for the authority to implement the opening moves of the conflict at this moment. He wavered momentarily. 'The same thing was said by our predecessors. Shortly before the war with Russia.'

The chairman nodded gravely. 'I know. And I cannot counter your comment in any way, except to remind you that there is one great difference between then and now.'

'And what is that?'

'Seven years ago our predecessors underestimated Jack Ryan.'

Wei leaned back in the chair now, gazing at the ceiling for several seconds before chuckling without real mirth. 'We certainly will not make *that* mistake.'

'No. We will not. And if you agree to sanction me to initiate our opening moves, there is one more thing I would like you to consider. I have been speaking about the need to act in the South China Sea to protect our core interests for years. I am known, above everything else I have ever said or done, as the man who wants to take back the territory for China. If we begin our movements without your speaking out, I fear some in the West will feel these actions have been set in motion by me without your consent.'

Su leaned forward, and in a friendly, imploring tone he said, 'I do not want you to be marginalized. I think you should speak out strongly. Show the world you are in command.'

Wei said, 'I agree. I will speak out about our core interests in the South China Sea.'

Su was pleased by this. He smiled. 'So, let's be clear. You are authorizing my initial military actions?'

'Very well. You do what you think is best. You have my

blessing to initiate initial preparations. But I warn you now, Chairman, that if this plot of yours is uncovered, and this threatens our enterprise, then I will ask you to cease your operation immediately.'

Su fully expected such a lukewarm sanction. 'Thank you. The actions we begin now will soften the enemy's blows if hostilities ensue later. You can rest easy knowing that your decision tonight has helped our endeavor greatly.'

Wei Zhen Lin just nodded.

Su left the meeting knowing good and well that Wei Zhen Lin had no idea what he had just authorized.

Chairman Su was back in his office twenty minutes later. He'd asked Xia, his two-star adjutant, to personally put a call through for him, and when Xia leaned in through the doorway and said, 'He's on the phone,' the big chairman nodded curtly and waved his adjutant back out the door with his fingertips.

When the door shut, Su lifted the phone to his ear. 'Good evening, Doctor.'

'Good evening, Comrade Chairman.'

'I have important news. This call serves to initiate your sanction authorizing Operation Earth Shadow.'

'Very well.'

'When will you begin?'

'Physical assets are in place, as you requested, so action will begin immediately. Once these are completed, in a week, two weeks at most, we will begin cyberkinetic operations. Things will proceed very quickly after that.'

'I understand. And how are the preparations for Operation Sun Fire?'

There was no pause. 'Preparations will be complete as soon as we receive a shipment of hardware on the way from

146

Shenzhen, and bring it online. In ten days we will be ready. I await your orders.'

'And I await mine.'

'Comrade Chairman?'

'Yes, Doctor?'

'I feel it my duty to remind you, once again, that key aspects of Earth Shadow, once initialized, are beyond my capability to rescind.'

Chairman Su Ke Qiang smiled into the phone. 'Doctor . . . I am *relying* on our inability to reverse course once Earth Shadow begins. Civilian leadership has sanctioned us to tip the first domino in the row as if we can simply stop the momentum before the second and third dominoes fall. The will of our president is strong at the moment, here before the onset of adversity. If he wavers under pressure, I will stress to him that the only way is forward.'

'Yes, Comrade Chairman.'

'You have your orders, Doctor. Do not expect to hear from me again until I contact you with sanction to initiate Sun Fire.'

'I will continue to report through channels.'

'I wish you fortune,' Su said.

'*Shi-shi.*' Thank you.

The phone went dead in Chairman Su's hand, and he looked at it with a chuckle before placing it back in its cradle.

Center was not one for small talk.

15

Silicon Valley is home to Intel and Apple and Google and Oracle and dozens of other major technology companies. In support of these firms, hundreds if not thousands of smaller businesses have sprung up in the area in the past twenty years.

Menlo Park, California, is in the Valley, just north of Palo Alto, and its office buildings and business parks house hundreds of high-tech start-ups.

In a midsized complex on Ravenswood Drive, just up the road from mega-tech research firm SRI, a sign on a glass door reads *Adaptive Data Security Consultants*. Below this, the sign claimed the company shared the same daytime hours of operation as all the other small tech start-ups that shared the business park. But the night security officer who drove by the business in his golf cart at four a.m. was not surprised to find several cars in the lot that had been there since his shift started six hours earlier.

The principals of ADSC, Lance Boulder and Ken Farmer, were well accustomed to working long hours. It came with the territory.

Lance and Ken had grown up next door to each other in San Francisco, and they all but lived on their computers in the early days of the Internet. By the time they were twelve the boys were building machines and customizing software, and at age fifteen the two friends had become accomplished hackers.

The hacking subculture among intelligent teenage boys

was a powerful force for Ken and Lance, and they began working together to break into the computer networks of their high school, local universities, and other targets around the world. They did no great damage, they weren't involved with credit card fraud or identity theft, nor did they sell data hauls to others – they were more in the game for the excitement and the challenge.

Other than a few graffiti attacks on website homepages for their school, they did not cause any harm.

But the local police didn't see it that way. Both boys were picked up for computer graffiti that was tracked back to them by their junior-high computer teacher, and Lance and Ken immediately confessed.

After a few weeks of community service they decided to reform their ways before they became adults, when such brushes with the law would stay on their records and could seriously affect their future prospects.

Instead they focused their talents and their energies in the right direction, and gained admittance to Caltech, majored in computer science, and then took jobs for computer software companies in Silicon Valley.

They were model citizens, but they were still hackers at heart, so in their late twenties they left the corporate world to start their own company, specializing in penetration testing, or 'pentesting,' known in the computer networking world as 'ethical hacking.'

They hired themselves out to the IT departments of banks, retail chains, manufacturers, and others, and then endeavored to break into their clients' networks and hack their websites.

And soon they boasted a one hundred percent success rate hacking their customers' systems.

They developed a reputation as some of the best 'white

hat' hackers in Silicon Valley, and the big antivirus companies, McAfee and Symantec, tried to buy them out several times, but the two young men were determined to grow their company into a powerhouse of its own.

Business grew along with their reputation, and soon they began pentesting networks under government contract, attempting to break into so-called bulletproof systems run by top-secret government contractors, looking for ways in that the black-hats – the malicious hackers – had not yet found. Lance and Ken and their two dozen employees had excelled in this task and, flush with fresh government contracts, ADSC was poised to expand again.

The two owners had come a long way in five years, but Lance and Ken still knew how to work twenty hours a day when a project demanded it.

Like tonight.

They and three more of their staff were working overtime because they had found a new exploit in a Windows server component that could be potentially calamitous for any secure government network. It had revealed itself during penetration testing on the network of a government contractor headquartered in nearby Sunnyvale, California.

Lance and Ken had discovered the vulnerability in the software, then they had built their own Trojan, a malware that leeches on to a legitimate process, and used it to climb into the secure network. From here they were astonished to find they could execute an 'upstream attack,' using the company's connection to the U.S. Department of Defense's secure network to make their way into the bowels of the U.S. military's most secure information databases.

Everyone at ADSC knew the implications for what they had found. If a smart and determined hacker discovered the vulnerability before Microsoft patched it, the black-hat could build his own virus to steal, alter, or erase terabytes of crucial data necessary for war fighting.

Lance and Ken had not alerted their customers, the DoD, or their colleagues at Microsoft's Digital Crimes Unit yet; they knew they had to be certain about their findings, so they tested through the night.

And this critical project would be going at full steam, even now at four in the morning, if not for one significant snag.

The power had just gone out in the entire office park.

'Well . . . that blows,' Lance said as he looked around the dark office. The glow from the monitors in front of the five men working there was the only light in the room. The computers were still running; the backup battery power supply attached to each machine kept the men from losing their data, although the batteries would keep the devices juiced for only an hour, so the men would need to power down if the electricity did not come back on soon.

Marcus, one of ADSC's lead data-flow analysts, grabbed a pack of cigarettes and a lighter from the drawer in his desk and stood up. As he stretched his arms and shoulders over his head he said, 'Who forgot to pay PG and E?'

Pacific Gas and Electric was the local utility, and none of the five young men in the room thought for a second the culprit was a missed payment. The office had two dozen workstations, several high-capacity servers in the basement server farm, and dozens of other electronic peripherals, all of which drew power from the grid.

This was not the first time they'd tripped a breaker.

Ken Farmer stood up, then took a quick swig of luke-warm Pepsi from a can. 'I'm going to take a leak and then I'll go down and flip the breaker.'

Lance said, 'I'm right behind you.'

Data-flow analysts Tim and Rajesh stayed at their machines, but put their heads in their hands to rest.

A resilient, powerful, and utterly secure computer network was a necessity for a company whose business plan consisted of tracking down computer hackers, and ADSC had the tools and the protocols in place to make sure that any cyber-attacks targeting their company did not make it through.

Lance and Ken focused great attention on making certain ADSC had all but bulletproofed its network.

But they did not place the same attention on the physical security of their property.

One hundred twenty yards from where Lance and Ken and their three employees stretched and smoked and pissed, a lone individual walked in the heavy mist hanging between trees alongside dark and quiet Ravenswood Drive, approaching the business park that housed ADSC. Other than the early hour and a slight altering of his path to stay out of the direct light of the streetlamps, the figure in no way appeared out of the ordinary.

He wore a black zip-up raincoat with the hood down, his gloved hands were empty, and his pace was a leisurely stroll.

Some thirty yards behind him, a second man walked the same path, but his pace was faster and he closed on the man ahead of him. He too wore a dark raincoat with the hood down.

And twenty yards behind the second pedestrian, a third man jogged up the path, rapidly gaining on the two ahead of him. He wore dark running clothes.

All three men formed together just a few yards in front of the parking lot of the complex, the jogger slowed to match the pace of the other two, and here the three turned as one and stepped onto the property.

With a continued air of nonchalance the men flipped the hoods of their jackets over their heads. Each man also wore a black fleece gaiter around his neck, and simultaneously they pulled these up with gloved hands until their faces were covered from the bottoms of their eyes down.

They stepped onto the small parking lot that would have been illuminated if not for the power outage.

All three reached under their jackets and pulled Belgian-made semiautomatic pistols, FN Five-seveNs. Each weapon carried twenty-one rounds of 5.7x28-millimeter ammunition, a potent handgun caliber.

Long silencers protruded from the muzzles of their guns.

A man with the call sign of Crane was in charge of the small unit. He had more men – seven in total served under him – but he felt his ingress would not require his full squad, so he brought along only two of his assets for this phase of the mission.

And he was correct. ADSC was not a hard target by any stretch of the imagination.

A single security guard worked on the premises, patrolling the office complex in a golf cart at this time of the early morning. He was cocooned in a zippered plastic weather enclosure to keep the mist off him.

When the lights had not come on after thirty seconds or so, the guard reached to his belt and pulled off his iPhone. He knew that of the six companies with offices here on the property, only a few guys at ADSC were actually on site early this morning. He decided he'd call them to see if they needed him to come over with a flashlight.

As the guard scrolled through his contact list, movement in the dark outside his plastic shell caught his eye. He glanced up and to his left.

*

Crane fired a single round through the clear plastic enclosure and into the forehead of the security guard at a range of five feet. Blood and brain matter splattered inside the enclosure, and the young man slumped forward. A mobile phone slid out of his fingertips, and it fell between his feet.

Crane unzipped the plastic, felt around in the pockets of the dead security guard, and retrieved a set of keys.

The three men then continued around the side of the building. It was dark back here, except for the single orange glow of a cigarette.

'Hey,' came an uncertain voice from behind the glow.

Crane raised his Five-seveN and fired three suppressed rounds into the darkness there. From the flashes of the muzzle blast he saw a young man tumbling back through an open doorway that led to a small kitchen.

Crane's two hooded assets ran forward and pulled the dead man back outside, and then they closed the door.

Crane pulled a walkie-talkie from his coat. He clicked the push-to-talk button three times.

Together the three men waited at the side door for thirty seconds. Then a black Ford Explorer appeared in the parking lot, racing forward with its lights off. It slowed and parked, and five more assets, all dressed the same as those already at the door but also wearing large backpacks, poured out of the Explorer.

The unit members had designated call signs, each man named after a different type of bird – Crane, Grouse, Quail, Stint, Snipe, Gull, Wigeon, and Duck. Crane was trained to lead, and the others were trained to follow, but each and every man in the team was trained to kill.

They had memorized the layout of the property from the

building's blueprints, and one of them had with him a schematic for the server farm in the basement, and together they entered through the kitchen door, moving silently in the darkness. They left the kitchen, headed up a hallway, and entered the front lobby. Here they split into two forces. Four men went to the stairwell; four more headed straight back, past the elevators, and toward the main lab.

Lance Boulder had pulled a flashlight from a toolbox in a closet near the kitchen, and he used this to head up the hall toward the stairwell to check the UPS system, the uninterruptable power supply battery unit that would be keeping his servers running. He hoped like hell that the breaker was, in fact, the culprit. He decided to check to see if power was out at the entire office park, so he took his BlackBerry from his belt and began typing a text message to Randy, the night security guard on the premises.

When he looked up from the BlackBerry he stopped dead in his tracks. There, just a few feet in front of him, his flashlight shone on a man dressed head to toe in black. Behind him were more men.

And then he saw the long handgun in the hand of the man in front.

Only a slight gasp passed his lips before Crane shot him twice in the chest. The silenced rounds barked in the hall. Lance's body slammed into the wall on his right and he spun to his left, then pitched over facedown.

His flashlight fell to the floor and illuminated the way ahead for the four killers, and they advanced toward the lab.

Ken Farmer was taking advantage of the power outage in his building. He had not left his desk or his computer for more than six hours, so now he was just finishing up in the bathroom. The emergency lights did not reach the hallway by the bathroom so, as he opened the door to return to his office, he literally had to feel his way for a few feet.

He saw the silhouettes of the men ahead, and he immediately knew they were not his colleagues.

'Who are you?' he asked. He was too shocked to be scared.

The first man in the group walked up to him quickly, then placed the hot tip of a pistol's silencer on his forehead.

Ken raised his hands slowly. 'We don't have any money.'

The silencer pushed him back, and he walked backward into the dark lab. As soon as he entered he saw black forms move around him, past him, and he heard the shouts of Rajesh and Tim, and then he heard the loud thumps of suppressed gunfire and the tinkling sounds of spent casings bouncing on the tile floor.

Farmer was led back to his desk, turned around, and placed in his chair by rough gloved hands, and from the light of the monitors in the room he saw Tim and Raj both lying on the floor.

His mind could not process the fact they had just been shot dead.

'Whatever you want . . . it's yours. Just please don't –'

Crane moved the silencer of his Five-seveN to Ken Farmer's right temple and then, at contact distance, he fired a single round. Bone and tissue sprayed the carpet, and the body fell onto the red mess.

Within seconds Stint called on the radio. In Mandarin he said, 'Building secure.'

Crane did not respond on the walkie-talkie, but instead he took a satellite phone out of his jacket. He pressed a single button, waited a few seconds, and then, speaking Mandarin himself, said, 'Power on.'

Within fifteen seconds the electricity returned to the building. While four of Crane's assets stood guard at the entrances to ADSC, three more assets went downstairs to the basement.

Crane sat at Ken's desk and opened Ken's personal e-mail. He began a new message, then added everyone on Ken's contact list to the address line, which ensured more than one thousand different addresses would receive the note. Crane then reached inside his jacket and pulled a small notepad, upon which a letter had been written in English. He transcribed this into the e-mail, his gloved fingertips slowing his typing speed to a crawl.

Family, Friends, and Colleagues,

I love you all, but I cannot go on. My life is a failure. Our company has been a lie. I am destroying everything. I am killing everyone. I have no other options.
I am sorry.

Peace, Ken

Crane did not hit send; instead he spoke into his walkie-talkie. Still in Mandarin, he said, 'Ten minutes.' He stood and stepped over Farmer's body and headed to the basement, where the three others there had already begun the process of attaching a dozen homemade explosives in and around all of the servers. Each device was carefully placed near the hard drives and memory boards of the servers, ensuring that no digital records would remain.

Wiping the drives clean would have taken hours, and Crane did not have hours, so he had been ordered to take a more kinetic approach to his task.

In seven minutes they were finished. Crane and Gull returned to the lab, Crane passed his pistol to Gull, and then he leaned back to Farmer's keyboard and clicked send with the mouse, distributing the disturbing mass e-mail to 1,130 recipients.

Crane pocketed the notebook with the original letter, and he looked at Ken Farmer's body. Gull had placed his Five-seveN pistol in the dead man's right hand.

A few extra pistol magazines went into Farmer's pocket, and within a minute the four men were out of the lab. One of the team lit the fuses in the basement, and they headed back out the kitchen door and climbed into the waiting Explorer.

The four-man security team was already in the vehicle.

They drove out of the parking lot calmly and slowly, just thirteen minutes after entering the property. Four minutes after they turned off Ravenswood onto the highway, a massive explosion lit the early-morning sky behind them.

16

Jack Ryan, Jr, drove his black BMW 335i into D.C. for a morning run around the National Mall. Melanie was with him; she'd spent the night at his place. They were dressed in running clothes and running shoes, and Melanie wore a fanny pack on her hip that contained a water bottle, her keys and wallet, and a few other small odds and ends. They passed a thermos back and forth, sipping the coffee for a little more energy before their run.

Ryan pulled into the parking lot just north of the Capitol Reflecting Pool, and they finished their coffee while listening to NPR's *Weekend Edition*. There was a brief report about a murder-suicide with five victims the previous morning at a software company in Menlo Park, California.

Neither Jack nor Melanie commented on the piece.

When the news ended they climbed out of Jack's Beamer and walked to the Reflecting Pool, where they spent a few minutes stretching, sipping water, and watching the sunrise over the Capitol building and the morning joggers moving in all directions.

Soon they set off to the west. Though both Melanie and Jack were in excellent condition, Melanie was the all-around better athlete. She'd started playing soccer when her father, an Air Force colonel, had been stationed in Egypt during her teenage years, and she'd taken to the sport, earning herself a full-ride scholarship to American University, where she played as a tough and dependable defender and even led her team as captain her senior year.

She'd kept her fitness up in grad school and in the two years since college with running and many angry hours spent in the gym.

Jack had gotten used to three- or four-mile jogs a few mornings a week, and this helped him keep pace with Melanie for much of the run, but he found himself sucking wind after the end of the fourth mile. As they passed the Smithsonian he fought the urge to ask her to slow down; his ego would not allow him to admit he was struggling.

He noticed her looking over at him several times just past the fifth mile, and he knew his face would be showing the strain he felt in every part of his body, but he did not acknowledge her.

She spoke in a relaxed tone. 'Should we stop?'

'Why?' he asked, his voice clipped between hard gulps of air.

'Jack, if you need me to slow down a bit, all you have to do is say –'

'I'm fine. Race to the finish?' he asked, picking up the pace slightly and getting in front of her.

Melanie laughed. 'No, thanks,' she said. 'This pace is comfortable for me.'

Jack slowed back down a little, silently thanking God she did not call his bluff. He felt her eyes on him for another fifty yards or so, and he imagined she could see right through him. She was doing him a favor by not pushing him any further this morning, and he appreciated her for that.

All in all, they covered just over six miles. They finished at the Reflecting Pool, where they started, and as soon as they stopped, Jack doubled over, his hands on his knees.

'You okay?' she said as she put her hand on his back.

'Ye-yeah.' He struggled to recover. 'I might have a little cold coming on.'

She patted his back and pulled her water bottle from her fanny pack and offered it to him. 'Have a sip. Let's go home. We can stop and get oranges on the way and I'll make juice to go along with the omelet I am going to make you.'

Jack rose back up, squeezed a long stream of water into his mouth, and then kissed Melanie softly. 'I love you.'

'I love you, too.' Melanie took her bottle back and took a long gulp of water, and then, as she looked down the length of the bottle, her eyes narrowed.

A man in a trench coat and sunglasses stood a hundred feet farther along the Capitol Reflecting Pool, facing her. He was looking at them both, and he made no effort to avoid Melanie's gaze.

Jack was unaware of the man behind him. 'Ready to head back to the car?'

Melanie looked away from the man quickly. 'Yes. Let's go.'

They walked toward Pennsylvania Avenue, away from the direction of the man in the trench coat, but had gotten no more than twenty yards when Melanie reached out and took Jack by the shoulder. 'You know what? I hate to do this, but I just remembered I need to get home this morning.'

Ryan was surprised. 'You aren't coming back to my place?'

Her face registered disappointment. 'No, I'm sorry. I've got something I have to take care of for my landlord.'

'You need help? I'm handy with a screwdriver.'

'No . . . no, thanks. I'll take care of it.'

She saw Jack's eyes flick around, as if he was looking for a clue as to what really caused her to change her mind.

Before he could question her further about the sudden change of plans, she asked, 'We're still having dinner tonight in Baltimore with your sister, aren't we?'

Jack nodded slowly. 'Yes.' He paused. 'Is something wrong?'

'No, not at all. Other than the fact I forgot I had some things I needed to take care of around my place. I also have some stuff to do for work on Monday.'

'Something you can work on in your apartment, or are you going to Liberty Crossing?' Liberty Crossing was the name of the building complex that housed the ODNI, Melanie Kraft's place of employment.

'Just open-source stuff. You know how I am always moon-lighting.' She said it with a smile that she hoped did not appear as forced as it felt.

'I can give you a lift home,' he said, clearly not buying the story, but playing along.

'No need. I'll just jump on the Metro at Archives, I'll be home in no time.'

'All right,' said Jack, and he kissed her. 'Have a good day. I'll pick you up around five-thirty.'

'I can't wait.' As he headed off to his car, she called out to him: 'Pick up some OJ on the way home. Take care of that cold.'

'Thanks.'

Minutes later Melanie walked north past the Capital Grille toward the Archives Metro Station. As she turned the corner onto 6th Street, she found herself face-to-face with the man in the trench coat.

'Miss Kraft,' the man said with a polite smile.

Melanie stopped in her tracks, stared at him for several seconds, and then said, 'What the hell is wrong with you?'

Still smiling, the man asked, 'What do you mean?'

'You can't just appear like this.'

'I *can*, and I *did*. I need just a moment of your time.'

'You can go to hell.'

'That's not very polite, Miss Kraft.'

She began walking again up the hill toward the Metro. 'He saw you. Jack saw you.'

He followed now, matching her brisk pace. 'Do you know that, or do you just suspect that?'

'I assume it. You caught me off guard. I had to give him an obvious brush-off because I didn't know if you were going to walk right up to us. He picked up on the fact that something was going on. He's not an idiot.'

'Intellect doesn't have anything to do with one's ability to detect surveillance measures. That comes from training, Melanie.'

Kraft did not respond; she only continued walking.

'Where do you think he would have gotten that training?'

Melanie stopped now. 'If you needed to talk, why didn't you just call me?'

'Because I wanted to talk in person.'

'About what?'

Now the man affected a crooked smile. 'Please, Melanie. This won't take any time at all. I'm parked up on Indiana. We can find someplace quiet.'

'Dressed like this?' she asked. She looked down at her skintight Lycra running shorts and a form-fitting Puma jacket.

The man looked her up and down now, taking a little too long to do so. 'Why not? I'd take you anywhere looking like that.'

Melanie groaned to herself. Darren Lipton was not the first lecherous asshole she had met while working in the federal government. He was, however, the first lecherous asshole Melanie had met who was also a senior special agent in the FBI, so she reluctantly followed him to his car.

17

They walked together down the ramp of an underground parking garage that was nearly empty so early on a Saturday morning, and, at Lipton's direction, they climbed in the front seats of his Toyota Sienna minivan. He put the key in the ignition, but he did not turn the engine over, and they sat in the silence and the near darkness of the garage. Only the faint light of a fluorescent bulb on the concrete wall illuminated their faces.

Lipton was in his fifties, but he wore his gray-blond hair in a boyish flop that somehow did not make him look any younger, just less put together. His face was pocked with acne scars and frown lines and he looked like he enjoyed sitting in the sun as much as he enjoyed drinking – Melanie pictured him doing a lot of both at the same time. He wore his aftershave so heavy that Melanie wondered if he filled his bathtub with it and took a dip each morning. He talked too loudly and too quickly, and, she had noticed the first time they met face-to-face, he went out of his way to stare at her chest while they talked, clearly taking pleasure from the fact that she knew what he was doing.

He reminded Melanie of the uncle of an ex-boyfriend she had when she was in high school who spent way too much time staring at her and complimenting her athletic physique in a way that was obviously perverse but also carefully worded so as to be deniable.

In short, Lipton was a creep.

'It's been a while,' he said.

'I haven't heard from you in months. I assumed you had moved on.'

'Moved on? You mean out of the FBI, out of the National Security Branch, or out of Counterintelligence Division?'

'I mean away from your investigation.'

'Away from Jack Ryan, Jr? No, ma'am. On the contrary, just like you, we are still very interested in him.'

'You obviously don't have a case.' She said it with derision in her voice.

Lipton drummed his fingers on the steering wheel. 'The Justice Department's inquiry is just an intelligence-gathering operation at this point; whether or not an indictment comes from this is yet to be determined.'

'And you are running it?'

'I am running *you*. You don't really need to know anything more than that at this stage.'

Melanie looked out the windshield at the concrete wall as she spoke. 'When I first heard from you in January, after DD/CIA Alden was arrested, you said exactly the same thing. The FBI's National Security Branch was looking into Alden's concerns about Jack Junior and Hendley Associates, suspicions that Jack and his coworkers were getting classified intelligence about national security affairs to make illegal trades on world financial markets. But you said it was all speculation, and no determination had been made by CID that any crime had been committed. Are you telling me that here we are, six months later, and nothing has changed?'

'Things *have* changed, Miss Kraft, but they are things you are not privy to.'

Melanie heaved a sigh. This was a nightmare. She had hoped she'd seen the last of Darren Lipton and Counterintelligence Division. 'I want to know what you have on him. I want to know what this is all about. If you want my help, you need to fill me in.'

The older man shook his head, but he retained his little smile. 'You are CIA on loan to the Office of the Director of National Intelligence, and you are, for all intents and purposes, my confidential informant in this inquiry. That does not get you a look at the case file. You have a legal responsibility to cooperate with the FBI on this, not to mention a moral one.'

'What about Mary Pat Foley?'

'What about her?'

'When we met, you told me she was part of the inquiry into Hendley Associates as well, so I could not reveal any information to her. Have you at least managed to clear her in . . . in this yet?'

Lipton just said, 'Nope.'

'So you think Mary Pat and Jack are somehow involved in a crime?'

'It's a possibility we have not ruled out. The Foleys have been friends with the Ryans for over thirty years. In my line of work you realize that tight relationships like that mean people talk to one another. We don't know the details of the relationship between Junior and Director Foley, but we do know they have met a number of times over the past year. It is possible that, with her clearances, she could be communicating classified information through Jack to benefit Hendley Associates.'

Melanie leaned her head back against the headrest and let out a long sigh. 'This is fucking crazy, Lipton. Jack Ryan is a financial analyst. Mary Pat Foley is . . . hell, she's an American institution. You just said it yourself. They are old friends. They go to lunch once in a blue moon. I usually go with them. Even entertaining the possibility that they are involved in some national security crime against the U.S. is outlandish.'

'Let me remind you what you told us. When Charles Alden asked you for information tying John Clark to Jack Ryan, Jr, and Hendley Associates, you indicated your belief that they were, in fact, involved in something more than trading and currency arbitrage. You told me, in only our second conversation, that you believed Ryan was in Pakistan during the events that transpired there last winter.'

She hesitated for a moment. 'I *thought* he was. He reacted very suspiciously when I mentioned it. There was other . . . circumstantial evidence at the time that made me think he was lying to me. But nothing I could prove. But even if he was lying to me, even if he *was* in Pakistan . . . that does not prove anything.'

'Then you need to dig a little deeper.'

'I'm not a cop, Lipton, and I'm definitely not an FBI national security agent.'

Lipton smiled at her. 'You'd be a damn good one, Melanie. How 'bout I talk to some people?'

She did not return the smile. 'How 'bout I pass?'

His smile faded. 'We have yet to get to the bottom of this. If there is a crime being committed by Hendley Associates, we need to know.'

'I haven't talked to you for . . . what? Six months? Why haven't you been doing anything for the past half a year?'

'We have, Melanie, via other means. Again, you are just one tiny piece of the puzzle. That said, you are our inside man . . . I should say "woman."' He said the last part with a grin and a quick glance down at Melanie's tight Puma jacket.

She ignored his misogyny and said, 'So, what has changed? Why are you here today?'

'What, you don't like our little visits?'

Melanie just stared at Lipton. Her look said *Eat shit*. It was a look he'd received from many beautiful women in his life.

Darren gave her a little wink. 'My superiors want movement on this. There has been talk of wiretaps, location-tracking equipment, even a surveillance team put on Ryan and some of his coworkers.'

Melanie shook her head emphatically. 'No!'

'But I told them that was not necessary. Due to your . . . *intimate* relationship with the subject, any close surveillance would be an invasion of your privacy as well. My superiors were not moved by this. They don't think you have been that helpful to date. But in the end, I bought you a little time to get us some actionable intel on your own, before the FBI orders a full-court press.'

'What do you want?'

'We need to know where he is, twenty-four-seven, or as close as you can get us to that. We need to know of any trips he takes, flight times and flight numbers, hotels he stays in, people he meets with.'

'When he travels for business, he doesn't take me with him.'

'Well, you will just have to get more out of him through subtle questions. Pillow talk,' he said with a wink.

She did not respond.

Lipton continued, 'Have him e-mail you his itinerary when he travels. Tell him you miss him and want to know where he's going. Get him to send you his e-mail confirmation from the airline when he books his travel.'

'He doesn't fly commercial. His company has a plane.'

'A plane?'

'Yes. A Gulfstream. It flies out of BWI, but that's all I know. He's mentioned it a few times.'

'Why don't I know about this?'

'I have no idea. I told Alden about it.'

'Well, you didn't tell me. I'm FBI, Alden was CIA, and Alden is under house arrest at the moment. He sure as hell isn't working with us anymore.' Darren winked again. 'We're the good guys.'

'Right,' she replied.

'We need you to get intel on his coworkers as well. Who he travels with, primarily.'

'How?'

'Tell him you are jealous, suspicious he has other lovers. Whatever it takes. I saw the two of you together just now. You have him wrapped around your finger. That's great. You can use that.'

'Fuck you, Lipton.'

Lipton smiled wildly; she could see he enjoyed the repartee. 'I can arrange that, my dear. *Now* we're on the same page. Let me just lower the seat here. Not the first time the Sienna's suspension has gotten a workout, if you know what I mean.'

He was joking, but Melanie Kraft wanted to puke. Almost instinctively she reached out and slapped the middle-aged FBI agent across the jaw.

The hard contact between the palm of her hand and Lipton's fleshy face sounded like a rifle shot in the enclosed minivan.

Lipton recoiled in pain and surprise, and his sly smile disappeared.

Melanie shouted at him, 'I'm done with you! Tell your bosses that they can send another agent to talk to me if they want, I can't stop them, but I'm not saying one more word to you!'

Lipton touched his fingertips to his lip, looked down at a small spot of blood from Melanie's strike.

Melanie glared at him. She considered just getting out of

the minivan and walking to the Metro. Whatever Jack was involved in, it wasn't anything that was hurting the United States. She'd done what they'd asked of her back in January.

Now the FBI could kiss her ass.

As she turned to reach for the door handle, Lipton spoke again. His tone was soft but grave. He sounded like a different person.

'Miss Kraft. I am going to ask you a question. I want you to answer me truthfully.'

'I told you. I'm not talking to you anymore.'

'Answer this, and you can leave if you want, and I won't follow.'

Melanie slumped back in the seat. Stared straight ahead out the windshield. 'Fine. What?'

'Have you, Miss Kraft, ever been employed as an agent for a foreign principal?'

Now she turned to him. 'What in God's name are you talking about?'

'A foreign principal is a legal term that refers to the government of a country other than the United States of America.'

'I know what a foreign principal is. I *don't* know why you are asking me that.'

'Yes or no?'

Melanie shook her head. Genuinely confused. 'No. Of course not. But if you are investigating *me* for something, I want a lawyer from the Agency here to –'

'Has any member of your family ever been employed as an agent for a foreign principal?'

Melanie Kraft stopped speaking. Her entire body stiffened.

Darren Lipton just looked at her. A fresh drop of blood glistened on his lip from the light of a fluorescent lamp outside the van.

'What . . . are you . . . what *is* this?'

'Answer the question.'

She did so, but more hesitantly than before. 'No. Of course not. And I resent the accusation that –'

Lipton interrupted her. 'Are you familiar with Title Twenty-two of the United States Code? Specifically Subchapter Two, section six hundred eleven?'

Her voice cracked as she shook her head and softly replied, 'I am not.'

'It's called the Foreign Agents Registration Act. I could recite it for you chapter and verse if you like, but let me just give you the takeaway from that little piece of American federal law. If someone is working for another country, as a spy, for example, and does not register with the U.S. government as such, they are subject to a sentence of up to five years in prison for each act as a representative of the other country.'

A hesitant and confused 'So?' from Melanie Kraft.

'Next question. Are you familiar with Title Eighteen of the USC?'

'Again, Agent Lipton, I do not know why –'

'That one is awesome. My personal favorite. It says – and this is paraphrased, of course, but I can quote it backward and forward – that you can get five years in a federal lockup for lying to a federal officer.' Darren smiled for the first time since Kraft had slapped him. 'A federal officer like me, for instance.'

Melanie's voice had none of the bluster and insolence it did two minutes ago. 'So?'

'*So*, Melanie, you just lied to me.'

Melanie said nothing.

'Your father, Colonel Ronald Kraft, passed top-secret military information to the Palestinian Authority in 2004. This makes him an agent of a foreign principal. Except he sure as hell never registered as such, and he was never arrested, never prosecuted, never even suspected by the U.S. government.'

Melanie was dumbfounded. Her hands began to shake, and her vision narrowed.

Lipton's smile widened. 'And you, sugar, know all about it. You knew about it at the time, which means you just lied to a federal officer.'

Melanie Kraft reached for the door handle, but Darren Lipton took her by the shoulder and spun her back around violently.

'You also lied on your application to the CIA when you said you had neither knowledge of nor contact with agents of a foreign government. Your dear old dad was a treasonous motherfucking spy and you *knew* it!'

She lurched again for the door handle, and again Lipton spun her back to him.

'Listen to me! We're a quarter-mile from the Hoover Building. I can be at my desk in ten minutes working up an affidavit, and I can have you arrested by lunch on Monday. There is no parole for federal crimes, so five years means five fucking years!'

Melanie Kraft was in shock; she felt the blood rushing from her head and leaving her hands. Her feet felt cold.

She tried to speak, but she had no words.

18

Lipton's voice softened again. 'Honey . . . calm down. I don't care about your piece-of-shit dad. I really don't. And I don't even care all that much about his poor pitiful daughter. But I do care about Jack Ryan, Junior, and it's my job to use every last tool in my toolbox to learn everything I need to know about him.'

Melanie looked up at him through puffy, tear-clouded eyes.

He continued, 'I don't give two shits if Jack Ryan, Junior, is the son of the President of the United States. If he and his fat-cat financial management company up there in West Odenton are involved in using classified intelligence to make themselves rich, I *will* take them all down.

'Are you going to help me, Melanie?'

Melanie stared at the dashboard ahead of her, sniffed back tears, and gave a slight nod.

'There's no need for this to take long. You need to make a point of noting things, writing them down, getting them back to me. No matter how insignificant they might seem. You are a CIA officer, for crying out loud; this should be child's play for you.'

Melanie sniffed again and wiped her eyes and nose with the back of her bare arm. 'I'm a reports officer. An analyst. I don't run agents, and I don't spy.'

Darren smiled at her for a long time. 'Now you do.'

She nodded again. 'Can I go now?'

Lipton replied, 'I don't have to tell you how politically sensitive this is.'

She sniffed back tears. 'It is personally sensitive, Mr Lipton.'

'I get it. He's your man. Whatever. Just do your job and this will be wrapped up in a couple of weeks. If nothing comes from this investigation, you two lovebirds will be planted in your picket-fence house in no time.'

She nodded now. Compliant.

Lipton said, 'I've been working counter-intel operations for most of thirty years. I've worked ops against Americans working for foreign nations, Americans working for organized crime, or just Americans committing acts of espionage for shits and grins – assholes who leak classified docs onto the Internet just because they can. I've been at this long enough to where the little hairs on the back of my neck stick up when I'm being lied to, and I put people in federal prison for telling lies.'

His voice had softened, but now the menace returned.

'I swear to God, young lady, if I get so much as a twitch in the hairs on the back of my neck that you are not shooting straight with me, you and your father will be cellmates at the shittiest, tightest facility the DOJ can find for you. You got me?'

Melanie just looked off into space.

'We're done,' Lipton said. 'But you can be sure I'll be in touch.'

Melanie Kraft rode nearly alone on the Yellow Line Metro, across the Potomac and back toward her little carriage-house apartment in Alexandria. Her face was in her hands for most of the way, and though she did her best to control her tears, she sobbed from time to time as she thought about her conversation with Lipton.

It had been almost nine years since she'd learned that her father was a traitor to the United States. She had been a senior in high school in Cairo, she had her scholarship to American in hand, and already she planned to major in international relations and go into government service, she hoped at the Department of State.

Her dad was attached to the embassy, working in the Office of Military Cooperation. Melanie had grown up proud of her father, and she loved the embassy and the people there, and wanted nothing more than to make that her own life, her own future.

A few weeks before Melanie's graduation, her mother was away, back in Texas tending to a dying aunt, and her father had told her he would be spending a few days on temporary duty in Germany.

Two days later Melanie was out driving her Vespa on a Saturday morning and she saw him leaving an apartment building in Maadi, a southern neighborhood full of tree-lined streets and high-rise apartments.

She was surprised that he had lied to her about leaving town, but before she could drive up to confront him she saw a woman step out of the building and into his arms.

She was exotic and beautiful. Melanie had an immediate impression that she was not Egyptian; her features had some other Mediterranean influence. Perhaps Lebanese.

She watched them embrace.

She watched them kiss.

In her seventeen years she had never seen her father hold or kiss her mother like that.

Melanie pulled into the shadow of a shade tree across the four-lane street and watched them for a few moments more. Then her father climbed into his two-door and disappeared in traffic. She did not follow him. Instead she sat down in the shade between two parked cars and watched the building.

As she sat there, tears in her eyes, her mind filled with rage, she pictured the woman walking out the front door of the apartment building, and she pictured herself crossing the street, walking up to her, and beating her onto her back on the sidewalk.

After thirty minutes she had calmed down slightly. She rose to get back on her bike and leave, but the beautiful Mediterranean woman appeared on the curb in front of the building with a rolling suitcase. Seconds later a yellow Citroën with two men inside pulled up next to her. To Melanie's surprise, they loaded her luggage in the trunk and she climbed in.

The men were young toughs, with heads on a swivel and conspiratorial movements. They pulled back into traffic and raced off.

On a whim she followed the car; on her Vespa it was easy to keep up with the yellow Citroën in traffic. She cried as she steered the little bike and thought of her mother.

They drove for twenty minutes, crossing the Nile River on the 6th October Bridge. When they entered the Dokki district, Melanie's broken heart sank. Dokki was full of foreign embassies. Somehow she now knew her father was not just having an affair, but was having an affair with some diplomat's wife or other foreign national. She knew his position was sensitive enough that he could be court-martialed or even thrown in jail for this act of utter foolishness.

Then the yellow Citroën pulled into the gates of the Palestinian embassy, and she knew, again, she just knew, that this was not just an affair.

Her father was involved in espionage.

She did not confront the colonel at first. She thought of her own future; she knew if he was arrested there would be no chance she could ever get a job working for the Department of State, the daughter of an American traitor.

But the night before her mother returned from Dallas, Melanie walked into his study, up to the edge of his desk, and she stood there, in front of him, on the verge of tears.

'What's wrong?'

'You know what's wrong.'

'I do?'

'I saw her. I saw you together. I know what you are doing.'

Colonel Kraft denied the allegations at first. He told her his travel plans were changed at the last minute and he'd gone to meet an old friend, but Melanie's razor-sharp intellect defeated lie after lie and the forty-eight-year-old colonel became more and more desperate to extricate himself from his deceit.

He broke down in tears next; he confessed to the relationship, told Melanie the woman's name was Mira and he had been having a clandestine affair for some months now. He told her he loved her mother and he had no excuse for his actions. He buried his face in his hands at his desk and asked Melanie to give him some time to get himself together.

But Melanie was not through with him.

'How could you do it?'

'I told you, she seduced me. I was weak.'

Melanie shook her head. It wasn't what she was asking. 'Was it for the money?'

Ron Kraft looked up from his hands. 'The *money*? *What* money?'

'How much did they pay you?'

'Who? How much did *who* pay me?'

'Don't tell me you did it to help their cause.'

'What are you talking about?'

'The Palestinians.'

Colonel Kraft sat up fully now. From cowed to defiant. 'Mira isn't Palestinian. She's Lebanese. A Christian. Where did you get the idea that –'

'Because after you left your love nest two men picked her up and then drove to the Palestinian embassy on Al-Nahda Street!'

Father and daughter stared at each other for a long time.

Finally he spoke, his voice low and unsure: 'You are mistaken.'

She just shook her head. 'I know what I saw.'

It soon became clear that her father, the Air Force colonel, had no idea that his mistress was using him.

'What have I done?'

'What did you tell her?'

He put his head back in his hands and sat there, silently, for some time. With his daughter standing over him, he thought back to every conversation he'd had with the beautiful Mira. Finally he nodded. 'I told her things. Little things about work. About colleagues. About our allies. Just conversation. She hated the Palestinians . . . She talked about them all the time. I . . . I told her about what we were doing to help Israel. I was proud. Boastful.'

Melanie did not respond. But her father said what she was thinking.

'I am a fool.'

He wanted to turn himself in, to explain what he had done, damn the consequences.

But seventeen-year-old Melanie screamed at him, told him that by attempting to make peace with his own foolishness, he would destroy the lives of both herself and her mother. She told him he needed to be a man and break off the relationship with Mira and never speak again of what he had done.

For her sake and the sake of her mother.

He agreed.

She had not spoken to him since she left for college. He

retired from the military, broke off contact with all his friends and colleagues from the Air Force, and he and his wife moved home to Dallas, where he took a job selling industrial solvents and lubricants.

Melanie's mother died two years later of the same cancer that had killed her aunt. Melanie blamed her father, though she could not say why.

In college Melanie did her best to push it all out of her mind, to compartmentalize those few anomalous days of hell from a happy life that had led her inexorably toward her own future as an employee of the U.S. government.

But the event had had a powerful effect on her. Her desire to work in diplomacy turned into a desire to work in intelligence, a natural evolution for her to fight back against the enemy spies who nearly ripped her family, and her world, apart.

She told no one about what she saw, and she lied on her CIA application and in her interviews. She told herself that she was doing the right thing. She would not allow her life, her future, to be cursed by the fact that her father could not keep his pants on. She could do so much good for her country, so much good that could not be appreciated now.

She was surprised when the lie detector did not pick up on her deception, but she decided that she had so thoroughly convinced herself that her father's transgressions had nothing to do with her that her heart rate did not even change when she thought about it.

Her career in service to the United States would rectify all her father had done to damage their country.

Though she lived with the shame of what she knew, she had long since grown comfortable in the knowledge that no one else would ever know.

But when Darren Lipton confronted her with his knowledge of the incident, it was like she'd been grabbed by the ankles and pulled underwater. She panicked, she could not breathe, she wanted to get away.

Now that she knew people in the FBI were aware of her father's act of espionage, she saw her world ending, her future in doubt. She now knew that at any time this could come back to haunt her.

She decided, as the Metro conductor announced her stop over the PA, that she would get Lipton what he needed on Jack. She had her own suspicions of her boyfriend. His rushing off out of the country, his deception as to where he was going and vagueness about his work. But she knew the man, she loved the man, and she did not believe for a second that he was stealing classified information to line his own pockets.

She would help Lipton, but it would come to nothing, and soon Lipton would be gone and this would all be over and behind her, another compartmentalized piece of her life. But unlike Cairo, she told herself, this would never come back to haunt her.

FBI Senior Special Agent Darren Lipton turned his Toyota Sienna onto U.S. 1 and headed south for the 14th Street Bridge. He crossed the Potomac at nine a.m., his heart still beating heavily from the encounter with the sexy piece of ass from the CIA as well as in anticipation for where he was now headed.

Things had gotten physical with Kraft, although certainly not in a way that he had anticipated. When she struck him he wanted to grab her by the throat and pull her into the backseat and punish her, but he knew that his superiors needed her.

And Lipton had learned to do what he was told, despite the urges that nearly consumed him.

The fifty-five-year-old knew he should get back home

now, but there was a massage parlor operating out of a flea-bag motel by the airport in Crystal City that he frequented when he couldn't splurge on a high-class call girl, and a dump like that would be open for business this early in the morning. He decided he would let off a little of the pressure Miss Melanie Kraft built up in him before heading back home to Chantilly to his bitchy wife and his checked-out teenagers.

He would then report on today's meeting to his superior, and await further instructions.

19

It is estimated that nearly half a billion people tune in for China Central Television's seven p.m. news hour. The fact that all local stations in China are ordered by government mandate to carry the program likely has much to do with this high number, but frequent announcements that the president would be making an important national address this evening ensured even higher ratings than normal.

Wei Zhen Lin's address was also simulcast on China National Radio for those in the outer provinces who could not receive a television signal or could not afford a television, as well as China Radio International, ensuring immediate and widespread coverage around the globe.

The female news anchor opened the show by introducing President Wei, and then on televisions all across the country the image switched to the handsome and cool Wei walking alone toward a lectern centered on a red carpet. Behind him was a large monitor displaying the Chinese flag. On both sides of the small set, gold silk curtains hung from the ceiling.

Wei wore a gray suit and a red-and-blue regimental tie; his wire-rimmed glasses were a little low on his nose so that he could read a prepared statement from the teleprompter, but before he spoke he greeted nearly half of his countrymen with a wide toothy smile and a nod.

'Ladies, gentlemen, comrades, friends. I am speaking to you from Beijing, with a message for everyone here in China, in our special administrative regions of Hong Kong and

Macau, in Taiwan, to the Chinese abroad, and to all our friends around the globe.

'I address you all today to deliver proud news about our nation's future and the development of the socialist course.

'I am announcing with great joy our intentions regarding the South China Sea.'

Behind Wei, the image on the monitor changed from the Chinese flag to a map of the South China Sea. A line of dashes, nine in all, descended south from China into the sea. On the east it drooped just west of the Philippines, turned west at its southernmost point to run north of Malaysia and Brunei, then headed north, just off the shore of Vietnam.

The line of dashes formed a deep bowl that contained virtually the entire sea.

'Behind me you see a representation of Chinese territory. This has been Chinese territory for as long as the People's Republic of China has been in existence and well before, though many of our friends and neighbors refuse to accept this fact. China has indisputable sovereignty of the South China Sea and sufficient historical and legal backing underpinning claims for this territory. These important waterways are a core interest of China, and for too long we have allowed our neighbors to dictate their terms to us, the fair claimants of this property.

'Before he became chairman of the Central Military Commission, my colleague, comrade, and friend Chairman Su Ke Qiang had been an outspoken critic of our reluctance to press the issue of the South China Sea. As a four-star general and an expert on military history, he was in a position to know how vulnerable we had become by allowing our neighbors to dictate to us our movements, fishing rights, and mining and drilling authorities in these waters that belong to us. Chairman Su has made rectifying this injustice a key component of his long-term military modernization. I applaud Chairman Su on his brilliant foresight and initiative.

'It is I addressing you today, and not Comrade Chairman Su, because I want to show that I agree with his assessment, and I personally authorize upcoming naval actions that will advance our territorial claims.

'It would be a serious miscalculation for other nations to assume there exists disagreement between Chairman Su and myself in any regard, but specifically with regard to our bilateral relations with our neighbors in the South China Sea region. I fully support the chairman's recent clear remarks on China's historical claim to these waters.'

Wei paused, took a sip of water, and cleared his throat.

He returned to his teleprompter. 'I have a business and a political background, I am not a soldier or a sailor. But as a businessman I understand the value of property and the legal exercise of proprietary rights. And as a politician I represent the will of the people, and I, in whatever capacity I possess, claim the property of our ancestors for today's China.

'Ladies and gentlemen, facts are not something to be accepted or rejected. Facts are truths, and behind me on the map, you see the truth. For nearly one thousand years these seas, and the land that exists within them, have been the historical property of China, and it is time for the historical injustice of the theft of this property to end.

'So with our territorial claim established, now comes the question of what to do with those peoples who reside and make commerce illegally in our territory. If a man is living in your house uninvited, if you are a good person you don't just throw him out. You tell him he must leave before taking further action.

'My predecessors have made such notifications for some

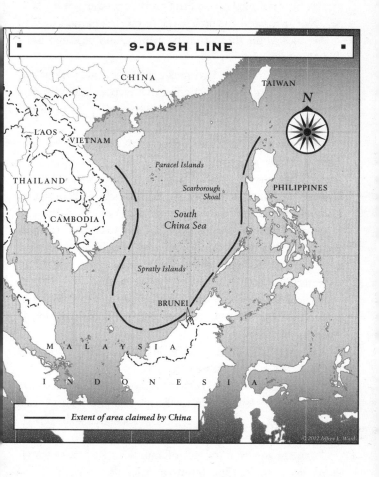

9-DASH LINE

CHINA

TAIWAN

N

LAOS

VIETNAM

THAILAND

Paracel Islands

*Scarborough
Shoal*

PHILIPPINES

CAMBODIA

*South
China Sea*

Spratly Islands

BRUNEI

M A L A Y S I A

I N D O N E S I A

―――― *Extent of area claimed by China*

© 2012 Jeffrey L. Ward

sixty years. I see no reason I should do the same. As the people's leader, I see my role in this long-standing injustice as putting those nations in our territory on immediate notice that we will be reclaiming our rightful property in the South China Sea. Not at some vague time in the future, but immediately.'

Wei looked up, directly at the camera, and repeated himself: 'Immediately.

'If the use of force becomes necessary in this endeavor, the world at large must recognize that responsibility for this lies with those entrenched on Chinese territory who ignored repeated polite requests to remove themselves.'

Wei pushed his glasses up higher on his nose, addressed the camera directly again, and smiled. 'We have worked very hard for very many years to establish good relations with countries all over the world. Currently we do business with over one hundred twenty nations, and we consider ourselves, first and foremost, friends to our business partners. Our movements in the critical area of the South China Sea should be recognized as our attempt to make sea lanes safe for everyone, and it is in the interest of world commerce that we do this.'

He said the next line with a wide smile and in halting but understandable English. 'Ladies and gentlemen, China is open for business.'

And then he switched back to Mandarin. 'Thank you very much. I wish you all prosperity.'

The president stepped off to the side and out of the room, giving the full camera shot to the map of the South China Sea, including a line of dashes, nine in total, that all but encircled the sea.

As the image on hundreds of millions of Chinese televisions stood static, 'The Internationale,' the anthem of the Communist Party of China, played in the background.

20

At ten a.m. on the Monday morning after President Wei's national address, there was a full house in the Oval Office. Twelve men and women sat on the two sofas and six chairs, and President of the United States Jack Ryan had rolled his own chair around in front of his desk to be closer to the action.

President Ryan at first considered having the meeting in the conference facility in the Situation Room in the basement of the West Wing. But he decided the Oval Office would be the proper venue, as China had not actually done anything yet, other than make vague threats in diplomatic-speak. Also he decided to get everyone together today in the Oval Office because his intention was, in part, to rally his troops so that they would all be focused on a task that, Ryan thought, he and his administration had not focused on sufficiently in the first year of his new administration.

And the Oval Office commanded suitable authority for this purpose.

On the sofa in front of Ryan and to his right, Secretary of State Scott Adler sat next to the director of national intelligence, Mary Pat Foley. Next to them was Vice President Rich Pollan. Across the coffee table on the other sofa, the director of the CIA, Jay Canfield, sat between Secretary of Defense Bob Burgess and Ryan's chief of staff, Arnie van Damm. National Security Adviser Colleen Hurst sat on the wingback chair on the far side of the coffee table. On other chairs arrayed on either side of her were the chairman of the Joint Chiefs of Staff, General David Obermeyer, the U.S. ambassador to China, Kenneth Li, and Attorney General Dan Murray.

Farther back, ahead of Ryan on his left and right, were the head of the NSA and the secretary of commerce.

Also present was the commander of U.S. Pacific Command, Admiral Mark Jorgensen. Secretary of Defense Burgess had asked permission to bring Jorgensen along, as he knew China's capabilities in the SCS better than anyone.

As everyone settled into their seats with soft greetings to one another, Ryan looked to Ambassador Kenneth Li. The United States' first Chinese-American ambassador had been recalled the day before from Beijing, and his plane had only just landed at Andrews after a seventeen-hour flight. Ryan saw that though Li's suit and tie looked crisp and fresh, the ambassador himself had puffy eyes and slightly slumped shoulders. 'Ken,' said Ryan, 'all I can offer you right now is an apology for rushing you back so quickly and free refills on the coffee.'

There were chuckles around the room.

Kenneth Li smiled a tired smile and replied, 'No need for the apology, I'm glad to be here. I do truly appreciate the coffee, Mr President.'

'Glad to have you.' Ryan now addressed the room, looking over narrow glasses that were propped just above the tip of his nose. 'Ladies and gentlemen, President Wei got my attention and I sure as hell hope he got yours. I want to know what you know, and I want to know what you think. As always, be clear about which is which.'

The men and women around the Oval Office nodded, and Jack Ryan could see in their eyes that Wei's proclamation was ominous enough for everyone here to recognize its importance.

'Let's start with you, Ken. Until twenty hours ago I looked at President Wei as a bit of a hard-liner at home, but also as a man who knew what side his bread was buttered on. He has been absolutely the most pro-business, pro-capitalist leader we could have hoped for. What has changed?'

Ambassador Li spoke loud enough to be heard by everyone in the room. 'Frankly, Mr President, nothing has changed with regard to his desire to do business with the West. He wants our business, and he needs our business. Considering the economic problems China is facing, he needs us more than ever, and he knows that better than anyone.'

Ryan posed the next question to the ambassador as well. 'We know about Wei's public persona in the West versus his "tough guy" pro-Party stance at home. What can you tell us about the man? Is he as good as many think he is, or is he as bad as many fear he is, especially in light of all the protests going on in China these days?'

Li regarded the question for a moment before answering: 'The Communist Party of China has forced the population of China to swear allegiance to the CPC since 1949. The Tuidang movement that is getting limited press abroad is seen as a huge cultural phenomenon at home, especially among the old party guard. They are seriously worried about it.

'Additionally, there have been strikes, human rights protests, growing unrest in the provinces, even some small-scale acts of rebellion far from the capital in the past couple of months.

'For the past forty years or so, the prevailing thinking in the West has consistently been that with the growth of capitalism and increased engagement with the rest of the world, the nation of China would, slowly but surely, come over to a more liberal way of thinking. But this "liberal evolution" theory has sadly not panned out. Instead of embracing political liberalization, the Communist Party of China has grown more resistant, more paranoid about the West, and more hostile to liberal values.

'Even though Wei has been at the forefront of economic liberalism, he also leads the charge in fighting back against Tuidang and personal liberty.'

Scott Adler, secretary of state, said, 'Wei has always worn two faces. He believes in the party, in the devotion to the central government. He just doesn't believe in the communist economic model. Since he came into power he has been crushing dissent, backing off on freedoms of travel between provinces and pulling the plug on more websites per day than his predecessor pulled per month.'

Ryan said, 'He just does it all with a wide grin on his face and a regimental tie that makes him look like an Ivy Leaguer, so he gets a pass from the world's press.'

Ambassador Li said, 'Maybe not a full pass, but he sure gets a mulligan or two.'

Jack shook his head. He thought, but did not say, that the world's press liked Wei Zhen Lin more than it did John Patrick Ryan.

'What are his intentions? Why the saber rattling? Is it just to fire up his party and his military? Scott?'

The secretary of state replied, 'We don't see it as that. We have witnessed major speeches by generals and admirals for that purpose, and they seem to work quite well at whipping up nationalist pride and animosity against their regional rivals. Having their decidedly nonmilitant president and general secretary taking up the bully pulpit to echo the generals, Wei has to know, will just create ill will with the rest of the world. This was not done for the purpose of political grandstanding. This seems to be an aggressive policy shift, and we should accept it as such.'

'So you are saying,' Ryan asked while leaning forward, 'that this actually *means* they are going to use the People's Liberation Army-Navy to control the South China Sea?'

'We at State are very concerned that it does mean the PLAN will be reaching out to the south to exert more influence.'

Ryan turned his head to the director of national intelligence. As the chief of all seventeen U.S. intelligence agencies, Mary Pat Foley was well positioned to fill in any details.

'What does it mean, Mary Pat?'

'Honestly, sir, we are taking this at face value. We expect them to land troops on some of the nondefended but contested islands, to push their Navy out further, and to claim international waters, not just with rhetoric but with gunboats.'

'Why now?' Ryan asked. 'Wei is an economist; he's shown no evidence of this militancy.'

Secretary of Defense Bob Burgess said, 'True, but Chairman Su has real clout. He had, arguably, one-third of the power before the coup. After he pulled Wei's butt off the grill over the summer by sending tanks to his compound to stop the Ministry of Public Security from effecting Wei's arrest, you have to assume Su's stock went through the roof.

'Wei can't think he's going to help his economy by taking control of a bigger portion of the South China Sea. Sure, there is oil and there are minerals and fish, but the headaches that it will generate for him with the West just aren't worth it.'

Regina Barnes, secretary of commerce, said, 'If anything, sir, significant military action in the SCS will destroy them economically. They rely on safe passage of freighters and tankers, and that passage will be disrupted if things get ugly in those waters. Saudi Arabia is the largest supplier of oil to China, which should surprise no one. What is surprising, perhaps, is that Angola is the second-largest supplier. Both nations deliver oil through the SCS via tankers. Any disruption of sea traffic in the South China Sea would be devastating for the Chinese industrial machine.'

Foley said, 'Look at the Strait of Malacca. That is the choke point, and the Chinese know it. It's their Achilles' heel. Seventy-five to eighty percent of all oil heading to Asia passes through the Strait of Malacca.'

Ambassador Ken Li offered, 'Maybe, sir, Wei is not doing this to help the economy. Maybe Wei is doing this to protect himself.'

'From what threat?'

'From Chairman Su. Maybe he is going along with this to placate Su.'

Ryan looked to a point on the far wall of the Oval Office. The crowd of people in front of him sat silently.

After a moment Jack said, 'I agree that's part of it. But I think Wei has something up his sleeve. He knows this will hurt business. If you look at his entire career, you can't point to a single thing he has ever done to jeopardize trade with the West, unless it had something integral to do with his internal domestic situation. I mean, yes, he's been involved with some hard-line Standing Committee decisions to put down insurrection in ways that were bad for business, but these were things he saw as necessary to keep the party's hold on power absolute. I believe there must be something else to his comments.'

Admiral Mark Jorgensen lifted a hand slowly to get the President's attention.

'Admiral?'

'Sir, just speculation.'

'Speculate,' Ryan said.

Jorgensen made a face like he was sucking a lemon as he

hesitated. Finally he said, 'Su wants to take Taiwan. He's been as clear as any Chinese government figure has ever been. Wei wants to strengthen his economy, and Taipei under Chinese rule could arguably do that. Area denial of the South China Sea is a necessary first step for the Chicoms before they can make a play for Taiwan. If they don't control their unfettered access to the Strait of Malacca, we could shut off their oil spigot, and their entire country would grind to a halt. It just may be that this is step one in their bid to finally suck Taiwan back into their control.'

It was perfectly silent in the Oval Office for several seconds. Then Jorgensen added, 'Just throwing that out there, sir.'

Scott Adler was not buying this line of thinking. 'I don't see it. Cross-strait relations between China and Taiwan are good economically, or better than they were, anyway. Direct flights, business deals, visitations of offshore islands . . . normal peacetime engagement. There is one hundred fifty billion a year in Taiwan money invested in mainland China.'

SecDef Burgess interjected, 'Mutual prosperity doesn't mean that nothing bad will happen.'

President Ryan sided with Burgess. 'Just because everyone is making money does not mean that the Chicoms won't muck it up. Money has never been their only aim. There are other paths to power over there. You may be absolutely right, Scott, especially in light of all the good tidings at the moment between the mainland and Taiwan. But don't forget that this rapprochement is reversible by the Communist Party of China in a heartbeat. The CPC leadership is not satisfied with the status quo with relation to Taiwan. They want it back, they want the Republic of China in Taipei gone, and a few direct flights between Shanghai and Taipei isn't going to change that long-term goal.'

Adler conceded this point.

Ryan sighed. 'So . . . the admiral has outlined a worst-case scenario that I want everyone to keep in mind while we work on this. We thought Wei's term would be the most friendly toward Taiwan, but the attempted coup and Chairman Su's strength have, possibly, changed the equation.'

Ryan could see most people in the room thought Jorgensen was being overly pessimistic. He himself felt Wei's going after Taiwan was doubtful, even with Su urging him forward, but he didn't want his top people caught napping if that happened.

The United States had officially recognized Taiwan, and the United States could easily be forced into war if fighting broke out between the two nations. And though Jack Ryan was called a warmonger in much of the world's press, he sure as hell hoped open war in the Pacific was not on the horizon.

Ryan next said, 'Okay. President Wei said China owns the sea due to some historical precedent. What about international law? Laws of the sea, whatever. Do the Chinese have *any* rights at all to make these claims?'

Secretary of State Adler shook his head. 'None whatsoever, but they are smart. They have made a point to not join binding agreements that could allow their neighbors to band together to gang up on them on this or on any other issue. To the Chinese, the South China Sea is not an international issue; they call it a bilateral issue with whichever country they are up against in the region. They won't let this go to the UN or any international body. They want to fight their arguments one by one.'

'Divide and conquer,' Jack said under his breath.

'Divide and conquer,' agreed Adler.

Jack stood and began pacing around his desk. 'What do we know about what is happening inside China?'

This opened the meeting up to the various members of the intelligence services present.

For the next twenty minutes, the national security adviser and the head of the CIA, as well as the director of national intelligence, spoke about covert technical means of espionage. Aircrafts and ships that monitored the country flew and sailed just offshore, satellites raced by overhead, and radio signal interception means were positioned to pick up much Chinese unsecure communication within the country.

It all left Ryan comfortable that America's electronic eyes were turned toward the Middle Kingdom. Signals intelligence, measurement and signatures intelligence, and electronic intelligence means were well represented in America's intelligence community's coverage of China.

But something was missing. Jack said, 'I've heard a good bit about SIGINT, MASINT, ELINT. What *human* intelligence assets do we have in the PRC?' The question was, naturally, posed to the head of the CIA.

Director Canfield said, 'HUMINT is sadly lacking, sir. I wish I could report we were well positioned inside Zhongnanhai, Mr President, but, in truth, we have very few human assets in place other than officers working out of the U.S. embassy in Beijing who control relatively low-level agents. There have been quite a few arrests in the past year of our best assets.'

Ryan knew about this. After a ring of agents spying for the U.S. was rolled up in China in the spring, there was a rumor of a mole in the CIA working for the Chinese government, but an internal investigation revealed that to be unlikely.

Ryan asked, 'We don't have nonofficial cover assets in Beijing anymore?'

'No, sir. We have a few NOCs in China, but none in Beijing,

and no agents I would classify as highly placed. We have been working tirelessly at getting more agents in the PRC, but our efforts have been met by surprisingly robust counterintelligence operations.'

Robust counterintelligence operations. Ryan said the term to himself. He knew it was a polite way of saying the fucking Chinese had been executing anyone they thought might be spying for the United States.

The President said, 'Back in the last go-around with Beijing we had a NOC that gave us a mother lode of intel from inside Politburo meetings.'

Mary Pat Foley nodded. 'Who knew that those were the good ol' days?'

Many of those in the room knew the story, but Ryan explained for those who had either not been in the government at the time or else did not have a need to know. 'When Mary Pat was deputy director at CIA, she had an officer who worked for NEC, the computer company. He sold a bugged computer to the office of a minister without portfolio, one of the premier's closest confidants. At the height of the conflict we were getting nearly daily reports on the leadership's plans and mind-set. It was a game changer, to say the least.'

Mary Pat said, 'And then, a couple months after the war, Minister Fang had to go and have a fatal aneurism while boffing his secretary.'

'Damn inconvenient of him,' agreed Ryan. 'The case officer who pulled this off. Chet Nomouri, was it?'

Mary Pat nodded. 'That's correct, Mr President.'

'He must be a station chief by now.'

CIA Director Jay Canfield shook his head. 'He left the Agency a long time back. Last I heard he took a job with a West Coast computer firm.' With a shrug he said, 'More money in the private sector.'

POTUS mumbled, 'Don't I know it?'

That earned a burst of laughs from a room that was in need of a light moment.

Secretary of Commerce Barnes said, 'Mr President. I hope we don't forget what Wei said in his speech. "China is open for business."'

Jack countered, 'You mean you hope *I* don't forget how much we need China's business.'

She shrugged apologetically. 'Fact is, sir, they own a big chunk of us. And they could call in those chips at any time.'

'And be destroyed,' said Ryan. 'They hurt us economically and it only hurts them economically.'

The secretary of commerce came back with a quick retort of her own: 'Mutually assured destruction.'

Jack nodded at this but said, 'Hey, it was ugly, but you can't say MAD didn't work.'

Barnes nodded.

'Let's finish up with talk about capability,' Ryan said as he turned to his secretary of defense. 'If they wish to exert themselves in the South China Sea, what exactly can they do?'

'As you well know, Mr President, China has added over twenty percent to their military budget every year for nearly two decades. We estimate they spend over two hundred billion a year on their offensive and defensive weaponry, logistics, and manpower.

'China's Navy has been growing by leaps and bounds. They have thirty destroyers, fifty frigates, seventy-five or so submarines. The Chinese have two hundred ninety ships in their Navy, but not much in the way of a blue-water capability. Not yet, anyway.'

Chairman Obermeyer said, 'They have also been focusing on fourth-generation aircraft. They get SU-27s and SU-30s from Russia, and they have their own J-10 fighter, which is made locally although, at this juncture, they are buying their engines from France. Additionally, they have about fifteen SU-33s.'

Burgess said, 'But it's not just their Navy and Air Force; they have expanded in all five war-fighting domains: land, sea, air, space, and cyber. It could be argued, and I would agree with this assessment, that of the five, land has gotten the least attention in the past five years or so.'

'What do we make of that?'

Burgess said, 'China does not see enemies attacking its turf, nor does it see large wars with its neighbors. It does see, however, small conflicts with neighbors and large conflicts with major world powers who are too far away to land armies on China's shores.'

'Especially us,' the President said. It was not a question.

'Exclusively us,' the SecDef replied.

'What about their aircraft carrier?'

The chairman of the Joint Chiefs said, 'Mr President, the *Liaoning*, China's carrier, is a source of national pride, but that is *all* that it is. It is no exaggeration when I say we have three mothballed aircraft carriers, the *Ranger*, the *Constellation*, and the *Kitty Hawk*, that are still in better condition than that old piece of retrofitted junk they bought from Russia.'

Ryan said, 'Yes, but despite its bad condition, is that carrier giving them the *impression* that they have a blue-water Navy? Could that make them dangerous?'

Obermeyer answered, 'That might be their assumption, but it is an assumption that we can relieve them of quite easily if this should turn into a shooting war. I don't want to sound overly boastful, but we could put that carrier on the bottom of the sea on day one.'

Ryan said, 'Short of sinking their aircraft carrier, what

other options do we have to show that we take their threats seriously?'

PacCom Admiral Jorgensen said, 'The *North Carolina* is in the SCS right now. She's a *Virginia*-class fast-attack boat. One of our most stealthy.'

Ryan gave Jorgensen a long look.

The admiral said, 'I'm sorry, Mr President, I did not mean to patronize. You know about *Virginia*-class boats?'

'Yes, and I know about the *North Carolina*.'

'Apologies. I briefed your predecessor . . . and sometimes I had to fill in some details.'

'I get it, Admiral. You were saying about the *North Carolina*?'

'Yes, sir. We could have her make an unscheduled port visit at Subic Bay.'

Ryan liked that. 'Just surface right there in the danger zone to show China we aren't going to lie down and play dead.'

Secretary of Defense Burgess liked it, too. 'And show the Filipinos we support them. They will appreciate the gesture.'

Scott Adler held a hand up. Clearly he did not like the idea. 'Beijing will see that as a provocative act.'

'Shit, Scott,' Ryan said. 'If I eat Italian tonight instead of Chinese, Beijing will see that as a provocative act.'

'Sir –'

Ryan looked to the admiral. 'Do it. Make all the typical statements about how the port visit has been scheduled for some time and the timing is in no way meant to signify blah, blah, blah.'

'Of course, sir.'

Ryan sat on the edge of his desk and addressed all his guests now. 'We've said for some time that the South China Sea was the most likely place for bad stuff to happen. As you can imagine, I am going to want a lot of information from all of you on this one. If you have anything you need to discuss with me personally, just get with Arnie's office.' Jack looked to Arnie van Damm. 'This subject goes to the top of the batting order. If someone in this room wants a few minutes of my time, I don't want you sending me on a meet-and-greet with the Girl Scout who sold the most Thin Mints last year.'

The room laughed, as did Arnie, but he knew his boss was serious.

21

The annual DEF CON Conference in Las Vegas, Nevada, is among the largest underground computer hacking conventions in the world. Each year as many as ten thousand computer security professionals, cybercriminals, journalists, federal employees, and other tech enthusiasts come together for several days to learn about new techniques, products, and services and to enjoy speaker presentations and competitions pertaining to all aspects of hacking and code breaking.

It is an annual Woodstock for top-level hackers and tech geeks.

The conference is held at the off-strip Rio Hotel and Casino, and most attendees stay there or at one of the many nearby hotels, but each year a group of old friends pitch in together to rent a house a few miles to the east in Paradise.

Just before eleven p.m. Charlie Levy pulled his rented Nissan Maxima into the driveway of the luxury vacation home at the end of South Hedgeford Court, in a neighborhood of quiet residential streets full of zero-lot vacation rentals. He stopped at the gate, rolled down his window, and pressed the intercom button.

While he waited he looked around him at the high iron fence lined with palm trees and the landscaped driveway that led up to the six-bedroom house. He and a group of long-time DEF CON attendees had rented this same home for ten years now, and it was good to be back.

After a beep from the call box a nasal voice said, 'Dark-God? What's the password, you fat bastard?'

'Open, sez me, you piece of shit.' Levy said it with a laugh, and seconds later the driveway gate silently opened.

Charlie stomped on the gas pedal and burned rubber in the drive, squealing his tires loud enough to be heard by those up in the house.

Charlie 'DarkGod' Levy was not a founding member of the DEF CON conference, but he'd been coming since 1994, the year after it started, and as a member of the old guard, he was something of a legend.

Back in '94 he'd been a freshman at the University of Chicago, as well as a self-taught hacker who cracked passwords for fun and wrote code as a hobby. His first DEF CON had been an eye-opening experience. He found himself a part of a huge group of like-minded enthusiasts who were careful to not ask anyone what they did for a living, but instead treated everyone with equal measures of suspicion and bonhomie. He'd learned a lot that first year, and more than anything, he learned that he had an intense desire to impress his peers with his hacking exploits.

After college Levy was hired by the computer gaming industry as a programmer, but he spent the majority of his downtime on his own computer-related projects: building and configuring computer software and working on new malware and penetration tactics.

He hacked every device with a processor known to man, and each year he took his trip to Vegas to show his friends and 'competition' what he had done. He became one of the major presenters at the conference and garnered something of a cult following; his exploits were discussed on Web chat boards for the rest of the year.

Each year Charlie Levy had to outdo himself, so he worked

harder and harder in his time away from the office, dug deeper and deeper into operating systems code, and sought bigger and bigger victims to attack.

And after his presentation at this year's conference, he was sure, the whole world would be talking about Charlie Levy.

He climbed out of the Maxima and greeted five friends whom he hadn't seen since last year's meeting. Levy was only thirty-eight, but he looked a lot like Jerry Garcia, short and heavy, with a long gray beard and thinning gray hair. He wore a black T-shirt with the white silhouette of a busty woman and the phrase 'Hack Naked' written underneath it. He was known for his funny T-shirts that stretched across his fat frame, but this year he had been careful to pack a few button-down shirts as well, because he knew that after his presentation on day one of the conference, he would be doing a lot of media interviews.

He unpacked his suitcase in his room and then met his friends down at the beautiful backyard swimming pool. He took a Corona from a full ice chest, made a few minutes of small talk about what everyone else had been up to in the past twelve months, and then stood by himself near the rock waterfall so he would not have to answer questions about his own activities or what he had in store for tomorrow.

Looking around him, Charlie Levy saw tech royalty. Two men were Microsoft execs who flew in from Washington state this afternoon. Another guy was a technical director at Google; he was worth more than the Microsoft guys combined. The remaining two were just mere millionaires; one worked the hardware side at AT&T and the other ran the IT department of a French bank.

Charlie was accustomed to feeling a bit like the odd man out at these annual get-togethers.

Charlie was a video-game programmer, and it paid well,

but he had turned down a decade's worth of promotions because he did not want to be rich.

No, Charlie Levy wanted to be a legend.

And this would be his year.

Tomorrow he would reveal during his presentation his discovery of a zero-day vulnerability he had exploited that allowed him to infiltrate JWICS, the Joint Worldwide Intelligence Communications System – known as 'Jay-Wicks,' and through it Intelink-TS, the top-secret secure intranet used by the U.S. intelligence community to transfer their most highly classified data.

Charlie 'DarkGod' Levy had – and he planned to use this as a punch line during his opening comments – wormed his way inside the CIA's brain.

Although the CIA's website had been brought down several times by 'denial-of-service attacks,' Levy would be the first to claim, and to prove publicly, that he had hacked into actual top-secret CIA cables, thereby reading classified information sent between CIA Langley and CIA stations and officers abroad.

This would be huge news in the amateur hacking world, that a 'garage hacker' had infiltrated America's spy agency, but this was not the most interesting part of Levy's discussion, for the very simple reason that Levy would also announce that he had proof that he was not the first to do this.

When Charlie entered Intelink-TS and began poking around he discovered that another entity had beat him to it, and was, at that very moment, reading CIA message traffic via a RAT, a remote-access Trojan.

Charlie had the screen shots of the intrusion, the code, a thumbnail sketch of the entire brilliant RAT itself.

It was clear to Charlie that the malware was brilliant and

he had already decided he would not mention that the RAT the other hacker used was several orders of magnitude more advanced than the code he had managed to put together to access the zero-day vulnerability.

This was an absolute bombshell, and in the thirty-five days since Levy had made this discovery, he'd told no one about it.

He looked around the pool deck at the glitterati of DEF CON here with him, and he knew that in twenty-four hours they'd have to take a number to talk to him.

This DEF CON would be his coming-out party.

Of course Levy knew it was inevitable that he would catch a lot of grief from the government about not only his successful hacking, but his revelation that he knew good and well that someone else was privy to America's deepest, darkest secrets, and he had not alerted the authorities. He thought he might get harassed by the Feds for what he had done, but he also pictured tens of thousands of members of his community coming out in support of him and standing up against the government.

Getting harassed by the Feds was a rite of passage.

There was one more chapter to Charlie Levy's story, and this he would also reveal at tomorrow's presentation.

The mystery hacker on the CIA network had discovered Levy's intrusion. His RAT had been so well built it was able to recognize when someone pushed into the network by the same means as had he.

How did Charlie know this? Because the hacker contacted him via instant messaging two weeks ago, offering DarkGod money to work remotely for him on other projects involving JWICS and Intelink-TS systems.

Levy was stunned when he realized he had been identified, but he knew there was no way in hell the mystery hacker had ID'd him through Intelink-TS. Levy was confident in his methods of attack concealment; he performed his digital breach of the CIA network over a complicated series of hops and proxies that would completely mask the machine of origin. The only explanation he came up with for how he was discovered was his research into JWICS, Intelink-TS, and the protocols and architecture used by the networks. Some of this research had been performed on open networks that, theoretically, could have been monitored by the mystery hacker.

Somehow, the mystery hacker was smart enough, and his visibility over the Internet was pervasive enough, that he'd deduced Levy's involvement.

When Levy declined the offer to work with the other entity – Levy did not want to be someone else's hired gun – his computer came under heavy persistent attack from a wide variety of sophisticated cyberthreats. The mystery hacker was doing his best to infiltrate Levy's computer. But Dark-God was no mere mortal when it came to computer security, and he took up the challenge as if he was playing chess with the mystery hacker and he had, for the last two weeks, anyway, managed to keep all malware off his machine.

Charlie Levy fully expected his new nemesis to be present at DEF CON, or else at the Black Hat conference, a more corporate convention for security professionals that would take place the following week here in Vegas.

Charlie hated to think that the son of a bitch might try to steal his thunder.

It took a while for Levy to loosen up with the rest of the guys, but by three a.m. he'd downed close to ten Coronas and he was feeling no pain. It was always like this on the first night, when the booze flowed out at the pool. Although all of the other guys were married with children now, they came to Vegas with the dual objectives of getting as drunk as possible and carrying on and even expanding their legendary exploits around DEF CON.

The Google guy had just stumbled off to bed, but the rest of the crew was still out by the pool, drinks in hand. Levy reclined on a chaise longue with a fresh Corona while the Microsoft guys smoked Cohibas next to him and AT&T and French Bank reclined on pool floats in the water with their drinks and their laptops.

While the party slowly died down at the South Hedgeford Court home, at another vacation rental five doors down on East Quail Avenue the glass patio door slid silently open. The home was pitch black and appeared unoccupied, but out of the darkness eight men stepped into the moonlit backyard, walked around the covered swimming pool, and made their way to a wooden fence.

Each man carried a black backpack on his back and a handgun equipped with a long suppressor in a holster on his hip. One at a time they climbed the fence and dropped down into the next yard, their movements stealthy and quiet.

AT&T looked up from his laptop while he floated on the pool chair. 'Hey, DarkGod. We've all talked about our presentations, but you haven't said shit about your topic.'

One of the Microsoft guys blew out Cohiba smoke and said, 'That means Charlie's talk is either really good or really bad.'

'Wouldn't you like to know?' replied Charlie, slyly.

French Bank shook his head; he paddled with his hand to turn himself toward the men on the deck. 'If it's anything like two years ago when you cracked into the Bellagio's physical plant and increased the pressure on the fountain pumps, I'll pass. Squirting a few dozen tourists is not my idea of – Hi. Can we help you?'

The rest of the men at the pool turned their heads, following the direction French Bank was looking. There, in the moonlight just out of the lights of the pool deck, several men stood in a row, facing the pool.

Charlie sat up. 'Who the hell are you guys?'

The Corona in Charlie's hand exploded with a pop, and he looked down. His 'Hack Naked' shirt was ripped, and blood drained from his chest. A second hole next to the first appeared as he watched.

A third round struck him in the forehead, and he flipped back on the chaise, dead.

The two men in the deck chairs were sluggish from the alcohol, but they both managed to stand and turn. One made it a few feet up the deck toward the house, but both were cut down by suppressed handgun rounds to the back.

One of them tumbled into the swimming pool; the other fell back over his chair into a small rock garden.

The two men on the pool floats were helpless. They both screamed out, but they were gunned down where they lay, their dead bodies draining blood into the clear water along with the blood from the Microsoft man floating facedown nearby.

When everyone at the pool was dead, Crane, the leader of the unit, turned to Stint. In Mandarin he said, 'There should be one more. Find him.'

Stint ran into the house with his pistol in front of him.

The Google man had slept through it all, but Stint found him in his bed, and put a single round through the back of his head.

Out by the pool, three of the men used small flashlights to

pick up the spent shell casings, while three more men went back inside, checking room by room to find DarkGod's luggage. They went through it and took his laptop and all his peripherals, his papers, thumb drives, DVDs, mobile phone, and anything else other than clothing. In place of all this, they left a handful of DVDs and thumb drives of their own, and a mobile phone spoofed with Levy's number and data that they downloaded from his device.

All this took more than ten minutes, but Crane had been given several objectives, and he'd been ordered to be perfectly thorough.

Soon all four were back out on the pool deck. The swimming pool water was bright pink now. On Crane's command, Wigeon unzipped his backpack and took out three small bags of high-quality cocaine. He tossed these in the grass near the fence, with the intention that the drugs would be found with the bodies and this entire event would appear to be a nefarious deal gone bad.

That none of the men had any drugs in their bodies could be explained by the fact that the deal had gone belly-up and the guns came out before anyone had time to partake in the drugs.

Finally Crane ordered everyone but Snipe back to the safe house, and the six men departed.

After they gave them time to get clear, Crane and Snipe stood on the side of the beautiful pool and unscrewed the silencers from their FN Five-seveNs. These they slipped into their backpacks. Then they aimed their weapons high above the horizon to the south, just below the hazy half-moon, and then both men opened fire.

They fired individual rounds and short volleys in a chaotic cadence, until both weapons were empty and the handguns' slides locked open. They then quickly reloaded, holstered their guns, and kicked the fallen spent shell casings in all directions. Some of the hot brass fell into the bloody pool, where it sank to the bottom; other casings rolled into the grass; and more rolled farther away along the decorative concrete deck.

As dogs barked in the neighborhood and lights flipped on up and down East Quail Avenue and South Hedgeford Court, Crane and Snipe walked calmly but quickly down the driveway. They used a pedestrian gate by the main drive gate and then walked out onto the street.

The front door of a home across the street opened, a woman in a bathrobe stood backlighted by the overhead fixture in her entryway, and Snipe drew his pistol and fired twice at her, sending her back inside, crawling frantically to safety.

In seconds a gray panel truck pulled up and the two men climbed into the van. It rolled north, heading to I-15. While Grouse drove and the other men sat silently, Crane pulled out his phone and pressed a few buttons. After a long wait for a connection and an answer, he said, 'All objectives achieved.'

22

Sitting alone in front of a bank of glowing computer monitors in a glass office that overlooked a massive floor of open cubicle workspaces, a forty-eight-year-old Chinese man in a rumpled white shirt and a loose necktie nodded in satisfaction at Crane's news.

'Begin uploading data as soon as you can.'

'Yes, sir,' said Crane.

'*Shi-shi*' – thank you – the man in the office replied.

Dr Tong Kwok Kwan, code name Center, tapped the secure voice-over Internet earpiece in his right ear to disconnect the call. He looked out past his monitors toward the open office floor and considered his next play. He decided to make the quick walk across the operations floor to the workspace of his best coder to let him know DarkGod's data would be coming in shortly from America.

Normally he would simply touch a button on his desk and talk to the young man via videoconference, but he knew a personal visit would encourage the coder to take this matter seriously.

Tong looked around his spotlessly clean office. Though there were no pictures of family or other personal items in view, a small, unframed cardstock sign hung from the glass door to the hallway.

It was written in flowing Chinese calligraphy, the characters one above the other in a single vertical row. Taken from the *Book of Qi*, a history of China from AD 479 to 502, the line was one of the thirty-six stratagems, an essay about deception for politics, war, and human interaction.

Tong read the words aloud: *'Jie dao sha ren.'* Kill with a borrowed knife.

Although his unit of operatives in the United States had just killed on his behalf, Tong knew he himself was the borrowed knife.

Not much gave him pleasure, his brain had been virtually programmed by the state so that it did not respond to such banal stimuli as pleasure, but his operation was on track, and this satisfied Dr Tong.

He stood and left his dark office.

Tong Kwok Kwan was from Beijing originally, the only child of a union between two Soviet-trained mathematicians who worked in China's then-fledgling ballistic missile program.

Kwok Kwan had no Princeling pedigree, but his brilliant parents pushed academics upon him relentlessly, focusing his attention and his studies on mathematics. He consumed workbooks and textbooks as a child, but he reached adolescence in the early days of the personal computer, and his family saw immediately that his future lay in the near limitless power of the incredible machines.

Because of his good grades, the state sent him to the best schools, and then to the best universities. He went to the United States to heighten his abilities in computer programming, to MIT in 1984, and then to Caltech for his master's in 1988.

After Caltech, Tong came home and taught programming for a few years at China's University of Science and Technology, before beginning a doctoral program in computer science at the prestigious Peking University in Beijing.

By now the concentration of his studies was the Internet

and the new World Wide Web – specifically, their vulnerabilities and the ramifications of these vulnerabilities in any future conflict with the West.

In 1995, while a thirty-year-old doctoral candidate, he wrote a paper titled 'World War Under Conditions of Informationization.' Almost immediately the paper made its way from the world of Chinese academia to the People's Liberation Army and the Ministry of State Security. The Chinese government classified the document top-secret, and immediately MSS operatives fanned out into any institutions of higher learning where the paper had been distributed, picking up hard copies, retrieving floppy disks containing the work, and giving long, intense, and intimidating talks with any professor or student who had come into contact with it.

Tong was immediately brought to Beijing, and within weeks he was lecturing the military and intelligence communities on how to leverage cyberoperations against China's enemies.

The generals, colonels, and spymasters were in over their heads in Tong's lectures, since the arcane terminology used by the brilliant young man was difficult for them to follow, but they realized they had, in Tong, a valuable resource. He was handed his doctorate and placed in charge of a small but powerful cyberwarfare testing, training, and development group within the MSS, and he was also given responsibility over PLA and MSS computer defensive operations.

But Tong was not content to run teams of government computer network operators. He saw more potential for power in the harnessing of the individual and independent Chinese computer hacker. He formed an organization of independent Chinese hackers in 1997 called the Green Army Alliance. Under his direction they targeted websites and networks of China's enemies, achieving intrusions and registering some damage. Although their impact was relatively minor, it showed that his academic paper could, in fact, be implemented in the real world, and it only increased his cachet even more.

Later he started the Information Warfare Militia, a collection of civilians in the technology industry and academia who worked independently but under the direction of PLA's Third Department (Signals Intelligence).

In addition to this unit, Tong formed the Red Hacker Alliance. By courting or threatening hundreds of China's most accomplished amateur computer coders via online bulletin boards frequented by the hackers, and then organizing them into a purpose-driven force, he used the men and women to penetrate industry and government networks around the globe to steal secrets for China.

But Tong and his army developed the means to do more than steal digital data. During a public dispute between China's state-owned petroleum organization and an American oil company over a pipeline contract in Brazil, Tong came before the leadership of the MSS and asked them, quite simply, if they would like his Red Hacker Alliance to destroy the oil company.

He was asked by the ministers if he intended to destroy the American oil company's dominance in the marketplace.

'That is not what I mean. I mean, physically ruin them.'

'Shut their computers down?'

Tong's impassive face did not let on what he thought of these foolish ministers. 'Of course not. We need their computers. We have obtained command-level control of their pipelines and oil-drilling capacity. We have kinetic capabilities at their locations. We can cause actual real-world destruction.'

'Breaking things?'

'Breaking things, blowing things up.'

'And they can't stop you?'

'There are manual overrides for everything at the site, at the physical location. I am just assuming this, of course. Some human being can get in the way and close a pump or cut power to a control station. But I can do so much, so quickly, that there is no way their humans can stop me.'

No physical action was taken on the oil company. The Chinese government recognized, instead, the importance of Tong and his capabilities. He was not just a valuable resource, he was a potent weapon, and they would not waste this capability on ruining a single firm.

Instead he and his team hacked into the oil company's website and read sensitive internal communications between the oil company's executives about the acquisition attempt of the Brazil pipeline. Tong passed this on to China's state-owned National Petroleum Corporation, which used the information to underbid the Americans and win the contract.

Later, when K. K. Tong was tasked with stealing the plans for the U.S. Navy's quiet electric drive for its submarines, Tong and his hackers had the plans, representing five billion dollars in research by the U.S. Navy, in less than six weeks.

Dr Tong next personally extracted more than twenty terabytes of data from the Department of Defense's unclassified database, handing over to the PLA the names of all American Special Forces operators and their home addresses, the refueling schedules for every ship in the Pacific, and the training and leave rotations of virtually all military units.

He and his men also stole the plans for America's next-generation fighter, the F-35.

Shortly before the end of the decade, Tong, along with the heads of the PLA's Third Department (Signals

Intelligence) and Fourth Department (Electronic Counter Measures and Radar), developed the computer network operations component to the PLA policy of INEW, Integrated Network Electronic Warfare, the formal name of China's entire electronic warfare strategy. INEW would rely on electronic warfare to jam, deceive, and suppress America's ability to receive, process, and distribute information, and it was clear to all in the PLA by now that K. K. Tong and his civilian hacker army would be critical to INEW's success.

He and his minions infected millions of computers around the world, creating a robot army, a botnet, that could then be directed to attack a website or a network, overloading it with requests and denying service to anyone who attempted to log on. He directed his botnets to attack China's adversaries with devastating results, and the owners of the nodes on the robot army never knew their hardware was working for the PRC.

Unlike the rest of China, Tong operated in a constant state of war against the United States. Via espionage or harassing actions, he and his force of men and women, most of whom worked from home or their 'day job' workstations, endeavored to compromise American computer network operations at every turn and build a massive target portfolio in case a shooting war broke out.

There was only one problem with Tong and his endeavors, as far as the Chinese were concerned. He was too successful. He'd been given nearly free rein to go seek out access to U.S. networks, and eventually, the Americans began to notice. The U.S. government realized someone was, in effect, attaching a vacuum cleaner to their data and sucking it out.

They called the persistent attacks into their government and industrial networks at first Titan Rain, and a second series of attacks they called Shady Rat, and the Americans tasked hundreds of investigators with finding out who was behind them. China was suspected from the beginning, and as Tong's operation grew in scope and importance, the MSS and the Politburo insiders who knew of the cyberprogram grew worried that some of the more high-profile attacks could be positively attributed to China.

The United States made a series of arrests of hackers involved in the operation, and some of them were ethnic Chinese. This worried the Chinese greatly, and pressure was put on the PLA and MSS to do a better job covering their tracks in the future.

When the full scope of Tong's vulnerability became apparent to the PLA and the MSS, the decision was made that he needed to be protected at all costs, and his organization needed to be completely sequestered and distanced from the Chinese government. Deniable computer network operations were critical in this time of declared peace, and to remain deniable there could be no comebacks to China itself.

But Tong had become known in the United States as a key civilian computer operations official working for the PLA. The investigators in the FBI and NSA looking into China cyberoperations referred to his influence over cyberstrategy as the Tong Dynasty, and when the Chinese realized Tong had been outed to such a degree, they knew they had to act.

After much discussion, the decision was made by the head of the Ministry of State Security that K. K. Tong, whose official title of director of technological training for the Chengdu Military Region First Technical Reconnaissance Bureau belied his field-marshal level of influence on one of war fighting's five domains, would be arrested on false charges of corruption, and then he would 'escape' from custody.

Then Tong would relocate to Hong Kong and go under the protection of the 14K Triads. 'Triad' was something of a catchall title referring to an organization with many unaffiliated branches, but the 14K was the largest and most powerful branch in Hong Kong. The MSS and the 14K had no operational relationship with each other. Triad activity had long been a thorn in the side of the Chinese government, but Tong would 'sell' himself and his army of hackers to the Triads, and then repay them for their protection with money from any of the dozens of financial schemes his men and women ran around the globe.

The 14K would, of course, know only that Tong had escaped prison on the mainland and now was working in computer-related embezzlement and blackmail operations – black-hat computer crime.

The Triads would have no idea that ninety percent of the Tong organization's productivity involved cyberespionage and cyberwarfare, all on behalf of the Communist Party of China, the enemy of the Triads.

Tong was 'arrested,' and a short notice of his charges was printed in the *People's Daily*, a newspaper in China that served as a mouthpiece for the government. He was charged with computer crimes, and the article described an effort by Tong to embezzle electronically from ICBC, the state-owned Industrial and Commercial Bank of China.

The article was written to show the West that the mysterious Dr Tong was out of favor with Beijing, and it was written to show the Triads in Hong Kong that this mysterious Dr Tong had skills that could make them a great deal of money.

Tong was sentenced to the firing squad, but on the day of his scheduled execution, rumors came out of the prison that he had escaped with inside help. To enhance the ruse, prison officials ordered several guards shot the next day for their 'collaboration.'

The 14K Triads, the largest and most powerful underworld organization in Hong Kong, and the largest Triad in the world, took K. K. Tong in weeks later. He rebooted the army of civilian hackers that he had cultivated, and he reacquired his botnet army, and within months he was generating money for the Triads by using tens of thousands of nodes from his botnet to swindle credit card numbers with phishing e-mails.

Tong then started a new endeavor. With the 14K's blessing, though without any understanding of what he was really up to, Tong purchased hundreds of computers and recruited top-level hackers from the mainland and Hong Kong to operate them, bringing them slowly into Hong Kong and into the fold of his new operation.

K. K. Tong adopted the handle 'Center' and called the physical hub for his new worldwide operation, his nerve center, the Ghost Ship. It was housed on the eleventh through the sixteenth floors of a Triad-owned office building in Mong Kok, a gritty high-density and lower-income portion of Kowloon, well to the north of Hong Kong's lights and glamour. Here the Triads watched over Tong and his people night and day, although they remained oblivious of his true mission.

Tong employed dozens of the best coders he could find, mostly men and women from his earlier hacker 'armies.' The rest of his employees he called controllers – these were his intelligence officers, and they all used the handle 'Center' when dealing with their assets. They operated from workstations on the operations floor of the Ghost Ship, and they communicated via Cryptogram instant messaging with the hackers and physical assets who unknowingly worked for them around the world.

The controllers used cash payments, coercion, and false flag trickery to co-opt thousands of individual hackers, script kiddies, criminal gangs, intelligence operatives, government employees, and key tech-industry personnel into a massive intelligence organization the size and scope of which the world had never seen.

Tong and his top lieutenants patrolled the hundreds of Internet forums used by Chinese hackers, and from here they found their army. One man and one woman at a time were discovered, vetted, approached, and employed.

The Ghost Ship now had nearly three hundred employees working in the building itself, and thousands more working on its behalf around the world. Where language was a problem they posted in English or used high-quality language-translation software. Tong recruited foreign hackers into his network, not as Ghost Ship operators but as proxy agents, none knowing they were working for the Chinese government but many certainly recognizing that their new employers came from Asia.

The physical agents came last. Underworld organizations were recruited to work on 'meat space' ad hoc projects. The best of these received regular assignments from Center.

The Libyan organization in Istanbul was an example of this, although their controller saw almost immediately that natural selection would work against the fools, especially their communications officer Emad Kartal, a man who did not follow his own security protocols.

The controller overseeing the cell in Istanbul had discovered that a group of Americans who worked for the company Hendley Associates was conducting surveillance on the Libyans. With Dr Tong's blessing the controller allowed the assassination of the entire five-man cell, all for the objective of planting a virus on the closed network of Hendley Associates so that the Ghost Ship could learn more about them. The plan had failed when the masked Hendley Associates gunman took the entire computer with him instead of doing what the controller had hoped, pulling media off the machine and returning to the States to place it on his own network.

Still, Tong's controllers had already been working other avenues to learn about the true nature of the curious organization Hendley Associates.

Other criminal organizations hired by Center included Triad groups in Canada and the United States, as well as Russian *bratva*s, or brotherhoods.

Soon Tong began active recruitment of more high-level espionage professionals to work as field assets. He found Valentin Kovalenko and decided he would be perfect for this task, used one of his Russian *bratva*s to get him out of prison, and then used blackmail to retain the strong-willed ex-assistant *rezident*.

As with many other spies, Center started Kovalenko out slowly, monitored his success and his ability to keep himself undetected, and then he began giving him more and more responsibility.

Tong also had another type of spy unwittingly under his command.

The converted spy.

These were turned employees in government agencies around the world, in businesses like telecommunications and finance, and in military contractor and law enforcement positions.

None of these co-opted members of the organization had any idea they were working on behalf of the Chinese government. Many of these assets felt the same as did Valentin Kovalenko, that they were conducting some sort of industrial espionage on behalf of a large and unscrupulous foreign technology concern. Others were convinced they were in the employ of organized crime.

Dr K. K. Tong was in control of the entire operation, taking directives from the Chinese military and intelligence communities, and so directing his controllers, who then directed their field assets.

It helped, perhaps more than anything else, that Dr K. K. Tong was a sociopath. He moved his humans across the earth much as he moved 1's and 0's across the information superhighway. He had no more regard for one than the other, though the failings of human beings caused him to look with more respect at the malicious code he and his hackers developed.

After two years of Ghost Ship activity, it became clear to Tong that his near-omnipotent control was not enough. Word was getting out about brilliant new viruses, worldwide networking of cybercrime, and successful penetrations of industry and government networks. To combat the spread of information, Tong told the PLA and MSS leadership that in order for his cyberoperations to have maximum effect, he would need additional kinetic assets, a unit of soldier-spies in America, not duped assets but men dedicated to the Communist Party of China and completely beholden to Center.

After argument, deliberation, and finally the involvement of senior military officials, the computer operations man Tong was given command authority over a team of PLA special-operations officers. Everything Tong did worked, they reasoned. His two years of running proxy assets around the world had greatly empowered the PLA and strengthened the Chinese cause. Why not allow him a small unit of additional deniable forces?

Crane and his team, eight men in all, came from Divine Sword, a special-operations unit of the Beijing Military Region.

They were highly trained in reconnaissance, counterterrorism, and direct action. The team sent to the United States to follow the instructions of Center was given additional vetting for bravery, pure ideological thought, and intelligence.

They were infiltrated into Vancouver Triad crime for a few months before making their way south over America's porous border with Canada. Here they lived in safe houses rented or purchased by Ghost Ship front companies, and they had documentation, thanks to Center and his ability to generate resources of all types.

Crane and his cell, if captured or killed, would be explained away as a team of Triad gangsters from Vancouver, working for computer criminals somewhere in the world. Certainly not at the behest of the CPC.

As in the operation in Menlo Park and the operation in Las Vegas, Crane and his men performed wet operations, killing people who represented a threat to Center's operations and stealing code and records necessary to further Ghost Ship activities.

Those few highly placed individuals in the PLA and the MSS who knew about Center and his Ghost Ship were pleased. The Chinese had their weapon, and their plausible deniability. They could steal secrets from American government, military, and industry, and they could prepare the battle space for any upcoming conflict. If Tong and his organization were ever discovered, well, he was an enemy of Beijing, working with the Triads – how could anyone make the claim that he and his people were working *for* the Chinese Communists?

It was a short walk from Tong's office up a well-lit linoleum-floored hallway to a set of double doors, guarded on either side by hard local men with space-age-looking QCW-05 submachine guns hanging from their chests. The guards wore no uniforms; one wore a scuffed leather jacket and the other a blue polo shirt with the white collar turned up to his ears.

Dr Tong did not address the men as he passed through the doorway, but this was nothing out of the ordinary. He never spoke to them. Tong did not make small talk with any of his underlings, much less the thirty or forty local Triads on and around the premises who had been tasked with protecting him and his operation.

A strange relationship, to be sure. A strange relationship that Tong himself did not care for, though he understood the strategic necessity of leaving his homeland to come to Hong Kong.

Through the double doors K. K. Tong walked down the middle of the open operations floor, passing dozens of men and women hard at work at their desks. Twice someone stood and bowed to Center and asked him for a moment of his time. Both times Dr Tong just held up a hand as he passed, indicating he would get back with them momentarily.

Right now he was looking for someone specific.

He passed the banking and phishing department, the research and development department, the social media and engineering department, and made his way to the coders' department.

This was where the men and women worked who did the actual computer network hacking.

At a workstation in the back corner of the room, next to a floor-to-ceiling window that, had it not been covered over with red velour drapes, would have given a southerly view over Kowloon, a young man with dramatically spiked hair sat in front of a bank of four monitors.

The young Chinese punk stood and bowed when Tong appeared behind him.

The older man said, 'Kinetic operation complete. You should be receiving data shortly.'

'*Sie de, xiansheng.*' Yes, sir. With a bow the man turned back to his desk and sat down.

'Zha?'

He quickly stood back up and turned around.

'Yes, sir?'

'I want a report on what you find. I don't expect Dark-God's code will reveal anything you can use to optimize your RAT before we attack DoD, but keep an open mind. He did well to get as far as he did in the CIA Intelink network with his limited resources.'

The punk rocker said, 'Of course, sir. I will look at Dark-God's code and report to you.'

Tong turned and headed back through the operations room without another word.

The young punk rocker's name was Zha Shu Hai, but he was known in cyberspace as FastByte22.

Zha was born in China, but his parents immigrated to the United States when he was a child and he became a U.S. citizen. Like Tong, he was something of a child prodigy in the computer sciences, and also like Tong, he went to Caltech, graduating at age twenty. When Zha was twenty-one years old he obtained a U.S. government security clearance and began working in the research-and-development department of General Atomics, a high-tech defense contractor in San Diego, and the manufacturer of unmanned aerial vehicles for the military and intelligence industries. Zha was tasked with testing secure and encrypted networks to see if the systems could be hacked into.

After two years of work, Zha reported back to General Atomics that such hacking was virtually impossible without specific knowledge of the networks, the communications gear that transmitted signals to the drones, and incredibly sophisticated equipment.

And then the young Chinese-American tried to make contact with the Chinese embassy in Washington, D.C., telling them that he would like to offer them his specific knowledge of all these things, and then help them build incredibly sophisticated equipment to help them exploit this knowledge.

Unfortunately for Zha, a routine polygraph required to maintain his clearance picked up strong indications of deception, and a search of his computer picked up the correspondence with the Chinese embassy. The young General Atomics penetration tester was arrested and sent to prison. As soon as Tong started the Ghost Ship, however, he used his resources to help the young man make his way out of the United States so he could join Tong in his operation in Hong Kong.

With Zha's knowledge of computer code and penetrating secure networks, he developed the Ghost Ship's powerful remote-access Trojan, the malware that allowed Center to steal data covertly, as well as see through the cameras and listen through the microphones of every machine it infected.

Zha's virus was as insidious as it was brilliant. It began by performing a port scan, looking for computer security's version of an unlocked window. If it found the exploitable port, it then began a series of common password attempts to make entry on the machine.

All this happened in the span of a few hundredths of a second. No one operating the computer at the time, unless they were watching the machine's resources carefully, would notice anything amiss.

If the worm succeeded in getting into the machine's subconscious, it then performed an ultra-high-speed reconnaissance, taking note of the applications installed and the quality of the processor and motherboard. Low-quality or older machines were rejected; the worm would instantly relay information back to the hacker that the node was not worth probing further, and then it would delete itself. High-end machines, on the other hand, were invaded further by the malware, the brain of the computer was taken over by the virus, and the message would go back to the hacker that another member of the robot army was reporting for duty.

Once the computer had been taken over by the Ghost Ship, a subroutine designed by FastByte22 himself would go into the system's machine code and remove any vestige of the delivery system.

Or so Zha thought. In truth, his subroutine missed a single strip of code, and this is what Gavin Biery detected on the Istanbul Drive.

With this virus Zha had been the first to break into the CIA's Intelink-TS network router for cable traffic, but on one of his maintenance forays into the source code, he realized he was not alone. He traced the other hacker, narrowing down the man's identity by monitoring research done at open source bulletin boards and technical directories, discovering he was a well-known amateur hacker in the United States named Charlie Levy. And then Center's controllers went to work trying to convince Levy to work for his organization so he could exploit the man's knowledge.

That attempt had failed, so Tong then tried to exploit Levy's knowledge by hacking into his machine.

That also failed. So Crane and his men got the information the old-fashioned way, by killing Charlie Levy and stealing it.

Tong knew Zha was cocky, and would not think DarkGod had anything in his virus that would improve on Zha's own work.

Tong, on the other hand, appreciated how much could be learned by pooling intellectual resources of individual hackers, even hackers who did not give up their intellectual resources willingly.

Zha may not have believed that Levy had anything to add to his code, but Tong felt he had been forceful enough to make clear to the young man that he would be expected to give the data stolen from DarkGod his full attention.

23

Thirty-four-year-old Adam Yao sat behind the wheel of his twelve-year-old Mercedes C-Class sedan and wiped his face with a beach towel he kept on the passenger seat. Hong Kong was hot as hell this fall, even at seven-thirty in the morning, and Adam wasn't running the air conditioner because he did not want his engine's noise to draw attention to his surveillance.

He was close to his target location, too close, and he knew it. But he had to park close. He was dealing with the lay of the land, the bend in the road and the close proximity of the parking lot to the target.

He was pushing his luck parking here, but he had no choice.

Adam Yao was on his own.

When most of the sweat was off his brow he brought his Nikon camera back to his eye and zoomed in on the lobby door of the high-rise condominium tower across the street. The Tycoon Court, it was called. Despite the cheesy name, it was opulent inside. Adam knew the penthouse digs, located here in the lush Mid-Levels neighborhood of Hong Kong Island, must have cost an arm and a leg.

He used his lens to scan the lobby, searching for the target of his surveillance. He knew it was unlikely the man would be standing around in the lobby. Adam had been coming here for days and each morning was the same. At about seven-thirty a.m. the subject would shoot out of the penthouse elevator, walk purposefully across the marble floor of the lobby, and step outside and duck into an SUV in the middle of a three-vehicle motorcade.

And that was as far as Adam Yao had been able to track the man. The windows of the SUVs were tinted, and the subject was always alone, and Adam had not yet tried to tail the motorcade through the twisting narrow streets of the Mid-Levels.

Doing that alone would be nearly impossible.

Adam wished he had support from the leadership of his organization, just some resources and personnel he could call on in times like this to lend a hand. But Adam worked for CIA, and pretty much every CIA officer in Asia knew one thing about the organization: there was a breach. Langley denied it, but it was clear to the men and women on the sharp edge over here that the PRC was getting tipped off about CIA plans and initiatives, sources and methods.

Adam Yao needed some help with this surveillance operation, but he didn't need it bad enough to risk compromise, because Adam Yao, unlike most every other CIA officer in China and HK, was working without a net. He was a CIA nonofficial cover officer, which meant he had no diplomatic protection.

He was a spy out in the cold.

Not that he wouldn't mind something cold at the moment. He reached for his beach towel and wiped more sweat off his face.

A few days ago Yao had been alerted to the presence here at the Tycoon Court of a man from the mainland, a known manufacturer of counterfeit computer hard drives and microprocessors that had made their way into critical systems of U.S. military equipment. His name was Han, and he was director of a large state-owned tech factory in nearby

Shenzhen. Han was in HK for some reason, and was getting picked up each morning by three white SUVs and driven off to an unknown location.

But even though this counterfeiter had managed to get his counterfeit devices into U.S. military equipment, to the CIA this was a commercial case, and commercial espionage was not something CIA put a lot of focus on over here.

Chicom cyberespionage and cyberwarfare were a big deal. Industrial computer crime was small potatoes.

But despite knowing good and well that Langley would show little interest in his initiative, Adam pushed ahead in this new investigation, for the simple reason that he very much wanted to know just who the hell the counterfeiter was meeting with on *Adam's* turf.

Yao had been holding the camera to his eye for so long that the rubber eyecup over the viewfinder was filling up with sweat. He started to lower it from his eye, but then the penthouse doors in the lobby opened and, true to his daily ritual, the Shenzhen knockoff computer hardware maker stepped out alone and walked across the lobby. Just then three white SUVs rolled by Yao's car and stopped under the awning of the Tycoon Court.

Each day the vehicles picking up the man were the same. Adam had been too far up the street to read the license plates on his earlier attempts, but today he was close enough to get a good angle and he had plenty of time to snap pictures of the tag numbers.

The back door to the second vehicle was opened from the inside, and the counterfeiter ducked in. In seconds the three SUVs rolled off, east on Conduit Court, disappearing around a hilly turn.

Yao decided he would attempt to tail the SUVs today. He would not get too close and it was unlikely he'd be able to follow them for long before he lost them in the thick traffic, but as far as he was concerned, he might as well head off in the same direction as they had on the offhand chance he'd get lucky and track them to a major intersection. If so, and assuming they took the same route each day, he could position himself farther along the route tomorrow and tail them a bit closer to their ultimate destination.

Any success using this technique would be a slow process and a long shot. But it beat coming here every morning, sitting here, day after day, which was beginning to look pointless.

He lowered his camera to the passenger seat and reached for his keys, but a loud rapping on his driver's-side window made him jump.

Two police officers peered in the window, and one used the plastic antenna of his walkie-talkie to knock on the glass. *Great.*

Yao rolled down the window. *'Ni hao,'* he said, which was Mandarin, and these cops likely spoke Cantonese, but he was pissed about wasting his morning, again, so he did not feel like being helpful.

Before the officer at the window said anything he looked past Yao to the passenger seat of the Mercedes, where the camera with the two-hundred-millimeter zoom lens sat next to a directional microphone with a set of headphones, a set of high-quality binoculars, a tiny notebook computer, a small backpack, and a legal pad full of handwritten notes.

He looked up at Adam now with suspicion. 'Step out.'

Adam did as he was told.

'Is there a problem?'

'Identification,' the officer demanded.

Adam reached carefully into his pants and pulled out his wallet. The cop a few meters back watched him closely as he did so.

Adam passed his entire billfold over to the officer who requested it, and he stood quietly while the man looked it over.

'What's all that in your car?'

'That is my job.'

'Your job? What, are you a spy?'

Adam Yao laughed. 'Not quite. I own a firm that investigates intellectual property theft. My card is right next to my license there. SinoShield Business Investigative Services Limited.'

The cop looked the card over. 'What do you do?'

'I have clients in Europe and the U.S. If they suspect a Chinese firm is manufacturing counterfeit versions of their goods over here, they hire me to investigate. If we think they have a case they'll hire local attorneys and try to get the counterfeiting stopped.' Adam smiled. 'Business is good.'

The cop relaxed a little. It was a reasonable explanation for why this guy was sitting in a parking space taking pictures of the comings and goings next door.

He asked, 'You are investigating someone at the Tycoon Court?'

'I'm sorry, officer. I am not allowed to reveal any information about an ongoing investigation.'

'The security office over there called about you. Said you were here yesterday, too. They think you are going to rob them or something.'

Adam chuckled and said, 'I'm not going to rob them. I won't bother them at all, though I wish I could sit in their lobby and enjoy the air-conditioning. You can check me out. I've got friends at HKP, mostly in B Department. You could call and get someone to vouch for me.' The Hong Kong Police B Department was the investigative branch, the detectives and organized crime force. The officers, Adam knew, would be A Department, the division under which the patrol cops worked.

The officer looking Adam over took his time. He asked Yao about some B Department police he knew, and Yao answered comfortably until a connection was made.

Finally satisfied, the two policemen headed back into their patrol car and left Adam by his Mercedes.

He climbed back inside his car and slammed his hand on the steering wheel in frustration. Other than tag numbers that would probably lead him nowhere, it had been a wasted day. He'd learned nothing about the counterfeiter and his activities he had not already known yesterday, and he'd been compromised by some damn security guard at a condominium tower.

Adam was once again, however, greatly appreciative of his fantastic cover for status. Running a private investigation firm gave him a ready-made excuse to be doing just about anything he could imagine being caught doing while in performance of his clandestine duties for the Agency.

As far as CIA nonofficial-cover 'white side' jobs were concerned, Adam Yao's SinoShield Business Investigative Services Ltd. was as solid as they came.

He drove off, down the hill and back toward his office near the harbor.

24

Jack Ryan, Jr, woke next to Melanie Kraft and immediately realized his phone was ringing. He had no idea of the time at first, but his body told him it was well before his normal internal clock's wake-up call.

He grabbed the ringing phone and looked at it. *2:05 a.m.* He groaned. He checked the caller ID.

Gavin Biery.

He groaned again. 'Really?'

Melanie stirred next to him. 'Work?'

'Yeah.' He did not want her to be suspicious, though, so he followed that with: 'The director of the IT department.'

Melanie laughed softly and said, 'You left your computer on.'

Jack chuckled, too, and started to put the phone back down.

'Must be important, though. You should take it.'

Jack knew she was right. He sat up and answered. 'Hello, Gavin.'

'You have got to come in right now!' said a breathless Gavin Biery.

'It's two a.m.'

'It's two-oh-six. Get here by two-thirty.' Biery hung up.

Jack put the phone back on the nightstand, fighting off a very strong urge to hurl it against the wall. 'I've got to go in.'

'For the IT guy?' Melanie's tone was incredulous.

'I've been helping him on a project. It was important, but

not "come in the middle of the night" important. But he seems to think this warrants a two-thirty a.m. meeting.'

Melanie rolled over, away from Jack. 'Have fun.'

Jack could tell she did not believe him. He sensed that a lot from her, even when he was telling her the truth.

Jack pulled into the parking lot of Hendley Associates just after two-thirty. He came through the front door and gave a tired wave to William, the night security officer behind the front desk.

'Morning, Mr Ryan. Mr Biery said you'd be staggering in looking like you just woke up. I've got to say you look a lot better than Mr Biery does during normal business hours.'

'He's going to look even worse after I kick his ass for dragging me out of bed.'

William laughed.

Jack found Gavin Biery in his office. He fought his mild anger over Biery's intrusion into his personal life and asked, 'What's up?'

'I know who put the virus on the Libyan's machine.'

This woke Jack up more than the drive from Columbia. 'You know the identity of Center?'

Biery shrugged dramatically. 'That I can't be sure of. But if it's not Center, it's somebody working for or with him.'

Jack looked over at Biery's coffeemaker, hoping to pour himself a cup. But the machine was off and the pot was empty.

'You haven't been here all night?'

'No. I was working from home. I did not want to expose the Campus network to what I was doing, so I did it from one of my personal machines. I just got here.'

Jack sat down. It was sounding more and more like Biery had had a very good reason to call him in after all.

'What have you been doing from home?'

'I've been hanging out in the digital underground.'

Jack was still tired. Too tired to play twenty questions with Gavin. 'Can you just fill me in while I sit here quietly with my eyes closed?'

Biery had mercy on Ryan. 'There are websites one can visit to conduct illegal business in cyberspace. You can go to these sort of online bazaars and buy fake IDs, recipes to build bombs, stolen credit card information, and even access to networks of previously hacked computers.'

'You mean botnets.'

'Right. You can rent or buy access to infected machines around the world.'

'You can just put in your credit card number and rent a botnet?'

Biery shook his head. 'Not your credit card number. Bitcoin. It's an online currency that is not traceable. Just like cash but better. It's all about anonymity out there.'

'So are you telling me you rented a botnet?'

'Several botnets.'

'Isn't that illegal?'

'It's illegal if you do something illegal with them. I did not.'

'What did you do?' Jack found himself playing twenty questions with Biery again.

'I had this theory. You know how I told you the string of machine code left on the Istanbul Drive could lead us to whoever the culprit was?'

'Sure.'

'I decided I would reach out in the cyberunderground, looking for other infected machines that also have the same lines of machine code that I found on the Libyan's machine.'

'That sounds like looking for a needle in a haystack.'

'Well, I figured there would be many machines out there with this virus. So it's more like looking for any one of a bushel of needles in a haystack, and I did what I could to make the haystack smaller.'

'How so?'

'There are a billion networked computers in the world, but the subset of hackable machines is much smaller, maybe a hundred million. And the subset of machines that have been hacked is probably a third of that.'

'But still, you had to check thirty million computers to –'

'No Jack, because malware that good isn't going to just be used on a couple of machines. No, I figured there were thousands, tens of thousands, or even hundreds of thousands of nodes out there with this same remote-access Trojan on them. And I narrowed it down further by only renting botnets of machines using the same operating system as the Libyan machines and high-quality processors and components, because I figured Center wouldn't fool around with any old machine. He'd want to break into the machines of important people, companies, networks, et cetera. So I just grabbed botnets of high-caliber players.'

'They rent out botnets of different quality?'

'Absolutely. You can order a botnet that is fifty machines at AT&T, or one that is two hundred fifty machines from offices of the Canadian Parliament, or a ten-thousand-node botnet of Europeans who have at least one thousand friends each on Facebook, twenty-five thousand computers that have industrial-quality security cameras attached to them. Pretty much any variable can be purchased or rented.'

'I had no idea,' admitted Jack.

'When I found botnets for sale possessing all the attributes I wanted, I just cast as wide a net as I could afford, rented them, and then ran some diagnostics on the hacked machines to pare them down further. Then I wrote a multithreaded program that took a peek at that location in each machine to see if that line of code was present.'

'And you found a computer with the Istanbul Drive code on it?'

The IT man's smile widened. 'Not *a* computer. One hundred twenty-six computers.'

Jack leaned forward. 'Oh my God. All with the identical piece of malware you found on the Libyan's drive?'

'Yes.'

'Where are these machines? What physical locations are we talking about?'

'Center is ... I don't want to sound too dramatic, but Center is *everywhere*. Europe, North and South America, Asia, Africa, Australia. All inhabited continents were represented in the infected machines.'

Jack asked, 'So how did you find out who he is?'

'One of the infected machines was being used as a relay to the command server. It was pushing traffic from the botnet to a network in Kharkov, Ukraine. I penetrated the network servers and saw that they hosted dozens of illegal or questionable websites. The sickest porn imaginable, online marketplaces for buying and selling fake passports, card skimmers, stuff like that. I hacked into each of these sites easily. But there was one location I could not get into. All I got was the name of the administrator.'

'What's the name of the administrator?'

'FastByte Twenty-two.'

Jack Ryan deflated. 'Gavin, that's not a name.'

'It's his computer handle. No, it's not his Social Security number and home address, but we can use it to find him.'

'Anybody can make up a handle.'

'Trust me, Jack. There are people out there who know

the identity of FastByte Twenty-two. You just have to find them.'

Jack nodded slowly, and then he looked at the clock on the wall.

It was not even three a.m.

'I hope you're right, Gavin.'

25

CIA nonofficial cover operative Adam Yao leaned against the entrance of a shuttered shoe store on Nelson Street, in Hong Kong's Mong Kok district, eating dumplings and noodles with chopsticks from a cardboard bowl. It was nearly nine o'clock in the evening, the last of the day's light had long left the sliver of sky between the tall buildings that ran down both sides of the street, and Adam's dark clothing made him all but invisible under the shadow of the doorway.

The pedestrian crowd was not what it was during the day, but there was still a good bit of foot traffic, mostly coming to or going from the nearby street stall market, and Adam welcomed the crowd, because he felt his chances of avoiding detection were higher with more people strolling about.

Adam was on the job, conducting a one-man surveillance on Mr Han, the counterfeit-chip maker from Shenzhen. After he took photos of the plates on the SUVs that picked Han up at Tycoon Court earlier in the week, he'd called a friend at the Hong Kong Police B Department and talked him into running the tags. The detective told Adam the owner of the vehicles was a real estate company in Wan Chai, a seedy neighborhood on Hong Kong Island. Adam looked into the company on his own and found it to be owned by a known Triad figure. This particular personality was a member of 14K, which was the biggest and the baddest Triad in HK. That explained the origin of the security goons protecting Han, but Yao found it very curious this high-tech computer manufacturer would involve himself with the 14K. The Triads as a whole kept their crime dirty – prostitution and protection rackets and drugs mostly – and the 14K were no more refined than the rest of the Triads. Any criminal operation Han would be involved in, on the other hand, would necessitate high-tech equipment and personnel.

This guy coming to HK and hanging around the 14K made no sense.

Once Adam knew Han was getting picked up each morning by gangsters, he spent the next few days moving around 14K-owned restaurants and strip clubs frequented by the vehicle's owner, until he found all three gleaming white SUVs parked in a covered lot outside a hot-pot restaurant in Wan Chai. Here, with an abundance of skill derived from working in two separate jobs that required such a technique, he slapped a tiny magnetized GPS tracking device under the rear bumper of one of the trucks.

The next morning he sat in his apartment and watched while a blinking dot on his iPhone moved across a map of Hong Kong, first up to the Mid-Levels to Tycoon Court, and then down into Wan Chai. The dot disappeared, which Adam knew meant the SUV was traveling under Victoria Harbour through the Cross-Harbour Tunnel.

Adam ran outside and leapt into his Mercedes, knowing where Han was headed.

He was going to Kowloon.

Yao ultimately tracked the SUV here, to the big office building that held the Mong Kok Computer Centre, a several-story-tall warren of tiny storefronts selling everything from knockoff software to brand-new original high-tech motion-picture cameras. Anything electronics-related, from printer paper to mainframes, could be purchased here, though much of it was counterfeit and much more of it was stolen.

Above the Computer Centre were two dozen more floors of office space.

Adam did not go inside the building. He was a one-man band, after all, and he did not want to reveal himself to his quarry this early in the investigation. So he sat outside this evening, waiting for Han to leave, hoping to get pictures of everyone who came and went at the entrance of the building in the meantime.

He had attached a remote miniature camera with a magnet to the outside of a closed magazine stand on the sidewalk, and he had a wireless device in his pocket with which he could pan and zoom the lens and snap off rapid-fire high-quality pictures.

So he sat just up the street and watched, slurped noodles and dumplings from his bowl, and took pictures of all activity at either the front of the building or a side alley entrance right next to him.

For three consecutive nights he had photographed more than two hundred faces. Back in his office he ran the images through facial-recognition software, looking for anyone interesting he might link with Mr Han or the sale of military-grade computer equipment to the United States.

So far he'd come up with nothing.

It was boring work, for the most part, but Adam Yao had been doing this for a long time, and he loved the job. He told himself that if he were ever moved into an embassy position with the CIA's National Clandestine Service he would leave the Agency and start his own company, doing just exactly what his cover organization did, business investigations in China and Hong Kong.

Operating undercover in the streets was exciting, and Adam rued the day when he would be too old or too settled down to worry about anything more than his mission.

Four men appeared out of the dark alley that ran alongside the building that housed the Mong Kok Computer Centre. They passed close by Adam, but he looked down at his bowl and scooped dumplings and noodles into his mouth with his chopsticks. After they passed his position he looked up and immediately pegged three of their number as Triad soldiers. They wore open jackets on the warm evening, and Adam suspected they would be carrying small machine pistols under them. Along with them, a fourth man walked; he was slighter than the others and he wore his long hair spiked and gelled. He was dressed oddly, a tight purple T-shirt and tight jeans, a half-dozen bracelets on his arm and a gold chain around his neck.

He looked less like a Triad and more like a punk rocker.

It appeared to the American in the dark doorway that the three Triads were watching over this kid, much like the detail that protected Mr Han.

Adam stuck his hand into the pocket of his slacks and found the remote control for the camera affixed to the magazine stand, and then he looked down to his smart phone and the image from the camera's lens. He pushed a tiny control stick on the remote, and the camera rotated ninety degrees, more or less centering itself on the quickly moving punk rocker. Adam depressed a button all the way down on the control box and, at a range of only two meters, the camera started recording high-definition images, four per second.

The pictures clicked off automatically, but Yao had to pan the camera via the control stick to keep the subject in the frame. In seconds the four men had moved up Nelson Street and out of range, and then they turned left on Fa Yuen Street and disappeared from Adam Yao's sight.

He had no idea if they would be returning tonight. He pushed himself back in the doorway to wait for Han, but as he sat back down with his noodles he decided to take a quick look at the images he had just recorded.

The camera was connected via Bluetooth to his iPhone, and it was a quick and easy thing to review the last set of images. The camera had night-vision capability, so the faces, while not perfectly clear, were a hell of a lot better than they would have been if they were shot without a flash with a normal camera in this nighttime street.

He scrolled through them. He saw the first two meatheads pass by; they had the requisite 'Fuck off' expressions of gangsters who thought they owned the sidewalk on which they walked. Behind them was the third security man; he looked to be as much of a thug as the others, but Adam noticed the man's left hand was low on the elbow of the punk rocker, leading him along as they walked up the street.

The kid was odd, and it was not just his clothes. He held a handheld computer with both hands and thumbed it furiously. Whether he was playing a game or working on his thesis, Yao could not tell, but he was intense and completely unaware of his surroundings. It looked to Adam as if the kid would walk into moving traffic without the three men in front of him guiding him up the street.

Adam looked at the young man's face now, illuminated via night-vision enhancement. He scrolled back and forth between the two closest and most in-focus images on his phone. Back and forth.

Back and forth.

The American CIA man could not believe his eyes. He muttered to himself, 'I know this asshole.'

Yao stood quickly and headed off in the direction of the four men. As he passed his magnetic remote camera, he deftly reached up and pulled it off the magazine stand without breaking stride.

Adam found the group ahead of him in the crowd, and he stayed a full city block behind them as they walked, but he managed to keep them in view for a few minutes, until they turned and went into the Kwong Wa Street post office.

Normally the young CIA officer would not chance a close encounter, but adrenaline was racing through his body, and it encouraged him forward. He walked right into the post office. It was closed for the evening, but the P.O. boxes and mail slots were still accessible, as was a stamp machine.

Adam walked right by the four men, he felt the eyes of the 14K goons on him as he passed, but he did not meet their gaze. Instead he pulled some HK dollars out of his pocket and bought stamps.

As he waited for the stamps to be dispensed he glanced over his shoulder, taking a mental snapshot of what he saw. The punk rocker had unlocked a P.O. box on the wall and was going through the mail on a wooden table. Adam could not hope to read the box number from across the room, but on a second glance, this one as he exited the post office, he took another quick mental snapshot.

He stepped back out into the street. He did not smile; he would not think of breaking his cover like that. But he *was* happy.

He got it.

The young man's P.O. box was the largest of the three sizes along the southern wall, four from the left, two from the bottom.

He walked deeper into the night, some eighty meters away from the building, and then he turned around.

The four men left the post office and headed in the opposite direction, and then turned into an apartment building, the Kwong Fai Mansion.

Yao looked up at the building. It was easily thirty stories

high. There was no chance in hell he could tail anyone inside that building. He turned and headed back for his car, still somewhat in shock by tonight's revelation.

It wasn't every day, after all, that Adam Yao stumbled upon a fugitive.

The kid's name was Zha Shu Hai, and Adam first heard of him more than a year earlier, when he was e-mailed a bulletin from the U.S. Marshals Service asking him to be on the lookout for an escaped felon who, both Marshals and FBI suspected, would be heading to China.

Zha was an American citizen who'd been arrested in San Diego for trying to sell the Chicoms classified engineering secrets from his employer, General Atomics, the makers of unmanned aerial vehicles for the Air Force. He'd been caught red-handed with hundreds of gigabytes of design information about the secure networks on which communications and GPS information was sent, and he'd bragged to the Chinese embassy that he knew how to bring the system down by hacking into its sat link, and how to obtain deep persistent access into the Department of Defense's secure network by building a RAT that could infect a government contractor's network and then swim upstream. The Feds did not believe him, but they weren't sure, so they offered him partial immunity if he told General Atomics everything he knew about the system's vulnerabilities.

Zha refused, and was sentenced to eight years in prison.

After just one year in a minimum-security federal correctional facility, however, he walked away from a work-release program and disappeared.

Everyone in the States knew Zha would try to slip back to China. Adam had been working in Shanghai at the time, and he'd received the BOLO, or 'Be on the lookout' notice, from the Marshals Service because there was a reasonable expectation that some high-tech firm in Shanghai would employ Zha if he did make it to the mainland.

Adam had all but forgotten about it, especially after he moved from the mainland to Hong Kong.

Until tonight. It was clear Zha had done much to change his appearance; the booking photo on the BOLO showed a nondescript young Chinese man, not a spiky-haired flamboyant punk rocker, but Adam Yao recognized him nonetheless.

As Adam climbed into his car, he wondered about this strange relationship. Why the hell would Zha be here, in the protection of the Triads? Much like his discovery that Mr Han had a relationship with the local street thugs, Zha was, if everything the Feds said about his abilities as a top-level black-hat hacker were to be believed, seriously out of the 14K's league.

Yao had no idea what this meant, but he knew he'd be placing all of his other work on hold in order to find out.

One other thing was certain, though. He would not be shooting an e-mail to the U.S. Marshals Service or the FBI.

Adam Yao was a NOC; he wasn't exactly a team player. He knew that a call to the Marshals Service would bring marshals and embassy staff here to the post office on Kwong Wa Street and the Mong Kok Computer Centre, and he also knew good and well that Zha and the 14K would see all the white guys with earpieces, they would leave the area, and that would be that.

And there was another reason Adam decided to sit on this news for now.

The obvious breach at CIA.

In the past few months several CIA initiatives had been thwarted by the MSS. Well-placed agents in the government were arrested, dissidents in contact with Langley were imprisoned or executed, electronic operations against the PRC were discovered and shut down.

At first it appeared to be just bad luck, but as time went on, many were sure the Chinese had someone working in Beijing Station.

Adam, the one-man band, had always played his cards close to his vest. It came with being a NOC. But now he really was operating out on his own. He sent Langley as little cable traffic as possible and had no communication whatsoever with either Beijing Station or the CIA field officers at the U.S. consulate in Hong Kong.

No, Adam would sit on his discovery of Zha Shu Hai, and he would find out on his own what this guy was doing here.

He just wished he had a little help. Being a one-man band made for long hours and frustrating setbacks.

That said, it was a hell of a lot better than getting burned.

26

It might come as a surprise to many of the patrons of the Indian Springs Casino on Nevada's Route 95 to know that America's most distant and most secret wars are fought from a cluster of single-wide trailers a little more than a half-mile from the blackjack tables.

In the Mojave Desert northwest of Las Vegas, the runways, taxiways, hangars, and other structures of Creech Air Force Base serve as home to the 432nd Air Expeditionary Wing, the only wing dedicated to unmanned aircraft. From here, within sight of the Indian Springs Casino, pilots and sensor operators fly drones over denied territory in Afghanistan, Pakistan, and Africa.

Drone pilots don't climb into a cockpit for takeoff; instead they enter their ground-control station, a thirty-foot-by-eight-foot trailer in a parking lot on the grounds at Creech. Detractors, often 'real' pilots, refer to the 432nd as the Chair Force, but even though the men and women of Creech are some 7,500 miles from the battle space over which their aircraft fly, with their state-of-the-art computers, cameras, and satellite control systems they are as connected to the action as any fighter pilot looking out a canopy.

Major Bryce Reynolds was the pilot of Cyclops 04, and Captain Calvin Pratt served as the aircraft's sensor operator. While Reynolds and Pratt sat comfortably at the far end of their ground-control station, their drone, an MQ-9 Reaper, flew just inside the Pakistani border, twenty thousand feet over Baluchistan.

A few feet behind the pilot and sensor-operator seats in the GCS was master control, a lieutenant colonel overseeing the Reaper's mission, coordinating with units in the Afghanistan theater, the UAV's physical base at Bagram in Afghanistan, and intelligence operatives monitoring the flight in both hemispheres.

Though this evening's flight was designated reconnaissance and not a hunter/killer mission, the Reaper's wings carried a full weapons loadout, four Hellfire missiles and two five-hundred-pound laser-guided bombs. Reconnaissance flights often came upon targets of opportunity, and Cyclops 04 was ready to wreak destruction, should the need arise.

Reynolds and Pratt were three hours into their six-hour mission, monitoring ground traffic on Pakistan's National Highway N-50 near Muslim Bagh, when the flight's master controller voice came over their headsets.

'Pilot, MC. Proceed to the next waypoint.'

'MC, pilot, roger,' Reynolds said, and he tilted the joystick to the left to give Cyclops 04 twenty degrees of bank, then looked down to take a sip of his coffee. When he glanced back up he expected to see his monitor displaying the downward-looking infrared camera indicating a bank to the west.

But the monitor showed the vehicle was continuing its straight path.

He looked at the attitude indicator to check this, and saw the wings were level. He knew he did not have the autopilot engaged, but he checked again.

No.

Major Reynolds pushed the stick a little harder, but none of the relevant displays responded.

He tried banking to the right now, but still there was no response from the bird.

'MC, pilot. I've got a dead stick here. Not getting any positive reaction. I think we've got a lost link.'

'MC copies, understood Cyclops 04 has gone stupid.' *Gone stupid* was a term UAV pilots used to indicate the platform was no longer responding to operator commands. It happened sometimes, but it was a rare enough occurrence to warrant immediate attention from the base's technicians.

Sensor operator Captain Pratt, seated on Reynolds's right, said, 'Sensor confirms. I'm not getting any response from the UAV.'

'Roger,' said master control. 'Wait one. We'll troubleshoot.'

While Reynolds watched his aircraft fly due north, the heading he had given the Reaper several minutes earlier, he hoped to hear the MC report back that they had identified some glitch in the software or the sat link. In the meantime, there was nothing he could do but watch the screens in front of him, as uninhabited rocky hills passed by twenty thousand feet under his drone.

The Reaper software contained an important fail-safe that the pilot in the GCS expected to see initiated in the next few moments if the technicians were unable to get the UAV back online. Once Cyclops 04 went a certain amount of time with a broken link to the GCS, it would execute an autopilot landing sequence that would send the vehicle to a predetermined rally point and put it safely on the ground.

After a few more minutes of flying untethered to the GCS and unsuccessful attempts by technicians to find what was going on with the Linux-based software, Reynolds saw the attitude indicator move. The starboard wing lifted above the artificial horizon, and the port wing dropped below it.

But the emergency autopilot landing fail-safe had not kicked in. The drone was making a course correction.

Major Reynolds let go of the joystick completely to confirm he was not affecting the Reaper accidentally. The wings continued to tilt; all camera displays showed the vehicle was turning to the east.

The UAV was banking at twenty-five degrees.

Captain Pratt, the sensor operator, asked softly, 'Bryce, is that you?'

'Uh . . . negative. That is *not* my input. Pilot, MC, Cyclops 04 just altered course.' As he finished his transmission he saw the wings level out. 'Now it's holding level at zero-two-five degrees. Altitude and speed unchanged.'

'Uh . . . repeat last?'

'Pilot, MC. Cyclops flight is doing its own thing here.'

A moment after this, Major Reynolds saw that the speed of Cyclops 04 was ticking up quickly.

'Pilot, MC. Ground speed just went up to one-forty, one-fifty . . . one-sixty-five knots.'

While a nonresponsive aircraft that had temporarily 'gone stupid' was not unheard of, a UAV executing its own turns and increasing speed without controller input was something never seen before by the operators in the GCS or any of the technicians in communication with them.

For the next several minutes the pilot, the sensor operator, and the MC worked quickly and professionally but with a growing level of concern. They cycled through programs on multiple screens, clearing out autopilot commands and way-point coordinates and loitering information, all trying to clear some glitch command that had caused their armed air-craft to stray off course.

Their monitors showed the infrared image on the ground as the UAV proceeded to the east. None of their attempts to retake control had worked.

'Pilot, MC. Tell me we've got someone working on this?'

'Roger that. We've . . . we're trying to reestablish link.

We've established comms with General Atomics, and they are troubleshooting.'

The UAV made several more speed and course corrections as it neared the border with Afghanistan.

Sensor Operator Cal Pratt was the first man at Creech AFB to say aloud what everyone aware of the situation was thinking. 'This isn't a software glitch. Somebody's hacked the PSL.' The primary satellite link was the satellite umbilical cord that sent messages from Creech to the Reaper. It was – theoretically, at least – impossible to disrupt and take over, but there was no other explanation anyone on the ground could come up with for what was happening to the UAV 7,500 miles away.

The GPS readout indicated that Cyclops 04 crossed the border into Afghanistan at 2:33 local time.

Reynolds plotted the current course. 'Pilot. At present heading and speed, in fourteen minutes Cyclops 04 will arrive over a populated area. It will pass two klicks east of Qalat, Afghanistan.'

'MC copies.'

'Sensor copies.'

After a few more seconds: 'MC. We are in contact with intelligence assets at Kandahar . . . They advise there is a forward operating base two kilometers east of Qalat. FOB Everett. U.S. and ANA forces on the ground there.'

'We'll be passing directly overhead.'

It was quiet in the GCS for several seconds. Then Captain Pratt said, 'Surely to God . . .' He paused, not even wanting to say the rest aloud. But he did say it. 'Surely to God it can't launch ordnance.'

'No,' answered back Reynolds, but he did not sound so sure. 'Pilot, MC. Do we want to . . . uh . . . ascertain whether or not we have any air assets in the area that can, uh, shoot down the UAV?'

There was no response.

'Pilot, MC, did you copy my last? It is clearly in someone else's hands and we do not know their intentions.'

'Copy, pilot. We are getting in contact with Bagram.'

Reynolds looked to Pratt. Shook his head. Bagram Air Force Base was too far away from Cyclops 04 to be of any use.

Within moments there was more activity in the GCS, the images on several displays changed, and the onboard cameras began switching through color mode to infrared/black-hot mode and then to infrared/white-hot mode. The display cycled through all settings multiple times but not at a constant speed. Finally it settled on infrared/white-hot.

Reynolds looked over at Pratt. 'That's a human hand making those inputs.'

'No doubt about it,' confirmed the sensor operator.

'MC, pilot. Bagram advises there is a flight of F-16s inbound. ETA thirty-six minutes.'

'Shit,' said Pratt, but he wasn't transmitting. 'We don't have thirty-six minutes.'

'Not even close,' confirmed Reynolds.

The camera lens display on the primary control console began adjusting, finally zooming in on a distant hilltop, upon which several square structures lay in a circular pattern.

'MC. That's going to be Everett.'

A green square appeared on the primary control console around the largest building on the hilltop.

'It's locked up,' Pratt said. 'Somebody has access to all capabilities of Cyclops.' He feverishly tried to break the target lock with keyboard controls, but there was no response from the vehicle.

Everyone in the GCS knew that their drone was targeting the American base. And everyone knew what would come next.

'Do we have somebody who can get in contact with this FOB? Warn them that they are about to receive fire?'

The MC came over their headsets. 'Kandahar is on it, but there is going to be a lag.' He followed that with, 'Anything that's about to happen is going to happen before we can get a message to them.'

'Christ Almighty,' said Reynolds. 'Fuck!' He jammed his joystick hard to the left and right, and then forward and back. There was no reaction on the screen. He was nothing more than a spectator to this looming disaster.

'Master arm is on,' reported Captain Pratt now.

And then he began reading off information as it appeared on his displays. There was nothing else he could do but provide narration for the disaster. 'Midstore pylons, selected.'

'Pilot copies.'

'Sensor, pilot,' Pratt said, his voice quavering slightly now. 'Hellfire is spinning up. Weapon power is on. Laser is armed. Weapon is hot. Where are those goddamned F-16s?'

'MC, sensor. Thirty minutes out.'

'Damn it! Warn the fucking FOB!'

'Laser fired!' This would give the exact range-to-target information to the UAV. It was the last step before launching a Hellfire.

Seconds later the Reaper let loose a missile. Its five-hundred-pound warhead raced away at the lower edge of the monitor, the flame behind it whiting out the camera for a moment before the screen cleared up and only a bright, fast-moving speck was visible.

'Rifle!' Reynolds shouted. *Rifle* was the term used to indicate the pilot had fired a missile, but there was no term to use for a phantom launch, so he said it anyway. He then read aloud the targeting data on his PCC. 'Time of flight, thirteen seconds.'

His stomach tightened.

'Five, four, three, two, one.'

The impact of the Hellfire whited out the center of the monitor. It was a massive detonation, with several secondary explosions, indicating that munitions or fuel had been hit by the missile.

'Son of a bitch, Bryce,' muttered Pratt from his seat on Major Bryce Reynolds's right.

'Yeah.'

'Shit!' Pratt said. 'Another Hellfire is spinning up.'

Thirty seconds later Reynolds called 'Rifle!' again. 'Looks like the same target.'

A pause. 'Roger that.'

Together they sat, watching the feed through the eyes of their aircraft as it attacked friendly forces.

All four Hellfires launched from the Air Force Reaper, striking three different prefabricated buildings in the FOB.

The two bombs then dropped, detonating on an unoccupied rocky hillside.

After the launching of all its weapons, Cyclops 04 made an abrupt turn, increased speed to two hundred knots, virtually the UAV's top speed, and shot south toward the Pakistan border.

MC gave updates on the location of the F-16s; they were twenty minutes out, they were ten minutes out, they were just five minutes from having the drone in range of their AIM-120 AMRAAM air-to-air missiles.

At this point it was not about saving lives. At this point it was about destroying the Reaper before it 'escaped' into Pakistan, where it could end up in enemy hands.

The drone made it over the border before they could bring it down, however. The F-16s hopped the border themselves in a desperate attempt to destroy the sensitive equipment, but the drone dropped to five thousand feet and arrived over the outskirts of heavily populated Quetta, and the flight of F-16s were ordered to return to base.

Finally the men and women at Creech, along with the men and women in Afghanistan and at CIA and at the Pentagon who were now watching real-time feeds from the runaway Reaper, watched in dismay as Cyclops 04 circled a wheat field just a few hundred meters from the Quetta suburb of Samungli.

The pilots could tell that even the crash was a controlled setup. The descent had been nearly perfectly executed, the airspeed had decreased as the phantom pilot backed off on the throttle, and the Reaper had made a forward scan of the landing site with its cameras. Only at the last instant, as the UAV floated sixty feet above the ground alongside a well-trafficked four-lane road on final approach, did the phantom pull hard on the control stick, pitching the drone into a left down attitude and removing all lift. Then the aircraft dropped from the sky, hit the field, cartwheeled in the hard dirt a few times, and came to rest.

The men and women at Creech, at Langley, and in Arlington who possessed a front-row seat to this nightmare lurched back in unison at the violence of the surprise intentional crash at the end of a smooth flight.

At the GCS at Creech Air Force Base, Major Reynolds and Captain Pratt, both men stunned and furious, pulled off their headsets, walked outside into a warm, breezy afternoon, and waited to hear casualty reports from FOB Everett.

Both men were covered in sweat, and their hands shook.

In the end, eight American soldiers and forty-one Afghanis were killed in the attack.

*

An Air Force colonel at the Pentagon stood in front of the seventy-two-inch monitor that had, up until the screen went black two minutes earlier, displayed the entire event.

'Suggest we demo in place,' he said.

He was asking his higher-ups for permission to send a second UAV into the area to launch enough munitions onto the downed UAV to demolish it where it lay, destroying every shred of evidence that it was an American drone. With a little luck – and with a lot of Hellfire missiles – the UAV might just cease to exist completely.

There were expressions of agreement throughout the room, though many in attendance remained silent. There were protocols in place for destroying a UAV that crashed over the border in Al-Qaeda country so that they could keep its secrets hidden and remove the enemy's propaganda value.

Secretary of Defense Bob Burgess sat at the end of the long table. He tapped his pen on a legal pad in front of him while he thought. When the beating of the pen stopped, he asked, 'Colonel, what assurances can you give me that the follow-up UAV will not be hijacked and put down right alongside Cyclops 04 or, worse, fly over the border and attack blue forces?'

The colonel looked at SecDef, and then he shook his head. 'Frankly, sir, until we know more about what just happened, I can't give you any assurances whatsoever.'

Burgess said, 'Then let's save our drones while we still have some left.'

The colonel nodded. He didn't like SecDef's sarcasm, but the man's logic was solid.

'Yes, sir.'

SecDef had been spending the past half-hour conferring with admirals, generals, colonels, CIA execs, and the White House. But of all his communications since this rapid crisis had begun, his most informative conversation had been with a General Atomics technician who happened to be in the Pentagon at the time and had been rushed into a five-minute meeting with SecDef before being put in a holding area, awaiting further consultations. When the scope of the crisis was explained to him he declared, in terms forceful enough to get his point across, that however the hacking of the UAV had been accomplished, it would be dangerous to presume that there were *any* technological limitations to the geographical reach of the perpetrator. No one in the military or at General Atomics could say, at this early stage, that an operator who takes control of a drone in Pakistan could not also take control of a U.S. drone flying over the Mexican/American border or a drone flying in Southeast Asia or in Africa.

Secretary of Defense Burgess used this information when he announced to the room, 'We don't know where the attacker is, or what his access points are into our network. Therefore I am ordering, at this moment, a full ground stop of all Reaper drones.'

A colonel involved with UAV operations raised his hand. 'Sir. We do not know if the access point is limited to the Reaper system and fleet. It may well be that someone with the capability we just witnessed might have the ability to hack into the other UAV frames.'

SecDef had thought about this. He stood, grabbed his suit coat from the back of his chair, and slipped it on. 'For now, just the Reaper. Between us and CIA and Homeland Security we have, what? A hundred drone ops running at any one time?' He looked to a subordinate. 'I need that number for POTUS.'

The woman nodded and rushed out of the room.

Burgess continued, 'There are a hell of a lot of soldiers, border patrol, and others who owe their safety to the situational awareness those UAVs provide. I'm heading over to the White House and will talk it over with the President. I will give him both sides of the argument on this, and he'll make the call as to whether or not we shut down all UAVs world-wide until we figure out what this . . . until we figure out what the hell is going on. Meanwhile, I need information. I need to know who, how, and why. This incident is going to be an ugly mess for all of us, but if we can't answer those three questions asap then it's only going to get uglier and last longer. If you and your people are not working on getting me answers to those three questions, then I don't want you bothering me or my people.'

There was a crisp round of *Yes, sir*s from the room, and Bob Burgess left, an entourage of suits and uniforms moving out behind him.

In the end, President of the United States Jack Ryan did not have time to decide whether or not it was necessary to shut down all of the UAVs in the U.S. military and intelligence. As the secretary of defense's black Suburban pulled through the White House gates one hour after the crash of the Reaper in Pakistan, a massive Global Hawk drone, the largest unmanned vehicle in the U.S. inventory, lost contact with its flight crew while flying at sixty thousand feet off the coast of Ethiopia.

It was another hijacking – this became clear as the phantom pilot disengaged the autopilot and began making gentle adjustments to the pitch and roll of the aircraft, as if testing out his control of the big machine.

The men and women watching the feed recognized quickly that either the phantom pilot of this incident was not as experienced as the one who expertly operated the Reaper over eastern Afghanistan, or else it was the same pilot, but his familiarity with this larger and more complex airframe was not as good. For whichever reason, within moments of the hijacking the Global Hawk began to lose control. Systems were shut off incorrectly and restarted out of sequence, and any chance to right the aircraft was lost while it was still several miles in the air.

It crashed in the Gulf of Aden like a piano falling from the sky.

This was seen, by virtually everyone cleared to know about it at all, as a message from the hackers. Your entire unmanned fleet is compromised. Continue to operate your drones at your peril.

27

CIA officer Adam Yao was dressed in a black baseball cap, a white T-shirt, and dirty blue jeans. He looked like most every other male his age in Mong Kok, and he moved through the street crowds like a man who lived here in the lower-income neighborhood, not like he lived in Soho Central, one of the ritziest parts of Hong Kong. He was playing the role of a local merchant coming to get the mail for his shop, like any one of hundreds of other men in and out of the Kwong Wa Street post office.

Of course he had no shop, and he had no address in Mong Kok, which also meant he had no mail at Kwong Wa. In truth he was there to pick the lock of Zha Shu Hai's P.O. box and to get a look at the young man's mail.

The post office was crowded; it was shoulder to shoulder coming through the door. Adam elected to arrive just before noon, during the busiest part of the day here in always congested Mong Kok, hoping to use the chaos to his advantage.

Adam had always operated in the field with a simple credo: 'Sell it.' Whatever he was doing, whether he was playing the part of a homeless person or a high-flying young trader on the Hong Kong Stock Exchange, Adam embraced his role totally. It allowed him to get into and out of buildings without proper credentials, to walk right past Triad gunmen without them giving him a second glance, and it meant secretaries in line for noodles and tea on their lunch break might well chat about work within earshot of Adam without knowing, allowing him to learn more about a company and its secrets during lunch hour than he would by breaking into the company over the weekend and rummaging through file cabinets.

Adam was an actor, a con man, a spy.

And he was selling it now. He had a set of lock picks in his hand, and he pushed into the post office, walked directly up to Zha Shu Hai's P.O. box, and knelt down. With men and women within inches of him on both sides, no one paid an instant's attention to him.

Yao picked the lock in under ten seconds. He slipped his hand inside and found two pieces of mail, one a business envelope and the other a small package containing a Bubble-Wrapped item. He pulled both pieces of mail out, closed the door to the box, and then pulled out the pick holding the tumblers up, which instantly relocked the door.

He was out in the street a minute later, and he did a quick surveillance detection run to make sure he had not been followed from the post office. Once satisfied he was in the clear, he descended into the MTR underground station and headed back to his office on Hong Kong Island.

Soon, he was back at his desk dressed in his suit and tie, and had placed the small package and the envelope in the ice tray portion of a small refrigerator/freezer he kept near his desk. After letting them chill for an hour, he reached into the freezer and removed the envelope, and opened it with a sharp knife. The sealant had frozen solid, and this allowed the knife to cut through it without tearing the paper, and it would also make it easy to reseal the envelope once it had thawed out.

When he had it opened, Adam read the address on the outside. It had been sent from mainland China, from a town in Shanxi Province that Yao did not recognize. The address was handwritten not to Zha Shu Hai, but to the P.O. box.

The return address was a woman's name; Yao wrote it down on a pad on his blotter, and then he reached inside the envelope.

He was somewhat surprised to find a second envelope inside the first one. This envelope had no writing on it at all. He cut it open in the same manner as the first, and inside found a letter handwritten in Mandarin by a shaky hand. Adam read it quickly, and by the third paragraph he understood what it was.

The author of the letter was Zha's grandmother. From her note he could tell she was in the United States, and she had posted this letter to a relative in Shanxi Province so as not to tip off the U.S. Marshals Service, which she knew was hunting her grandson.

The relative from Shanxi had forwarded this on to the P.O. box without adding any note of his or her own.

The grandmother talked about life in northern California and a recent surgery and other members of the family and some old neighbors. She closed with an offer to help Zha with money or to put him in contact with other family members who, she said, had not heard from him since he'd arrived in China a year earlier.

It was a typical letter from a grandmother, Adam saw, and it told him nothing other than a little old Chinese lady in the States was likely involved with aiding and abetting a fugitive.

He put the envelope and the letter aside, and he reached back into the freezer for the package. It was small, not larger than a paperback book, and he quickly opened it before the sealant began to thaw. Once it was open, he checked the mailing address. Again, it was sent just to the P.O. box without a name, but the return address was an address in Marseille, France.

Curious, Adam reached inside and pulled out a small

Bubble-Wrapped disk roughly the size of a silver dollar. It had pins coming out of the sides as though it attached to a computer motherboard or some other electronic device.

Along with the item was a several-page data sheet explaining that the device was a low-power superheterodyne receiver. The paper went on to explain that the device was used in keyless entry systems, garage door openers, remote security alarms, medical devices, and many other devices that receive external radio frequency transmissions as commands to perform mechanical functions.

Adam had no idea what Zha would want with the device. He turned to the last of the pages and saw that it was a chain of correspondence between two e-mail addresses.

Both parties wrote in English; the man in Marseille was clearly an employee of the technology company that manufactured the device. He was corresponding in the e-mails to someone named FastByte22.

Adam read it again. 'FastByte Twenty-two. Is that Zha?'

The e-mails were concise. It seemed FastByte22 had made contact with this employee on the Internet and asked him to sell him a sample of the superheterodyne receiver because the company would not export it to Hong Kong. The two then negotiated payment in Bitcoin, an untraceable online currency that Adam knew was used for computer hackers to barter services and for criminals to buy and sell illicit goods on the Internet.

The e-mails went back a number of weeks, and they gave no indication as to what FastByte22 needed with a little gadget that could be used for anything from a garage door to a medical device.

Adam took out his camera and began photographing everything, from the letter from Zha's grandmother to the high-tech receiver. He'd have to spend most of the rest of the day retracing his steps. From repackaging the envelope and the package to returning to Mong Kok to breaking back into the P.O. box to drop the two items back in before Zha had reason to suspect they had been taken.

It would be a long afternoon, and he did not yet know what he had accomplished today.

Other than finding a potential alias for Zha Shu Hai.

FastByte22.

28

The conference room of the White House Situation Room is smaller than most people imagine. The narrow oval table seats ten, which means for many sensitive meetings the assistants of the principals arc lincd up standing along the walls.

The scene in the conference room was chaotic as the Situation Room staff prepared for the meeting. The walls were full of men and women, many in uniform, some arguing with one another and others desperately trying to get last-minute information about the events of the morning.

Half the seats were empty, but CIA Director Canfield and Secretary of Defense Burgess were in their places. The director of the NSA as well as the director of the FBI were present, but they stood and conferred with underlings, sharing details of anything new learned in the past ten minutes.

It was a fluid situation, to be sure, and everyone wanted to be ready to answer all POTUS's questions.

Time ran out on those trying to prepare for POTUS when Jack Ryan walked through the door.

He came to the head of the table and looked around the room. 'Where is Mary Pat?'

Director of National Intelligence Foley stepped into the room behind the President, a slight breach of protocol, though everyone in Ryan's White House, from the house-keepers to the vice president, knew Ryan did not give a whit about ceremony.

'Excuse me, Mr President,' she said as she took her place.

'I've just found out there has been a third hijacking. A Homeland Security Predator drone working customs and enforcement on the Canadian border went rogue twenty minutes ago.'

'In the U.S.?'

'Yes, sir.'

'How the hell did this happen? I ordered a ground stop of UAVs. Homeland Security was notified.'

'Yes, sir. This Predator was on the tarmac at Grand Forks AFB in North Dakota. It had been prepped for a mission along the border today, but the mission was canceled per the ground stop. They were about to push it back into the hanger when the craft initiated its systems, rolled away from ground control, and took off from a taxiway. Presently it's flying south at twenty thousand feet over South Dakota.'

'Jesus. Where is it going?'

'Unknown at this time. FAA is tracking it, rerouting air traffic. We have a flight of two Air Force interceptors en route to take it down. There are no weapons on board, of course, but it could be used as a low-yield missile. They might try to impact another aircraft or a building or even vehicles on the highway.'

'This is unreal,' muttered National Security Adviser Colleen Hurst.

Ryan said, 'I want every last UAV in the U.S. inventory, regardless of ownership, model, or manufacturer, at home or abroad, physically dismantled in whatever way necessary to where it cannot take off.'

SecDef Burgess said, 'Yes, sir. That process is under way on our end.'

Homeland Security and CIA both agreed they were doing the same thing with their drones.

Jack looked to Scott Adler, Secretary of State. 'We need

your office telling all of our allies who possess UAVs that they need to follow our lead until we have more information.'

'Yes, sir.'

'Good. What do we know about this cyberattack so far?'

Mary Pat said, 'NSA is in the process of bringing in all of their people to look at how this was done. I've already been warned that we will not get answers in hours, and they only hope to know something in days. I am told that this was a very sophisticated attack.'

'What *do* they know?'

'They suspect someone jammed the frequency of the drone's communications to its satellite, which caused the Reaper to revert to autopilot. It does this anytime there is a break in communications.

'Once the aircraft was not under our control, someone used their own equipment to impersonate the valid secure signal. In order for them to do this, they had to have access deep inside the Department of Defense's most secure network.'

'Who could have done this?'

CIA director Canfield said, 'We're looking at Iran.'

Mary Pat said, 'Mr President, keep in mind, it does not have to be a state actor.'

Ryan thought about this for a moment. 'What you're saying is that our threat matrix needs to include terrorist and criminal organizations, private businesses . . . hell, even rogue operators in our own government.'

CIA director Canfield said, 'All we can do right now is look at the actors who had the motive and the means. Regarding the Afghanistan attack, that would be Al-Qaeda, the Taliban, and Iran, as they all have been meddling in our Afghan operations for some time. When it comes to means, on the other hand, you can dismiss the Taliban. They have just about zilch in the technical-know-how department.

'Al-Qaeda is light-years ahead of the Taliban, which means they might be able to do some low-level website attacks at best. But they did *not* do this.'

'So you think it was Iran?'

'If anyone in that part of the world did it, it was Iran.'

Ryan asked, 'They are only hacking one UAV at a time. Does that mean anything about how they are doing this? Is that due to technical ability or because they only have one pilot trained to fly the drones?'

'Could be either, sir. Might just be that they have only set up one flight control center. I've got to say that considering the capability we witnessed today, I find it hard to believe there is a technical reason they can't fly more than one UAV at a time.'

'Someone is sending us a message. As much as I'd like to send them a message right back, I think we need to be in receive mode at the moment.'

Mary Pat said, 'I agree, sir. We'll get to the bottom of just how this happened before we can start placing blame.'

Ryan nodded, then turned to SecDef. 'You guys have been hacked before, right?'

Bob Burgess said, 'Twenty-fourth Air Force detected a virus six months ago in the Reaper system software upgrade on the network at Creech. We executed a rolling stand-down of the fleet while we checked each and every drone. None had been infected. Nevertheless, we had to wipe clean every hard drive in every GCS at Creech and start from scratch.'

Ryan said, 'The Defense Department's secure network is not supposed to be connected to the Internet. How the hell did a virus infect the Reaper software?'

Burgess said, 'Yes, it's true there is what is called an "air gap," physical space between our secure network and the Internet, that should preclude this happening.'

'But?'

'But human beings are involved, and human beings are fallible. We found the virus on a portable drive used to update map software in one of the ground-control stations. It was a breach of protocol by a contractor.'

CIA Director Canfield said, 'Iran has done this sort of thing before. A couple years back the Iranians successfully hacked into a Predator feed and downloaded videos from the cameras.'

DNI Foley interjected, 'Grabbing the video off a camera's sat transmission is not the same thing as taking total control of the unit, aiming and firing the weapons, and then crash-landing the UAV. That is several levels of magnitude more complicated.'

Ryan nodded, taking it all in and reserving judgment for now. 'Okay,' he said. 'I expect you to let me know when you learn anything of value about the investigation.'

SecDef said, 'Mr President, as you know, we lost eight members of First Cavalry Division, and forty-one Afghan Special Forces soldiers. We have not released information about the casualties yet, but –'

'Do it,' Ryan said. 'And admit the UAV was involved and there was a technical malfunction. We need to get out in front of this and tell the world that we got hacked and American and Afghan servicemen were murdered.'

Burgess said, 'Sir, I recommend against that. Our enemies will use that against us; it makes us look weak.'

DNI was shaking her head, but Ryan was ahead of Mary Pat. 'Bob, whoever hacked the drone is going to have the video feed from the cameras. They can show themselves defeating our technology whenever the hell they want. If we do anything to cover this, it's just going to compound the problem.'

Ryan added, 'In this case, ladies and gentlemen, we are going to have to take this on the chin. I want you to release a statement saying that while on a sensitive mission in Afghanistan airspace, at the invitation of the Afghan government, an unknown force wrested control of our hunter/killer drone and attacked an American forward operating base. Our attempts to destroy the weapon before it crossed into Pakistan were unsuccessful. We will find the perpetrators, the murderers, and we will bring them to justice.'

Burgess did not like it, Ryan could tell. SecDef would be thinking about how, within hours of that announcement, the Taliban would be on Al Jazeera with some bullshit story about how they did it themselves.

He said, 'I don't like us sharing our vulnerabilities with the world. It will encourage more people to try it.'

Ryan retorted, 'I'm not thrilled about it, either, Bob. I just see the alternative as being worse.'

At that moment the phone beeped in the center of the conference table. President Ryan himself tapped it. 'Yes?'

'Sir, we just heard from Homeland Security. The Predator drone has been shot down over western Nebraska. No casualties reported.'

'Well, thank God for that,' Ryan said. It was the first good news all day.

29

Computer hardware territory sales manager Todd Wicks sat in a pizzeria with a slice of cheese pizza greasing up a waxed paper plate in front of him.

He had no appetite, but he could not fathom any reason why he should be sitting here, right now at three p.m., that did not involve him eating pizza.

He forced himself to take a bite. He chewed slowly, swallowed tentatively, worried he would not be able to keep it down.

Todd thought he was going to puke, but it wasn't the pizza's fault.

The phone call setting up the meeting had come at eight o'clock that morning. The caller did not give a name, nor did he say what the meeting would be about. He just gave a time and a place, and then he asked Todd to recite back the time and the place.

And that was it. Since the call, Wicks's stomach had felt like he'd eaten a live cat; he'd stared at the walls in his office and he'd looked at his watch every three or four minutes, at once wanting three o'clock to never come and to hurry up and get here so he could get this over with.

The man who contacted him was Chinese, that much was clear from his voice over the phone, and that, along with the short and cryptic conversation, was enough reason for him to worry.

This man would be a spy, he would want Todd to commit some act of treason that could get him killed or thrown in prison for the rest of his life, and, Todd knew already . . . that whatever it was, he would fucking do it.

When Todd got home from Shanghai after the episode with the hooker and the Chinese detective, he considered telling the inevitable agent who contacted him to go fuck himself when he came calling about his bullshit spy mission. But no, he could not do that. They had the videotape and the audiotape and he only had to think back to that fifty-two-inch TV in the Shanghai suite and his lily-white sweaty ass bouncing up and down to know that the Chinese had him by the fucking balls.

If he balked when the Chinese came calling, then there was no doubt that within a few days, his wife, Sherry, would open an e-mail containing an HD video of the entire event.

No fucking way. That's not happening. He'd told himself this at the time, and since then he'd waited on the call and dreaded whatever would come after the call.

At five minutes past the hour an Asian man carrying a shopping bag walked into the pizza joint, bought a calzone and a can of Pepsi from the one man behind the counter, and then brought his late lunch toward the small seating area in the back.

As soon as Todd realized the man was Asian, he tracked his every move, but when he neared Todd's table the computer hardware salesman looked away, down at his greasy cheese pizza, assuming eye contact would be a definite no-no in a situation such as this.

'Good afternoon.' The man sat down at Todd's little bistro table, violating the protocol Wicks had just established.

Todd looked up and shook the hand offered by the Chinese man.

Wicks was surprised by the look of this spy. He certainly did not seem ominous. He was in his twenties, younger than

Todd would have predicted, and he seemed almost nerdish in appearance. Thick glasses, a white button-down shirt, and slightly wrinkled black Sansabelt slacks.

'How is the pizza?' the man asked with a smile.

'It's okay. Look, shouldn't we go somewhere private?'

The young man in the thick glasses just shook his head with a little smile. He bit into his calzone and winced at the hot cheese. He gulped Pepsi and then said, 'No, no. This is fine.'

Todd rubbed his fingers through his hair. 'This shop has security cameras. Just about every restaurant does. What if someone goes back and –'

'The camera is not working at the moment,' the Chinese spy said with a smile. He started to take another bite of his lunch, but then he stopped. 'Todd, I am beginning to wonder if you are looking for a bad excuse to avoid helping us.'

'No. It's okay. I'm just . . . worried.'

The younger man took another bite, then another sip from his can. He shook his head and waved a hand dismissively. 'Nothing to worry about. Nothing at all. We would like to ask a favor of you. It is very easy. One favor, and that's it.'

Todd had spent the past month thinking about little else other than this 'favor.'

'What is it?'

With his continued nonchalance, the Chinese spy said, 'You are planning on making a delivery to one of your customers in the morning.'

Fuck, thought Wicks. He was due at Bolling Air Force Base at eight a.m. to drop off a pair of motherboards at DIA. Panic shot through his heart. He would be spying for the Chinese. He would be caught. He would lose everything.

But he had no alternative.

Todd lowered his head halfway to the table. He wanted to cry.

The Chinese man said, 'Hendley Associates. In Maryland.'

Todd's head came back up quickly.

'Hendley?'

'You *do* have an appointment with them?'

Wicks did not even wonder how it was the Chinese knew about his dealings with this particular customer. He was elated that he was being asked to do something involving corporate espionage as opposed to something involving the U.S. government. 'Right. Eleven a.m. Dropping off a new high-speed drive from a German manufacturer.'

The young Chinese man who had not given his name slid the shopping bag under the table.

'What is that?' Todd asked.

'It is your product. The drive. It is exactly the same product you would deliver. We want you to make that delivery but substitute this drive. Do not worry, it is identical.'

Wicks shook his head. 'Their IT director is kind of a security freak. He is going to run all sorts of diagnostics on your drive.' Todd paused, unsure if he should say out loud what was obvious. After a moment he blurted out, 'He is going to find whatever you put on there.'

'I did not say we put anything on there.'

'No. You did not. But I'm sure you did. I mean . . . why else would we be doing this?'

'There is nothing on there that any IT director can find.'

'You don't know this guy, or his company. They are top-notch.'

The Chinese man smiled as he bit into his calzone. 'I know Gavin Biery, and I know Hendley Associates.'

Wicks just looked at him for a long moment. Behind them, a group of high school kids entered, talking loudly to one another; a boy put another in a headlock as they stepped up to the counter to order, and the rest of the group laughed.

And Todd Wicks sat in the middle of this normalcy, knowing that his life was not normal at all.

An idea popped into his head. 'Let me take the unit and run my own diagnostics on it. If I can't find anything on it, then I'll deliver it to Gavin.'

The Chinese man smiled yet again. He was all smiles. 'Todd. We are not entering into a negotiation. You will do as you are told, and you will do it when you are told to do it. The product is clean. There is nothing for you to worry about.'

Todd took a bite of his pizza, but he let the food sit in his mouth. He wondered when he would feel like eating again. He realized that he had to trust the Chinese.

'I do this and I am done?'

'You do this and you are done.'

'Okay,' he said, and then he reached down and brought the shopping bag closer to him.

'Excellent. Now just relax. You have nothing to worry about at all. This is just business. We do this sort of thing all the time.'

Todd picked up the bag and stood up. 'Just this once.'

'I promise.'

Wicks left the restaurant without another word.

30

Adam Yao had been working all day at his 'white side' job as president, director, and sole employee of SinoShield, his one-man intellectual property rights investigation firm. As much as duty called with the CIA, it was also his job to maintain the front company that kept him over here in Hong Kong, kept him in touch with members of the local police and government, and gave him a ready cover for his CIA surveillance activities.

But it was nine p.m. now and, with the twelve-hour difference between Langley and Hong Kong, Adam decided to check in on the 'black side' of his duties via his secure e-mail link.

He had not wanted to send the message yesterday afternoon; he knew somewhere in the Asia sector of CIA's National Clandestine Service there existed a leak.

But he had to send the message.

Yesterday the entire U.S. drone fleet, military, intelligence, Homeland Security, the entire enchilada, had been shut down full stop, because someone had hacked into the network or the satellite signals or both, which was the prevailing opinion in the NSA's prelim tech reports about the incident Adam had read.

As soon as he heard about the UAV incident in Afghanistan, Adam knew he would have to come out of the dark and let Langley know that, over here in Hong Kong, he was tailing Zha Shu Hai, a Chinese drone hacker and American fugitive.

No, he couldn't very well sit on that information.

Yao knew his cable to Langley was going to be a tough sell. His supposition, that a young Chinese hacker who had stolen UAV software code two years earlier might somehow be involved in this week's computer attack and hijacking of several American drones, was not based on any hard evidence.

On the contrary, there seemed to be some evidence that Zha Shu Hai was not working on anything as high-level as drone hijackings. Yao did not mention the Triads in his cable, but hacking drones and killing American soldiers in Afghanistan hardly seemed like the modus operandi of the 14K. No, hacking banking software or other forms of computer embezzlement seemed like it would be the more likely aim of Zha if he was, in fact, employed by 14K.

But Adam needed to be sure, and he had asked only for some additional resources to help him dig deeper into whatever was going on above the Mong Kok Computer Centre.

But Langley had declined his request, explaining that all assets in Asia were tied up at the moment and assets at Langley were similarly otherwise engaged.

The response Adam received had been reasonable, he had to admit, even if it pissed him off. The reply from Langley had explained simply that, in the unlikely case that China was involved with the UAV incidents, it would come from inside China. All intelligence out of China indicated that offensive computer network operations of a military nature on the scale of a UAV attack would originate from the PLA's General Staff Department, Fourth Department. These were China's elite cyberwarriors.

A well-coordinated attack on the United States would originate with them, not with a hacker or group of hackers in Hong Kong.

The cable went on to explain to Adam Yao, in what he saw as a patronizing tone, that Zha working in Hong Kong in an office building was not a threat to the Department of Defense's secure computer network.

After all, Hong Kong was not China.

'No shit,' Adam responded to the message on his monitor. He knew the situation he described in his cable was highly unusual, but his evidence, his on-the-ground intelligence collection, though circumstantial, surely warranted a closer look.

But his superiors, the CIA's analysts, did not agree.

So Adam did not get his assets, but that was not the worst news in the cable from Langley. His superiors in the National Clandestine Service indicated that they would pass on the helpful information about the location of Zha Shu Hai to the U.S. Marshals Service.

That meant, Adam was certain, that within a few days a couple of four-doors would show up in Mong Kok and a team of deputy marshals would climb out. They would be identified as a threat by the Triads, the Triads would get Fast-Byte22 out of town, and that would be the last Yao saw of Zha.

Adam logged off the secure e-mail system and leaned back in his chair. 'Shit!' he shouted to the small empty room.

Zha Shu Hai had never been in Center's office before. Few of the employees of the Ghost Ship, even the important ones like Zha, had personally been inside the surprisingly cramped and spartan work area of their leader.

Zha stood with his hands at his sides and his knees locked, an affected military stance because Center had not asked him to sit down. The rock-hard gel in his spiked hair shone and sparkled in the light from the flat-screen displays on Center's desk. Center himself was in his chair in front of his monitors, his ever-present VOIP earpiece in his ear and his rumpled demeanor on display here just as it always was on the operations floor.

He said, 'Three American drones were downed before the Americans ceased all flights.'

Zha just stood there at semi-attention. *Was that a question?* Center cleared up the confusion. 'Why just three?'

'They were quick to land their other UAVs. We managed to break into one more in Afghanistan within minutes of the crash of the first one, but it had landed before our pilot achieved input control and the weapons had been offloaded. As soon as I realized that, I took the Global Hawk off the coast of Africa. That is a very valuable and technologically advanced machine. It will show the Americans that the capacity is there for great harm to them.'

'The Global Hawk crashed into the ocean.' Center said it in a way that Zha could not read.

'Yes. It is a Northrop Grumman product, and my software was optimized for the Reaper and Predator platforms from General Atomics. I had hoped that the pilot could have crashed it into a ship, but he lost control soon after I passed responsibility to him.

'The third vehicle I took was on the American mainland, for the obvious effect of causing them great concern.'

Zha was proud of himself for all three hacks. He wanted more appreciation from Center than he was getting.

'We should have had more pilots,' Center said.

'Sir. I felt it necessary to be personally involved with each hijack. I could have captured the signal and given control to different pilots, but there were many technical nuances with each operation. The pilot was not trained to maintain the signal.'

Tong looked over a report Zha had sent him with details of each operation. He looked like he was going to comment further, but instead he laid the paper down.

'I am satisfied.'

Zha breathed a long inward sigh. He knew that was Center's highest compliment.

The older man then said, 'I'd hoped for five, or even more, but the three UAVs you took were well chosen for maximum impact.'

'Thank you, Center.'

'And the Trojan in their network?'

'It remains. I have provided them with the false trail, they will find this within the week, but the actual Trojan is ready to go to war again as soon as they fly their drones.'

'The false trail should focus their attention on Iran?'

'Yes, Center.'

'Good. The PLA has hopes the Americans will attack Iran over this. That is their ultimate goal. I, however, think they are underestimating the abilities of the NSA to recognize the misdirection. Still, every day Washington's understanding of China's involvement in Earth Shadow remains unclear is another day closer our forces are to achieving their goals.'

'Yes, Center.'

'Very well,' said Center, and Zha bowed, then turned to leave the office.

'There is one other item.'

The young man snapped back to attention, facing Dr Tong. 'Sir?'

The older man picked another sheet of paper up off his desk and looked it over for a moment. 'It seems, Zha, that you have been under surveillance by the Central Intelligence Agency. There is a spy from their organization here in Hong Kong, and he is watching you. No, don't worry. You aren't in trouble. Even with your disguise we knew it was possible that someday you would be recognized. He has your name, and he has your computer handle. Do not use the name FastByte Twenty-two again.'

Zha said, 'Yes, Center.'

'But the local CIA man does not seem to have any other concrete details about our operation. CIA leadership has told him you are not a concern of theirs at the moment, although they may notify police to try and bring you back to America.'

The young man with the spiked black hair did not speak now.

After a moment Center waved a hand in the air. 'This is something I will bring up with our hosts. They should be taking better care of us. They are making a lot of money from our banking operations, after all.'

'Yes, Center.'

'You should limit your activities around town, and I will insist your guard is doubled.'

Now Zha asked, 'What will we do about the Americans?'

It was clear Center had already given this consideration. 'For now? Nothing other than warn Fourteen-K to be on the lookout. This is a critical time in Operation Earth Shadow; we can't do anything overly' – he searched for the word – 'kinetic to this operative without receiving too much scrutiny from the Americans.'

Zha nodded.

'We will wait for now. Later, when there is no longer any reason for us to remain in the shadows, we will leave Hong Kong and we will have our friends here take care of Mr Adam Yao of the CIA.'

31

Jack Ryan, Jr, dropped into the chair in his cubicle at eight-thirty a.m., as he did each workday.

He had fallen into a predictable morning routine. Up at five-fifteen, coffee with Melanie, a jog or a workout, a kiss good-bye, and the fifteen-minute drive to work.

Once in the office, normally he would start his day by picking through overnight traffic sent from the CIA down in Langley up to NSA in Fort Meade. But that had changed since the cyberhijacking of three American drones. Now he spent more time watching traffic flow in the opposite direction. The cybersleuths at NSA were delivering daily updates to CIA about their investigation into the attack.

Jack read the information from NSA each morning, hoping the folks over there would get to the bottom of the affair quickly, but the drone hijackings were not something The Campus was working on officially. No, Jack and the other analysts were still digging into the investigation of the Istanbul Drive, but he read every bit of data he could understand from NSA to see where they were with the investigation.

He'd even had a long conversation with his girlfriend about the events. He'd become something of an expert on keeping his tone light and only semi-interested when he discussed Melanie's work, although in truth he wanted to pick her brain like the highly skilled intelligence analyst he was. She was working on the matter for Mary Pat Foley, but at this point the computer forensic people at NSA were running lead in the investigation.

There was a new development this morning. Hard evidence, as far as Ryan could tell from the data, that Iran was involved in the UAV attack.

'Damn,' said Ryan as he took notes down on a legal pad for his morning meeting. 'Dad is going to have a coronary.' Jack's father had fought it out with the United Islamic Republic several years ago, kicked Tehran's ass and assassinated its leader. Even though Iraq and Iran were once again two separate nations, Ryan wasn't surprised to see that the Iranians were still causing trouble.

Ryan figured his dad would take this news out of NSA and start preparing his retaliation.

Jack spent much of the morning reading NSA-to-CIA traffic, but when he'd finished going through all the new data from Fort Meade he quickly thumbed through CIA internal communication. He did not see much here regarding the UAV matter, but he noticed that one of his data-mining targets had received a flag.

Jack clicked on the program to launch it.

Ryan used data-mining software to hunt through CIA traffic for key terms, and daily he got anywhere from ten to one hundred hits on terms such as 'Libya JSO operatives,' 'computer hacking,' and 'assassination,' and as he waited to see what flagged term had just appeared in CIA traffic, he hoped it was something that would help him get the operational stand-down lifted on The Campus.

When the software launched, he blinked his eyes several times in surprise.

The flagged term was 'FastByte22.'

'I'll be damned,' Jack said. The hacker of the Istanbul Drive had shown up in a CIA cable.

Quickly Ryan read the cable. A CIA nonofficial cover operative named Adam Yao, based in Hong Kong, had found an American computer hacker of Chinese descent named Zha Shu Hai living and working in a Hong Kong neighborhood. Zha, Yao explained, may also be using the computer handle FastByte22 in cyberspace, and he is definitely a fugitive from American justice.

Yao pointed out in his cable that the hacker had been a penetration tester for defense contractor General Atomics, and had been imprisoned for offering to sell secrets about drone hacking and classified network penetration to the Chinese.

Jack said it again: 'I'll be damned.'

Adam Yao suggested that CIA send a team to Hong Kong to follow Zha to learn more about his actions, associations, and affiliations in HK to determine if he may have been involved in the recent computer penetration of the Department of Defense's secure information network.

Jack Ryan, Jr, had read thousands – no, *tens* of thousands – of CIA cables in his four years working at Hendley Associates. This particular correspondence seemed to him to be very thin on details about how Yao found Zha, how Yao linked Zha to the name FastByte22, and what sort of activities Zha was now engaged in. This Adam Yao fellow seemed to be offering up just a small piece of the puzzle to Langley.

Langley declined Adam Yao's request for support in surveillance of Zha Shu Hai.

Jack reached into CIA records to look into this NOC Adam Yao. While they were accessing he looked down at his watch; the morning meeting would be starting in just a few minutes.

Twenty minutes later Jack was on the ninth floor, addressing the rest of the operatives, Gerry Hendley, Sam Granger, and Rick Bell. 'NSA says they have a long way to go, but they have found a Trojan on their secure network at Creech Air Force Base in Nevada. One of the lines of code steals the software for flying the drones, and then orders the software to be sent to a server on the Internet.'

Bell said, 'If the DoD network isn't attached to the Internet, then how can the software get exfiltrated to an Internet server?'

Ryan explained, 'Anytime somebody uses a remote hard drive, which they have to do to update software or to put new data on the network, the Trojan sneaks pilfered data onto hidden portions of the drive automatically, without the user knowing. Then, when this drive is later plugged into a computer with Internet access, the data immediately is snuck out to a command server controlled by the bad guys. If the malware is any good, then it all happens on the down low.'

Domingo Chavez said, 'The old way to defend your position was called "the Three G's." Gates, guns, and guys. That method doesn't slow these guys down a bit.'

Sam Granger asked, 'Where was the data sent?'

'The data was sent to a network server, a physical computer, at Qom University of Technology.'

'Qom?' Caruso did not recognize the name.

Ding Chavez blew out a sigh. 'Iran.'

'Those sons of bitches,' muttered Sam Driscoll.

Sam Granger said, 'Looks like CIA's suspicions are confirmed.'

Jack said, 'That's not exactly true, Sam. This virus wasn't controlling the drone; this virus is a Trojan that recorded every bit of the control software and exfiltrated it back out. The Trojan points to a university in Iran, but in order to fly the Reaper they would have had to spoof the signal. They would need a ton of equipment and some expertise, but that doesn't mean they couldn't do it.'

'So, was it Iran?'

'I don't know. The more I think about it, the more I am suspicious. This line of code makes it so obvious, it looks to me like whoever set this whole operation up *wants* Iran to be implicated.

'I'd like to bring Gavin into the meeting to get his take on it,' Jack said. 'This is pretty much all that Gavin Biery thinks about.'

Rick Bell balked. 'True though that might be, he is not an analyst.'

'No, not at all. He doesn't have the training, nor does he have the patience or temperament to deal with voices that disagree with his own, which is something any analyst worth a damn needs to possess. But still, I say we look at Biery like a source.'

'A source?'

'Yeah. We give him everything the NSA knows about the attack. Starting with this information about the exfiltration server.'

Rick Bell looked to Gerry Hendley to make the call.

Gerry said, 'Gavin knows his stuff. Let's bring him in and ask for his take on this. Jack, why don't you go down and talk to him when we're finished here?'

'Sure. And there is more news from CIA this morning. I would have told Gavin this already because it relates to him, but I had to get up here first.'

Granger said, 'What is it?'

'There is a NOC in Hong Kong who says FastByte Twenty-two, the guy who is involved with the Istanbul Drive, is living there in Hong Kong. He says he's been watching him for several days.'

'What is he doing?' asked Hendley.

'That isn't really explained in the cable. The NOC is trying to get some resources to expand surveillance because, he says, the hacker worked on the software for some of the UAV drones that were attacked. He thinks he might be involved with what's going on.'

'What does Langley say about that?'

'They said, "Thanks, but no thanks." My guess is CIA is looking at Iran too hard to put much stock in this lead in Hong Kong. They made some good points refuting his argument.'

Hendley said, 'But we're sure it's the same FastByte Twenty-two?'

'It's the only one that has turned up anywhere. Open source, classified intel, LexisNexis. I think he's our guy.'

Sam Granger saw a look on Ryan's face. 'What's on your mind, Jack?'

'I was thinking, Gerry, that maybe we could go over and help this Adam Yao out.'

Sam Granger shook his head. 'Jack, you know The Campus is in operational stand-down.'

'The Campus is, but Hendley Associates is not.'

Chavez said, 'What are you talking about, Jack?'

'This NOC, Adam Yao, runs a front company over there that is a business investigation firm. I was thinking we could go over there as representatives of Hendley and say this FastByte character has been trying to break into our network. Just play dumb like we don't know Adam Yao is already tailing the guy in his clandestine duties for the CIA.'

It was quiet in the conference room for a good fifteen seconds.

Finally Gerry Hendley said, 'I like it.'

'That's a great idea, kid,' admitted Chavez.

Granger said, 'Okay, but let's keep it small. Ryan and Chavez can go to Hong Kong and meet with Yao. See what you can find out about FastByte Twenty-two and report in to us.'

Jack nodded, but Ding said, 'Sam, I'm going to throw something out there, and I hope you'll consider it.'

'Shoot.'

'Ryan and I are going to be out of our element when it comes to this hacking stuff. I mean, even conceptually. I don't know what these servers look like, how many people it takes to run them, who does what, et cetera, et cetera.'

'Yeah. Me, either,' admitted Ryan.

Chavez said, 'I suggest we take Biery with us.'

Granger almost spit his last sip of coffee out with that suggestion.

'Gavin? Out in the field?'

Chavez said, 'I know, I don't like thinking about it too much, but he's one hundred percent reliable and has all the intel we need to sell our situation to the NOC working this. I think he can help us with our cover for status as well.'

'Explain.'

'We go to this company like we're chasing a hacker, but only Gavin can represent the problem we face. Hey, I've got a master's and Jack is a freaking genius, but if the guy on the ground starts questioning us too much we are going to show ourselves as out of our element. We're going to look like a couple of knuckle draggers compared to the computer geeks.'

Sam nodded. 'Okay, Ding. Request granted. I need you guys to keep him safe, though. He will be a babe in the woods if things get dicey.'

'Roger that. I will say that since the Agency is going to notify the U.S. Marshals, there's a good chance that we don't have a lot of time to act. If they go over there and arrest FastByte, and he enters the justice system, we may never know who he was working for.'

Chavez said, 'And he might have loose lips about our operation here in order to bargain for a reduction in sentence.'

Hendley said, 'Why don't you guys go over tonight?'

'Sounds good,' said Ryan.

Chavez did not respond.

'Ding?' asked Granger. 'Something wrong?'

'Patsy is out of town this week, in Pittsburgh for some training till tomorrow. I've got JP in school and then an after-school program, but I have to pick him up at five.' He thought for a moment. 'I can get a sitter. No problem.'

'What's Biery going to say about going to Hong Kong with the operatives?' Caruso asked.

Jack stood up. 'I guess the only way to know is to ask him. I'll go talk to him and ask him to come to our afternoon meeting and we'll get his take on the Iran angle and let him know he's heading to Hong Kong.'

32

Todd Wicks was not sweating, and he felt like his pulse and blood pressure were low. In fact, he felt calmer than he had in years.

Three Valium saw to this.

He sat in his Lexus in the parking lot of Hendley Associates, giving the pills every last second available before his appointment so they could have plenty of time to do their work. He'd also applied three times the antiperspirant that he normally wore, and he'd forgone his normal quad latte at Starbucks this morning so that he wouldn't have his normal midday jitters.

He'd even listened to a half-hour of cool jazz satellite radio on his drive from DC up to West Odenton, thinking that might put him in an extra-mellow frame of mind.

At eleven a.m. he determined himself to be as prepared as he was going to get, so he climbed out of his luxury car, popped the trunk, and pulled out a small plastic box that contained his delivery for Hendley Associates.

He knew very little about this company; he had nearly one hundred accounts, so it was impractical to dig too deeply into what each and every one of them sold or offered or serviced. Half of his clients were government-agency IT departments, and the other half were companies like Hendley that, as far as Todd Wicks knew, traded stocks or invested or something like that.

He knew Gavin Biery, and kind of liked the rumpled computer nerd, even if Gavin could be a bit of a curmudgeon.

And Biery didn't fight him on his pricing. Hendley Associates was a good account, and Wicks hated to do anything that might hurt them, but he had resigned himself to the fact that it was necessary.

He knew a thing or two about industrial espionage; he read *Wired* magazine and he worked in an industry where fortunes were won and lost by the secrets that companies keep. The Chinese would have some sort of spy software hidden on the German-made drive, probably in the master boot record. He had no idea how they did it, or why they were so interested in Hendley Associates, but it was no great surprise to him. The Chinese were immoral bastards when it came to stealing industrial secrets, especially high-tech or financial secrets from Western companies.

Wicks was sickened that he was helping the Chinese, but he did have to admit to himself that he was getting off lightly.

It beat spying against the government.

He carried the shopping bag containing the drive and entered the front door of Hendley Associates right on time, stepped up to the reception desk, and told the security officers in blue blazers that he had an appointment with Gavin Biery.

He stood in the lobby while he waited, a little wobbly on his knees from the muscle relaxers, but he felt good.

He actually found himself more relaxed now than he had been the day before.

'What the hell, Wicks?'

Todd jerked back into reality, spun around, and found himself face-to-face with an angry-looking Gavin Biery. Behind him, the two security men stood at the reception desk.

Shit, shit, shit.

'Wha-what's wrong?'

Biery said, 'You *know* what's wrong! You always bring doughnuts! Where are my damn doughnuts?'

Todd sighed all the air out of his lungs, but he felt sweat forming on the back of his neck under his suit. He forced a toothy smile. 'It's almost lunchtime, Gavin. Usually I'm here a lot earlier.'

Biery replied, 'Where is it written that doughnuts are just for breakfast? I've enjoyed many a bear-claw lunch, and more than my share of apple fritters for dinner.'

Before Todd could think of a funny reply, Gavin said, 'C'mon up to IT and let's take a look at the new toy you brought me.'

Wicks and Biery stepped out of the elevator on the second floor and headed toward Biery's office. Wicks would have loved to have dropped off the drive and then left immediately, but he always went up to IT to talk shop for a few minutes with Gavin and some of the other Hendley IT staff. He did not want today to appear any different than normal, so he agreed to the quick visit to the computer department.

They'd made it only a few yards when Todd saw a tall young man with dark hair heading toward them.

'Hey, Gav. I was looking for you.'

Biery said, 'I leave my department for five minutes a week, and that's when I get a visitor. Jack, this is Todd Wicks, one of our hardware vendors. Todd, this is Jack Ryan.'

Todd Wicks extended his hand, had already begun greeting the young man, when he realized he was face-to-face with the son of the President of the United States.

Instantly panic washed through his body, his knees locked, and his back stiffened.

'Nice to meet you,' Ryan said.

But Wicks was not listening. His mind was racing with the

realization that he was doing a job for Chinese intelligence against the workplace of the son of a man who went to war with the Chinese in his first term, and was now back in the White House.

He stammered out a 'Nice to meet you' before Biery told Ryan he would call him when he was free.

Jack Ryan, Jr, headed back to the elevator.

As Gavin and Todd continued up the hall, Todd Wicks put his hand against the wall to steady himself.

'Crap, Wicks. You okay?'

'Yeah. Fine.' He recovered a little. 'Just a little starstruck, I guess.'

Gavin just laughed.

They sat down in the office and Biery poured coffee for them both.

'You didn't tell me the President's son works with you.'

'Yeah. 'Bout four years or so. I don't make a point of saying anything about it. He doesn't like a lot of attention.'

'What does he do here?'

'Same stuff most all the other folks who aren't in IT do.'

'Which is what, exactly?'

Biery said, 'Financial management, currency trading. Jack's a good egg. He's got his dad's brain.'

Wicks was not going to tell Biery he'd voted for Ed Kealty in the last election.

'Interesting.'

'You really *are* starstruck. Hell, you look like you just saw a ghost.'

'What? No. No. Just surprised. That's all.'

Biery looked at him for another moment, and Todd did his best impersonation of someone who was calm, cool, and collected. He caught himself wishing he'd popped a fourth Valium before getting out of his car. He tried to think of a different line of small talk, but fortunately he did not have to.

Biery opened the plastic box containing the hard drive and said, 'There she is.'

'Yes, that's it.'

Gavin took the board out of its protective sheath and looked it over. 'What was the deal with the delay?'

'Delay?' Wicks asked nervously.

Biery just cocked his head. 'Yeah. We ordered this on the sixth. Usually you guys get off-the-shelf items to us in a week.'

Todd shrugged. 'It was on back order. You know me, buddy, I get it to you as fast as I can.'

Biery just looked at the salesman. He smiled while he shut the box. '"Buddy"? What, you trying to butter me up? Sell me a few mouse pads or something?'

'No. Just being friendly.'

'An ass-kissing is a poor substitute for a box of dough-nuts.'

'I'll remember that. I hope your system wasn't inconvenienced by the back order.'

'No, but I will install the hard drive myself in the next day or two. We need the upgrade.'

'That's great. Really great.'

Biery looked up, away from the component that Wicks knew could get him thrown in prison. He asked, 'You feeling okay?'

'Fine. Why?'

Biery cocked his head. 'You seem a little out of it. I can't tell if you need a vacation or if you just got back from one.'

Todd smiled now. 'Funny you say that. I'm taking the family down to Saint Simons Island for a few days.'

Gavin Biery suspected his vendor had started his vacation a little early in his head.

*

297

Biery finished his meeting with Todd Wicks, and within twenty minutes found himself sitting in the conference room off Gerry Hendley's office. Where the other seven men in the room looked crisp and clean, Gavin looked like he'd climbed the stairwell up to the ninth floor on his hands and knees. His pants and shirt were wrinkled, except where his significant paunch pulled them tight, his hair was unkempt, and his baggy eyes made Ryan think of an old Saint Bernard.

Jack told Biery about the NSA's discovery of the connection between Iran and the drone attacks, going into detail about how the pilfered data was exfiltrated to a command server at the Qom University of Technology.

Instantly Biery declared, 'I'm not buying that for a minute.'

Rick Bell said, 'You're not? Why not?'

'Think about it. Whoever managed to break into the secure Air Force network and exfiltrate the data back out would most definitely hide the origin of the attack. There is no way in hell the Iranians would have put a line of code in the virus that sent data to a drop point in their own borders. They could put that server anywhere on the planet and then use other means to get the data there.'

'So you don't think Iran had anything to do with this?'

'No. Somebody wants us to think they did.'

'But,' asked Ryan, 'if it wasn't the Iranians, who –'

'It was the Chinese. No doubt in my mind. They are the best, and something like this took the best.'

'Why the Chinese?' It was Caruso asking. 'The Russians are good at cyberstuff, too. Why can't this be them?'

Gavin explained: 'Here is a good general rule of thumb for you guys to keep in mind when it comes to cybercrime and cyberespionage. The Eastern Europeans are damn good. The Russians, Ukrainians, Moldovans, Lithuanians, and so on. They have tons of great technical colleges, and they train computer programmers of high quality and in high numbers. And then, when these kids get out of school . . . there are no jobs over there. No jobs over there except in the underworld. Some get recruited in the West. As a matter of fact, Romanian is the second most spoken language at Microsoft's headquarters. But still, that's a small subset of the total number of the East and Central European talent pool. Most of the rest go into cybercrime. Stealing banking info and hacking into corporate accounts.

'In China, on the other hand, they have amazing technical universities, as good as or better than in the former East Bloc states. They also have special training in the military for young programmers. And then, when these young men and women get out of school or out of military vocational training . . . each and every one has a job. In one of many military information warfare battalions around China, or working for their Ministry of State Security's cyberdirectorate. Or else they go to work for the state in telecom or something like that, but even these programmers are organized for offensive and defensive CNO, that's computer network operations, because the government has cybermilitias that conscript the best and brightest minds into working for the state.'

Hendley strummed his fingers on his desk. 'So, it sounds to me like the Chinese are more organized and ready to act against us.'

Gavin said, 'Yes. A Russian hacker will steal your ATM card number and your pin. A Chinese hacker will blow out the electrical grid in your city and send your commercial aircraft into a mountainside.'

It was silent in the conference room for several moments.

Chavez asked, 'But why would the Chinese do this? We aren't operating drones against them in any number. This happened in Afghanistan and Africa and in the U.S.'

Biery thought about this for a moment. 'I don't know. The only thing that comes to mind is they want to distract us.'

'From what?' asked Ryan.

Gavin said, 'From whatever it is that they are really doing.' He shrugged. 'I don't know. I'm just the computer guy. You guys are the spooks and the analysts.'

Sam Granger leaned forward on the desk. 'Well, now. That is a good segue into the next order of business.'

Biery looked around. Quickly he noticed everyone smiling at him.

'What's up, guys?'

Chavez said, 'Gavin, we need you to get on a plane with us tonight.'

'A plane to *where*?'

'Hong Kong. We have located FastByte Twenty-two, and we need your help to go over there and learn a little more about him and who he's working for.'

Gavin's eyes widened.

'You found FastByte Twenty-two?'

'The CIA did, actually.'

'And you want me in the field? With the operators?'

Ryan said, 'We think you could be a crucial part of this operation.'

'There is no question about that,' Gavin said with immodesty. 'Do I get to carry a heater?'

Chavez cocked his head. 'A *what*?'

'A heater. You know. An iron. A piece.'

Ryan started laughing. 'He means a gun.'

Chavez groaned. 'No, Gavin. Sorry to disappoint you, but you don't get a heater.'

Biery shrugged. 'It was worth a shot.'

*

John Clark sat on his porch, looking out over his back pasture at the blustery autumn afternoon. In his left hand he held a paperback book that he'd been trying to read for the last few days, and in his right hand he held a racquetball.

He closed his eyes slowly and concentrated on squeezing down. His three functional fingers exerted enough pressure to slightly deform the rubber ball, but his index finger just wiggled a little.

He threw the ball into the backyard and returned his focus to the paperback.

His mobile rang, and he found himself happy for a temporary diversion from his boring afternoon, even if it was probably some telemarketer.

He read the name on the phone and his mood perked up instantly. 'Hey, Ding.'

'Hey, John.'

'How's it going?'

'Good. We got a lead on the Istanbul Drive.'

'Excellent.'

'Yeah, but still a lot of work ahead. You know how it is.'

Clark knew how it was. He felt incredibly out of the loop at the moment. 'Yeah. Anything I can do to help?'

There was a pause on the other end.

'*Anything*, Ding,' Clark reiterated.

'John, this sucks, but I'm in a bind.'

'Say the word.'

'It's JP. Patsy is in Pittsburgh till tomorrow and I'm heading up to BWI on my way to Hong Kong.'

A babysitter, Clark said to himself. Ding was calling him because he needed a babysitter. John recovered quickly and said, 'I'll pick him up from school. He'll stay with us until Patsy gets back tomorrow.'

'I really appreciate it. We've got a lead but there is no time –'

'Not a problem at all. Found a new fishing hole that I've been wanting JP to check out with me.'

'That's great, John.'

'You guys watch your backs in HK, you hear me?'

'Absolutely.'

33

President of the United States Jack Ryan opened his eyes, focused them quickly in the darkness, and found a man standing over him at his bedside.

This would startle the average person, but Ryan merely rubbed his eyes.

It was the night-duty officer, a uniformed member of the Air Force, in this case. He stood uncomfortably over Ryan, waiting for him to wake up.

Presidents are rarely woken because something so wonderful has happened that the night officer just had to pass it on, so Jack knew this would be bad news.

He did not know if the man had shaken him or called out to him. These guys always looked like they worried about imposing on the President's sleep, no matter how many times Ryan told them he wanted to be made aware of important news and not to worry about something as inconsequential as a middle-of-the-night 'shake and wake.'

He sat up as quickly as he could and grabbed his eyeglasses from the bedside table, and then he followed the night-duty officer out of the bedroom and into the West Sitting Hall. Both men moved silently so that they wouldn't wake up Cathy. Jack knew she was a light sleeper, and their years in the White House were filled with his late-night rousings, which, more often than not, disturbed her sleep as well.

There were nightlights on the walls, but otherwise the hall was as dark as the master bedroom.

'What's up, Carson?'

The Air Force officer spoke softly: 'Mr President, Secretary of Defense Burgess asked me to wake you and let you know that roughly three hours ago, Chinese PLA forces landed an engineering battalion as well as an element of combat troops in the Philippines' Scarborough Shoal.'

Jack wished he were surprised by the act. 'Was there resistance?'

'A Philippine coastal patrol boat, this according to the Chinese, fired on the landing craft. The vessel was sunk by a Chinese *Luda*-class destroyer. No word yet on casualties.'

Jack blew out a tired sigh. 'All right. Tell SecDef to come on over; I'll be in the Situation Room in thirty minutes.'

'Yes, Mr President.'

'I want Scott Adler, PACOM Jorgensen, Ambassador Li, DNI Foley either there in the meeting or attending via videoconference. And' – Ryan rubbed his eyes – 'Sorry, Carson. Who am I forgetting?'

'Uh . . . the vice president, sir?'

Jack gave a quick nod in the low light of the Sitting Hall. 'Thanks. Yeah, alert the veep.'

'Yes, sir.'

President Ryan sat at the conference table and took his first sip of what he knew would be many cups of coffee. The adjoining Situation Room was bustling, and the conference room had filled before he arrived.

Bob Burgess and several of his military minds from the Pentagon had just arrived. They all looked like they had been up all night. Mary Pat Foley was here as well. Arnie van Damm was in the room, but the commander of the Pacific Fleet, the vice president, and the secretary of state were out of town and attending remotely, though men and women from their offices stood along the walls.

'Bob,' Ryan said. 'What's the latest?'

'The Philippines say there were twenty-six sailors on the boat that sank. They are fishing some out of the water alive, but there will be fatalities. There are other Philippine warships in the area, but they are heavily outgunned and probably won't engage the Chinese.'

'And Chinese troops are on Philippine soil?'

'Yes, sir. We have satellites overhead, and we're collecting images. The engineering battalion will already be fortifying positions.'

'What do they want with the shoal? Is there any military objective at all, or is this about fishing rights?'

Mary Pat Foley said, 'It's simply to increase their footprint in the South China Sea. And to gauge reaction, Mr President.'

'My reaction.'

'Indeed.'

President Ryan thought for a moment. He then said, 'We need to send an immediate message, let them know we aren't wringing our hands just watching their actions over there.'

Scott Adler spoke on the monitor across the room. 'The submarine that made the call in Subic Bay a couple of weeks ago. The Chinese will claim that provocation had something to do with this.'

Jack said, 'I do not believe for a moment that we are the ones driving this thing. Short of us opening fire on the Chinese, they are going to make their moves on their time frame.'

Adler said, 'But we don't want to fall into the trap of giving them an out. An excuse to inflame the situation.'

'Point taken, Scott, but *no* response is also an out. That will look like an all-clear from us. I'm *not* giving them an all-clear.'

Ryan looked to Burgess. 'Suggestions, Bob?'

Bob turned to Admiral Jorgensen on the monitor. 'Admiral,

what assets are we prepared to move quickly into the area? Something to show them that we are serious?'

'The *Ronald Reagan* is in the East China Sea, heading up Carrier Strike Group Nine. We can move it and its elements west today. Put it off the coast of Taiwan by the end of the week.'

'I recommend against that,' said Adler.

Arnie van Damm seconded that motion. 'I do, too. You've been getting hammered in the press for antagonizing the people who own our foreign debt.'

Ryan reacted angrily. 'If Americans want to subjugate themselves to the Chinese, then they need to put somebody else in here to oversee that.' Jack ran his fingers through his gray hair as he calmed himself. He then said, 'We aren't going to war over the Scarborough Shoal. The Chinese know that. They will expect us to move carriers closer to our allies. We've done it before. Do it, Admiral. And make sure the carrier group has everything they need.'

Jorgensen nodded, and Burgess turned to one of the other Navy officers against the wall and began conferring.

Jack said, 'This is not the endgame. This battalion taking the shoal is just one tiny step. We protect Taiwan, we reach out to our friends in the SCS, and we stress to China that we aren't going to take anything lying down. I want information about their intentions and their capabilities.'

The men and women in the Situation Room conference room had their instructions. It was going to be a long day.

Valentin Kovalenko liked Brussels in the fall. He'd spent a little time here when working for the SVR, and he found it beautiful and cosmopolitan in a way London could not quite reach and Moscow could not even imagine.

When Center ordered him to Brussels he'd been pleased,

but the reality of this operation had kept him from enjoying the city.

Right now he sat in the back of a hot van full of crypto gear, looking out the rear window, watching well-heeled lunchtime patrons enter and exit an expensive Italian eatery.

He tried to stay on mission, but he could not help but reflect back to a time in the not-too-distant past when he would have been inside the restaurant, enjoying a dish of lasagna with a glass of Chianti, and he would have made some other bastard sit in the van.

Kovalenko had never been much of a drinker. His father, like many men of his generation, was a world-class consumer of vodka, but Valentin preferred a glass of fine wine with dinner or an occasional aperitif or digestif. But since his experience in the Moscow prison and the pressure of working for his shadowy employer, he'd picked up the habit of having a few beers in the refrigerator at all times or a bottle of red that he tipped each evening to help him sleep.

It did not affect his work, he reasoned, and it helped keep his nerves settled.

Valentin looked over at his partner today, a sixtyish German technical assistant named Max who had not said one word all morning that was not mission-critical. Earlier in the week, when they met in a parking lot at the Brussels-Midi train station, Kovalenko had tried to draw Max into a conversation about their mutual boss, Center. But Max would not play. He just held up a hand and said he'd need several hours to test the equipment and their safe house would need to have a garage with ample electrical outlets.

The Russian sensed the mistrust in the German, as if Max thought Valentin somehow would report whatever he said back to Center.

Valentin assumed Center's entire enterprise maintained

organizational security on the principle of mutual distrust.

Much like Valentin's old employer, the SVR.

Right now Valentin could smell the garlic wafting out of the entrance of the Stella d'Italia, and it made his stomach rumble.

He did his best to push it out of his mind, but he hoped like hell his target would finish soon and head back to his office.

As if on cue, just then an impeccably dressed man in a blue pinstripe suit and cherry wingtips stepped out through the front doors, shook hands with two other men who'd come out with him, and then began heading to the south.

Valentin said, 'That's him. He's heading back on foot. Let's do it now.'

'I am ready,' confirmed Max with his typical brevity.

Kovalenko hurriedly crawled past Max, through the van and toward the driver's seat; around him electronics buzzed and hummed and warmed the still air. He had to push himself all the way against the wall for part of the crawl, as a metal pole jutted up into the ceiling of the van. The pole contained wiring that attached to a small antenna that extended out over the roof, and could be directed by Max in any direction.

Valentin made his way behind the wheel and began following his target at a distance down Avenue Dailly, turning slowly behind him as he made a left on Chaussée de Louvain.

The man, Kovalenko knew, was the acting assistant secretary for public diplomacy of the North Atlantic Treaty Organization, or NATO. He was Canadian, in his mid-fifties, and he was in no way, shape, or form a hard target.

Though he worked for NATO, he possessed no military bearing. He was a diplomat, a suit, a political hire.

And though Valentin had not been informed of this by

Center, the assistant secretary was about to be Center's access into NATO's secure computer network.

Kovalenko did not understand the technology humming and buzzing in the van behind him; he had Max for that. But he did know that the tiny roof antenna could pinpoint and then receive leaking radio signals off a mobile phone or, more specifically, the chip in the mobile phone that performs the encryption calculations that make the device secure. By taking these leaked signals, received initially as a series of peaks and valleys in the radio waves and then converted by the computer in the van into the 1's and 0's that make up any electronic signal, the phone's encryption key could be deciphered.

As they followed the assistant secretary, Kovalenko was happy to see the man pull his phone from his jacket pocket and make a call.

'Max. He's on.'

'*Ja.*'

As Kovalenko drove, he listened to Max flip switches and type on his keyboard. 'How long?' he called back.

'Not long.'

The Russian was careful to stay close enough to the target for the antenna to pick up the signal and far enough back to where any odd glance over the shoulder would not alert his target to the presence of an ominous-looking beige van rolling slowly at his five-o'clock position.

The assistant secretary ended his call and put his phone back in his pocket.

'Did you get it?'

'Yes.'

Valentin turned to the right at the next intersection and left the neighborhood behind.

They parked in a lot by the train station and Kovalenko climbed into the back to watch the technician at work.

The smart phone, Kovalenko knew, used a common cryptographic algorithm called RSA. It was good, but it wasn't new, and it was easily breakable with the tools at the technician's disposal.

Once the German had the key, the software told him that it could now spoof the device. With a few clicks, he opened the website for NATO's secure Brussels command network, and then sent the encryption information taken from the Public Diplomacy Department man.

He then impersonated the smart phone with his software and logged on to the NATO Communication and Information Systems Services Agency's secure network.

It was the responsibility of Max and Valentin to get into the network, just to test the access. They would do no more, other than return to the safe house and e-mail the encryption information for the diplomat's smart phone to Center. The German would leave immediately, but Valentin would take a day or two to break down the van and sanitize the safe house, and then he would get out of Brussels.

Easy work, but that was nothing new. Kovalenko's job, he had determined over the past month, was little more than child's play.

He would bide his time for now, but before much longer, Valentin Kovalenko had decided he would make a break. Leave Center and his organization behind.

He still had friends, he was certain of it, in the SVR. He would reach out to someone at an embassy somewhere in Europe, and they would help him out. He knew better than to go back to Russia. There the government could pick him up and 'disappear him' with little trouble, but he'd reach out to an old friend or two working at a foreign posting, and he'd start laying the groundwork to allow for his return.

But this travel and this waiting would take money, and for

that Kovalenko would continue to work for Center until he was ready to make his move.

Though he'd been warned by the Russian mobster that Center would have him killed, he was not worried. Yes, Center contracted out the unpleasantness at Matrosskaya Tishina prison, but Kovalenko felt that staying out of Russia would keep him relatively safe from those thugs.

This was an organization of computer hackers and technical surveillance specialists. It's not like the Center organization were killers themselves, after all.

34

Captain Brandon 'Trash' White looked away from his instruments, turned his attention outside his canopy, and saw nothing other than the black night and the streaking raindrops lit up by the lights of his aircraft.

Somewhere out there, off his eleven o'clock and several hundred feet below him, a tiny postage stamp of deck in the middle of the sea bobbed up and down on heaving swells. He closed on it at one hundred fifty miles an hour, except when the swirling winds at this altitude slowed him down, sped him up, or knocked him left and right.

And in just a couple of minutes he would, God willing, land on that erratically moving postage stamp.

This was a Case Three landing, night ops, and this meant he'd been 'flying the needles,' watching the Automatic Carrier Landing System needles projected on the heads-up display in front of him. He kept his aircraft lined up in the center of the display as he neared the carrier, which was easy enough, but he was about to get passed off from radar control to the landing signals officer for the last few hundred feet to the deck, and he almost wished he could fly around up here in the shit a little while longer to compose himself.

The winds were said to be 'down the angle' at deck level, meaning blowing from bow to stern, and this would help things a bit as he got lower, but up here he was getting knocked all over the damn place and his hands were sweating inside his gloves from the effort of keeping lined up.

Still, it was safe up here, and it was dicey as hell down there on the deck.

Trash hated carrier landings with a white-hot passion, and he hated nighttime carrier landings a hundred times more. Adding awful weather and an angry sea to the equation ensured that White was having one hell of a shitty evening.

There. Down there past all the digital information projected on his heads-up display, he saw a tiny row of green lights with a yellow light in the middle. This was the optical landing system, and it grew in brightness and size in his HUD.

A voice came over his radio an instant later, loud enough to be audible through the heavy sound of his own breathing coming through the intercom. 'Four-oh-eight, three-quarter mile. Call the ball.'

Trash pressed his transmit key. 'Four-oh-eight, Hornet-ball, Five-point-niner.'

In a calm and soothing voice the LSO answered, 'Roger ball. You're lined up left. Don't go any higher.'

Trash's left hand drew the throttle back just a hair, and his right hand nudged the stick a touch to the right.

Marines on carriers. Why? Trash thought to himself. He knew the answer, of course. Carrier integration, they called it. Marines had been flying off carriers for twenty years as a result of some bright idea thought up by some officer sitting motionless at a desk. It was a manifestation of the thinking that anything Naval Aviation could do Marine Corps Aviation was supposed to be able to do as well.

Whatever.

As far as Trash White was concerned, just because the Marine Corps *could* do it, it didn't necessarily mean the Marine Corps *should* do it. Marines were meant to fly off flat runways cut out of jungles or deserts. They were meant to sleep in tents under camo netting with other Marines, to walk through the mud to their aircraft, and then to take off and support their fellow jarheads in battle.

They were not meant to live on and fly off of a damn boat.

That was Trash's opinion, not that anyone had ever asked him for it.

His name was Brandon White, but no one had called him that in a long time. Everybody called him Trash. Yes, it came from a play on his last name, but the Kentucky native wasn't really what anyone but the most blue-blooded Northerner would call white trash. His father was a doctor with a successful podiatry practice in Louisville, and his mother was a professor of art history at the University of Kentucky.

Not exactly trailer-park material, but his call sign was part of him now, and, he had to admit, there were worse call signs out there than Trash.

He knew a pilot in another squadron named Mangler, for example, which sounded cool as hell to Trash until he learned the poor guy received the moniker after one night chugging margaritas in a Key West bar. On his stagger out of the men's room the young nugget zipped his balls in his fly, couldn't get them out, and was rushed to the hospital. The medical term the ER nurse wrote down on his paperwork was 'testicular mangling,' and though the young lieutenant recovered from the unfortunate incident, he was damn sure never going to be allowed to forget that night in the Keys, since it became his permanent call sign.

Earning a call sign as a play on one's last name, as Trash White had done, seemed like a hell of a lot less trouble.

As a boy, Brandon had wanted to be a NASCAR driver, but by his mid-teens a ride-along in a friend's father's crop duster set his life's course. That one morning he spent streaking low over soybean fields in a 'two-holer,' a two-seat open biplane, showed him that the real excitement was not on the oval track but rather in the wide-open sky.

He could have gone into the Air Force or the Navy, but a friend's big brother joined the Marines, and then sold Brandon on the Corps the night he came home from Paris Island and took his kid brother and his friend out to McDonald's and regaled them with stories about what a badass he was.

Now White was twenty-eight, pilot of an F/A-18C Hornet tactical fighter, an aircraft about as far away from that first Air Tractor crop duster as one could get.

Trash loved flying, and he loved the Marine Corps. He'd been stationed in Japan for the past four months, and had enjoyed himself as much as anyone could. Japan wasn't as much fun as San Diego or Key West or some other places he had been stationed, but still, he had no complaints.

Not until the day before yesterday, when he was told his squadron of twelve aircraft would be heading out to the *Ronald Reagan* to make haste toward Taiwan.

The day after the U.S. announced the *Reagan* was moving closer to the Republic of China, People's Liberation Army Air Force warplanes began harassing Taiwanese aircraft around the Strait of Taiwan in retaliation. Trash and his Marines were ordered to the carrier to bolster the Navy Super Hornets already on board. Together the Navy and Marine aviators would be flying combat air patrol missions on the ROC side of the centerline of the Strait of Taiwan.

He knew the Chinese would probably go ape shit when they saw American aircraft protecting the ROC, but Trash didn't care. He welcomed the opportunity to mix things up with the Chinese. Hell, if there was going to be action and F/A-18Cs were going to be involved, Trash damn well wanted the Marine Corps there, and he damn well wanted his own aircraft in the thick of it.

But he hated boats. He'd qualified on carriers – every Marine has to qualify on carriers – but he had fewer than twenty traps under his belt, and all twenty of those were more than three years ago. Yes, for the past couple of weeks, he'd been on FCLP, field carrier landing practice, at a field in Okinawa, where he landed on a stretch of runway fixed with arresting wires just like on a carrier, but that flat stretch of concrete hadn't been Dutch rolling in the dark in a rainstorm like the deck of the *Reagan* below him.

FCLP was a long way from what he was going through now.

Two minutes ago Trash's flight lead, Major Scott 'Cheese' Stilton, touched down on the deck and caught a four-wire for a long but acceptable landing. The other ten Marine F/A-18C pilots coming in this evening had all landed before Cheese. Trash was the last one in the sky tonight, with the exception of the refueler, and this sucked for Trash, because the weather was getting worse by the minute and Trash was down below six thousand pounds of fuel, meaning he would get only two passes at the deck before he'd have to refuel and try again, making everyone down there in flight ops on USS *Ronald Reagan* wait.

'Power. You're low,' the landing signals officer coached Trash in over the radio.

Trash had backed off the throttle too much. He goosed it forward again, which pushed his jet too high.

Too high meant he'd either catch the four-wire, the last wire on the deck, or he'd bolter, meaning he'd miss all four wires and roll down the deck. In the case of a bolter he'd fly right off the end, climb back into the soupy black sky, and reenter the landing pattern.

Too high would not be good, but it was a hell of a lot better than too low.

Too low, not catching the one wire but *really* too low, meant a ramp strike, which was carrier-ops speech for slamming into the back of the boat, killing yourself and sending your burning wreckage rolling across the deck in a fireball that would turn into a video to be used in carrier training curriculums as a bright and shining example of what *not* to do.

Trash didn't want to bolter, but it sure as shit beat the alternative.

Trash was focused on the meatball now, the illuminated amber bulb in the center of the OLS that helped pilots maintain the proper approach angle down to the deck. As much as every human instinct told him to eye the deck itself as he approached it at one hundred fifty miles per hour, he knew he had to ignore his impact point and trust the meatball to bring him down safely. He was on the ball now, it was nice and centered in the middle of the OLS, indicating a good glide path, three-point-five degrees of descent, and he was just seconds from touching the deck. It looked like he was on his way to a safe three-wire, a nice landing considering the weather.

But just a few moments before his wheels and his tail hook touched down, the amber ball rose above the center horizontal green datum lights on the OLS.

The LSO said, 'Easy with it.'

Trash quickly pulled back on the throttle, but the ball rose higher and higher.

'Shit,' Trash said between two heavy breaths. He came off the power even more.

'Power back on,' admonished the LSO.

It took Trash a moment to realize it, but that was only because he wasn't a Navy pilot used to carrier landings. He *had* been lined up perfectly, but now the pitching deck was dropping away as the *Ronald Reagan* sank between massive ocean swells.

Trash's wheels touched down on the deck, but he knew he was long. He shoved his throttle forward to the full power detent, and his speed shot up. He raced down the deck toward the impenetrable darkness ahead.

'Bolter! Bolter! Bolter!' called the LSO, confirming something Trash already knew.

In seconds he was back in the black sky, climbing over the sea, reentering the bolter/wave-off pattern with his plane as the sole aircraft.

If he could not land on this next pass, the air boss on the carrier, the officer in charge of all flight operations, would send him to gas up behind the F/A-18E that was circling around ahead and to the left of the bow of the *Reagan*.

Trash had a strong suspicion the pilot of the refueler didn't want to be up here in this black soup any more than Trash did, and was probably wishing that a-hole Marine pilot would put his jet on the deck already so he could call it a night.

Trash concentrated on his instruments as he leveled out and began a series of turns that would put him back on final.

Five minutes later he was lined up on the carrier once more.

The LSO came over the radio, 'Four-oh-eight, this is Paddles. The deck is pitching a bit. Concentrate on a good start and avoid overcontrolling in the middle.'

'Four-oh-eight, Hornet-ball, Five-point-one.' He watched the ball, it was just about the only damn thing he could see at this point, and he could tell he was high.

The LSO said, 'Roger ball. High again. Work it down.'

'Roger.' Trash pulled back slightly on the throttle.

'You are high and lined up left,' called the LSO now. 'Easy with it. Right for line up.'

Trash's left hand twitched the power back again and he pushed the stick to the right.

He centered nicely on the deck ahead and below, but he was still too high.

He was moments away from another bolter.

But just then, as he crossed the threshold of the rear of the massive carrier, he saw the lights of the deck rising underneath him, he watched the deck push up into the black sky toward the bottom of his aircraft like it was on a hydraulic lift.

His tail hook caught the three-wire, and the arrester cable yanked him to a stop with the effect of bringing a loaded semi-trailer traveling at a hundred fifty miles an hour to a complete halt in under three seconds.

Trash jerked to a violent but welcome stop on the deck of the *Ronald Reagan*.

An instant later the air boss came over his headset. 'Well, if you can't come to the *Reagan*, the *Reagan* will come to you.'

Trash gave an exhausted chuckle. His landing would be scored; all carrier landings are scored. It would be judged fair, which was fine with him, but the air boss made it clear he knew that the only reason he'd not boltered again was that the boat had reached up and snatched him out of the sky.

But he was glad to be on the deck. 'Yes, sir,' he said.

'Welcome aboard, Marine.'

'Semper Fi, sir,' Trash said with a bit of false bravado. He took his gloved hands off the stick and throttle and held them up in front of his face. They shook a little, which did not surprise him in the slightest.

'I hate boats,' he said to himself.

35

The office of SinoShield Business Investigative Services Ltd was located on the thirty-third floor of IFC2, Two International Finance Centre, which, at eighty-eight stories, was the second-tallest building in Hong Kong, and the eighth-tallest office building in the world.

Gavin, Jack, and Domingo were dressed in high-dollar business suits, and they carried briefcases and leather folios; they fit in perfectly with the thousands of office workers and clients moving through the hallways of IFC2.

The three Americans checked in with the receptionist for the floor, and she called Mr Yao and spoke to him briefly in Cantonese.

She then said, 'He will be here right away. Won't you sit down?'

They got the impression that several small companies shared the check-in desk, the receptionist, and all of the common areas here on the thirty-third floor.

After a few minutes a young handsome Asian man walked up the carpeted hallway into the common space. Unlike most Chinese businessmen, he was not wearing his suit coat. Instead his lavender dress shirt was somewhat wrinkled and his sleeves were rolled up to his elbows. As he closed on the three men in the waiting area, he ran his hands over his shirt and straightened his tie.

'Good morning, gentlemen,' the man said with a tired smile and an extended hand. He possessed no hint of any accent, save perhaps a touch of southern California. 'Adam Yao, at your service.'

Chavez shook his hand. 'Domingo Chavez, director of corporate security.'

'Mr Chavez,' Yao replied politely.

Both Jack and Ding recognized immediately that this kid was probably a great intelligence officer, and likely a hell of a poker player. Every last member of CIA's Clandestine Service would know the name Domingo Chavez in a heartbeat, and they would also know the man would be in his middle to late forties. The fact that Yao did not bat an eyelash and let on that he recognized a CIA legend was a testament to his good tradecraft skills.

'Jack Ryan, associate financial analyst,' Jack said as the two men shook hands.

This time, Adam Yao did show genuine surprise.

'Whoa,' he said with a bright smile. 'Jack Junior. All I knew about Hendley Associates was that Senator Hendley was running the show. I didn't know you were –'

Jack interrupted, 'Yeah, I try to stay pretty low-key. I'm just one of the grunts working a keyboard and a mouse.'

Yao gave a look like he found Jack's comment to be just modesty.

After Yao was introduced to Gavin Biery, he led all three back toward his office.

Chavez said, 'I'm sorry about springing this meeting on you like this out of the blue, but we were in town with a problem and needed somebody who knew the lay of the land.'

Yao said, 'My secretary said representatives from your company were in town and asked for a brief consult. I honestly wish I could offer you more than twenty minutes, but I am slammed. As I bet you can imagine, intellectual property investigations in HK and China keep a guy in my profession busy. I'm not complaining, even if I am reduced to catching catnaps on the love seat in my office instead of going home and having a life.' He waved a hand over his slightly wrinkled shirt, making an excuse for his worn look.

As they entered his small and spartan office, Jack said, 'We appreciate any time you have to talk to us at all, we really do.'

Yao's secretary brought coffee service for the four men and placed it in a small sitting area in front of Adam's messy desk.

Jack wondered what was going on in Yao's head. Having the son of the President of the United States in his office must have been somewhat cool, as laid-back as Jack was about his family name, he recognized at least that much. But meeting and chatting with Domingo Chavez would be, Ryan had no doubt, one of the seminal events in this CIA officer's life.

'So,' Yao asked, 'how did you guys find out about me?'

Jack said, 'There was an article that named your firm along with a couple others a few months ago in *Investor's Business Daily*. When our own problems brought us over here to Hong Kong, we dug it out and gave your office a call.'

'Ah, yes. A case we worked on last year involving some high-tech patents being counterfeited in Shenzhen. Happens all the time, but it was nice to get the free advertising.'

'What sorts of projects are you taking on these days?' Jack asked.

'Could be anything, really. I have clients in the computer industry, in the pharmaceutical industry, in retail, publishing, even in the restaurant business.'

'Restaurants?'

Adam nodded. 'Yep. There's a prominent chain in southern California, over sixty locations. Turns out they have eleven more locations over here that they didn't know about.'

'You're kidding,' said Biery.

'Nope. Same name, same signs, same menu, same little hats on their heads. Except the owners of the chain don't see a dime of the profits.'

'Incredible.'

'It's happening more and more. They just busted a ring of fake Apple stores over here selling Mac knockoffs. Even the employees thought they worked for Apple.'

'Must be tough shutting them down,' Ryan said.

Yao smiled pleasantly. 'It is tough. I enjoy the investigation part, but dealing with Chinese bureaucracy is . . . What's the word I'm looking for?'

'Bullshit?' Jack said.

Yao smiled. 'I was going to say "tedious," although "bullshit" is a better description.' He regarded Ryan with a smile. 'So, Jack. Why don't I see a couple of square-jawed security guys in black suits and earpieces standing behind you?'

'I rejected my Secret Service detail. I like my privacy.'

Chavez added with a smile, 'I watch his back, when necessary.'

Yao chuckled, took a sip of his coffee, and shuffled in his chair. Jack caught him looking at Chavez for a moment. 'Well, gentlemen, what sort of mischief has China made for your financial management firm?'

Gavin Biery said, 'It's cybercrime, essentially. My network has been getting hit with a series of very well thought-out and organized hacking attempts. They managed to get in and to steal our client lists. Obviously this is extremely sensitive data. I was able to trace the source of the intrusion back to a command server in the U.S., and I hacked into that server.'

Adam said, 'Good for you. I like a company that's willing to fight back. If everybody did that, we'd sure as hell be in a better place as far as commercial theft. What did you find on the server?'

'I found the culprit. There was data on there that told me who was behind the attack on it. Not a real name but his online handle. We also were able to establish that the attack originated here in Hong Kong.'

'That's interesting, and I'm sure that was tough to trace them all the way back here, but there's something I don't get. Once these folks get the data they are looking for off your network . . . there is no point getting it back. It's out there, they've used it, copied it, compromised you. What's your objective coming over here?'

Chavez stepped in. 'We want to catch the guy who did this so he can't do it again. Prosecute him.'

Yao gave the three men a look like they were hopelessly naive. 'My professional opinion, gentlemen, is that that is *highly* unlikely. Even if you could prove this crime, the criminals won't be prosecuted here, and if you're thinking about extradition, you can forget about it. Whoever this guy is, he is working here in HK because this is a damned convenient place to commit such crimes. It's getting better, HK is not the Wild West it once was, but you guys are in over your heads. I hate to be blunt, but better I tell you honestly before you burn a hell of a lot of money over here finding out the same thing.'

Jack said, 'Maybe you could take us on as a client, just to investigate a bit. If nothing comes from it, well, it's our money to burn, right?'

Adam said, 'The problem is, these cases are built very slowly and methodically. Right now I'm working on a case that's four years old. I wish I could tell you things over here moved faster, but it won't serve anyone's purposes to mislead you about what you are faced with.

'On top of all that, I'm much more versed with the intellectual-property side of fraud over here. Cybersecurity is a growing problem, but it's not my specialty. I honestly think I'd be somewhat out of my lane.'

Chavez asked, 'Do you have any contacts or resources at all? As Mr Biery said, we've got a user name for the perpetrator. We were hoping there might be someone over here with a database that could get us a little more information on this character's operation.'

Yao smiled, a little patronizing to the older man, though not intentionally. 'Mr Chavez, there are probably ten million hackers across China involved with computer fraud to one degree or another. Any one of these guys probably has multiple user names. There is not a database that I am aware of that keeps up with that rolling landscape.'

Jack said, 'This guy is pretty good. Surely somebody knows about him.'

Yao sighed a little but kept a polite smile, then stood and went behind his desk. He pulled his keyboard to him. 'I can send an instant message to a friend up in Guangzhou who's a bit more up-to-date on cyber-financial crime. It's going to be a needle in a haystack, I promise you, but it won't hurt to ask him if he's ever heard of the guy.'

As Adam Yao typed he asked, 'What's the handle?'

Gavin and Jack looked at each other. With a conspiratorial smile from Ryan that said, *Let's blow this guy's mind,* he gave Gavin the go-ahead.

Biery said, 'His handle is FastByte Twenty-two.'

Yao stopped typing. His shoulders stiffened. Slowly he turned back toward his three guests. 'You've got to be kidding me.'

Chavez had joined the game with his two colleagues. He asked, 'You *know* him?'

Yao looked across his desk. Ryan could feel a mild suspicion on the part of the CIA covert operator, but above this, the thrill in the young man's eyes was obvious. He seemed to recover a bit before replying, 'Yeah. I know him. He's . . . he's a subject of interest in another case in which . . . in which I am tangentially involved.'

Jack tried not to smile. He liked this guy, he was smart as hell, and it was clear by everything Jack had seen that Yao worked his ass off out here, essentially by himself. He enjoyed watching Adam Yao squirm trying to find the right words to hide his excitement that he might finally get some more intel about a target that had, until now, not been on anyone's radar but his own.

'Well, then, maybe we can work together to combine our efforts,' Chavez said. 'As Jack said, we are willing to put some money into this operation to see if we can track him down.'

Yao said, 'The tracking down is free of charge. He's working out of offices in the Mong Kok Computer Centre up in Kowloon.'

'You've seen him? In person?'

'I have. But it's a complicated situation.'

'How so?' asked Ding.

Yao hesitated for several seconds. Finally he asked, 'Where are you guys staying?'

Jack answered, 'We're right across the harbor at the Peninsula.'

'Are you three free for drinks tonight? We can talk it over a bit more, maybe come up with a plan.'

Chavez spoke for the group: 'Eight o'clock?'

36

Melanie Kraft sat on the sofa in the living room of her carriage-house apartment on Princess Street in Alexandria's Old Town. It was seven in the evening, and normally she would be up at Jack's place or even working late, but tonight Jack was out of town and she just wanted to sit on her couch in the dark, watch TV, and think about something else other than her problems.

She flipped channels, decided against a Discovery Channel program about the Middle East and a History Channel program about the life and career of President Jack Ryan. Both of these shows would normally be interesting to her, but right now she just wanted to vegetate.

She settled on an Animal Planet show about wildlife in Alaska. She felt sure that would keep her attention and take her mind off everything that was going on.

Her mobile buzzed, moving across the coffee table in front of her. She looked down, hoping it would be Jack. It wasn't. She did not recognize the number, but saw the area code was D.C.

'Hello?'

'Hey, girl. What you up to?'

It was Darren Lipton. He was the last person on earth she needed to talk to tonight.

She cleared her throat, put on her business voice, and said, 'What can I do for you, Special Agent Lipton?'

'Senior Special Agent, but I'll let it slide.'

He seemed like he was in a good mood – jovial, even.

It occurred to Melanie almost immediately that he was probably drunk.

'Senior Special Agent,' she corrected herself.

'Listen, we need to get together for a quick powwow. Might take all of fifteen minutes.'

She knew she could not say no. But she was not ready to say yes. She wanted Lipton to think she was not his puppy, his personal property that would come whenever he called. Even though that's exactly how Melanie felt now that he'd revealed that he was holding her entire future in his hands.

She said, 'What's this about?'

'We'll discuss it tomorrow. How 'bout we get a cup of coffee. Seven-thirty a.m. I'll come to you. Starbucks on King Street?'

'Fine,' she said, and she hung up the phone, then went back to watching grizzly bears catch salmon, her mind heavy with new worries.

Melanie and Lipton sat at a table outside on a cool and windy fall morning. Her hair whipped around her face while she sipped her tea to keep warm. Lipton drank coffee, his black trench coat was open to show a dark blue suit, and he wore sunglasses even though the sky was overcast.

She wondered if he was trying to hide bloodshot eyes. In any case, with the shades and the blue suit and the black trench coat, he screamed Fed to anyone in the coffee shop or walking by on the sidewalk who paid attention.

After a minute of one-sided small talk, Lipton got down to business. 'My boss needs more from you. I tried to placate him, but you haven't given us anything since our last conversation.'

'I don't know any more now than I did then. It's like you want me to catch him passing nuclear secrets to the Russians or something.'

'Or something,' Lipton said. He plucked his flop of gray-blond hair out from under his shades and then reached into his jacket. He pulled out a sheaf of papers and held it up.

'What's that?'

'Court order to put a locator on Ryan's cell phone. FBI wants to track his day-to-day movements.'

'What?' She snatched it out of his hand and began reading the documents.

'We have evidence he's been conducting some highly suspicious meetings with foreign nationals. We need to be there and see what's going on.'

Melanie was furious that the investigation was continuing. But something else occurred to her. 'What does this have to do with me? Why are you even telling me?'

'Because you, my fair lady, are going to put the beacon on his phone.'

'Oh no I'm not!' Kraft said testily.

'I'm afraid you are. I've got the card you need to use. There is no physical device that he might find, it's all done through the software. You just poke the little card in his phone, let it load, and then pop it back out. A thirty-second operation.'

Melanie looked off into the street for a moment. 'Don't you have assets for this?'

'Yes. *You* are my asset. My asset with assets, if you know what I mean.' He looked down at her chest.

Melanie looked at him in disbelief.

'Uh-oh,' Lipton said with a barking laugh. 'Am I about to get another right hook to the teeth?'

Melanie picked up from his tone and his facial expressions that he had somehow enjoyed it when she hit him.

She told herself she wouldn't do *that* again.

She took a moment to compose herself. She knew, with the information the FBI had about her and her father, that

Lipton could make her do whatever he wanted. She said, 'Before I agree to do this, I want to talk to someone else at National Security Branch.'

Lipton shook his head. 'I'm running you, Melanie. Deal with it.'

'I'm not saying I need a new handler. I just want to confirm things with someone other than you. Someone *above* you.'

Now the special agent's nearly constantly leering smile wavered. 'That thing in your hand is a court order. Signed by a judge. What more confirmation do you want?'

'I'm not your slave. If I do this, I want some sort of assurances from the FBI that you won't keep using me. I do this, and I'm done.'

'I can't make that promise.'

'Then find me someone who can.'

'It's not happening.'

'Then I guess we're finished.' She stood.

He uncrossed his legs and bolted to his feet. 'You realize how much trouble I can make for you?'

'I'm just asking for someone else to talk to. If you can't make that happen, then I hardly believe you have the clout to send me to prison.'

She stepped into the morning crowd heading up King Street toward the Metro.

The Peninsula hotel is on the southern tip of Kowloon, overlooking Victoria Harbour in a high-end retail district called Tsim Sha Tsui. A five-star property, the Peninsula opened in 1928 and proudly wears its old-world colonial charm.

Past the fleet of fourteen green Rolls-Royce extendedwheelbase Phantoms at the front of the building, past the huge ornate lobby and a short hallway, an elevator whisks patrons to the top of the hotel. Here, the ultramodern and chic Philippe Starck-designed Felix restaurant serves modern European cuisine in front of floor-to-ceiling windows that look out over Victoria Harbour to Hong Kong Island. A small bar sits at the top of a spiral staircase overlooking the restaurant, and here four Americans sat together in a back corner, sipping bottled beer and looking out over the lights.

Chavez said, 'You said this morning that the FastByte situation was complicated. What did you mean by that?'

Yao took a swig of his Tsingtao. 'FastByte Twenty-two's real name is Zha Shu Hai. He's twenty-four years old. He's from the mainland, but he moved to the USA as a child and became an American citizen. He was a hacker when he was a kid, but he got a security clearance and was hired by a government contractor to do penetration testing of their systems. He figured how to break in, tried to give the information to China, and then was caught and sent to prison.'

'When did they let him out?'

'They didn't. He was doing time at a federal correctional institution – that's minimum security – in California. He was on work release, teaching computer skills to senior citizens, and then one day . . . *poof.*'

'He split?' asked Chavez.

'Yep. The Feds canvassed his home and all his old known contacts, and he never turned up. Escapees just about always return to their old life, even if it is just making contact with family, but Zha did not. The U.S. Marshals Service came to the conclusion that the Chinese helped get him out of the U.S. and back to the mainland.'

Biery was confused. 'This isn't the mainland.'

'No, it's not. It's a surprise that he's turned up here, but there is one thing even more surprising than that.'

'What's that?'

'He's now with the Fourteen-K.'

Chavez cocked his head. 'Fourteen-K? The Triads?'

'Exactly.'

Ryan was surprised Ding knew about this organization. He had never heard of 14K. 'A gang?'

Chavez said, 'Not like a gang in the States. Here, just admitting you are a member is against the law. Isn't that right, Adam?'

'Yeah. Nobody admits they are Triad in HK. Just being in management will get you fifteen years in jail.'

Ding explained for Ryan and Biery: 'There are over two and a half million members of the Triads around the world. The actual name of the organization is San He Hui, the Three Harmonies Society. The Fourteen-K are just one of many offshoots, but they are the most powerful around here these days. There are probably twenty thousand members of Fourteen-K here in Hong Kong alone.'

Adam said, 'I'm impressed.'

Chavez waved the compliment away with a hand. 'In my business it pays to know who the agitators are when you go into a new territory.'

'So,' Ryan asked, 'FastByte Twenty-two is a member?'

'I don't think he's a member, but he definitely associates with them.'

'If he isn't a member of the Triads, what is his relationship with them?' Ryan asked.

'It might be some sort of a protector-protected relationship. A guy like him can print money. He can sit at his computer and then, within a couple of hours, steal the credit card numbers of ten thousand people. The kid is worth his weight in gold as far as his ability to conduct cybercrime, so the Fourteen-K could be watching over him due to his value.'

Chavez said, 'How good are the Fourteen-K guys at protecting him?'

'They keep a couple of enforcers around him twenty-four-seven. There are Fourteen-K on him when he goes to work; when he gets off work, they guard his office and they hang outside of his apartment building, too. He does like to go shopping, out to the clubs at night, and he does this primarily in Fourteen-K bars and neighborhoods, and always with goons by his side. I've done my best to watch him to see who he moves with, but, as you can see, I am a small operation here. I thought I was doing a good job keeping my distance, but just the other day it became clear they burned me.'

'Any idea how?' Ding asked.

'None at all. One morning he just had more security and they were most definitely hunting for a specific threat. They must have made me the evening before.'

Ding said, 'It sounds to me like you need a couple new bodies in your operation to help you watch him.'

Yao raised his eyebrows. 'You volunteering?'

'Absolutely.'

Yao asked, 'Have you done any surveillance work?'

Ding smiled. 'I've done a fair bit. Ryan's helped me out once or twice. He enjoys it.'

Jack nodded. 'It's in my blood, I guess.'

'I imagine it would be.' Ryan still detected a hint of suspicion from Adam Yao. The guy was clearly a dialed-in observationalist. He said, 'Just out of curiosity, what sort of surveillance, I mean, other than this situation here, does Hendley Associates get itself involved with?'

Ding said, 'Typical business-intelligence stuff. I can't really go into it.'

Adam seemed to accept this, and then he looked at Gavin Biery.

'Mr Biery, will you be joining us?'

Chavez answered for him: 'Gavin will stay here at the Peninsula and support us.'

Adam Yao reached into his pocket and pulled out his iPhone. He punched up a photo, and then passed the phone around.

'Zha Shu Hai,' Yao said.

His spiked hair, jewelry, and punk rock clothing surprised Ding and Jack. 'Not exactly what I expected,' said Ding.

'I was picturing a younger Chinese version of Gavin Biery,' admitted Ryan.

Everyone, Gavin included, laughed.

Yao said, 'Lots of hackers in China think they are counterculture rock stars. The truth is, even the civilian ones like Zha usually work for the Chicoms, so they are pretty much the opposite of counterculture.'

Ryan asked, 'There's no way he could be working for the Chicoms, is there?'

Yao shook his head. 'Being here in HK and not on the mainland, and moving around under the protection of the Triads, those are two pretty big strikes against the theory that this kid is shilling for the PRC.'

Ryan had to admit that Yao's logic seemed sound on that point.

With that settled, Yao finished his beer. 'Okay, guys. We can pick Zha up when he leaves the Mong Kok Computer Centre tomorrow evening. With three of us, we might catch a break and get some pictures of his contacts.'

Everyone agreed.

'First, though,' said Adam, 'we need to do some dry runs through the city, just to get a feel for how we will work together. Why don't we meet early to do some practice tails for an hour or two?'

'Good idea,' said Ding, then he drained his beer and called for the check.

As the men headed out through the restaurant, a young American dining with an attractive female stood and quickly rushed over toward Jack. Ding put himself between Ryan and the man and held a hand up to stop him.

The diner said, a little too loudly, 'Junior?'

'Yeah?'

'Big fan of your dad's! Great to see you! Man, you've grown up.'

'Thanks.' Jack smiled politely. He did not know the man, but Jack's dad was famous, meaning Jack himself was recognized from time to time.

The guy had been smiling himself, but the small and tough-looking Hispanic man giving him the stink eye had blunted his excitement to some degree.

Jack shook the man's hand. He expected to be asked for an autograph or a picture, but he could tell Chavez was having a cooling effect on the encounter.

Yao, Ryan, Chavez, and Biery headed back down to the lobby. Adam said to Jack, 'I bet that gets old.'

Ryan chuckled. 'Getting recognized? It's not a big problem. I don't get noticed one-tenth as much as I used to.'

Gavin said, 'I had a vendor in the office the other day who didn't know Ryan worked with us. When I introduced him I thought the guy was going to crap his pants, he was so thrilled. Must have been a big Jack Ryan, Senior, fan.'

Everyone laughed. The Campus team wished Adam a good evening, and Adam headed out into the night to catch a ferry across Victoria Harbour, back to his apartment.

37

Melanie Kraft sat at a fast food restaurant in McLean, just a couple blocks from her office at Liberty Crossing, picking at her salad. She did not have much of an appetite after her conversation with Special Agent Lipton that morning. She worried that at any time, carloads of FBI agents could appear to arrest her, and she even caught herself looking out through the glass of the shop more than once when a car pulled up.

She thought, not for the first time, about sitting Jack down and telling him what was going on. She knew it would destroy his trust in her, and he would be justified in never speaking to her again, but maybe if she explained the situation, the entire situation, he would understand enough that he would not hate her for the rest of his life. She'd done very little, after all, in her mission to spy on him for the FBI. In fact, other than a couple of phone calls about his trips abroad, Lipton was correct when he said she was basically useless as an agent.

Her phone rang, and she answered it without looking. 'Hello?'

'Hey, hon.' It was Lipton. 'Okay. You get what you want. Come on over and you can meet with my boss, Special Agent in Charge Packard.'

'Come over? Come over *where*?'

'To J. Edgar. Where else?' The J. Edgar Hoover Building, on Pennsylvania Avenue, was the headquarters of the FBI.

Melanie balked. She did not want to be seen walking into the Hoover Building. 'Can we meet someplace else?'

'Sugar, do you think SAIC Packard's got nothing better to do than to drive out to McLean this afternoon?'

'I'll take the afternoon off and come to D.C. Right now. You tell me where. Anyplace but the Hoover Building.'

Lipton blew out a long sigh and said, 'Let me call you back.'

An hour later Melanie entered the same underground garage where she had met with Lipton previously. Unlike that early Saturday morning, it was now packed with cars.

She found two men standing next to a black Chevy Suburban with government plates.

Packard was younger than Lipton by a few years, though his hair was fully gray. He passed Melanie his credentials, which she looked at briefly to confirm his name and title, and then he handed her all the paperwork Lipton had shown her that morning.

Packard said, 'What we are asking of you, Miss Kraft, is very simple. Place a software location tracker on Mr Ryan's phone without his knowledge, and then stand down. We are not telling you we won't require your services again, but we will not require you to provide us updates on his whereabouts.'

Melanie said, 'I have not gotten a straight answer from Special Agent Lipton, maybe you can provide me with one. Just what evidence do you have that he has committed any crimes?'

Packard took a moment. 'It's an ongoing investigation, of which Mr Ryan is a subject of interest. That's really all I can tell you.'

Melanie was not satisfied. 'I can't just indefinitely spy on my boyfriend. Especially if I have no reason to believe he's done anything wrong.'

Packard turned to Lipton now. 'Darren, can you give us a minute?'

Lipton looked like he was going to argue. Packard raised a single bushy eyebrow, and Lipton shuffled off through the parking garage, headed up the ramp to street level.

Packard leaned back against his Suburban. 'First things first. I know Special Agent Lipton is a little rough around the edges.'

'That's putting it mildly.'

'He's damn good at what he does, so I give him some leeway, but I know this must be difficult for you for many reasons.'

Melanie nodded.

'I'm sorry about this entire situation. Hell, to tell you the truth, Jack Ryan, Senior, is my hero. The last thing in the world I want to do is expose his son in some sort of illegality. That said, I swore an oath, and I go where the law points me.

'I know Lipton has, essentially, threatened to expose your father's involvement with that Palestinian thing in Egypt if you don't play ball with us. Sometimes our job gets a little dirty like that.'

Melanie looked down to her hands.

'I'll be honest with you. I approved him making that threat. But we only did that because we know there is no way we can conduct this investigation without your help. I mean, of course we can put a twelve-man surveillance team on him, get federal wiretaps, and a search warrant for his home and office. But you and I know that is going to make a lot of news in this town, and we want to avoid that. If nothing comes out of this, we don't want to do anything to harm his reputation, or the reputation of his father. So we want to do this with all the sensitivity the situation warrants.

'You get that, right?'

After a moment Melanie said, 'Yes, sir.'

'Great. If you can plant the tracking software that the judge has allowed us to use, then we can be aware of his movements without doing the dog-and-pony show that's going to make the front page of *The Washington Post*.'

'And my situation?' she asked.

'Nobody needs to know about that. You have my personal assurance that those sleeping dogs will continue to lie where they are.' He smiled. 'Help us, and we'll help you. It's a win-win, Miss Kraft.'

'All right,' said Melanie. 'He's out of town right now, but when he gets back I'll download the thing onto his phone.'

'That's all we need.' Packard handed her his business card. 'If Darren gives you too much trouble, feel free to give me a call. I can't make him go away; the last thing anyone wants to do is bring someone else into this situation. But I will have a talk with him about his colorful behavior.'

'I appreciate that, Agent Packard.'

The two shook hands.

Adam Yao, Ding Chavez, and Jack Ryan, Jr, met at the Peninsula in the early afternoon. Yao had traded vehicles with a neighbor, allowing the neighbor to drive his Mercedes in exchange for using the man's maroon Mitsubishi Grandis, a seven-seat mini-van common in Asia. He had no idea if his own car had been spotted by the Triads, but he did not want to take any chances, and he liked the idea of having a little extra room in his vehicle for lugging around the men from Hendley Associates.

They drove up Nathan Road a few blocks, and Yao parked in an hourly lot. 'I thought we could get our operation set up for this evening, maybe work out any kinks in our surveillance process.'

Chavez said to Yao, 'You are in charge here. Just let us know what you want us to do.'

Adam hesitated. Ryan knew the CIA man must surely feel intimidated by running Domingo Chavez in a surveillance operation. Ding had fifteen years more experience in these sorts of things than did Yao. But of course Adam Yao could not reveal his discomfort to the businessmen working with him.

'Okay,' he said. 'First thing first. Everybody put on your Bluetooth headsets and dial in to this number.'

Ding asked, 'What number is this?'

'This will set all three of us up on a conference call. We will be in constant communication this way.'

They all logged in to the conference call and checked that they were in touch with one another.

Then Adam reached into his glove compartment and pulled out two small devices, each not much larger than a matchbox. He handed one to each of the two Hendley Associates men.

'What are these?' Jack asked.

'It's called a slap-on. It's a magnetic GPS beacon. I use them to track vehicles, mostly, but I can track you with them just as easily. Just stick it in a pocket, and I can monitor you on the map on my iPad. I will stay way behind you guys in the car while you do the foot follow, and I'll navigate for you.'

'Cool,' admitted Jack.

Ding and Jack exited the Mitsubishi and headed off to the south. Yao stayed in communication with them as they headed up opposite sides of a busy pedestrian street. Chavez picked a passerby at random to begin following, and he stayed well behind her as she window-shopped along Nathan Road.

Ryan managed to fight his way through the thick pedestrian traffic, and he got ahead of her on the other side of the tree-lined street. He was waiting inside a clothing store, watching her through the window as she passed.

'Ryan has the eye,' he said.

'Copy that,' replied Chavez. 'She seems to want to continue heading south. I'm going to get on the far side of the street and head to the next decision point.'

Now Yao came over their headsets. 'Ding, that's going to be the Austin Road intersection. There is a 7-Eleven there. You can go inside and retain visual on the subject as she makes that corner.'

'Copy that.'

Yao controlled both men from the map on his tablet computer. He moved his car ahead of the surveillance more than once to be in position to pick the woman up if she climbed into a vehicle.

They continued their coverage for an hour. The unsuspecting woman shopped, stopped for coffee, talked on her phone, and finally returned to her hotel room on the fifth floor of the Holiday Inn, all completely oblivious to the three-man team that kept her under constant surveillance.

Adam was impressed with the abilities of the American businessmen. Of course, it was no surprise to him that Domingo Chavez possessed such skills, but Ryan's abilities were, frankly, suspicious, considering the fact that he was an analyst in a financial management and currency trading concern.

POTUS's kid knew how to operate in a foot follow without being compromised.

They all rallied back at the car, which was now parked in an underground lot near the Jordan Road MTR station.

Yao went over his observations and talked about how things would be that night. 'The Triads are running counter-surveillance measures, so we'll have to back off a little from what we got away with today.'

Chavez and Jack agreed, but Yao could tell Ryan did not seem satisfied.

'Jack, something bothering you?'

'My only problem was that I was recognized a couple of times. Add that to the guy in the Peninsula last night, and that's three times in about eighteen hours. I almost never get recognized at home.'

Adam chuckled. 'HK is incredibly crowded, and it's one of the hubs of world finance. On top of that, there is a lot of connection with the West here. Everybody knows who your dad is. A few know who you are.'

'Not much I can do about it.'

Adam said, 'That's not exactly true. You want people to stop noticing you, the solution is easy enough.'

'I'm in your hands.'

Yao reached into his backpack and pulled out a paper air mask that attached to the face with rubber bands that went behind the ears.

Jack had seen hundreds of people walking the streets of Kowloon wearing these paper masks. Both Avian Flu and SARS had hit Hong Kong hard, which was no surprise, considering the dense population. Many people, especially those with compromised immune systems, took no chances and wore masks to help filter the air.

Adam placed the blue paper mask over Ryan's face. Then the Chinese-American dug in the pack again, and retrieved a black baseball cap. This he positioned on Ryan's head. He took a step back and looked at his handiwork.

'You are a little tall for a local, but look around, a lot of Chinese men are over six feet these days, and there is still a huge British population here. All in all, you will blend in just fine in that getup.'

Jack wasn't crazy about wearing a mask over his face, especially in the stifling heat and humidity of Hong Kong. But he understood that getting recognized at the wrong time on this foot follow could prove disastrous.

'One less thing to worry about, I guess,' he said to Yao.

'That's right. This will help with the Westerners, but to most people around here, even with the mask, you're still a *gweilo*.'

'A *gweilo*?'

'Sorry. A foreign devil.'

'That's harsh.'

Adam nodded. 'Yeah. It would serve you to remember that the Chinese are a prideful people. They think, in general, that they are superior to foreign races. They aren't an inclusive society, overall.'

'I'm not planning on buying a condo here. Just tailing Zha.'

Adam chuckled. 'Let's get back to the Mong Kok Computer Centre. Zha will be leaving work in about an hour.'

38

At eight-thirty p.m. Zha Shu Hai left the side exit of the Mong Kok Computer Centre with a security detail of four. Chavez had the eye; he was up the street in the 7-Eleven, heating up some frozen dumplings in the microwave. He started to turn away to announce to Ryan and Yao that the bird had left the nest, but he saw Zha stop suddenly and turn on his heels, as if someone had called out to him. He moved with his entourage back to the entrance of the building, and there he all but snapped to attention like a lance corporal. Chavez caught a glimpse of a man just inside the light from the streetlamps. Zha was talking to him with obvious deference. Ding knew this could be important, so he risked blowing his cover for action in the convenience store, pulled his big Nikon camera with a three-hundred-millimeter lens from his backpack, and took a picture of the men fifty yards up the street. Quickly he looked away from them, walked to the back of the 7-Eleven, and checked the digital image in the viewing pane of the camera. It was fair, at best. He could sort of make out Zha, and he could make out the one Triad sentry who was facing the 7-Eleven, but he could not see many features of the man in the dark.

Quickly he used the e-mail function on the camera, sent the image to Gavin Biery back in the suite in the Peninsula, and then took himself off the eye.

'Ryan, move in, I need to back off for a bit.'

'Roger that.'

He headed up the street and called Gavin.

'What's up, Domingo?'

'I just sent you an image.'

'Looking at it right now.'

'I need a favor.'

'You need photography lessons.'

'Yeah. Right. Anything you can do to make that clearer?'

'No big deal. I'll send it to all of your phones in a few minutes.'

'Great. From the way our boy FastByte leapt to attention when this guy called him, we may be looking at the MFIC.'

'MFIC? I don't know that acronym. Is that from the Chinese military or something?'

Chavez said, 'Just work on the pic and send it back to us.'

'You got it.'

Five minutes later the three Americans were back in the Mitsubishi Grandis, following the white SUV carrying Zha 'FastByte22' Shu Hai and his six 14K minders as it left the gritty streets of Mong Kok and headed south through late-rush-hour Kowloon into Tsim Sha Tsui.

The SUV stopped at a corner in a chic retail area. Five of Zha's security men climbed out, and then Zha himself appeared. He wore black jeans with silver studs running up the side, a bright pink tank top, and a black studded leather jacket. His detail, on the other hand, all wore the same blue jeans and drab T-shirts under denim jackets.

Zha and his entourage entered a clothing store as a group.

A steady rain had begun to fall; this did nothing for the oppressive heat but only added uncomfortable moisture to the mix. Adam pulled his car over to the side of the road two blocks past the store, then produced four collapsible umbrellas and passed one black and one red umbrella to each man. Ding and Jack slipped the red one in the small of their backs under their shirts and went with the black. This would virtually double their chances of remaining covert, as they could switch out umbrellas to reduce the risk that someone who spotted them earlier would notice them a second time.

As the two Hendley Associates men climbed out of the Mitsubishi, Adam called to them, 'Remember, for some reason Zha's security has been alerted that he's under surveillance. You'll have to watch yourselves. Don't push it, stay back, if we lose them tonight we'll pick them up tomorrow night.'

Jack and Ding split up immediately and took turns passing the shop every few minutes. The darkness, the heavy crowds on the sidewalks, and the large glass windows of the clothing store made keeping an eye on the young hacker easy work, even when one of the 14K men stood outside the shop to smoke and scan the pedestrians passing by.

Zha and the others left without making a purchase a few minutes later, but they did not climb back into the SUV. Instead the five guards popped umbrellas, one covered Zha with his, and they headed south, stepping into and out of several stores along the way.

Zha spent half the time window-shopping or looking at clothes and electronics inside the various shops, and the other half of the time either talking on his phone or using a tiny handheld computer as the man on his arm led him through the busy streets.

He bought some cables and a new laptop battery in a small store on Kowloon Park Drive, and then he and his goons ducked into an Internet café on Salisbury Road, near the entrance to the Star Ferry port.

Ryan had the eye at the time. He transmitted to Yao. 'Should I go in?'

'Negative,' said Yao. 'I've been in that place. It's a small, narrow space. He might be meeting someone, but we can't risk compromise by sending you in.'

Ryan understood. 'I'll hang back at the Star Ferry entrance with visual on the front.'

Yao said, 'Ding, that place has a back door. If he takes it he'll end up on Canton Road. Hustle over there in case they are trying to shake a tail.'

'Copy that.' Ding had been two blocks behind Ryan, but he picked up the pace and made a right on Canton. He put himself on the far side of the street and stood in the rain, his umbrella shielding his face from the streetlamps above.

Just as Yao suspected, Zha and his entourage appeared on Canton road a few minutes later. 'Chavez has the eye. Headed south on Canton.'

Adam had noticed that the Triads had been doing SDRs, surveillance detection runs, more and more in the last few days. The American CIA operative still had no idea how he had been burned, but whatever he'd done to expose himself, he was damn glad to have the help from Chavez and Junior.

Just minutes after Ding announced he had the eye, Jack saw Zha and the others, moving under a tight pack of umbrellas, approaching his position near the ferry entrance.

Jack said, 'Looks like they are getting on the ferry.'

'Excellent,' said Yao. 'He's probably going to Wan Chai. That's where the bars are. He's done that several times in the last week, hitting the girlie bars around Lockhart Road. I don't think he gives a shit about naked girls, but the Fourteen-K run most of those clubs, so it's probably where his guards feel comfortable taking him.'

'Can we go in without being compromised?' Jack asked.

'Yeah, you'll just have to watch yourselves. There will be other Triads in the crowd. They may not be working on the Zha detail, but they are a rough bunch when they are drinking.'

Jack said, 'Don't they all know martial arts?'

Yao chuckled. 'It's not one long Jackie Chan movie over here. Not everybody is a kung fu master.'

'Well, that's comforting.'

'It shouldn't be. They all carry pistols or knives. I don't know about you, but I'd rather take a donkey kick to the chest than a nine-millimeter round to the chest.'

'You got a point there, Yao.'

'Jack, you go ahead and get in line for the next ferry across. They shouldn't suspect you if you are in front of them, but be careful where you position yourself.'

'Roger.'

'Ding, I'm en route to pick you up. We'll take the tunnel to the other side and be there waiting when they get off the boat.'

The old Star Ferry boat bobbed and swayed in the choppy Victoria Harbour as it crossed between thick harbor traffic on its eight-minute journey to Hong Kong Island. Jack sat well behind the 14K men and the computer hacker as they rode at the front of the covered deck.

He was confident he had not been spotted by the opposition, and he was also confident they were not meeting anyone on the boat, as no one had approached.

But something else caught Jack's eye about midway through the crossing.

Two men entered the passenger cabin and walked right past Jack's position. They sat down several rows behind Zha. They were fit men in their late twenties or early thirties; one had a red polo and jeans, and on his right forearm was a tattoo that said 'Cowboy Up.' The other wore an untucked button-down and cargo shorts.

They looked – to Jack, anyway – like Americans, and both men had their eyes trained on the back of Zha's head.

'We may have a problem,' Ryan said softly as he looked out the window in the opposite direction of the Triad group.

'What's up?' asked Chavez.

'I think there are two more guys, two American guys, who are watching the target.'

'Shit,' said Yao.

'Who are they, Adam?' asked Chavez.

'I don't know. They could be U.S. marshals. Zha is a wanted man in the USA. If so, they won't know their way around HK. They won't know how to blend. They won't know that Zha and the Fourteen-K are watching for a tail. They *will* get burned.'

Ryan said, 'They are a little too close, but otherwise they aren't being obvious just yet.'

Yao countered, 'Yeah, but if there are two on him now, there will be a half-dozen on him soon enough. There's only so many wide-eyed Americans you can stick in one place over here without the Triads figuring out their protectee has grown a tail.'

The ferry docked on Hong Kong Island a few minutes later, and Ryan was the first off, well ahead of Zha and his crew. He walked down a long ramp into the Central neighborhood, then disappeared down an elevator to the MTR without ever regarding his targets.

He did not need to. Chavez was positioned at the exit to the ferry, and he followed Zha and company as they climbed into a taxi van. They headed off to the south.

Adam had seen this from the Mitsubishi minivan. He announced over the conference call, 'I'll tail them. Ding, get down in the MTR with Jack and take a train to Wan Chai Station. I'd bet money that's where they are going. You can be there ahead of them if you hustle, and I'll guide you to wherever they are.'

'En route,' said Ding, and he disconnected from the conference call and ran down to the MTR entrance to meet Jack.

As Chavez and Ryan rode in the long subway car, Jack disconnected his phone from Adam and leaned into his superior's ear. 'If the marshals get too close, Zha's going to bolt. If he does that, then we'll never know about Center and the Istanbul Drive.'

Chavez had been thinking the same thing. 'Yep.'

But he had not been thinking anything along the lines of what Ryan said next: 'We need to grab him.'

'How, Jack? He's got a significant security detail.'

'Manageable,' declared Ryan. 'We can orchestrate something quick and nasty. Look how big the stakes are. If FastByte Twenty-two did the UAV hack, then he's got blood on his hands. I'm not going to lose sleep over wasting a couple of his henchmen.'

'*Then* what, kid? We're going to take FastByte back to the Peninsula and interrogate him over room service?'

'Of course not. We slip him out on the Gulfstream.'

Ding shook his head. 'We stick with Adam Yao for now. If an opportunity arises that looks good, we consider taking him, but right now the best thing we can do is support the Agency guy who knows his way around.'

Jack sighed. He understood but worried they would miss their opportunity to bag FastByte and learn who he was working for.

39

The two Campus operatives exited the MTR at Wan Chai Station, and by then Adam had tracked the taxi carrying the five men to a strip club called Club Stylish on Jaffe Road, just a few blocks away. Yao warned the two Hendley Associates men that the girlie bar was a known 14K hangout, and there would be, among the crowds of lonely businessmen and Filipino waitresses and strippers, some presence of heavily armed and heavily drinking 14K mobsters.

Jack and Ding suspected they had a different definition for 'heavily armed' than did Adam Yao, but neither Jack nor Ding was carrying any weapons whatsoever, so they told themselves they would keep their heads on a swivel and do nothing to raise the ire of the locals in the establishment.

Jack and Ding found the entrance to Club Stylish to be just a narrow dark doorway at the street level of a high-rise ramshackle apartment building on a two-lane street one block over from Lockhart Road, the nicer and more touristy section of Wan Chai. Ryan pulled off his paper mask and entered first, passing a bored-looking bouncer, then descended a little staircase lit only by Christmas lights strung along the ceiling. The staircase seemed to go down at least two stories, and at the bottom he found a large basement nightclub with a high ceiling. On his right was a long bar along the wall, in front of him was the floor of the establishment, full of tables and lit by candles, and on the far wall was a raised stage made out of see-through plastic tiles over garish amber lighting that gave the entire room an odd golden glow. Above it, a large spinning disco ball created thousands of swirling white lights that painted the crowd.

Four stripper poles stood near the corners of the raised dance floor.

The establishment seemed to be running at about twenty percent capacity, and a strictly male audience sat around at the tables, in booths along the walls, and at the bar. Some talked to the bored-looking dancing girls who milled between them. Jack saw Zha and his group of four Triads sitting in a large booth in the corner of the far wall, to the right of the stage on the other side of the entrance to a darkened hallway that led out the back of the club. Jack assumed there would be restrooms back there, but he did not want to pass so close to Zha to get a better lay of the land. Instead, he saw a spiral staircase off to his left, and he climbed to find a little mezzanine over the back bar area. Here a few businessmen sat in groups and looked out over the paltry action. Ryan liked it up here – he could watch Zha while keeping a low profile with the dark and deep booths. He sat alone, and he ordered a beer from a passing cocktail waitress a few minutes later.

Within moments two young Filipino exotic dancers took the stage and went through the well-practiced motions of dancing seductively to loud, thumping Asian-influenced techno music.

Zha and his security detail remained in their booth stage left of the strippers. Jack saw that the young man remained more interested in his handheld computer than he was in the semi-naked women twenty feet away from him, and he barely glanced up at them as he typed furiously with his thumbs.

Jack thought about how much he'd love to get his hands on that handheld device. Not that he'd know what the hell to do with it, but Gavin Biery would likely have a field day cracking its secrets.

Domingo Chavez entered the club a few minutes later, and he sat back by the downstairs bar near the entrance. He had a good view of the stairwell up to street level and a decent view of the 14K entourage, but mostly his job was to back up Jack, the eye in the surveillance.

They communicated with Adam through their tiny earpieces. Yao was sitting out in the borrowed Mitsubishi, positioned in a back alley that ran between the rear of the high-rises on Jaffe and the high-rises on Gloucester, just blocks from the northern shore of Hong Kong Island. Here he parked in a small lot and had a view of the back exit of Club Stylish, which was good, but he was parked next to dozens of full garbage bins outside a seafood restaurant, meaning a foul rotten stench and the scuffling feet of rats were all he had to keep him company back there.

Adam informed the Hendley Associates men how lucky they were, via the conference call. Chavez sipped his first beer of the evening and regarded the women working for tips on the stage and the other dancers milling about the crowd.

He assured young Adam that he was not missing much.

The two mysterious Americans who had been on the ferry entered the club a few minutes later, confirming Jack's suspicions that they were, in fact, tailing Zha. Ding reported this to Ryan, and Jack saw them from his overwatch on the mezzanine when the men sat down in plush chairs in a dark corner, far from the stage. They bought Budweisers from a cocktail waitress and sipped them while rejecting advances from the strolling bar girls.

As Chavez turned and scanned the stairwell, two more Western men, both in blue blazers and ties, entered together.

There were a dozen other Westerners in the bar, Ding and Jack and the two younger guys from the ferry included, but these guys stood out to Ding. They looked like Feds, and Chavez could ID Feds easily, which wasn't saying much, because they had a way of standing out. The two men sat down just a few tables from the Triad entourage, positioning themselves awkwardly so that they had a better view of Fast-Byte22 than they did of the stage.

'Looks like a damn weatherman convention in here,' Chavez said softly, hiding his moving lips behind his beer bottle before taking a swig.

Adam Yao's voice came over the headset. 'More Americans?'

'Two suits. Could be DOJ guys from the consulate, here trying to confirm Zha's presence.'

Yao said, 'Okay, maybe we should think about backing off. By my count there are now six *gweilo*s in there with eyes on Zha. That's too many.'

Chavez said, 'I hear you, Adam, but I've got another idea. Wait one.' He reached into his jacket and pulled out his mobile phone, then opened a video camera feature. He put the conference call with Ryan and Adam on hold and called Gavin Biery at the Peninsula.

Gavin answered on the first ring. 'Biery.'

'Hey, Gavin. I'm sending you video transmission from my phone. Will you get on your laptop and check that you are receiving?'

'I'm already on. I'm picking it up.' A few seconds later he said, 'How 'bout you zoom in on that stage for me?'

Ding placed the phone on the table, propped it against a small glass candleholder, and turned it toward Zha's table.

Ding said, 'I need you to focus on the target, not the dancing girls.'

'Oh, all right. Zoom in a bit.'

Chavez did so, and then recentered the image.

'Got it. What am I looking for?'

'Just keep tabs on them. You've got the eye. I'm pulling Ryan out, and I'm turning away from them. There is too much surveillance in this room already.'

'Got it.' He laughed. 'I'm on a mission. Well ... a *virtual* mission anyway. Hey, by the way, I'm sending you that cleaned-up image of the guy you photographed back at the Mong Kok Computer Centre. You should be able to see the man in the dark now with no problems.'

Domingo brought Gavin into the conference call with the other two and then explained to Jack and Adam what he'd done. Jack left the club and went out front, crossed Jaffe and sat at a tiny noodle bar open to the street. From here he could see the stairway entrance to Club Stylish.

Yao, Chavez, and Ryan simultaneously received e-mails on their phones. They opened them to see a good picture of a quarter-shot of Zha's face and three-quarters of the back of his head, as he spoke to an older Chinese man in a white shirt and a light blue or gray tie. The older man's face was clear enough, but none of the three recognized him.

Chavez knew Biery had special facial-recognition software on his computer, and he would be trying to get a match right now.

Yao said, 'He's not familiar to me, but you think he looked important, Ding?'

'Yes. I'd say you might be looking at the MFIC there.'

Yao responded, 'The what?'

'The Motherfucker in Charge.'

Ryan and Yao just chuckled.

Gavin Biery's voice came back over the headsets of the team a minute later. 'Domingo, pan the camera to your left.' Chavez reached out and did so as he kept his eyes in the opposite direction, toward the bartenders.

'What do you see?'

'I noticed that the tough guys around Zha were all looking at something or somebody. I think it's those two white guys in blue blazers. One of the Triads just pulled out his phone and made a call.'

'Shit,' said Ding. 'I'd be willing to wager that the consulate guys made it obvious they aren't here to watch the dancers. Adam, what do you think Fourteen-K is going to do?'

'My guess is they will bring in a few reinforcements. If they were really worried they would shuffle Zha out the back door, but all is quiet back here. Ryan, what's going on at the front?'

Jack noticed a group of three Chinese men entering the club. Two were young, early twenties or so, and the third was perhaps sixty. Jack thought nothing of it, people were coming and going with regularity.

'Just regular traffic out here.'

'Okay,' said Yao. 'Be on the lookout for more Fourteen-K, though. If those guys just called in a potential threat, things might get tight in there.'

'Our boy has visitors,' Biery said a minute later, when the three newest patrons to the bar, the older Chinese man and his two friends, slid around Zha into the booth. 'I'm sending a screen shot to your phones so you can see.'

Adam waited for the picture to arrive, and looked at it closely. 'Okay. The older guy is Mr Han. He's a known smuggler of high-end computer equipment. He's the one I was tracking when I ran into Zha in the first place. I don't know what his relationship to Zha is. Not sure who the other two are, but they aren't Fourteen-K. They are too puny and bewildered-looking.'

Gavin came over the call: 'I'm running their faces through

facial-recognition software against a database of known Chinese hackers.'

No one responded to this for several seconds.

At the noodle shop, Ryan cursed to himself, and at the bar in the strip club, Chavez groaned inwardly. It was going to be a hard sell to Adam Yao that this database, which The Campus had pulled from a classified CIA database, would be something a financial management firm, even one hunting for a Chinese hacker, could just call up on a laptop.

Ryan and Chavez waited to hear what Yao said next.

'That's pretty handy, Gavin. Let us know.' His voice was overtly sarcastic.

Gavin was clueless about what he had done, and it was clear he did not pick up on Yao's sarcasm. 'I'll let you know. And by the way, I ran the other guy, the MFIC, too. No match at all,' he said, a tinge of frustration in his voice.

Yao said, 'Hey, Domingo. Any chance you could meet me around back of the club for a quick chat.'

At the bar by the entrance to the strip club, Ding rolled his eyes now. This young NOC was about to take Ding to the woodshed, and he knew it.

And at the noodle shop, Jack Ryan put his face in his hands. As far as he was concerned, their cover was blown to the CIA man.

Chavez said, 'I'll be right out, Adam. Ryan, why don't you come on back in and take the eye up on the mezzanine? Keep a soft surveillance. Just make sure nobody joins the entourage without getting a look at them.'

'Got it,' said Jack.

It took a few minutes to get Jack into position and Chavez back out the front, up the block, and back around into the small street behind the nightclub and high-rise apartment buildings, but finally Ding climbed into the passenger door of the Mitsubishi.

He just looked at Adam and said, 'You wanted to talk?'

Yao said, 'I know you are ex-Agency, and I checked you out. You retain your TS security clearance.'

Chavez smiled. The sooner they got this charade over with, the better.

'You've done your homework.'

Yao was not smiling. 'You have friends at the Agency, friends all over. And I am going to go out on a limb here and say that you know good and damn well that I am Agency, too.'

Ding nodded slowly. 'I'm not going to lie to you, kid. I am aware that you wear two hats.'

'Are you going to tell me the real reason you guys are here?'

'No mystery to that. We're here to find out who the hell Zha is. He is trying to get into our network.'

'Trying to? He has not succeeded?'

'Not that we know of.' They had lied to Yao about that. 'Sorry, kid. We needed your help, and we wanted to help you. I fed you a little bullshit along the way.'

'Fed me a little bullshit? So you came all the way to Hong Kong to tail a hacker who is trying to hack your network? It sounds like you have me on a steady diet of bullshit.'

Chavez sighed. 'That's *part* of the reason. We are also aware he is a person of interest in the UAV attack. We see our interests, and America's interests, dovetailing nicely here, and we wanted to support you in your investigation.'

'How do you know he was involved in the UAV attack?'

Chavez just shook his head. 'Word gets around.'

Yao did not seem satisfied by this answer, but he moved on. 'What is Jack Junior's role in this?'

'He's an analyst at Hendley Associates. Simple as that.'

Yao nodded. He didn't know what to make of Hendley Associates, but he knew Domingo Chavez had as much or more credibility than anyone who had ever worked in the U.S. intelligence community. Chavez and company were providing him with the assets he needed to tail and, he hoped, identify some of the people working with Zha. He needed these guys, despite the fact they weren't exactly part of his team.

'The Agency is not buying into the fact that Zha is part of the UAV attack. They think it was a state actor of some sort, maybe China, maybe Iran, and since Zha clearly isn't working for either of them over here, they figure he's not involved.'

'We figure differently, and, apparently, so do you.'

'I do.'

Just then Gavin Biery called Chavez, and Ding turned on his speakerphone so Yao could hear. 'Bingo. We have a match on one of the young men, the guy in the black shirt. His name is Chen Ma Long. It says he lives in Shaoxing, on the mainland. He was a known member of an organization called the Tong Dynasty.'

'The Tong Dynasty?' Yao said with surprise.

'What's that?' asked Chavez.

'That's an unofficial name the NSA gave to an organization that was around from about 2005 to 2010. It was run by Dr K. K. Tong, sort of the father of China's offensive cyberwar systems. He used tens of thousands of civilian hackers, developed them into a kind of army. This kid must have been part of that group.'

'Where is Tong now?'

'He was thrown in prison in China for corruption but escaped. No one has heard from him in a couple of years. Word is the Chicoms want him dead.'

'Interesting. Thanks, Gavin,' said Chavez. He ended the

call with Biery and then turned his attention back to Yao.

'We aren't going to learn anything more than what we already know about whatever the hell is going on over here, because it's not going to take any time at all for the Triads to pick up on the fact that Zha has grown a really long tail. Once they see these guys following Zha, Zha is going to disappear.'

'I know.'

'You need to check with Langley one more time. If they want him, they better take him right fucking now, because he will either run to the mainland, in which case you'll never find him, or else the Marshals Service is going to arrest him, in which case he'll enter the justice system. If he does that he'll get a lawyer, a pat on the ass, and three hots and a cot. The Agency won't learn a damn thing about who he's working with.'

Adam nodded. Chavez could tell the prospect of losing Zha Shu Hai was eating the young NOC up.

'I already talked to Langley. They said they didn't think Zha was involved, but they would kick it over to the Pentagon, since it was their system that got hacked,' said Adam.

'And what did the Pentagon say?'

'I have no idea. I try and communicate with Langley as little as possible.'

'Why is that?'

'Pretty much everybody knows that there is a leak at Beijing Station. The Pentagon is aware CIA is compromised in its affairs in China, too, so I doubt they would let us know if they were interested in Zha.'

'A leak?'

'I have been living with that reality for a while. Too many Agency initiatives involving China have foundered in ways that we can only figure were due to inside information about our activities. I try to keep most of my activity very low-profile. I don't like letting Langley know what I'm up to, in case the Chicoms do something to stop me. Even though HK isn't the mainland, per se, there are Chinese spies all over.'

Chavez said, 'Maybe that leak is the reason Fourteen-K doubled their guard on Zha and started doing SDRs every couple of hours.'

Yao said, 'That only makes sense if the Fourteen-K are working with the Chicoms, and that just does not track with everything I've seen or heard about the Triads.'

Ding's phone beeped. It was Ryan, and Ding put the call on speaker.

'What's up, Jack?'

'The two younger Americans, the guys I saw on the ferry, just paid their tab and hit the road.'

'Good. Maybe they are calling it a night. And the two suits?'

'Still in the same place, still glancing over at Zha and company every thirty seconds like clockwork. Pretty obvious.'

'Okay,' said Ding. 'I'm heading back in. Wait for me to take the eye, and then you can go back out front.'

'Roger that,' said Jack.

Chavez entered the club through the back door. It led to a long narrow staircase that descended to a hallway. Chavez passed doors to bathrooms and a kitchen area, and then he stepped back into the club, walked past Zha and his entourage in the corner, and returned to the bar. Ryan left through the front entrance and went back to the noodle shop on Jaffe and ordered a Tsingtao beer.

A minute after Ryan returned to his post he announced, 'Here come the Fourteen-K. I've got close to a dozen goons who just got out of a pair of silver SUVs; they are all wearing jackets and it's eighty degrees, so I'm going to guess they are packing. They are heading through Club Stylish's door.'

Yao said, 'Shit. Ding, you think we should back out of the area?'

Chavez replied, 'It is your call, but I am not compromised at all here at the bar, other than the fact I've been mumbling to myself every few minutes. How 'bout I just sit tight to make sure the consulate guys don't get into any trouble with all the new muscle around.'

'Roger that, but be careful.'

After a few moments the Triad presence increased all around Club Stylish. A dozen obvious gunmen fanned out and took up positions in the corners and around the bar.

Ding spoke softly behind his beer. 'Yep . . . the new goons are eyeballing the two guys in the suits. This might get ugly, Adam; let me stick around for a minute in case someone needs to call in the cavalry.'

Adam Yao did not respond.

'Ding for Adam, do you read?'

Nothing.

'Yao, you receiving?'

After a long moment, Adam Yao responded in a whisper. 'Guys . . . Things are about to get *really* ugly.'

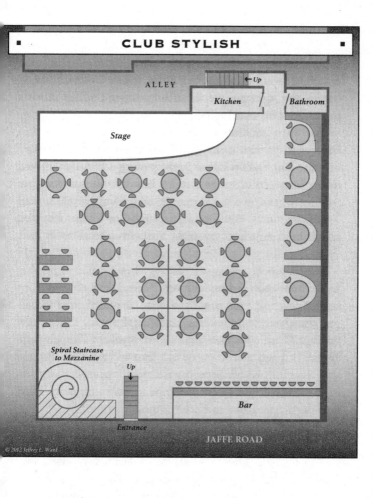

40

Adam Yao had lowered the backrest of his driver's seat in the Mitsubishi minivan all the way back, and he lay flat, his body out of the sight line of the windows. He did not move a muscle, but his mind raced.

Just thirty seconds earlier, a large twelve-passenger van had rolled up with its lights off, forty feet away in the alley, not far from Yao's position in the parking lot. Adam ducked down before the driver noticed him in the minivan, but Adam did get a look at the man behind the wheel. He looked American, he wore a baseball cap and had a radio headset, and behind him in the vehicle Yao saw several other dark figures.

'Adam, what's going on?' It was Ding's voice in his earpiece, but Adam did not answer. Instead he reached for his backpack in the front passenger seat. He pulled out a rectangular hand mirror, and carefully raised it above the driver's-side window. Through it he could see the twelve-passenger van. It had stopped near the exit to the strip club, and the side door had opened up. Seven men slipped out silently; they all held black rifles close to their bodies, and they wore small backpacks, sidearms, and body armor.

As he lay silent and still, Ding's voice came over his earpiece yet again. 'What is it, Adam?'

Yao replied, 'There's a fucking A-Team back here. Not Marshals, not CIA. These guys are probably Jay-Sock.' JSOC, Joint Special Operations Command, and pronounced 'Jay-Sock' by those aware of the organization, was the Department of Defense's direct-action special-mission units, SEAL Team Six or Delta Force. Yao knew that the Pentagon would not send anyone else to do this job but JSOC. 'I think they are about to come in through the back door, and it sure doesn't look like they're heading in to watch boobs jiggle.'

'Shit,' Ding said. 'How many?'

'I count seven operators,' Adam said.

Jack said, 'There are probably four or five times that number of armed Triads in there. You need to stop them before they get slaughtered.'

'Right,' Adam said, and he quickly opened his door and slid out of the Mitsubishi. The Americans at the back door were facing the other direction, seconds away from moving into Club Stylish. Yao decided to call out to them, but he'd taken no more than one step when he was knocked to the ground from behind. His earpiece flew from his ear and he crashed face-first onto the wet alleyway, his breath knocked from his lungs.

He did not see the man who took him down, but he felt the weight of a knee on his back, he felt the burn in his shoulders as his arms were yanked roughly behind him, and the sting in his wrists as his hands were secured with flexi-cuffs. Before he could speak, he heard someone tearing electrical tape from a roll, and the tape was wrapped tightly around his head several times at the mouth, gagging him roughly.

He was dragged by his feet in the parking lot; he fought to keep his face from rubbing against the asphalt. In seconds he found himself on the other side of the Mitsubishi van, shoved into a sitting position, the back of his head slammed against the side of the minivan. Only then did he see that a single person had done all this to him. A blond-haired man with a beard and tactical pants, a combat vest of body armor and ammo mags and an automatic pistol, and a short-barreled rifle that hung over his shoulder. Adam tried to speak through the tape, but the American just patted him on the head and slipped a hood over him.

The last image Yao had was of the man's forearm, and his 'Cowboy Up' tattoo.

Adam heard the man run off, around the van, obviously to join his mates near the door.

Chavez had spent ten of the past twenty seconds trying to raise Adam Yao on the conference call, two more seconds cussing violently to himself, and finally the last eight seconds barking soft but authoritative orders into his headset as he walked through the strip club toward the restroom in the back.

'Gavin, listen up. I need you in a cab on your way over to our position. Wave every scrap of money on your person to get the cabbie to haul ass!'

'Me? You want me out there with –'

'Do it! I'll update you when you get close.'

'Oh. Okay. I'm on the way.'

'Ryan, I want you to hotfoot it around back to see what happened to Adam. Put your mask on.'

'Understood.'

Chavez passed several Triads standing around the bustling nightclub as he headed toward the restroom by the back door. He knew he would have to try to stop the men here to snatch Zha before they walked right into a bloodbath.

It was clear to him what had happened. The two young men Ryan spotted on the ferry and then here in the club were spotters for this team of SEALs, or Delta, or whoever the hell they were. They'd seen Zha and a manageable crew of security men sitting in a booth by the hallway that led to the back door and they'd radioed the snatch team to tell them that now was the time to make the grab.

The spotters left the area at the last possible moment, probably to get geared up and armed to take part in the hit. This was not standard operating procedure; but they surely weren't expecting a crew of 14K reinforcements to show up in that tiny time window when Zha was without coverage.

This was a clusterfuck in the making, Chavez knew, and the only way he could stop it was to get to the back door before it start–

From the darkness of the hall that led to the stairs at the back of the club, a group of armed men appeared in a tight neat row, their weapons' laser targeting devices causing red pinpricks of light to move around ahead of them, dancing through the dim amber lighting of the club like the twinkling sparkles of the disco ball hanging from the ceiling.

Chavez was caught in the center of the club, too far away to stop the men but not back far enough to be clear of the impending gun battle. Just twenty feet ahead and to his right, Zha sat at a table full of his computer-crime colleagues and armed 14K gunmen. In front of Ding to his left, the lighted stage was full of naked women, and all around him, a dozen 14K sentries were standing around, most of them looming over two very uncomfortable-looking men from the U.S. consulate who, Ding was certain, had no idea a team of commandos was about to fly into the room with guns high and voices loud.

Chavez spoke into his mic, and he made a solemn announcement: 'It's on.'

Chief Petty Officer Michael Meyer, team leader of this DEVGRU (SEAL Team Six) JSOC element, was second in line in the tactical train, his HK MP7 Personal Defense

Weapon aimed just over the left shoulder of the special warfare operator in front of him. They broke into teams as they left the hallway and entered the nightclub, with Meyer and the first man breaking right, shining their lasers on the dance floor and the patrons in front of it.

Just to his left, two operators covered the club toward the rear bar, and directly behind him now, three of his men were taking down Zha and holding their guns on his protection detail.

Meyer felt almost immediately that his zone was clear of danger. There were strippers and a few businessmen, but the action was back by the bar and behind him at Zha's table, so he left the other SEAL and turned around to help with the takedown.

The team had hoped to execute this takedown after Zha left the club with his minders, and they had been waiting a few blocks up the street to do just that. But the two men Meyer had tasked with following Zha had reported that another pair of Americans were here, two suited and blow-dried guys from the consulate, by the looks of them, and they worried that Zha would be rushed away under heavy guard.

So Meyer exerted his execute authority to do the unexpected and snatch the target right here in the back of the club by the alley.

It wasn't anyone's idea of a perfect situation. DEVGRU normally operated with a much larger force, with better command and control and communications, and a much better sight picture of the target area. But this was what was referred to in the business as an 'in extremis op,' a rush job, to be sure, and the first rule of in extremis ops was to make the best of an imperfect situation.

The two-man SEAL recon team had left the building not

five minutes earlier, but it became clear to Meyer almost instantly that things had changed in the past five minutes. Where he expected to see four or five bodyguards at the round corner booth, he now saw ten.

They were tough, jacketed men with short haircuts and hard stares, men standing around the table with no drinks in their hands.

Meyer then heard a shout from one of his men on the right, and it was the last thing he had hoped to hear tonight from his men scanning the crowd.

'Contact front!'

Things went bad quickly. A single 14K soldier back by the bar near the entrance was partially shielded by a group of businessmen standing there, and he took the opportunity to yank a .45 pistol from his waistband. With the protection of the cover provided by the civilians, he raised his weapon and squeezed off two rounds at the first armed gunman through the door, grazing the man once on the left arm and once squarely on the ceramic body-armor plate on his chest.

The Navy SEAL closest to the wounded operator dispatched the Chinese shooter with a three-round burst of tiny but hard-hitting 4.6x30-millimeter bullets to the forehead, blowing the top of the man's head off and over the crowd of men around him.

Within the next two seconds, throughout the strip club some twenty 14K Triads went for their guns.

And all hell broke loose.

When Chavez found himself in no-man's-land as the firefight started, he did the only thing he could – he went into self-preservation mode. He dropped flat on the floor, rolled to his left, knocking chairs and people down along the way, trying like hell to get himself out of the crossfire between the Americans and the Triads. Along with other men who had been sitting along the raised dance floor, he made his way through the tables there and then pressed himself tight against the edge of the riser.

He wished like hell he had a pistol. He could pick off some of the opposition and help the JSOC men in their mission. But instead he covered his head as men in tailored suits and dancers in thongs and body glitter crashed on top of him, desperately trying to scramble away from the gunfire.

Through this he did what he could to maintain his situational awareness. He peered into the crazed crowd, saw pistols and sub-guns firing here and there, and heard the mammoth boom of a shotgun blast from up near the bar. The crowd looked like rats scattering in the amber lighting, with the SEALs' red laser targeting devices and the sparkle from the disco ball providing additional frantic movement to the scene.

Chief Petty Officer Meyer realized in seconds he had led his team into a hornets' nest. He had been prepared for resistance from Zha's bodyguards, but he intended to mitigate that resistance with speed, surprise, and overwhelming violence of action. But instead of a manageable fight against an equal number of bewildered opponents, Meyer and his force of six other operators found themselves in the middle of a shooting gallery. Adding to this, the large number of civilians in the club, in the crossfire, forced his men to check their fire unless they saw a gun in the hand of one of the figures moving in the dark of the club.

Two of the chief petty officer's men had already pulled Zha over the top of the big round table in the corner and onto the floor in front of the booth. The spiky-haired Chinese man was down on his face on the ground; one SEAL jammed his knee in the back of his neck to hold him still while the SEAL's rifle scanned for targets across the club at the long bar near the entrance.

He fired two quick bursts at the origin of a gunshot near the entrance, then dropped his rifle to its sling and went back to work on securing his captive, while Meyer himself took a 9-millimeter round to the chest plate of his body armor, tipping him back for a moment. The CPO recovered, went prone on the floor, and then fired at the flash of a handgun blast back at the bar.

Jack Ryan found Adam Yao 'tagged and bagged,' still struggling against his bindings next to his vehicle. The Mitsubishi's passenger door was unlocked, so Jack reached in and grabbed a folding knife from Yao's backpack, and he cut the CIA officer's wrist bindings free in seconds.

Popping handgun fire and short, disciplined bursts from automatic weapons came from the nightclub. Ryan pulled the hood off Yao and then yanked the smaller man to his feet.

Jack shouted, 'Any guns in the van?'

Adam pulled the tape off his mouth with a wince. 'I'm not issued a weapon, and if I got caught with –'

Ryan turned and ran unarmed toward the back door of the club.

Chavez had found fair cover from the crossfire, flat on his face, pressed up against the side of the stage. He was completely out of view of the SEALs, and completely exposed to armed Triads who had taken positions of concealment or cover behind tables, at the long bar at the front of the establishment, or mixed between the civilians in the crowd. As the gunfire raged around him, Ding was not a combatant in this, and he looked and acted like any of the other terrified businessmen huddling in the center of this maelstrom, trying to ride out the gunfight by thinking small.

Ding wondered if the commandos would be able to make it back down the hall, up the stairs, and out into the alley before they were cut down by all the 14K shooters. Their original objective, capturing Zha Shu Hai alive, seemed out of reach from his admittedly poor view of the action.

Chavez figured that if they could exfiltrate at all, they would be exfiltrating back out through the hall and up the back staircase. He shouted into his earpiece between bursts of fire in the room.

'Ryan? If you are out back, get your ass to cover! This shit looks like it's about to spill out into the alley!'

'Roger that!' Ryan said.

Just then, a Triad armed with a stainless-steel Beretta 9-millimeter pistol crawled up beside Chavez, using the stage to remain hidden from the American commandos.

Chavez recognized that the man could make it to within ten feet of where the JSOC snatch team was positioned by the back hall without them seeing him. There, he could simply stand up and dump rounds from his Beretta at point-blank range into the men who would be more focused on all the shooters at the long bar some hundred feet away from them.

Chavez knew the young tough with the pistol wasn't going to squeeze off more than a few of his gun's seventeen rounds before he was sawed in half by return fire, but it was a good bet he'd kill an American or two first.

The 14K goon rose to a crouch, his tennis shoes just inches from Chavez's face, and he started moving closer to the commandos, but Ding reached out and grabbed the man's gun hand, pulled him off balance and then down onto the floor. Ding yanked him back behind an overturned table, fought for the handgun from the surprisingly strong Chinese man, and finally rolled on top of him, twisted the Beretta back, broke two of the Triad's fingers in his right hand, and peeled the gun free.

The Triad screamed, but his screams were lost in the gunfire and shouting in the club. Ding head-butted the man twice, breaking his nose the first time and knocking him senseless the second.

Ding stayed low behind the table, concealed from the Triads shooting up at the bar, and he dropped the magazine out of the butt of the Beretta, checking how many rounds he had. It was nearly full, fourteen bullets, plus one in the chamber.

Now Domingo Chavez had a gun.

Chief Petty Officer Meyer's problems were compounding by the second, but he'd been in this line of work for too long to allow fear, confusion, or mission overload to take control of his faculties. He and his men would keep their heads in the game as long as they still had a pulse and still had a mission to accomplish.

Zha had been flexi-cuffed and dragged back into the hall, part of the way by his shirt and the rest of the way by his spiked hair. As soon as he was at the foot of the stairs up to the rear exit, Meyer's team began collapsing back, covering for one another as they reloaded.

Two of the SEALs had taken rounds to their body armor, but it was Special Warfare Operator Kyle Weldon who caught the first serious injury. A 9-millimeter round hit him square in the kneecap, sending him face-planting in the hall. He dropped his HK PDW, but it remained attached to his body by the sling, and he quickly fought off the pain enough to spin around so that one of his mates could grab him by the pull straps on his body armor.

Seconds later his mate was himself shot. Petty Officer Humberto Reynosa took a ricocheted round through his left calf as he dragged Weldon, and he fell down in a heap next to his buddy. As Chief Petty Officer Michael Meyer provided cover up the hallway and out into the club, two more SEALs scrambled back to grab both operators and pull them closer to safety.

Meyer slipped in the blood as he backed up the stairs behind them. He then regained his footing and centered his laser-aiming device on a 14K gunman wielding a pistol-grip shotgun, who appeared at the mouth of the hall. The American fired a three-round burst into the man's lower torso before the Triad managed to get a shot off.

SWO Joe Bannerman, nearest to the back door up the stairs and farthest from the fight, somehow managed to take a bullet in the back shoulder from a Triad who leapt out of the restroom with his gun spraying lead. The bullet pitched Bannerman forward, but he stayed on his feet and kept going, and Petty Officer Bryce Poteet blasted the Triad with a twelve-round spray of jacketed lead.

Ryan had done as instructed by Chavez and sought cover. He'd just crossed the alleyway and dived between several reeking garbage cans when headlights from the mouth of the alley approached. It was the black twelve-passenger van that dropped off the SEALs just a few minutes earlier; no doubt it had gotten the call to come back around and pick them up.

No sooner had the van slammed on its brakes at the exit to the club when the door flew open. Jack watched from between two plastic bins as a bearded American with a bloody right shoulder raced out into the alley and began scanning for targets in the opposite direction. A second man came out and scanned with his rifle high back toward Jack and beyond.

Moments later Jack saw FastByte22, or at least someone wearing the same clothes as FastByte22. He was hooded and his wrists were tied, and he was being shoved forward by an American operator.

Meyer was last out of the door. He spun toward the van in time to see Zha thrown into the open side door of the vehicle; then men jumped, limped, or were helped in after him.

Meyer kept his weapon trained down the staircase until the door closed, then followed his mates into the van.

As he made it into the vehicle, he spun around to check his 'six' while still crawling across his prostrate colleagues.

The back door to the club burst open and two men in black leather jackets stepped out. One wielded a black pistol and the other a 12-gauge shotgun with a pistol grip.

CPO Meyer dumped a half-magazine into each man, sending them and their weapons tumbling into the alley as the door closed again behind them.

'Go!' Meyer shouted, and the van accelerated up the alley to the east.

As soon as the van moved past him, Jack emerged from between the garbage cans and rushed toward the back door, desperate to check on Chavez. 'Ding? Ding?' he said into his headset.

When he was still twenty-five feet from the door, a white SUV turned into the alley from the west on squealing tires. It raced closer, accelerated after the panel van holding Zha and the Americans.

Jack had no doubt this SUV would be full of 14K reinforcements. He made it to the shotgun lying by the dead Triad, picked it up off the ground, and then stepped into the center of the alleyway. He raised the weapon and fired a single shell

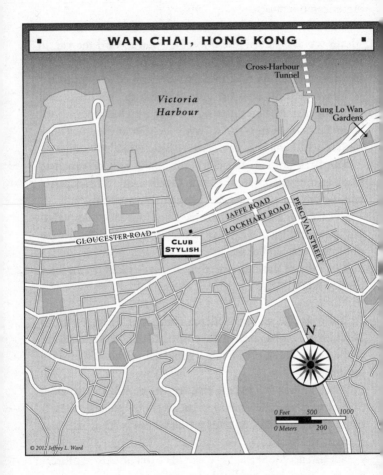

into the street just in front of the approaching vehicle. Buckshot ricocheted off the asphalt and shredded both of the front tires, sending the SUV veering off to the left and crashing through the glass windows of an all-night market.

Jack heard a noise close on his right, turned, and saw Adam Yao running toward him. He continued on past Jack to the back door of Club Stylish. As he ran he said, 'There will be more where they came from. We have to go through the club to get out of here. Throw down the gun and follow me. Keep that mask on!'

Jack did as he was told and followed Adam.

Yao opened the door and immediately saw blood streaked down the stairs. In Mandarin he shouted, 'Is everybody okay?'

He made it just a few steps down before being confronted by a man pointing a pistol in his face. Instantly the gunman realized he was looking at two unarmed men in civilian dress, not geared-up shooters. 'Where did they go?' he demanded.

Adam replied, 'West. I think they are going to the Cross-Harbour Tunnel!'

The Triad lowered the weapon and ran past them up the stairs.

Down in the strip club, Adam and Jack were met by a scene of carnage. A total of sixteen bodies lay on the floor. Some moved in the throes of agony, and others lay still.

Seven 14K Triads lay dead or dying, with three more less gravely wounded. Six club patrons were dead or injured as well.

Adam and Jack found Chavez, who himself was heading toward the stairs up the hallway. When he saw them he held up a small handheld computer. Jack recognized it as belonging to Zha Shu Hai. Ding had picked it up off the ground where FastByte had been bound by the SEALs.

Ding slid it into the inside pocket of his sport coat.

Adam said, 'We need to keep moving. Go out the front like everyone else.'

The CIA officer led the way, and Ding and Jack followed him.

Ryan could not believe the inside of the nightclub. Every table and every chair was flipped on its side or upside down, broken glass was everywhere, and blood seeping out of bodies or smeared on the tile floor shimmered in the spinning light from the disco ball that, somehow, managed to stay intact and operational.

The shrill wail of sirens got louder and louder out on Jaffe Road.

Yao said, 'It's going to fill up with police around here quickly. They always move in when the fighting is done over here in the Triad neighborhoods.'

As they headed up the stairs, Jack said, 'Whoever those guys were, I can't believe they pulled it off.'

Just then the sound of gunfire erupted once again. This time it came from the east.

Ding looked at Jack. Softly he said, 'They haven't pulled it off yet. Go back down and grab a gun off of one of those bodies.'

Jack nodded, turned, and rushed down the stairs.

Yao asked Chavez, 'What are we going to do?'

'Whatever we can.'

Adam then said, 'The van. My keys are in it, and it's unlocked. Maybe Biery can pick it up.'

Chavez nodded and called Gavin, who was in a cab on the way to the scene. 'I need you to get Adam's maroon Mitsubishi Grandis out of the alley behind Club Stylish. When you get it, give me a call, I'm sure we'll need a pickup.'

'Okay.'

41

Meyer and his team of shot-up SEAL Team Six operators managed to make it six blocks before the 14K closed in on them.

From the moment the first gunshots rang out at the club on Jaffe Road five minutes earlier, all across Wan Chai mobile phones chirped and text messages were received. Word spread quickly to 14K gunmen that their turf was under some sort of attack, and they were all ordered to descend on the corner of Jaffe and Marsh, the location of Club Stylish.

Coordination between the various groups of 14K was a disjointed mess, especially so in those first minutes, but the sheer number of goons on foot, on motorcycles, in cars, and even in the MTR rushing to the area ensured that Meyer and his team would be outnumbered fifteen to one. The Triads did not know Zha had been kidnapped – in fact, only a small fraction of them would know who Zha was in the first place. All they knew was that there was a shoot-out at the club and a group of heavily armed *gweilo*s were trying to get away. Someone reported they were in a black van, and that made it just a matter of time before Meyer and his element were caught like roaches in the light on the narrow, crowded streets of Wan Chai.

They had driven east up the alley until it ended at Canal Road, then took that south until they could go east again on Jaffe. As they passed shuttered businesses and high-rise office and apartment buildings, the driver of the van, Special Warfare Operator Terry Hawley, veered left and right to avoid slow-moving and oncoming traffic.

In the back of the van, Zha was facedown and still tied and hooded, the injured men were busy wrapping quick bandages around their gunshot wounds, and Meyer was in comms with the extraction team, telling them his element was minutes away.

But things went south as soon as Meyer finished the transmission. They rolled into the intersection of Jaffe and Percival, less than a half-mile from the shoot-out and into the ultra-ritzy Causeway Bay area, when an automatic rifle was fired by a plain-clothed man in the backseat of a Ford Mustang convertible. Special Warfare Operator Hawley was hit in both arms and the chest, and he slumped forward over the steering wheel.

The twelve-passenger van swerved in the rain, skidded perpendicular to the road, and then flipped onto its side, sliding thirty yards until it crashed into the front of a light bus, a sixteen-passenger vehicle used for public transportation.

Hawley was killed by rifle fire, and another special warfare operator broke his shoulder in the crash.

Meyer was dazed, and broken glass had cut his chin, cheeks, and lips, but he kicked open the back door of the van and rallied his men. The dead and the wounded were either carried or helped along, and the prisoner was held on to, and the men shuffled into an alleyway that led toward the water, some four hundred yards to the north.

They had not been out of the street for more than a few seconds when the first of dozens of police cars raced to the scene and began pulling bewildered Hong Kongers out of the public light bus.

Three hundred yards west of the crash, Chavez, Ryan, and Yao ran through the rain, pushing past late-night crowds and leaping out of the way of emergency vehicles of all types that either raced toward Club Stylish or headed toward the popping gunfire to the east.

Crossing the eight lanes of traffic at Canal Road, Adam caught up to Chavez and said, 'Follow me! There is a pedestrian walkway between those condo towers there, we can head north of Jaffe and come up from a quieter street.'

'Let's do it,' Ding said.

As they ran on, Yao asked, 'What's the plan when we get there?'

Domingo answered back, 'We wing it.' Then he clarified, 'We can't do too much for those boys, but I'll bet they'll take any help we can give them.'

The seven surviving SEALs were overtaxed with responsibilities. Two men carried their dead comrade; one man kept a firm gloved hand on FastByte's collar, pulling the young hacker along, and his other hand on his SIG Sauer pistol. The two operators with serious leg wounds were helped along by the SEALs still able to walk under their own power, even though one of the ambulatory SEALs himself had a broken shoulder. He had dropped all his gear, and now all he was able to do was help the man with the wounded knee hobble along while at the same time doing his best to fight his body's urge to go into shock from the pain of the broken shoulder.

CPO Meyer helped Reynosa, who had lost a sizable chunk of meat out of the back of his left calf.

Meyer and one other operator were still able to use their small, suppressed HK PDWs as a primary weapon. Two more men had their pistols in their hands, but the other three surviving men could not even get a gun into the fight because they were fully engaged, either dragging someone or dealing with their own injuries.

Meyer's team's ability to fight had been depleted more than sixty percent in five minutes.

They struggled along as fast as they could, winding through parking lots and back alleys, doing their best to stay away from police vehicles racing through the streets, and pockets of 14K who gave their positions away by screaming and shouting, wild from the chase.

The rainfall and the late hour kept passersby to a minimum here, a few blocks from the lively restaurant and bar location of Lockhart Road, so Meyer knew that any fighting-age males grouped together were likely a threat.

As they approached a shuttered row of shops at the foot of a skyscraper under construction and cocooned in a latticework of bamboo, Bannerman called out, 'Contact left!' and Meyer fixed his laser onto three young men running up a side street with rifles in their hands. One of the toughs fired a wild burst from a folding-stock AK, sending sparks and asphalt off the street and into the air near the SEAL element, but Meyer and Petty Officer Wade Lipinski each opened fire with their MP7s, killing all three combatants in a matter of seconds.

The threat was eliminated, but the gunfire from the AK and the eruption of car alarms on the street were bad news for Meyer and his team. The roving bands of Triads would be able to pinpoint them easily.

They kept moving, heading north toward the water and doing everything they could to stay under cover, as thumping jet-powered helicopters circled overhead and spotlights whipped across the high buildings all around them.

It seemed to Jack Ryan as if every damn siren in Hong Kong was now in operation in or around Wan Chai. Even before the short barking of rifle fire echoed through the canyons of skyscrapers a few seconds ago, Jack's ears were ringing from police and fire department sirens, as well as from his firing the shotgun back in the alley behind the club.

He ran on through the pedestrian walkway, following Adam, who had taken the lead, and he felt the weight and bite of the Beretta 9-millimeter tucked inside his belt. Without Adam, Ding and Jack would have run straight into police roadblocks and racing gangs of 14K crews every few seconds. So far they had passed only one group of five or six men, whom Adam identified as probable 14K gunmen. Jack wondered if he would see these guys again when and if he made contact with the JSOC operators who had kidnapped FastByte.

From the sound of a new volley of shooting it was clear the American direct-action team was still heading north. They were just a few blocks from Victoria Harbour.

As they ran, Jack asked, 'A boat? Should we get them a boat?'

Ding turned to Yao, 'What's closest to us at the shoreline?'

Yao said, 'There's a private marina over there, but forget about it. There will be twenty-five harbor-patrol craft with spotlights ready to stop them as soon as they go to the water, and the choppers overhead will have a perfect line of sight. Those guys aren't going to Jet Ski out of this shit.'

Chavez tapped his earpiece as he jogged. A moment later, Gavin answered.

'Where are you?' Chavez asked.

'I'm approaching the rear of the club, but there are a lot of people back there. Some of them are going to be Fourteen-K.'

'Gavin, we *need* those wheels.'

'Okay, but no promises. I'm not even sure I –'

'This is life and death! Do what you have to do.'

'But there are police and –'

'Figure it out and call me back!' Chavez hung up.

Suddenly all three men stopped running. Just up ahead they heard a weapon firing cyclic. It was a suppressed HK MP7; both Ding and Jack were familiar with the sound.

The JSOC operators were close.

Jack stepped into a small concrete courtyard between four identical buildings. The only light illuminating the scene was from red Chinese lamps strung across the courtyard over metal picnic tables and a small fenced-in playground. Just on the other side of the courtyard, Jack watched the group of men he saw back at the girlie bar emerge from a breezeway that passed under one of the buildings.

Ryan stepped back around the corner, knelt down, and took another peek.

The men looked like they'd just hit Omaha Beach. Every man Ryan could see was either seriously wounded or assisting someone who was. Two men carried what appeared to be a dead body.

Ding looked out quickly, and then pulled himself and Ryan back around the corner to cover. Keeping himself shielded, Chavez whistled loudly, then shouted, 'Listen up! You've got friendlies over here! A three-man OGA unit! We're ready to help if you can use us!' OGA was how CIA personnel often referred to themselves in the field. It stood for Other Governmental Agency, and it was safer than saying 'Agency' or 'Company,' common nicknames for CIA.

Chavez knew, whether these guys were JSOC or CIA or any other U.S. paramilitary unit, they would understand this term.

Meyer looked down to Reynosa to make sure he had actually heard what he thought he heard. The wounded operator nodded distantly, then propped himself against the wall of the courtyard and raised his gun to cover the area in case it was a trap.

Meyer shouted back, 'Step out, one at a time, hands high and empty!'

'Coming out,' shouted Chavez, and he raised his hands and stepped into the dim light under the paper lanterns.

Jack Ryan and Adam Yao did the same, and within thirty seconds the SEALs had help from three able-bodied men.

Meyer said, 'We can talk while we move.'

Ryan rushed over to grab the man with the bloody bandages around his left calf, and Adam Yao relieved the ashen-faced SEAL with the broken shoulder from his responsibility, helping the man with the bullet wound in his knee.

Chavez lifted the dead SEAL off the ground in a fireman's carry, so the two men carrying his body could once again wield their HKs.

Together the ten surviving Americans and the flexi-cuffed and hooded Zha Shu Hai started again for the north. They still moved way too slow, but they were faster now than before.

Police sirens wailed all around and lights flashed in all directions; helicopters flew high overhead and spotlights reflected off windows. Fortunately for the SEALs, the two Campus operators, and Adam Yao, the high apartment buildings kept the helos from getting their spotlights near the action.

Five minutes later they had found refuge hiding in the trees and darkness in Tung Lo Wan Garden. All around them on the street, police cars raced by in all directions, and several cars full of young tough-looking men passed by, often slowing to shine flashlights in the park.

All the men lay flat in the grass, though Petty Officer Jim Shipley kept half of his body over Zha Shu Hai to keep him still and quiet.

Chavez called Biery and was pleasantly surprised to learn that the IT director had managed to pass his first challenge in the field. He'd argued his way past a police barrier to get 'his' minivan out of the parking lot, and Ding directed him to their position.

CPO Michael Meyer checked on his wounded men and then crawled over to the three new guys in his group. He did not know who these men were, really. The short Hispanic guy was oldest, he was doing all the talking; the tall younger American kept a sweat-soaked paper mask over his face; and the Asian guy looked both worn-out and freaked-out.

Meyer motioned to Yao. 'We saw you behind the target location. I had Poteet bag you. Didn't know you were OGA. Sorry about that.'

Yao shook his head. 'No problem.'

'Wish we could have hooked up with you from the beginning, but we were told you guys have a massive breach over here, so there would be no coordination.'

Yao said, 'Can't argue with the thinking on that. There is a breach, but it's not out of Hong Kong. Trust me, no one knows where I am or what I'm doing right now.'

Meyer raised an eyebrow behind his ballistic eye protection. 'Okay.'

Chavez asked, 'Who are you guys?'

'DEVGRU.'

Chavez knew that U.S. Special Warfare Development Group, or DEVGRU, was the organization formerly known as SEAL Team Six. He wasn't surprised to learn this element was pulled from one of America's most elite special-mission units. Hell, even with all the damage they'd taken, they'd probably wasted twenty enemy in the past twenty minutes and were on the way to completing their mission objective, though Ding had been around enough to know that Meyer would remember this event only as the mission where he lost a man.

The Navy team leader reloaded his HK. 'With all our injuries and all the helos in the air, our exfil is going to be a bitch. You boys know the area better than we do. You got any bright ideas about extricating ourselves from this bullshit?'

Now Chavez leaned over. 'I've got a guy on the way in a minivan. If we squeeze we can fit everyone. Where is your rally point for the exfil?'

The SEAL said, 'North Point Ferry Pier. A couple klicks from here. We've got RIBs coming to pick us up.'

Chavez realized these guys must have come into the harbor via boat or submarine, and then had their guy already on the shore pick them up in the van, while their other two colleagues kept their eyes on Zha. It was a pretty quick and dirty op for a busy city like Hong Kong, but Ding knew the DoD was desperate to stop the cyberthreat that was plaguing their network.

Meyer turned to Chavez. 'I pulled my two guys out of the bar because I wanted to do the takedown with seven operators, and one man behind the wheel. They said there were four or five armed guards and that was it.'

Ding said, 'There *were* only four, but things went tits-up pretty quickly. Some suits from the consulate came into the club, probably watching Zha for the DOJ. They spooked Zha's protection detail of Triads, so the Fourteen-K called in a van-load of backup right before you guys hit the back door.'

'Shit,' Meyer said. 'We should have known.'

Chavez shook his head. 'Murphy's Law.'

Meyer nodded. 'Gets you every time.'

Just then the headlights of a vehicle entered the road that

ran through the little park. The vehicle slowed down to a crawl but continued closer.

Ding called to Gavin, 'Where are you?'

'I'm heading east. I . . . I am really turned around. I don't know where the hell I am.'

'Stop right where you are.'

The vehicle on the road stopped.

'Flash your lights.'

The lights flashed.

'Good. We've got you. Pull up about two hundred yards on the double, then scoot into the back. Make room, we've got to fit a dozen bodies in there.'

'A *dozen*?'

Chavez was behind the wheel now and heading northeast, following Yao's instructions from the front passenger seat. In the back, nine living men and one body were pressed together like cordwood. The men grunted and groaned with each jolting bump in the road, and every turn pressed air from the lungs of the men at the bottom. SO Lipinski, the ST6 medic, valiantly fought to check bandages on any wound he could access with his one free hand in the scrum. The rest of the wounds just had to remain unattended.

Ding kept his speed down and his lane-switching to a minimum, but at a red light on Gloucester Road a 14K spotter walked into the street and looked right at him. The man pulled a mobile phone out of his pocket and brought it to his ear.

Chavez looked straight ahead. He said, 'Damn. This isn't over yet.'

As the light turned green he accelerated forward, doing his best to not just haul ass, hoping against hope that the spotter would make the decision that the maroon minivan was not, in fact, full of armed *gweilo*s escaping the scene.

But his hopes were in vain.

As they moved east through the rain on a side street running parallel to King's Road, a small two-door car rolled into the intersection with its headlights off. Chavez was forced to swerve to avoid being sideswiped.

As the car drove alongside Chavez's side of the minivan, a man rose out of the passenger-side window, sat on the door, and then swung an AK-47 rifle over the roof of the car, pointing it toward Chavez.

Ding drew the Beretta pistol in his waistband and fired through his window, across his body, while he held the wheel with his left hand.

Several AK rounds tore into the minivan before Chavez struck the driver of the two-door with a bullet into the side of the neck. The car swerved violently and slammed into the wall of an office building.

'Who's hit? Who's hit?' Chavez yelled, certain that, with this many men in this small vehicle, multiple men would have been struck by the powerful 7.62-millimeter rounds.

Everyone checked in, the wounded men proclaimed they were in no more pain than before, and even FastByte22 answered Adam that he was okay when he asked him if he'd been shot.

It was a small miracle that the four rounds that hit the side of the minivan struck the dead special warfare operator pressed against the wall of the vehicle.

Chavez raced to the east faster than before, but still he was careful to not draw any more attention than was necessary.

After consulting with Adam Yao about the best place to be picked up by boat that was far enough away from the site of the hit, Meyer struggled to get his radio mic to his mouth under the crushing weight of the other bodies on top of him. Finally he established comms with his extraction and told them they would do the pickup several miles to the east in Chai Wan.

Chavez made it to the location just after three a.m., found a secluded rocky beach, and everyone struggled to get out of the tight minivan.

Here, behind the cover of high boulders, Lipinski, the element's medic, rebandaged all the wounded men. Both Reynosa and Bannerman had lost a lot of blood, but they were stable for now.

While they waited for the SEALs' rigid inflatable boats to come for the pickup, Jack leaned over to Ding and spoke softly: 'How about we hold on to FastByte's little computer?'

Chavez just looked at him. 'Way ahead of you, kid. We'll give Gavin a crack at it and then find a way to get it over to DoD.'

Suddenly three Zodiac boats materialized in the black water at the shoreline.

Chief Petty Officer Michael Meyer got his men together, both the living and the dead, and quickly shook Yao's hand. 'Wish we worked with you from the beginning.'

Adam said, 'You would have had more problems that way. We are leaking like a sieve. Glad we were able to help. Sure as hell wish we could have done more.'

Meyer nodded, thanked Ryan and Chavez, and then joined his men as they loaded into the RIBs.

The Zodiacs turned away from the beach and disappeared in the night.

As soon as the SEALs were gone, Gavin Biery called out to Adam Yao, 'Any idea where a guy can get some pancakes around here?'

Yao, Ryan, and Chavez just chuckled exhaustedly as they climbed back into the Mitsubishi.

42

Dr K. K. Tong, code-named Center, sat at his desk and watched the recorded feeds from dozens of security cameras, both municipal and privately held. It was a video montage created by his Ghost Ship security staff showing the events of the previous evening.

From inside Club Stylish he watched the white men appear from the hallway, he watched a crazed, disjointed crowd react to the gun battle, and he watched young Zha being dragged over the top of the table, tied up, and pulled back into the dark.

From a 7-Eleven security camera pointed toward the street he watched the crash of the black van, the men climbing out and pulling Zha and a dead commando from the wreckage, and then rushing into a dark alley.

He watched the feed from a traffic camera at the intersection off King's Road that showed the maroon minivan as it swerved to avoid the two-door with the armed man, and then he saw the car veer off and crash, and the minivan holding Zha and his kidnappers race off into the night.

Tong exhibited no emotion over any of this.

Standing over his shoulder and watching the violent montage was the leader of the Ghost Ship's own security staff. He was not a Triad, but he was responsible for coordinating with the Triads. He said, 'Twenty-nine members of Fourteen-K were killed or wounded. As you can see from the feeds here, members of the opposition force suffered casualties as well, but none of them turned up in any local hospitals.'

Tong did not comment on this. He only said, 'CIA.'

'Yes, sir, their local man, Adam Yao, the one we have been aware of for the past week, is clearly captured here on the video.'

'We are reading CIA communications. We know Yao is present in HK and operating surveillance on our operation. Why did you not prevent this?'

'If the CIA used CIA paramilitary forces or coordinated this kidnapping directly, we would have been aware of it and we would have been prepared. But the Pentagon used American military forces, apparently members of their Joint Special Operations Command. We do not have deep persistent access into JSOC communications.'

'Why did CIA use JSOC? Do they suspect a leak in their cable traffic?'

'Negative. From what we've determined monitoring CIA cable traffic after this hit, this element of commandos happened to be training in South Korea and was able to move over here very quickly yesterday when an in extremis opportunity arose to kidnap Zha. No one at JSOC told the CIA they were coming.'

'And yet the local CIA operative was present.'

'I . . . I have not determined how that occurred.'

Tong said, 'I am very dissatisfied that this happened.'

The security manager said, 'I understand, sir. Visualization of the kidnapping after the fact does not help us much. Preventing it would have been ideal.'

'Have you reported this to our colleagues in Beijing?' Tong asked.

'Yes, sir. They ask you to contact them as soon as you can.'

Tong nodded. 'Our time in Hong Kong is over.'

He watched the violent movie on his main monitor a second time. Quickly he reached out and pressed a button, stopping as the driver of the minivan fired a handgun out the driver's-side window. As the window shattered, a brief but relatively clear image of the driver emerged as the vehicle passed close to the camera.

Tong pulled a frame capture, and in seconds he had sharpened it up greatly with software on his machine.

'This man was in Club Stylish at the beginning of the sequence, before the attack. He was not part of the attacking force.'

'Yes, I think you are correct.'

Together Tong and the security manager went through raw feed of Club Stylish, both before and after the kidnapping. They saw the unknown man sitting at the bar before the attack; he was all alone. But after the kidnapping, he was met by two other men. Together the three left through the front entrance. One was tall, with a common paper mask on his face.

And the other man was Adam Yao.

Tong found a good image of the short, slightly dark man as he entered the club for the first time, passing directly in front of a security camera at the entrance. He cleaned the image up even more, and zoomed in on the man's face.

'I know who this man is,' said K. K. Tong.

He pressed buttons on his computer and brought up a videoconference. A woman with a headset on was sitting at her desk, somewhere on the operations floor of the Ghost Ship.

She was surprised to find herself on camera. She sat up straighter and bowed in her seat. 'Desk forty-one.'

'Come in my office.'

'Yes, Center.'

A few moments later the controller entered Tong's dark office, stood next to the security manager, and gave a quick bow before standing at attention with her eyes straight ahead.

'Look at this image capture.'

She peered past Center at the screen for several seconds, and then returned to standing erectly once again. She said, 'That appears to be subject Domingo Chavez of the Maryland, America, company Hendley Associates. Wife, Patsy Chavez. One son, John Patrick Chavez. Domingo Chavez served in the U.S. Army and then in the CIA's Special Activities Division. After leaving –'

'I know who it is,' Tong interrupted. 'Hendley Associates is a target of interest, is it not?'

'Yes, Center.'

'They assassinated Kartal and his band of Libyan misfits in Istanbul a few months ago, did they not?'

'Yes, Center.'

'You seem to know all about Chavez and Hendley Associates.'

'Yes, Center.'

'Did you also know Mr Chavez and at least one colleague of his were here in Hong Kong last night, helping the CIA and the U.S. military capture Zha Shu Hai, chief of our coders department, and killing a large number of our Fourteen-K hosts in the process?'

The young woman's eyes moved to Center, and her white skin seemed to turn gray as blood left her face. Softly she said, 'No, Center.'

'Do we have deep persistent access into the Hendley Associates network yet?'

'No, Center.'

'I ordered this months ago.'

The woman said, 'With help from MSS assets in Shanghai and in Washington we have placed a RAT on a drive that was delivered to Hendley Associates last week. The Trojan has not reported in as of yet.'

'Perhaps the Hendley Associates people discovered the RAT and did not install the device?'

The woman blinked hard. 'It is possible, sir.'

With the tip of his pen, Tong flipped to a different photograph. It was Adam Yao, Domingo Chavez, and a tall man with dark hair wearing a paper mask. 'Is this Jack Ryan, son of the President of the United States? He works at Hendley, you know.'

The woman looked at the image. 'I . . . I do not know, Center. I cannot see his face.'

'If we had access into their network, we would know exactly who that was, wouldn't you agree?'

'Yes, Center.'

Tong thought for a few moments. Finally he said, 'You will be reassigned. You are dismissed.' The woman bowed and left the room. Tong initiated another videoconference before she was out the door, this time with the director of the Ghost Ship's controller department.

'Replace desk forty-one with your best English-speaking controller, and instruct them to immediately take control of your best English-speaking field operative, whoever that is and wherever in the world they are working, and send him or her to Washington, D.C. Come to my office in thirty minutes with this done, and I will give you further instructions.'

Without waiting for a response he disconnected the videoconference and then swiveled in his chair to the director of his security staff. 'Where has the U.S. military taken Zha?'

The man looked down at a notebook in his hand. 'We are working on getting this information. Surely to the United States, likely to Andrews Air Force Base. From there he will probably be turned over to the CIA for debriefing. They will use a safe house, since they will want to debrief him before placing him in official U.S. custody.'

Tong nodded. 'I want an address.'

'I will get it for you.'

Valentin Kovalenko had been working full days and many nights for Center in the past few weeks. He'd planted bugs in corporate offices, pilfered wireless communications from tech companies, stolen RFID credit card information, and performed a number of other tasks.

Tonight, however, he was not working for Center. He had spent the day here in Barcelona getting pictures of a British politician who was on vacation in sunny Spain with a girlfriend while his wife was back in gray London with four kids.

But that was today. Tonight he was on a mission of his own. He'd purchased a prepaid cell phone from a convenience store several kilometers away from his Boulevard Rosa flat, then he went to an Internet café to look up a phone number he did not know from memory. After he wrote it down on a sheet of paper, he stopped in a bar and drank two quick glasses of Rioja to settle his nerves, then returned to his flat, locked the door, and sat down to make his call.

He looked at his laptop on his desk. Cryptogram was open and flashing.

Shit.

He headed to the little desk. He would check in with Center first, then he would be free to call his father, Oleg Kovalenko, in Moscow.

His father did not own a computer; he did not own a cell phone. He was, effectively, off the grid and out of the reach of the Center organization.

Valentin planned on telling his father as little as possible about his predicament, then sending the old man to the SVR in Moscow to talk to his old friends and explain the situation.

His arrest for the John Clark episode. His escape from prison and his coerced recruitment into the Center organization.

His dad and his old friends would help him out of this.

He decided on this course of action after going to the Russian embassy in Barcelona, passing by a couple of times on foot, and then deciding it was not safe for him to make contact with anyone directly there. His father could do it for him, in Moscow, where Valentin knew many people and could direct his father to any one of a dozen friends who could help him.

But first he clicked on Cryptogram. Typed, 'I'm here.' He pulled the card out of his camera and slid it into the side of the laptop. Typed, 'Uploading images now.'

He initiated the upload on Cryptogram, and Center accepted the file.

But Center's reply, when it came, was incongruous to Kovalenko's message. The words 'Everyone makes a mistake' appeared on the screen.

Kovalenko cocked his head. He typed, 'What does that mean?'

'You made a mistake by deciding to contact your father.'

Instantly sweat formed on the back of Kovalenko's neck. His fingers began to type some sort of denial, but he stopped himself.

How the fuck did Center know?

After a delay he typed instead, 'He is my father.'

'That is irrelevant to us, and he is irrelevant to your assignment. You will not have any contact with anyone from your past life.'

'He is no longer with the government. He will tell no one.'

'Irrelevant. You need to follow instructions.'

Kovalenko looked over at the new mobile phone. No, there is no way that Center could have some sort of tracking or listening device planted on every new phone in every blister pack in the world.

The Internet café? Could they really be looking at every machine in every Internet café in Barcelona? In Europe? On earth? That was unfathomable.

Impossible.

Wait. Kovalenko pulled his own mobile phone out of his jacket. He had been working for Center long enough to put together some of the technological pieces of any operation they might be running against him. Maybe his phone was bugged with a GPS beacon of some sort. His movements could be tracked; if Center was really on the ball he could have seen him go to the Internet café. Then he could have – Kovalenko supposed – looked at the traffic coming out of those computers. The Internet search of the Moscow phone book. They could have recognized the name or done some other follow-up search to determine that he was trying to contact his father.

They could have monitored him at the market where he purchased the phone.

Is that how they did it?

Not a simple thing, but somewhat less than omnipotent.

Shit. He'd been stupid. He should have tried harder, come up with some more remote way to get his father's number.

He typed, 'I have been working for you for three months. I want to return to my life.'

The response he received from Center was not what he expected: 'You will continue doing as you are instructed. If you had managed to contact your father successfully, he would be dead by now.'

Kovalenko did not respond.

A new paragraph of text appeared on Cryptogram an instant later. 'Documents will be dead-dropped to you in Barcelona today. You will use them to go to the United States.

You will leave tomorrow. There you will rent suitable habitation in Washington, D.C., and you will operate from there. You have two days to get into position and to report in prepared to receive operational instructions.'

D.C.? Kovalenko was surprised and more than a little concerned.

'I do not have a good relationship with the current administration.' This flat declaration by Valentin Kovalenko could not have been more of an understatement. One year prior, Kovalenko had conspired with billionaire Paul Laska, a U.S. citizen, to destroy the election chances of Jack Ryan. Laska and Kovalenko had failed, and while Laska seemed to have gotten off scot-free, Valentin became an embarrassing inconvenience for the Kremlin, so he'd been thrown in a rat hole.

Kovalenko had no trouble believing that the Ryan administration knew all about him. Flying into Washington, D.C., to work for a shadowy criminal organization seemed like a terrible idea.

Center responded, 'We know about your relationship with the John Clark episode and, by association, with President Ryan. The documents, credit cards, and cover for status we will give you will ensure your ability to get into the country and situated. Your own OPSEC and tradecraft will ensure your continued safety once there.'

Kovalenko looked at the screen for a moment before typing, 'No. I do not want to go to America.'

'You will go.' That was all. Just a demand.

Valentin typed 'no,' but he did not press the enter key. He just looked at it.

After several seconds he removed the 'no' and typed, 'How long an assignment?'

'Unknown. Likely less than two months, but all depends on your skill. We feel you will do well.'

Kovalenko spoke aloud in his flat. 'Yes. Threats and flattery. Kick an agent in the ass and then give him a blow job.' He knew nothing about Center, but he could easily deduce that the man was a seasoned spymaster.

The Russian typed, 'And if I refuse?'

'You will see what will happen to you if you refuse. We suggest you do not refuse.'

43

The life of a CIA officer in the field had its moments of raw adrenaline and pure excitement, but there existed many more moments like this.

Adam Yao had spent the night in the small waiting room of an auto body shop in Sai Wan on Hong Kong Island, just a few kilometers from his flat. He'd brought his neighbor's Mitsubishi minivan here the previous evening, and he'd paid the shop owner and his assistant handsomely to work through the night to clean blood off the upholstery, to fill in and buff out the bullet holes, to repaint the vehicle, and to replace the broken windows.

It was seven a.m. now, and they were wrapping up, which meant Adam would, he hoped, just be able to get the minivan back in time to park it in its place in the parking garage before his neighbor came down from his flat to head for work.

None of this was a thrilling postscript to the excitement of the past few days, but these things happened, and Yao could not very well just give the Mitsubishi back to his friend as it was.

His neighbor, a man Adam's age named Robert Kam, had three kids and owned the minivan out of necessity. He had been driving Adam's Mercedes for the past two days, and he had not complained one bit. Though Adam's car was a dozen years old, it was in fine condition, and a hell of a lot better ride than the Mitsubishi Grandis minivan.

The body shop owner tossed Yao the keys, and they inspected it together. Adam was impressed – he could see no evidence of the damage to the car's body, and they had replaced the side windows with tint that perfectly matched the tint on the windshield and back glass.

Adam followed the manager to the counter and paid his bill. He made sure to get an itemized receipt. It had cost an arm and a leg to get the vehicle repairs expedited, and he'd paid with his own money. He had every intention of sending the invoice to Langley, and to pitch a white-hot fit if he wasn't reimbursed for this expense.

But he was not going to be sending that invoice in anytime soon. He was still over here, in the field, operating under a strong suspicion that there was a leak in the pipeline of information between Asian-based CIA officers and Langley.

The last thing he wanted to do was send a cable that revealed the fact he had been involved in the shoot-out the night before last.

Adam raced home in the minivan now, checking his watch every minute, hoping he could get the Mitsubishi back in time for his neighbor to find it in his parking place.

Adam's place was in Soho, a trendy and pricey area of Central on Hong Kong Island built into a steep hillside. Yao could never afford his small but modern flat on his CIA salary, but his place fit his cover as president and owner of a business investigation firm, so he justified it to Langley.

His neighbor Robert, on the other hand, was a banker with HSBC, and he probably raked in four times Adam's salary, though Adam could imagine that the expense of having three boys would cut into Robert's discretionary income.

Adam made it back to his building and pulled up the ramp into his parking garage just after seven-thirty a.m., and he made the turn to go find the Mitsubishi's numbered parking space.

Up ahead of him, at the end of the lane of cars, Adam saw Robert stepping up to Yao's black Mercedes with his briefcase in his hand and his suit coat over his arm.

Shit, Adam thought. He could still switch out cars with him, but he'd have to come up with some excuse why he was just getting the vehicle home right now. Adam's fertile brain started working on something as he headed up the parking lot to Robert's numbered space a row over from his own.

He saw Robert open the door of the Mercedes, then sit down, just as Adam pulled Robert's Mitsubishi into its parking space facing him across the lane.

The CIA officer put the minivan in park as Robert looked up and noticed him. Adam smiled and waved sheepishly, an apologetic grimace for not having the minivan back until now.

Robert smiled.

And then Robert Kam disappeared in a flash of light.

The Mercedes exploded right in front of Adam Yao's eyes, fire and shrapnel and a shock wave visible as a wall of dust rocked the parking garage, the new windows of the Mitsubishi shattered, and Adam's head was slammed back against the headrest with the violent blast.

A hundred car alarms of luxury vehicles began whining and screaming and chirping, and pieces of car and concrete from the ceiling of the lot rained down on the minivan, cracking the windshield further and tearing holes in the hood and roof. Adam felt the trickle of blood on his face where auto glass cut into him, and the choking smoke of the explosion in the enclosed parking lot threatened to suffocate him.

Somehow he forced his way out of the damaged Mitsubishi and stumbled toward his Mercedes.

'Robert!' he screamed, and he tripped over an I-beam that had fallen from the ceiling. On his hands and knees he pushed and kicked through the twisted metal of other cars, his head pounding from the concussion he just received and his face dripping blood freely now. 'Robert!'

He climbed on the hood of the Mercedes, looked into the burning interior, and he saw the charred remains of Robert Kam in the driver's seat.

Adam Yao turned away with his hands on his head.

He'd seen Robert with his wife and his three young boys in the elevator or climbing into or out of their minivan a hundred times in the past year. The image of the kids in their soccer uniforms laughing and playing with their father rolled over and over in Yao's mind as he stumbled and fell away from the burning wreckage of his car, back over the broken concrete and shattered Audis, BMWs, Land Rovers, and other twisted wrecks of hot metal that had been, seconds before, rows of luxury automobiles.

'Robert.' Adam said it this time, he did not shout it. He fell to the ground dazed and bloodied, but he fought his way back to his feet, then wandered through the dust and smoke for a minute, his ringing ears assaulted by the car alarms. Finally he found a clear lane to the exit through the smoke and dust, and he walked to it.

Men and women from the street ran up to him on the drive and tried to help him, but he pushed them away, pointing toward the scene of the blast, and they ran on to look for more survivors.

Adam was on the street a moment later. It felt cool here this morning high on the hill, above the congested streets of Central and the air thick with humidity down by Victoria Harbour. He walked away from his building, down a steep decline; he wiped blood from his face as emergency vehicles raced past him, up the winding roads toward the black smoke now two blocks behind him.

He had no destination, he just walked.

His thoughts were on Robert, his friend, a man just about Adam's own age who had sat down in Adam's own car and taken the full brunt of the bomb that had clearly been meant not for Robert Kam but for Adam Yao.

When he was five blocks from home, the ringing in his ears lessened and the pounding from the concussion abated just enough for him to start to put salient thoughts together about his own situation.

Who? Who did this?

The Triads? How the fuck would the Triads know who he was, where he lived? What car he drove? The only people who knew his identity and who knew he was CIA, other than CIA, were the Hendley Associates men and whoever was managing to compromise cable traffic out of Hong Kong and China.

No way in hell the Triads were getting intel directly from the CIA. The Triads ran hookers and pirated DVDs, they did not assassinate CIA officers and compromise tier-one intelligence agencies.

If it wasn't the Triads, then it *had* to be the PRC. Somehow, for some reason, the PRC wanted him dead.

Had FastByte been here in China working *with* the Triads *for* the PRC?

None of that tracked with anything Adam understood about the way these organizations worked.

As confused as Adam was about what had just happened and what he'd stumbled onto, there was one matter on which the bruised and bloodied CIA operator was crystal fucking clear.

He wasn't calling in to CIA; he wasn't saying one damn thing to anybody about anything. Adam was a one-man band, and he was getting the fuck out of here on his own.

He continued staggering down the hill, toward the harbor, wiping blood out of his eyes as he walked on.

44

Brandon 'Trash' White checked the seal of his oxygen mask over his mouth, saluted the catapult officer on the deck to his right, then placed his gloved left hand on the throttle of his F/A-18 Hornet. With some reluctance he wrapped his right hand around the 'towel rack,' a metal bar handgrip high on the canopy in front of his head. He was just seconds from being airborne, and it was his natural inclination to keep his hand on the controls of his aircraft, but carrier rules were different. The catapult shot would shove Trash's body back hard against his seat, and if his hand was holding on to his stick, there was a high probability his hand would fly back with the high g-forces, pulling the stick along with it and pitching the airplane up and out of control on takeoff.

So Trash held on to the towel rack and waited to be shot off the boat like a marble from a slingshot.

To his immediate right, the F/A-18 of Major Scott 'Cheese' Stilton, call sign 'Magic Two-One,' sprang forward toward the bow ahead of the steaming catapult track and flame-red engines. He was flying an instant later, banking to the right and climbing into a beautiful blue sky.

And then Trash was moving. Really moving. He went from zero to one hundred sixty-five miles an hour in two seconds along a three-hundred-foot-long cat-track toward the end of the boat. His helmet pressed into the headrest and his raised right arm pulled back to him, but he held on, waited to feel the thump of his nose wheel popping up at the end of the deck.

The thump came and he was over water, hurled screaming from the deck with no control over his aircraft. He quickly reached down for the stick, pulled his nose up slightly, and banked gently to the left for a clearing turn.

'Trash is airborne. Hoorah,' he said coolly into his inter-flight-comm radio, letting Cheese know he was in the air and flying, and he climbed into the sky on his way to the strait one hundred miles to the northwest.

The F/A-18s of the *Ronald Reagan* had been patrolling the Taiwan Strait for four days now, and Trash and Cheese had flown two sorties each of those days. Fortunately for Trash's blood pressure, all his flights so far had been during daylight hours, but he doubted his luck would hold in that regard.

His blood pressure *had* spiked a few times from close encounters with PLA pilots. Trash and Cheese had been flying combat air patrols on the Taiwanese side of the strait, manning a sector just offshore of Taipei, at the northern part of the island. Republic of China F-16s flew most of the sorties over the rest of the strait, and they, just like the aircraft from the *Reagan*, were careful not to pass over the centerline of the strait into Chinese territory.

But the Chinese were not playing by the same rules. Some sixteen times in the past four days flights of PLAAF Su-27, J-5, and J-10 jets took off from their air base in Fuzhou, directly across the hundred-mile-wide strait from Taiwan's capital, Taipei, and then raced directly toward the centerline. A dozen times so far the Chinese fighters actually locked on to American or Taiwanese aircraft with their radars. These 'spikes' were considered aggressive, but even more aggressive were the three instances where Chinese Su-27 and J-5 fighters actually flew over the centerline before returning to the north.

It was a threatening flexing of Chinese muscle, and it kept

Trash and the rest of the pilots working the strait on their toes and ready for action.

Trash and Cheese were sent to their patrol area by a naval flight officer in the *Reagan*'s Combat Information Center, known as the CIVIC, and they also received updates on other aircraft in their area of operations from a combat air controller flying in the back of an E2-C Hawkeye airborne early-warning aircraft patrolling far to the east of the strait, with visualization of the area via their powerful radar and computers.

As the distant eyes and ears for the pilots in the strait, the Hawkeye could track aircraft, missiles, and even surface vessels for hundreds of miles in all directions.

Once on station, Trash and Cheese flew a racetrack pattern at twenty thousand feet over the water. Trash manipulated his throttle and stick instinctively to stay in a loose combat formation with his flight lead, and he monitored his radar and listened to the comms from the Hawkeye and the CIVIC.

There were broken clouds well below him, but nothing but brilliant blue sky all around. He could see bits of the Chinese mainland when his racetrack took him to the north, and he could easily make out Taipei and other large cities on Taiwan anytime the clouds broke up enough to the south.

Even though the tension in the strait was palpable, Trash felt good being right here, right now, comfortable in the fact he had the best training, the best support, the best flight lead, and the best aircraft in this entire conflict.

And it *was* a magnificent aircraft. The F/A-18C was fifty-six feet long, with a forty-foot wingspan. When 'slick,' or operating without weapons or extra fuel, it weighed only ten tons, because of its aluminum-steel composite construction. And its two beastly General Electric turbofan engines generated roughly the same amount of power as three hundred fifty Cessna 172 aircraft, giving it an excellent power-to-weight ratio that meant it could hit Mach 1.5 – or thirteen hundred miles per hour – and stand on end and fly vertically like a rocket launching off a pad.

Trash's fly-by-wire aircraft did a lot of the work for him now while he scanned the sky and the screens in front of him – the left data display indicator and the right DDI, the up-front control display, and the moving map display low in front of him, almost between his knees.

There were five hundred thirty switches in his cockpit, but most every input Trash needed to fly and fight could be made from sixteen buttons on his stick and throttle without even taking his eyes off the HUD.

The thirty-million-dollar C was one of the best fighter air-frames in the air, but it wasn't exactly the newest kid on the block. The Navy flew the newer, bigger, and more advanced Super Hornet, which cost a good twenty million dollars more.

Trash had just turned to follow Cheese back to the south, trailing his flight leader in an echelon formation, when his headset came alive with a transmission from the Hawkeye.

'Contact bull's-eye, zero-four-zero. Forty-five miles, heading southwest, single group, two bogeys, southeast of Putian. Heading, two-one-zero. They appear to be heading toward the strait.'

Cheese's voice came into Trash's headset: 'Coming our way, brother.'

'Hoorah, aren't we popular?' Trash responded, a tinge of sarcasm in his voice.

The two Marines had heard similar notifications multiple times over the past four days of patrols out here. Each time Trash and Cheese found themselves in the sector where a potential incursion might occur, the Chinese fighters raced toward the centerline only to bank back around to the northwest, and then return to the coast.

The PLAAF was feinting up and down the length of the strait, for what purpose other than to incite some sort of response, no one knew.

Cheese acknowledged the Hawkeye's transmission, and then immediately listened to a report of a contact just south of the Marines' sector. Two more bogeys were headed into the strait. This area was patrolled by two ROC F-16s, who were getting their information from the U.S. Hawkeye as well.

Cheese radioed Trash: 'Magic Two-Two, let's descend to angels fifteen, tighten up our pattern so we can be close to the centerline in case the bogeys make an incursion.'

'Roger that,' said Trash, and he followed Cheese's descent and turn. He did not think for a moment that the two Chinese pilots were going to do anything more than what he'd seen the past four days, and he knew Cheese felt the same, but Trash also knew Cheese was careful enough to not get caught with his pants down, finding himself and his wingman out of position if the Chinese fighters entered Taiwanese airspace.

The Hawkeye updated Cheese. 'Magic Two-One. Bogeys zero-two-zero, four-zero miles, ten thousand . . . climbing.'

'Magic Two-One, roger,' responded Cheese.

A moment after this transmission, the Hawkeye air combat officer notified Cheese that the bogeys approaching the Taiwanese F-16s to the south were following a similar flight path.

Trash said, 'Looks like this could be coordinated.'

'Doesn't it, though?' replied Cheese. 'That's a different tactic from what they've been doing. They've been sending up flights of two. I wonder if two flights of two at the same time in adjacent sectors means they are raising the stakes.'

'We're about to find out.'

Cheese and Trash widened their formation and pulled out of their descent at fifteen thousand feet. The Hawkeye divided its time between sending them updates on the two unknown bogeys heading toward them and passing on information to the ROC Air Force F-16s forty miles to the south of the Marines' sector over the strait.

Just after the Hawkeye announced that the two bogeys heading toward Magic Two-One and Magic Two-Two were twenty miles away, the ACO added, 'They are still heading toward the centerline of the strait. At current speed and heading they will breach in two minutes.'

'Roger,' said Cheese. He squinted into the distance to try and pick them out in front of the white clouds and gray of the mainland in the distance.

'Magic Two-One, Hawkeye. New contact. Four bogeys taking off at Fuzhou and approaching the strait. Climbing rapidly and turning south, angels three and climbing.'

Now things were getting complicated, Trash realized. He had two Chinese fighters of unknown type heading directly toward him and his flight leader, two more threatening the sector just south of him, and now four more bogeys heading in behind the first group.

The ACO announced he had a flight of four Navy F/A-18 Super Hornets finishing up air-refueling over the east of Taiwan Island, and he would expedite moving them to the Marines' sector in support just as soon as he could.

Cheese said, 'Trash, I've got the bogeys on radar, they are just off my nose. Are you tally?'

Trash clicked a button and removed most of the digital data projected on his heads-up display and his helmet-mounted cueing system, then squinted as he peered ahead out past the HUD into the sky.

'No joy,' he said, but he kept looking.

Cheese said, 'Sixty seconds to intercept, let's fly heading zero-thirty, a twenty-degree offset so they can see we aren't threatening them.'

'Roger that,' replied Trash, and he tipped his wing to the right, following Cheese's turn so that the bogeys were no longer directly on their nose.

Within a few seconds Cheese said, 'Bogeys are jinking left to come back on an intercept course. Descending, let's speed it up.'

'Sons of bitches,' said Trash, and he felt a new level of tension instantly. The Chinese pilots were screaming toward the centerline and overtly pointing their noses, which meant their radars and their weapons, directly at the two Marine aircraft.

With an intercept speed of more than twelve hundred miles an hour now, Trash knew things were about to start happening very, very quickly.

Cheese said, 'Turn heading three-forty; let's pull away from them again.'

Trash banked with Cheese back to the left, and within ten seconds he could see on his radar that the Chinese were mirroring the maneuver. He reported, 'Bogeys are jinking back to us, bearing oh-one-five, two-eight miles. Fourteen thousand.'

Trash heard the Hawkeye ACO acknowledge this and then immediately divert his attention back to the ROC F-16s, who were seeing similar moves from their bogeys.

'Spike,' said Cheese now, indicating that one of the bogeys had locked on Cheese's plane with his radar.

Trash heard the spike warning for his own jet just a moment later.

'I'm spiked, too. These guys aren't fucking around, Cheese.'

Cheese gave the next order with a tone of seriousness that

Trash seldom heard from the major: 'Magic Two-Two, Master Arm on.'

'Roger,' said Trash. He flipped his Master Arm into the armed position, ensuring all his weapons were hot and he had the launch of his air-to-air missiles at his fingertips. He still did not think he was about to get into a fight, but the level of threat had gone up precipitously with the enemy's radar lock, and he knew he and Cheese needed to be ready in case this devolved from an incident into a fight.

The ACO announced almost simultaneously that the Taiwanese had reported a spike.

Trash followed Cheese's turn yet again, away from the centerline and away from the approaching aircraft. He looked out the side of his canopy now, using his 'Jay-Macks,' his joint helmet-mounted cueing system, a smart visor on his helmet that gave him much of his heads-up information even when he looked left, right, and above his HUD. Through it he saw two black specks streaking in their direction over a backdrop of a puffy white cloud.

He spoke quickly and energetically, but he was a pro, there was no unnecessary excitement in his voice. 'Magic Two-Two. Tally two bandits. Ten o'clock, just slightly low. Possible Super 10s.' No American had ever come up against China's most advanced operational frontline fighter, the Chengdu J-10B Super 10, a newer version of the J-10 Annihilator. Trash knew the J-10 airframe used composite materials just like his own and its reduced radar signature was designed to make a radar missile lock difficult. The B model supposedly had an upgraded electronic warfare suite that helped in this regard as well.

It was a smaller aircraft than the F/A-18 and it possessed only a single engine to the Hornet's two, but the Russian-built turbofan gave the nimble fighter plenty of power for air-to-air engagements.

'Roger that,' said Cheese. 'Guess it's our lucky day.'

The Chinese had more than two hundred sixty J-10s in service, but probably fewer than forty B variants. Trash did not respond; his game face was on.

Cheese said, 'They are turning back hot! Thirty seconds from the centerline and displaying hostile intent.'

Trash expected to hear the Hawkeye ACO acknowledge Cheese's transmission, but instead he spoke in a loud voice, 'Magic flight, be advised. ROC flight south of you is under attack and defensive, missiles in the air.'

Trash spoke with astonishment into his radio: 'Holy fucking shit, Scott.'

Cheese saw the J-10s in front of him now and reported that he had visual. 'Tally two on my nose. Confirmed Super 10s. Hawkeye, are we cleared hot?'

Before the Hawkeye answered, Trash said, 'Roger, two on your nose. Tell me which one to take.'

'I've got the one on the left.'

'Roger, I've got the guy on the right.'

Cheese confirmed, 'Roger, Two-Two, you have the trailing aircraft on the right.'

Now Trash's HUD and his missile warning system announced that a missile launch had been detected. One of the J-10s had just fired at him. He saw in his HUD that the time-to-target of the inbound missile was thirteen seconds.

'Missile in the air! Missile in the air! Breaking right! Magic Two-Two defensive!' *Motherfucker!* Trash banked his aircraft away from Cheese and went inverted. He pulled back on his stick, and with his canopy showing nothing but blue water, he increased his speed and descent.

The legs of his g-suit filled with air, forcing the blood in the upper part of his body to stay there so his brain would continue to think and his pounding heart would continue to pound.

He grunted against the g-forces.

The Hawkeye announced belatedly, 'Magic flight, you are cleared to engage.'

At this stage of the game Trash didn't give a rat's ass if someone safe over the horizon line gave him the authorization to shoot back. This was life and death, and Trash had no intention of doing peaceful lazy-eights out here until he was blown out of the sky.

Hell, no, Trash wanted those other pilots dead, and he would shoot every missile he had if that's what it took, regardless of instructions from the Hawkeye ACO.

But for right now, he had to stay alive long enough to shoot back.

45

Trash rocketed his Hornet toward the water, twelve thousand feet below him now but filling his windscreen quickly. Knowing the distance between himself and the J-10 when the other plane fired, the American was certain he was being chased down right now by a PL-12, a medium-range air-to-air radar-guided missile with a high-explosive warhead. Trash also knew that, with the missile's top speed of Mach 4, he would not be outrunning this threat. And he was also well aware that with the missile's ability to make a thirty-eight-g turn, he would not be outturning it, since his body could not pull more than nine g's before G-LOC, g-induced loss of consciousness, knocked him out and ended any chance he had to get himself out of this mess.

Instead Trash knew he'd have to use geometry as well as a few other tricks he had up his sleeve.

At five thousand feet he yanked back on the stick, pulling his nose directly toward the oncoming threat. He could not see the missile; it was propelled by a rocket using smokeless fuel, and it raced through the sky nearly as fast as a bullet. But he kept his head through his maneuver and retained the situational awareness to know the direction from which the missile had been fired.

Just coming out of the dive was a challenge for the twenty-eight-year-old captain. It was a seven-g turn, Trash knew this from his training, and to keep enough blood in his head for the high-g turn he used a hook maneuver. As he tightened every muscle in his core, he barked out a high-pitched 'Hook!' that tightened his core even more.

In his intercom he heard his own voice. 'Hook! Hook! Hook!'

Bitching Betty, the audio warning announcements delivered by a woman's voice, too calm considering the news she delivered, came through Trash's headset: 'Altitude. Altitude.'

Trash leveled out now, and he saw on his radar warning receiver that the threat was still locked on. He deployed chaff, a cloud of aluminum-coated glass fibers that dispersed via a pyrotechnic charge into a wide pattern around and behind the aircraft, hopefully decoying the radar of the incoming missile.

Simultaneous with his deployment of chaff, Trash banked right, pulled back on the stick, and rocketed sideways only twenty-three hundred feet above the water.

He deployed more chaff as he raced away, his right wing pointing to the water, his left wing pointing to the sun.

The PL-12 missile took the bait. It fired into the floating aluminum and glass fiber, losing its lock on the radar signature of the F-18, and it slammed into the water moments later.

Trash had beat the medium-range missile, but his maneuvers and his concentration on this threat had allowed the J-10 to get in behind him now. The Marine leveled his wings at eighteen hundred feet, looked around the sky on all sides of his cockpit, and he realized he'd lost sight of his enemy.

'Where's he at, Cheese?'

'Unknown, Magic Two-Two! I'm defending!'

So Cheese was in a fight for his life himself, Trash now realized. Neither man could help the other; they were both on their own until they either killed their enemy or were joined by the Navy Super Hornets, still several minutes away.

Trash looked at the DDI above his left knee. The small screen showed him the top-down view of all the aircraft in the area. He saw Cheese to his north, and far to the south he saw the two ROC F-16s.

He looked as far back over his left shoulder as he could, and now he saw the black silhouette of an aircraft bearing down on him at his seven-o'clock high, some two miles distant. The aircraft was far to the left of his HUD but he could still target it via his Jay-Macks visor.

The J-10 turned in on Trash's six o'clock, and Trash banked hard to the left, shoved his throttle forward, and dove toward the deck to pick up more speed, all to keep the enemy pilot from getting behind him.

But the J-10 anticipated Trash's move and worked his way to the Marine's six, and closed to within a mile and a half.

The Chinese pilot fired his twin-barreled 23-millimeter cannon. Glowing tracer rounds passed within a few feet of Trash's canopy as he reversed his turn to the right and dropped down even lower. The rounds looked like long laser beams, and Trash watched them turn the blue-green water into geysers of foam ahead of him.

Trash juked hard to the left and right, but he kept his nose flat now; he was only five hundred feet above the water, so he could not dive, and he did not want to lose airspeed by pulling up. In the cool jargon of combat aviation this was referred to as 'guns-d' or 'guns defensive,' but Trash and his fellow pilots called it 'the funky chicken.' It was a desperate, ugly dance to stay out of the line of fire. Trash jacked his head up left and right as far as he could, straining his neck muscles to keep his enemy in sight behind him while he banked and yawed all over the sky. He caught a glimpse of the J-10 banking to follow his last evasive move, and Trash knew the Chinese pilot was almost in place for another shot.

After another burst of cannon rounds went high, the Marine saw in the small mirror on the canopy next to the towel rack that the Super 10 had closed to under one mile, and he was perfectly lined up to take Trash out with his next volley.

Trash did not hesitate; he had to act. He 'got skinny' by turning his aircraft to show the smallest dimension, the side, and as the J-10 closed range, Trash pulled his nose up. His body was shoved down farther, both forward against the straps and deep into his seat. His lumbar spine ached from the maneuver, and his eyes lost focus as they bulged in their sockets.

His last-ditch maneuver had increased the closure on the enemy fighter, not by slowing but by simply turning perpendicular to his line of flight at the perfect moment. He grunted and clenched his teeth, and then looked straight up through his canopy's glass.

The J-10B had been concentrating on his cannon, and he had not reacted to the maneuver in time. He shot past, just one hundred feet above Trash's Hornet.

The Chinese pilot was clearly doing his best to bleed off all his excess speed and to stay in the control zone, but even with his speed brakes on and his throttle back to idle he could not match Trash's deceleration.

As soon as the shadow of the Chinese fighter passed over Trash's aircraft, the American tried to pull into the control zone behind his enemy for a guns solution, but his enemy was good, and he knew better than to make himself an easy target. The J-10 got its nose up and its engine generating thrust once again, and he came off his speed brakes and went vertical.

Trash overshot his target low and instantly found himself in danger. To avoid having the J-10 get behind him, Trash shoved the throttle forward, past the detent and into afterburners, and his F/A-18 reared back like a mustang and launched toward the sun on two pillars of fire.

Trash accelerated upward, gradually getting his nose up to seventy degrees, passing three thousand feet, four thousand, five thousand. He saw the J-10 above him in the sky, saw the enemy's wingtips turning as the pilot tried to find the American plane somewhere below him.

Trash reached ninety degrees of pitch – pure vertical – and shot upward at a speed of forty-five thousand feet a minute.

In sixty seconds, he could be nine miles above the water.

But Trash knew good and well he did not have sixty seconds. The J-10 was up here with him, and the enemy pilot was likely slamming his head all over his cockpit trying to find where the hell in the sky the Hornet had run off to.

At ten thousand feet Captain White brought the throttle out of afterburner and tipped the nose of his jet over. He could tell that the enemy pilot still did not see him, a few thousand feet below and behind. The Chinese pilot rolled inverted and turned back toward the water.

Like a loop on a roller coaster, Trash rocketed in the direction of his enemy; in seconds he saw the Super 10 passing through a cloud below him. The pilot was using a split-S maneuver, trying to turn back toward the F/A-18 with a high-speed nose-low turn.

Trash thumbed a small trackball-like input on his flight stick and switched to his cannon. As soon as the aiming pipper appeared on his HUD, the J-10 descended right into it, just eight hundred yards away.

Trash fired one long and then two short bursts from his six-barreled Vulcan 20-millimeter cannon.

His long burst passed well in front of the Super 10; his second spray of cannon fire was closer but still ahead of the jet.

His last short burst, just a fraction of a second, nailed the enemy jet on the starboard wing. Bits of smoking aircraft broke free. The Chinese pilot broke hard to the right. Trash mimicked the maneuver just six hundred feet away, rolling toward dark smoke.

The Chinese plane dove for the water, and Trash fought to line up the pipper for another gun shot, 'hooked' with the hard-jerking g-forces he put on the plane to position himself behind.

In front of him a flash moved his focus from his pipper to his target. Flame poured from the wing and the engine, and almost instantly he knew the plane in front of him was about to die.

The rear of the J-10B exploded and the doomed aircraft spun hard to the right, corkscrewing toward the sea below.

Trash broke off the attack, banked hard to the left to avoid the fireball, and then struggled to level his wings up above the water. He had no time to look for a chute from the pilot.

'That's a kill. Splash one. Pos, Cheese?' 'Pos' was a request for the other jet's position.

Before his flight leader responded, Trash looked down at his DDI and saw he was heading toward Cheese. He looked up through several small clouds and saw the glint of sun off gray metal, as Magic Two-One, Cheese's aircraft, shot from right to left.

Cheese's voice came over the radio. 'Defensive. He's on my six, about two miles back. He's got me locked. Get him off me, Trash!'

Trash's eyes tracked quickly back to the north and saw the surviving Super 10 just as he launched a missile at Cheese's jet exhaust.

'Break right, Two-One! Missile in the air!'

Trash did not watch the missile, nor did he look back over at Cheese. Instead he switched his weapons to select a

Sidewinder short-range heat-seeking missile. Trash had a 'tally' on the Chinese Super 10, meaning that he could see him through his helmet-mounted sight.

Inside his headset he heard a loud electronic buzz indicating that his Sidewinder was searching for a suitable heat signature.

The buzz changed to the high-pitched lock tone as the J-10 passed by just three miles off Trash's nose, indicating the AIM-9's infrared homing system had found the hot engine of the Chinese aircraft and was tracking it.

Trash pressed the air-to-air launch button on his stick and fired the AIM-9 Sidewinder. It streaked away on a trail of smoke and homed in on the Super 10.

The missile was fire and forget, so Trash turned to the left to position himself behind the enemy fighter if the Sidewinder missed.

Quickly he found Cheese in the sky. Trash's flight leader was banking hard to the south; behind him his automatic flares deployed out of both sides of his aircraft and arced to the earth.

The Chinese missile dove into the hot flares and exploded.

Trash looked back to his target and saw the J-10 launch his own flares as he banked hard to the left. 'Get him, get him, get him,' Trash said aloud, urging his missile toward the flaming engine of the Chinese aircraft. But the Sidewinder was duped by the flares fired by the Super 10.

'Shit!'

Trash switched back to guns, but before he could get his pipper on his target, the enemy jet dove for the deck.

Trash followed him down, hoping to get behind him for another kill.

In his headset he heard, 'Magic Two-One is engaging bandits approaching from the north. Fox three.'

Trash had not even had time to check what happened to the four other approaching aircraft, but clearly Cheese was firing radar-guided missiles at them from a distance.

'Cheese, I'm engaged, pushing this guy to the deck.'

'Roger, Trash, Navy Super Hornets two minutes out.'

Trash nodded, then focused intently on his enemy, the Chinese pilot and his aircraft.

'Fox three!' said Cheese as he fired another AIM-120 AMRAAM at the bandits approaching from the north.

Trash and the Super 10 he had engaged spent the next sixty seconds in a tight, wild chase, each pilot jockeying to get in position to fire on the other while, at the same time, doing everything in his power to prevent his enemy from getting position on him.

This was known, in the lexicon of air-to-air combat, as a 'phone booth.' It was a small area to operate in, and getting smaller with the corrections both pilots made to jockey for advantage in the air.

Trash felt the bone-crushing pressure of high positive-g turns and the eye-popping, nausea-inducing dives of negative g's.

A minute into the dogfight White slammed the stick to the right, following the enemy's high-g turn above the water. Trash got his nose inside the turn slightly, but the PLAAF man reversed course suddenly and removed Trash's advantage.

The sheer number of inputs entering Trash's brain was unimaginable. His aircraft moved on three axes as he tried to remain in an offensive position against another aircraft moving on three axes. His mouth delivered information to his flight lead and the Hawkeye as he tracked the targets and the deck below, and both of his hands moved left, right, backward, and forward as his fingers flipped switches and pressed buttons on his throttle and stick. He read a dozen different readouts on his constantly moving HUD, and he occasionally brought his focus inside the cockpit to give quick glances to his navigational display to see where he and his lead were in relation to the centerline over the strait.

Sweat poured down the back of his neck and the muscles in his jaw quivered and spasmed from the tension of the moment.

'Can't get a bite on him!' Trash announced into his mic.

'I'm engaged, Magic Two-Two. He's yours.'

Cheese had fired a third missile at the inbound fighters, which he had determined to be Russian-built Su-33s. One of the three AMRAAMs hit its target, and Cheese announced, 'Splash two.'

The PLAAF fighter banked left and right, spun upside down, and performed a high reverse-g maneuver that Trash replicated, causing his eyes to bulge and his head to fill with blood.

He tightened his core muscles, his abs and low back turned to rocks, and he 'hooked' over and over.

He forced himself to lessen his turn angle, helping his body but causing him to lose his position behind the enemy.

'Don't lose sight. Don't lose sight,' he told himself as he tracked the J-10 through white puffy clouds.

The other pilot kept the bank going, however, and Trash craned his neck all the way behind him, then spun it back to check the mirrors high on the canopy.

The other jet was getting in behind him for a kill shot. Trash had lost his offensive advantage.

Not good.

The Chengdu J-10 pilot did make his way behind Trash and fired a short-range PL-9 missile at his tail, but Trash managed to defeat it with his automatic flare deployment and a seven-point-five-g bank that nearly knocked him out cold.

He needed his speed, but it was bleeding off on the turn. 'Don't bleed it! Don't bleed it!' he shouted to himself between grunting through the g-forces.

The two planes were corkscrewing down through the sky. Seven thousand feet, six thousand, five thousand.

At just three thousand feet Trash reversed direction quickly, pulled himself into an eight-g turn, and switched to guns.

The Chinese aircraft did not recognize what happened, and he kept his downward spiral going for critical seconds while Trash prepared to meet him head-on.

Trash saw the Super 10 at one mile, and he used his rudders to line up for a gun shot. He slammed his feet down, left and right, all the way to the firewall to make the necessary corrections in the very short time he had before the Super 10 passed.

There. At two thousand feet separation and a closing speed of more than one thousand miles per hour, Trash slammed his right index finger down on the trigger on his stick.

A long burst of tracers from his Vulcan cannon reached out from the nose of his aircraft. He used the laserlike light to guide him toward the enemy.

At five hundred feet the Super 10 burst into a fireball. Trash disengaged, pulled up on the stick violently with a hook to avoid an air-to-air collision or an FOD flameout, because foreign-object damage from the explosion could easily get sucked into his plane and destroy one or both engines.

Once he was clear, he confirmed the kill by going inverted and looking up in the canopy.

Below him the J-10 was nothing but small pieces of black

wreckage and burning, smoking debris, all falling toward the water. The pilot would be dead, but Trash's elation at having survived trumped any sympathy he could possibly feel in this moment.

'Splash three,' he said.

The Super Hornets arrived in time and committed on the three remaining Su-33s attacking from over the centerline, but Magic Flight was not finished. To their south, one of the two Taiwanese Air Force jets under attack by the other pair of J-10s had already disappeared from radar.

Cheese said, 'Magic Two-Two, heading two-four-zero, combat spread. Let's help out that surviving ROC F-16 before it's too late.'

'Roger that.'

Trash and Cheese raced to the southwest while the Navy Super Hornets chased the Su-33s back over the centerline and back to the Chinese coast.

A moment later, Trash got a radar lock on the J-10s, still forty miles away. He immediately fired an AMRAAM missile.

'Fox three.'

He doubted his missile would hit the Chinese fighter. The pilot of the enemy aircraft would have a hell of a lot of defensive tricks up his sleeve that he could deploy easily with such a distance between them, but he wanted to give the attacker something to focus on other than killing the Taiwanese F-16.

His AMRAAM might not knock the Chinese jet out of the sky, but it would screw with the pilot's attack.

The attack worked as he had hoped, one J-10 disengaged, but they were not in time to save the Taiwanese pilot. The ROC F-16 was hit by a short-range missile and blown to bits over the western coast of Taiwan.

The two Chinese planes immediately turned and raced back to the mainland before Trash and Cheese could engage them.

The two Marine F/A-18s were low on fuel, so they flew west, then lined up behind a refueler on station over Taipei to gas up before heading back to the carrier. Trash felt the tremors in his hand as he delicately jockeyed his aircraft in position behind the refueling drogue.

He chalked the shakes up to pure exhaustion and leftover adrenaline.

When they were back on the carrier, when their aircraft were chocked and chained and their parking brakes were set, when both men had climbed out of their cockpits, climbed down the stepping platforms on the side of the fuselage, returned to their ready room, and shed the survival gear off to reveal flight suits soaking wet from sweat, only then did the two men shake hands and hug.

Trash's knees shook now, but he felt good. Happy to be alive, mostly.

They learned only when they got back to the ready room that up and down the Taiwan Strait there had been several air-to-air encounters. Nine ROC aircraft had been shot down, versus five PLAAF fighters.

Trash and Cheese recorded three of those five kills, with Trash getting two Super 10s and Cheese shooting down one Su-33.

No one understood the audacity or aggression of the Chinese, and the squadron commander told his pilots that they could expect to be back up in the skies in combat within hours.

The Marines on the boat treated Trash and Cheese like heroes, but when the two men made it back to their quarters, Major Stilton could tell something was bothering Captain White.

'What's wrong, man?'

'I should have done better. That phone booth I was in, the second engagement ... I can already think of about five things I could have done differently to take that guy down faster.'

'What are you talking about? You got him, and your situational awareness out there this afternoon was outstanding.'

'Thanks,' Trash replied.

But Cheese could tell he was still brooding.

'What's really bothering you?'

'We should have nailed those other two J-10s before they wasted the F-16s. We took too long with our bandits, and the ROC guys got wasted. We come back here to the *Reagan* and everybody is acting like we're fucking rock stars. Those two ROC pilots are dead, and I'm just not feeling the joy.'

Cheese said, 'We did damn good today, bro. Were we perfect? Nope. We're just men. We do our best, and our best today took down a couple of enemy aircraft, saved our own asses, and showed the Chinks that they don't own the skies over the strait.' He reached over and flipped off the light to their quarters. 'That's going to have to be enough.'

Trash closed his eyes and tried to go to sleep. As he lay there he realized he was still trembling. He hoped like hell he'd be able to get some rest before he headed back into the unfriendly skies tomorrow.

46

Dr Tong Kwok Kwan stood in his new glass-enclosed office, looking out over the massive floor of low cubicles, and he decided that he was satisfied with his reconstituted, if temporary, Ghost Ship. He left his office, walked down a short hallway, and exited a locked door that opened to a twelfth-floor balcony. Here, breathing smoggy air that was not nearly as humid as the air he had left behind in Hong Kong, he looked out over a sprawling city, flat and wide around a river that snaked from the southeast to the northwest.

Below him in the parking lot were armored personnel carriers, machine gun emplacements, and troops patrolling on foot and in jeeps.

Yes, he thought. *This arrangement will do for now.*

Dr Tong and his entire operation had moved from Hong Kong's Mong Kok neighborhood to Guangzhou's Huadu district, some one hundred miles to the northwest. They were within the borders of mainland China now, safe from the CIA, and it was clear to Tong that the PLA had spared no expense to protect them and provide them with whatever they needed.

The Ghost Ship had spent the last two years operating under the pretense that it was not part of China's cyberwarfare infrastructure. The MSS would have liked to keep it that way, but the event in Hong Kong – the exposure of Zha Shu Hai by the CIA and his kidnapping by an American special-mission unit – had necessitated a quick change of plans. Tong had been ordered to move his entire operation up to the mainland and then to increase his cyberkinetic attacks on the United States immediately.

The 14K Triads had failed to keep his operation safe in Hong Kong, and now the 14K were wondering what the hell had happened to their cash cow. Four nights earlier, some sixty Chinese paramilitaries of the Guangzhou Military Region's 'Sharp Sword of Southern China' unit were dispatched into Mong Kok in a dozen civilian vehicles. There was a short standoff at the Mong Kok Computer Centre between the soldiers and the 14K, but a phone call from the colonel leading the unit to the head of the 14K in his suite at a casino in Macau made clear to the man that, unless his street goons walked away immediately, there was going to be another bloodbath in the streets, and, for the second time this week, the 14K would be supplying the majority of the blood.

The 14K backed down; they assumed that PLA forces had recaptured Tong and would take him and his people back to the mainland to be tried and executed.

In fact, the entire Ghost Ship – personnel, computers, communication gear, everything – was moved to a large China Telecom building just a few blocks away from the PLA's Technical Reconnaissance Bureau in Guangzhou, one of the hubs of the Army's cyberwar capability. All of China Telecom's operations were relocated, which meant mobile phone service in the Guangzhou area would be spotty or nonexistent for a few days, but the PLA's wishes took precedence over the needs of the citizenry.

Here Tong and his people were guarded by Guangzhou Military Region Special Forces Units 24/7, and in less than four days they were back in business, pressing the attack against the United States.

It was a temporary solution. Eventually the PLA wanted

Tong and his facility protected by a hardened bunker, but there were no available facilities anywhere in China in possession of both the networking resources and the structural requirements, so until something suitable was built, the China Telecom building surrounded by crack troops would have to suffice.

Tong stepped back through the doors and off the balcony. His quick break was over; it was time to get back to work. In his office he sat at his new desk and opened a file sent to him by one of the controllers he had monitoring CIA cable traffic. Tong scrolled through the transcript of a CIA cable and found what he was looking for.

He tapped out a preprogrammed number to a voice-over-Internet phone currently in the United States. He sat silent and still, waiting for the call to be answered.

'This is Crane.'

'Crane, Center.'

'Go ahead.'

'Prosper Street, number 3333, Washington, D.C.'

A pause. Then, 'Do you have any more information on the location and disposition of forces there?'

'I will have the local controller tasked to obtain and provide more intelligence in advance of your arrival. That will take a day, so prepare to act within two days. Time is of the essence.'

'Very well. What is the target at that location?'

Center replied instantly, 'Your target is every living thing at that location.'

'Understood. Will comply.'

'*Shi-shi.*'

Tong hung up and put the matter out of his mind. Now he checked his messages from his controllers. He glanced at a few, ignored a few others on subjects in which he was not interested, and then settled on a subject that he found extremely interesting.

Hendley Associates, West Odenton, Maryland, USA.

Tong had tasked a new controller on this case, and ordered that a field asset be brought in to supplant his understanding of just what this company had to do with the American CIA. He had watched Hendley Associates months earlier when they began tracking a team of Libyan ex-intelligence officers one of his controllers had hired to do some ad hoc work in the Istanbul area. The Libyans were not terribly competent and were responsible for getting discovered, so when the controller told Tong that one of his proxy teams of field personnel had been compromised, Tong ordered his controller to take no action other than to monitor the attack and find out more about the attacking force.

Soon it became clear that men from the American company Hendley Associates were involved.

It was a strange company, Hendley. Tong and his people had been interested in them for some time. The President's own son worked there, as had, until just weeks prior, John Clark, the man involved in the Jack Ryan affair during the election the previous year. A former U.S. senator named Gerry Hendley ran the organization.

A financial management firm that also assassinated people and seemed to support the CIA. Of course, killing the Libyans in Istanbul had been a curiosity to Tong; it did not slow his operation down in the slightest. But their participation in the kidnapping of Zha the previous week was deeply concerning to Tong.

Tong and his people had their eyes and ears on hundreds of companies around the world that were on a contract basis for intelligence organizations, militaries, and other secretive government bureaucracies. Tong suspected Hendley Associates was some sort of deniable off-the-books operation set up with the knowledge of the U.S. government.

Much like Tong and his Ghost Ship.

He wanted to know more, and he was investigating Hendley via different avenues. And one of those avenues had just opened up. This new report in his hand explained that the virus implanted on the Hendley Associates network had reported for business. Within the next very few days the manager on the project expected to have a better understanding of just what Hendley's role was in the American intelligence community. The IT director of the company – Tong scanned down to see the man's name again, Gavin Biery, strange name – had been evaluated by Tong's coders, and they had determined him to be highly competent. Even though their RAT was in the network, it would take more time than normal to carefully exfiltrate information.

Tong very much looked forward to that report.

He had considered just dispatching Crane and his men to terminate Hendley's operation. If he had known they would come and help the CIA take Zha from him, he would have done just that, either in Istanbul or at their offices in West Odenton. But now Tong considered them 'the devil he knew.' He was inside their network, he could see who they were, what they were doing. With visualization of their operation he could control them.

Of course, if Hendley Associates became problematic again to his operation, he could always send Crane and the other men of the Divine Sword.

The speech by Chairman of the Central Military Commission Su Ke Qiang was delivered to students and faculty of the Chinese Naval University of Engineering in Wuhan, but the men and women in the audience were just props. The message was clearly intended for international consumption.

Unlike President Wei, Chairman Su had no interest in presenting himself as charming or polished. He was a big man, with a big chest full of medals, and his projection of personal power mimicked his plans for his nation and his aspirations for the ascendance of the People's Liberation Army.

His opening remarks extolled the PLAN, the People's Liberation Army-Navy, and he promised the students he was doing everything in his power to make sure they had all the equipment, technology, and training they would need to meet China's future threats head-on.

Those watching in the West expected yet another Chairman Su speech, full of bluster and vague ominous warnings to the West, thinly veiled threats about Chinese territorial claims without any concrete details.

The same speech, more or less, he had been giving since he was a three-star in the General Staff Department shortly after the war with Russia and the USA.

But today was different. Today he drew specific lines.

Reading from a printed page and not a teleprompter, he discussed the recent air-to-air encounters over the Taiwan Strait, framing them as inevitable results of America's sending warplanes into a crowded but peaceful part of the world. He then said, 'In light of the new danger, China is hereby excluding all international warships from the Strait of Taiwan and the South China Sea other than those in national-border waters or those with permission to traverse Chinese territory. All nations other than those with national boundaries in the SCS will be required to apply to China for permission to pass through its territory.

'This, of course, includes all undersea warships, as well.

'Any warship entering this exclusion zone will be considered an attacking vessel, and it will be treated as such. For

434

the good of peace and stability, we encourage the world community to oblige. This is China's sovereign territory I am speaking about. We will not steam our ships up the Thames River into London or up the Hudson River to New York City; we only ask that other nations offer us the same courtesy.'

The students and faculty present at the Naval University of Engineering cheered, and this led to an extremely rare event. Chairman Su looked up from his speech and smiled.

Excluding non-indigenous warships from the South China Sea created immediate difficulties for a few nations, but none more so than India. India was two years into a contract with Vietnam to conduct exploration for oil and natural gas in a part of Vietnam's Exclusive Economic Zone in international waters off their coast. To date, the exploration had not been particularly fruitful, but India had two corvettes, the *Kora* and the *Kulish*, as well as the *Satpura*, a larger frigate, protecting more than one dozen exploration vessels in the South China Sea only one hundred thirty miles from the Chinese coast.

PLAAF aircraft flown from Hainan Island, on the southern tip of China, began flying low and threatening over the Indian ships the day after Chairman Su's speech, and three days after the speech a Chinese diesel sub bumped the *Kulish*, injuring several Indian sailors.

India did not take this provocation lying down. New Delhi announced publicly that one of their aircraft carriers had been invited by the Vietnamese to make a port call at Da Nang, Vietnam's third-largest city. The carrier, already off the western coast of Malaysia, would enter through the Strait of Malacca along with a few support vessels, and then head up the coast of Vietnam.

The infuriated Chinese immediately demanded the Indians keep their carrier out of the SCS, and a second bump of an Indian corvette by a Chinese sub indicated that the PLAN meant business.

In Washington, President Ryan saw nothing good coming out of India's carrier cruise of the South China Sea, and he sent his secretary of state, Scott Adler, to New Delhi to implore the prime minister of India to cancel the action and to move their other naval vessels in the SCS into Vietnamese territorial waters until a diplomatic solution to the situation could be found.

But the Indians would not back down.

47

Melanie Kraft and Jack Ryan, Jr, had enjoyed their first night out together in more than a week. She had been working late into the evening at ODNI and he had been out of town. He'd told her he was in Tokyo; he'd been there on business before, and it seemed like it would explain his slight jet lag upon his return.

Tonight they'd eaten at one of Jack's favorite restaurants, the Old Ebbitt Grill, right next door to the White House. Ryan had come here often with his family when he was younger, and it became a weekly get-together place for him and his friends when he was at Georgetown. This evening the food was just as good as he remembered it, perhaps even more so because in Hong Kong he'd not had the opportunity to sit down and enjoy a good meal.

After dinner Jack invited Melanie back to Columbia, and she'd readily agreed. As soon as they were back at his place they went to the sofa. They watched TV for a while, which for them meant making out through fifty percent of the programs and one hundred percent of the commercials.

Around eleven, Melanie excused herself to go to the bathroom. She took her purse with her, and when she was alone she reached in and removed the small drive with the iPhone connector on the end. The device was no larger than a matchbook, and Lipton had explained that she need not do anything but attach Jack's phone to the device, and then the upload would happen automatically in about thirty seconds.

Her hands were perspiring with nerves and her mind was nearly overtaken with guilt.

She had had a week to think about this and to justify what she was doing. She recognized that having a locator on his phone would be preferable to having an entire surveillance team following him twenty-four hours a day, and since she did not believe he was involved in anything illegal or even unethical, she knew nothing would come out of a few days of tracking that led nowhere.

But in those moments of guilt when she allowed herself to be honest, she recognized fully that she was doing this for her own self-preservation.

This was not something she would do were she not being coerced and threatened by her past.

'Get yourself together,' she whispered to herself, then slipped the tiny device into the pocket of her slacks, and flushed the toilet.

She was out on the couch with Jack a few minutes later. She wanted to add the tracker before they retired to the bedroom, because Jack was a very light sleeper and she did not think for a second she could get around to his side of the bed and attach the device without him stirring. Right now his iPhone was under the lamp on the end table by him; she just needed him to go to the bathroom or the kitchen or back to the bedroom to change into his warm-ups.

As if on cue, Jack stood. 'I'm going to make a nightcap. Can I get you something?'

Her mind raced. What could she request that would keep him busy for a minute?

'What are you having?'

'Maker's Mark.'

She thought it over. 'Do you have any Baileys Irish Cream?'

'Sure do.'

'On ice, please.'

Jack disappeared through the open kitchen door, and Melanie decided this was her moment. She would easily be able to hear him grabbing ice from the refrigerator for their drinks. She knew she would not have to worry about him popping back out into the living room until then.

She vaulted over to the other side of the couch, glanced down to pull the phone off the end table, and then took the FBI tracker from her pocket. With one hand on each device, she attached them together, all the while keeping her eyes on the door to the kitchen.

Thirty seconds. She counted in her head, even though Lipton had explained to her that the device would vibrate gently when the upload was complete.

In the kitchen she heard the opening and closing of cabinets, and the sound of a bottle being placed on the counter.

Come on! She willed the damn transfer to go faster.

Fifteen, sixteen, seventeen . . .

Jack cleared his throat, and it sounded like he was at the kitchen sink.

Twenty-four, twenty-five, twenty-six . . .

The eleven-o'clock news came on; the first story was about U.S. Navy jets engaging Chinese fighter planes over the Strait of Taiwan.

Melanie looked toward the opening to the kitchen, worried Jack might run out to catch the news if he heard about it.

Thirty. She started to take the device off the phone, but then realized she had not felt the vibration.

Damn it! Melanie forced herself to wait. She had not heard the sound of ice cubes yet, so she told herself Jack would be in the kitchen for a moment more.

The device in her left hand buzzed, and instantly she separated the two gadgets, slipped the FBI tracking drive into her pocket, and reached to put the phone back on the table. As she was placing it there, she stopped herself suddenly.

Had it been up or down?

She could not remember. *Shit.* She looked at the table and the phone, tried to remember which way it had been lying when she grabbed it. After no more than a second, she flipped it upside down, then placed it back on the table.

Done.

'What are you doing with my phone?'

Melanie jumped as she looked back to the kitchen. Jack stood there with a glass of Baileys in his hand.

'What?' she asked, her voice croaking a little.

'What were you doing to my phone?'

'Oh. Just checking the time.'

Jack stood there, looking at her.

'What?' she asked. Perhaps too defensively, she realized.

'Your phone is right there.' He nodded to the side of the couch where she had been sitting. 'Seriously. What's going on?'

'Going on?' Melanie felt her heartbeat, and she was certain Jack must have heard it.

'Yeah. Why were you looking at my phone?'

The two just stared at each other for several seconds while the news report discussed the air war over Taiwan.

Finally, Melanie said, 'Because I want to know if there is someone else.'

'Someone else?'

'Yes. Come on, Jack. You go away on trips all the time, we don't talk while you're out of town, you can never say when you are coming back. You can tell me, I'm a big girl. Do you have someone else?'

Jack shook his head slowly. 'Of course not. My job . . . my job takes me places suddenly from time to time. It always

440

has. Before last week I hadn't traveled anywhere in a couple of months.'

Melanie nodded. 'I know. It's stupid. It's just that this last time, I would have liked to have heard from you.'

Jack sighed. 'I'm sorry. I should have made time to call. You're right.'

Melanie stood and walked across the room to him, embraced him tightly. 'I'm just stressed out right now. Hormones. I'm sorry.'

'Nothing to be sorry for. I really didn't know it bothered you.'

Melanie Kraft reached for the glass in his hand and took it. She smiled.

'Did you forget the ice?'

Jack looked at the glass. 'The bottle was in the freezer. It's basically a milk shake as is. Thought that would work.'

Melanie sipped it. 'Oh. Yeah, that's great.'

She turned with her drink to go back to the couch, but Jack stood there for a moment, his eyes on his phone.

He'd known she was suspicious of him, and he'd given her much to be suspicious about. He didn't like the fact that he'd just caught her checking up on him, but he could not say he didn't understand it. He let it go, told himself he needed to be careful to keep her happy, and put the matter out of his mind.

Valentin Kovalenko sat at the little desk in the furnished rental flat he'd acquired in Washington, D.C. He had just logged in to Cryptogram to let Center know he was in place and ready for instructions, and he was waiting for a reply.

The past two days had been a whirlwind. He'd cleared out of Barcelona, then trained to Madrid and flown from there to Charlotte, North Carolina. He was stressed about his trip to the USA; he knew there were dangers there for him on a par with what he faced in his own country. To combat the shakes he'd developed worrying about passing through U.S. immigration, he'd gotten himself good and drunk on the plane, and he passed through the airport control formalities in a calm, collected stupor.

In Charlotte he rented a car and then drove up the coast to D.C. He spent a night in a hotel, and moved into this base-ment apartment underneath the front staircase of a brownstone in upscale Dupont Circle.

He had actually been ready to work since noon today, and it was eight p.m. now, but before he even pulled his laptop out of his backpack or turned on his mobile phone he'd attempted to contact an acquaintance at the Russian embassy here. He wasn't sure if the old SVR colleague was still posted in Washington, so he found a pay phone outside a post office and then called local directory assistance.

The man was not listed under his own name, which was no big surprise, but Kovalenko checked a couple of aliases the man had used on operations abroad, and only then did he accept the fact he would not so easily wend his way out of his obligations with the Center organization by phoning a friend for help.

After a lengthy surveillance detection run he went to the Russian embassy on Wisconsin Avenue, but he did not dare get too close. Instead he remained a block away and watched men and women come and go for an hour. He had not shaved in a week, and this helped him with his disguise, but he knew he needed to limit his exposure here. He did another SDR on his way back to his neighborhood, taking his time to get on and off public transportation.

He'd dropped by a liquor store on 18th Street just around the corner from his place and picked up a bottle of Ketel

One and a few beers, returned to his flat, then put the vodka in the freezer and downed the beers.

His afternoon, then, was a complete bust, and now he found himself sitting at his computer and waiting on Center to reply.

Green text appeared on the black screen. 'You are in position?'

'Yes,' he typed.

'We have an operation for you that is most urgent.'

'Okay.'

'But first we need to discuss your movements today.'

Kovalenko felt a twitch of pain in his heart. *No. No way in hell they tracked me.* He'd left his phone on his desk in his apartment, and his laptop had not even been unpacked. He'd used no computer, he'd not seen anyone tracking him through his SDRs.

They were bluffing.

'I did exactly as you asked.'

'You went to the Russian embassy.'

The pain in his heart increased; it was just panic, but he fought it. They were still bluffing, he was certain. It would be easy for them to guess he would try to make contact with SVR associates as soon as he got to Washington. He had been a good one hundred yards from the embassy.

'You are guessing,' he wrote, 'and you guessed wrong.'

A photograph appeared on his Cryptogram window without warning. It was Kovalenko, surveillance quality, and he was sitting in a small park across from the Russian embassy on Wisconsin Street. Clearly it was taken this afternoon, perhaps from a traffic camera.

Valentin closed his eyes for a moment. They *were* everywhere.

He stormed into his kitchen and took the bottle of Ketel

One out of the freezer. Quickly he grabbed a water glass from his cabinet and poured two fingers of the chilled vodka. He polished off the glass in a few gulps and then filled it again.

A minute later he sat back down at the desk. 'What the fuck do you want from me?'

'I want you to obey your directives.'

'And what will you do if I don't? Send the Saint Petersburg mob after me? Here in America? I don't think so. You can hack a security camera, but you can't touch me here.'

There was no response for a long moment. Valentin looked at his computer while he drained the second glass of vodka. Just as he put the glass back on the tiny desk, there was a knock on the door behind him.

Kovalenko bolted upright and spun around. Sweat that had formed on his forehead in the past minutes dripped into his eyes.

He looked down at the Cryptogram window. There was still no response.

And then . . . 'Open the door.'

Kovalenko had no weapons; he was not that kind of intelligence officer. He ran into the little kitchen off the living room, and he pulled a long kitchen knife out of a butcher's block. He returned to the living room, his eyes on the door.

He rushed over to the computer. Typed with shaking hands, 'What's going on?'

'You have a visitor. Open the door or he will break it down.'

Kovalenko peered through the small window next to the door, and he saw nothing but the steps up to street level. He unlocked the door and opened it, his knife low to his side.

He saw the figure now in the darkness, standing next to the garbage can under the stairs up to the brownstone. He

444

was a man, Kovalenko judged from the stature, but he stood as still as a statue, and Valentin could not make out any of his features.

Kovalenko backed into his living room, and the figure moved toward him, came near the doorway, but did not enter the apartment.

From the light of the living room Kovalenko saw a man, perhaps in his late twenties. He was solidly built and fit-looking, with an angular forehead and very pronounced and high cheekbones. He looked to the Russian like some sort of cross between an Asian and an American Indian warrior. Serious and stern, the man wore a black leather jacket, black jeans, and black tennis shoes.

'You are not Center.' Valentin said it as a statement.

'I am Crane,' was the response, and Kovalenko instantly could tell the man was Chinese.

'Crane.' Kovalenko took another half-step back. The man was intimidating as hell; he looked to the Russian like a stone-cold killer, like an animal not fit for civilized society.

Crane unzipped his jacket and opened it. A black automatic pistol was tucked in his waistband. 'Put down the knife. If I kill you without sanction, Center will be angry with me. I do not want Center angry.'

Valentin took another half-step back and bumped into the desk. He placed the knife on the desk.

Crane did not reach for his gun, but he clearly wanted it displayed. He spoke in heavily accented English. 'We are here, close to you. If Center tells me to kill you, you are dead. Do you understand?'

Kovalenko just nodded.

Crane motioned to the laptop computer on the desk behind the Russian. Valentin turned and looked at it. At that moment a new paragraph appeared on Cryptogram.

'Crane and his men are force multipliers for our operation. If I could realize all my schemes from a computer keyboard, I would do that. But sometimes other measures must be taken. People like you are used. And people like Crane are used.'

Kovalenko looked away from the computer toward Crane, but he was gone. Quickly Kovalenko shut the door and locked it.

He returned to the desk and typed, 'Assassins?'

'Crane and his men have their tasks. Making sure you follow directives is one of their tasks.'

Valentin wondered if, all this time, he'd been working for Chinese intelligence.

When he thought it over, some of the pieces fit. But others did not.

He typed, his hands still shaking, 'It is one thing to work with the mob in Russia. It is very different to control teams of assassins in the United States. This has nothing to do with industrial espionage.'

The uncharacteristically long pause by Center was disquieting. Valentin wondered if he should have kept these suspicions close to his vest.

'It is all business.'

'Bullshit!' shouted Kovalenko to his apartment, but he did not type this.

When he did not respond, a new line popped up on Cryptogram. 'Are you ready to hear your next assignment?'

'Yes,' Kovalenko typed out.

'Good.'

48

He who conquers the sea is all powerful.' It was the motto of the INS *Viraat*, the Indian aircraft carrier that docked in Da Nang one week to the day after Chairman Su Ke Qiang ordered all foreign warships out of the South China Sea.

The *Viraat* began its life in 1959 as Britain's HMS *Hermes* and sailed under the Union Jack for decades before it was sold to India in the 1980s. No one could argue that the carrier was still cutting-edge, but a recent refitting by the Indian Navy had extended the *Viraat's* life a few years, and, new technology or old, it was an important symbol of the Indian nation.

At just under thirty thousand tons, it was significantly less than a third the size of the *Nimitz*-class *Ronald Reagan*. There were 1,750 sailors and pilots on board, as well as fourteen Harrier fighter jets, and eight Sea King attack helicopters.

On the second day after the carrier arrived in Da Nang, one of its Sea King helicopters was patrolling in India's oil exploration zone when it spotted a Chinese *Song*-class submarine moving to within ramming range of an Indian oil exploration vessel. The sub struck and damaged the ship minutes later, sending the thirty-five civilian crew members of the exploration ship into lifeboats. The Sea King began ferrying the crew to other vessels nearby, but not before calling in the antisubmarine-warfare-capable INS *Kamorta*, a corvette that had moved into the SCS along with the *Viraat*. The *Kamorta* raced to the area and got a radar fix on the *Song*-class sub.

The *Kamorta* fired one 213-millimeter rocket from its deck-mounted RBU-6000, a Soviet-designed antisubmarine rocket launcher. The rocket sailed from the horseshoe-shaped launcher, flew through the air for five kilometers, and then dove into the water. It sank to a depth of two hundred fifty meters but exploded prematurely, inflicting no damage on the sub, which had dived to a depth of three hundred twenty meters.

A second missile also failed to find its target.

The *Song*-class sub escaped the encounter. But this was the excuse the Chinese were waiting for.

Three hours after the attack on the Chinese submarine, just after dark, the *Ningbo*, a Chinese guided-missile destroyer on station between Hainan and the Vietnamese coast, went to battle stations. It launched four SS-N-22 missiles, NATO classification Sunburn, a Russian-developed anti-ship missile.

The Sunburns streaked over the water at Mach 2.2, three times faster than the American Harpoon anti-ship missile. The radar and guidance systems in the nose of the weapons kept them on target as they closed on the biggest ship within range.

The *Viraat*.

As the lightning-fast flying three-hundred-kilogram armor-piercing warheads neared their target, anti-missile defensive SAMs on board the *Viraat* fired in a desperate attempt to shoot down the Sunburns before impact. Miraculously, the first SAM out of its launch tube struck the first incoming missile just four kilometers from impact, but within moments all three of the remaining SS-N-22s slammed into the starboard-side hull of the big ship, with the second missile striking high enough to send three Sea King helos into the air in a fireball and to destroy two of the Harriers on the deck with the resulting shrapnel.

The carrier did not sink – three three-hundred-kilogram warheads were not enough ordnance to put the thirty-thousand-ton ship on the ocean floor, but the missiles succeeded in effecting a 'mission kill' – a naval term for rendering a vessel useless as a war-fighting instrument.

Two hundred forty-six sailors and airmen were killed as well, and the *Viraat*'s support ships all raced to the aid of the carrier to help put out fires and to pull crew members from the black water.

Two Harrier pilots in the air at the time of the accident found themselves with nowhere to land, as they were too low on fuel to make it to their divert airfields in Vietnam. Both pilots ejected into the ocean and survived, though their aircraft were lost to the waves.

While the PLAN immediately declared the attack a defensive response to India's attack on the submarine earlier in the day, it became abundantly clear to the world that China had determined that the South China Sea was worth killing for.

Valentin Kovalenko rented a white Nissan Maxima from a rental lot near Ronald Reagan Airport and drove it north over the Francis Scott Key Bridge and into Georgetown.

He was on yet another milk run for Center, or so he deduced from the instructions that Center gave him the evening before, shortly after his face-to-face introduction to Crane.

Kovalenko did not imagine today's work would be as dramatic as last night's events. He was to pick up a car, and then conduct surveillance on a location just two miles from his flat.

As usual, Kovalenko did not know a single thing about his operation past his instructions.

He drove through Georgetown for a few minutes before

he went to his target location, just to make certain he had not acquired a tail. It was good tradecraft, of course, but Valentin was not just looking for enemy surveillance. He spent as much time keeping his eyes peeled for Center, or someone from the organization he worked for, as he did for the local police or American counterintelligence operatives.

He turned off Wisconsin and onto Prosper Street, a quiet two-lane row of big Federal and early Victorian homes with tiny front yards, as well as an elementary school and some small retail shops. Kovalenko kept just slightly below the speed limit as he scanned for the address he was looking for.

3333.

He found it on the right. It was a two-centuries-old two-story home on a small piece of hilly land hemmed in tight on both sides by a redbrick school and a two-story duplex. A black wrought-iron fence surrounded it, and the front of the house was covered in leafy trees and bushes. It looked like a zero-lot haunted mansion. There was a garage down at street level, and winding stone steps led from the gate at the sidewalk in the front of the property to the home above.

Valentin drove around the corner, pulled into the small parking lot of a dry cleaner's, and here he used a digital audio recorder to help him remember as many details about the property as possible. When finished, he drove around back and looked at the street to the north of 3333 Prosper. Here he found that a back alley went behind the property, between the two streets.

For his third pass he went by on foot, parking his car on Wisconsin and doing a full circle of the block, taking time to look over many different properties, not just his target location.

He walked down the back alleyway, past the school grounds, and he found there was a small gate that provided access to the target location.

In all his passes on all sides he did not see any hint of movement in or around the home, and he noted there were dry autumn leaves on the steps leading to the front door that looked like they had been there for a while. While he could not see inside the garage, and he had no idea if there was direct access to the house from inside the garage, it was his best estimate that the property was not occupied at the moment.

He could not possibly fathom what Center wanted with this location. Maybe he was looking for some local real estate. As vague as his handler had been about what he needed to know about the place, Valentin wondered if all his subterfuge was unnecessary.

Maybe he should have just walked up to the front door and knocked and asked for a tour of the place.

No. That was not Kovalenko's style. He knew the best thing for him personally was to keep his interactions with others to a minimum.

He returned to his car on Wisconsin and headed back to the airport to return the rental. He'd go home, report his findings to Center via Cryptogram, and then get good and drunk.

John Clark stood still as a stone on his back pasture, and a cold autumn wind blew oak leaves across his field of vision, but he did not focus on them as they passed.

Suddenly he moved; his left hand whipped across the front of his body, to his waistband under the right side of his leather bomber jacket, and then it drew back out, pulling with it a black SIG Sauer .45-caliber pistol with a short, stubby silencer attached. The pistol rose to John's eye level, centered on a steel disk the width of a grapefruit that hung from a metal chain at chest level ten yards off, just in front of a backstop of hay bales.

John Clark fired one-handed at the small target, a double tap that cracked the cold air despite the suppressor.

A pair of satisfyingly loud metal 'pings' echoed across the pasture as the bullets exploded against the steel.

All this took place in under two seconds.

John Clark used his right hand to move his jacket aside, and then he resecured the pistol back in his cross-draw appendix holster.

Clark had come a long way in a week of daily handgun drills, but he was not satisfied with his performance. He'd like to cut his time in half. And he'd like to achieve his hits from twice this distance.

But that would take both time and commitment, and though John had the time – he had nothing but time these days – for the first time in his adult life he wondered whether he really had the commitment he needed to achieve an objective.

As disciplined an individual as he was, there was something about a strong likelihood that you would need your gunfighting skills to save your own life in the future that tended to focus your energies into being an excellent student.

And John knew he would not be shooting his gun in anger anymore.

Still, he had to admit, the movements and the gun smoke and the feel of the weapon in his hand – even in his *left* hand – felt damn good.

John reloaded a magazine on the small wooden table next to him, told himself he'd run through a few more boxes of ammo before lunch.

He had nowhere else to be today.

49

President Ryan felt like he was spending as much time in the Situation Room as he was in the Oval Office.

The usual suspects were there. Mary Pat Foley and Scott Adler on his right. Bob Burgess and Colleen Hurst on his left. Filling the rest of the table were Arnie van Damm, Vice President Pollan, Ambassador Ken Li, and various high-ranking generals and admirals from the Pentagon.

On the monitor at the far end of the room, Admiral Mark Jorgensen, commander of the Pacific Fleet, sat at a conference table with a laptop open in front of him.

Ambassador Li's visit to Washington was the main reason for the meeting. The day before, he had been summoned by China's foreign minister and given a message to be hand-delivered to the President of the United States.

Li had flown through the night, arrived the next day, and done as China asked.

The message had been succinct. China was directly warning the United States to move its *Ronald Reagan* carrier group three hundred nautical miles from the coast of China or risk 'accidental and regrettable incidents.'

At present the *Reagan* was ninety nautical miles northeast of Taipei, meaning it could easily send its aircraft into the strait on patrols. Pushing it back to three hundred miles meant that the strait would be out of range for most regular flight operations.

Ryan did not want to do it, he wanted to show support to Taiwan, but he also recognized the *Reagan* was in the line of fire of virtually hundreds of missiles as powerful as, or more powerful than, those that had hit the *Viraat* in the South China Sea.

Secretary of Defense Burgess started the meeting by first updating everyone on Chinese aggression in the South China Sea in the days since the attack on the INS *Viraat*. PLAN warships had been seen as far south as Indonesian waters, and small landing parties had come ashore on several unoccupied islands in the Philippines. China's one aircraft carrier, the *Liaoning*, set sail from Hainan into the South China Sea, surrounded by a full complement of missile frigates, destroyers, refuelers, and other support ships.

The secretary of defense said, 'This is a flexing of muscle, but it is a pretty pathetic show.'

'What's pathetic about it?' asked Ryan.

Burgess said, 'The carrier doesn't have any airplanes.'

'*What?*' Jack asked in astonishment.

'It's carrying about twenty-five attack and transport helicopters, but the Chinese don't have even one squadron of jets that are carrier-qualified. This cruise by the *Liaoning* is . . .' He hesitated. 'I was going to say it was just for show, but I can't say that. They will likely go out and attack some things and kill some folks. They just aren't operating it like a real aircraft carrier, because they don't have the capability.'

Ryan said, 'I have a strong suspicion that China state media will forget to mention that the carrier isn't operating with fixed-wing aircraft on board.'

Kenneth Li said, 'You can take that to the bank, Mr President. Most of China will react with fierce pride that, as far as they know, the *Liaoning* has set sail to claim the SCS.'

Ryan next asked, 'Have there been more attacks over the Strait of Taiwan?'

'Not since the attack on the *Viraat*, but don't expect that to hold. There has been some bad weather over the strait; that's probably got more to do with it than any feeling by China that they have gone too far,' Burgess replied.

Ryan turned to Ambassador Li. 'What does your gut tell you about what is going on, Ken?'

The Chinese-American ambassador said, 'The attack on the *Viraat* had very little to do with the conflict between China and India, and much more to do with the conflict between China and the United States.'

Ryan said, 'It was a signal to our Navy. A signal to me.'

Li nodded and said, 'A signal that said, "Stay away."'

'As messages go, killing two hundred and forty-something souls is pretty loud and clear.'

Li agreed.

Ryan said, 'Wei singles us out, tells us not to meddle in affairs that don't concern us. What specific thing are they pointing to when they threaten us like this? Just the carrier?'

'Partially they are pointing to our increased engagement in the region. But much of it is guilt by association, Mr President. The countries there that are our allies, and that is virtually everyone in the SCS region, are hyping their relationship with us, insinuating that we will protect them in any conflict with China. This doesn't help matters over there. Standoffs between Chinese and Philippine vessels have been increasing. Ditto with Indonesia and Vietnam.'

'The Chinese really feel the entire South China Sea belongs to them?'

'Indeed they do,' Li said. 'They are doing everything in their ever-expanding power to extend Chinese sovereignty. They are pushing the Navies of Vietnam, the Philippines, Indonesia, and India out of what they see as their own territory, and they do not care about international law. At the same time, they are doing their best to foment armed conflict in the strait with the air-to-air attacks.'

Li paused, but Ryan could tell he had something else he wanted to say.

'Speak up, Ken. Your input is very valuable to me.'

Li said, 'China's hegemonic aspirations are not the only reason for the current conflict. The thing is, Mr President, you can't underestimate the strength of the animosity against you personally in the top echelons of the military.'

'You are saying they hate my guts.'

'I . . . I am saying that. Yes, sir. They were humiliated by the war, and if you read the statements by the Chinese generals that are made for local consumption, you will see that they want glory against the United States.'

Ryan looked to Admiral Jorgensen on the monitor. 'Admiral, what do you think about the message from the Chinese? Do we move the *Reagan* back to three hundred miles?'

Jorgensen, of course, knew he would be asked the question. His answer was measured. 'Mr President, the Chinese have been acting irrationally for the past month. I think it would be suicide for them to attack the *Reagan* or any of its support ships, but I am not going to say that I don't think they will do it. If you had asked me a month ago whether the PLAAF would fire on U.S. Navy and Marine fighters flying over international waters, I would have said that I regarded that as incredibly unlikely.'

'Do they have the capability, technology-wise, to hit the *Ronald Reagan*?'

Without an instant's hesitation Jorgensen said, 'Oh, yes, sir. It can be done. We have anti-missile defensive measures, and they are effective, but not against a sustained barrage of ballistic and cruise missiles fired from the land, air, and sea. If the Chinese really want to sink the *Reagan*, I am not going to tell you we can prevent it.'

Jorgensen continued, 'But if they wanted to affect our capability to stand and fight on their turf, they would not have to hit the *Reagan*. They could much more easily take out crucial support ships that are not as well protected.'

'Explain.'

'Our nuclear-powered carriers and subs can operate for years without refueling, but the rest of the fleet, all those support ships, they are all being fueled by only six tankers in the Pacific Ocean. It would not be impossible for the Chinese to target those tankers and severely degrade the mobility of the Seventh Fleet. Our ability to project power would be limited. We will be like a bear chained to a tree. The tree would be Pearl Harbor, and we would not be able to venture very far. We have two hundred eighty-five ships deployed around the world, and fifty percent of them are in the Western Pacific. These anti-ship missiles China possesses are a real danger.'

Mary Pat Foley said, 'With China's anti-access/area-denial capabilities, the balance of power has tilted away from the U.S. and our allies in the region, and they know it. They think we would be idiots to challenge them in their territory.'

Burgess said, 'We are thinking that that is what is going on here. Getting us into a short, intense fight on their turf, bloodying our nose, so that we will go home and stay home.'

Ryan said, 'Then they make a play for Taiwan.'

Mary Pat said, 'That's the golden ring, isn't it? The Chinese are trying to destroy the Taiwanese government. They do that successfully, and then they move in and pick up the pieces.'

'You don't mean literally move in?'

'No, not immediately. They will not invade Taiwan. Instead, they want to put their own people in positions of power, weaken the anti-PRC parties, damage the economy and the island's political relationships with its allies. They do that, and they don't have to invade. They just have to mop up. They think they can end the ROC by slowly, over time, reabsorbing it into the PRC.

'They have been accepting more risk in Taiwan lately. Pulling out all the stops in getting informants and spies. Buying off politicians sympathetic to the PRC.'

President Ryan discussed the matter a few minutes more, and then he sat quietly at the end of the table for a moment. Finally he looked up at Jorgensen. 'Push the *Reagan* back to three hundred miles exactly, but also bring the *Nimitz* battle group closer. Move her into the East China Sea.

'Send a message that we aren't going to play into whatever the hell they are trying to goad us into doing at the same time, but we are not running away.'

Burgess said, 'If we pull the *Reagan* out to three hundred miles, Mr President, we won't be able to patrol the Taiwan Strait. The ROC will be on its own.'

Ryan's eyes settled on Bob Burgess. 'Is there any way we can covertly move air support to Taiwan?'

'Covertly?'

'Yes.'

Foley spoke up: 'Espionage cases out of the ROC have shot through the roof in the past couple of years. China is now dumping money into its spy services, bribing everyone with access to political or military information who will play with them. It's a tough place to do anything without the PRC knowing about it.'

Jack said, '"Tough" means it will be difficult. That was not my question. My question was: Can it be done?'

Burgess said, 'There are contingency plans worked up. We have a plan to put in limited numbers of Marine fighter pilots, outfitting them in ROC aircraft. We aren't talking about large numbers. But it would be a show of support for the ROC government.'

President Ryan nodded. 'Do it. But do it right. Don't just throw a couple of guys out there without cover or support. If they are detected by the PRC, it just might be the provocation they need to attack Taiwan.'

'Yes, Mr President. I understand the stakes.'

Jack Ryan stood and ended the meeting by saying, 'Send in the Marines.'

50

Su did not like the way Wei had summoned him today. He had meetings scheduled all day at Zhongnanhai, but shortly before noon his office contacted him and told him President Wei demanded his presence in his living quarters at lunch.

Su bristled at the intemperance of his coequal demanding anything of him, but he cut short his noonday meeting and went to Wei's quarters without delay.

It was not as if he needed time to prepare for the conversation with the president. He knew *exactly* what the man would say.

The men embraced and called each other Comrade and asked after their family members, but these pleasantries were dealt with in seconds, not minutes.

In short order, Wei sat down with Su and spoke in a concerned voice. 'This is not at all how I pictured events unfolding.'

'Events? I take that to mean events in the South China Sea and the strait?'

Wei nodded and said, 'I feel like you have manipulated me to some degree, taking my initial program for economic improvement and folding it into your own agenda.'

'General Secretary, we have a saying in the military: "The enemy gets a vote." What you have seen over the past weeks – the aggression by India despite our clear warnings, aggression by the United States as we executed carefully calculated maneuvers in the Taiwan Strait to display our readiness to act against any show of force by the ROC – these situations were brought on by our adversaries. Of course, if all my . . . excuse me, if all *our* forces stayed at their bases or in their ports, well, then certainly none of this would have happened, but in order to achieve our territorial objectives, which will, in so doing, help us achieve our economic objectives, we had to make these forays into contested areas.'

Wei was almost overcome by all the rhetoric. He lost his train of thought for a moment. Su was known as a firebrand, not as an orator, but Wei felt the man had just manipulated time and space in order to win his argument.

'The cyberattacks against America –'

'Have no connection to China.'

Wei was surprised. 'Are you saying we are not involved?'

Su smiled. 'I am saying they cannot be connected to us.'

Wei hesitated again.

Su took the opportunity to add, 'Within the past hour my naval intelligence service has notified me that the *Ronald Reagan* carrier group has begun moving to the northeast.'

Wei cocked his head in surprise now. 'And we think this is a reaction to our demand that they move back to three hundred nautical miles?'

Su said, 'I am certain of it.'

This brightened President Wei immediately. 'So Jack Ryan can be reasoned with, after all.'

Su fought to keep a calm gaze. No, of course Ryan could not be reasoned with. He could only be threatened or beaten. But Wei chose to look at this military brinksmanship as some sort of moment of détente.

Idiot, Su thought.

'Yes,' he said. 'President Ryan only wants what's best for his country. Quitting the region is what's best for him as well as us. He is learning slowly, but moving the *Reagan* shows us he *is* learning.'

And with that, Wei's anger seemed to dissipate. He talked for the next half-hour about his plans for the future of the economy. About potential state-run enterprise opportunities in the SCS and his hope that the transition in Taiwan back to mainland rule would be even quicker and more painless than his greatest hopes.

Su parroted Wei's ambitions, and struggled not to look at his watch.

Finally Wei drew the meeting to a close. But before Su left Wei's quarters, the president regarded the chairman for a long moment. Clearly he hesitated to ask the next question. 'If the circumstances change. If we decided the time is not right . . . will we still be able to stop this?'

'Stop China's growth? China's only prospect for growth?'

Wei vacillated. 'I mean the most extreme military measures. Some of the larger cyberattacks you hinted at in our earlier discussions and the naval attacks and air attacks.'

'Are you thinking of stopping this?'

'I merely asked the question, Chairman.'

Su smiled thinly. 'I am at your service, General Secretary. I can do whatever you wish. But I will remind you, there is much at stake. The way forward was never going to be without roadblocks.'

'I understand.'

'I hope you do. Adversity is part of the process. As I said before, the enemy gets a vote.'

Wei nodded, his face solemn now.

Su, on the other hand, smiled. He said, 'But Comrade, remember, America voted today, and they voted to get out of our way.'

The five men working at the CIA safe house at 3333 Prosper Street in Georgetown were enjoying a mid-morning break, but they were not enjoying it as much as the young man locked in the soundproof room on the second floor.

Three of the five were armed security, one kept his eyes out the kitchen window toward Prosper Street, and a second stayed on a chair moved to a second-floor bedroom that looked through a magnolia tree and down to the old carriage lane converted into an alley that ran behind the property.

The third security officer stayed downstairs. He was positioned at a kitchen table with a bank of monitors, and here he monitored the radio and the home's robust security system. He kept his eyes on the monitor showing the feed from the four security cameras.

The other two men stayed upstairs, either with their subject or in a small office where they met to plan the next 'interview' with their subject. Several times a day, one or the other of the men would enter the soundproof room with a recording device and a notepad and pen, and he would go through a long list of questions that, so far, the subject had done his best not to answer.

Zha Shu Hai had not been tortured in any physical sense, but he'd been kept awake through the night and subjected to dozens of rounds of interrogations at all hours. Different people asked him the same things in different ways so many times that Zha could not even recall most of the conversations.

He felt certain, however, that he'd said nothing at all about Tong, the Ghost Ship, the UAV hacking, or his breaking into the classified government networks.

He knew he could not hold out indefinitely, but he felt confident he would not have to.

He'd asked for a lawyer at least two hundred times since arriving here in the United States, and he could not understand why one had not been given to him. He'd done time in prison here in America before, and it wasn't bad at all, really, but he knew that was a minimum-security facility and he was now likely in a hell of a lot more trouble because of the UAV attack.

But he was in trouble only if they managed to make the charges against him stick, and Zha had spent enough time in the U.S. system during his previous trial and incarceration to know that right now they didn't have anything on him nearly as explosive as everything *he* had on *them*. The illegal kidnapping, the shooting of the 14K guys in Hong Kong, the sleep deprivation, and so on, and so on.

Zha Shu Hai knew he had to hold out for only a little longer, to use his superior intelligence – the benefit of coming from a superior race – and then the Americans would determine he would not crack.

Zha was exhausted, but that was just a nuisance. He was better than these fools, and he would beat them; he only had to keep his mouth shut. They wouldn't beat him or kill him. These were Americans.

One of the interrogators came back into the room and beckoned Zha to the table. As he climbed off his sleeping mat and reached for the plastic chair, all the lights in the room flickered and then went dark.

'Shit,' said the interrogator as he stepped backward to the door, keeping his eyes on his subject in the dim. He pounded on the door with his fist.

Zha Shu Hai's heart began beating with excitement. He sat down at the chair, placed his hands flat on the table.

He did not expect this. Despite himself, he smiled brightly.

'What's so funny?' asked the interrogator.

Zha had not spoken yet that day, but now he could not hold his tongue. 'You will see what is so funny.'

The man did not understand, but he banged again on the

locked door to the soundproof room. He knew the locks were mechanical, not electrical, so there was no reason why his partner wouldn't let him right out.

After a third time banging against the door, the interrogator went to the one-way observation window. He could not see out, of course, but his partner should have been looking in.

He waved back and forth, and then he heard the bolt lock of the door disengage.

The door opened.

The interrogator began walking out. 'Did we blow a fuse, or is the whole neighborhood –'

An Asian man in a black jacket stood in the doorway; a suppressed handgun was extended out in front of him. He looked down through the sights with cold black eyes.

'What the –'

Crane shot the CIA interrogator through the forehead. His body landed with a muted thud on the floor of the soundproof room.

Zha was careful to keep his hands on the table. He bowed quickly. 'Crane, I have not spoken. I have not said a –'

'Center's orders,' Crane said, and he shot Zha Shu Hai through the forehead as well.

FastByte22's body tumbled out of the plastic chair and onto the floor. He came to rest facedown next to his interrogator.

51

Valentin Kovalenko was walking back to his apartment from the liquor store when he realized that multiple sirens were blaring to the southwest. It occurred to him that they had not just begun; maybe they had been sounding even before he stepped into the tiny soul food café to pick up some carry-out lunch prior to stopping at the liquor store for a fresh bottle of Ketel One.

Almost immediately he had a sinking feeling in the pit of his stomach. He did his best to shake it off as he continued down 17th Street, but well before he turned onto Swann Street he heard helicopters in the air.

'*Nyet,*' he said to himself. '*Nyet.*'

He kept a leisurely pace up Swann Street to his basement apartment, but once inside the door he shot across the living room to the television, dropped his bottle and the take-out food on the sofa, and turned the TV on to a local station.

A soap opera was playing. He switched the channel to another local station and saw a commercial.

He sat down on the couch, his eyes riveted to the screen, waiting for the noon news, which was coming up in five minutes.

While he waited he listened to the distant sirens' wail, and he poured two fingers of lukewarm Ketel One into a glass he'd left on the coffee table the night before.

He chugged it down and poured another.

He almost made himself believe his fears had been unfounded. Until the news began, and they opened with a live

466

helicopter shot over Georgetown. Valentin saw the smoke pouring out of the home on the wooded lot on Prosper Street.

The news anchor knew little, except there were fatalities, and neighbors reported the sound of gunshots from inside the house and a mysterious van.

Kovalenko's first inclination was to drink, and he did so, straight from the bottle this time. His second inclination was to run. To just get up and go, to make tracks in the opposite direction of the sirens.

But he fought this urge, stood, and went to his laptop. His hands were shaking as he typed into Cryptogram: 'What have you done?'

He was surprised by how fast the green letters appeared on the black window in front of him: 'Explain your question.'

Explain my question? Kovalenko's hands hovered over the keys. Finally he typed, '3333.'

The delay was only a few seconds, then, 'You and your work have not been compromised.'

The thirty-six-year-old Russian looked to the ceiling in his room and shouted, 'Fuck!' He typed, 'Who did you kill?'

'That is not connected to you. Stay focused on your daily instructions.'

Kovalenko typed furiously: 'Fuck you! You had me go over there!!!! I could have been seen. I could have been filmed. Who was in the house? Why? *Why?*' He grabbed the Ketel One bottle and hugged it close to his body as he waited for an answer.

Now there was a long pause for the response. Valentin pictured Center waiting to send a message just to give the angry man on the other end of the connection time to calm down.

Finally, 'I am monitoring police and other official traffic.

There has been no mention of you. I assure you there were no CCTV recordings of you or your rented vehicle anywhere around Prosper Street. You do not have anything to worry about, and I do not have time to placate every one of my agents.'

Kovalenko wrote, 'I live less than two miles away. I will have to relocate.'

'Negative. Stay where you are. I need you near Dupont Circle.'

Kovalenko wanted to ask why, but he knew he needn't bother.

Instead he drank for a minute, felt the effects of the vodka calming him somewhat, and then asked, 'The people at 3333? Who were they?'

No response came.

Valentin typed: 'It will be on the news soon enough. Why not just tell me?'

'One was a problem.'

That told Valentin nothing. He started to type a line of question marks, when a new line of green type flashed on the screen.

'The other five were employees of the Central Intelligence Agency.'

Kovalenko just stared at the screen blankly, his mouth slightly open.

He whispered, *'Ni huya sebe'* – Oh, fuck – and held the vodka bottle tight against his heart.

Jack Ryan learned directly from CIA's Intelink-TS network that the biggest news story of the month in D.C., the murder of six men that morning in Georgetown, would have been an even bigger news story if the truth got out.

Traffic between CIA and NSA revealed 3333 Prosper

Street to be a CIA safe house, and communications confirmed that five of the dead were CIA employees and the sixth was the main suspect in the UAV attack.

FastByte22, the guy Jack Ryan and his colleagues helped identify and capture.

Needless to say, Ryan had the entire Campus operational and managerial staff convene in the conference room so he could disseminate the news.

Chavez could not believe the audacity of the crime. 'So the Chinese really have the balls to send a wet team into Georgetown to kill CIA officers?'

'I don't know that it was actually the Chinese who did it,' Director of Analysis Rick Bell said as he walked into the conference room. 'We just intercepted a CIA message to U.S. Cyber Command at Fort Meade. In one of FastByte's interrogations, apparently one where he was severely sleep-deprived, he mentioned the name Tong Kwok Kwan as the true identity of Center. Maybe Center did it as punishment for giving up his real name.'

'What do we know about this Tong guy?' Granger asked.

Ryan said, 'That's Dr K. K. Tong. Adam Yao said he was the father of China's cyberwarfare community.'

Granger couldn't believe it. 'What the hell was he doing in HK working with FastByte and the hackers? He should be in Beijing or in a military installation somewhere.'

Ryan shook his head. 'He had a falling-out with them. He's a wanted man in China.'

Chavez said, 'Maybe they kissed and made up and he's working with the Chinese again. The PLA. I can't believe for a second that some ad hoc computer hacking organization is doing all this just for their own murky objectives. This act today sounds like it has state sponsorship, just like the UAV hack.'

Gerry said, 'Whoever they are, they had to kill Zha to silence him.'

Jack said, 'But they did not silence him. Gavin has Zha's computer, and you can bet we'll hear a lot from Zha when Gavin reveals what's inside.'

As elite Marine fighter pilots, Major Scott 'Cheese' Stilton and Captain Brandon 'Trash' White had experienced much more in their lives than average thirty-one- and twenty-eight-year-olds, but neither man could say he had ever experienced anything like what they had been up to for the past twenty-four hours.

Just over one day earlier, both men were awakened in the middle of the night by Naval intelligence officers, and then led, bleary-eyed, into the squadron room with the rest of their squadron as well as another squadron of Marines on the *Reagan*. The twenty-four pilots stood at attention when a lieutenant commander entered from the Office of Naval Intelligence. He asked them to sit back down, then told them they would all be flying to Japan at first light, air-refueling along the way. The squadron would land at Marine Air Corps Station Iwakuni, and there they would receive further instructions.

To a man the Marines were both angry and disappointed. The action had been out here in the middle of the East China Sea and the strait, not all the way over in Japan. But the *Reagan* was pulling back, out of range of the strait, which Trash saw as a retreat. And now they had been ordered to leave the carrier altogether and go even farther from the action.

None of the pilots liked leaving the *Reagan*, but all these young men had been in the Marine Corps long enough to know military orders did not need to make a damn bit of sense to be lawful, so they sat there, waiting to be dismissed.

But the lieutenant commander surprised them again when he told them that they would need to volunteer to go on an extremely dangerous mission. They would learn more details in Iwakuni, and then further details at their final destination.

Confused, intrigued, and excited, every man in the room volunteered.

They landed in Iwakuni before lunch, and as soon as they climbed out of their flight gear they were handed civilian clothing and led into a briefing room. Here Trash, Cheese, and the rest of the two squadrons found themselves in front of a Defense Intelligence Agency civilian who did not offer his name.

Trash was floored when the man told them they would all be issued packed luggage and false passports, and they would climb in a helicopter and be flown to the international airport in Osaka. There they would board a commercial flight to Taipei, Taiwan.

Trash and his squadron were going to sneak onto Taiwan, an island with no U.S. military presence.

The Taiwanese Air Force had recently taken delivery of two dozen F/A-18 Hornets. The Marines would be sent to Taiwan, placed in the airplanes, and they would then run combat air patrols in the Taiwan Strait.

The United States had not placed military fighting forces on Taiwan since 1979, as it would have been seen by the mainland Chinese as an overt provocation to do so. The conventional wisdom had always been that U.S. forces on Taiwan would freak the PRC out enough for them to launch missiles at the tiny island and forcibly repatriate it. America did not want to give China such an excuse, so America had stayed away.

The Marines, the DIA man told the pilots, had been chosen because they were versatile, able to operate with less support than Navy forces, and all the men in the room had spent the previous two weeks going head-to-head with the PLAAF in the strait.

They were battle-hardened, as it were.

The covert squadron would be getting some support staff, mechanics, and flight operations personnel from here in Iwakuni, but the bulk of the ground crew would be Taiwanese Air Force men and women secretly moved to the base.

Trash knew he and twenty-three other guys were not going to fight off the Chinese if they attacked Taiwan. He wondered if this entire exercise was nothing more than politics, showing the ROC government that even though the *Reagan* and the other carrier in the Pacific weren't getting too close to the danger, the United States was willing to stick a few of its own boys right there in the middle of the strait.

It pissed him off to think of himself and his friends as pawns in a geopolitical chess match, but he had to admit, he was glad for the opportunity to get back in the action.

The flight to Taiwan Taoyuan International Airport went without incident, other than the fact twenty-four American men, age twenty-six to forty-one, all with military haircuts, sat in ones and twos throughout the cabin and ignored one another. On the ground they passed breezily through customs, and then met up in the lobby of an airport hotel.

A couple of guys whom Trash took for DIA operatives led them to a bus, which shuttled them to a closed portion of the big international airport.

They flew in a ROC C-130 transport aircraft from Taipei to Hualien Airport, a commercial airport in the middle of an active military base on Taiwan's eastern shore. The ROC Air Force flew F-16 fighters off the runway year-round, and the civilian portion of the airport had been closed indefinitely for 'military training maneuvers.' Trash and the other Marines had been told they would be kept away from the vast majority of base personnel to minimize the possibility of leaks.

A Hawkeye owned by the ROC Air Force was also staffed with American air combat officers, and it provided command and control for the flights.

The Americans were ushered into a large bunker built into a hillside near the runway, where they found twenty-two used, but in good condition, F/A-18C Hornets, as well as living quarters and operational areas set up for the Americans.

Thirty-three hours after being awakened in the middle of the night on the *Ronald Reagan*, Captain Brandon 'Trash' White and Major Scott 'Cheese' Stilton walked out of the secure area with their helmets over their heads, following the operational security orders given to them by the DIA.

On the tarmac they both inspected their aircraft one last time, and Trash climbed into the cockpit of 'his' Hornet, 881. Cheese climbed up the ladder and stepped into the cockpit of his assigned aircraft, 602.

Soon they were back in the air, flying CAPs over the strait, and – and this was the best part for Trash and the other Marines – returning after their mission to land on a real runway – a long, wide, flat, unmoving piece of asphalt, not a bobbing postage stamp in the middle of the ocean.

52

Gavin Biery had spent the past week since returning from Hong Kong locked in his laboratory picking apart the secrets of FastByte22's handheld computer.

Now that FastByte22 was dead, Gavin knew the only clues the young hacker would ever reveal were locked within the circuitry, and it was his job to expose them.

The device had been difficult to crack. On the first day of working on it, he realized FastByte22 had booby-trapped the machine with a virus that would launch against any computer, Bluetooth-receiving device, or other peripheral that was attached to it in any way. The virus would then deliver a RAT payload into the infected device that would take a snapshot of the user on the other side.

It was an ingenious piece of code, and it took Gavin two full days to circumvent it.

Once inside the drive and through the encryption, he found a treasure trove of information. Almost all of the notes he found were in Chinese characters, of course, and Zha was a note taker. Biery was terrified about the possibility that the machine had other virus booby traps installed, so he had a Mandarin-speaking translator from the third floor come into the room after submitting to a pat-down, and this poor young man then had to hand-transcribe hundreds of pages of document files onto a legal pad for translation back at his desk.

While the documents were being transcribed, Biery looked through the executable files and discovered other secrets.

A complicated custom-coded file-uploading system on the device was at first a mystery to Biery. Looking through the source code of the program, he could not for the life of him discern what made it different from all the commercial file-uploading applications available for free. It seemed to be an overly complicated Rube Goldberg piece of software.

He was certain there was something to it; FastByte22 was not the kind of hacker to build something so bloated just to pass the time, but he put it aside and kept hunting through the device.

In the end, the Chinese translator unlocked the secret of FastByte22's computer. The Mandarin notes, it seemed, were ruminations that Zha had in his time away from work. Ryan had explained to Gavin that when they tailed FastByte through the streets of Hong Kong, and even when he sat in the strip club, he seemed to always be typing away on the computer. Biery understood the kid; he was the same way. In his time away from work Gavin was always on his laptop at home or making little audio notes to himself in his car, ideas that just came to him in that moment that he wanted to record for later.

Most of Zha's notes were just his ideas, and many of them were silly or downright weird: 'I want to break into the website of Buckingham Palace and place a picture of Chairman Mao over the Queen's head,' and 'If we were able to fire the stabilizing rockets on the International Space Station, could we hold the world for ransom to prevent the ISS from crashing into a satellite?'

There was also a detailed plan to take control of a diabetic's insulin pump remotely by going through the attached low-power superheterodyne receiver and hacking into it with a directional antenna, presumably for the purpose of increasing the flow of insulin into the person's bloodstream to kill him from up to one hundred feet away. It was clear from the notes that FastByte22 had done some testing on the equipment itself and had recently ordered a receiver from a company in Marseille to be sent to a P.O. box in Mong Kok.

Many of Zha's notes revealed to Gavin that the dead Chinese hacker had possessed a brilliant mind with a fertile imagination.

But many more of the notes contained important pieces of intelligence value. 'Discuss with Center the discovery regarding the hydroelectric dam fail-safe measures.' And 'Ukrainian command servers are only as stable as the local power grid. Kharkov = better than Kiev. Discuss with Center the need for Data Logistics to reroute traffic away from Kiev before adopting next phase.'

Most of the notes posed more questions than they provided answers for Biery, but he did find the explanation for the large, complicated file-uploading application. From a note Zha had made just one week before his capture by Navy SEALs, Gavin learned the software was a handmade piece of malware Zha created that would allow a hacker to upload a virus via Cryptogram, the instant-messaging system Center used that was thought to be virtually hackproof. Gavin had studied Cryptogram when it came out, but he'd not delved deeply enough into the software to where he could easily recognize the code Zha wrote. Once he had the simple explanation from the Mandarin text document, he went back into the code and saw there was nothing at all simple about the uploader itself. It was brilliant and intricate, and Biery saw in the different way the code was written that a large team of coders had been involved in constructing it.

That was interesting. Back in Hong Kong, Zha had been seen with other well-known Chinese hackers. Here was more evidence that they were, in fact, working together on high-level computer malware.

The second big revelation from FastByte's handwritten notes was even more of a bombshell. The young Chinese hacker used code words to signify people and general names to signify places, and Gavin realized quickly that he would not be able to break the code without being inside Zha Shu Hai's head. But Zha slipped up in one of his documents. He had mentioned the 'Miami command server' four times earlier in a long note to himself about exfiltrating data from an unnamed U.S. defense contractor, but the fifth time he referred to the location as the 'BriteWeb command server.'

Gavin immediately left his sterile lab, rushed to his office, went online, and searched for BriteWeb in Miami. He got an instant match. It was a Web-design and data-hosting outfit located in Coral Gables. A little more digging showed him the business was owned by a holding company on Grand Cayman.

Gavin picked up his phone, called in one of his employees, and told him to drop everything and dig into the holding company.

An hour later Gavin was back on the phone, this time calling Sam Granger, director of operations.

'Morning, Gavin.'

'How soon can you get everybody into a conference room?'

Granger replied, 'You've got something?'

'I do.'

'Come up in twenty minutes.'

Twenty-five minutes later, Gavin Biery stood at the end of the conference table. In front of him was the entire complement of Campus operators, along with Gerry Hendley and Sam Granger.

'What do you have for us?' Hendley asked as soon as everyone was settled.

'I've got a long way to go before I've unlocked all the secrets on the device, but in the meantime, I've located one of Center's command servers.'

'Where is it?' asked Chavez.

'Miami. Coral Gables. Southwest Sixty-second Place.'

'Miami?' Granger was clearly surprised. 'So this is the command-and-control location of the hacking operation? *Miami?*'

'No. This is one of the places a botnet run by Zha and Tong sends data that it steals from hacked machines. It looks as though this is not just some benign server being hacked as a data drop location, though. You can tell by how the company is set up that the owners of this server knew good and well they were going to be using their hardware for nefarious purposes. It's an underground-economy server. Definitely run by shady bastards. They have a drop point nearby, so they can pick up cash and goods.'

'We are talking about criminal acts?'

'Yes,' Gavin said, 'there is no doubt. They are hiding the identities of the owners of the server behind front companies and bogus registry information. The owner of the company is Russian, his name is Dmitri Oransky, he incorporated in the Caymans, and he lives in the U.S.'

'Shit,' said Granger. 'I was hoping . . . expecting it to be somewhere out of the country.'

Gavin replied, 'There will be other command servers in a botnet this large. Some will likely be in the U.S., others will be overseas. But this one is definitely part of the operation, and the guys running it definitely aren't playing by the rules.'

Driscoll said, 'If it's attacking the U.S., why would it be here in the U.S.? Don't they know that makes it easier for us to shut it down?'

'Bad guys *love* putting their servers in the U.S. We've got a stable power grid, we've got cheap and widespread broadband, and we've got pro-business policies that cut out a lot of red tape that the gangsters don't like. They can be pretty sure that a truckload of soldiers or cops isn't going to show up in the middle of the night and haul them and their equipment in without the Feds jumping through months of legal hurdles that give them time to pull up stakes and hit the road.'

Gavin saw most of the men at the table did not really understand. 'They think they can hide the origin of their command servers, so why not put them right under our noses? The fact is that it works pretty damn well ninety-nine percent of the time.'

Dom Caruso said, 'Even if Miami isn't the nerve center of the entire operation, it's clear this Coral Gables address is a piece of the puzzle, and we need to check it out.'

Sam Granger put up a hand. 'Not so fast. I'm leery about sending you guys on an op on U.S. soil.'

'Not like we haven't done it before.'

'True, the Nevada op, for example. But that was a different situation. We know Tong and his people, whoever the hell they are, have targeted us directly, and they have evidence that could close us down easily. This isn't the time to be running and gunning against Americans in America. None of Jack's dad's pardons will do us any good if you get ID'd and picked up on a local or state rap.'

'Look,' Jack Ryan said, 'our enemy is foreign, that much is clear. Just some of their resources are here. I say we just go down and take a look. I'm not talking about gearing up in body armor and hitting the place, just some recon. We get a couple of snapshots of the guys working down there, poke around into their backgrounds and known associates, and that can lead us to the next link in the chain.'

Granger shook his head. 'I wish we could, but that's a slippery slope. Your dad did not set up this operation so that we could spy on Americans.'

Jack said, 'Assholes are assholes, Sam. It doesn't matter what color their passport is.'

Sam smiled at this, but it was clear his mind was made up. 'We tip off the FBI about the command server. We'll figure out the details of how we are going to go about notifying them. But in the meantime, The Campus stays out of it.'

Dom and Jack both nodded. Neither man really got it, but Sam was their boss, so that was that.

The meeting broke up soon after, but Gavin Biery asked Ryan to follow him back down to his office. Once there, Biery said, 'I didn't want to discuss this in the meeting, because at this point all I have is a theory, but I wanted to tell you about it, because it may necessitate some work on the operations side of The Campus.'

Jack said, 'Lay it on me. Since we can't go to Miami and investigate, I'd appreciate some work.'

Gavin held up a hand. 'This is nothing for you to do now. This may take days and days. But with a lot of work, I might be able to reverse-engineer two pieces of malware I found on Zha's computer and, with it, make a pretty powerful weapon.'

'What kind of weapon?'

'Zha built a covert delivery system that allows someone to sneak malware through Cryptogram, and he booby-trapped his device with a virus that infects any device that connects to it with a version of his RAT software.'

'The thing that makes it where he can see through the camera.'

'Right.'

Jack slowly understood. 'So . . . you are saying you might be able to construct a new virus that could be delivered through Cryptogram to infect the computer on the other side, and then take a picture of what's on the other side?'

Biery nodded. 'Again, this is theoretical. And on top of that, you would have to find a computer that someone uses to connect with Center. Not Zha's handheld, because Center will know that device is burned and he would never establish communications. And not the Istanbul Drive, for just exactly the same reason. But a new device, used by someone Center trusts. If Center opened up a Cryptogram conversation, accepted the digital handshake of the other party, then accepted a file that was uploaded by another party . . . then we might be able to get a look at Center.'

Normally Jack saw Gavin light up when he talked about what he could do with computer code, but Gavin seemed to be a lot more subdued than usual.

Jack wanted to encourage him. 'You do realize how important that would be for The Campus? Shit, how important it would be for America?'

Gavin said, 'No promises, though. It's not going to be easy.'

Jack patted him on the arm. 'I've got faith in you.'

'Thanks, Ryan. I'll work on the code, you work on finding one of Center's people stupid enough to play along.'

Two hours later Ryan was at his desk. He felt a presence, then looked up to find Dom standing behind him with a smile on his face.

'Hey, cuz. Any big plans for the weekend?'

Ryan shook his head. 'None. Melanie says she'll be

working Saturday. Figured I'd come in here and mess around. I guess we'll hang out after that. Why, what's up?'

'How long has it been since the two of us have gone on vacation together?'

Jack looked up from his monitor. 'Have we *ever* gone on vacation together? I mean, other than when we were kids?'

Tony Wills, Jack's cubicle mate, was away to lunch, so Caruso slid his empty chair over and sat down in it. He moved closer to Ryan. In a conspiratorial tone he said, 'Too long, then.'

Jack sensed trouble. 'What's on your mind, dude?'

'We've been working hard. I was just thinking we might push off early this afternoon, do a quick weekender somewhere. Just two guys blowing off a little steam.'

Jack Ryan cocked his head. 'Where were you thinking about blowing off this steam?'

Dom Caruso did not reply. He just smiled.

Jack answered his own question: 'Miami.'

'Why the hell not? We fly down commercial, get a couple of rooms in South Beach, eat some good Cuban food . . .' He trailed off at the end, and again, Ryan finished the thought.

'And we pop over to Coral Gables, maybe do a quick peek at Southwest Sixty-second Place. Is that your plan?'

Dom nodded. 'Who's gonna know? Who's gonna care?'

'And we don't mention it to Granger?'

'Do we have to tell Granger what we're doing every weekend?'

'If we aren't going to tell Granger or anybody else here, what's the point of going?'

'Look, we won't get too close, we won't compromise ourselves. We just go for a little look-see. Maybe get tag numbers in the parking lot, follow some computer nerd back to his computer-nerd apartment and get an address.'

'I don't know,' said Jack. He knew, as Dom said, the two of them could do what they wanted with their downtime.

But he also knew this was violating the spirit of Sam Granger's instructions, if not the actual instructions. Even though they wouldn't be working for The Campus on their trip, that was a pretty fine line.

'You want to go home and sit on your ass this weekend, or do you want to do something that just might make a difference? Again, if nothing comes of it, no harm, no foul. But if we do get some actionable intel, we take it to Sam and give it to him with apologies. You know how it is. Sometimes it's better to ask forgiveness than permission.'

That hit home with Jack. He saw himself sitting around wondering what he could accomplish if he took his cousin up on his offer. He thought it over a little more, then smiled slyly. 'I have to admit, cuz, that I love a good mojito.'

Caruso smiled. 'That's my boy.'

53

Dominic and Jack arrived in Miami late on Friday afternoon. They'd flown commercial, coach, and it felt a bit like the Stone Age to them compared with the Hendley G-550, but the flight was on time and both men had slept most of the way.

They had no guns on them, although bringing a gun along on a commercial flight in the United States is not against the law. Since licensed concealed carry of a handgun was permitted in Florida, they could have flown into Miami with locked, unloaded guns in their checked luggage, but that entailed forms and delay, and, both men decided, this wasn't that type of a trip. They were under orders not to initiate a formal surveillance operation of the command server location, and they also knew if Sam somehow found out, the fact they hadn't even brought their pieces along might serve in their defense, indicating they weren't down there on 'official business.'

It was splitting hairs, and Jack didn't feel great about it, but he did feel that The Campus operators should get their own eyes on the command server location.

They rented a nondescript Toyota four-door and drove it to Miami Beach, where they found a cheap one-and-a-half-star motel. Dominic rented two rooms for two nights and paid cash for them while Ryan waited in the car. They found their adjoining rooms, tossed their overnight bags onto their beds, and headed back out to the Toyota in the parking lot. Within thirty minutes of checking in they were walking down Collins Avenue on foot, making their way through the throngs of beachgoers and weekend tourists. They headed two blocks over to Ocean Drive and sat down at the first bar they saw, which, like most nightspots on a Friday night in Miami, had an impressive amount of beautiful women.

When each man had drained a mojito and ordered a second, they talked about their plan for the weekend.

'First thing in the morning we head down to Coral Gables,' Dom said.

'A daylight drive-by?' asked Jack.

'Sure. Just a soft recon. We're not going to get away with much else on this trip. You saw the street on Google Maps, there's not going to be an opportunity to disappear around there, so we'll have to stay mobile, either on foot or in the car.'

'Sure you don't want to go by there right now?'

Dominic looked around the bar at the beautiful women. 'Cuz, *you* may not be single anymore, but I am. Have a heart.'

Ryan laughed. 'I'm still single. I'm just not looking at the moment.'

'Right. I see how you melt when she calls. Hell, dude, your voice goes up half an octave when you talk to her.'

Jack groaned. 'No. Please tell me it doesn't.'

'Sorry. She's got you whipped.'

Jack was still reacting to the possibility that guys in the office could tell when he was talking to Melanie on the phone. But he sighed, then said, 'I got lucky with this one.'

'It's not luck. You're a good guy. You deserve her.'

They sat in silence for a few minutes while they sipped their drinks. Ryan was bored; he checked his phone for any texts from Melanie, while Dom eyed a Colombian beauty at the bar. She smiled back, but a few seconds later her boyfriend appeared, kissed her, and sat down at the bar stool next to her. He looked like a linebacker for the Dolphins. Caruso shook his head with a chuckle, then finished his mojito with a slurp.

'Fuck it, cuz. Let's go check out the command server.'

Ryan had a pair of twenties out of his wallet a second later. He tossed them on the table and they headed back to get their rental.

It was almost midnight by the time they found the address.

They drove past the building slowly, both men eyeing the parking lot and the entrance. The sign said BriteWeb was a data-hosting company for individuals as well as small businesses. There were a few lights on inside the two-story building, and a few cars in the small lot.

They turned the corner and looked into a small, lighted breezeway that went through the middle of the building.

Instantly Jack felt the hair stand up on the back of his neck.

Dominic just whistled. He said, 'Those don't look like computer nerds.'

Two young men stood by the door in the breezeway, smoking cigarettes. Both men wore tight-fitting T-shirts and khaki cargo pants; they were well over six feet tall and muscular. They had dirty-blond hair, square jaws, and wide, Slavic noses.

'Did those guys look Russian to you?'

'Yeah,' said Jack. 'But I doubt either one of those guys is Dmitri Oransky, the owner of the place. They looked like security.'

Dom said, 'Might be Russian mob. They are all over South Florida.'

'Whoever they are, they are going to see us if we keep rolling by here at this time of night. Let's come back in the a.m.'

'Good call.'

'How 'bout we both pick up two new vehicles, just to make sure we don't get compromised? Different makes and models. This is South Florida, so we'll have tinted glass, which will help. With two cars it will double our time on target without raising any red flags with the goons watching the street. We need to get pictures of everyone coming and going.'

'Roger that.'

Nine thousand miles away, in a fourteen-story building in Guangzhou, a twenty-three-year-old woman leaned forward to check an image on her monitor. Five seconds later she tapped a button on her keyboard, and she heard a short, low beep in her headset.

She sat quietly, watching the real-time image from Miami while she waited for Center to accept her videoconference. She had seen Center walking by a few minutes earlier, so he might well have been in the conference room and not in his office. If so, he would take the call on his VOIP headset instead of on the videoconference feature on his computer. Even though he might have been here in the room, she did not call out to him. If everyone did that the room would sound like the trading floor of the Chicago Mercantile Exchange.

The image of Dr Tong appeared on her computer monitor next to the image in Coral Gables.

He looked up from his desk. 'Center.'

'Center, desk thirty-four.'

'Yes?'

'Target Hendley Associates, Maryland, United States. Personality Jack Ryan, Junior, and personality Dominic Caruso.'

'Have they arrived in Florida?'

'Affirmative. They are conducting surveillance on the command server at the location there. I have them in real time in a rented vehicle just a block from the BriteWeb location.'

'Alert local assets. Notify them that an unknown force has compromised the command server. Give them their hotel information, vehicle identification, and descriptions. Do not reveal identities of personalities to local assets. Instruct local assets to terminate the targets. We have allowed this to continue long enough.'

'Understood.'

'Then tell Data Logistics to divert data flow from the Miami command server. That operation is closed as of now. With the death of Jack Ryan, Junior, there will be close scrutiny of the incident, and we must not leave any trackbacks to the Ghost Ship.'

'Yes, Center.'

'Data Logistics can route through the Detroit command server until they can find a permanent solution.'

'Yes, Center.'

The twenty-three-year-old controller disconnected the call and then opened the Cryptogram application on one of her monitors. In seconds she was patched through to a computer in Kendall, Florida. It was owned by a thirty-five-year-old Russian national living in the U.S. on an expired student visa.

Twelve minutes and thirty seconds after Center spoke to his desk officer, a cell phone rang in the pocket of a Russian U.S. citizen at a nightclub in Hollywood Beach, Florida.

'*Da?*'

'Yuri, it's Dmitri.'

'Yes, sir?'

'We have a situation. Are the boys with you?'

'Yes.'

'Grab a pen and write down this address. You guys get to have some serious fun tonight.'

Jack and Dom made it back to the fleabag motel and drank a beer together on the tiny back patio adjacent to Ryan's room. At about one-thirty they finished their beers, and Dom started to head to his room but decided he'd go buy a bottled water from the vending machine in the breezeway first.

He opened the door to head out into the breezeway and found himself staring down the barrel of a long black automatic pistol.

Ryan was still out on the patio. He looked up in time to see two men come over the low fence. They both carried pistols that they waved in Ryan's face.

'Back inside,' said a man with a pronounced Russian accent.

Jack raised his hands.

Two aluminum patio chairs were brought in from the patio by one of the Russians, and Ryan and Caruso were forced down into them. The smallest of the three goons had a canvas gym bag with him, and from it he pulled out a huge roll of wide duct tape. While both of the other men stood on the far side of the room, the Russian taped first Jack's and then Dom's legs to the legs of the chairs, and then their hands behind the backs of the chairs.

Ryan had been too stunned to speak at first; he knew he had not been followed back to the motel, so he could not imagine how they had been tracked here.

The three guys looked serious, but they also looked like simple muscle. Jack could tell these were not the brains behind this operation, or any operation more complicated than tying their shoes or shooting their pistols.

These would be Dmitri's thugs, and by the looks of things, Dmitri wanted Ryan and Caruso dead.

Dom tried to talk to the men. 'What's this all about?'

The obvious leader of the trio said, 'We know you are spying on us.'

'I don't know what the hell you are talking about. We just came down to the beach for the weekend. We don't even know who –'

'Shut up!'

Every fiber of Ryan's being was focused on readying himself to act. He knew once his feet were tied together it would be over, he'd have no way to move or fight.

But he did not see any opening. The two men holding the pistols on them were on the other side of the bed, easily ten feet away. Jack knew there was no way in hell he could get to those guns before the men fired them.

Jack said, 'Look. We don't want any trouble. We were just following orders.'

The man in charge said, 'Yeah? Well, your boss is going to have to get a new crew, because you two pretty boys are about to die.'

The smaller man with the gym bag pulled out a length of black wire and handed it across to his boss. It took Ryan only a moment to see the loops at each end, and to understand what he was looking at.

It was a garrote, an assassination device designed to be placed around the neck and then pulled tight from behind to strangle the victim.

Ryan continued speaking more quickly: 'You don't understand. Our boss is the same as your boss.'

'What are you talking about?'

'Center sent us. He says Dmitri is stealing from the wire

transfer that is supposed to be split evenly among you. That's why we're here.'

'What are you talking about?'

Caruso followed Jack's lead: 'Center hacked your boss's computer and his phone, and you boys are getting ripped off.'

One of the men on the other side of the bed said, 'They are just making up some shit so we don't kill them.'

Jack said, 'I've got proof on my laptop. A Cryptogram conversation where Center tells Dmitri how much to pay you guys. I can show you.'

'You aren't showing us shit,' said the same guy. 'You are lying. Why would Center care what we are getting paid?'

'Center demands that his agents do what he says. You guys *must* know that. He tells your boss to pay you a certain amount, he damn well expects that to happen. Dmitri is skimming off your cut, and Center sent us down to take care of it.'

Caruso chimed in again: 'Yeah. A few months back he sent us to Istanbul to take out some guys who were cheating him.'

The lead Russian against the wall said, 'Dmitri told me Center wanted you guys taken care of.'

Jack and Dom looked at each other. Center knew they were here in Miami? How?

But Jack recovered quickly. 'That's what Dmitri told you? I can *prove* that's bullshit.'

'How?'

'Let me log on to Cryptogram. I can be talking to Center inside of two minutes. You can confirm with him.'

The three goons started speaking in rapid-fire Russian. One asked, 'How will we know if it's really him?'

Jack shrugged in his bindings. 'Dude. It's Center. Ask him

anything. Ask him about your organization. Ask him what ops you've done for him. Hell, ask him what your birthday is. He'll know.'

That sank in with the Russians, Ryan could tell.

After another conversation between them, one of the three holstered his pistol and walked over to the desk. 'Give me your password. *I'll* check with Center on your computer.'

Ryan shook his head. 'That won't work. He can see through the webcam. Shit, how long have you guys been on the job? He'll see it's not me and he won't authenticate the conversation. He'll lock out the machine and, knowing Center, he'll probably send another crew down to Miami to kill everybody down here working for him, starting with the idiot that logged on to my machine.'

'You are exaggerating,' the Russian at the desk said. Still, he took a step back from the laptop, away from its camera.

'Trust me,' said Jack. 'The Chinese take their security seriously.'

'Chinese?'

Jack just looked back at the man.

'Center is Chinese?' one of the other Russians asked.

'Are you serious?' Jack said, then looked at Dom. Dom just shook his head like he was in the presence of idiots.

'Are you guys new?'

'No,' said the smaller man in the crew.

With a barking order from the man by the desk, one of the other two pulled a butterfly knife from his jacket and whipped it open with a flourish. He cut the tape from Ryan's ankles and wrists, and Jack got up from the metal chair. As he moved the ten feet he looked back over his shoulder at Caruso. Dominic gave nothing away with his look. He just sat there watching.

Ryan looked to the head goon now. 'Let me connect with

him, explain the situation, and then bring you into the conversation.'

The Russian nodded, and Jack could tell that he'd successfully tricked the three armed men who just a minute before had been about to kill him and his cousin.

He knelt in front of his laptop, painfully aware of three sets of eyes on him right now. The closest man was just two steps away on his right, another was still on the other side of the bed with his weapon low by his side, and the third, the man who had just cut Ryan free, stood next to Caruso with his butterfly knife in his hand.

Jack had a plan, but it was an incomplete plan. He knew he wasn't going to be talking to Center on Cryptogram, he did not even have the software on his machine, so he was seconds away from a full-on fight here in the room. And while he felt reasonably certain he could take care of one of these three thugs in a mano-a-mano brawl, there was no way he would make it across the room to the guy on the other side of the bed.

He needed a gun, and the closest gun was in the holster under the shirt of the man next to him.

Jack looked up at him from his kneeling position in front of the computer.

'Well?' said the Russian.

'Maybe I won't check with Center,' Jack said, his tone a lot sharper than when he was taped to the chair.

'Why not?' asked the Russian.

'You guys aren't going to do anything to us. You're just bluffing.'

'Bluffing?' The man was confused. The American in front of him just spent several minutes trying to talk him into letting him use his computer. Now he was saying he would not. 'I am not bluffing.'

'What, are you going to have your little buddies beat me up?'

The leader shook his head and smiled. 'No, they will shoot you.'

'Oh, I see. You have these guys with you to do the shit you are too scared to do yourself.' Jack shook his head. 'Typical Russian pussy.'

Draw your gun! Jack's inner voice screamed it. It was the only chance he and Dom had to survive the next few seconds.

The man's face reddened with fury, and he reached under his red silk shirt to his appendix area.

Bingo, thought Jack, and he launched up from his knees, both of his hands going for the weapon that was just now coming out from under the silk.

The man tried to take a step back and away, but Ryan had spent many hours working on weapon takeaways, and he knew what he was doing. As he used his body to slam into the Russian, knocking him back, he pushed the pistol's muzzle down and to his left to get out of the line of fire in case the Russian got a shot off. With the same motion he both pulled on the Russian's gun and twisted it against his trigger finger, snapping the appendage. As the man screamed, Jack got his own finger in the trigger guard and twisted the gun back nearly a hundred eighty degrees, with the Russian's hand still holding it. Jack pressed the Russian's broken finger against the trigger.

Both rounds slammed into the armed Russian on the far side of the bed. The man spun on his heel and fell to the floor.

As the closest Russian fell back toward the bed, Jack pulled the gun all the way free, found a combat grip on it, and shot the man twice in the stomach at a distance of less than three feet. The Russian mob goon was dead before he hit the bed.

He spun toward the man standing near Dom on his right, but before he could line the gun up for a snap shot he knew he was in trouble. As he came out of his turn he saw the man's hand arcing over his head, and Jack realized the guy was throwing his knife right at him.

Jack dropped to the floor without firing; he did not want to risk shooting his bound cousin by squeezing off indiscriminate rounds while dodging a knife.

The spinning steel whirled over his head and buried itself into the wall.

The Russian drew his handgun from his pants as Jack looked up. The man was fast . . . a faster draw than Jack.

But Ryan already had his Glock in his hand. He fired two rounds into the man's chest, and the Russian slammed back against the wall, then fell onto the floor between Dom's chair and the bed.

Caruso fought his bindings while Ryan took a moment to make sure all the men were dead.

Dom said, 'Good thinking, great shooting.'

Jack cut Dom free quickly. 'We need to be out the door in sixty seconds.'

'Got it,' Dom said, and he leapt across the bed, grabbing his carry-on and slinging personal items into it.

Ryan pulled mobile phones and wallets from the dead men, then grabbed his own bag, stuffed his laptop into it, and ran into the bathroom, where he grabbed a towel. He took ten seconds to wipe down any surfaces he may have touched, and then another ten seconds to check the room for anything left behind.

As they hustled through the dark parking lot, Jack said, 'Security cam?'

'Yep, the box is behind the counter, I've got it.'

'I've got the car.'

Caruso entered the lobby. There was just one man on duty, and he looked up from the telephone as Dom approached the counter with purpose.

The man hung up the phone. Nervously he said, 'I just called the cops. They are on the way.'

'I *am* the cops,' replied Caruso, then he vaulted over the counter, pushed by the clerk, and punched the eject button for the hotel's security camera recording equipment. 'And I'm going to need to take this into evidence.'

The clerk clearly did not believe him, but he made no move to stop him.

Jack pulled the Toyota up to the front door of the lobby, and Dom climbed in quickly. They headed out of the parking lot well in advance of the police.

'What now?' asked Ryan.

Caruso slammed his head back against the headrest in frustration. 'We call Granger, tell him what happened, and then we go home and get yelled at.'

Ryan groaned and squeezed the wheel, the adrenaline still coursing through him as he drove.

Yeah. That sounded exactly like the way it would go down.

54

The call between President of the United States Jack Ryan and President of the People's Republic of China Wei Zhen Lin had been Ryan's initiative originally; he wanted to attempt a dialogue with Wei, because, regardless of what Wei had been saying publicly, Ryan and most of his top advisers felt that Su was pushing the conflict in the strait and the SCS way past what Wei was comfortable with.

Ryan felt he could reach out to Wei and stress the perilous path his country was traveling down. It might not make a difference, but Ryan felt like he should at least try.

Wei's staff had contacted Ambassador Ken Li the day before, and arranged a time the following evening, China time, for the two presidents to talk.

Jack found himself in the Oval Office before the call, meeting with Mary Pat Foley and CIA Director Jay Canfield, trying to decide if he should bring up the Georgetown killings with the Chinese president.

Zha had been killed, both Foley and Canfield were certain, to silence him before he revealed China's involvement in the cyberattacks going on in the West, especially in America.

Little was known about Dr K. K. Tong and his scheme, but the deeper the NSA dug into the operation, the more certain they were that this was Chinese-run, and not some Triad/cybercrime nexus run out of Hong Kong. Zha's involvement with the UAV hacking seemed clear, the Iranian misdirection in the code had been discounted by the geeks at NSA, and more and more attacks against critical U.S. government networks bore the hallmark of Zha's code.

Their evidence was circumstantial but persuasive. Ryan believed China was behind the network attacks and the UAV attacks, and he also felt the Georgetown killing was a government operation, meaning China.

On top of this, Canfield and Foley wanted blood for the death of the five intelligence officers, and this Jack understood very well, but now he found himself playing the role of devil's advocate. He told them he needed more concrete proof that the PLA and/or the MSS were directing the Center network before he could publicly accuse the Chinese of anything.

He decided he would not bring up the Georgetown killings in this morning's phone call. Instead he would keep the focus on actions China could not deny, which meant everything that had happened in the South China Sea and the Taiwan Strait.

Both Ryan and Wei would be using their own translators. Jack's Mandarin speaker was located in the Situation Room, and his voice was piped into one of Jack's ears via an earpiece while Jack could listen to Wei's own voice through the telephone. This would make for a slow conversation without much spark, Ryan thought, but that did not bother him at all.

He would be doing his best to choose his words carefully; a little extra time to think through what he would say next might just keep him from challenging President Wei to a fistfight.

The conversation started out as all high-level diplomatic conversations do. It was polite and stilted, made even more so by the others in the chain of communication. But soon enough Ryan treaded into the main topic of conversation.

'Mr President, it is of great concern that I must discuss with you your nation's military actions in the South China

Sea and the Strait of Taiwan. The past month of aggression by the PLA has left hundreds dead, thousands displaced, and it has hurt the flow of traffic through the region, degrading the economies of both of our countries.'

'President Ryan, I too am concerned. Concerned about your actions off the coast of Taiwan, sovereign territory of China.'

'I ordered the *Ronald Reagan* pulled back to three hundred miles, as you requested. I had hoped it would deescalate the situation, but so far I see no evidence your aggression has been halted.'

Wei said, 'You also, Mr President, have brought your *Nimitz* close to the three-hundred-mile limit. This is thousands of miles from your territory – what reason would you do this if not to cause provocation?'

'American interests are in the area, and it is my job to protect those interests, President Wei.' Before Wei's translator finished the sentence, Ryan added, 'Your nation's military maneuvers, as bellicose as they have been in the past few weeks, can still be repaired with diplomacy.' Ryan continued speaking while the translator spoke to Wei softly. 'I want to encourage you to make certain nothing happens, that you *allow* nothing to happen, that diplomacy cannot fix.'

Wei's voice rose. 'Are you threatening China?'

Ryan, in contrast, was calm and measured in his tone. 'I am not talking to China. That is your job, Mr President. I am talking to you. And this is no threat.

'Much of statecraft, as you know, involves trying to determine what your adversaries will do. I will relieve you of that burden in this phone call. If your nation attacks our carrier groups in the East China Sea, jeopardizing some twenty thousand American lives, we will attack you with everything we have.

'If you fire ballistic missiles at Taiwan, we will have no choice but to declare war on China. You say you are open for business? I assure you that war with us will be bad for business.'

Ryan continued: 'I value the lives of my fellow country-men, Mr President. I cannot make you understand this, and I cannot make you respect this. But I can, and I must, make you acknowledge that this is the case. If this conflict turns into open war, then it will not make us run away, it will force us to respond with fury. I hope you realize Chairman Su is quickly taking China down the wrong path.'

'Su and I are in total accord.'

'No, President Wei, you are not. My intelligence services are very good, and they assure me that you want economic improvement and he wants war. Those two things are mutu-ally exclusive, and I believe you are beginning to realize that.

'My assets tell me it is likely that Chairman Su is promising you we will not escalate past what he is doing and if he strikes out against us we will disengage and quit the region. If that is indeed what Su has told you, you have been given very bad information, and I worry you will act on that bad information.'

'Your disrespect for China should not surprise me, Mr President, but I admit that it does.'

'I mean China no disrespect. You are the largest nation, with one of the largest territories, and you possess a brilliant and hardworking workforce with whom my country has done good business for the past forty years. But that is all in danger.'

The conversation did not end there. Wei went on for a few minutes about how he would not be lectured, and Ryan expressed the wish that they keep this line of communica-tion open, as it would become very important in case of emergency.

When it was over, Mary Pat Foley, who had been listening

in, congratulated the President and then said, 'You told him your intelligence services were giving you information on high-level military decisions. Do you have some other intelligence service that I am not aware of?' She said it with a sly smile.

Jack answered, 'I've been doing this for a while, and I thought I detected some indecision in his words. I played a hunch about the discord between the two camps, and I tried to turn his worry into paranoia with the comment about our intelligence services.'

Mary Pat said, 'Sounds like armchair psychology, but I'm all for it if it makes life harder for the Chicoms. I have some funerals to go to this week for some great Americans, and I feel certain Wei, Su, and their minions are responsible for these men's deaths.'

55

Jack Ryan and Dominic Caruso sat in Gerry Hendley's office and faced the ex-senator and the director of operations for The Campus, Sam Granger.

It was eight o'clock on Saturday morning, and while Jack imagined Sam and Gerry did not like getting dragged into the office so early on a Saturday, he was pretty sure that was not going to be their number-one complaint once they heard everything that had taken place the evening before in Miami.

Hendley leaned forward with his elbows on his desk and Granger sat with his legs crossed while Dom explained everything that happened the evening before. Jack chimed in here and there, but there was not much to add to the story. Both young men freely admitted that they knew their 'vacation' down to Miami was in violation of the spirit, if not the letter, of Granger's order not to conduct surveillance on BriteWeb, the Russian data-hosting company.

When Dom's story was finished, when it became clear to Gerry and Sam that three men were left dead in a motel room in Miami Beach a few hours earlier, and neither of their two operatives could either explain how Center knew they were down in Miami or promise that there was not a single fingerprint, camera-phone image, or CCTV recording that would tie Caruso and Ryan to the event, then Gerry Hendley just sat back in his chair.

He said, 'I am glad you two are alive. That sounds like it was a pretty close thing there for a few moments.' He looked to Sam. 'Your thoughts?'

Sam said, 'With operators ignoring direct orders, The Campus will not be around for much longer. And when The Campus falls, America will suffer. Our country has enemies, in case you didn't know, and we all, you guys included, have done a fine job in fighting America's enemies.'

'Thank you,' said Jack.

'But I can't have you guys doing stuff like this. I need to know I can count on you.'

'You can,' said Ryan. 'We screwed up. It will not happen again.'

Sam said, 'Well, it won't happen this week, because you guys are both on suspension for the week. Why don't you both go home and spend a few days thinking about how close you came to compromising our very important mission?'

Dom started to protest, but Jack reached out and grabbed his arm. He spoke for both of them when he said, 'We understand totally. Sam. Gerry. We thought we could just pull it off without exposing ourselves. I don't know how they found out about us being there, but somehow they did. Still, no excuses. We fucked up, and we're sorry.'

Jack stood and headed out of the office, and Dominic followed.

'We deserved that,' Ryan said as they walked out to their cars.

Caruso nodded. 'We did. Hell, we got off light. It's a shitty time to be on suspension, though. I sure as hell would like to be involved if we figure out who took down Zha and the CIA guys. The thought of the Chinese having assassins right here in D.C. makes my blood boil.'

Ryan opened the door to his BMW. 'Yeah. Same here.'

Caruso said, 'You want to hang out later?'

Jack shook his head. 'Not today. I'm going to call Melanie and see if she can meet for lunch.'

Caruso nodded, then turned to walk away.

'Dom?'

'Yeah.'

'How did Center know we were in Miami?'

Caruso shrugged. 'I don't have a clue, cuz. You figure it out, then let me know.' He walked to his car.

Jack sat down in his BMW, started the engine, and then reached for his phone. He started to dial Melanie's number, but then he stopped.

He looked at the phone.

After a long moment, he dialed a number, but it was not Melanie Kraft's.

'Biery.'

'Hey, Gavin. Where are you?'

'I'm in the office on a Saturday morning. What a thrilling life I lead, huh? Been working all night on the little trinket we brought back from HK.'

'Can you come out in the parking lot?'

'Why?'

'Because I've got to talk to you, I can't do it over the phone, and I've been suspended, so I can't do it in your office.'

'Suspended?'

'Long story. Come out in the parking lot and I'll take you to breakfast.'

Gavin and Jack went to a Waffle House in North Laurel and managed to get a booth in the back corner. As soon as they sat down and ordered, Gavin tried to get Jack to tell him what he did to earn a week's suspension, since Jack had refused to speak during the ten-minute drive.

But Jack interrupted him.

'Gavin. What I'm about to say stays between you and me, okay?'

Biery took a swig of coffee. 'Sure.'

'If someone took my phone, could they upload a virus to it that could track my movements in real time?'

Gavin did not hesitate. 'That's not a virus. It's just an application. An application that runs in the background so the user doesn't know about it. Sure, someone could put that on your phone if they had control of it.'

Ryan thought for a moment. 'And could they make it to where it recorded everything I say and do?'

'Easily.'

'If such an app was on my phone, could you find it?'

'Yes. I think so. Let me see your phone.'

'It's still in the car. I didn't want to bring it in.'

'Let's eat, then I'll take it back to the lab and check it out.'

'Thanks.'

Gavin cocked his head. 'You said someone took your phone? Who?'

'I'd rather not say,' Jack answered, but he was pretty sure his worried face gave away the answer.

Gavin Biery sat up straight. 'Oh, shit. Not your girl.'

'I don't know for sure.'

'But you obviously suspect something. Let's skip breakfast. I'll take it back right now.'

Jack Ryan sat in his car in the parking lot of Hendley Associates for forty-five minutes. It felt strange not having his phone with him. As with most people these days, his mobile had become an extension of himself. Without it he just sat quietly and thought uncomfortable thoughts.

His eyes were closed when Biery came back out to the car. Gavin had to tap on the window of Jack's black BMW.

Ryan climbed out of the car and shut the door.

Gavin just looked at him for a long time. 'I'm sorry, Jack.'

'It was bugged?'

'Location software and a RAT. I left it in the air-gapped lab so I can study it more. I'll have to go through the source code to see the details of the malware, but trust me, it's there.'

Jack mumbled out a few words of thanks, then got back in his car. He headed toward his apartment, but changed his mind, drove to Baltimore, and got a new cell phone.

As soon as the clerk set it up to accept calls from his phone number, he saw he had a voice mail.

As he walked through the mall he listened to the message.

It was Melanie. 'Hey, Jack. Just wondering if you are around tonight. It's Saturday, and I'll probably only work till four or so. Anyway . . . give me a call. I hope I get to see you. I love you.'

Jack disconnected the call, and then sat down on a bench in the mall.

His head was spinning.

Valentin Kovalenko had been hitting the bottle more and more in the days since the Georgetown murders; later and later into the night he was up with his Ketel One and his American television. He did not dare surf the Internet, as he knew with certainty that Center was watching his every online move, and there were no sites he wanted to troll bad enough to do so with some Chinese über-geek spook looking over his shoulder.

Late nights of pizza, booze, and channel surfing had caused him to slack off on his morning runs in the last week or so. This morning he did not roll out of bed until nine-thirty, a near-cardinal sin for a health nut and gym rat like Kovalenko.

With bleary eyes and bed head he made coffee and toast in his kitchen, and then sat down at his desk, opening his laptop

– he'd been careful to shut it when he wasn't using it, because he suspected Center would sit around looking at his living room throughout the night if he did not.

He was paranoid, he knew this, but he also knew what had brought him to this state of being.

He checked Cryptogram for this morning's instructions and found that Center had sent him a message at five-twelve a.m., ordering him to wait outside the Brookings Institution this afternoon and to take covert pictures of the attendees of a symposium on cybersecurity.

Easy, he said to himself before shutting down his laptop and changing into his running clothes.

He decided that since he had his morning free, he might as well go for a run. He finished his coffee and breakfast, changed into his running attire, and then finally stepped outside his rented apartment at five minutes until ten and turned to lock his door only to find a small envelope taped on the knob. He looked up past the staircase at the residential street, and then around the side of his building toward the back parking lot.

There was no one in sight.

He pulled the envelope off the knob and stepped back inside his apartment to open it.

The first thing he noticed as he opened it was the Cyrillic script. It was a handwritten note, just a line of scribbled text, and he did not recognize the handwriting.

'Dupont Circle fountain. Ten a.m.'

It was signed 'An old friend from Beirut.'

Kovalenko read it again, then put it on his desk.

Instead of leaving for his run, the Russian sat down slowly on his couch to think over this strange change of events.

Kovalenko's first posting as an SVR illegal had been in Beirut. He'd spent a year there around the turn of the century, and though he did not work in the Russian embassy there, he remembered many Russian contacts from his time in Lebanon.

Could this be someone from the embassy who saw him the other day and was reaching out to help, or could it possibly be some sort of a trick by Center?

Kovalenko decided he could not ignore the message. He checked his watch and realized he'd have to hurry if he was going to make the meet on time.

At ten o'clock on the nose, Kovalenko crossed the street into Dupont Circle and walked slowly toward the fountain.

The walkway around the fountain was ringed with benches, which were full of people either alone or in small groups, and the park around the benches had many people sitting around even on this chilly morning. Valentin did not know whom he was looking for, so he just wandered in a large circle, tried to recognize any faces from his past.

It took a few minutes, but he saw a man in a beige trench coat standing under a tree on the southern side of the circular park. The man was alone, removed from the other people enjoying themselves, and he faced Valentin.

Kovalenko walked toward him warily. As he got closer he recognized the face. He could not believe it. 'Dema?'

Dema Apilikov was SVR; he'd worked with Valentin in Beirut many years ago, and then he'd been posted under Valentin in London more recently.

Kovalenko had always thought Dema to be a bit of an idiot; he'd been a substandard illegal for a couple of years before becoming a paper pusher for the Russian spy service in the embassy, but he'd been honest enough and never so awful in his job as to get the ax.

Right now, however, Dema Apilikov looked pretty good

to Valentin Kovalenko, because he was a lifeline to the SVR.

'How are you, sir?' asked Dema. He was older than Valentin, but he called everyone sir, as if he was nothing more than a paid servant.

Kovalenko glanced around again, searching for watchers, for cameras, for little birds Center might have sent to follow his every move. The area looked clean.

'I'm okay. How did you know I was here?'

'People know. Influential people. I've been sent with a message.'

'From who?'

'Can't say. Sorry. But friends. Men at the top, in Moscow, who want you to know that they are working to extricate you from your situation.'

'My situation? Meaning?'

'I mean your legal troubles at home. What you are doing here in Washington, it is supported, it is considered an SVR op.'

Kovalenko did not understand.

Dema Apilikov clearly saw this and said, 'Center. We know about Center. We know how he's using you. I'm told to tell you that you have SVR sanction to continue, to see it to the end. This could be very helpful for Russia.'

Kovalenko cleared his throat and looked around. 'Center is Chinese intelligence.'

Dema Apilikov nodded at this. 'He's MSS, yes. He's also working for their military cyberwarfare directorate. Third Branch.'

This made instant and perfect sense to Valentin, and he was elated that the SVR knew all about Center. Indeed, apparently Dema knew more about Center than Kovalenko himself did.

'Do you have a name for this guy? Any idea where he's working out of?'

'Yeah, he's got a name, but I can't give it to you. Sorry, sir. You're my old boss, but officially you are outside the system. You are an agent, more or less, and on this op, I've got a script to give you and that's it.'

'I understand, Dema. Need to know.' He looked around at the sky and it seemed bluer, the air cleaner. The weight of the world had been lifted from his shoulders. 'So . . . my orders are to keep working for Center until I get pulled out?'

'Yes. Keep your head down but carry out all orders to the best of your ability. I am allowed to tell you that while you may not go back to PR Directorate when you come back to work with us, due to the risk of exposure having you traveling abroad, you will have your pick of high-level postings in Directorate R.' PR Directorate was political intelligence, Kovalenko's old posting and career track. Directorate R was operational planning and analysis. While he'd much prefer to return to his life as an assistant *rezident* in London, he knew that was out of the question. Working at the Kremlin for R, developing worldwide SVR ops, was a plum position for anyone in SVR. If he could get away from Chinese intelligence and back to SVR, he would not complain about Directorate R one damn bit.

Already he was thinking about going home to Moscow as a hero. What an incredible reversal of fortune.

But quickly he cleared his mind and got back to his situation. 'Do you . . . do you know about Georgetown?'

Dema nodded. 'Doesn't concern you. The Americans will work out that the Chinese are doing this, and they will go after the Chinese. We are in the clear. You are in the clear. The Americans have enough on their plate at the moment.'

Kovalenko smiled, but his smile faltered. There was something else.

'Listen, one more thing. Center had a Saint Petersburg

mafia group break me out of Matrosskaya. I had nothing to do with the death of the –'

'Relax, sir. We know. Yes, it was Tambovskaya Bratva.'

Kovalenko knew a little about this particular *bratva*, or brotherhood. Tambovskaya were tough guys who operated all over Russia and in many other European countries. He was relieved to know that the SVR knew that he had not been involved in the escape.

'That is a great relief, Dema,' he said.

Apilikov patted Kovalenko on the shoulder. 'Just stick with this for now, do what they tell you to do. We'll pull you out before too long, and get you back home.'

The men shook hands. 'Thank you, Dema.'

56

On the third morning of his weeklong suspension, Jack left Columbia and drove with rush-hour traffic toward Alexandria.

He wasn't sure what he was doing, but he wanted to spend some time outside Melanie's apartment while she was at work. He wasn't thinking about breaking in – at least he wasn't *seriously* thinking about breaking in – but he was considering peeking through the windows and checking though her garbage can.

He wasn't proud about any of this, but for the past three days he'd done little but sit at home and stew.

He knew Melanie had done something to his phone back at his apartment before he went to Miami, and when Gavin told him, in no uncertain terms, that a bug had been put on the device, he realized he would be nothing more than a lovesick fool to think she had nothing to do with it.

He needed answers, and to get them he decided to go to her house and dig in her trash.

'Nice one, Jack. Your dad the CIA legend would be really damn proud.'

As he passed through Arlington at nine-thirty a.m., however, his plans changed.

His phone rang. 'This is Ryan.'

'Hi, Jack. Mary Pat.'

'Director Foley, how are you?'

'Jack, we've talked about this. It's still Mary Pat to you.'

Jack smiled despite himself. 'Okay, Mary Pat, but don't think that means I'm going to let you call me Junior.'

She chuckled at the joke, but immediately Jack got the impression that things were about to get serious.

She said, 'I was wondering if we could meet.'

'Of course. When?'

'How does right this minute suit you?'

'Oh . . . okay. Sure. I'm in Arlington. I can run right over to McLean.' Jack knew this was big. He could not imagine everything the director of the Office of National Intelligence had on her plate at the moment. This definitely would not be a social get-together.

Next she said, 'Actually, I need to keep this low-key. How about we meet someplace quiet. Can you come over to the house? I can be there in a half-hour.'

Mary Pat and Ed Foley lived in the Adams Morgan neighborhood of D.C. Jack had been over many times; in the past nine months most of his visits had been with Melanie.

'I'll head that way. Ed can keep me company until you get there.' Jack knew Ed was retired.

'Actually, Ed is out of town. I'll be there as quick as I can.'

Jack and Mary Pat sat at a patio table on the deck out in back of her Adams Morgan colonial. The backyard was a garden of thick trees and other foliage, mostly brown with the autumn cold. She'd offered him coffee and he'd declined, simply because he could see the urgency on her face as soon as she pulled up in her car. She'd asked her security officer to remain in the house, which surprised Jack even more.

As soon as they sat down she pulled her chair close to him and spoke softly. 'I called John Clark this morning. I was surprised to learn he wasn't working at Hendley anymore.'

'His own choosing,' said Jack. 'We hated to lose him, that's for sure.'

Mary Pat said, 'I get it. The man has served his country,

sacrificed a lot, for a long, long time. A few years of normal life can start to look mighty appealing, and he has most definitely earned them, especially after what he went through last year.'

Ryan said, 'You called Clark, found out he was out of the business, so you called me. Am I to assume there is something you wanted to share with us?'

She nodded. 'Everything I am about to say is classified.'

'Understood.'

'Jack, it is time the U.S. intelligence community faces up to the reality that we have a serious compromise with respect to assets in China.'

'You have a leak.'

'You don't seem surprised.'

Jack hesitated. Finally he said, 'We've had our suspicions.'

Foley regarded his comment, and then continued: 'We've had a number of opportunities to liaise with people in China – local dissidents, protest groups, disaffected government and military employees, and others well positioned in the CPC. Every last one of these opportunities has been discovered by Chinese intelligence. Men and women over there have been arrested, chased into hiding, or killed.'

'So your eyes and ears on the ground in China are lacking.'

'I wish they were just lacking. No, our HUMINT assets are virtually nonexistent in China right now.'

'Any idea where the leak is coming from?'

Mary Pat said, 'It's at CIA, we know that. We *don't* know if they have some sort of visualization into our cable traffic or if it is someone on the inside. Beijing Station or Shanghai Station or maybe even someone at Asia desk at Langley.' She paused. 'Or someone higher.'

Jack said, 'I'd be looking hard at their cybercapabilities in light of everything else that's going on.'

'Yes, we are. But if it is coming from our traffic, then they have been masterful at hiding it. They have been using the information very judiciously, confining it only to certain aspects of counterintelligence with respect to China. Obviously there is a lot of information traveling across our wires that could be beneficial for China, but we don't see that level of exploitation.'

'How can we help you?' he asked.

'A new opportunity has popped up.'

Ryan raised an eyebrow. 'Popped up from your leaky CIA?'

She smiled. 'No. At this point I can't trust any organization in the U.S. intelligence community, nor can I trust any service under the DoD, in light of what they are going through over there at the Pentagon.' She paused. 'The only people I trust with this information are outsiders. Outsiders with an incentive to keep quiet about it.'

Jack said, 'The Campus.'

'Exactly.'

'Go on.'

Mary Pat scooted her chair even closer. Jack leaned in to within inches of her face. 'Several years ago, when Ed was in charge at CIA, back during your father's last run-in with the Chinese, I ran a CIA officer over in Beijing who proved instrumental in resolving that conflict. But there were other options presented to us at that time. Options that we decided against pursuing because they were ... what's the word? I suppose the word is *unseemly*.'

'But now it's all you've got.'

'Right. There is organized crime inside China. I'm not talking about Triads, which are active outside of mainland China, but organizations that exist in secret within the Communist state. Being arrested as a member of one of these gangs in China will earn you a perfunctory trial, and then a bullet in the back of the neck, so only the most desperate or most evil join these groups.'

Jack could not imagine being in an organized criminal gang in a police state, which essentially meant the government was a gang of organized criminals itself – in China's case, a gang with an army of millions of soldiers and trillions in military equipment.

Mary Pat continued. 'One of the most heinous organizations over there is called Red Hand. They make their money in kidnapping, extortion, robbery, human trafficking. These are some real sons of bitches, Jack.'

'Sounds like it.'

'When it became clear to me that our HUMINT in China was compromised, I talked to Ed about Red Hand, a group we considered using during the last war as additional intelligence assets in China. Ed remembered that Red Hand had a representative in New York City, living in Chinatown. This man wasn't in the CIA database or in any way tied to U.S. intelligence; he's just someone we learned about back then but never approached.'

Jack knew Ed Foley, former director of the CIA, was out of town. He said, 'You sent Ed to see him.'

'No, Jack. Ed sent himself. He drove to New York yesterday and spent last evening with Mr Liu, the Red Hand emissary. Liu made contact with his people on the mainland, and they have agreed to help us. They can put us in touch with a dissident organization in the city who claims to have contacts in the local police and government. This group is committing armed acts of rebellion in Beijing, and the only reason they haven't been rolled up like so many others is the CIA hasn't reached out to them.

'Ninety-nine percent of the dissident groups over in China

516

these days exist only on the Internet. But this group, if Red Hand is to be believed, is the real McCoy.'

Jack raised an eyebrow. '"If Red Hand is to be believed"? No offense, Mary Pat, but that sounds like the flaw in your thinking.'

She nodded. 'We are offering them a great deal of money, if and only if they deliver what they promise. An active insurgent group with some connections. We aren't looking for George Washington's Continental Army, but something legitimate. We don't know what we are dealing with until someone goes and checks them out.

'We need someone on the ground there, in the city, to meet with these people, far from any American or Chicom eyes, and get a feel for who they are. If they are anything more than a group of well-intentioned but inept fools, we will support them to get intelligence about what's going on over there in the city. We don't expect large-scale insurrections, but we need to be ready to provide clandestine support if the opportunity presents itself.'

She added, unnecessarily, 'This is totally off the books.'

Before Jack could speak she defended herself from what she expected him to say. 'This is undeclared war, Jack. The Chinese are killing Americans. I am very comfortable supporting locals fighting back against that evil regime over there.' She pointed to Jack's chest for emphasis. 'But it is not my intention to create more cannon fodder. We have done enough of that with our intelligence leaks.'

'I understand.'

She handed Ryan a piece of paper she pulled from her purse. 'This is the Red Hand contact in New York. His name is not in any computer, he has not met with anyone from the government. You commit the name and the number to memory, and then destroy this.'

'Of course.'

'Good. And understand this. You, Jack, are *not* going to China. I want you to talk to Gerry Hendley and, if he thinks this is something your organization can help us with, quietly, then he can send Domingo Chavez or one of the other operators. Having the President's son captured in Beijing working with rebels there will make all of our problems exponentially worse.'

'I get it,' Jack said. *Not to mention it would give my dad a coronary.* 'I will talk to Gerry about it as soon as I leave.'

Mary Pat gave Jack a hug and started to get up.

Ryan said, 'There is one more thing. I don't know if I am stepping out of my lane on this, but . . .'

Mary Pat sat back down. 'Speak up.'

'Okay. The Campus was involved with the Zha arrest in Hong Kong a couple of weeks ago.'

Mary Pat looked genuinely surprised. 'Involved?'

'Yes. We were over there, working with Adam Yao, CIA's NOC who identified him in Hong Kong.'

'Okay.'

'Yao did not know us as The Campus. We sold ourselves as a business trying to track Zha down because he hacked our network. His white-side cover is as a business-intelligence investigator.'

'I have read CIA's reports about Adam Yao and the Zha incident in Hong Kong. The SEALs said they had CIA support. We suspected Yao had two local assets helping him.'

'Anyway, I just wanted to say this: I suppose you know hundreds of great officers in the U.S. intelligence community, but Adam seemed very well dialed-in over there. An extremely sharp guy. He knew about the CIA leak, and he was working his ass off, staying low-profile to avoid getting caught up in the leak while still getting the job done at the same time.

'It's not my place to say, but I really think he is the type of guy who needs your full support, especially at a time like this.'

Mary Pat said nothing.

After an uncomfortable moment, Ryan said, 'I apologize. I know you have more irons in the fire right now than you know what to do with. I just thought –'

'Jack. Adam Yao disappeared two weeks ago, after someone tried to blow him up in his car but instead killed his next-door neighbor.'

Ryan reeled with this news. 'Oh my God.'

Foley said, 'It's possible he just took himself off-grid for his own PERSEC. Hell, I couldn't blame him if he was running from us because of the leak. But our people over there at the consulate in HK think the Fourteen-K Triads got him.' She stood up to leave. 'Their best guess is that he's at the bottom of Victoria Harbour.

'I'm sorry. We failed Adam, too.'

She went back inside the house, while Jack sat there in the cold, sitting on the patio chair with his head in his hands.

57

Adam Yao had spent the first two weeks after the shootout in Wan Chai on Lamma Island, part of Hong Kong territory a forty-minute ferry ride from his home. It was quiet and peaceful here, which was just what he needed. He did not know a soul, and the locals thought he was just some tourist here to enjoy the beach and the bars.

He had made no contact with anyone. Not CIA, not SinoShield clients or colleagues, not relatives in the States or friends in Soho. He'd lived in a tiny monthly vacation rental off the beach, he paid cash, and he took all his meals in the attached restaurant.

His life had changed drastically in the past couple of weeks. He had not used his credit cards, and he had thrown his cell phone in a dumpster in Kowloon. He'd sold a few personal items for cash on the street, and he spent a few days with no cash, but he was not too worried about money. Adam's 'day job,' his SinoShield cover company, had put him in contact with all sorts of local crooks, smugglers, counterfeiters, and other profiteers, and he had cordial dealings with many of them. Occasionally he had to make friends in low places in order to do his job, and he had called in a few markers with some of these friends. He knew he could find temporary work on a dock or in a counterfeit basement handbag shop or any number of other shitty jobs, that, even though they were shitty jobs, were a hell of a lot better than getting burned to a crisp like his poor friend Robert Kam.

He waited two weeks; he wanted the people after him to

think someone else had gotten him or that he'd gotten away, and he wanted anyone from the CIA to stop looking for him as well. Adam knew it would be a big deal at Langley that a NOC had disappeared, especially under the circumstances following the SEAL mission, but he knew CIA assets in the area were just about nonexistent, and, anyway, Langley had bigger fish to fry these days.

Once two weeks had passed, Adam returned to Kowloon, now wearing a full beard and mustache. Within twenty-four hours he owned new dark sunglasses, a new mobile phone, and a new suit and accessories. His suit was impeccable; everyone in Hong Kong who so desired wore a great suit, as Hong Kong tailors had a reputation that rivaled Savile Row, and were known for making beautifully bespoke suits for one-fourth the cost of their London counterparts.

Adam knew he could have left Hong Kong and returned to the States. It would be safe there, certainly from the Triads and almost certainly from the PRC.

But he was not leaving HK until he found out more about the shadowy hacker group that he'd stumbled onto, leading to the deaths of God knows how many. The Americans had Zha, this was true, but this Center character Gavin Biery had spoken of must surely still be in operation.

Adam wasn't going anywhere till he found Center.

The MFIC.

With a few deep breaths and some whispered self-affirmations, Adam then walked into the Mong Kok Computer Centre like he owned the place, asked to speak to the leasing manager of the building, and told the woman he was looking to rent a large space to house a new call center for a Singapore-based bank.

He handed her his business card, and that was all the ID he needed to convince her of his cover for action.

The leasing manager told him, much to her delight, that two floors had just been vacated two weeks earlier, and he asked to take a look. She led him through the carpeted rooms and hallways, and he inspected them carefully, taking pictures and asking questions.

He also asked her questions about herself, which was not his original plan, but going out to dinner with the woman and getting information on the company that just left was to Adam Yao much preferable to his original plan, which was dumpster-diving, hoping against hope to find a scrap of paper that might be a clue about the big group Zha had been a part of.

That evening at dinner the woman spoke freely about Commercial Services Ltd., the large computer company that had just left, mostly about how they were a 14K-owned business and they used an insane amount of electrical power and installed an alarming number of very unattractive antennas on the roof of the building, some of which they did not have the decency to remove when they left in the middle of the night, led away in trucks by armed men who seemed to be security police.

Adam took in all the information, and it made his head spin.

'That was very nice of the Fourteen-K to move all their equipment for them.'

She shook her head. 'No. The people who worked in the offices packed up their own things, and then a shipping service came and took it away.'

'Interesting. I'll need someone who can work quickly to deliver my computers from Singapore. Would you remember the name of the shipping service?'

She did, and Adam committed it to memory and then

spent the rest of the evening enjoying his time with the leasing agent.

The next morning he walked through the doors of Service Cargo Freight Forwarders, at the Kwai Tak Industrial Centre in Kwai Chung, in the New Territories north of Hong Kong. It was a small outfit, only one clerk was present, and Adam Yao presented the man with a beautifully professional business card claiming him to be the leasing manager of the Mong Kok Computer Centre building.

The clerk seemed to believe the cover, though he was hardly impressed. He barely looked up from his television.

Yao said, 'The day after your company picked up the Commercial Services Limited equipment from our building, two pallets of tablet computers that had been delayed in customs arrived for them. The shipment is in our warehouse right now. I checked the packing list and it was listed as a complete shipment, but someone screwed up and didn't realize these two pallets had not yet been delivered. Someone is going to be very unhappy if those goods don't sail with the rest of the shipment.'

The clerk could not possibly have looked less interested. 'That's not my problem.'

Yao was undaunted. 'No, it will be my problem, except for the fact you guys signed off on the incorrect manifest. If they come to me looking for the three hundred sixty units that you signed for, I could just tell them the shipper must have lost them.'

The clerk eyed Yao with annoyance.

Adam smiled. 'Look, man, I just want to do what's right.'

'Leave the pallets here. We'll get them to the client as soon as they note the discrepancy.'

'I hope I don't look that stupid. I'm not giving you one million HK dollars' worth of product that's already been legally imported from China. You could just sell it yourselves on the street and then tell the customer I never delivered it.

'I want to keep our client happy, and you should, too. We made a little screwup, these things happen, and I am just trying to rectify it quietly. If you can do me the personal favor of telling me the port of disembarkation and the name of the person who signed for the goods, I can go directly to them without involving the customer in this at all.'

Adam most often got what he wanted with the incredible social-engineering skills that most good spies possessed. He presented himself professionally, he was polite, and he carried himself with a calm air of self-assuredness. It was hard for anyone to tell him no. But occasionally Adam achieved success in social engineering more from the fact that he could be annoyingly persistent.

This was such a time. The shipping clerk determined, after several minutes of 'No,' that his own laziness and strict adherence to company policy was not going to be enough to get rid of the bothersome young man in the nice suit.

The clerk slid over to his computer, making a show of how much trouble it was to do so. He clicked through a few screens, then settled on one, used his pen to look down at the data. 'Okay. It sailed on the eighteenth. Right now it is one day out of Tokyo.' The man kept looking at the computer.

'Where is it heading?'

'USA next, then Mexico.'

'The cargo. Where will the fourteen pallets disembark?'

The man cocked his head to the side. 'It's already off the vessel. It was offloaded on the nineteenth, in Guangzhou.'

'Guangzhou?'

'Yeah. That makes no sense. You said this stuff was imported from the mainland, which means all the duties, taxes, tariffs, were paid. And then they turn it around and send it back to China? Who the hell does that?'

No one does that, Adam knew. But it told him where Center had moved his organization.

Center was in China. There was no other explanation. And there was no way in hell he could run such a huge operation on the mainland without the Chicoms knowing about it.

Things fell into place quickly in Yao's mind while he stood at the shipping desk. Center was working for China. Zha had been working for Center. Zha orchestrated the UAV attacks.

Was the Center group some sort of false flag operation set up by the Chinese?

The prospect was chilling, but Yao was having a hard time coming up with alternative explanations.

Yao only wished he could tell someone at CIA what he had just learned, and what he was about to do. But Adam Yao wanted to stay alive even more than he wanted a pat on the back or a helping hand.

He'd make his way over the border. He would find Center and his operation. And then he would figure out what to do.

Valentin Kovalenko was up early this morning. He took the Metro from D.C. across the river to Arlington, did a brief surveillance detection run, and then entered the Ballston Public Parking Garage at 7:15 a.m.

Today's instructions were clear, though unusual. For the first time since he'd arrived in D.C. he would be running an agent himself. This would be, it had been explained to him by Center, his priority assignment here in the United States, so he should take it seriously and see it through.

Today was set up as just a brief meet-and-greet, but there

was a subtext to it, which Center had conveyed via Cryptogram the evening before. This agent was a government employee and a willing accomplice of Center's, though he did not know Center's identity, and he himself was running an unwitting agent.

Kovalenko's job was to get the man to turn up the heat on his agent and get some results.

All this seemed to be child's play when Center relayed the mission the evening before; at least it certainly did not seem to be anything along the lines of being involved with the killing of five CIA officers.

But Kovalenko could not really say how sensitive this operation would be, for the simple reason that he was not allowed to know who the ultimate target was. As usual, Center kept things so damn compartmentalized that Valentin knew only that he was to lean on his agent to be harder on his agent, who, in turn, was responsible for compromising the ultimate target.

'No way to run an effective intelligence operation,' Kovalenko had said aloud the night before.

Still, the SVR wanted Valentin to go along and get along, so he was here in a chilly parking garage early this morning, waiting to meet with his agent.

A Toyota minivan pulled into the lot and parked next to Kovalenko, and he heard the snap of the doors being unlocked. He climbed into the passenger seat and found himself sitting next to a large man with a ridiculous flop of gray-blond hair dangling into his eyes.

The man reached out a hand. 'Darren Lipton. FBI. How the hell are you?'

58

Kovalenko shook the man's hand, but he did not identify himself. He only said, 'Center has asked me to work with you directly. To help you find access to resources you may need in the furtherance of your objective.'

This wasn't really true. Valentin knew this man was an FBI agent in the Bureau's National Security Branch. He would have access to a hell of a lot more resources than Valentin would. No, Kovalenko was here to pressure him for results, but there was no sense in starting out the conversation or the relationship, short-lived though Kovalenko expected it to be, with threats.

The American just stared at him for a long time without speaking.

Kovalenko cleared his throat. 'That said, we expect results immediately. Your objective is crucial to the –'

The big man interrupted with a booming shout: 'Are you *fucking* kidding me?'

Kovalenko recoiled in surprise. 'I beg your pardon?'

'Really? I mean . . . *really*?'

'Mr Lipton, I do not know what –'

'The goddamned *Russians*? I've been working for the goddamned motherfucking *Russians*?'

Kovalenko recovered from his shock. Actually he empathized with his agent. He knew what it felt like to have no idea whose flag it was you risked your life and liberty for.

'Things are not as they appear, Special Agent Lipton.'

'Is that right?' Lipton said, and then he slammed his hand

on the steering wheel. 'I sure as hell hope not, because you *appear* to be a fucking Russian.'

Kovalenko just looked down at his fingernails for a moment. He continued. 'Be that as it may, I know your agent has planted a bug on the mobile phone of the target. But we are not getting further GPS updates. We assume he has discarded the phone. We will be going forward with physical surveillance if we don't see immediate results. That will involve you, me, and perhaps others. I don't have to tell you that this would entail long hours of uncomfortable work.'

'I can't do that. I have a job and a family to come home to.'

'Obviously we won't do anything to cause suspicion with the FBI. You will not have to conduct surveillance at times you need to be at your office. Your family, on the other hand, is your problem, not ours.'

Lipton stared at Kovalenko for a long moment. 'I could snap your scrawny little fucking neck.'

Now Kovalenko smiled. He may not have known anything about Lipton's agent, or Lipton's agent's target, but he *did* know a thing or two about Darren Lipton. Center had sent him everything. 'If you try to break my fucking neck, Special Agent Lipton, you will fail. But whether or not you fail or you succeed, your past will come back to haunt you very quickly, because Center will be angry with you, and we both know what Center will do.'

Lipton turned away, and looked out the windshield of the minivan.

Kovalenko said, 'Child pornography, Mr Lipton, on one's computer, certainly of the quantity and variety that was found on *your* personal computer, is something that will put you behind bars very quickly. And I do not know how things are in your country, but I would imagine an incarcerated former federal agent would have a difficult time in prison. Add to that' – he leaned forward toward Lipton menacingly – 'and trust me, we *will* add to that, the knowledge of your specific crimes, and I should think prison life for you would be especially . . . brutal.'

Lipton bit his lip while he looked out the windshield. His fingers began drumming on the steering wheel now. 'I get it,' he said softly, a tone much different than his tone earlier in the conversation. Again he said, 'I get it.'

'Excellent. Now it's time to put all pressure possible on your agent.'

Lipton nodded, still not looking at the Russian in his passenger seat.

'I'll be checking in on you.'

Another nod. Then, 'Is that it?'

Kovalenko opened the door and climbed out of the minivan.

Lipton started the engine, then regarded Kovalenko before he closed the car door. With a shake of his head he muttered, 'The goddamned Russians.'

Kovalenko closed the door, and the Toyota backed out, then drove toward the exit ramp of the parking garage.

'You fucking wish,' Valentin Kovalenko said softly as he watched the car's taillights disappear.

Darren Lipton met Melanie Kraft at the Starbucks at King Street and Saint Asaph. She was rushed this morning; she was on a task force set up at the office of the Director of National Security to evaluate any security leaks that might have led the Prosper Street safe house to be compromised, and there was an eight-o'clock meeting that she could not be late for.

But Lipton had been beyond insistent, so she told him she'd give him ten minutes before she caught the bus for work.

She could tell immediately he was more stressed-out than usual. He wasn't leering over her like he usually did. Instead, he was all business.

'He dumped his phone,' Lipton said as soon as they sat down.

This made Melanie nervous. Had Jack found the bug? 'Really? He didn't say anything to me.'

'Did you tip him off? Did you say anything about the FBI locator?'

'Are you kidding? Of course not. You think I can just confess this whole thing to him over a beer?'

'Well, *something* made him get rid of it.'

'Maybe he suspects,' Melanie said, her voice trailing off as she thought about how distant he had been to her all weekend. She'd called him to do something Saturday night, but he had not called her back. When she called the next morning he said he had not been feeling well, and had planned on taking a couple days off work. She offered to come over and take care of him, but he'd told her he just wanted to sleep it off.

And now Lipton was telling her it was possible – likely, even – that Ryan had discovered the bug.

She shouted at him, 'That tracker was supposed to be impossible to detect!'

Lipton put his hands up. 'Hey, that's what they told me. I don't know. I'm not a tech.' He smiled a little. 'I'm a people person.'

Melanie stood up. 'I did exactly what I was told to do. No one said anything about me getting burned in the bargain. You can tell Packard or I will tell him, I'm done with you guys.'

'Then you and your dad will go to jail.'

'You don't have anything on my father. If you did he would have been arrested years ago. And if you don't have anything on him, that means you don't have anything on me.'

'Sweetheart, it doesn't matter, because we are the FBI, and we have the best polygraph technicians and equipment on planet earth, and we will take your little ass into a room and hook you up to that whoopee cushion, and we will ask you about Cairo. You will be the one that sends both you and your dad to prison.'

Melanie turned away and stormed up King Street without another word.

It was called a hot seat. Trash and Cheese ran out onto the tarmac and stood below two Hornets that had just landed as the other Marine pilots climbed out and the refueling team gassed them up, leaving one engine on so that they would not have to refire all the aircraft systems. Then Trash and Cheese climbed aboard the jets, slid into the cockpits, still warm from the last pilots. They quickly strapped themselves in, hooked up communications lines and air hoses, started the second engine, and taxied back to the runway.

Three days ago, when they first started their CAPs over the Taiwan Strait in ROC aircraft, there had been as many planes as there had been pilots. But the heavy use had taken a toll on the older C-model Hornets, and four of the aircraft had been taken off the flight line for maintenance, necessitating the hot seat.

One more had been shot down; the young pilot had successfully ejected and was picked up by a Taiwanese patrol boat full of sailors shocked to scoop an American out of the water. Another jet slammed into debris after it shot down a Chinese J-5, and this pilot had to crash-land at an airport on the southern tip of the island.

The pilot had survived but with serious injuries, and the word was his flying days were over.

In the past three days the United States had suffered one real combat loss, and they had inflicted nine kills on the PLAAF. The ROC F-16s had lost eleven aircraft and six pilots, a painful toll for the small force but a small fraction of what it would have been if there hadn't been two dozen American fliers in country doing everything in their power to keep the menacing Chinese at bay.

Things were getting dicey at sea level as well. A Chinese anti-ship missile had sunk a Taiwanese cruiser. The PLA claimed to have done this only after the cruiser sank a Chinese diesel sub, but all signs indicated the sub had sunk itself while laying mines in the strait when one of the mines was improperly set and exploded against the submarine's hull.

There were more than one hundred fatalities on both sides in the two sinkings. This was still something less than open war, at this point anyway, but the losses of men and material were increasing by the day.

Trash and Cheese were ordered to fly south this morning; storms were predicted, and the Chinese had not been sending up as many harassing flights in bad weather, but the two young Americans knew better than to assume they would have a quiet CAP.

Cheese had recorded his second kill the day before. With Trash as his wingman supporting and watching his 'six,' Cheese had fired a radar-guided AIM-120 AMRAAM missile that took down a J-5 attacking a flight of Taiwanese F-16s thirty miles to the north of Taipei.

That meant the two Marines had four total combat kills, and Trash's two gun kills of Super 10s were already becoming a source of legend around the Corps. That very few knew, even among the Marine Corps, that this squadron was here in Taiwan still flying against the Chinese was a bit annoying to the men, especially so to Cheese, who would not get to paint the record of the kill on his own aircraft when he returned to his base in Japan.

Still, through the fear and the stress and the danger and the exhaustion, the two young American fighter pilots would not trade their predicaments with anyone else on earth. Flying, fighting, and protecting the innocent were all in their blood.

Their Hornets took off from Hualien air base and flew south toward the strait, toward the storm.

59

Gavin Biery sat at his desk rubbing his tired eyes. He looked like a beaten man, which he was, and the feeling of loss and hopelessness manifested itself in his slumped shoulders and his hung head.

Two of his top engineers were with him; they stood above him, and both men reached out. One patted him on the back, the other gave him an awkward hug. The men left the room without saying another word.

How? How can this be?

He blew out a long hiss of air and picked up his phone. Pressed a button and shut his eyes as he waited for it to be answered.

'Granger.'

'Sam. It's Biery. Got a second?'

'You sound like someone died.'

'Can I get a quick meeting with you, Gerry, and the Campus operators?'

'Come up. I'll get them together.'

Gavin hung up, stood slowly, and left the office, flipping the light off as he left.

Biery addressed the assembled group with solemnity. 'This morning one of my engineers came to me to tell me that after a random security check he detected an uptick in outbound network traffic. It began immediately after I returned from Hong Kong, and it did not follow a strict pattern, though each incident of increased activity lasted exactly two minutes and twenty seconds.'

Biery's announcement was met with a roomful of stares.

He continued: 'Our network is targeted with computer attacks tens of thousands of times a day. The vast, vast majority of these attacks are nothing, just stupid phishing schemes that are pervasive on the Internet. Ninety-eight percent of all the world's e-mail activity is spam, and most of it is hacking attempts. Every network on earth is hit by these things all the time, and moderately competent security measures are sufficient to protect them. But in the midst of all this low-level stuff, our network has been singled out for very serious and smart cyberattacks. It's gone on for a long time, and only by the admittedly draconian measures I've been using have we kept the bad guys outside the wire.'

He sighed again, like a balloon deflating. 'After I got back from Hong Kong, the low-level attacks continued, but the high-level attacks just stopped.

'Unfortunately, this uptick in outbound transfer activity means there is something inside our network. Something has been set up to send out data, our data, our *secure* data.'

Granger asked, 'What does that tell us?'

'They are inside. We have been compromised. We have been hacked. The network has a virus. I dug into a couple of locations, and I regret to say I have found the FastByte Twenty-two fingerprint on our network.'

Hendley asked, 'How did they do it?'

Biery looked off into space. 'There are four threat vectors. Four ways for a network to be compromised.'

'What are the four?'

'A remote threat, like a network attack over the Web, but that didn't happen. I'm firewalled here, meaning there is no direct line to the Internet that someone can use to access the network.'

Granger said, 'Okay. What else?'

'A proximate threat. Like someone hacking into a wireless network from close range. Again, we're as bulletproofed as we can be against that.'

'Okay,' said Chavez, urging Biery on.

'The third threat vector is the insider threat. That would be someone here in the building, working for the enemy, compromising our system.' Biery shook his head. 'I can't believe anyone here would do that. My hiring and vetting process is as tough as I can possibly make it. Everyone in this building has worked in top-secret —'

Hendley waved away the thought. 'No. I don't believe this was an inside job. What's the fourth threat vector?'

Biery said, 'Supply chain.'

'Meaning?'

'Compromising hardware or software that then makes its way onto the network. But again, I have safeguards against that. We monitor everything that comes in, every peripheral connected to the system, every —'

He stopped talking mid-sentence.

'What is it?' asked Chavez.

Biery stood quickly. 'The German hard drive!'

'What?'

'Todd Wicks at Advantage Technology Solutions delivered a drive I ordered. I checked it out myself. It was legit. Clear of known viruses. But maybe there is something new. Something hidden in the master boot record that no one knows how to detect. I did not install it till I got back from HK, and that's exactly when the virus began reporting back.'

'What do you want to do?'

Biery sat back down. He put his elbows on the table and

dropped his head in his hands. 'Step one? Shoot the hostage.'

'What?' Hendley exclaimed.

'We call it shooting the hostage. They have my network. That is the advantage they hold on us. But I can shut it all down. The entire network. Just go dark. That removes their advantage. Kill everything.'

Granger nodded. 'Okay. Do it. Step two?'

'Step two? You send me down to Richmond.'

'What's in Richmond?'

'Todd Wicks. If his board had been compromised, he would know about it.'

Hendley asked, 'Are you sure he knew?'

Gavin thought back to Todd's visit to Hendley Associates. He seemed overly friendly, a little nervous, especially when he met Jack Junior.

Biery said, 'He knew.'

Chavez stood up quickly. 'I'll drive.'

Todd Wicks watched his kids play on the swing set in the back-yard. Even though it was only forty-five degrees, they were enjoying the last of the daylight outside, and he knew they would enjoy the hamburgers he was grilling up even more.

Sherry was out here on the deck with him, talking on her phone with a client while she reclined on the chaise longue, bundled up in a polar fleece and ski pants but looking beauti-ful nonetheless.

Todd was feeling good about the day, about his family, about his life.

Through the constant din of the playing children, Wicks heard a new noise, and he looked up, away from the grilling burgers, and saw a black Ford Explorer pull up in his drive-way. He didn't recognize the vehicle. He flipped the four burgers on the grill quickly and called out to his wife.

'Honey, are you expecting anybody?'

She could not see the driveway from where she lay back on the chaise. She pulled the phone away from her ear. 'No? Is someone here?'

He did not answer, because now he saw Gavin Biery climbing out of the passenger side of the Explorer, and he did not know what to do.

His knees went weak for a moment, but he fought his panic, put the spatula down, and took off his apron.

'Couple of guys from work, babe. I'll talk to them inside.'

'Can I meet them?'

'No,' he said, a little more forcefully than he would have liked, but he was worrying about what was going to happen.

Deny, deny, deny, he told himself. *You don't know anything about a virus.*

He rushed off the deck and down to the driveway, catching Gavin and the Hispanic-looking man before they made it into the backyard. *Play cool,* he told himself over and over. He smiled widely. 'Gavin? Hey, buddy. How's it going?'

Gavin Biery did not return the smile. The Hispanic guy stood stone-faced next to him. 'Can we go inside and talk for a minute?'

'Sure.' *Good. Get them out of the damn driveway and into the house where Sherry can't hear.*

A minute later they were in Wicks's living room. All three men remained standing. Todd asked his guests to sit down, but neither man complied, so Todd just stood there nervously, looking hot and uncomfortable while telling himself over and over to be cool.

'What's this about?' he asked, and he thought he hit the right tone.

Biery said, 'You know what this is about. We found the virus on the drive.'

'The *what*?'

'"The what?" That's the best you can do? C'mon, Todd. I remember how you just about shit your pants when I introduced you to Jack Ryan. What must have been going on in your mind at that moment?'

Chavez stared Wicks down.

'Who are you?' Wicks asked.

The Hispanic man did not answer.

Wicks looked at Biery. 'Gavin, who the hell is –'

Biery said, 'I know the hard drive was infected with malware. In the master boot record.'

'What are you talking –'

Chavez spoke now: 'Best you don't lie. We can see right through you. And if you lie, I *will* hurt you.'

Wicks's face went even paler, and his hands began to shake. He said something, but his voice cracked, and Ding and Gavin looked at each other. Chavez said, 'Speak up!'

'I didn't know what was on there.'

'How did you know *anything* was on there?' asked Chavez.

'It was the . . . the Chinese. Chinese intelligence.'

Gavin asked, 'They gave you the drive?'

'Yes.' Todd started to cry.

The Hispanic man rolled his eyes. 'Are you fucking kidding?'

Between sobs, Wicks asked, 'Can we please sit down?'

Over the next ten minutes Todd told the two men everything. The girl in Shanghai, the entourage of cops, the detective who said he could help Todd stay out of jail, the agent in the pizza parlor in Richmond, and the hard drive.

Chavez said, 'So, you got taken by a dangle.'

'A what?' asked Wicks.

'It's called a dangle. They dangled this girl, Bao, for you to go after, and then they caught you in a honey trap.'

'Yes. I guess that's about the size of it.'

Chavez looked at Biery. The doughy computer geek looked like he wanted to kill Todd Wicks. The Hendley/Campus network was Gavin Biery's great love, and this guy had slipped through the defenses and brought it down. Ding wondered if he would have to pull Gavin off the younger, fitter Wicks, who right now did not look like he would be able to defend himself from a house cat, much less a rage-filled computer geek.

'What are you going to do to me?' Wicks asked.

Chavez looked to the broken man. 'Don't ever say another word about this to anyone as long as you live. I doubt the Chinese will contact you again, but if they do, it might just be to kill you, so you might want to think about grabbing the family and running like hell.'

'*Kill* me?'

Ding nodded. 'You saw what happened in Georgetown?'

Wicks's eyes widened. 'Yeah?'

'Same guys that you've been working for, Todd. What happened in Georgetown is just an example of how they go about tying up loose ends. Might want to keep that in mind.'

'Oh my God.'

Chavez looked out the window at Wicks's wife. She was pushing the children on the swings and looking back into the kitchen window, no doubt wondering who the two men were that her husband did not want her to meet. Chavez gave her a nod and then turned around to Todd Wicks. 'You don't deserve her, Wicks. Maybe you want to spend the rest of your life trying to rectify that obvious fact.'

Chavez and Biery left through the garage door without another word.

60

Gavin Biery and Domingo Chavez arrived at Jack Ryan, Jr's apartment just after ten o'clock in the evening. Jack was still under suspension, but Gavin and Ding wanted to fill him in on the day's events.

Chavez was surprised when Ryan said he did not want to talk in his house. Jack handed each man a Corona, then led them back downstairs to the parking lot, and then across the street to a golf course. The three of them sat in the dark at a picnic table and sipped beer along a fairway shrouded in mist.

After Biery told Ryan about the visit to Wicks's house and the revelation that Chinese intelligence agents had a hand in putting the virus on the Hendley Associates computer network, Jack searched for some explanation. 'Is there any way at all that these guys weren't working for the MSS? Could they have been foot soldiers for Tong that slipped into mainland China to compromise this computer guy?'

Ding shook his head. 'This happened in Shanghai. Center couldn't bug a hotel room, bring a big crew of cops, uniformed and plain-clothed, and pull this off without the knowledge of the MSS. Hotels in China, especially luxury and business-class hotels, are all ordered by law to do the bidding of the MSS. They are bugged, surveilled, staffed with agents working for state security. It just is not possible this was anything other than an MSS operation.'

'But the virus is Zha's RAT. The same one on the Istanbul Drive. The same one on the UAV hack. The only explanation is that Zha and Tong were working for China in Hong Kong when they were under the protection of the Triads.'

Chavez nodded. 'And this also means that the Chinese government knows about Hendley Associates. Just think about what's on our network that they infiltrated. Names and home addresses of our employees, data that we've pulled from CIA and NSA and ODNI chatter. Obvious linkages to anyone with half a brain that we are an off-the-books spy shop.'

Jack said, 'The good news, on the other hand, is what is not on the network.'

'Explain,' said Chavez.

'We don't record our activities. There's nothing on there that talks about any of the hits we've done, the operations we've been engaged in. Yes, there is more than enough there to target us or to prove we're getting access to classified data, but nothing to tie us to any particular operation.'

Ding gulped his Corona and shivered. 'Still, anybody in China picks up a phone and calls *The Washington Post*, and we're toast.'

'Why hasn't that already happened?' Jack asked.

'No idea. I don't get it.'

Ryan gave up trying to figure that one out. He asked, 'Has there been any more talk about sending operatives over to Beijing to meet with Red Hand?'

Chavez said, 'Granger is working on getting us into the country. As soon as we have a way in, me and Driscoll are wheels up.'

Jack felt incredibly isolated. He wasn't working, he wasn't talking to Melanie, and now he did not even want to communicate with his mom and dad, because he felt, at any moment, the Chinese would reveal information about him that could bring down his father's presidency.

Gavin Biery had been silent this whole time, but suddenly he stood up from the picnic table and said, 'I see it.'

'You see what?' asked Ding.

'I can see the big picture now. And it's not pretty.'

'What are you talking about?'

Gavin said, 'Tong's organization is a group that works in the interests of its host nation, uses the assets of its host nation to some degree, but it is a sub rosa outfit that is self-directing. I'd also bet they are self-funding, since they can generate so much cash from cybercrime. Moreover, Center's organization has the incredible technological means that he uses to get intelligence to fulfill his mission.'

Jack saw it now, too. 'Holy shit. They are us! They are almost the same as The Campus. A deniable proxy operation. The Chinese could not let the cyberattacks lead back to them. They set Center up with his own operation, like my dad did with The Campus, to free them up to be more aggressive.'

Chavez added, 'And they have been watching us since Istanbul.'

'No, Ding,' Jack said, his voice suddenly grave. 'Not since Istanbul. Before Istanbul. *Way* before.'

'What does that mean?'

Jack put his head in his hands. 'Melanie Kraft is a Center asset.'

Chavez looked at Biery and saw that he already knew. 'What the hell are you talking about?'

'She bugged my phone. That's how Center knew Dom and I were in Miami investigating the command server.'

Chavez could not believe it. 'She bugged your phone? Are you sure?'

Jack just nodded and looked off into the mist.

'That's why we are sitting out here in the cold?'

Jack shrugged. 'I've got to figure she's planted bugs all over my house. I don't know, I haven't swept for them yet.'

'Have you talked to her? Confronted her?'

'No.'

Ding said, 'She's CIA, Ryan. She's passed a hell of a lot more background checks than you have. I don't believe she's working for the fucking Chicoms.'

Ryan slammed his hand on the table. 'Did you hear what I just said? She bugged my phone. And not just some off-the-shelf spy shit. Gavin found Zha's RAT, or a version of it, on the device, along with a GPS tracker.'

'But how do you know she wasn't duped somehow? Tricked into planting it.'

'Ding, she's been acting suspiciously for a long time. Ever since I got back from Pakistan in January. There have been signs; I was just too whipped to see them.' He paused. 'I was a damn idiot.'

''*Mano*, there are reasons to be suspicious of you. A girl as smart as her has a bullshit meter cranked up to eleven. As for the bug on your phone . . .' Chavez shook his head. 'She's being played. Somebody socially engineered that. I find it hard to believe she is a spy for China.'

Biery said, 'I agree.'

Jack said, 'I don't know *why* she did it. I only know *that* she did it. And I know I am the one who compromised our entire operation letting her do it.'

Ding said, 'Everybody at The Campus has got loved ones on the outside who don't know what we do. We're at risk every time we let someone new into our life. The question is, what are you going to do about it?'

Jack turned his hands up on the table. 'I'm open to suggestions.'

'Good. You're on suspension, which you can use to your

advantage. You've got some time. Use it to find out who the hell is pulling her strings.'

'Okay.'

'I want you to make a covert entry on her place, and do it carefully. She's not a spook, she's an analyst, but don't take any chances. Be on the lookout for any countermeasures or telltales. See what you can find, but don't bug her place. If she is working for the other side, she might be running security sweeps and detect it.'

Jack nodded. 'Okay. I'll slip in tomorrow morning when she goes to work.'

'Good,' said Chavez. 'You might want to follow her for the next couple of evenings. See if she's doing anything out of the ordinary. Meeting anyone.'

Gavin added, 'Eating Chinese food.'

It was a joke, but Ding and Jack just responded to it with cold stares.

'Sorry,' he said. 'Not the time.'

Chavez continued: 'Obviously give your laptop to Gavin to have it checked out. We'll have a team from Science and Technology on the fifth floor come by your place and sweep for bugs. Ditto your car.'

Gavin said, 'I checked his car earlier today – it's clean.'

Chavez nodded. 'Good.'

Ding's phone chirped on his belt, and he grabbed it. 'Yeah? Hey, Sam. Okay. I'm in the neighborhood, actually. I'll be right there.'

Chavez got up from the table quickly, draining his beer while he stood. 'I'm going in to the office. Granger thinks he has a way to get me and Driscoll into China.'

'Good luck,' Ryan said.

Ding looked at the younger man, then put his hand on his shoulder. 'Good luck to *you*, kid. Keep an open mind with

Miss Kraft. Don't let your emotions convict her before you figure out what's going on. That said, even if she is not wittingly working for Center, she is another piece of the puzzle. You have to exploit that, *'mano*. If you do this right, we can find out from her more about Center than we already know.'

'I'll get it done.'

Chavez nodded to Biery, then turned and disappeared in the mist.

Dr K. K. Tong stood at desk thirty-four, looking over the shoulder of the controller as she typed into Cryptogram. He knew most managers were intimidated by his presence at their desk while they worked, but this woman was extremely competent, and she did not seem to mind.

He was satisfied with her performance so far.

He had been making his rounds through the Ghost Ship when she called him on his VOIP headset and asked him to come over. Tong supposed he walked some ten kilometers a day between all the nodes in the building, and on top of this he probably had somewhere in the neighborhood of fifty daily videoconferences.

When the woman at desk thirty-four finished what she was working on she turned around to face him, began to stand, but he stopped her. 'Remain seated,' he said. 'You wanted to see me?'

'Yes, Center.'

'What is happening at Hendley Associates?'

'We lost tracking and remote access to Jack Ryan's phone on Saturday. This afternoon our deep persistent access into the company network ceased. It appears as if they detected the intrusion and took the entire network offline.'

'The entire network?'

'Yes. There is no traffic coming from Hendley Associates.

Their e-mail server is not accepting messages. It looks as if they simply pulled the plug on everything.'

'Interesting.'

'My field asset, Valentin Kovalenko, is very good. I can have him meet again with his agent, Darren Lipton, and force him to apply pressure to his agent, Melanie Kraft, to find out how the intrusion was detected.'

Tong shook his head. 'No. Hendley Associates was a curiosity. We hoped to learn their role in the American intelligence hierarchy. But then they became a problem in Hong Kong. Then came Miami, where they were even more of a nuisance. Our measures against them have been insufficient. I do not have time to devote to unraveling the mystery of Hendley Associates. If they have detected our presence on their network, then they might have more information about us than we know. It is time for larger measures.'

'Yes, Center. As was always the case, we can covertly report them to the American authorities, or direct one of our proxy assets in the American press to investigate them.'

Tong shook his head. 'They know about us. Revealing them to the world reveals us to the world. No, we can't do that.'

'Yes, Center.'

Tong thought for a moment more and then said, 'I will call in Crane.'

'Yes, Center. Shall I end our relationship with Lipton?'

'No. He is FBI. He might still be useful. His agent, though . . . the girlfriend of the President's son?'

'Melanie Kraft.'

'Yes. She has proved worthless, and she can compromise our asset Lipton. Send her details to Crane. I will have him remove that compromise.'

'Yes, Center.'

61

Domingo Chavez and Sam Driscoll sat in Gerry Hendley's office with Gerry and Sam Granger. For the first time in the two years Chavez had worked for The Campus, Hendley's laptop was not open on his desk. Instead he'd zipped it up in a leather bag and put the bag in his closet. It seemed a little paranoid to Ding, but there was a lot of that going around these days.

It was after eleven p.m., but no one commented on the late hour. The only topic of discussion was the potential to follow Mary Pat Foley's request for help inside China.

Granger said, 'We've found a way to get you into Beijing, and I talked to the Red Hand representative and let him know we might be requesting their help.'

Driscoll asked, 'What's our access?'

'The Propaganda Department of the PRC is conducting a major charm offensive with other nations around the world. Trying to rally support for China and pull support away from the United States. They are inviting foreign media outlets to come to Beijing to learn about China from a Chinese perspective, not what Hollywood says about it.'

Chavez said, 'I've used media credentials as cover for status on more than one occasion in my career.'

'Yeah, the Propaganda Department is pledging free movement of the press in China throughout this conflict.'

Chavez said, 'Yeah? I've heard other dictatorships say the same shit.'

Granger conceded the point. 'You can figure that every step you take will be with a government minder on your arm and clandestine surveillance will be monitoring your every move.'

Driscoll said, 'That sounds like it might interfere with our plans to work with a group of cutthroat criminals to link up with a group of armed rebels.'

Chavez chuckled.

Granger laughed, too, then said, 'Red Hand has a plan to get you away from the minders.' He looked down at his notepad. 'In Beijing the Ministry of Culture will offer you the opportunity to go on a number of media excursions. One of the excursions will be to the Great Wall. There is a main location where they visit, and a secondary, less traveled location. The name of it is listed here. You are to ask to see that portion of the wall.'

Driscoll asked, 'And then what?'

'Somehow they will get you away from the minders, at which point they will take you to the rebels.'

'Tell me what you know about the rebel force.'

'One of their number is a cop, and he's been alerting them to police crackdowns, government movements, and the like. They have been doing small-scale harassing actions against the government out in the provinces. They set some government vehicles on fire, blew up a couple of rail lines.

'So far Chinese state-run media has covered it up. No surprise there. But they are planning on acting next inside of Beijing, where there is a lot of international media and foreigners who can spread the word. That's their main goal, starting a small fire that will grow and grow like the protests grew.

'They claim to have a well-trained force of over three hundred rebels, as well as small arms. They want to hit back against the Chicoms.'

Chavez was incredulous. 'They want to take on the Army? Are they insane?'

Driscoll echoed the sentiment: 'Excuse me if I don't faint from excitement. They sound like lambs to the slaughter.'

Granger shook his head. 'Obviously they are not going to topple the government with a counterinsurgency. Not with three hundred guys. Hell, not with three hundred thousand guys. But maybe we can use them.'

'Use them for what?' Ding asked.

'If a shooting war starts, Mary Pat wants assets in the capital city. These rebels are in place and might be just what we need. It's hard to get a straight read on how successful they've been. The Chinese government makes out like they are a couple of mosquito bites, and the rebels are proclaiming that they are a gnat's-ass distance from toppling the Communist government.'

Driscoll groaned. 'I think we have to go on the assumption that, on this one issue, the official word from Beijing is closer to the truth.'

'I agree. But even if the rebels aren't exactly an organized and elite fighting force, if we get over there with the right equipment and intelligence, we will provide a force multiplication effect.'

Ding asked, 'What are their politics?'

Granger shrugged. 'Confused. They are against the government – on that they all agree. Otherwise they are just a disparate band of students. Plus there are some criminals in the mix, folks on the run from the cops, AWOL soldiers.'

Chavez asked, 'Are our document guys good enough to get us into Beijing?'

'Yeah. We can get you into the country, but you'll be going in light.'

Gerry Hendley added, 'Shit, you'll be going in naked. You will be foreigners in a city that is wary of foreigners.'

Chavez said, 'We'll need to bring Caruso back for this. He can play Italian, at least in front of the Chinese.'

Hendley nodded, looked to Granger. Sam did not seem happy about it, but he said, 'Do it. But not Ryan. Not there.'

Chavez said, 'Okay. We get Caruso, and I'll go. What about you, Sam?'

Driscoll was not sold. 'Just trust the killers and thieves of Red Hand to take us to some untested rebel force. Is that the plan, basically?'

Granger replied, 'You don't have to do this.'

Driscoll thought it over and then said, 'Under normal conditions, this would be way too thin to chance it. But I think we have to give it a shot.' He sighed. 'What the hell, I'm in.'

Hendley nodded appreciatively, then said, 'Damn lot of unknowns on this, guys. I am not prepared to green-light you for any action, but I will let you three go over there and sniff around. You meet with the rebels, send me your best impressions of what is going on, and together we'll decide if this is something that we can pursue.'

'Sounds good to me,' said Chavez, and he looked at the other two men on his side of the desk.

'Works for me,' said Driscoll.

Granger stood up, signifying the end of the meeting. 'Okay. Head down to operations and order a full identification portfolio for all three of you. Tell ops to double-time the credentials but do their best work. No one down there goes home until you have what you need. I don't care if they are here all night, you will get your credos. Catch any flak and have them give me a call.'

Ding stood and shook Sam's hand. 'Thanks.'

Hendley shook the men's hands and said, 'You guys just be careful. Pakistan in January was no cakewalk, I know, but the Chinese are several orders of magnitude more competent and dangerous.'

'Roger that,' said Ding.

62

'Mr President?'

Jack Ryan woke to see the night watch officer standing over his bed. He sat up quickly; he was, after all, getting used to this. He followed the Air Force officer out into the hall before Cathy woke.

He joked softly as they walked: 'I get more news overnight than during the day.'

The NWO said, 'The secretary of state wanted me to wake you. It's all over television, sir. The Chinese are saying American pilots are flying covert missions in Taiwanese aircraft.'

'Shit,' said Ryan. It was his idea, it was secret, and now it was on the news. 'Okay, get the gang together. I'll be down in a few minutes.'

'How did they find out?' Ryan asked the table full of his best military and intelligence advisers.

Mary Pat Foley said, 'Taiwan is full of Chinese spies. Word leaked somehow. A Marine pilot was shot down and then rescued by a fishing trawler. That one event probably doubled the number of people who knew about the covert operation.'

Jack knew the real world had a habit of intruding on his best schemes.

He thought it over for a moment. 'I'm reading the daily reports on our pilots' activities. They are providing a real benefit to the ROC. Taiwan would have suffered tremendous losses to the Chinese if not for our operation.'

Burgess agreed. 'Taiwan is there for the taking. A couple dozen American pilots can't change that. But if the PLAAF had racked up another twenty-five air-to-air kills, the morale in the ROC would have already hit rock bottom, and there would be a groundswell of Taiwanese ready to throw in the towel. I'm very glad we've got our well-trained jet jocks over there giving it back to the Chinese.'

Roger said, 'We neither confirm nor deny the story. We just refuse to comment on China's allegations. And we keep our guys over there.'

Everyone agreed, though Adler looked worried.

The Commander of the Pacific Fleet, Mark Jorgensen, had excused himself from the videoconference just as Ryan entered the room. Ryan had been around long enough to know that admirals did not usually tell the President they had something more important to deal with unless it was indeed more important.

Now he was back on-screen. His voice was loud, almost angry, as he interrupted the secretary of state, who had been speaking about the situation in Taiwan. 'Mr President, my apologies. The Chinese have fired more anti-ship cruise missiles against another Taiwanese ship. They struck the *Tso Ying*, a destroyer that was on patrol in the Taiwan Strait, with two Silkworm missiles. This boat was the USS *Kidd* before we sold it to the ROC some years back. The *Tso Ying* is currently disabled, burning and adrift. It has crossed the centerline of the strait and is heading toward Chinese territorial waters.'

Burgess muttered, 'God damn it.'

Jorgensen continued, 'Chairman Su has ordered the United States to stay out of the area. He just publicly threatened to launch an anti-ship ballistic missile, apparently the Dong Feng 21, against the USS *Ronald Reagan* or *Nimitz* carrier groups, if they move within the three-hundred-mile exclusion zone Su imposed last week.'

There were gasps around the room.

Ryan asked, 'What is the range of the DF 21?'

'Nine hundred miles.'

'Jesus Christ! We could move the *Reagan* back to Tokyo Bay and they could still hit it.'

'That is correct, sir. And it is a true carrier killer, sir. One DF 21 would sink a *Nimitz*-class carrier, and likely kill most everyone on board.'

'How many of these weapons do the Chinese have?'

Mary Pat Foley answered this one: 'Our best guess is eighty to one hundred.'

'Mobile launchers?'

'Yes, Mr President. Land-based wheeled mobile launchers, as well as submarines.'

'Okay, what about our subs? We are operating undersea in the strait, yes?'

Jorgensen said, 'Yes, sir.'

'Can we help with the Taiwanese destroyer?'

Bob Burgess said, 'You mean with the rescue?'

'Yes.'

Burgess looked to Jorgensen. The admiral said, 'We can launch cruise missiles against the PLAN if they attack the wounded ship.'

Ryan looked around the room. 'That's open naval warfare.' He drummed his fingers on the table.

'All right. Scott, get Ambassador Li on the line right now. I want him to go to the Chinese foreign ministry this second and tell them that any further attack on the *Tso Ying* will be resisted by U.S. force.'

Scott Adler stood and headed out of the conference room.

Jack Ryan addressed the others: 'We are on the verge of

open war in the strait now. I want every U.S. asset in the East China Sea, the Yellow Sea, anywhere in the Western Pacific, on the absolute highest state of readiness. If one of our subs attacks a Chinese vessel, then we can expect all hell to break loose.'

Valentin Kovalenko climbed into the passenger seat of Darren Lipton's Toyota Sienna at six in the morning. The Russian had instructions from Center. As always, he did not know the reason behind the message he was about to deliver, but he was placated in the fact that his Russian colleagues at the embassy had given him the go-ahead to do what he was told, so he did not question his directive.

He said, 'You are to make an appointment with your agent immediately.'

Lipton responded with his usual anger. 'She's not a trained pet. She doesn't come the moment I call. She will be at work, she won't meet with me until after she gets off.'

'Do it now. Have her come before work. Be persuasive. Tell her to take a taxi to this address, and you will meet her there. You'll have to convince her it is crucial.'

Lipton took the printed address and looked at it while he drove. 'What's there?'

'I don't know.'

Lipton looked at Kovalenko for a moment, then put his eyes back on the road.

'What do I tell her when she gets there?'

'Nothing. You will not be waiting for her. Someone else will.'

'Who?'

'I don't know.'

'Packard?'

Kovalenko did not respond. He had no idea who Packard

was, but Lipton did not need to know this. 'I don't know if it will be Packard or someone else.'

'What's this all about, Ivan?'

'Just get the woman to the location.'

Lipton eyed Kovalenko for a moment while he drove. 'You don't know what's going on, do you?'

Kovalenko saw that Lipton could see right through him. He said, 'I do not. I have my orders. You have yours.'

Lipton smiled. 'I get it, Ivan. I see it now. Center has something on you, same as me. You aren't his man. You are his agent.'

Kovalenko spoke in a tired voice: 'We are all cogs in a system. A system we do not fully understand. But we understand our own mission, and that is what I need you to focus on.'

Lipton pulled over to the side of the road. 'Tell Center I want more money.'

'Why don't you tell him yourself?'

'You're Russian. He is obviously Russian. Even though you are his errand boy, just like me, he's more likely to listen to you.'

Kovalenko smiled wearily. 'You know how it is. If an intelligence organization pays its agent a lot of money, then the agent won't need money anymore, and he will be less incentivized to help.'

Lipton shook his head. 'You and I both know what my incentive is to work for Center. It's not money. It's blackmail. But I am damn well worth more money.'

Kovalenko knew this was not true. He had read the man's file. Yes, blackmail had been the short-term impetus to get him to begin spying. He had images on his computer that Center had found that could get him thrown in prison.

But he now was very much in it for the money.

The quantity and quality of his whores had gone through

the roof in the year that he had been working for the mysterious employer who gave him simple instructions every week or two.

His wife and kids had not seen a dime of the money he'd made; he'd opened a private account, and almost every penny of it had gone to Carmen and Barbie and Britney and the other girls who worked the hotels in Crystal City and Rosslyn.

Kovalenko had no respect for the man, but he did not need to respect an agent to run him.

He opened the door and got out. 'Have your agent arrive at that location at nine a.m. I will talk to Center about your compensation in the meantime.'

The Chinese government's State Security Law compels China's citizens to comply and cooperate with all government security employees, mandating that hotels and other businesses give unrestricted access to all operations.

This meant, in short, that most business-class hotels in China were bugged with audiovisual equipment that was piped to Ministry of State Security employees who monitored it for intelligence value.

There were many commercial secrets the Chinese could learn just by flipping a switch and posting a translator with a notepad at a radio receiver.

Chavez, Caruso, and Driscoll knew their Beijing hotel would be bugged, and they agreed on their game plan while still in the States. During their time in their suites they would stay in character, their cover-for-status would remain in place.

As soon as they checked in after their interminably long commercial flight from the U.S., Ding turned the shower on its hottest setting and then stepped out of the bathroom, closing the door behind him. He flipped on the TV and then began undressing, just a tired businessman, worn-out from a brutal flight, looking to grab a quick shower before crawling into bed. He walked around while he took off his shirt, stood in front of the TV, doing his best to act naturally, although in truth he was scanning carefully for cameras around the room. He checked the television set itself, and then the wall opposite his bed. He laid his shirt and undershirt on the desk next to his carry-on bag, and while doing this he peered carefully at the lampshade.

Ding was familiar with at least two dozen of the most common miniature cameras and audio receivers; he knew what to look for, but so far he had found nothing.

He noticed the overhead lights were recessed in the ceiling. To him this looked like a great place to secrete a camera. He stood directly under the lights, but he did not climb onto a bed or a chair to check for them.

They were here, he was sure enough. If he went out of his way to look for them, the MSS goons watching him would notice, and this would ensure even more attention on his room.

When he was undressed he stepped back into the bathroom. By now it was completely fogged, and it took a minute for the fog to clear enough for him to get a good look around. The first place he checked was the large bathroom mirror, and he found what he was looking for immediately: a foot-square portion where the glass had not fogged up.

That, Ding knew, was because there was a recess on the other side of the glass where a camera was positioned. There was probably a Wi-Fi radio there, too, which sent the camera's signal and the signal for the audio equipment hidden somewhere in the suite back to wherever it was the MSS guys were.

Ding smiled inwardly. Standing there naked, he wanted to wave at the camera. He suspected ninety-nine percent of the businessmen and -women who stayed in this hotel and dozens more like it in Beijing had absolutely no idea they were on candid camera every time they took a shower.

In two other suites on the same floor, Dominic Caruso and Sam Driscoll were doing their own hidden countersurveillance of their rooms. All three Americans came to the same easy conclusion: they would all have to be careful to do nothing, to say nothing, and to act in no way different from the average hotel guest, lest they compromise their operation.

All three men had been in the field in hostile environments many times before. The Chinese were hard-core in their spying tactics, but all three men knew they could play their roles and do nothing to alert the bored men and women monitoring them that they were up to something here in Beijing.

Ding had just settled in to bed to catch a few hours' sleep when his satellite phone rang. It was encrypted, so he wasn't worried about anyone listening in electronically, although there were no doubt microphones in the room.

He turned on the TV, walked out to the balcony, and then closed the glass door behind him.

'*Bueno?*'

'Uh . . . Ding?'

'Adam?' Chavez said, his voice barely more than a whisper.

'Yeah.'

'I'm glad you called. People are wondering what happened to you.'

'Yeah. Just went off-grid for a while.'

'I get it.'

Yao said, 'I've found where Center is operating from.'

'By yourself?'

'Yep.'

'Where?'

'It's in Guangzhou, about two hours north of Hong Kong. I don't have an address, but I've narrowed it down. It's near the TRB, the Technical Recon Bureau. He's in mainland China, Ding. He was working for the Chicoms the entire time.'

Chavez looked around nervously. It occurred to him that Beijing was a really bad place to take this phone call.

'Yes. We put that together ourselves. You have to find a way to let your employer know.'

'Look, Ding. I'm done sending cables back to Langley. They've got a leak, and that leak is getting back to the PRC. I tell Langley and it's a good bet Center just moves again.'

'What are you going to do?'

'I'm going to work without a net.'

Chavez said, 'I like your style, Adam, but that's not going to be good for your career.'

'Getting killed isn't good for my career, either.'

'Can't argue with that.'

'I could use some help.'

Chavez thought it over. There was no way he could spare either Driscoll or Caruso right now, and no way they could just take off without having the Chinese minders become very suspicious.

'I'm in the middle of something I can't leave right now, but I can get Ryan on the way to help you.' Chavez knew sending Jack into mainland China was questionable, at best. But he knew Tong was at the center of the entire conflict with China, and Guangzhou was close to the Hong Kong border, anyway, unlike Beijing.

At least, Ding told himself, he wasn't sending Jack to Beijing.

'*Ryan?*' Yao said, no attempt to hide his disappointment.

'What's wrong with Jack?'

'I've got too much to do to have to watch out for the Junior Pres.'

'Jack's an asset, Yao. Take my word for it.'

'I don't know.'

'Take it or leave it.'

Yao sighed. 'I'll take him. At least he knows people who can make things happen. Have him go to HK, and I can meet him at the airport and get him over the border.'

'Okay. Call me back in ninety minutes and I'll put the two of you together.'

63

Jack Ryan, Jr, drove across the Francis Scott Key Bridge, his eyes fixed on a taxi in the traffic one hundred yards ahead.

It was just after seven in the morning, and Jack had tailed the cab since it left Melanie's Alexandria carriage-house apartment twenty minutes earlier.

Today was the third day in a row he had shown up at her place before dawn, parking his car several blocks over from Princess Street and then finding a secluded spot in a tiny garden across the street. Each day he watched her windows with his binoculars as soon as there was enough light in the sky to do so, and he stayed there until she left for work, walking up the street to catch the Metro.

Then, for the past two days anyhow, he'd checked her mailbox and her trash, but he'd not found anything of value. He'd left within minutes of her departure for work, and he'd spent the rest of the day trying to figure out how he was going to confront her about Center.

Today his plan had been to break into her flat once she left; he knew he could pick her door lock with ease, but his plan had been derailed when a cab pulled up to her door at six-forty and she'd rushed out, already dressed for work.

Jack hurried back to his car, and then caught up to the taxi on the Jefferson Davis Memorial Highway. He'd recognized early on that she wasn't going to her job in McLean, but instead was heading into D.C.

Now, as he followed her off the bridge and into George-town, he thought about the murder of all the CIA officers two weeks earlier, and it sickened him to think she might have somehow been involved.

'Unwittingly, Jack,' he said, telling himself aloud she would not be working either against him or for the Chinese without being seriously duped.

He wanted to believe it, anyway.

His phone chirped in the console. He touched the hands-free button on the steering wheel.

'Ryan.'

'Jack, it's Ding.'

'Hey. Are you in Beijing?'

'Yes. Sorry, no time to talk. I just called the Gulfstream. You need to be at BWI in an hour.'

Shit. He was almost an hour away from Baltimore as it was. He'd have to break off his tail of Melanie's car and haul ass. But then something else occurred to him. 'I'm on suspension, remember?'

'Granger rescinded it.'

'Okay. Roger that. I'm in D.C., en route to BWI. Where am I heading?'

'Hong Kong.'

Jack knew it was unlikely Ding's satellite call was being monitored, and Gavin and his team had spent hours searching his car for trackers or listening devices, but he also knew there was no point in saying anything more that could give away operational intel, so he asked no more questions.

'Okay,' he said, and he hung up. He was thick in the streets of Georgetown now, and the best way north to Baltimore was up ahead, so he continued following Melanie's cab until he could turn off.

He could not see the taxi at the moment because a dry-cleaning van had pulled out of a drive on P Street directly behind it.

As Jack drove he thought about just calling Melanie and talking to her. If he was going to Hong Kong he would not get any answers about what was going on for days, at least, and that worried him greatly. But he also worried that if he did talk to her, she might pick up on the fact he was leaving town, and this could be dangerous to his mission.

Because Center would know.

As they crossed over the Rock Creek Parkway, Jack resigned himself to the fact that he would get no answers, but then he saw the taxi turn onto the on-ramp for the parkway. Jack realized she would be heading north, too, which was odd, because he could not imagine why she had the cab run her into Georgetown just to leave D.C.

He accelerated as he crossed the overpass to make the turn on the ramp, but ahead of him he saw the dry-cleaning van pull up alongside Melanie's cab, as if it was trying to pass her on the steeply graded one-lane looping on-ramp.

'Idiot,' he said as he watched from some seventy-five yards back.

Just then, as the van pulled directly next to the taxi, its side door opened. It was such an odd sight that Ryan did not know what was happening at first, and he was slow to recognize danger.

Until he saw the barrel of a submachine gun appear from the dark interior of the van.

Before his eyes, the gun fired a long automatic burst, flame and smoke blew from the barrel, and the front passenger-side window of the cab exploded in a cloud of glass dust.

Jack screamed inside his BMW as Melanie's cab veered hard to the left, drove off the ramp on the inside of the turn, and then flipped and rolled down the hill, coming to rest on its roof.

The dry-cleaning van stopped lower on the ramp, and two armed men leapt out of the back.

Jack was armed with his Glock 23, but he was too far back to stop his car here and engage the men at the bottom of the ramp. Instead, acting more on impulse than anything else, he drove the BMW 335i off the ramp at speed, launched through the air, hit the grassy hill, and then skidded sideways as he lost control, careening down to the bottom of the hill toward the upside-down taxi.

Jack's airbag deployed and slammed him in the face; his arms flew through the air helter-skelter as the BMW bottomed out and then bounced back into the air. He sideswiped a tree on the hill, skidded through grass and mud, and then slammed down again at the bottom of the hill and came to rest. The windshield was badly cracked, but through it Ryan realized he was facing the two gunmen, fifteen yards ahead and approaching the taxi.

Jack was dazed, and his field of view was obstructed by dust and the cracked windshield, but the gunmen were slowed as well, and they looked directly at him. They apparently did not recognize the BMW as a threat; they assumed, obviously, that another motorist had crashed his car behind all the commotion on the on-ramp from the overpass.

Jack Ryan fought through the fog of his daze. Just as the gunmen refocused their attention on the crashed cab, kneeling down to look inside the inverted vehicle with their submachine guns at the ready, Jack drew his Glock, raised it with unsteady hands, and then fired through the smashed windshield.

Over and over and over he dumped rounds at the two men in front of him. One flipped back into the grass, his weapon tumbling away from his crumpled body.

The other man fired back, and the windshield just to Ryan's right blew in, spitting bits of safety glass into Jack's face. Jack's own spent casings bounced around the inside of his car, singeing his face and arms when they pinged off him on their way to the backseat or down to the floorboard or passenger seat in the front.

Ryan emptied his pistol at the two threats, firing thirteen rounds in total. When his gun locked open he executed an emergency reload, pulling a spare magazine from inside his waistband on his left and slamming it into the butt of the gun. As he got his weapon back into battery and aimed it, he saw the surviving gunman retreating back to the van, falling twice on the way, obviously wounded.

And then the van screeched out into high-speed traffic on the Rock Creek Parkway. It sideswiped an SUV, sending the other vehicle crashing into the center divider. The dry-cleaning van then raced off to the north.

Jack climbed out of his BMW, stumbled in a daze, and then raced over to the taxi. He knelt down. 'Melanie!' He saw the cabdriver, a young Middle Eastern man, still strapped in his seat belt, and he was obviously dead. Part of his forehead was missing, and blood drained down onto the roof of the car below him. 'Melanie!'

'Jack?'

Ryan turned around. Melanie Kraft stood behind him. Her right eye was dark and puffy, and there were cuts on her forehead. She had climbed out of the other side of the cab, and Jack was relieved to see her on her feet, with only minor scrapes. But looking in her eyes he saw complete shock, a dazed look that told him she was lost, confused.

Jack grabbed her by the wrist and pulled her to his BMW, pushed her into the backseat, and then leapt into the front.

'C'mon, baby! Please start!' Jack said as he pushed the ignition button.

The luxury sedan fired up, and Jack slammed it into gear and then sped off to the north, pieces of the smashed vehicle tumbling around the passenger seat, and small pieces of safety glass blowing off the broken windshield, hitting him in the face as he raced away.

Melanie Kraft woke up to find herself lying on her side in the back of Jack's car. All around her was broken glass and spent shell casings. She sat up slowly.

'What's happening?' she asked. She touched her hand to her face and found a little blood, then put her hand to her right eye and felt the swollen eyelid. 'What just happened, Jack?'

Ryan had pulled off the parkway, and now he turned onto a series of back roads, using his in-car GPS to keep his journey off the main roads to avoid being noticed by law enforcement.

'Jack?' she repeated.

'Are you okay?'

'Yes. Who were they? Who were those men?'

Ryan just shook his head. He pulled his phone out of his pocket and made a call. Melanie listened to his side of the conversation.

'Hey. I need your help. It's serious.' A short pause. 'I need to meet you somewhere between D.C. and Baltimore. I need a car, and I need you to watch over someone for a while.' Another brief pause. 'It's a fucking mess. Come armed. I knew I could count on you, John. Call me back.'

Ryan put the phone back in his pocket.

'*Please*, Jack. Who were they?'

'Who were they? Who were they? They were Center's people. Who the hell else would it be?'

'Who is Center?' Melanie asked.

'Don't lie to me. You have been working with Center. I know it. I found the bug on the phone.'

Melanie shook her head slowly. It made her head hurt to do so. 'I don't . . . Is Center Lipton?'

'Lipton? Who the hell is Lipton?'

Melanie was so confused. She just wanted to lie down, to throw up, to get out of the moving car. 'Lipton is FBI. National Security.'

'He's with the Chinese?'

'The Chinese? What's wrong with you, Jack?'

'Those men back there, Melanie. They work for Dr K. K. Tong, code name Center. He's a proxy agent for Chinese Ministry of State Security. Or at least I think he is. Pretty sure of it, anyway.'

'What does that have to –'

'The bug you put on my phone. It came from Center, it told Center where I was, and it listened in on my calls. He tried to kill me and Dom in Miami. They knew we were there because of the bug.'

'What?'

'The same group killed the five CIA operatives in Georgetown. And today they tried to kill you.'

'The FBI?'

'The FBI my ass!' Jack said. 'I don't know who Lipton is, but you have *not* been dealing with the FBI.'

'Yes! Yes, I have! FBI. Not the Chinese! Who the hell do you think I am?'

'I don't *fucking* know, Melanie!'

'Well, I don't know who you are! What just happened back there? Did you just kill two men? Why were they after me? I was doing what I was ordered to.'

'Yes, by the Chinese!'

'No! The FBI. I mean, at first Charles Alden with the CIA told me you were working for a foreign intelligence agency; he just asked me to find out what I could. But when he was arrested, Lipton called me, they showed me the court order, he introduced me to Packard. I had no choice.'

Jack shook his head. Who was Packard? He did not understand what was going on, but he believed Melanie. He believed *she* believed she was working for the FBI.

'Who are you?' She said it again. This time, however, it was softer, less panicked, more imploring. 'Who do you work for, and don't tell me you are in fucking finance!'

Jack shrugged. 'I haven't exactly been honest with you.'

She looked at him in the rearview for a long moment before saying, 'No shit, Jack.'

Jack met John Clark in a parking lot behind a furniture store that was not yet open for business for the day. Melanie said little. Jack had talked her into giving him the benefit of the doubt for a short while so he could get her somewhere safe, and then they could talk.

But after a several-minutes-long consultation with Clark, out of Melanie's earshot, Jack returned to the damaged BMW. Melanie sat in the back, looking straight ahead, still dazed by what she had gone through.

Jack opened her door and knelt down. When she did not look his way he said, 'Melanie?'

She turned slowly. He was glad she wasn't any more out of it than she was.

'Yes?'

'I need you to trust me. I know that's hard right now, but I'm asking you to think back over everything that's ever happened in our relationship. I won't say that I've never lied to you, but I swear to you I have never, ever done anything to hurt you. You believe that, don't you?'

'I do.'

'I'm going to ask you to go with John Clark. He'll take you

back to his farm in Maryland, just for the day. I need to know that you are somewhere safe, somewhere where those guys can't get you.'

'And you?'

'I have to leave town.'

'Leave town? You've got to be kidding.'

He winced; he knew this looked bad. 'This is very important. I will explain everything when I get back, a couple days at most. Then you can decide if you still believe in me. At that point, I'll listen to anything you have to say. You can tell me about this guy Lipton who you think is with the FB–'

'Darren Lipton *is* with the FBI, Jack.'

'Whatever. We'll discuss it. All I am saying is, for now, let's try to trust each other. *Please* go with John, and let him take care of you.'

'I need to talk to Mary Pat.'

'John and Mary Pat have been friends since before you were born. We need to lie low for right now, we don't want to get MP involved just yet.'

'But –'

'Trust me, Melanie. Just for a couple of days.'

She did not seem happy about it at all, but after a moment she just nodded.

Clark drove Melanie away in the BMW. He knew a lake he could dump it in, and he already had Sandy heading there in her car to pick them both up.

Jack climbed in John's Ford truck and headed to BWI to meet the Hendley Associates Gulfstream that would take him to Hong Kong.

64

Dom, Sam, and Ding met their minder in the lobby of their hotel at seven a.m. for what the government media office termed a 'cultural excursion.'

The minder introduced himself as George. He was a jovial man, as well as, all three Americans knew, a trained inform- ant for Chinese intelligence. George would be taking these 'journalists' on the day's tour.

They were heading to the Mutianyu section of the wall, some fifty miles north of Beijing. Even before the minder ushered the men out to the covered drive of the hotel and into the van waiting to take them there, he explained in his halting English that they were wise to choose this portion of the wall to see, as the rest of the media contingent had opted for a closer site that had, unfortunately, changed much in the last years because of renovation.

Chavez nodded and smiled as he climbed into the van, and in a Spanish accent that he thought was neither Argentine- sounding nor terribly necessary, he told his minder he was glad his producers had been so wise as to suggest this por- tion of the Great Wall for their feature story.

In truth, Chavez did not give a shit about the Great Wall of China. Not the Mutianyu section, not *any* section. Sure, if this had been a vacation and he'd been over here with his wife and son, it would have been amazing to see. But at the moment he was operational, and this operation was not tak- ing him to the Great Wall.

The Red Hand contact had directed him to request a trip to this location.

Ding assumed Red Hand had some plan to get himself and his two colleagues away from their minder and the driver. He did not have any details from the organization; he was putting his faith in a band of criminals that he neither trusted nor held much respect for, but this mission was of such great stakes that he, Dom, and Sam had decided to roll the dice and hope like hell Red Hand could orchestrate something that would get them away from government watchers, while at the same time not get them killed.

Sam Driscoll nudged Ding on the knee while they rode in the back of the van. Ding looked over at Sam and then followed his eyes to a point on the vehicle's dashboard near the windscreen. He had to squint to make it out, but there he saw a tiny microphone positioned. There was likely a camera somewhere in the van as well. The Chinese would be watching them – if not now, then they would be able to view a recording of whatever incident Red Hand had in store.

Ding nudged Caruso and leaned into his ear. He whispered, 'Cams and mics, '*mano*. Whatever goes down . . . stay in character.'

Dom did not react to the instructions. Instead he just looked out the window at the brown hills and gray sky.

While their chatty government minder from the Propaganda Department droned on and on about everything from the quality of the highway upon which the van drove, to the bumper crop of wheat harvested from the fields they passed, to the amazing feat of engineering that was the Great Wall's construction, Chavez looked back over his shoulder nonchalantly. Some fifty yards behind the van he saw a black two-door following them. In the front seats were two men who were dressed similarly to the government minder.

These would be armed guys from the ministry here to make sure the foreign media were not harassed by protests or highway thieves or any other local difficulties.

They surely thought they were in for a boring day.

Chavez was pretty sure that they were wrong in that assumption.

About forty minutes outside Beijing's city limits, they came to the first traffic light they had seen in some time. The van's driver stopped his vehicle at the red light, and a black truck that had pulled onto the road from a gas station a block back pulled up alongside the government van.

With no warning the driver's-side door of the van opened, just next to where the minder was sitting in the passenger seat, continuing to proclaim to the foreign journalists in the back that China was the worldwide leading supplier of wheat and cotton.

Ding saw the barrel of a rifle an instant before it fired. He yelled to Dom and Sam, 'Get down!' The window next to George's head shattered, and then his head slumped down, his seat belt holding his body in place.

The driver next to him slumped over dead, as well.

All three men did their best to get their heads as low as possible, shoving their faces between their knees and their hands over their heads just as another burst of automatic fire shattered glass in the front of the vehicle.

'Shit!' yelled Dominic.

None of the three were going to find it necessary to put on much of an act to appear terrified and helpless. Unknown assholes firing automatic rifles into their minivan helped them stay in character. The camera and the mic were going to record this event, and the three men in the backseat looked legit.

Ding heard shouting outside the broken windows now. The frenzy of barking Chinese, rushed footfalls of men running around in the street. More cyclic rifle fire close to the van.

Someone tried to open the sliding back door, but it was locked. None of the Americans moved to help, they just kept their heads down between their knees.

A rifle butt shattered the rest of the window glass of the door. Ding imagined someone reaching in to unlock the door, but he did not look up to confirm this. When the door slid open a moment later he did look up quickly, and he caught a glimpse of three or four masked men in the street, their weapons held high and their movements fast and nervous. Ding saw one man place a white cotton bag over Caruso's head and then jerk him out of the van.

A second hood was shoved over Chavez's head, and now he was pulled into the street. He kept his hands up as he was pushed around roughly to the back of the other vehicle.

Crazed-sounding shouts of Mandarin came from all around him. Instructions from the Red Hand team leader to his men, or barking arguments between them, Domingo could not tell, but he felt a hand shove him forward, and a second hand grabbed his jacket and pulled him up and into the back of the black truck.

He did not know if the journalists in the vans behind were watching or perhaps even filming all this action. But if they were getting this, he felt it was a sure bet this would look just like a brutal third-world roadside kidnapping.

This was about as realistic as anyone could make it. Likely because, it occurred to Chavez, Red Hand had done this sort of thing before.

The truck lurched forward on squealing tires. Domingo fell over with the momentum, and only then did he feel two men sitting next to him.

'Who's that?'

'Sam.'

'And Dom.'

'You guys okay?'

They both said they were, though Dom complained his ears would be ringing for a while because one of the Red Hand jackasses had let loose a full magazine dump just a couple of feet from Caruso's ear.

The hoods stayed on the men as the truck continued. Chavez tried to talk to the Chinese men in the back with them, but they clearly did not speak English. He heard at least two men speaking back and forth, and they ignored the Americans.

Fifteen minutes after they left the scene of the fake kidnapping, the truck stopped. Dom, Ding, and Sam were led out the back, their hoods still in place, and they immediately found themselves pushed into the back of what seemed to be a small four-door sedan.

They were moving again in seconds, pressed tightly against one another as they took tight turns and went up and down steep roads.

It was a long, nausea-inducing drive. The blacktop underneath them turned to gravel, and the sedan slowed and then stopped. The three Americans were led out the back and inside a building. Ding smelled the unmistakable scent of livestock, and he felt the cold damp of a barn.

There were a few minutes of conversation around him as he stood there with his teammates. Several men were in conversation, and then Ding was surprised by a woman's voice. An argument erupted, he could not fathom what it was about, but he just stood there, silently waiting to be addressed by someone in the room.

Finally the barn door shut behind him, his hood was removed, and he looked around.

Dom and Sam were with him; they had also just had their hoods removed. Together the three of them looked across the dark barn interior at about two dozen men and women. They were all armed with rifles.

A young woman walked up to the three Americans. 'I am Yin Yin. I will be your translator.'

Chavez was confused. The people in front of him looked like college kids. They did not look like criminals. Not one of them had an ounce of muscle on their bodies, and they looked scared.

It was pretty much the opposite of what Ding had hoped to find.

'You are Red Hand?' he asked.

She made an expression of distaste and shook her head vigorously. 'No, we are not Red Hand. We are Pathway of Liberty.'

Ding, Sam, and Dom looked at one another.

Sam said what was on the other men's minds: '*This* is our rebel force?'

Dom just shook his head in disgust. 'We do any direct action with this gang, and we are condemning the entire movement to slaughter. Look at them. These folks couldn't fight their way out of a paper bag.'

Yin Yin heard this, and she stormed over to the three Americans. 'We have been training.'

'On Xbox?' asked Driscoll, coolly.

'No! We have a farm where we have practiced with our rifles.'

'Awesome,' muttered Dom. He looked to Chavez.

Chavez smiled at the woman, doing his best to be the diplomat in the room. He excused himself and his colleagues, took Dom and Sam to a corner of the barn, and said, 'Looks like Red Hand sold CIA a bill of goods. They passed us off to some coffee-shop student movement.'

'Son of a bitch,' said Caruso. 'These guys aren't ready for prime time. That didn't take long to figure out.'

Chavez sighed. 'I don't really see how we can just walk out of here at this point. Let's keep an open mind and spend some time with them to learn what they have accomplished. They may be just a gaggle of kids, but they sure as shit are brave to be standing up to the Chicom government in Beijing. We owe them some respect, guys.'

'Roger that,' said Dom, and Driscoll just nodded.

65

Valentin Kovalenko watched the news reports of another wild shooting on the streets of Washington, D.C. This time there were two fatalities, a Syrian cabdriver and an unidentified Asian man in his thirties. Witnesses said two vehicles fled the scene, and 'dozens' of shots rang out during the gunfight.

Valentin did not waste a moment wondering if this had something to do with the Center organization. He knew. And while it was apparent Center's assassins had failed to eliminate their target, it was also obvious that their target was Darren Lipton's agent.

The address Kovalenko had given Lipton to pass on to his agent was less than a mile from the location of the shoot-out. That a submachine gun was used by the dead Asian made it even more obvious that this was a crew of Center's people. Whether or not the dead man was Crane himself, Valentin had no idea, but it did not matter.

Valentin understood the larger meaning of the news story.

Center kills his own agents when he has no further use for them.

Which was why Kovalenko turned off the television, went into the bedroom, and began throwing his clothes in a suitcase.

He came out a few minutes later and went into the kitchen. He poured a double shot of cold Ketel One into a glass, and then drained it as he began packing items in the living room.

Yes, he had SVR sanction, and yes, Dema Apilikov had

told him to see this through, but he'd already seen enough through, and he knew that at any moment Crane or his goons could show up at his door and kill him, at which point his promise of a plum position in Moscow at R Directorate would lose its ability to motivate him onward.

No. Valentin needed to run, to get away. From a place of safety he could negotiate with SVR for a return to active service, he could point to all the time he put his life on the line while going solo, working in Russia's interests by following Center's commands.

That would get him back in the good graces of SVR.

He reached to turn off his computer, and he saw Cryptogram was open and a new message was blinking. He figured Center was watching him right now, so he opened it and sat down.

The message read: 'We need to talk.'

'So talk,' he typed.

'On the phone. I will call.'

Kovalenko's eyebrows rose. He had not spoken to Center before. This was indeed odd.

A new Cryptogram window opened on his computer, and on it was the icon of a telephone. Kovalenko plugged a set of headphones into his laptop and then double-clicked the icon.

'Yes?'

'Mr Kovalenko.' The voice was a male in his forties or fifties, and he was most definitely Chinese. 'I need you to remain in Washington.'

'So you can send your people to kill me?'

'I do not want to send my people to kill you.'

'You just tried to kill Lipton's girl.'

'That is true, and Crane's men failed. But that was because she stopped working for us without permission. I suggest you do not follow her path, because we will find her and the next time we will not fail.'

Kovalenko needed some leverage, so he played the only card he had. 'SVR knows all about you. They sanctioned me to continue helping you, but I am pulling the plug on this right now and getting out of here. You can try to send your Chinese wrecking crew to find me, but I will return to my former employers, and they will –'

'Your former employers in SVR will shoot you on sight, Mr Kovalenko.'

'You aren't listening to me, Center! I met with them, and they said –'

'You met with Dema Apilikov on October twenty-first in Dupont Circle.'

Kovalenko abruptly stopped talking. His hands squeezed the edge of the desk so tightly it seemed the wood would break off in his hands.

Center knew.

Center *always* knew.

Still, that did not change a thing. Kovalenko said, 'That's right, and if you think about touching Apilikov, you will have the entire illegals department after you.'

'*Touch* Apilikov? Mr Kovalenko, I *own* Dema Apilikov. He has been working for me, providing details of SVR communications technology, for over two and a half years. I sent him to you. I could see that you were losing your vigor for the operation after the Georgetown action. I knew that the only way to bring you back into the program to the extent that you would follow orders was if you thought your efforts would earn you a glorious return to SVR.'

Kovalenko slid off his chair, sat on the floor of his apartment, and cradled his head between his knees.

'Listen to me very, very carefully, Mr Kovalenko. I know

that now you are thinking that there is no more incentive to follow my instructions. But you are wrong about that. I have wired four million euros into a bank account in Crete, and the money is yours. You won't be able to return to SVR, but with four million euros you can do much with what is left of your life.'

'Why should I believe you?'

'Think back over our relationship. Have I ever lied to you?'

'Is that a fucking joke? Of course you –'

'No. I had others deceive you, yes. But I do not lie.'

'All right, then. Give me the access code to the account.'

'I will give it to you tomorrow morning.'

Kovalenko just stared at the floor. He didn't really care about the money, but he did want to be free of Center.

'Why not give it to me now?'

'Because you have one more task. One more very important task.'

The Russian on the floor of the basement apartment in Dupont Circle heaved a long sigh. 'What a fucking surprise.'

President Ryan was running on fumes at five in the afternoon, after having been up and hard at work since three a.m. The day had been full of diplomatic and military crises; often success in one arena was offset by setbacks in another.

In the South China Sea a pair of Chinese Z-10 attack helicopters flying off China's aircraft carrier shot down two Vietnamese Air Force aircraft monitoring activity in Vietnam's Exclusive Economic Zone. Just an hour and a half later, several companies of PLA paratroopers dropped in Kalayaan, a tiny Philippine island with a permanent population of only three hundred fifty, but also an island with a mile-long airstrip. They took the airfield, killing seven, and within a few hours more Chinese troops began landing in transport aircraft.

American satellites had detected Chinese attack aircraft landing on the island as well.

The Taiwanese destroyer that had been hit by the Silkworm missiles sank in Chinese waters, but the PLA had allowed the Taiwanese to enter China's side of the strait for recovery of survivors. China very publicly claimed it had acted in self-defense, and Jack Ryan had gone before cameras at the White House to express outrage about China's actions.

He announced he would be sending the *Nimitz*-class carrier *Dwight D. Eisenhower*, currently with the Sixth Fleet in the Indian Ocean, farther to the east, to the mouth of the Strait of Malacca, the narrow waterway through which some eighty percent of Chinese oil passes. His rationale, delivered in measured tones to convey strength yet composure, was that America wanted to ensure the safe passage of world commerce through the strait, as if the *Ike* would go simply to ensure that the spigot of world trade continued to flow nicely. What he did not say, but which was clear to all with understanding of ocean commerce, was that the *Ike* could shut off the flow of Chinese oil much more easily than it could ensure the safe passage of container ships up the entire length of the South China Sea.

It was a threatening gesture, to be sure, but it was a measured response, considering all China's actions of the past few weeks.

The Chinese, quite predictably, went ballistic. Their foreign minister, ostensibly the most diplomatic person in a nation of 1.4 billion, blew a gasket on Chinese National Television, and called the USA a world power run by criminals. The chairman of the Central Military Commission, Su Ke Qiang, released a statement saying America's persistent interference with a Chinese internal security matter would cause an immediate and unwelcome response.

The unwelcome response came at five minutes after five in the afternoon, when the NIPRINET, the Department of Defense's unsecure network, went down under the weight of a massive denial-of-service attack. The entire U.S. military global supply chain – and a vast amount of its ability to communicate between bases, departments, forces, and systems – simply ceased to function.

At 5:25, the secure DoD network began having drop-offs in bandwidth and problems with communications. Public military and U.S. government websites went down completely or were replaced with pictures and videos of American forces being killed in Afghanistan and Iraq, a sick and violent loop of images of exploding Humvees, sniper victims, and Jihadi propaganda.

At 5:58, a series of cyberkinetic attacks on critical infrastructure in the United States began. The FAA's network went down, as did the Metro systems in most major cities along the eastern seaboard. Mobile phone service in California and Seattle became spotty or nonexistent.

Almost simultaneously, in Russellville, Arkansas, the light water pumps at Arkansas Nuclear One, a pressurized-water-reactor nuclear power plant, suddenly shut down. A backup system failed as well, and the core temperature at the plant quickly began to rise as the fuel rods radiated more heat than the steam turbines could handle. As the system neared a potential meltdown, however, the Emergency Core Cooling System did function properly, and a crisis was averted.

Jack Ryan walked the length of the Situation Room conference room, manifesting his anger in his movements instead of his tone. 'Someone explain to me how the hell the Chinese are able to turn off equipment at our nuclear facilities?'

The head of Cyber Command, General Henry Bloom,

answered on video link from his crisis center in Fort Meade. 'Many nuclear facilities, for purposes of efficiency, have linked their secure plant computer systems to their less secure corporate networks. A chain is only as strong as the weakest link, and many of our links are weakening instead of strengthening, as technology improves, because there is actually more integration, instead of more security.'

'We have managed to keep the news of the attack at the plant secret for now, have we not?'

'For now, sir. Yes.'

'Tell me we saw this coming,' Ryan said.

The head of Cyber Command said simply, 'I've seen it coming for a long time. I've been putting out papers for a decade describing just exactly what we are all witnessing today. America's cyberthreatscape, the spectrum of possible threats, is vast.'

'What can we expect next?'

Bloom said, 'I would be stunned if Wall Street's systems operated normally tomorrow morning. Banking and telecom are ripe targets for an attack of this magnitude. So far the electrical grid has not been attacked like it easily could be. I suspect large power outages across the country sooner rather than later.'

'And we can't stop it?'

'We can fight back with whatever electronic resources they don't rob from us. Something this large and well coordinated will take some time to combat. And there is something else you should know.'

'What's that?'

'The networks that are not down, and I'm speaking of Intelink-TS, the CIA network, for example, are suspect.'

'Suspect?'

'Yes, Mr President. I see their capability by what they have accomplished this evening. Anything left standing is only left standing because they are using it to spy on us.'

'So they are inside the CIA's digital brain?'

Bloom nodded. 'We have to operate under the assumption that they have deep persistent access to all our secrets.'

Ryan looked to CIA Director Canfield and DNI Foley. 'I would take General Bloom's comments seriously.'

Both Foley and Canfield nodded.

Ryan then asked, 'Why the hell are we so far behind the Chinese on cybersecurity? Is this more of the aftermath of Ed Kealty's gutting of defense and intelligence?'

General Bloom shook his head. 'We can't blame Ed Kealty for this, sir. The simple fact is that China has millions of very smart people, many of whom were trained here in the U.S. and then went home to essentially do the modern equivalent of taking up arms against us.'

'Why don't those smart people work for us?'

'A key reason is, the average hacker we need on our side in order to even the playing field is a twenty-something born in Russia or China or India. He's gone to the right schools, has the language and the math background.'

Ryan understood the problem before Bloom said it. 'But there is no way in hell the foreign kid can obtain a Top Secret, Sensitive Compartmented Information full-scope polygraph clearance.'

Bloom said, 'No way in hell, sir.

'And another reason is that America's strong suit has never been dealing with things that have not happened yet. Cyberwar has been a distant vague concept, a fantasy . . . until this morning.'

Ryan said, 'When the power goes out, the water turns to sludge, and when the fuel stops flowing . . . America is going to expect us to fix this.'

Ryan continued. 'We have been focusing on low-impact, high-probability events. China taking the South China Sea and Taiwan is seen as a high-impact, low-probability event. Cyberwar against America is seen as a high-impact, low-probability event. We have not had our eyes on these areas as we should have in the past few years. Now both of these things are happening at once.

'General Bloom, what would be the quickest, best way we can help you right now?'

The Air Force general thought it over for a second. He said, 'A kinetic response to the command-and-control centers in China that are effecting this cyberattack.'

'A *kinetic* response?'

'Yes, Mr President.'

'Combat their cyberwar with a shooting war?'

General Bloom did not blink. 'War is war, Mr President. People will die from this here in America. Plane crashes, traffic accidents, little old ladies freezing to death in a home without electricity. You can, and I believe you *should*, look at what happened in Russellville, Arkansas, as a nuclear attack on the United States of America. Just because they did not use an ICBM and just because the warhead did not detonate this time, it doesn't mean they did not try, they will not try again, and they won't succeed the next time. The Chinese have changed the method of attack, but they did not change the type of ordnance.'

Ryan thought for a moment. 'Scott?'

Secretary of State Adler responded, 'Yes, Mr President.'

'Bloom is right, we are a hair's breadth away from a full-on shooting war with the Chinese. I want you to help me come up with every last diplomatic card we can use to avoid this.'

'Yes, sir.' Adler knew the stakes; there existed no greater

use of diplomacy than preventing war. 'We start with the United Nations. Without positive attribution of the Chinese in the cyberattack, I think we pull out all the stops in going after their encroachment into the SCS and their attacks on the ROC.'

'Agreed. It's not much, but it has to be done.'

'Yes, sir. Then I go to Beijing, meet with the foreign minister, give him a direct message from you.'

'All right.'

'I can deliver your "stick" with no problem, but I'd like to have a carrot to offer as well.'

'Sure. I'm not wavering on Taiwan or open access to the SCS, but we can be flexible with some of our military movements in the region. Maybe we promise we won't renew a base over there somewhere that they don't like. I don't want to do that, but I sure as shit don't want this to blow up. We'll work this out with Bob before you go.'

Burgess did not look pleased, but he nodded at Adler.

Scott said, 'Thank you, sir. I'll put together a list of other diplomatic moves we can make to pressure or cajole the Chinese. They seem intractable, but we have to try.'

'That's right,' agreed Ryan. Then he looked to SecDef Bob Burgess. 'Bob, we can't depend on the Chinese being reasonable to our threats of the stick or our offers of the carrot. I want you back in here in seventy-two hours with your plan to combat the cyberattack with attacks in China. Get with all the war fighters, General Bloom at Cyber Command, and the NSA, and make it happen.'

'Yes, Mr President.' Ryan knew Burgess could not even communicate effectively with his staff at the moment, but there wasn't much Ryan could do to help him.

Ryan added, 'With no surface ships in the area, submarines will be crucial.'

Burgess said, 'Still, we are going to need pilots flying over the Chinese mainland.'

'That is going to be suicide,' Ryan said, rubbing his temples under his bifocals. 'Shit.' After a long hesitation he added, 'I'm not going to approve a target list. You don't need civilian leadership micromanaging your campaign. But Bob, I am personally putting this on your shoulders. Only the most critical targets for our flyboys, things that subs can't hit. I do not want one American life risked for any target that is not absolutely required to fulfill the overall mission objective.'

'I understand completely, sir.'

'Thanks. I don't wish your job on anybody right now.'

'I feel the same about you, sir.'

Ryan waved his hand. 'Okay, enough of our pity party. We might be sending people to fight and die, but we aren't the ones who are on the knife's edge.'

'That's a fair point.'

Jack thought about how powerless he had become, the president of a country under threat of being demolished by its dependence on computer networks.

Suddenly he had another idea. 'Scott?'

Secretary of State Scott Adler looked up from his notepad. 'Sir?'

'What does your communication situation look like? Can you talk with your embassy in Beijing?'

'Not via secure comms, sir. But I can pick up a phone and make a long-distance call. Who knows? At this point, it might have to be collect.'

There were a few stressed chuckles in the room.

Mary Pat Foley said, 'Scott, I can *guarantee* it will be a party line.'

That garnered some more stressed laughs.

The President continued: 'Make a call to Ambassador Li, have him arrange another phone call between Wei and me. Do it as soon as possible. I'm sure just your making the call will pass the message directly to the Chicoms.'

66

President Wei Zhen Lin received word from his Ministry of State Security that the American ambassador to China, Kenneth Li, would be requesting an urgent phone conversation between Wei and President Jack Ryan. Li had not yet made the request; clearly the MSS was listening in to his phone conversations, and Wei was glad for this, because it bought him a little time.

He had spent the day in his office, having his people bring him reports about military actions in the South China Sea and the Strait of Taiwan, and then about the situation in America with the cyberattacks.

To say Wei was furious did not properly express his mood. Wei saw very well what Chairman Su was doing, and he also knew that Su would know good and well that he would be angry.

Clearly Su just did not care.

The phone on Wei's desk beeped, and he touched the speaker. 'General Secretary, Chairman Su is on the phone for you.'

'On the phone? He was supposed to come to my office.'

'I'm sorry, sir. He said that he could not get away.'

Wei stifled his rage. 'Very well. Connect him.'

Su Ke Qiang said, 'Good morning, *tongzhi*. I apologize that I could not be in Beijing at the moment. I was called to Baoding today and will remain here until our Standing Committee meeting on Thursday morning.' Baoding was a city to the southwest of Beijing, as well as home of a large PLA base.

Wei did not acknowledge the lack of respect that he felt Su was expressing. Instead he said, 'This has been a most difficult day.'

'How so? I see nothing but success. The Americans are moving a carrier from the western Indian Ocean to the eastern Indian Ocean. *This* is their response to our sinking of the Taiwanese warship? You do see, don't you, that they are afraid?' Su chuckled. 'They are on a war footing in the Indian Ocean.' Su chuckled at what he saw as a feeble, empty attempt by the Americans to flex their muscles.

'Why was the ship sunk?'

'One thing leads to another in any military conflict.'

'I am not a soldier, not a sailor. Tell me what you mean by that.'

'I will boil down the events quite simply. We have been exercising our muscularity in the air over the strait as a precursor to naval actions there. This has led to dozens of air-to-air encounters with the Taiwanese and the Americans. We ordered the American aircraft carrier to move back, and they did so, but now we have found out they snuck American pilots, like spies, onto Taiwan. To retaliate for this, our submarines have laid some mines, and in so doing there was a conflict with a Taiwanese vessel. We destroyed the vessel. That is where we stand at present.'

Wei realized Su would show no contrition for the reckless escalation of events.

Wei said, 'But there is more to the story, is there not? I am learning of the cyberattacks in the United States from my advisers who are watching American television. Do you still maintain these will not be attributed to the People's Republic of China?'

'I do.'

'How can you possibly say that? On the day you make

threats of reprisals to the Americans, suddenly a very powerful computer attack damages their military and civilian infrastructure. Obviously, this was China's doing.'

'Obvious? Yes, I will grant you that. But attributable? No. There is no proof.'

Wei raised his voice: 'Do you think Jack Ryan wants to take us before a magistrate?'

Su chuckled again. 'No, Wei. He wants to see China in ashes. But he won't do anything but put a few pilots on Taiwan and sail his vulnerable ships out of range of our ballistic missiles. This is *exactly* what we wanted. Ryan will show a little bluster, but he will see his battle is lost before it has begun.'

'Why was it necessary to take such drastic steps? Why not attack the military networks only?'

'Wei, I've told you before, my experts inform me that in the very near future, inside of two years, perhaps, the United States will have a much more defendable electronic communications architecture. We have to act now, to escalate quickly. The Americans refer to it as "shock and awe." It is the only way forward.'

'But what will the Americans do to us?'

Su had been expecting the question. 'If we control the Taiwan Strait, as well as most of the SCS, the American response will be limited.'

'Limited?'

'Of course. Their carriers will be nowhere near any military activity. They know that our coastal anti-ship batteries can destroy them.'

'So they will not attack?'

'They will do what they can to protect Taiwan, but they understand that is a fool's errand. We can launch fifteen hundred missiles a day from our coast, to say nothing of our Air Force and Navy. They will back down.'

'We misjudged Ryan before. Are you misjudging him now?'

'I told you, comrade. I fully expect an American response.' He paused. 'And I fully expect it to fail.

'We will not allow China to lose power on any front during the next five years. We will overcome our current crises and we will grow, but we will not do it without some near-term sacrifice. It would be naive to imagine that President Ryan, a warmonger of the highest order, will simply respond with some sort of diplomatic or economic reprisals. Some continued armed response is inevitable.'

'What sort of armed response?'

'The PLA has been working on the answer to this question for some time. Our think tanks in Washington are actively involved in the evaluation of the Ryan administration, looking for signals in policy that can help discern just how far they will go.'

'Conclusions?'

'We have nothing to worry about.'

Wei then said, 'Tell me about the Ryan Doctrine.'

Su paused. 'The Ryan Doctrine is not relevant.'

'What do you know of it, Su?'

Su coughed into the phone, hesitating for a moment before responding: 'President Ryan has said publicly, and he has proven this by his deeds, that he holds the leadership of his enemies responsible for their actions. Personally responsible. Ryan is a monster. He has ordered the decapitation of governments. The assassination of leaders.' Su laughed into the phone. 'It that the reason behind your reluctance? Are you personally afraid of what Jack Ryan will do to you?'

'Of course not.'

'You have nothing to worry about, comrade.'

'I am not worried.'

'Then why did you bring it up?'

The line was silent for a moment as both men raged internally. Eventually Wei spoke; his words were clipped and tight as he tried to keep from shouting. 'I am an economist, and I see that we are doing more damage to our relationships than the business environment can sustain. What you are doing, the speed and intensity with which you are pushing the aggression, will force war, and it will destroy our economy.'

'And backing down now won't?' Su shouted at Wei, having no filter of charm with which to blunt the expression of his anger. 'You have pushed us across a bridge and burned it down! There is no turning back now! We have to see this through!'

'*I* have done that? *I* have?'

'Of course. You sanctioned my operation, and you are afraid to sit quietly and wait for Ryan to run away.'

Wei said, 'President Ryan will not run from a fight.'

Su said, 'He will run, because if he does not, then he will witness a nuclear detonation in Taipei, and the threat of further strikes in Seoul, Tokyo, and Hawaii. Trust me, if it comes to it, America will have no choice but to back off.'

'You are mad!'

'*You* were mad to think that you could blow navies out of the water while offering free-trade agreements to offset the damage. You only see the world as an economist. I promise you, Wei, that the world is not about business. The world is about struggle and force.'

Wei said nothing.

'We will discuss this in person when I come on Thursday. But understand this: I will address the Standing Committee, and they will back me. You should stay aligned with me, Wei. Our good relationship has served you in the recent past, and you would do well to remember that.'

The call ended, and President Wei took several minutes to

compose himself. He sat silently in his office, his hands on the blotter of his desk. Finally he pushed the button on his phone that connected him to his secretary.

'Yes, General Secretary?'

'Connect me with the President of the United States.'

67

President Jack Ryan held the phone to his ear and listened to the translator quickly and effortlessly convert the Mandarin into English. The conversation had already been going for several minutes, and Jack had endured a lecture in economics and history from the Chinese president. Wei said, 'You made Thailand and the Philippines "non-NATO major allies." That was very threatening. Moreover, the U.S. has worked tirelessly to expand intelligence and defensive contacts with India, and to bring them into the nuclear nonproliferation regime.

'America is doing its best to make India a global power. Why on earth would it be in one global power's interests to promote the emergence of another global power? I can answer that question, Mr President. America wants India's help in keeping China under threat at all times. How can we not feel endangered by this hostile act?'

Wei waited quietly for a response to his question, but Jack Ryan would not be giving ground to Wei tonight. He was on the phone to talk about the cyberattacks and the escalation of Chairman Su.

He said, 'Your nation's attacks on our critical infrastructure are an act of war, Mr President.'

Wei replied, 'The allegation by the Americans that China participated in any sort of a computer attack against them is groundless and exhibits yet another display of racism as your administration attempts to denigrate the good people of China.'

'I hold you personally responsible for the lives of Americans that are lost due to damage to our transportation infrastructure, our communications systems, our nuclear power facilities.'

'What nuclear power facilities?' Wei asked.

'Do you not know what happened this afternoon in our state of Arkansas?'

Wei listened to the translator. After a time he said, 'My country is not responsible for any computer attacks against your country.'

'You *don't* know, do you? Your cybermilitia, acting in your name, President Wei Zhen Lin, forced an emergency shutdown of a nuclear reactor in the middle of the United States. If this attack had been successful, thousands of Americans would have died.'

Wei hesitated before responding: 'As I said before, China had nothing to do with this.'

'*I* think you did, Mr President, and at the end of the day, *that* is what matters.'

Wei hesitated again, and then he changed the subject. 'President Ryan. You do realize, don't you, the leverage we have over you in the economic and commercial sectors?'

'That is not important to me right now. There is nothing you can do to us economically that we will not recover from. America has many friends and great natural resources. You have neither.'

'Perhaps not. But we have a strong economy and a strong military.'

'Your actions are destroying the first! Don't force me to destroy the second!'

Wei had no response to this.

'Recognize, Mr President, that you are inexorably linked to Chairman Su's war. My country will make no distinction whatsoever between the two of you.'

Still nothing from Wei. Ryan had been involved in hundreds

of translated conversations with state leaders in his years in the White House, and he had never known one to sit in stunned silence. Normally the two parties spoke prepared text or jockeyed for position in the conversation.

Jack asked, 'Are you there, President Wei?'

'I do not lead the military,' he responded.

'You lead the nation!'

'Nevertheless. My control is … It is not the same as in your country.'

'Your control over Su is the only chance to save your country from a war you cannot win.'

There was another long pause; this time, it was nearly a minute long. Ryan's national security team sat on the sofas in front of him, but they were not listening in to the conversation. It was being recorded, and they could listen after. Jack looked at them and they back at him, clearly wondering what was going on.

Finally Wei responded: 'Please understand, Mr President. I will have to discuss your concerns directly with Chairman Su. I would prefer to do this in person, but I will not see him again until he comes to the Politburo meeting Thursday morning, traveling with his entourage from the PLA base in Baoding. He will speak to the Standing Committee, and I will talk to him afterward about this conversation and other matters.'

Ryan did not answer for several seconds. Finally he said, 'I do understand, Mr President. We will speak again.'

'Thank you.'

Ryan hung up the phone, then looked at the group in front of him. 'Can I have a moment alone with Director Foley, Secretary Burgess, and Director Canfield?'

Everyone else filed out of the room. Ryan stood, but he did not step around his desk. There was an unmistakable look of astonishment on his face.

As soon as the door shut he said, 'That was something I can't say I expected.'

'What's that?' Canfield asked.

Ryan shook his head. He was still in a state of shock. 'I am reasonably certain that President Wei just purposefully fed me intelligence.'

'What kind of intelligence?'

'The kind that he wants me to use to assassinate Chairman Su.'

The two men and one woman standing in front of the President adopted the same bewildered expressions he wore.

President Jack Ryan sighed. 'It's a damn shame we don't have any assets to exploit this opportunity.'

Gerry Hendley, Sam Granger, and Rick Bell sat in Gerry's office on the ninth floor of Hendley Associates just after eleven o'clock in the evening. The three men had been here all evening, waiting for updates from Ding Chavez and the others in Beijing. Ding had checked in just a few minutes earlier to say his first impression of the rebels was that they were not ready for prime time, but he would reserve judgment for a couple of days while he, Dom, and Sam evaluated their capabilities.

The three senior executives were about to call it a night when Gerry Hendley's mobile phone rang.

'Hendley.'

'Hi, Gerry. Mary Pat Foley here.'

'Hello, Mary Pat. Or should I say Mrs Director?'

'You got it right the first time. I'm sorry to call you so late. Did I wake you?'

'No. Actually I'm at the office.'

'Good. There has been a new development I wanted to talk to you about.'

*

The home phone rang at the Emmitsburg, Maryland, home of John Clark. Clark and his wife, Sandy, were in bed, and Melanie Kraft was in a guest bedroom, sitting wide awake.

She had spent the day putting ice on her bruised eye and cheekbone and doing her best to pick the brain of John Clark about just what the hell Jack was doing. John was the wrong man to try to pull secrets out of, Melanie learned quickly enough, but he and his wife were nice enough, and they both seemed genuinely concerned about Melanie's well-being, so she decided to wait on Jack to return before seeking answers to her many questions.

Within five minutes of the ringing phone, Clark tapped on her door.

'I'm awake,' she said.

John stepped in. 'How are you feeling?'

'A little sore, but better than I would have been if you hadn't made me keep the ice on my face, I'm sure.'

John said, 'I have to go to Hendley Associates. Something critical has come up. I hate to do this to you, but Jack made me promise to stay with you at all times till he gets back.'

'You want me to go with you?'

'We've got a couple of beds there for data guys who work the night shift. It's not the Ritz, but neither is this.'

Melanie slid out of the bed. 'I finally get to see the mysterious Hendley Associates? Trust me, I don't plan on sleeping.'

Clark smiled. 'Not so fast, young lady. You'll get to see the lobby, an elevator, and a hallway or two. You'll have to wait for Jack to come back to get the VIP tour.'

Melanie sighed while putting on her shoes. 'Yeah, like *that* will happen. Okay, Mr Clark. If you promise to not treat me like a prisoner, I promise to not snoop around your office.'

Clark held the door open for her as she passed. 'It's a deal.'

68

Gavin sat in his office at one in the morning. On his desk in front of him was a technical manual from Microsoft that he'd been reading on and off for the entire day. It was not uncommon for him to work this late, and he imagined he'd be pulling a long string of all-nighters over the next few days while he rebuilt his system. He'd sent most of his staff home, but a couple of programmers were still somewhere on the floor; he'd heard them talking a few minutes earlier.

Since The Campus had men in the field he also knew there would be several guys up in Analysis, although there wasn't a hell of a lot they could do but doodle on notepads without a computer network to assist them.

Biery felt like he'd let everyone down by allowing the virus onto his system. He worried about Ding, Sam, and Dom in Beijing, and even Ryan in Hong Kong, and he concentrated on getting back online as quickly as possible.

Right now it looked like they would not be able to go live for at least another week.

The phone rang on Biery's desk.

'Hey, Gav, it's Granger. Gerry and I are up here in his office, waiting for word from Chavez. We figured you might be down there.'

'Yeah. Lots to do.'

'Understood. Listen, John Clark is coming into the office in just a few minutes. He is going to back up Chavez and the others on a new operation that is brewing in Beijing.'

'Good. Nice to know he's back with us, even if it's just temporary.'

'I was wondering if you could come up when he gets here and give him a ten-minute review of what happened in Hong Kong. It will help get him back in the loop.'

'I'd be glad to. I'll be here all night, all day tomorrow. I can spare a little time.'

'Don't burn yourself out, Gavin. Nothing that happened with that virus was your fault. I don't need you to fall on your sword over this.'

Gavin snorted a little. 'Should have caught it, Sam. Simple as that.'

Granger said, 'Look. All we can tell you is that we support you. Gerry and I both think you're doing a hell of a job.'

'Thanks, Sam.'

'Try and get some sleep tonight. You're no good to anyone if you can't function.'

'Okay. I'll catch some z's on my sofa as soon as I give Clark his briefing.'

'Good deal. I'll call you when he gets here.'

Gavin hung up the phone, reached for his coffee, and then, without warning, all the power in his office went off.

Sitting in the black, he looked out into the hallway.

'Dammit!' he shouted. The lights seemed to be out over the entire building.

'Son of a bitch!'

In the lobby of Hendley Associates, night security manager Wayne Reese looked out the glass doorway to the parking lot and saw the Baltimore Gas and Electric truck pull up to the door.

Reese reached down to the Beretta pistol on his hip, and

he thumbed the leather strap that secured it in the holster. This did not feel right.

One man walked up to the front door and held his ID badge up. Reese stepped up to the door, shone his flashlight on the badge, and determined that it looked legitimate. He turned the bolt lock and opened the door slightly.

'You guys sure are on the ball tonight. The power hasn't been off three –'

Reese saw the black handgun appear from the man's tool belt, and he knew he'd made a grave error. With all the speed he could muster he slammed the glass door, but a single round barked from the suppressed Five-seveN pistol, shot through the narrow opening, and hit him in the solar plexus, knocking him back onto the floor.

As Reese lay on his back, he tried to lift his head to see his murderer. The Asian man pushed through the unlocked door and stepped up to him. Behind him, several more men appeared out of the back of the van.

The shooter stood over Reese, raised his pistol to the wounded man's forehead, and then Wayne Reese's world went black.

Crane entered the building just as Quail shot the security officer a second time. Crane and five of his men shouldered their Steyr TMP machine pistols and took the stairs, leaving Grouse on the ground floor to watch the parking lot. One at the entrance was not optimal, but Grouse had a headset that kept him in constant touch with the rest of the operators, so he would serve more as a tripwire if there were any threats downstairs.

Crane knew tonight would be taxing on his small force. He had lost Wigeon this morning during the attempted assassination of Melanie Kraft on the Rock Creek Parkway.

Additionally, Grouse had been shot in the left thigh. He should have been out of action with this injury, but Crane had ordered him to come on this operation tonight, principally because the Hendley Associates building was quite large, and therefore Crane needed all the men he could muster.

The building was nine stories tall, impossible to clear and search with this force, but Crane knew from Ryan's phone intercepts and Center's research on the Hendley Associates network before it went dark the previous day that the second floor was IT, the third floor was the intelligence analyst staff, and the ninth floor was the location of the executive offices.

At the second-floor exit, three men peeled off of the six-man tactical train. They would search here and then on the third floor, while Crane and two others rushed directly up to the top floor.

Quail, Snipe, and Stint moved up the darkened second-floor hallway with their silenced machine pistols at the high ready.

A security officer walking with a flashlight in his hand came out of a room backward, locking the door behind him, and then he turned to head back to the stairwell. Stint shot the man four times, killing him instantly.

In a large office toward the back of the IT department, the three Chinese operators found a heavyset white man in his fifties at his desk. His office door said he was Gavin Biery, the director of information technology.

The men had been ordered to take everyone who did not offer resistance alive and keep them alive until the network system could be rebooted and the drives reformatted. There were references to Center, Tong, Zha, and several of the operations that linked Center to the Chinese PLA and MSS, and these needed to be scrubbed from the hard drives of the

604

servers before the company became front-page news after a mass murder there.

The data storage of Hendley Associates, it had been determined, was too large and well dispersed to simply blow up. Instead they needed to wipe the memory of the entire operation clean, and for that they would need employees of the company so they could find out passwords and the location of any offsite data storage.

After Biery was tied up they found two more IT men on the second floor, and then they headed up to the Analysis department on the third floor.

Crane, Gull, and Duck left the stairway on the ninth floor, and they too encountered a security officer in the hallway. This man recognized the threat immediately, however, and he moved laterally while drawing his Beretta pistol. Crane and Duck both got shots off but missed; then the guard fired two rounds up the hall, missing just high both times.

A second burst from Crane's Steyr TMP caught the guard in the lower torso, sending him spinning to the ground dead.

Without a word between them, the three Chinese men began sprinting up the hall.

'What in God's name was that?' exclaimed Gerry Hendley. He and Sam Granger were in the conference room, trying to work under dim emergency lights and lighting from a sliver of moon through the large windows.

Granger leapt to his feet and rushed to a small broom closet in the corner. 'Gunfire,' he said gravely. He opened the broom closet and retrieved a Colt M16 select fire rifle. It was loaded and kept here in case of emergency.

Granger had not fired a rifle in many years, but he deftly pulled back the charging handle, motioned for Hendley to stay right where he was, and then swung out into the hall with the gun raised in front of him.

Crane saw the man appear at the end of the hall some fifty feet away. The American saw Crane and his two operators at the same time, and he fired a short burst from his rifle. Crane dove for cover behind a planter by the elevator but then immediately rolled back out on the floor and fired an entire magazine from his machine pistol.

Sam Granger's knees buckled as the rounds tore into his chest. An involuntary muscle spasm in his arm and hand caused him to squeeze off another three-round burst as he fell backward into the conference room.

Crane looked back over his shoulder; Duck had been shot through the forehead by the suited man's M16 rifle. He now lay flat on his back, a pool of blood growing in the dark hall.

Gull and Crane rushed forward, leapt over the dead American, and entered the conference room. There, an older man in a tie and shirtsleeves stood near a table. Crane recognized him from a picture he'd been sent by Center. He was Gerry Hendley, director of Hendley Associates.

'Put your hands up,' Crane said, and Gull rushed in, knocked the old man onto his desk, and secured his hands behind his back.

69

Crane had his men bring everyone into the conference room on the second floor. There were nine individuals other than the three security officers and one executive they killed during the initial attack, and they were all bound at the wrists behind their backs and seated in chairs by the wall.

Crane called his controller and had the power restored to the building, and then he addressed the group in a monotone and heavily accented voice.

'We will bring your computer network back online. We need to do this quickly. I will require your passwords to the network and a description of each of your duties and access levels. There are many of you here; I do not need you all.' With the same monotone voice he said, 'If you refuse to help, you will be shot.'

Gerry Hendley spoke up: 'If you let everyone else go, I will give you whatever you want.'

Crane had been facing away, but he turned back to Hendley. 'No talking.' He lifted his machine pistol, pointed it at Hendley's forehead. He held it there for a moment.

His earpiece chirped. He put his hand to his ear and turned away. *'Ni shuo shen me?'* What did you say?

In the lobby, Grouse knelt down behind the reception desk and repeated himself softly: 'I said an old man and a girl are coming to the front of the building.'

Crane replied, 'Don't let them in.'

'He has a key. I see it in his hand.'

'Okay. Let them in then, and take them. Hold them down there until we have what we need here, in case they have passwords we require.'

'Understood.'

'Do you need me to send someone else down with you?'

Grouse winced with a fresh throb of pain in his wounded leg, but he quickly said, 'Of course not. It's an old man and a girl.'

John Clark and Melanie Kraft entered Hendley Associates' lobby, and immediately Grouse stood up behind the reception desk and pointed his Steyr machine pistol at them. He had them put their hands on their heads and turn back to the wall; then he limped over to them and frisked them with one hand while keeping the weapon trained on their heads.

He found a SIG Sauer pistol on the old man, which was a surprise. He pulled it out of a shoulder holster and stuck it in his waistband. On the woman he found no weapons, but he relieved her of her purse. He then had them stand against the wall in the elevator lobby with their hands on their heads.

Melanie Kraft fought waves of panic as she stood there, her fingers laced together on top of her brunette hair. She looked over at Mr Clark; he was doing the same, but his eyes were a flurry of activity.

She whispered, 'What should we do?'

Clark looked over to her. Before he said anything, the Chinese man said, 'No talking!'

Melanie leaned back against the wall, felt a quiver in her legs.

The armed man divided his attention between the two of them and the front of the building.

Melanie regarded the gunman now, and she saw no feeling, no emotion. He spoke into his headset once or twice, but other than that he looked and acted almost like a robot.

Except his limp. It was clear that he was having trouble with one of his legs.

Now Melanie's terrified eyes darted back to John, hoping to see some sign that he had a plan. But she saw instead that he looked different; he had changed in the past few seconds, his face had reddened, and his eyes seemed to bulge in their sockets.

'John?'

'No talking!' the man said again, but Melanie was not paying attention to him. All her focus was on John Clark, because it was apparent that something was wrong.

His hands came off his head and his face grimaced in pain and he clutched his chest.

'Hand on head! Hand on head!'

Clark slowly lowered to his knees. His face was beet-red now; she could see purple veins in his forehead.

'Oh my God!' she said. 'John, what's wrong?'

The old man took a half-step back and put his hand out to the wall.

'Don't move!' said Grouse, and he lifted his Steyr TMP machine pistol up to the man as he steadied himself against the wall. Grouse saw the man's face was red, and he saw the girl looking on with concern.

The Divine Sword commando spun his weapon's barrel to the girl. 'Don't move!' he repeated, principally because he did not know much English. But the dark-haired girl dropped to the floor next to the man, cradling him in her arms.

'John? John! What's wrong?'

The old *gweilo* put his hand to his chest.

'He's having a heart attack!' the girl said.

Grouse called on his radio in Chinese: 'Crane, this is Grouse. I think the old man is having a heart attack.'

'Then let him die. I'll send someone down to get the girl and bring her up here. Crane out.'

The white man was on his side on the tile floor, he was shaking and convulsing, his left arm was stuck out ramrod straight, and his right hand was pressed tightly against his heart.

Grouse pointed his gun at the girl.

'You move! Get up! Get back!' He knelt down slowly, the pain in his leg wound forcing him to adjust as he did so, and he grabbed her by her hair with his free hand. He started to pull her up and away from the dying old *gweilo*. He yanked her away, shoved her against the wall by the elevators, and then started to turn back to the man. As he did so, however, he felt an impact on his ankles, his feet flew out from under him, and he flipped backward. He crashed on his back on the tile floor right next to the white man, who no longer appeared to be dying.

The American's eyes were locked on him and intense with hate and purpose. The old man had used his legs to sweep Grouse off his feet, and now he had taken surprisingly strong hold of the Steyr's nylon sling, and he pulled it hard, and Grouse found himself pinned on his back on the cold tile floor. His finger had slipped out of the trigger guard of the weapon as his hand tried to break his fall, and as he scrambled on the tile, trying to free the sling from around his throat, he fought with the American for the grip of his gun.

The old man was fighting for it just as hard. He was alive and healthy and amazingly strong. The sling was around Grouse's neck, and the white man had it wrapped tightly around his wrist; every time Grouse tried to wrest control of the machine pistol, the sling was pulled to the side, yanking him off balance as he tried to sit up and take it.

Grouse looked to the stairwell, he tried to shout out for

help, but the old man pulled the sling even tighter, partially cutting off his windpipe and turning the shout into just a warbling gurgle.

One more vicious yank to the left by the American and Grouse fell all the way onto his back and lost his grip on the gun. His hands reached out desperately for the weapon.

Grouse felt himself weakening as he flailed and kicked.

The American had control now.

John Clark could not get his right hand inside the trigger of the gun because of his injury and limited mobility, but he had the sling perfectly positioned on the Chinese man's windpipe, so he cinched it tighter and tighter, strangling him to death.

When it was all over, some forty-five seconds after his feigned heart attack gave him the opening to fight back, he lay on his back panting next to the dead man for a few seconds.

But he knew he had no time to spare, so he sat up and went to work.

He felt quickly through the man's pockets and retrieved his SIG .45-caliber pistol and a mobile phone, and he pulled the headset off the man. He did not speak Mandarin, but he put the headset on, making certain the mute button was depressed so that his voice could not be heard.

Melanie just looked at him from across the floor. 'He's dead?' she asked, still not catching up to what she had just witnessed.

'Yes.'

She nodded. 'You tricked him? You faked a heart attack?'

He nodded.

'I needed him closer. Sorry,' Clark said as he hung the Steyr's sling over his neck.

'We have to call the police,' she said.

'No time,' said Clark. He looked the girl over quickly. Ryan had told Clark that Melanie had compromised him, apparently on the orders of a man she thought was an FBI agent. John was not sure who the young woman was working for or what her motivations were, but it seemed evident that this dead Chinese man on the floor was from the squad of assassins that had tried to kill her on the Rock Creek Parkway just hours earlier.

She was clearly not a confederate of theirs.

Clark had no idea how many more foreign killers there were in the building, nor how well armed and well trained they were, but if they were the group who took out the five CIA men in Georgetown, Clark was damn sure they were tier-one gunmen.

Clark did not trust Melanie Kraft, but he decided Melanie Kraft was the very least of his problems.

He held up his SIG pistol. 'Do you know how to use this?'

She nodded slowly while she looked at it.

He handed it to her and she took it, then adopted a two-handed combat grip, holding the weapon at the low, ready in front of her at the waist.

'Listen carefully,' Clark instructed. 'I need you to stay behind me. Far behind, but don't lose sight of me.'

'Okay,' she said. 'What are we going to do?'

'We're going upstairs.'

John Clark kicked off his shoes and entered the darkened stairwell. As he did so, he heard a door opening just one floor above.

70

Crane had ordered Snipe to go downstairs to retrieve the woman, and then he had his three other men, Quail, Stint, and Gull, wait with the prisoners in the conference room while he brought IT director Gavin Biery over to a node in the server room. The American had told them he would start up and then log in to the system, allowing the Chinese men administrator-level access to do whatever they wanted.

Twice Crane hit the big man in the back of the head for deliberately stalling, both times knocking him from his chair. A third time, when he saw hesitation on the part of the American, he told him he would go into the conference room and begin shooting prisoners.

Gavin reluctantly logged in.

John Clark stood over the limp body of a young, muscular Chinese man. The sixty-five-year-old American had heard the man descending the stairs, then hidden under the first-floor landing, waiting for him to come down. As he passed, Clark cracked him from behind with a vicious downward thrust of the butt of the Steyr TMP. The man fell forward onto the concrete, and three more heavy blows to the head knocked him out cold.

Melanie came out of her hiding place below the stairs, and she pulled off the man's belt, then used it to tie his hands behind his back. She pulled his jacket down to his elbows to make it even harder for him to get free. She took his machine pistol, but she did not know how to use it, so she just slung it around her neck and followed John upstairs with the pistol in her hand.

John slowly opened the door to the second floor and looked down a hallway, past a row of elevators, past the dead body of a security guard John recognized as an old friend named Joe Fischer, and toward the open door to the IT conference room at the end of the hall. As he did so he heard a transmission in Chinese in his borrowed headset. Of course he could not understand the words, but he had put the device on his head so he could get a heads-up when it became apparent to this crew of killers that members of their unit were not checking in.

And that time was now. The transmission came a second time, and then a third; each repetition was more alert- and alarmed-sounding than the one before. Clark quickly began walking up the hall with the TMP out in front of him in his left hand, his eye looking through the small glass sight.

He'd passed the elevators and was only fifteen feet from the entrance to the conference room when a man quickly stepped out, his gun rising but not yet fully raised. He saw John, tried vainly to yank his weapon up to a firing position, but Clark shot the man five times with a burst of automatic fire.

Now Clark was running; he entered the conference room as fast as he could, with no idea what he would find when he got there.

Before his eyes could take in the complete scene, an Asian man in black clothing fired a burst of bullets at him; John moved quickly to the side, lined up his gun on the threat, and saw that the man stood in front of a row of Hendley employees, all seated and tied. Clark did not hesitate – he fired a single round from the machine pistol, his left trigger finger pressed off another single round, and the man fell back onto Campus Analyst Tony Wills.

There was one more threat in the room. He had been facing

in the other direction when John came through the door, but now he was facing the old American with the Steyr. As he aimed to fire, Melanie Kraft came through the door, a pistol clutched in both hands in a firing grip, and she lined up her sights on the man. She fired a single round that missed high, but the Chinese assassin spun his machine pistol away from Clark and toward the girl, giving John the half-second he needed to refocus on this threat and drop the man dead with a long blast to the upper torso.

As soon as the Chinese operator dropped to the floor, Gerry Hendley said, 'There's one more. He's got Biery in the server room.'

Clark left Melanie with the eight Campus employees, and he rushed out of the conference room heading up a side hall that ended in the room where the servers were kept.

All the gunfire had been suppressed except for the single shot Melanie fired from John Clark's .45 SIG, but that noise got the attention of Crane. He called his men over and over on his headset, but while he did so he also grabbed Biery by the neck and pulled him out of his chair.

With the Steyr to Gavin's right temple and his arm around his neck, Crane yanked him into the hall, only to come face-to-face with an old man with gray hair and eyeglasses. The man had one of Crane's men's weapons held up in front of him, pointed directly at Crane's head.

'Put it down or I kill him,' Crane said.

The old man did not respond.

'I will do it! I will shoot him!'

The American with the machine pistol narrowed his eyes slightly.

Crane looked into the eyes. He saw nothing but focus, nothing but purpose, mission, intent.

Crane knew the look; Crane knew the mind-set.

This old man was a warrior.

Crane said, 'Don't shoot. I surrender.' And he dropped the Steyr on the floor.

Back in the conference room, Melanie had freed the Hendley Associates staff. She did not know what the hell was going on, but by now she had long since come to the obvious conclusion that her boyfriend, the President's son, did not work exclusively in the financial management field. Clearly this was some sort of super-secret government intelligence or security contractor, and clearly they had run seriously afoul of the Chinese.

She would make Jack tell her every last bit of detail about this place before she passed final judgment, if he allowed her the opportunity to talk to him ever again. His accusation that she was working for the Chinese, while it did not make any sense to her, had Melanie worried that the rift between the two of them might be too wide to repair with simple explanations.

Clark and three other men brought the two surviving Chinese men into the hallway by the elevators and tied them together, back to back. Crane, the leader of the group, spoke loudly, announced that he was a member of Divine Sword, a PLA special-missions unit, and he and his men demanded to be treated as prisoners of war. Clark responded to this by pistol-whipping the man behind the ear with his SIG, which shut him up quickly.

Other Hendley men began searching floor to floor for more victims and more killers; everyone was armed with pistols and machine pistols while doing so.

Clark had just searched Crane, pulling an odd-looking mobile phone from him, when the phone vibrated. He looked down at the device. Of course he did not recognize the number, but he got an idea.

'Gerry?' he called over to Hendley. 'Are there any Mandarin speakers here in the group?'

The ex-senator was shaken up, especially after the death of his friend Sam Granger, but Clark was glad to see the man retained his wits.

'Afraid not, but these two speak English.'

'I'm talking about whoever might be calling.' The phone buzzed again, and John looked down and saw the same number calling back.

Shit, John thought. This would be a great opportunity to get more intel on this organization.

Gerry said, 'If you need a Mandarin speaker, I think I know where we can get one quickly.'

Jack Ryan, Jr, rode in the passenger seat of a two-door Acura compact driven by Adam Yao. They had left Hong Kong and were now driving through the New Territories, heading north toward the border with China.

They had been on the road only a few minutes when Jack's mobile chirped. Ryan, a little punch-drunk from the jet lag of the seventeen-hour flight, answered it on the fourth ring.

'Ryan.'

'Jack, it's John Clark.'

'Hey, John.'

'Listen carefully, kid, I'm in a rush.' In the next thirty seconds Clark told Ryan what had happened that night at Hendley. Before Jack could even respond, he explained someone was calling the leader of the assassins, and he wanted to patch Yao through to the man's phone, call the number back, and then see if Yao could fake the caller into believing he was one of the Chinese killers.

Ryan quickly relayed the situation to Yao, and then put the earpiece in Yao's ear for him while he drove.

John said, 'You ready?'

Adam knew who John Clark was, but there was no time for a formal introduction. He just said, 'You don't know who will be on the other end?'

'No idea. You'll just have to wing it.'

'Okay.'

Winging it was what a NOC did for a living. 'Dial the number.'

It rang several times before it was picked up on the other end. Adam Yao did not know what he would hear, but he did not expect to hear someone speaking English with a Russian accent.

'Why did you not answer when I called?'

Adam was ready to answer in Mandarin. He switched to English but affected a strong Mandarin accent.

'Busy.'

'Are you clear?'

'We're at Hendley.'

A slight pause. 'Of course you are at Hendley. Is all the opposition dealt with?'

Adam was beginning to understand. This individual knew what was supposed to happen.

'Yes. No problems.'

'Okay. Before you erase data, I've been instructed to upload any encrypted files on the workstation of Gavin Biery, and then to send them to Center.'

Yao remained in character. 'Understood.'

There was a short pause. Then, 'I'm out front. I'll come through the front door. Alert your men.'

Holy shit, Adam thought. 'Yes.' Quickly he hung up and turned to Ryan. 'Some Russian guy is there, in the parking lot, apparently. He's coming through the front.'

Jack had Clark on speakerphone. Before Jack could relay the message, John said, 'Got it. We'll take care of it. Clark out.'

A minute later, Clark was still on the second floor, standing over the two prisoners, when Tony Wills came through the stairwell door, holding a .45 to the head of a bearded Caucasian man in a suit and tie. The man's hands were cuffed behind him, and his raincoat had been pulled down behind him to his elbows.

John made certain Biery had the Steyr machine pistol pointed at the ground in front of the two Chinese prisoners and his finger outside the trigger guard, and then he started up the hall to see what the new guy in the mix had to do with all this.

He had closed to within twenty feet when the bearded man's eyes widened in shock. *'You?'*

Clark stopped, looked harder at the man.

It took him a few seconds to recognize Valentin Kovalenko. *'You?'*

The Russian tried to back up, away from Clark, but he just pressed the back of his skull into Wills's .45.

Clark thought Valentin was going to faint. He directed Tony to take him into the IT conference room nearby, and then he sent Tony out to guard the prisoners with Biery.

When Clark and Kovalenko were alone in the room, John pushed the man roughly down into a chair and then sat down in front of him. He looked him over for a brief moment. Since the previous January, not a day had passed without Clark's thinking about snapping the neck of the little twerp sitting inches from him now. The man who had kidnapped him, tortured him, stolen from him his last few good years in the field by severely damaging his hand.

But John had other, more pressing objectives now.

He said, 'I'm not going to pretend like I know what the fuck you are doing here. As far as I knew, you were dead or else eating snow soup in a gulag somewhere in Siberia.'

John had been striking fear into the hearts of his enemies for forty years, but he doubted he'd ever seen anyone this terrified in his life. It was obvious from his reaction that Kovalenko had no idea John Clark had anything to do with his operation.

When Valentin still did not speak, John said, 'I just lost some good friends, and I intend to find out why. You have the answers.'

'I . . . I did not know –'

'I don't give a shit what you didn't know. I want to know what you *do* know. I'm not going to threaten to torture you. You and I both know there is no reason for me to threaten you. I will either break you apart, limb by limb, or not break you apart limb by limb, regardless of how helpful you are to me now. I owe you a lot of misery.'

'Please, John. I can help you.'

'Yeah? Then help me.'

'I can tell you everything I know.'

'Start talking.'

'Chinese intelligence is involved.'

'No shit! I've got dead and hog-tied Chinese soldiers all over the building. What is *your* involvement?'

'I . . . I thought it was industrial espionage. They blackmailed me, sprung me from prison, but made me an accomplice. The jobs started easy, but they got harder and harder. They tricked me, they threatened me, threatened to kill me. I could not get away.'

'Who do you report to?'

'He calls himself Center.'

'Is he waiting to hear from you?'

'Yes. Crane – that is one of the men still alive out there on the floor – was letting me come in to get some data, and I was to upload it, send it to Center. I had no idea anyone was going to be hurt or –'

'I don't believe you.'

Kovalenko looked to the floor for a moment. Then he nodded. '*Da, da,* you are right. Yes, of course I knew what was going on. The first people they killed, the other day in Georgetown? No, I did not know they would do that. And then again, when they killed the cabdriver and tried to kill the woman today. I did not know that was the plan. But by now? I am no fool. I thought I would come into this building and find a stack of dead bodies.' He shrugged. 'I just want to go home, John. I want no part of this.'

Clark looked him over. 'Cry me a fucking river.'

He got up and left the room.

Back in the hallway, Clark found Gavin Biery talking to Gerry Hendley. When Biery saw the older man, he rushed up to him.

'That guy in there. Does he work for Center?'

'Yeah. Says he does, anyway.'

Gavin said, 'We can use him. He will have a program on his computer that he uses to communicate with Center. It's called Cryptogram. I've created a virus that can go through Cryptogram and photograph the person on the other end.'

Clark said, 'But we have to get him to agree to help us, right?'

Biery said, 'Yes. You've got to convince him to log in to Cryptogram and get Center to accept an upload.'

Clark thought it over for a moment. 'Okay, come with me.'

Biery and Clark returned to the conference room.

Kovalenko had been sitting alone, his hands tied behind his back, his body positioned so that the two dead Chinese assassins were on the floor near his feet. This was by design. Clark wanted Valentin to sit there with dead men, to think about his own predicament.

Biery and Clark sat down at the table.

Before he could speak, Kovalenko said, 'I had no choice. They forced me to work for them.'

'You did have a choice.'

'Sure, I could have shot myself in the head.'

'You sound like a guy who wouldn't mind living through this.'

'Of course I do. But don't fuck with me, Clark. You, of all people, want to see me dead.'

'I'd get a few chuckles out of that, yeah. But what's more important is defeating Center before this conflict gets any bigger. There are millions of lives at stake. It's not just about you and me and a grudge.'

'What do you want?'

Clark looked at Gavin Biery. 'Can we use him?'

Gavin was still in a mild state of shock. But he nodded and looked at Kovalenko. 'Do you have Cryptogram on your computer?'

Kovalenko just nodded in reply.

Clark said, 'I am sure you have some security check you use to establish that it is actually you communicating with Center.'

'I do. But it's actually more complicated than that.'

'How so?'

'I am pretty sure that while we are talking on Cryptogram, he's also watching me through my camera.'

Clark's eyebrows rose, and he turned to Biery. 'Is that possible?'

Gavin said, 'Mr Clark, you have no idea what we've been dealing with since you left. If this guy told me Center had microchipped his brain I wouldn't bat an eyelash.'

Clark turned back to Kovalenko. 'We want to take you to your place and get you to connect with Center. Will you do that for us?'

'Why should I help you? You are going to kill me anyway.'

John Clark did not disagree. Instead he just said, 'Think back to a time before you were spying for a living. I don't mean for Center. I mean . . . before the SVR. There must have been some reason you went into this line of work. Yeah, I know your dear old dad was a KGB spook, but what did that get him? Even as a kid you must have seen him, the long hours, the low pay, the shithole postings, and you must have said to yourself, *No way in hell I'm going into the family business*.'

Kovalenko replied, 'It was different in the eighties. He was treated with respect. The seventies even more so.'

Clark shrugged. 'But you got into this in the nineties, long after the shine wore off the hammer and sickle.'

Kovalenko nodded.

'Did you, just maybe, think that someday you just might do some good?'

'Of course. I was not one of the corrupt ones.'

'Well, Valentin, you give us about one hour of help right now and you very likely might just stop a regional war from going global. Not too many spooks can say that.'

'Center is smarter than you,' Kovalenko said flatly.

Clark smiled. 'We're not going to challenge him to a game of chess.'

Kovalenko looked at the dead men on the floor again. He said, 'I feel nothing about these men. They would have killed me when this was over. I know that like I know my own name.'

'Help us destroy him.'

Valentin said, 'If you do not kill him – I don't mean his virus, his network, his operation – I mean *him*. If you do not put a bullet in Center's head, he will be back.'

Gavin Biery said, 'You can be that bullet. I want to upload something into his system that will give us his exact location.'

Kovalenko smiled slightly. 'Let's give it a shot.'

*

As Clark and Biery prepared to rush with Kovalenko to his apartment in D.C., Gerry Hendley came out of Gavin's office. 'John, I have Chavez on the phone from Beijing; he wants to talk to you.'

Clark took the satellite phone from Hendley. 'Hey, Ding.'

'You okay, John?'

'I'm fine. It's a nightmare, though. You heard about Granger?'

'Yeah. Shit.'

'Yeah. Did he talk to you about Chairman Su's motorcade Thursday morning?'

'Yeah. He said Mary Pat Foley got the intel directly from the PRC government. Sounds like somebody's not happy with what's going on in the South China Sea.'

Clark said, 'What do you think about your chances to pull it off?'

Chavez hesitated, then said, 'It's possible. I think we need to try, anyway, since there are no more American agency operatives in China in position.'

'So you guys are going to go ahead?'

Chavez said, 'There's one problem.'

'What's that?'

'We do this op, then we leave. Good for us. But you and I have both been around dictatorships long enough to know that some poor group of SOBs, some dissident group or other group of the citizenry, is going to take the fall for our actions. Not just these kids we're working with. We kill Su and then the PLA will find a fall guy, and the fall guy is going to fall hard.'

'They'll execute everyone with means and motive. There are hundreds of groups of dissenters around China. The PLA will make an example of them all so the country never rises up again.'

'Damn right they will. That doesn't sit well with me,' Chavez said.

Clark stood in the hallway, holding the phone to his ear with his right hand, thinking about the problem. 'You need to leave some evidence that proves it wasn't a group of local dissenters who did it.'

Ding answered back immediately: 'Thought of that, but any evidence will just tie the U.S. to the hit, and we can't let that happen. It's fine and dandy that the world will wonder if the Ryan Doctrine was in play, but if we left evidence the Chicoms could use to prove to the world that the U.S. was –'

Clark interrupted: 'What if you left evidence proving someone else did it? Someone who we wouldn't mind taking the fall for this.'

'What kind of evidence are you talking about?'

John looked down at the two Chinese assassins. 'What about a couple of dead Chinese special-forces guys left at the scene of the hit like they were part of the hit team.'

After a pause, Chavez said, 'Nice, *'mano*. That would kill two birds with one stone. You wouldn't happen to know where I could get any volunteers for that job, would you?'

'No volunteers. A couple of conscripts, though.'

Ding said, 'Just as good.'

Clark said, 'I'll be there in thirty hours with these two surviving Divine Sword assholes. We'll waste them at the scene.'

'*You?* You're coming to Beijing? How?'

'I still have a few friends in low places.'

'Russians? You have some Russian buddies that can get you in?'

'You know me too well, Domingo.'

71

An hour later, Clark, Biery, Kraft, and Kovalenko arrived at the Russian spy's Dupont Circle apartment. It was almost four a.m., nearly an hour after Kovalenko had been ordered to report in by Center. Kovalenko was nervous about the exchange to come, but more than that, he was nervous about what would happen to him afterward, at the hands of John Clark.

Before they entered the building John leaned in to Kovalenko's ear. He spoke softly. 'Valentin. Here is what you need to understand. You have one chance to get this right.'

'I do this and I walk?'

'You do this and you go into our custody. I let you go when it is all over.'

Kovalenko did not react negatively to this. On the contrary, he said, 'Good. I don't want to fuck over Center and be left alone.'

They entered the apartment; it was dark, but Valentin did not turn on any lights. The laptop was closed, and John, Melanie, and Gavin stood to the side of the desk, so that when the camera came on they would be out of the field of view.

Kovalenko stepped into the kitchen, and Clark rushed in after him, thinking he was trying to get a knife. But instead he reached into his freezer, pulled out a frosty bottle of vodka, and took several long swigs. He turned and headed out to his computer, his bottle in his hand.

He passed Clark with an apologetic shrug.

Biery had given the Russian a flash drive loaded with the

malware he built from FastByte22's file uploader and his RAT. Valentin slipped it into the USB port of the laptop, and then opened the machine.

In seconds he was logging in to Cryptogram, initiating a conversation with Center.

Kovalenko typed 'SC Lavender.' This was his authentication code. He sat there in the dark at his desk, tired and worn-looking, hoping like hell he could pull this off so that neither Center nor Clark killed him when this was all over.

He felt like he was walking a tightrope, with a long fall into the abyss on either side of him.

A green line of text on the black background: 'What happened?'

'There were men at Hendley Associates that Crane did not detect. After we entered and took the data from the server, they attacked. They are all dead. Crane and his men.'

The pause was shorter than Kovalenko had expected.

'How did you survive?'

'Crane ordered me out of the building while they fought. I hid in the trees.'

'Your instructions were to provide assistance if needed.'

'If I had carried out my instructions, you would have lost all your assets. If your assassins could not kill the Americans there, I surely could not do it, either.'

'How do you know they are dead?'

'Their bodies were removed. I saw them.'

Now the pause was long. Minutes long. Kovalenko imagined someone was getting directions from someone else on how to proceed. He typed a series of question marks, to which he received no immediate response.

A new Cryptogram window opened, and Valentin saw the phone icon, just like earlier in the day.

He put on the headset and clicked the icon. *'Da?'*

'This is Center.' It was definitely the same man as earlier in the day. 'Were you injured?'

'Not badly. No.'

'Were you followed?'

Kovalenko knew Center was listening to his voice, trying to detect signs of deception. He was also certainly watching him right then via the camera. 'No. Of course not.'

'How do you know?'

'I am a professional. Who can follow me at four in the morning?'

There was a long pause. Finally the man said, 'Send upload.' And he hung up.

Kovalenko uploaded Gavin Biery's file from the flash drive.

A minute later Center typed, 'Received.'

Valentin's hands were shaking now. He typed, 'Instructions?'

Softly, and barely moving his lips, he whispered to Biery, 'Is that it?'

Biery responded, 'Yes. It should work almost immediately.'

'You are certain?'

Biery was not certain. But he was confident. 'Yeah.'

A line of Cryptogram text appeared. 'What is this?'

Kovalenko did not respond.

'This is an application? This is not what was requested.'

Kovalenko looked at the camera.

Slowly he lifted his hand in front of his face in a fist and extended his middle finger.

Clark, Kraft, and Biery all stood to the side, mouths agape.

It took only seconds for a new line of text to appear on Cryptogram.

'You are dead.'

The connection terminated instantly.

'He's off,' Kovalenko said.

Biery smiled. 'Wait for it.'

Clark, Kovalenko, and Kraft all looked at him.

'Wait for what?' asked Valentin.

'Wait for it,' he repeated very slowly.

Melanie said, 'He logged off. He can't send any –'

A file popped up in the Cryptogram window. Kovalenko, still sitting in front of the machine, looked up to Gavin Biery. 'Should I . . .'

'Please do.'

Kovalenko clicked on the file, and a single picture expanded on the monitor. All four people in the dark apartment leaned forward to get a better look at it.

A young woman, with Asian features, eyeglasses, and short black hair, sat in front of the camera, her fingers resting on a computer keyboard. Over her left shoulder, an older Asian man in a white shirt and loose necktie leaned close, peering to a point just below the camera.

Valentin was confused. 'Who is . . .'

Gavin Biery touched the girl with his fingertip. 'I don't know who that is, but *that* guy, ladies and gentlemen, is the MFIC.'

Melanie and Valentin just looked at him.

Biery said, 'Dr Tong Kwok Kwan, code name Center.'

John Clark smiled and said, 'The Motherfucker in Charge.'

72

Adam Yao had documents to get him into mainland China, so he could come and go on the train or through the automobile border crossing.

Jack Junior, on the other hand, was not nearly so fortunate. Adam had a way across the border for him, but it necessitated some risk and discomfort.

Adam went first, driving through the crossing at Lok Ma Chau at five p.m. local time. He wanted to be in place on the other side for when Ryan made it over so Jack wasn't wandering mainland China as a *gweilo* with no papers, a scenario that would not have ended well for the son of the president.

Ryan took a cab to San Tin and then walked a few blocks to a hardware store parking lot, where he met the men who would take him across.

They were 'friends' of Adam's, meaning he had run across them working in his 'white side' job with SinoShield. They were smugglers, which made Ryan nervous when he was told they would be his access to China, but when he met them, he relaxed.

The smugglers were three small young men who seemed a hell of a lot more harmless than Ryan had spent the last sixteen hours imagining them to be.

Adam told him to not offer the men any money because he had taken care of them already, and although Jack had no idea what that meant, he trusted Adam enough to comply.

He sized them up as they stood there in the rapidly waning light. They clearly had no firearms on them. Jack had been trained to spot hidden pistols, and these guys weren't packing – not on their hips, under their arms, or on their ankles. He could not say for sure they did not have knives secreted somewhere on their person, but even if all three of these little guys came at him at once, Jack figured, he could bang their heads together and head for the border on his own.

That would not be the preferred outcome, however.

None of the men spoke a word of English, and this made things confusing for Jack as they stood next to their motorbikes and gestured toward his legs and feet. He thought they were admiring his Cole Haan loafers, but he could not be sure. The matter passed soon enough with a few chuckles from the men.

They had Ryan climb on the back of one of the bikes, which was not a great plan, considering Jack was six-two and he found himself riding tandem with a chubby young man who might have been five-four. He had to concentrate on his balance to keep upright as the little Chinese man fishtailed and lurched his straining, poorly tuned bike on the bad back roads.

After twenty minutes on the road Jack saw why the Chinese men were concerned about his leather shoes. They were surrounded by rice paddies that went all the way to a river, across which was the mainland. They would have to slosh in knee-deep water for a half-mile before even getting to the levee by the river. There was no way in hell his loafers would stay on his feet.

They parked their bikes and got out, and then one of the young men miraculously discovered an ability to speak English. 'You pay. You pay now.'

Ryan had no problem reaching into his money belt and thumbing off a few hundred bucks for the service these men provided, but Yao had been adamant that he not pay them.

Jack shook his head. 'Adam Yao to pay,' he said, hoping his nonconjugated verb might make comprehension easier.

Oddly, the men seemed not to understand this. 'Adam pay you,' Jack tried next.

The men just shook their heads like they did not understand, and said, 'You pay now.'

Jack reached into his pocket and pulled out a mobile phone he'd purchased that afternoon at the airport, and he dialed a number.

'Yeah?'

'It's Jack. They want money.'

Yao growled like an angry bear, which surprised Ryan. 'Put the smartest-looking of those three dumb shits on the fucking phone.'

Jack smiled. He liked Adam Yao's style. 'It's for you.' He handed the phone to one of the smugglers.

There was a quick conversation. Jack did not understand the words, but the facial expressions from the kid left no uncertainty as to who had the upper hand in the argument. The kid winced with Yao's words and fought to get his responses in.

After thirty seconds he passed the phone back to Ryan.

Jack held the phone up to his ear. Before he could speak, Yao said, 'That ought to be the end of that. We're back on, but don't show those bastards a dime.'

'Okay.'

They sloshed through the rice paddies as the sun set and the moon rose. Jack lost his shoes almost immediately. There was a little conversation at first, but as they neared the water all the talking stopped. At eight p.m. they arrived on the levee, and one of the men pulled a raft made of milk cartons and particle board out of tall grasses. Ryan and the smuggler climbed aboard, and the other two pushed them off.

It was only five minutes across the cold water to China. They landed in a warehouse district of Shenzhen, and they hid the raft in rocks and river grasses. The smuggler went with Ryan up to the street in the dark, they sprinted across just after a bus passed, and then Jack was told to wait in a tin storage shed.

The smuggler disappeared, and Jack dialed Yao again.

Adam answered, quickly. 'I'll be there in under a minute.'

Yao picked Jack up and immediately headed north. He said, 'We go through Shenzhen and then hit Guangzhou in about an hour. Center's building is in the northern part of the city, out in the suburbs near the airport.'

'How did you find it?'

'I tracked him from the movements of their supercomputers in Hong Kong. The servers traveled by ship, and I found the ship, the port, then the trucking company that brought them to the China Telecom building. I wasn't sure at first, but then I chatted up a girl at the new China Telecom office who said she came into work one morning and found out her entire building had been vacated overnight because the PLA needed the space.

'At that point I was pretty sure, so I got an apartment in a high-rise across a drainage culvert from the CT building. I can see the Army guarding the place, and I can see the civilians coming and going. They installed a satellite barn in the parking lot and have huge dishes on the roof. They must be using a ton of electricity.'

'What's the next step?'

Yao shrugged. 'The next step is you tell me who you really work for. I didn't ask you over here because I needed a friend. I need someone on the inside in the U.S., away from CIA. Someone who can make something happen.'

'Make *what* happen, exactly?'

Yao shook his head. 'I want you to be able to contact someone in the government, high up in the government not at CIA, and tell them what's going on. We will be able to prove it beyond a shadow of a doubt. And then when you do that, I want someone to come over here and blow it up.'

'You want me to call my dad.'

Yao shrugged. 'He could make it happen.'

Ryan shook his head. He had to keep his dad insulated, to some degree, from his operations. He said, 'There is someone else I can call. She'll get the message through.'

73

President Jack Ryan decided he would travel to the Pentagon to hear their plan to attack China's computer networking infrastructure and computer network operations capability. Most of America's top war-fighting strategists had been working on nothing else there in the building, doing their best to ad-lib parts of the tactical plan because the cyber-attack on America had hamstrung their capabilities to get information, advice, and a good picture of the battle space.

Napoleon is credited with saying an army marches on its stomach. But that was in Napoleon's time. Now it was clear to everyone affected by the attacks that the U.S. military marched on its bandwidth, and at the moment it seemed it could do little more than stand at parade rest.

And in the two days since his directive to draw up the plan, the situation had gotten worse. In addition to increased cyberattacks on the United States – attacks that had shut down two days of trading on Wall Street – the Chinese had exploited other attack vectors against the military. Many American military and spy satellites had been hacked and their signals corrupted, so critical data were not getting from the theater to the Pentagon. Those satellites still online were sending back data sluggishly or sporadically corrupted, meaning the picture of the situation over there was spotty at best.

The United States had lost visibility of the Chinese carrier in the South China Sea, and only received clues of its location again when an Indonesian Navy frigate, *Yos Sudarso*, was sunk eighty miles north of Bunguran Timur, reportedly by four missiles fired from a Chinese attack helicopter. Of the one hundred seventy sailors on board, only thirty-nine had been recovered alive as of twelve hours after the incident.

More air-to-air contests over the Taiwan Strait had resulted in the shooting down of five more ROC fighters and a Marine Hornet, compared with the loss of eight PLAAF aircraft.

Ryan sat quietly as colonels, generals, captains, and admirals briefed him on the options for a military strike or, more precisely, on the seeming lack of options for a military strike.

The most frightening aspect of building a target list, clearly, was the poor coverage of the area. The degradation of the satellite data, more than anything else, made much of their attack plan a crapshoot, and the men and women in the room admitted as much to the President.

Ryan asked, 'But some of our satellites are still functional?'

Burgess fielded this one: 'Yes, Mr President. But what you have to realize is, other than the dogfights over the Strait of Taiwan, the shooting war between the U.S. and China has not begun. Everything they've done to us to muddle our ability to fight, they've done with computer code. If we do attack, or if we do move carriers closer to attack or in any way show our hand, you can bet they will use shooting-war measures to disrupt those satellite feeds.'

Ryan said, 'Shooting down our satellites?'

Burgess nodded. 'They have shown their ability, in a test against their own equipment, to destroy a satellite with a kinetic missile.'

Ryan remembered the event.

'Do they have the capability to do that on a large scale?'

An Air Force general spoke up: 'Kinetic ASAT, or antisatellite weapons, are no one's first choice. They are bad for all parties with space platforms, because the debris from a strike can orbit for decades and fly into other equipment in space. It only takes a particle about one centimeter in length to mission-kill a satellite. The Chinese know that, so we don't think they will blow up our equipment in space unless they absolutely have to.'

Ryan said, 'They also can attack our satellites over China with an electromagnetic pulse weapon, an EMP.'

Burgess shook his head. 'The Chinese will *not* detonate an EMP in space.'

Ryan cocked his head. 'How can you be so sure, Bob?'

'Because it would damage their own equipment. They have GPS and communications satellites up above their own nation, of course, not far enough away from our platforms.'

Jack nodded. That was the kind of analysis he appreciated. The kind that made sense. 'Do they have other tricks up their sleeves?'

The Air Force general said, 'Yes, absolutely they do. The PLA also has the ability to temporarily blind satellites with the use of high-powered lasers. The technique is called "dazzling"; they have done it on the French and Indian satellites in the past two years with great success. In both cases they totally degraded the satellite's ability to see and communicate with the ground for three or four hours. We predict they will start with this, and if it does not give them the results they want, then they will start firing missiles into space to shoot down our communications and intelligence-collection platforms.'

Ryan shook his head in frustration. 'A couple months back I made a speech to the UN and said that any attack on a U.S. satellite was an attack on U.S. territory. The next morning half the news organizations in the country and three-fifths on the planet were running headlines saying I was claiming outer space for the United States. The *L.A. Times* had a caricature of me dressed like Darth Vader on their opinion page. America's chattering class does not get the stakes we're up against.'

Burgess said, 'You did the right thing. The future of warfare is going to be brand-new territory, Mr President. Looks like we're the lucky ones who get to blaze a trail.'

'Okay,' Ryan said, 'we're half blind in the sky; what does the picture look like at sea level?'

A Navy admiral stood and said, 'Anti-access/area-denial. A-two A-D, sir. China does not possess a great Navy, but they have the largest and most active land-based ballistic and cruise missile programs in the world. The PLA's Second Artillery Corps has five operational short-range ballistic missile brigades targeting Taiwan. DIA estimates they have over one thousand missiles.'

A captain stood in front of a whiteboard festooned with notes for the President to read in lieu of a PowerPoint presentation. 'Second Artillery Corps conventional anti-ship ballistic missiles also provide the PLA with an extra deployment option to enhance its anti-access/area-denial strategies against offshore threats.

'Their ocean surveillance system over-the-horizon radar will see a carrier battle group at a distance of one thousand eight hundred miles, and then their electronic signal-detection satellites will pinpoint and identify the ships.

'The battle group emissions are detected and the track is predicted, even through cloud cover.

'The Dong Feng 21D is their carrier-killer ballistic missile. It has its own radar, and it also pulls tracking information from Chinese satellite data.'

It continued like this for an hour. Ryan was careful to keep the momentum of the discussion up; he saw it as a waste of time for these men and women to be forced to explain the nuances of every weapons system of both sides to a man who had only to give a thumbs-up or a thumbs-down to the entire operation.

But he had to strike a balance. In his role as the man with the thumb, he owed it to America's war fighters to be as educated as possible on their options before ordering hundreds – no, thousands – of people into harm's way.

After an entire morning of back-and-forth, a Navy admiral, a former F-14 Tomcat pilot who'd led carrier wings and was now one of the Pentagon's top naval tacticians, took the President through the plan of attack on China. It involved nuclear subs in the East China Sea launching barrages of conventional missiles at PLA command-and-control centers and technical bureaus, as well as targeting electrical infrastructure that powered these locations.

Simultaneously, subs in the Taiwan Strait and off the coast of the Chinese city of Fuzhou would launch cruise missiles against PLAAF air bases, known fixed-missile batteries, and command-and-control facilities.

American strike aircraft would fly from the *Reagan* and the *Nimitz*, refuel while still far out to sea, and then strike up and down the Chinese coast near the Taiwan Strait, taking out SAM sites, warships in port and at sea, and a huge target list of anti-access/area-denial capabilities, including anti-ship ballistic missile sites that the Chinese maintained in the south of the country.

The admiral admitted that hundreds, if not thousands, of the PLA's best missiles were fired from mobile launchers, and the poor overhead picture of the area meant those missiles would survive any attack the Americans could mount.

Ryan was floored by the scope and obvious difficulties the Navy would face in this seemingly impossible task. He knew he had to ask the next question, but he feared the answer.

'What are your predictions as to losses to U.S. forces?'

The admiral looked at the top page of his notepad. 'To flight crews? Fifty percent. If we had better visualization, then that would be significantly less, but we have to deal with the battle space as it now exists, not as we had war-gamed it in the past.'

Ryan blew out a sigh. 'So we lose a hundred pilots.'

'Say sixty-five to eighty-five. That will go up if follow-on strikes are necessary.'

'Go on.'

'We will lose submarines as well. It's anyone's guess how many, but every one of those subs has to go shallow and reveal itself in waters where the PLAN is active and the PLAAF is overhead, so they will all be at risk.'

Jack Ryan thought about losing a submarine. All those young Americans, acting on his orders, and then dying a death that Jack had always considered to be about the most horrific imaginable.

He looked up at the admiral after a moment of contemplation. 'The *Reagan* and the *Nimitz*. They will be in imminent danger of a response from China.'

'Absolutely, sir. We expect the Dong Feng will be employed in combat for the first time. We don't know how good it is, frankly, but to say we are hoping it does not work as advertised would be about the biggest understatement anyone could make. Obviously we have a number of countermeasures that our ships will employ. But many of those countermeasures rely on networking and good satellite data, neither of which we have much of right now.'

All totaled, Ryan was told he could expect to lose between one thousand and ten thousand lives in the attack on China. The number could, and likely would, explode if Taiwan was attacked in retaliation.

The President asked, 'Do we think this will short-circuit the cyberattacks against America?'

Bob Burgess spoke up now: 'The best minds at Fort Meade's NSA and Cyber Command cannot answer that, Mr President. Much of our understanding of China's computer network attack infrastructure and bureaucratic architecture is, frankly, theoretical. We only hope to temporarily deteriorate their cyberattack capabilities and disrupt their conventional attack capabilities near Taiwan. Deteriorate and disrupt, temporarily, at the cost of upward of ten thousand lives.'

The Navy admiral spoke now, though this was not exactly his area of expertise: 'Mr President, with respect, the cyber-attacks on America will kill more than ten thousand people this winter.'

'That's a very good point, Admiral,' Ryan admitted.

Ryan's chief of staff, Arnie van Damm, stepped into the conference room and spoke in the President's ear.

'Jack, Mary Pat Foley is here.'

'At the Pentagon? Why?'

'She needs to see you. She apologizes, but says it's urgent.'

Jack knew she would not be here if she didn't have a good reason. He addressed the room: 'Ladies and gentlemen, let's break for fifteen minutes and pick back up where we left off.'

Ryan and Foley were shown to the anteroom of the secretary of the Navy's office and then left alone. They both remained standing.

'I'm sorry for barging in like this, but –'

'Not at all. What's so important?'

'CIA has had a nonofficial cover operative who had been working in Hong Kong, on his own initiative and without CIA support. He is the one who located the Chinese hacker involved in the UAV attacks.'

Ryan nodded. 'The kid who was killed in Georgetown with the Agency guys.'

'Exactly. Well, we thought we lost him, he disappeared a few weeks ago, but he just emerged and got a message to us from inside China.' She paused. 'He has located the nerve center of much of the cyberattack on the United States.'

'What does that mean? I just spent all morning listening to a room full of generals tell me China's cybernetwork operations were in bureaus and CIC centers all over the country.'

Mary Pat said, 'While that might be true, the architect of the overall strategy and the man in charge of the operation against us right now is located in a building in the suburbs of Guangzhou. He, a staff of a couple hundred hackers and engineers, and several mainframe computers are all in one place. One place that we have pinpointed. We are nearly certain that the vast majority of China's cyberwar is being fought out of that building.'

Ryan thought this sounded too good to be true. 'If this is, in fact, the case, Mary Pat, we could limit the scope of the planned naval attack considerably. We could save thousands of American lives. Hell, we could save thousands of innocent Chinese lives.'

'I agree.'

'This NOC. If he's inside China, how do we know they don't have him? How do we know this isn't some disinformation operation by the Chinese?'

'He is operational and not compromised.'

'How do you know this? And why isn't Director Canfield here giving me this intel? And how did this guy manage to communicate with Langley without getting compromised if Langley has a breach?'

Foley cleared her throat. 'The NOC did not communicate with Langley. He communicated this information to me.'

'Directly?'

'Well . . .' She hesitated. 'Through an asset.'

'Okay. So the NOC is not alone in the field?'

'No, sir.' Another clearing of the throat.

'Damn it, Mary Pat. What aren't you telling me?'

'Jack Junior is with him.'

The President of the United States went white. He said nothing, so Mary Pat continued: 'They both went on their own initiative. It was Junior who called me, who convinced me. He assures me they are both safe and absolutely not in harm's way.'

'You are telling me that right now my son is in fucking *China*?'

'Yes.'

'Mary Pat,' he said, but no more words would come.

'I talked to Junior. He confirmed that K. K. Tong and his entire operation are working out of a China Telecom building in Guangzhou. He has sent photos and geo coordinates. Communication with him is spotty, as you can imagine, but we have everything we need to target the location.'

Ryan just looked to a point against the wall. He blinked a few times, and then nodded. 'I think I can trust the source.' He smiled; there was no happiness, just resolve. He pointed to the entrance to the conference room. 'Get everything you have to those men and women. We can limit the attack, focus it on this nerve center.'

'Yes, Mr President.'

The two hugged. She said into his ear, 'We're going to get them back. We're going to get Junior home.'

74

John Clark flew on a private jet hired from the same fixed operating base where Hendley Associates kept its Gulfstream at BWI. Adara Sherman, Hendley's transportation manager, flight attendant, and aircraft security officer, arranged the entire early-morning flight to Russia while at thirty-five thousand feet over the Pacific, as the Gulfstream was still on its way back from Hong Kong after dropping off Jack Ryan, Jr

While Clark flew in the chartered Lear, he spoke via sat phone with Stanislav Biryukov, head of the FSB, Russian state security. Clark had done one hell of a big favor for Biryukov and Russian intelligence the year before, more or less single-handedly saving Moscow from nuclear annihilation. Director Biryukov had told Clark his door was always open to him, and a good Russian always remembers his friends.

John Clark put this to the test when he said, 'I need to get into China from Russia with two others, and I need to do it within twenty-four hours. Oh, and by the way, the two others are Chinese nationals who will be bound and gagged.'

There was a long moment of silence, and then a low, almost evil chuckle on the other end. 'Such interesting vacations you American pensioners take. In my country we prefer to go to the dacha to sunbathe after retirement.'

Clark just asked, 'Will you be able to help me?'

Instead of a direct reply, Biryukov said, 'And when you are there, John Timofeevich? Will you need assistance in the form of equipment?'

Now John smiled. 'Well, as long as you are offering.'

Biryukov did owe John a favor, but Clark knew any help he would get from the head of the FSB would be implied help for Clark's friend, the President of the United States. Biryukov knew that Clark would be working on behalf of America in its conflict with China, and he also knew Clark would not be working for the CIA, which was a good thing, as the FSB knew CIA was compromised in China.

John told Biryukov what items he would like to take with him into China, and the FSB director wrote them down. He told Clark to fly on to Moscow and he would have the gear and the military transport waiting for him, and that he would take care of all other details while John enjoyed his flight over.

'Thank you, Stanislav.'

'I suppose you will also need a way home afterward?'

John said, 'I sure hope so.'

Biryukov chuckled once again, understanding what Clark meant. If he did not need a way home, that would mean he was dead.

Biryukov hung up, called his top operations people, and told them their careers would be over if they could not make all this happen.

Clark and his two bound and hooded prisoners arrived in Moscow and then flew on a Tupolev transport to Astana, Kazakhstan. Here they were put on an aircraft loaded with munitions that were being delivered to China. The transporter, Russia's state-owned defense exporter Rosoboronexport, often flew covert missions into China, and they knew to do what FSB ordered and ask no questions.

Clark was shown to a pallet near the cargo door of the plane. On it were several green crates, and John waited until he was alone after takeoff to inspect them. Along with the crates was a bottle of Iordanov vodka and a handwritten note.

Enjoy the vodka as a gift from a friend. The rest . . . a repayment of a debt. Stay safe, John.

It was signed 'Stan.'

John picked up the subtext of the note and the gift. The FSB regarded this assistance as repayment in full for the help that Clark and America had provided Russia on the steppes of Kazakhstan.

The IL-76 transport flight landed in Beijing exactly thirty hours after Clark left Baltimore, and FSB agents at the airport collected the three men and the crates and drove them to a safe house north of town. Within an hour, Sam Driscoll and four men from Pathway of Liberty, the fledgling rebel force, arrived and drove them back to their barn hideout.

Domingo Chavez met John Clark at the door. Even in the low light Ding saw the circles under Clark's eyes, the discomfort on his face after the long journey and the fight in Maryland. He was a sixty-five-year-old man who had been traveling for more than thirty hours, crossing twelve time zones, and he looked every bit of it.

The men embraced, John took some green tea offered to him by Yin Yin, and a plate of noodles in a salty ground soybean sauce, and then he was shown to a cot in an upstairs loft. The two prisoners were placed in a locked stall in a basement, and two armed guards were set outside.

Chavez looked over the equipment Clark had brought in from Russia. In the first crate he found a Dragunov sniper rifle with an eight-power scope and a silencer. Ding knew this weapon well, and it immediately gave him ideas about the operation to come.

Next he opened two identical crates, each containing a single RPG-26 shoulder-fired anti-tank disposable grenade launcher.

These weapons would be perfect for knocking through an armored car.

There was also a large container with two RPG-9 rocket-propelled grenade launchers and eight finned grenades.

Other crates contained radios with high-tech digital encryption modules, ammunition, and smoke and fragmentation grenades.

Ding knew better than to hand over a grenade launcher or an anti-tank weapon to the Pathway of Liberty. He had quizzed them on their knowledge of their weapons and the tactics they would need to employ in order to use them effectively in an attack, and he decided that the twenty or so young Chinese would best be used either providing security for the escape route after the attack or else making a lot of noise with their guns during the attack.

Chavez discussed the feasibility of the operation to come with Dom and Sam. At first the three Americans discussed whether or not the mission had any chance at all for success.

Ding was not exactly a cheerleader for the exercise. 'No one has to go. It's going to be tough. Hell, we don't even know how many security will be in the motorcade.'

Driscoll asked, 'We're using them, aren't we? The Pathway of Liberty kids.'

Chavez did not disagree. 'We're using them to stop a war. I can sleep easy knowing that. I'm going to do what I can to keep them as safe as possible, but make no mistake, if they can get us close to Chairman Su, we take the shot, and then deal with the consequences. None of us will be safe after that.'

They brought the Chinese into the conversation, and

when Chavez told Yin Yin that they wanted to try to attack Chairman Su's motorcade as it came into the city from Baoding, she said she could help with advance information about the route.

They set up a large city map on a table in the barn, and the three Americans and the young rebel girl looked it over.

Yin Yin said, 'We have a confederate at the Beijing police department. He is reliable – he has given us information before when we want to target a procession.'

'Information to help you attack?'

'No. We have never attacked a government motorcade, but we sometimes hold signs off the overpass when they come by.'

'How does your guy at the police department know?'

'The Ministry of Public Security is tasked with sending motorcycle police officers to the overpasses, on-ramps, and off-ramps to hold the traffic along the routes. Our man at the police station will be on the detail, along with dozens of other police. They are only told at the very last moment, and there is a rolling system they use where they only are given their next blocking point at the time they are to go there.'

'There must be dozens of options the motorcade could take to Zhongnanhai.'

'Yes, this is true, but that is when they are already in the city. The police traffic blocks start when they hit the Sixth Ring Road, and continue on into the city. We cannot attack them before the Sixth Ring Road, because we won't know when he is coming. We can't wait too long after Sixth Ring Road, because then there are too many options. Even if we did know which road he was on, we would not have time to prepare an attack.'

Dom said, 'So it sounds like the Sixth Ring Road is where we need to set up the hit.'

Yin Yin shook her head. 'No. They will have much security there.'

Driscoll groaned. 'Sounds like our options are few.'

The girl nodded. 'But that is good. There are only two rational options for the motorcade to take right after passing the Sixth Ring Road. The Jingzhou Road or the G-Four. Once we know which one of these two motorways will be protected by police, we can have time to intercept them before they hit the city road network.'

'Sounds like a crapshoot.'

Chavez said, 'It's fifty-fifty. We'll have to position directly between them and haul ass to the right ambush point.'

On Wednesday evening the three Americans, Yin Yin, and two young Chinese men went to both locations in a small van with tinted windows. They would have loved to have been able to see the lay of the land in the daylight, but they didn't find a suitable location on the G-4 until nearly ten p.m., and it was after midnight when they came across a fair ambush point on the Jingzhou Road.

The G-4 location was the more ideal of the two. There was good cover from a tree line to the north, and a quick egress route via a road that led into open farmland and then hit a major intersection on the other side, meaning very quickly after the ambush Chavez and company and the Pathway of Liberty rebels could disperse into the city.

On Jingzhou Road, however, it was more open. Yes, there was a grassy hill that ran along the north side of the straight eight-lane thoroughfare, but the southern side was lower, just above the level of the street, and a congested mass of apartment blocks and streets behind it meant it would be difficult to race away during morning traffic.

Chavez looked over the layout of this potential ambush site and announced, 'We can hit from both sides, and put a gun way over on the pedestrian overpass to the north. Some-one will need to be on the highway at the rear of the convoy to keep them from backing out through traffic.'

Driscoll turned all the way around to face Ding in the darkness. 'I've seen my fair share of L-shaped ambushes. Never have heard of an O-shaped ambush. No offense, Ding, but I think there is a reason nobody's ever done that. It's so everybody doesn't shoot each other.'

Chavez said, 'I know, but hear me out. We'll be attacking from all sides, but if we watch our fire we should be okay. The guy on the overpass will be shooting down. The guy to the south on the highway will be firing from a vehicle, shooting below the level of the overpass. The Pathway of Liberty will be on the hill, shooting down into the motorcade, and I'll be on the other side with the scoped and suppressed sniper rifle, picking off people from the window of one of these apartments.'

'How are you going to get in an apartment?'

Ding shrugged. 'Details, *'mano.*'

They returned to the barn to find John Clark awake and examining the weapons he brought in from Russia.

Chavez had planned to leave Clark here at the barn during the attack and not have him there at the ambush site. He had a faint worry that Clark would want to go on the operation, but he told himself that John would recognize that a man his age, with one good hand, could do only so much.

Ding walked up to John while he inspected the row of weapons stacked on their crates. He seemed to take special interest in the two anti-tank weapons.

'How you holding up, John?'

'I'm fine,' John replied as he inspected the rifles leaning against the wall, the wooden cases of grenade launchers, the cans of ammo and grenades.

'What's on your mind, Mr C?' Ding asked, suddenly worried Clark thought he could have some role in the action to come. As far as Chavez was concerned, that was out of the question, but he was not looking forward to pulling rank on John Clark.

'I'm wondering where you want me tomorrow morning.'

Chavez shook his head. 'I'm sorry, John. But I can't let you go with us.'

Clark looked at Chavez now, and his eyes narrowed and hardened. 'Want to tell me why, son?'

Shit. 'It's going to be a rough one. I know you can hold your own. Hell, you proved that once again the other night in West Odenton against the Divine Sword. But our only shot of getting away from this is to be a fast hit-and-run. You know you can't run with the rest of us. Hell, I'm too old for this shit.' Ding said the last part with a smile that he hoped would defuse the angry glare he was getting from his father-in-law.

But Clark kept the look on his face as he said, 'Who's going to operate the anti-tank weapons?'

Chavez shook his head. 'I haven't figured that out yet. We'd have to have a shooter a good two hundred fifty yards back at least, and that would take one of our guns out of the fight, so I –'

Clark went from a hard look to a smile. 'Problem solved.'

'Come again?'

'I'll sit back with both twenty-sixes, back up the exfil route, and I will engage on your signal. As soon as I'm done, I'll head back to the trucks.'

'Sorry, John. The exfil route won't give you line of sight on the road.'

Clark walked to the map. Looked it over for about ten seconds, five seconds at each of the two circled ambush points. 'Well, then. This overpass gets me line of sight on everything if they hit here, and if they hit here, then this hilltop will do the trick.'

Ding saw Clark's idea instantly, and it was damn good. He was mad at himself for not seeing it, although he suspected he was just predisposed to keeping John out of the fight.

In retrospect, he should have known there was no way Clark would just wait at the barn.

'You're sure about this?'

Clark nodded; he was already kneeling down to look over the anti-tank weapons. 'These weapons might make the difference between success and failure. You need everyone to bail out of the cars in the motorcade. Boxing them in and picking them off with sustained RPG and rifle fire might just make them hunker down and hope their armor can absorb the damage until they are rescued. But if they see a couple of vehicles blown fifteen feet into the air, you can be damn sure everyone will want to get the hell out of their cars and trucks.'

'You can fire it left-handed?'

Clark snorted a short laugh. 'I've never even fired one right-handed. At least there is nothing to relearn.'

'What about the two Divine Sword men in the basement?' Sam Driscoll asked now.

Clark answered back with a question of his own: 'What about them? You're not getting squeamish, are you?'

'Are you joking? Those two fucks killed Granger and half the security staff. Plus five CIA officers, and they tried to whack Ryan's girlfriend. I was wondering whether we were going to draw straws or flip for the pleasure.'

Clark nodded. There would be no pleasure in executing the two Chinese special-forces men, but *they* were the ones who had killed in cold blood.

Chavez said, 'Sam, you'll drive the truck at the rear of the hit. You'll keep the prisoners with you, shoot them, and leave them in the vehicle.'

Sam just nodded. A couple years earlier he'd gotten in some trouble for shooting men in their sleep, even though it had been necessary. He did what he had to do then, and he'd do what he had to do now.

75

Fourteen Marine F/A-18C pilots took to the skies over Taiwan at midnight. They climbed into heavy cloud cover over the island and adopted flight paths to appear on PLA radars as if they were heading for regular CAP stations in the strait, just as they had done dozens of times before.

The ROC F-16s on station began leaving their sectors, as if the approaching flights would be relieving them, again to give the appearance to the Chinese that these radar signatures were just fighter planes on fighter missions, protecting the island from centerline incursions.

But not all the jets were flying as fighter planes tonight. Many of them, Trash's and Cheese's included, were equipped for a strike mission, and their destination was not a space of cold black sky over international waters.

No, their destination was the Huadu district of Guangzhou.

Fully laden with ordnance and extra fuel, Trash's F/A-18C weighed more than fifty thousand pounds, and the controls felt sluggish. This Hornet felt like a different species from the nimble dogfighter he had flown when getting his two gun kills, and this plane even felt different from how it did the day before, when he shot down his third enemy fighter, an Su-27, with an AIM-9 missile.

There was no way in hell he could dogfight with all the bombs and fuel; if any J-10s or Su-27s came after his flight, he and the others with a strike loadout would have to dump all the air-to-ground weapons from their pylons and concentrate on their survival.

That might save their lives, but it would also ensure they would fail their mission, and they had been told they would get only one crack at this.

As the fourteen aircraft – flying in flights of two and four – approached the strait as if to go on station, no Chinese planes came up to meet them, as the weather was bad tonight and there would be plenty of opportunities for air-to-air engagements during the day tomorrow.

They met a pair of ROC refuelers over the strait, and this might have seemed to be an anomaly to PLA radar officers, but it would not raise concern. It looked as if this group of flights would just be loitering on their CAPs a bit longer than normal, which would not have triggered any alarms for the Chinese.

Once Trash and the others topped off their tanks, they turned to the south, still looking like most every fighter signature to fly west of Taiwan for the past month.

And then things got interesting.

Trash and the thirteen other planes dove out of thirty thousand feet, down toward the deck, on a heading that took them to the west. Their speed increased, and they tightened up as much as they could in the dark night, and they adopted a heading that took them out into the South China Sea.

Trash and Cheese were two of the six jets on this mission tasked with dropping ordnance on the China Telecom building in Guangzhou, a target that neither of the men understood really, although they had been too busy in the past eight hours since their initial briefing to worry about the larger context of their roles.

Four other Hornets each carried two two-thousand-pound JDAMs, Joint Direct Attack Munitions. These were Mark 84 iron bombs with tailkits that increased the weapons' accuracy and the distance from the target the pilot could release his payload. The weapons were incredibly accurate, but no one on the flight knew if they would even be employed, as the GPS satellites that flew overhead were flicking on and off like table lamps with shorts in their wiring. The decision was made to outfit the fighters with the JDAMs for the simple reason that the survivability potential of aircraft dropping JDAMs at altitude from distance was better than the other option.

Dumb bombs dropped from low altitude.

That role went to the B-team on this mission, Trash and Cheese. If the first four Hornets could not get a GPS signal to allow them to drop their weapons, then the B-team would dive in. Both F/A-18s carried the two-thousand-pound Mark 84 iron bombs, two on each plane. The Mark 84 bomb had not changed at all since it was dropped by F4 Phantoms over Vietnam nearly fifty years earlier.

Trash found it ironic that with ultramodern aircraft in the U.S. inventory, such as the F-22 Raptor and the F/A-18E Super Hornet, and with ultramodern air-to-ground munitions, such as laser-guided bombs and pinpoint-accurate GPS weapons, he and his flight lead were flying into battle in twenty-five-year-old airplanes that carried fifty-year-old bombs.

In addition to the six planes designated for ground attack, six more had a strictly air-to-air role this evening. They were fully loaded with AIM-9s and AIM-120s, and they would fly out to meet any aggressors that approached the squadron.

The last two planes in the mission were loaded with HARMs, high-speed anti-radiation missiles, to take out enemy SAM sites along the route.

All the pilots wore NVGs, night-vision goggles, which gave them the ability to see both their HUDs and the terrain outside, although they all knew the NVGs brought an additional hazard to their already dangerous operation: if any of the men had to eject, they needed to remember to pull off their NVGs before punching out, as the weight of the device on the front of the helmet would snap their necks during the ejection.

At 1:30 a.m. the Hornets flew fast and low, screaming over the waves as they headed southwest. By now they all knew the Chinese had scrambled fighters and alerted their coastal defenses, but for a few moments more, at least, the PLA had no idea what the group of planes' intentions were.

After a heading change announced by the strike leader, the aircraft turned due north as one, directly toward Hong Kong.

Trash was the eleventh of the fourteen planes, and he kept his eyes on his HUD, making sure he didn't slam into the water or another aircraft as he made his turn at three hundred feet above the surface. With a quick smile he wondered how to say 'What the hell?' in Chinese, because he expected the phrase was being spoken in every radar room on every PLA base along the coast to the north.

Several flights of Chinese fighters took off from bases near the Taiwan Strait and headed out to meet the flight of Hornets racing over the South China Sea toward land. ROC Air Force planes flying combat patrols over Taiwan raced out to intercept them, launching AIM-120s from just south of the centerline, and then crossed it, heading into China's side of the strait. This broke up the attack on the Marine jets, but it created a massive air-to-air battle that lasted more than an hour in the strait.

More PLAAF planes from bases in Shenzhen and Hainan flew out to meet the approaching aircraft, thinking them to be flown by ROC pilots, not by U.S. Marines. Four of the Marine jets with air-to-air munitions left the formation to engage the Chinese, launching medium-range missiles from distance and shooting down three J-5s before the Chinese even fired back.

An F/A-18 was blown out of the sky just twelve miles off the coast of Hong Kong, the victim of a J-5's radar-guided missile, but two more J-5s were shot down by American missiles seconds later.

The remaining strike force flew on, low and fast, shooting over container ships at five hundred knots.

Four U.S. nuclear submarines had moved south of Hong Kong in the past forty-eight hours from their patrol areas in the Taiwan Strait. As the American aircraft approached Hong Kong, Tomahawk cruise missiles launched from all four subs sprang from the black water, arced into the sky, and flew toward SAM batteries along the coast.

The Tomahawks were successful, knocking out several AA launchers along the path into Victoria Harbour and beyond.

At 2:04 a.m. there were ten strike aircraft still together in a tight trail formation as they shot through Victoria Harbour in the center of Hong Kong. At an altitude of only three hundred twenty feet they passed the Peninsula hotel at five hundred miles an hour, and the roar of their twenty jet engines broke windows and woke virtually everyone asleep within a mile of the channel.

Their flight path took them through the center of Hong Kong for the simple reason that the hills to the north and the high buildings, as well as heavy sea traffic, would muddle the radar picture in China for a time, and Chinese missile defenses in Shenzhen would not be able to lock on and fire SAMs on the low aircraft until they crossed into the mainland.

But more frontline PLAAF fighters appeared on radar, sending the last two air-to-air fighters peeling off from the trail and heading to the northeast. A flight of six Su-27s engaged them over Shenzhen. Both Marine pilots scored air-to-air kills, and within ninety seconds of the fight starting, the two surviving F/A-18s that had been battling J-5s over the South China Sea joined the fray.

SAMs destroyed two Hornets over Shenzhen, but both pilots ejected safely. Two more Hornets were destroyed by air-to-air missiles; one Marine ejected, but the other pilot crashed into the side of Wutong Mountain and died.

The four Marine aircraft shot down six Chinese planes and slowed the others, putting them precious minutes behind the strike force.

The strike force of ten crossed the border to mainland China, and eight of the ten jets climbed off the deck and to ten thousand feet. Only Cheese and Trash stayed low, flying through the dark, focusing virtually all their attention on the green-hued terrain through their NVGs as it raced by below them.

Adam and Jack sat in their rented apartment in northern Guangzhou. They had been doing exactly the same thing, virtually nonstop, for the past two days: watching the China Telecom building. They had long-distance photos of K. K. Tong on his twelfth-floor balcony, as well as dozens of other personalities, many whom Ryan had been able to identify on the database on his laptop from photo-recognition software.

Jack's call to Mary Pat Foley the day before, coming on something like his thirty-fifth try to get a satellite call through, had been the culmination of Adam's work to hunt down the organization Zha had worked for in Hong Kong, an organization, it was clear, that was directing the attacks on America.

Since that time they continued to amass intelligence in the hopes that when Jack returned to Hong Kong and flew back to the United States, he could give it to Mary Pat and increase pressure on the Chinese government to arrest Tong or at least shame them into stopping the attacks.

Ryan had no expectations whatsoever of what was about to happen.

He was only half awake, propped in a chair by the window with the camera on a tripod in front of him and a wool blanket around him, when something caused his heavy eyelids to open. Off to the north, way beyond the China Telecom building by a mile or two, a flash of light came from rooftop level. Jack thought at first it was lightning – there had been rain on and off for days – but a second and a third flash appeared near the same area.

A low rumble made its way to him, and he sat up straighter.

More flashes, now to the northeast, and more noise, louder now.

'Yao!' he said, calling to Adam, who slept on a mat on the floor just a few feet away. The CIA man did not move at first, so Jack knelt down and shook him.

'What's up?'

'Something's happening. Wake up!'

Jack went back to the window and now he saw the unmistakable sight of tracer fire, anti-aircraft cannons shooting into the sky. Another flash to his north and an explosion now, and then a clear missile launch from the ground to the north.

'Oh my God!' Jack said.

'You don't think we're attacking, do you?' asked Yao.

Before Jack could answer, a sound like the sky being ripped apart came from behind their apartment building. It was a jet engine, or more likely *a lot* of jet engines, and the sky now was alive with more streaks of light.

Jack knew Mary Pat would have tried to warn him before an attack came, but he also knew that sat-phone communications were seriously degraded. He had also told her he was 'about a mile' away from the building, which was an exaggeration, but he knew Mary Pat had a near-direct line of communication with his father, and he knew his dad had more important things to worry about than his son's getting arrested in China near the nerve center of the Chinese cyber-attacks.

Now it seemed America was attacking a building less than a half-mile from where Jack Ryan, Jr, was staying.

While Ryan was still trying to process the images and sound around him, Adam Yao grabbed the camera and the tripod and said, 'Let's go!'

'Go where?'

'I don't know,' Yao said, 'but we're not staying here!'

They were prepared to bug out quickly in the event of a compromise; they had most everything in the apartment packed up in a pair of duffel bags, and Adam's car downstairs was gassed and ready to go. Together they threw the rest of their belongings in their bags and flipped out the lights, then began rushing to the stairs.

76

The two anti-SAM Hornets had peeled away from the four JDAM-carrying Hornets and fanned out, making themselves sitting ducks, but using their advanced electronic counter-measures and their HARMs to lock on to and destroy SAM sites as they revealed themselves.

Trash and Cheese were as low as they could possibly fly below and behind the eight other jets. They raced up the Pearl River, which went right through the center of down-town Guangzhou; they passed skyscrapers on either side of them, their wingtips sometimes not more than a hundred yards from the wall of a building. Then they broke north, turned over the city, and anti-aircraft guns began firing in their flight path. The sparkling tracers arced and whipped around the sky in front of them. Trash saw SAM launches in the distance, and he knew they were targeting the HARM Hornets above him, but he also knew if he was called in to drop his bombs, he'd have to expose himself and he'd have the worst of both worlds – the anti-air and terrain threats down here at the deck and the SAM threats a little higher.

The four strike fighters with the JDAMs came over the radio now one at a time, and announced they had no GPS signal, which was critical to guide their smart bombs all the way to impact. After just a few more moments Trash heard over the radio the plaintive calls of one of these Hornet pilots; he'd been hit by a SAM and was ejecting. An anti-SAM Hornet launched on the missile battery, but more SAMs raced into the air. Another strike pilot went defensive against a missile launch; he broke out of what remained of the group as he began jinking and diving and firing chaff.

Another pilot carrying JDAMs was forced defensive, and he dropped his weapons stores so he could maneuver. This pilot's wingman stayed in the flight, and he was the first to line up for a bomb run on the target.

He still could not get the GPS signal in his aircraft, and this told him his JDAM would be flying blind, but he could still drop it dumb and hope for the best.

He began a diving run on the target from fifteen thousand feet.

Four miles south of the China Telecom building, the Hornet was hit by anti-aircraft fire. Trash watched from his position over the river five miles to the south, as the aircraft erupted in a flash of light and then fell off to the side, its left wing tipped down toward the city, and then nosedived toward the buildings below.

Trash heard a clipped 'Ejecting!' and saw the canopy fire off, and then the pilot shoot into the air.

The tracer rounds only increased ahead with the success of the shoot-down. Another strike fighter had to dump his stores and escape back to the south.

Now Trash realized it was down to him and Cheese. The remaining JDAM Hornet would never get around for another attack run before he too had to dump his weapons and exfiltrate the area now that the frenzy of SAM and AA in the sky, along with a new report of approaching bandits from the east, had turned Guangzhou into nothing more than a threshing machine for American aircraft.

Just as Trash knew that he and his flight lead were up, Cheese's voice came over the radio.

'Magic Flight, commence attack run.'

'Magic Two-Two, roger.'

Trash and Cheese rose together to one thousand feet, switched to their bomb loadouts, and selected the mode to drop their Mark 84s nearly simultaneously. Trash knew four tons of iron bombs on a single twelve-story building would be devastating, though it would not bring it down to the ground. He just had to follow Cheese's flight in, and together they would slam a total of eight tons of high explosives, a four-ton impact point within a four-ton impact point, and completely devastate the building.

Cheese said, 'Ten seconds.'

A burst of flak right in front of Trash's canopy caused him to jack his head back reflexively. The wings of his aircraft wiggled and he lost a few feet of altitude, but he pulled back up and leveled off just as Cheese spoke.

'Bombs away.' Cheese dropped, and a second later both of Trash's Mark 84s separated with a clunk and the aircraft immediately felt lighter. High-drag chutes deployed from the tail section of each bomb, slowing them and allowing the Hornets to separate to a safe distance before detonation.

Trash raced away from the impending frag pattern.

He saw ahead of him the glowing jet engines of Cheese's Hornet bank hard to the left and head for the deck, trying to put distance between himself and the explosion to come.

A flash to the north caught his attention. 'Missile launch!' he said.

Cheese said, 'Magic Two-One is defensive! Missile tracking!'

From the parking lot of the apartment building Jack Ryan watched the dark planes race overhead. Ryan had seen no bombs drop, but almost instantly the China Telecom building a half-mile away exploded in a rolling ball of flame and smoke and debris.

A roar shook the ground under his feet, and a rolling mush-room cloud of fire and gray-black smoke rose into the air.

'Holy shit!' Jack said.

Yao screamed at him, 'Get in the car, Jack!'

Jack climbed in, and Adam said, 'I don't want to be the only guy driving an American around Guangzhou right now.'

As he fired the engine, both men looked up in the sky at the soft boom of an explosion miles to the north. In the distance, a burning fighter plane tumbled toward the city.

'Magic Two-One is hit!' Cheese said just moments after Trash dove his aircraft to the deck. 'Flight controls not responding! I've got nothing!'

'Punch out, Scott!' Trash shouted.

Trash saw Cheese's aircraft roll to the right and flip upside down, and then the nose tipped down, just eighty feet above the city.

He did not eject.

The aircraft slammed into the street, nose first, at more than four hundred miles an hour, and it broke apart in a cartwheel of disintegrating metal, glass, and composite material. An explo-sion of jet fuel arced behind it, swirled along with the cartwheel, and only died out when the plane rolled into a drainage culvert and foamy black water engulfed the wreckage.

'No!' Trash screamed. He had not seen an ejection or a chute; his rational mind would have told him there was no way Scott could have punched out without him seeing it, but still Trash looked up in the sky above him as he passed the wreckage at four hundred twenty knots, desperately search-ing the night sky for a gray canopy.

He saw nothing.

'Magic Two-Two. Magic Two-One is down, at my coordi-nates, I . . . I don't see a chute.'

The call back from the CIC was succinct: 'Roger Two-Two. Understood Magic Two-One down at your location.'

There was nothing Trash could do now for Cheese; he had to get the hell out of there. He shoved the throttle forward, past the full power detent, all the way to the max. Afterburners kicked in instantly, nearly standing the aircraft on end, and he felt his helmet pressed hard back against the headrest as his thrust increased and the twenty-five-ton jet rocketed into the night sky.

The young Marine's eyes darted around the displays in front of him. Altitude three thousand, four thousand, five thousand. The HUD spun like a slot machine.

He checked next on his vertical moving map display. He watched Guangzhou slip slowly below his aircraft. Far too slowly for Trash's taste. He wanted to put time, space, and altitude between himself and the scene of his action.

Six thousand feet.

At this moment all of Trash's focus was inside the aircraft. His threat indicators were clear at the moment, other than a flight of bogeys seventy miles to his east and heading away, no doubt toward the Navy F/A-18s attacking the ships in the strait.

Seven thousand feet.

He was over the southern part of the city now.

A beep in his headset brought his attention to his HUD.

He glanced down and saw that he had been lit up by a SAM radar to the southeast. Within two seconds another radar painted him from directly below his aircraft.

'Missile launch.'

He pulled hard to the left and then the right; he went inverted over downtown Guangzhou, pulled five g's as he leveled out and banked to the right, firing flares and chaff in a long wide arc.

It did not work. A surface-to-air missile exploded twenty-two feet from his left-side wing, sending shrapnel through the wing and fuselage.

'Magic Two-Two is hit! Magic Two-Two hit!'

His left engine fire light flicked on. It was followed instantly by an audio warning. 'Master Caution,' and then an instant later, 'Engine Fire Left. Engine Fire Right.'

Trash wasn't listening to Bitching Betty anymore. His HUD flickered off and on and off again, and he struggled to take in as much data as he could read when it was on.

Another SAM was in the air. His displays and his HUD were failing, but the warning came through his headset.

Trash fought to hold the aircraft level, and he pushed the throttle forward to the detent and beyond, trying like hell to gain a little more airspeed.

His stick felt sluggish, and his throttle had no effect.

The dead F/A-18 lost all lift, the nose pitched forward, and the aircraft rolled to port. Trash looked out through the blank HUD, past the canopy glass, and he saw his entire field of view filled with the twinkling lights of a city. As the plane tumbled down through the sky, however, his view out the canopy went dark. The lights were replaced by impenetrable blackness.

Somehow, in the terror of the moment and the fight to keep his head together and do what he had to do, Trash realized his plane was corkscrewing down to earth to the south of the city where the Pearl River Delta splayed out toward the sea.

The lights of Guangzhou and its suburbs.

The darkness of the river, its tributaries, and the farmland of the delta.

'Magic Two-Two is ejecting!'

Trash quickly removed his NVGs from their bracket on

his helmet and threw them to the side, then reached between his knees, grabbed the ejection control handle with both hands, and pulled up. This fired two gas impulse cartridges below him, and the gas shot through pipes throughout the cockpit and performed a variety of automatic functions. It turned on thermal batteries in the ejection seat, it pushed a piston to disconnect the emergency restraint system, it flipped internal switches to initiate the canopy jettison system, and it caused another impulse canister to fire, which pulled Trash's shoulder harness tight against his seat, holding him into the proper position to eject safely.

The last function of the gas was to spray through the inlet of the catapult manifold valve to fire the .75-second-delay cartridge-actuated initiator housed there.

This delay cartridge released its gas, which was piped to the ejection gun initiator.

The initiator fired the ballistic latches on the canopy and the catapult, and it pushed the seat up guide rails. The movement upward caused another impulse cartridge to be exposed, and this was fired by the head of the ejection gun initiator gas.

As Trash and his seat shot up the rails, his emergency oxygen turned on, his emergency beacon switched on, and leg restraints clamped down around his shins.

Till now, Trash had been propelled up by gases, but as his seat reached the top of the guide rails the rocket motor below him fired, shooting him out of his cockpit and launching him upward more than one hundred fifty feet.

A drogue chute deployed, pulling out the main canopy, which whipped in the cool air as Trash and his seat reached maximum altitude, hung there for a moment, and began to fall.

Trash spun through the air with his eyes clenched shut; a

scream left his lips because he felt only falling, falling, and he knew he was too low to fall much farther. If his chute did not deploy in the next second he would slam into the hard earth at one hundred miles an hour.

He squeezed every muscle in his body tight to prepare for an impact that, his rational brain knew, would kill him instantly.

Please, God, help –

The jolt of the harness arresting his fall grabbed at his balls and his chest and his back. He went from free-fall spin to swinging ramrod straight under his chute in the space of two seconds, and the shock of it blew the air from his lungs.

Before he'd even had time to suck a fresh breath of air into his lungs he crashed sidelong onto a metal building. It was a small tin-roofed fishing shack at the waterline, and the entire structure moved along with the force of his impact.

The momentum of his body and the pull of the chute yanked him across and then off the roof and he fell three meters to asphalt. He landed on his right side and heard the sickening sound of cracking bones in his forearm and wrist.

Trash screamed in pain.

A breeze pulled his chute taught, and he fought with it, his right arm hanging low by his side.

The chute pulled him onto a reedy bank, he rose to his knees, and a gust of wind pulled him forward, off his knees, and into the water. Once sensors in his harness detected water, the harness separated from his body, a lifesaving feature that had been built into his chute, but it did not free him in time to prevent him from being swept away by the river current.

As he plunged into the cold water, he heard the sound of sirens.

77

Adam Yao and Jack Ryan had been racing south through the city when they saw the Hornet hit by a SAM. They watched the plane fly on to the south, leaving the electric glowing haze over Guangzhou and entering the darkness over the Pearl River Delta, then it pitched down, and then they just barely caught a glimpse of the ejection at a distance of one mile before the pilot disappeared below the buildings between them and the aircraft.

Adam increased speed on Nansha Gang, desperate to get to the downed flier before the police or military, who would certainly be on their way. There were a few vehicles out at this time, but not many. Adam liked the wide-open road for purposes of making good time, but he worried that his little two-door stuck out like a sore thumb on the nearly empty streets.

This was a fool's errand and they both knew it, but they agreed they could not just leave without knowing the man's fate.

The PLA was out all over the city, as well as the local police, and this made the two Americans nervous, although there were no roadblocks or other barriers to travel. The attack was over now, and it was an attack the city had clearly been surprised by, so the military and police did little more than drive around, looking for the pilot or hassling pedestrians who came out into the streets to see what was going on.

But Adam and Jack had a head start on the civilians; they were out of the city now.

Big transport helicopters passed them, raced on to the south, and disappeared in the night.

'They're going the same place we're going,' Jack said.

'Guarantee it,' agreed Yao.

Twenty minutes after the jet crashed and the pilot ejected, Yao and Ryan rolled past the location of the crash, a field that ran along a tributary of the Pearl River. The helicopters had landed there, and troops had fanned out into a large copse of trees to the east. Ryan saw flashlight beams all through the trees.

Adam drove on by the crash site. He said, 'If the pilot is in those trees, they've got him. There's nothing we can do. If he made it to the river, though, he would have floated downstream. We can check it out at least.'

Adam turned at the river, passed row after row of storage sheds where the locals kept grains and fertilizer and other equipment for the nearby rice fields, and then they drove onto a narrow dirt road. Yao looked at his watch, saw it was just after three in the morning, and he knew it would be a miracle if they saw anyone or anything down here at all.

After ten minutes of driving very slowly along the water, the men noticed flashlights shining from a bridge just a few hundred meters on. Jack pulled Adam's binoculars out of his pack and looked at the scene, and saw there were four civilian cars on the bridge, and a group of men in civilian clothing were scanning intently into the water.

'Those guys had the same idea we did,' Jack said. 'If the pilot is in the river, he's going to pass right under them.'

Adam stayed on the gravel road until he made it to a parking lot next to a warehouse near the bridge; then he pulled in and parked.

'This place is going to be crawling with PLA or local cops.

I want you to stay right here, low in the back of the car. I'm going to head up to the bridge to see if I can see anything.'

Jack said, 'Okay, but call me if you do.'

Yao left the car, and he left Jack there in the pitch blackness.

Yao found himself in a group of a dozen civilians and two PLA soldiers on the bridge. They were cursing the damn pilot. Someone said they were Taiwanese aircraft that attacked the city, but others thought that man was a fool, because Taiwan would attack China only if it wanted to commit mass suicide.

They peered into the water, certain that the parachute was seen landing in the river, but Adam could not find anyone in the group who either saw the chute himself or spoke firsthand to a person who did.

It seemed like an exercise in angry groupthink, each man talking about what he would do to the pilot if he were the one to fish him out of the water. The soldiers had rifles, of course, but many of the other men on the bridge held rakes, pitchforks, lengths of pipe, or tire irons.

Yao knew that the pilot, if he had indeed survived the ejection and if he had indeed managed to avoid getting captured closer to the crash site, would be luckier to get caught by regular Army troops than to fall into this or any other group of vigilantes who would be up and down the river hunting for him.

One of the men in the group with a light had gone to the downstream side of the bridge, and there he scanned the water. With everyone else focusing upriver, thinking they could see a man in the water for a hundred yards before he passed, no one else adopted the downriver tactic.

But to Yao's astonishment the man called out, said he saw

something. Yao and the other men ran across the road to the railing, peered down into the light illuminating the brown river, and there was a man. All arms and legs were out, away from his body; he wore a green flight suit and a few other pieces of gear but no helmet. Adam thought the man looked dead, but he was faceup, so he could just be unconscious.

Yao pressed a button on his mobile to redial the last number he'd called, which he knew was Jack's phone.

As Yao stepped back away from the railing, one of the soldiers fired his rifle at the form as he floated downstream, leaving the light of the flashlight beam. A dozen other flashlights chased the pilot off into the darkness.

Everyone on the bridge began running to the bank or climbing into their cars, wild with the chase and desperate to be among the first to pull the devil out of the water.

Jack answered the phone, and Yao said, 'Get behind the wheel and head south now!'

'I'm on the way.'

Jack picked Adam up, and they raced down the gravel road along the riverbank. They quickly passed all the men on foot, but three cars were well ahead of them.

They'd gone no more than a quarter-mile when they saw the cars parked by the side of the road. The riverbank was another forty yards off on their right, and flashlight beams moved along the river grasses there.

'They've got him,' Yao said. 'Damn it!'

'The hell they do,' said Jack, and he pulled the car over next to the others. He reached into Adam's workbag and pulled out a folding knife, climbed out of the car quickly, and told Yao to follow him.

But he did not immediately run down to the shouting commotion at the riverbank. Instead he ran to each of the three cars and jabbed the knife into two tires on each vehicle.

High-pitched hisses filled the air as the two men then rushed through the dark toward the flashlight beams dancing at the water's edge.

Twenty-eight-year-old Brandon White was five feet, nine inches tall and one hundred fifty-three pounds. He was not a fearsome sight unless he was seated in the cockpit of his F/A-18 with his helmet on and his weapons at his fingertips. And at this moment, as he lay on the rocky, grassy riverbank surrounded by men who kicked and hit him, with a broken arm, pre-hypothermia, and pre-exhaustion, he looked like little more than a rag doll.

There were thirteen men in the scrum around him. He hadn't seen any faces before he took the first blow in the side of the head from a man's shoe. After that he'd kept his eyes closed; he'd tried to stand once, but there were too many men beating on him for him to even get a chance to make it up to his knees.

He had a pistol on his flight suit, strapped to his chest, but each time he tried to get his left hand up and awkwardly pull the weapon out of its right-sided retention holster, someone else would knock him down or snatch his arm away.

Finally someone pulled the weapon out of the holster and pointed the gun at Brandon's head. Another man knocked the gun away, insisting that the crowd be allowed to beat the pilot to death.

He felt a floating rib in his lower back crack, and then he felt a sharp, jabbing pain in this thigh. He'd been stabbed with a pitchfork, and he cried out, and he was jabbed again, and he kicked at the source of the pain, only striking the iron tool with the top of his boot, breaking a toe.

He then heard grunts of pain from someone else, which was odd, because he had been the only one around taking a

beating, and he opened his eyes in confusion to see a flashlight fall to the ground. One of his attackers fell down next
to him and then men shouted in Chinese and yelled in shock
and surprise.

The crack of a rifle at close range made him cringe his battered body. The gunshot was answered by another, and then
a PLA soldier fell down on top of him. Brandon lunged for
the man's rifle, got his noninjured arm out and his hand
wrapped around it, but he was not strong enough to wield it
with one hand. Still, shouting panicked men tried to pull the
gun away, but Brandon rolled on top of it, held it tight, protected it with every ounce of strength that remained.

Now the long burst of a fully automatic rifle pierced the
air, and he felt and heard the men around him scrambling,
falling, then getting back up and running away. He heard
men splash into the river, and others racing along the muddy
riverbank, their feet slapping the muck as they fled.

After another burst of automatic fire, Brandon opened
his eyes and saw flashlights lying all around the riverbank. In
the light of one of these beams he saw an armed man; he
was taller and broader than any of his attackers, and also
unlike them, he wore a paper mask over his face.

The man knelt over a PLA soldier whose lifeless form lay
in the grass, and he took a magazine of rifle cartridges from
his chest and reloaded the gun. Then the man turned away
and shouted to someone higher up on the bank: 'Get behind
the wheel. I'll carry him up there.'

Was that English?

The man knelt over White now. 'Let's get you home.'

Jack Ryan, Jr, helped the wounded pilot into the back of the
car, then climbed in behind him. Adam slammed his foot
down on the gas, and the little vehicle sped to the south,

passing several civilians by the road whom Ryan had just chased away from the pilot with the rifle taken from the hapless soldier whose throat Ryan had slit on the riverbank a minute earlier.

Adam did not know these roads, but he did know there was no way in hell they would make it long in a car that would be reported by a dozen men to the Army within moments.

He thought about helicopters in the air, about police roadblocks, about roving convoys of soldiers searching for the downed pilot and the spies who rescued him.

'We've got to get another car,' he announced to Ryan.

Jack said, 'Okay. Try and find a van, something where we can lay this guy out flat, he's hurt pretty bad.'

'Right.'

Jack looked into the eyes of the pilot. He could see the pain and shock and confusion, but he also saw that the guy was very much alive. His flight suit said *White* on the chest.

'White?' Jack said. 'Here's some water.' Jack opened a Nalgene bottle he pulled from Adam's bag and offered to pour it into the Marine captain's mouth.

The pilot took the bottle himself with his good hand and took a swig. 'Call me Trash.'

'I'm Jack.'

'Another aircraft went down. Before mine.'

'Yeah. We saw it.'

'The pilot?'

Ryan shook his head slowly. 'I have no idea. I didn't see what happened.'

Trash closed his eyes for a long time. Jack thought he'd passed out. But then he said, 'Cheese.'

Trash's eyes opened now. 'Who are you guys?'

Jack said, 'We're friends, Trash. We'll get you someplace safe.'

676

'Tell me whatever the hell we hit was worth it.'

'Whatever you hit?' Jack asked. 'You don't know what you bombed?'

'Some building,' Trash said. 'All I know is that me and Cheese nailed the fuck out of it.' The car hit a pothole, sloshing the two men in the back, and the Marine winced in pain. Adam then pulled onto a larger road, heading to the southeast for Shenzhen.

Jack fell to the side, but he sat back up and said, 'Captain, with what you did back there, you may have prevented a war.'

Trash closed his eyes again. 'Bullshit.' He said it softly.

Moments later Jack was sure he was asleep.

78

The morning started out typically Beijing gray, with a heavy mist and cloudy polluted skies that gave little hint of the sun's rise above them.

The force of twenty-five Chinese and Americans moved to their staging position in four vehicles. A sedan, a work truck, and two commercial minibuses.

Driscoll drove the heavy work truck. In the backseat were the two bound Divine Sword men, Crane and Snipe.

Once the morning rush-hour traffic began rumbling on the roads, rain started to fall, and Clark and Chavez positioned the force on Gongchen North Street, a north-south four-lane blacktop that ran between the two potential ambush points. A long row of municipal buses was parked on a quiet road that ran off to the north toward a concrete ditch high with rainwater that continued under the main highway.

The Americans felt incredibly exposed here. Their vehicles were loaded up with two dozen Chinese rebels, guns, ammunition, incriminating maps, and radios and other gear.

Not to mention two men tied up hand and foot and gagged with electrical tape.

If a single policeman pulled up on their little roadside get-together they would have to neutralize him somehow, which sounded clean and efficient, but which easily could get ugly in a hurry.

Though this particular road was secluded enough, dozens of high-rise apartments were just to the southeast of their location. As soon as the morning traffic got going, there were going to be a lot of eyes on Gongchen North.

Eight o'clock came and went, and then eight-thirty. The rain had picked up under dark gray clouds, and occasional lightning flashes to the north of the city preceded claps of thunder.

Twice Chavez ordered the two buses to relocate to other parts of the neighborhood. This would slow down their deployment at the ambush sites, but Ding was more concerned with being compromised before they even got the chance to hit the motorcade.

At eight forty-five Caruso stood by the rebel translator on the sidewalk next to the van. He said, 'Yin Yin. We *really* need to hear from your motorcycle cop friend.'

'Yes, I know.'

'One if by land, two if by sea,' Dom added.

Yin Yin cocked her head. 'It is land. It is definitely land. There is no sea here in Beijing.'

'Never mind.'

She held a radio, and he heard near-constant transmissions, but he'd given up on trying to pick even a single comprehensible word out of all the chatter.

A short, barking call from a male voice came through, and Yin Yin turned so quickly she startled Dom. 'Jingzhou Road!' she shouted.

Dom was on his radio within one second. 'Jingzhou! Everybody move out!'

Chavez broadcast to the unit as all the vehicles began heading to their objectives. 'We do it just like we talked about last night. Remember, the map is not the territory. When we get there it's not going to look like it did in the dark, and it's not going to look like it does on the map. You will have just minutes to set up. Don't look for the perfect situation, just the best situation you can make for yourselves in the time we have.'

Sam, John, and Dom said 'Roger,' and Ding went back to worrying about his own end of the operation.

Chavez drove in one of the minibuses with three rebels, none of whom spoke a word of English. Still, they had their instructions from Yin Yin, even if no ability to communicate with the American. They parked in front of a six-story apartment building and ran inside. Two men stayed downstairs to guard the entrance, while Ding and the last man carried long plastic bags and headed for the stairs.

They made it up the stairs to the fourth floor of the building and arrived at an apartment door on the northwest corner. The young Chinese man knocked on the door, and he pulled a small Makarov pistol from his jacket as he waited for it to be answered. After thirty seconds he knocked again. Chavez listened to the radio on his chest and shifted his weight nervously from foot to foot.

The rest of his ambush force was rushing to get into place before the target passed, and he was standing in a hallway, politely waiting for a door to be answered.

Finally Chavez gently moved the Chinese man out of the way and kicked in the door.

The apartment was furnished and lived in, but no one was home.

The Chinese man's job now was to protect Chavez from anyone coming into the apartment. He stayed in the living room and watched the door with his rifle at the ready while Chavez found a suitable sniper's nest.

He ran to a window in a corner bedroom and opened it, moved back deep into the dimly lit room, slid a heavy wood table against a back wall, and then lay down on the table, resting the sniper rifle on his backpack.

Through his eight-power scope he scanned the road, some

two hundred fifty meters away, a very makeable distance.

'Ding is in position.'

He scanned across the road to the low grassy hillside and saw the minibus there. The doors were open, and it was empty.

Dom Caruso crawled in the tall brown grass, wet from the morning storm, and hoped like hell everyone was still with him. He raised his head and picked his spot, fifty meters or so from the southbound lanes, and about sixty-five yards from the northbound lanes where the motorcade would pass in just moments. He positioned Yin Yin on his right and had her tell the other fifteen rebels with them to space themselves about two meters apart.

From here they could shoot down across southbound traffic and into the motorcade when it appeared.

'Dom, in position.'

Chavez spoke into his radio from his sniper perch southeast of the road. 'Dom, the rest of that gang over there with you is going to be spraying and praying. I want you firing that RPG carefully. You're going to make yourself a target each time you launch, so find some cover and move to a different part of the hill before firing again.'

'Roger that.'

Sam Driscoll was two kilometers south of the ambush point, parked alongside the road in a concrete block-laden four-door pickup truck. Crane and Snipe were hooded and bound next to him. The motorcade passed him in the morning traffic; it was seven black four-door sedans and SUVs, and two large green military trucks. Sam knew there could be fifteen to twenty troops in each of the trucks, and another twenty-five or so security in the other vehicles. He reported this over the radio, then drew a Makarov out of his waistband, got out of the truck, and then, by the side of the road, calmly shot both Crane and Snipe in the chest and head.

He pulled off their hoods and ripped off the tape binding them, and then tossed a pair of old Type 81 rifles onto the floorboards in front of them.

Seconds later he pulled his truck into traffic and raced to catch up to the convoy. Behind him a sedan with four more Pathway men followed.

John Clark wore a paper mask over his face and sunglasses that did not make much sense in this thunderstorm. He and his Chinese rebel minder walked with two large wooden crates between them, one stacked on the other. They entered the covered pedestrian overpass that crossed the eight-lane road two hundred fifty yards northeast of the ambush site. A single motorcycle policeman had dismounted and was walking well ahead of them. Dozens of men and women heading to work or public transportation pickup points on both sides of the road also were entering and exiting the walkway.

Clark's Pathway of Liberty man was tasked with holding a gun to the policeman and disarming him before Clark attacked the convoy. John hoped the frightened-looking young rebel would have the guts and the skill to pull this off, or the stomach to shoot the cop dead if he did not comply. But John had enough problems of his own to take care of, so when they arrived at their point directly above the north-bound lanes, he put the cop out of his mind and prepared himself for what was about to happen. He lowered the cases to the ground by the overpass railing, motioned for the young rebel to go handle the cop, and then John knelt down, opened both cases with his left hand, and reached into the top case to flip the safety off the first weapon.

He spoke into his radio at the same time.

'Clark in position.'

All around him, men and women walked by unaware.

''Bout thirty seconds out,' Driscoll said.

The chairman of the Central Military Commission of the People's Republic of China, Su Ke Qiang, was in the fourth vehicle of his nine-vehicle motorcade, surrounded by fifty-four men armed with rifles, machine guns, and grenade launchers. As always, he paid no attention to his protectors. His complete focus was on his work, and this morning that work consisted chiefly of the papers in his lap, the latest reports from the Taiwan Strait and the Guangzhou Military District.

He'd read them all before, and he would read them all again.

His blood boiled.

Tong was dead. That was not in the papers; Su had learned this at five o'clock this morning when his body was identified, pulled from the rubble in two large pieces. Ninety-two Ghost Ship hackers, managers, and engineers died as well, and dozens more were injured. The servers were blown to bits, and with that Su had learned almost immediately that America's secure Department of Defense network bandwidth increased, satellite communications came back online, and several of Center's initiatives in the United States, corruption of banking and telecom and critical infrastructure, had simply ceased or at least lost much of their designed impact.

Center's botnet operations, on the other hand, still executed denial-of-service attacks on America's Internet architecture, but the deep-persistent-access hacks and RATs in the DoD and intelligence community networks, while still in place, had no one monitoring the feeds or disseminating the information to the PLA or the MSS.

This was a disaster. The single most powerful counter-punch America could have delivered China. Su knew this, and he knew he had to admit this today when he went before the Standing Committee.

He did not want to acknowledge he should have had better security for the Tong network. He could roll out the excuse, the *valid* excuse, that the China Telecom building was a tempo-rary headquarters for the operation because there was nowhere else to put them on the fly after their compromise in Hong Kong. But he would not make excuses for the mistake. Yes, once this conflict was over and the South China Sea and Tai-wan and Hong Kong were back securely in China's grip, he would sack those in charge of Tong's relocation to Guang-zhou, but for now he needed to give his honest assessment of the damage Jack Ryan's strike the night before had caused.

He had to do this for one reason, and one reason only.

Today, at the Standing Committee meeting, he was going to announce his intention to attack the USS *Ronald Reagan,* the USS *Nimitz,* and the USS *Dwight D. Eisenhower* with Dong Feng 21 ballistic missiles.

There would be some reluctance from the Standing Com-mittee, but he did not expect anyone to really stand in his way. Su would explain carefully and forcefully that by dealing this devastating blow to America's blue-water Navy, Jack Ryan would be forced to disengage. Su would further explain that once American warships left the theater, China could press ahead for full regional hegemony, and with this domi-nance would come power, just as America had become powerful only by controlling its hemisphere.

If, for some reason, the attacks on the carriers were not successful, the next step would be a full ballistic- and cruise-missile attack on Taiwan, the launching of twelve hundred missiles targeting all the island's military sites.

Su knew Wei would yammer on about the damage this would do to the economy, but the chairman knew China's projection of power would help it at home now with the domestic situation, and eventually it would help them abroad, once their unrestrained hegemony was established and the world saw China as a force that must be dealt with as the leading world power.

Su was no economist, he admitted this to himself, but he knew quite securely that China would be just fine once it became the center of the world.

He put the papers aside and looked out the window, thinking about his speech today. Yes. Yes, he could do it. Chairman Su could take this awful event last night, this body blow to his attack against the United States, and he could parlay it into a way to get exactly what he wanted from the Politburo.

With the deaths of twenty thousand American sailors and the resulting degradation of the American blue-water Navy, there was no doubt in Su's mind America would leave the area, giving China complete control of the region.

Tong would be even more helpful in death than he had been in life.

Other than Driscoll, who was now trailing about one hundred yards behind the last troop transport truck, no one saw the motorcade in the rain until it neared the ambush point. Everyone was ordered to hold their fire until Clark launched an anti-tank rocket from the north. By the time Clark was sure he was looking at the motorcade, the first few cars had already passed by the position of Dom and his group of shooters.

Quickly Clark looked behind him to make sure the back blast area was clear. It was, so he adjusted his aim, lining the iron sight of the weapon on a white civilian car just in front of the motorcade. He knew, or at least he hoped, that by the time the rocket hit, the white car would have cleared that piece of road and the first SUV of the motorcade would occupy it.

He launched, felt the whoosh of the rocket motor as the weapon left the tube, then immediately dropped the spent tube to the asphalt on the overpass, and grabbed the second anti-tank rocket launcher from its case.

Only then did he hear the explosion two hundred fifty yards to his southwest.

He hefted the second weapon and saw that his first shot was a perfect bull's-eye. The SUV, the lead vehicle in the motorcade, was a burning, rolling, disintegrating fireball that bounced sideways up the highway. The vehicles behind were swerving left and right, trying like hell to get around it and out of the ambush zone.

John aimed at a clear spot just to the left of the wrecked SUV and about twenty yards closer to his position. He launched a second rocket, tossed the tube down, pulled a pistol out of his pants, and started running off the overpass back the way he came. Only then did he look down at the road and see his second shot hit just in front of a big sedan, cratering the concrete and setting the front of the vehicle on fire.

Behind it, the rest of the motorcade all slammed on their brakes and began reversing, trying to back away from the pedestrian overpass ahead and the missiles that came from it.

Sam Driscoll opened the door of his moving truck, threw a large canvas bag onto the road, and then leapt out next to it. He was one hundred yards behind the rear vehicle of the convoy, but his truck rolled on, big and heavy and slow, because he had looped a rope from the dash through the steering wheel, and the automatic transmission was still in drive.

Sam hit and then rolled along the wet street, ran back to

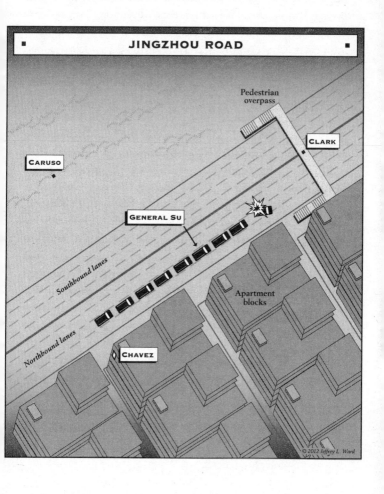

unzip his bag, and from it he removed an RPG-9 and an AK-47. By the time he leveled the launcher at the motorcade, he saw that several of the black cars were backing up or executing a three-point turn to reverse direction. The two big troop transports, however, were still in the process of slowing down. This compressed the motorcade, which was bad news for everyone in it.

Sam targeted the rear troop transport and fired. The finned grenade covered the distance in just over a second, and it impacted on the canvas walls over the bed. The vehicle erupted into a fireball, killing many in the back and sending others leaping and falling from the wreckage.

Quickly Sam checked his six-o'clock position. With the heavy rain, many motorists on the street could not see the melee until they were just a few hundred yards from Driscoll, which meant now a massive sliding car wreck was starting behind him. He put the slight danger of getting run over during this operation out of his mind, reloaded the launcher, and fired another grenade. This explosive shot right by the open driver's-side door of the rolling work truck and struck the second troop transport, which had just slammed its rear into the center dividing wall between the northbound and southbound lanes while trying to back up to reverse direction. The broadside hit of this grenade meant fewer soldiers were killed outright, but the truck was ablaze and blocking the road so the surviving vehicles in the motorcade now had no way to escape.

Sam ran off the southeastern side of the road, slid into a ditch containing two feet of cold, swiftly moving water, and began firing his AK at the soldiers who were still pouring out of the two burning trucks.

All along the wet, grassy hillside on Caruso's right, barking undisciplined rifle fire pierced the air. Dominic fired his rocket launcher three times. Two rockets hit high on the far side of the road, and the third made a glancing blow on an SUV, causing it to wreck into another vehicle but by no means destroy it. Dom grabbed a rifle off a dead rebel and, in contrast to his frantic comrades on the hill, carefully put his front blade sight on a running man seventy yards distant. He tracked him a few yards from right to left, then carefully pressed his rifle's trigger. It popped in his hand, and the man seventy-five yards away fell down dead.

He repeated the process with a soldier running north from one of the burning trucks.

And next to him fifteen other shooters, little Yin Yin included, poured inaccurate but energetic fire up and down the motorcade.

Domingo Chavez scanned the sedans in the middle of the motorcade, looking for officers. Giving up for the moment, he settled on a plain-clothed security guard who fled a wrecked SUV and then ran to the dividing barrier for cover. Ding shot the man in the lower torso while he ran, and then he took his eye off the scope while he changed out the spent magazine in his hot and smoking Dragunov. He took a half-second for a wide view of the battle space. To his left, the troop transport trucks were engulfed in rolling flames, and pouring black smoke rose into the sleet-gray sky. Bodies – from this distance they were just tiny forms on the ground – lay strewn near the truck.

The black SUVs and sedans were in front of the troop trucks and behind the two burning vehicles at the front. They had stopped in the road in an accordion fashion, and a half-dozen or more men in black suits and green uniforms lay prone behind the tires or crouched on the near side of the engine block. Many others from these three vehicles Ding had already shot dead.

Everyone had bailed out of the vehicles by now because the rocket-propelled grenades and the anti-tank weapons flying through the air showed them that a stationary vehicle was the last place to be at the moment.

Ding tucked his eye back behind his scope and scanned quickly, right to left, searching for Su. He estimated there were still at least thirty soldiers and security men on the road or on the shoulder. Those firing their weapons all seemed to be shooting off to the east, away from Chavez.

He swept his scope over the firing position of Dom and the rebels, about three hundred fifty yards from his position. He saw several bodies lying in the grass, and an impressive amount of mud, grass, brush, and other foliage was getting kicked up into the rain by the incoming fire from the Chinese in the road.

Domingo knew the tiny position of poorly trained fighters would be wiped out in another minute if he did not pick up the pace, so he lowered his scoped rifle back to the road and centered his crosshairs on the mid-back of a security man in a black raincoat.

The Dragunov spit fire, and the man pitched forward, tumbling across the hood of an SUV.

Caruso shouted over the sound of gunfire, 'Yin Yin is dead! I can't communicate with these people.'

'Keep pouring fire!' shouted Chavez.

Driscoll called over now, 'We've got police cars coming up the shoulder from the southwest!'

Ding said, 'Deal with them, Sam!'

'Roger that, but I'm going to run low on ammo in about a minute.'

Ding shouted back, his words punctuated by his sniper

rifle, 'If we aren't moving in a minute' – *boom!* – 'then we aren't moving!' *Boom!*

'Roger that,' shouted Driscoll.

General Su Ke Qiang crawled away from the cover of his sedan, and behind the row of men firing on the hillside to the west. To his left and right vehicles burned and bodies lay in the heavy rain, with blood running in long rivulets of rainwater off the road.

He could not believe this was happening. A few feet ahead of him he saw the slumped form of General Xia, his second-in-command. Su could not see his face; he did not know if he was dead or alive, but he clearly was not moving.

Su screamed as broken safety glass on the street ground into his hands and wrists as he crawled forward.

Chattering automatic fire came from the south, from the hills along the opposing lanes of traffic.

Two hundred fifty yards away, Domingo Chavez caught a quick flash of movement by the side of the road near the fourth vehicle. He centered his rifle's scope on a uniformed man crawling there, and without hesitation he pressed the taut trigger of the weapon.

The bullet left the barrel of the rifle, raced over the chaos of the motorcade attack, and slammed into the left scapula of Chairman Su Ke Qiang. The copper-jacketed round tore through his back, spun through his left lung, and exited into the asphalt below where he lay. With a plaintive cry of shock and pain, the most dangerous man in the world died on the roadside, facedown, next to young soldiers who poured hundreds of rounds in all directions in a desparate attempt to push back the attack.

Chavez did not know that the last man he targeted in the motorcade was Su; he only knew they had done their best and now it was time to get the fuck out of the area. He shouted into his radio, 'Exfiltrate! Everybody *move*! Go! Go! Go!' His command would be translated by those who understood for the benefit of those who did not, but anyone with radio contact could easily put together the message he was trying to convey.

Clark and his minder picked Chavez and his minders up four minutes later. Driscoll and three surviving men with him crossed all eight lanes of traffic and ran up the hill on the west side, met up with two of the Pathway of Liberty rebels who had run south instead of west, and they found Dom and two more surviving Chinese desperately trying to pull all the bodies off the hillside while staying in a gully that kept them clear of the sporadic fire from the road. Together they collected all the dead, and one man retrieved the minibus.

The thunderstorm helped with the escape. There were helicopters in the air, Chavez could hear them churning the black, soupy sky as they drove to the northwest, but their view of the ground was limited and there was so much carnage and congestion at the scene, just figuring out what the hell had happened took most of an hour.

The Americans and the ten surviving Chinese were back in the barn before noon. There were some wounds – Sam had a broken hand that he had not even felt when he was hit. Caruso had taken a ricochet off a rock that grazed his hip and bled heavily but wasn't serious, and one of the surviving Chinese had been shot in the forearm.

Together they all treated their wounds and hoped like hell neither PLA nor the police would find them before nightfall.

79

President of the United States Jack Ryan sat at his desk in the Oval Office, looked down to his prepared text, and cleared his throat.

To the right of the camera, just ten feet in front of his face, the director said, 'Five, four, three . . .' He held up two fingers, then one finger, and then he pointed to Jack.

Ryan did not smile for the camera; there was a perfect tone to hit, and the longer he played this damn game the more he recognized that the rules, while still annoying as hell, sometimes were there for a reason. He did not want to show outrage, relief, satisfaction, or anything else other than measured confidence.

'Good evening. Yesterday I ordered American strike air-craft to launch a limited attack on a location in southern China that was thought by American military and intelligence experts to be the nerve center overseeing the cyberattacks against the United States. Brave American pilots, sailors, and special-operations personnel were involved in the attack, and I am happy to report the attack was an unqualified success.

'In the past twenty-four hours we have seen major rever-sals in the potent assault on America's infrastructure and business capabilities. While we are a long way from repairing the extreme damage perpetrated on us by the Chinese regime, with the help of American government and business experts, working together across the full spectrum of attacks exe-cuted against us, we will see this crisis through and put in place measures to ensure this never happens again.

'In the attack in China, many Americans lost their lives, and several more were captured by Chinese forces and are currently being held prisoner. Here in the United States, deaths and injuries from the loss of electrical power, the loss of communications services, and the disruption of transportation networks will take some time to calculate.

'Additionally, eight American military personnel were killed in the opening salvo of the operation against us perpetrated by the Chinese, when the American Reaper drone was hijacked two months ago and missiles were fired on our soldiers and our allies.

'I have told you about the loss of American life. The loss of life to the Taiwanese, the Indians, the Vietnamese, the Filipinos, and the Indonesians by Chinese aggression also plays a large role in measuring this calamity.

'America and its allies have suffered needlessly, and we are all angry. But we do not want war, we want peace. I have consulted with Secretary of Defense Robert Burgess and others at the Pentagon to find a way to resolve this crisis with China that will preserve lives, not cost lives.

'To that end, starting at dawn tomorrow, the United States Navy will begin a partial blockade of oil shipments to China entering the Strait of Malacca, the gateway from the Indian Ocean to the South China Sea. China receives eighty percent of all its oil via this narrow waterway, and beginning tomorrow, we will restrict fifty percent of this oil.

'The leadership of China has an immediate choice to make. They can move their warships out of the South China Sea, remove their troops from the islands and shoals they occupied in the past month, and cease all centerline incursions in the Strait of Taiwan. As soon as they do this, the oil will once again flow unrestrained through the Strait of Malacca.

'On the other hand, if China continues to attack its neighbors, or launches an attack of any kind – land, sea, air, space, or cyber – on the United States of America, we will retaliate in kind, and we will shut off all of the oil to China through the Strait of Malacca.'

Ryan looked up from his text. His jaw stiffened. 'All of it. Every last drop.'

He paused, then adjusted his glasses and glanced back down at his copy. 'The United States has been a good friend and business partner to the People's Republic of China for over forty years. We have had our differences, but we retain our respect for the good people of China.

'Our quarrel now is with elements in the People's Liberation Army and the Communist Party of China. Clearly, we are not the only ones dissatisfied with the actions of the military's leadership. Indeed, there are factions within the PLA who are not happy with the aggressive actions China has taken.

'A few hours ago in Beijing, the chairman of the Central Military Commission and chief architect of the coordinated attacks by China on its neighbors and the United States was assassinated. Early reports suggest members of his own military were involved in the attack on his motorcade. There could be no greater underscoring of the dissatisfaction with the military's current path than the audacious killing of Chairman Su by his own men.

'President Wei has an important choice to make, and his choice will affect the lives of one-point-four billion Chinese. I call on President Wei to make the correct choice, cease all hostilities, call his military back to their bases, and work tirelessly to rectify the damage caused by China's actions over the past few months.

'Thank you, and good night.'

*

Wei Zhen Lin sat at his desk, his palms down on the blotter, and he looked straight ahead.

The Politburo Standing Committee wanted his head. Clearly, Wei thought, they wanted Su's head, but since Su was dead already, they were more than willing to destroy Wei as a substitute in order to channel their rage and distance themselves from the policies – economic, social, and military – that had failed so completely.

President Wei felt the stab of regret that Su had not just done what Wei had asked. With some saber rattling and bluster regarding the South China Sea, Taiwan, and Hong Kong, Wei felt certain, he could have made the region happy to align itself with the strong economy and future prospects of the People's Republic of China.

But no, Su wanted to have it all, to make a proper war out of it, to defeat the United States Navy and send it running for cover back home.

The man was a fool. Wei felt that, had he been chosen to lead the Central Military Commission, he would have done a better job than Su Ke Qiang.

But wishing things would have been different was a waste of time, and Wei had no time to waste.

He heard the heavy vehicles of the Ministry of Public Security outside his window. They had come to arrest him, just as they had done a few months earlier, except this time Su wouldn't show up to save him.

Save him? No, Su had not saved him back then. Su had only delayed Wei's fall long enough to further tarnish his legacy.

With a heart full of anger, regret, and insolence at those who still did not understand him, President and General Secretary Wei Zhen Lin took his right hand off the blotter, wrapped it around the grip of the pistol, and then quickly put the weapon to the side of his head.

In the end, he made a mess of it. He flinched with the anticipation of the gun's report, and the barrel jerked forward and down. He shot himself through the right cheekbone, and the bullet tore through his face, passing through his sinus cavity and exiting on the left side.

He fell onto the floor, grabbing at the indescribable pain, writhing around behind his desk, kicking over his chair and flailing in his own blood.

One of his eyes had filled with tears and blood, but the other remained clear, and through it he saw Fung standing over him, shocked and irresolute.

'Finish it!' he cried, but the words were unclear. The agony of the wound and the shame of rolling around on the floor of his office after failing such a simple task tore through his soul like the bullet had torn through his face.

'Finish it!' he yelled again, and again he knew he could not be understood.

Fung just stood above him.

'Please!'

Fung turned away, disappeared around the desk, and through his own screams and pleas Wei heard Fung shut the office door behind him.

It took the president four minutes to choke to death on his own blood.

Epilogue

China released the captured pilots after only three days, quietly putting them on chartered flights to Hong Kong, where they were picked up by DoD aircraft and flown home.

Brandon 'Trash' White was back in Hong Kong already. He had spent the first day after his crash in a small apartment in Shenzhen with the masked American named Jack and the Asian CIA man who called himself Adam, and here he was visited by a doctor from Hong Kong whom Adam seemed to know. The man treated Trash's wounds and prepared him for travel, and then, during the night, Jack and Trash crossed a river on a raft and then walked an hour through rice paddies before being picked up on the other side by Adam himself.

From there, Trash went to a Hong Kong hospital, where he was met by Defense Intelligence Agency personnel and ferried to Pearl Harbor. He would heal, and he would be back in the cockpit of the F/A-18 soon enough, although he imagined it would never again feel the same flying without Cheese as his flight lead.

John Clark, Domingo Chavez, Sam Driscoll, and Dominic Caruso spent nine days in Beijing, moving from safe house to safe house, being passed from Pathway of Liberty to Red Hand and back again, until a large cash payment, hand-delivered by Ed Foley to an old man in New York's Chinatown, really got things moving.

In the middle of the night the four Americans were taken to a building housing Russian pilots for Rosoboronexport,

Russia's state-owned weapons exporter, and they were covertly put aboard a Yakovlev heading to Russia after dropping off cluster bombs for the Chinese.

Clark had negotiated the return trip through Stanislav Biryukov, the head of the FSB. It went off without a hitch, though John knew that the favor Biryukov had owed him had now been paid in full, so he could not count on him again to be anything more than the head of a sometimes-enemy spy agency.

Valentin Kovalenko spent nearly a week locked in a room in a safe house belonging to Hendley Associates. He saw no one other than a couple of security men who brought him food and newspapers, and he spent his days staring at the walls and wanting to return home to his family.

But he never believed it would happen.

He feared, he expected, he was *certain*, that when John Clark returned he would walk into the room with a pistol in his hand and shoot Valentin Kovalenko in the head.

And Kovalenko could not say he blamed him.

But one afternoon a security man who called himself Ernie unlocked the door, handed Kovalenko a thousand dollars in cash, and said, 'I have a message from John Clark.'

'Yes?'

'Get lost.'

'Okay.'

Ernie turned and walked out of the room. Seconds later, Valentin heard a car start and pull out of the driveway.

The bewildered Russian stepped out of the building a minute later to find himself in a condominium complex somewhere in suburban D.C. Slowly he walked toward the street, wondering if he would be able to hail a cab, and where exactly he should tell the cabbie to take him.

*

After returning from Hong Kong on the Hendley Associates Gulfstream, Jack Ryan, Jr, went straight to the Alexandria apartment of Melanie Kraft. He'd called ahead, giving her time to decide whether or not she would be there when he arrived, and to decide what she would tell him about her past.

Over coffee at the bistro table in her tiny kitchen, he told her what she already knew. He was working for an intelligence organization running sub rosa, working in the interest of the United States, but free of the constraints of a government bureaucracy.

She'd had several days to process this since the Chinese attack at Hendley Associates; she saw the benefit of such an organization, while simultaneously seeing the obvious dangers that went along with it.

Then it was her turn in the confessional. She explained how her father had been compromised and how she'd learned of it, then decided she would not allow him to destroy her life with his mistake.

He understood her difficult situation, but he was unable to make her believe that this FBI man, Darren Lipton, must have been an agent for Center and not actually working on a real investigation.

'No, Jack. There was another guy with FBI. Lipton's boss. Packard. I still have his card in my purse. He confirmed everything. Plus, they had the court order. They showed it to me.'

Ryan shook his head. 'Center was running you since he intercepted phone calls from Charles Alden discussing how you were working for him, providing information about me and Hendley Associates to discredit John Clark.'

'Lipton is real. He knows about my father and –'

'He knows because Center told him! Center could have got that information from hacking into Pakistani intelligence files. His operation could do that easily.'

He saw that she did not believe him; she felt her entire life was about to fall down on her head when the FBI charged her for lying about her father's espionage.

Jack said, 'One way we can clear this up right now.'

'How?'

'We go pay Lipton a visit.'

It took a day to find him. He'd taken a leave of absence from work, and both Jack and Melanie worried he'd fled the country. But Ryan got Biery to hack into the man's bank records, and when he found out Lipton took out four hundred dollars from an ATM at a DoubleTree hotel in Crystal City just minutes earlier, Jack and Melanie headed over.

By the time they got there Biery had the room number for them, and minutes later Jack used a master keycard Melanie pilfered from a maid.

Ryan and Kraft came through the door and saw a half-naked Lipton and a fully nude hooker, and Jack told the girl to get her things, her four hundred bucks, and hit the road.

Lipton seemed scared seeing Ryan and the girl here, but he seemed in no great hurry to dress. Jack threw a pair of khakis at him. 'For the love of God, dude, put these on.'

Lipton slipped into the pants, but did not put a shirt on over his wife-beater.

'What do you want with me?' he asked.

Jack said, 'Center is dead, if you didn't already know.'

'Who?'

'Center. Dr K. K. Tong.'

'I don't know what you're –'

'Look, asshole! I know you were working for Center. We've got all the transcripts of your conversations, and we've got Kovalenko, who can finger you.'

Lipton sighed. 'The Russian with the beard?'

'Yep.'

It was a lie, but Lipton fell for it.

He gave up the ruse. 'Center was my handler, but I don't know K. K. Tong. I had no idea I was working for the Russians, otherwise I wouldn't –'

'You were working for the Chinese.'

Darren Lipton winced. 'Even worse.'

'Who was Packard?' Melanie asked.

Lipton shrugged. 'He's just some other poor schmuck that Center had by the balls. Just like me. He wasn't FBI. I got the impression he was a detective. Maybe D.C., maybe Maryland or Virginia. Center sent him to me when the phony court order didn't convince you to bug the phone. I dressed the guy up, gave him a fifteen-minute primer on the situation, and he did the good cop to my bad.'

'But you asked me to go to the J. Edgar Hoover Building to meet him. What if I said yes?'

Lipton shook his head. 'I knew you wouldn't walk through the front door of the Hoover Building.'

Melanie was so furious she had been played by this son of a bitch that, in a moment of fury, she hit him in the mouth. Instantly blood appeared on his lower lip.

Lipton licked at the blood, then winked at Kraft.

Her face reddened even more, and she growled. 'Jesus! I forgot. He gets off on that.'

Ryan looked at Melanie, understood what she meant, then turned to Lipton.

Jack said, 'Get off on this,' and he threw the most vicious right jab of his life, connecting with the FBI man's fleshy face. Lipton's head snapped back, and the big man went down in a heap. His jaw was swollen and purple within seconds.

Jack knelt down over him. 'You have one week to resign

from the FBI. Do it, or we come back for you. Do you understand?'

Lipton nodded weakly, looked up at Ryan, and nodded again.

The funerals for the Hendley Associates employees killed by the Divine Sword commandos took place all over Virginia, Maryland, and D.C. All of the Campus operators attended, as did Gerry Hendley.

Jack went to the funerals alone. He and Melanie had achieved some sort of détente in their relationship; they both understood why they had lied to each other, but trust was a precious commodity in a love affair, and trust had been thoroughly breached by both of them.

For whatever justifications, their relationship was tarnished, and they found they had little to say to each other.

Jack was not surprised to see Mary Pat Foley and her husband, Ed, at Sam Granger's funeral in Baltimore. When the Saturday-afternoon services were completed, Jack asked for a moment alone with the director of national intelligence. Ed excused himself to go chat with Gerry Hendley, and Mary Pat's security officer lagged far behind his boss and the President's son as the two walked alone through the cemetery.

They found a wooden bench and sat down. Mary Pat looked behind her to her security officer, gave him a nod that said 'Give us some space,' and he stepped back twenty yards and turned in the other direction.

'You okay, Jack?'

'I need to talk to you about Melanie.'

'Okay.'

'She's been informing on me, first for Charles Alden, last

year during the Kealty affair, and then, after Alden was arrested, she was approached by a guy at FBI, National Security Branch. He wanted intel on me and Hendley Associates.'

Mary Pat's eyebrows rose. 'NSB?'

Jack shook his head. 'It's not as bad as it sounds for us. This guy was actually a Center proxy agent.'

'Christ. What's his name?'

'Darren Lipton.'

She nodded. 'Well, he'll be out of a job by lunch on Monday, that's for damn sure.'

Jack cracked a strained smile. 'You won't find him in his office Monday. I think I broke his jaw.'

'I'm sure the Bureau of Prisons will be able to accommodate his liquid diet.' Mary Pat then looked off in the distance for a long time. 'Why did Melanie agree to inform on you? I mean, other than the fact she was working on orders from her superior and federal law enforcement.'

'A secret in her past. Something Center found out about her dad, something the FBI guy held over her.'

Mary Pat Foley waited for Ryan to explain. When he did not speak, she said, 'I'm going to need to know, Jack.'

Ryan nodded. Then he told her about her father, about her lie.

Mary Pat did not seem as surprised as Ryan had expected. She said, 'I've been doing this a long time. The drive and determination I saw in that young lady was something unique. I understand now, she was compensating, trying to outdo everyone else because she felt like she had to.'

Ryan said, 'If it helps at all, Clark says she saved lives at Hendley. Without her, we'd be going to a few more funerals.'

Mary Pat nodded, seemingly half lost in thought.

'What are you going to do?' Jack asked.

'She knows about The Campus. She's finished at CIA for

lying on her background investigation, but I sure as hell am not going to rake her over the coals. I'll head down to talk to her right now.'

'If you tell her to resign, she's going to know you are aware of The Campus. This could be a problem for you.'

DNI Foley waved her hand in the air. 'I'm not worried about me. It may sound hokey, but it's more important to me to preserve the integrity of American intelligence, and to preserve the security of the organization your father set up with the best of intentions. I've got to try to do that.'

Jack nodded. He felt like shit.

Mary Pat saw this and said, 'Jack. I'll go easy on her. She did what she thought was right. She's a good kid.'

'Yeah,' Jack said after a moment of reflection. 'She is.'

Mary Pat Foley's black Suburban pulled up in front of Melanie Kraft's Alexandria carriage-house apartment just after four in the afternoon. The temperature had dropped below freezing, and the low gray skies spit a light mix of snow and freezing rain.

The DNI's driver waited in the car, but her security officer walked with her to the front door holding an umbrella over her with his left hand. He stood beside her as she knocked on the door, with his free hand slipping inside his coat to his right hip.

Melanie answered quickly; there was nowhere in her flat more than ten steps to the front door.

She did not smile when she saw Mary Pat, who had become her friend as well as her boss. Instead she backed away from the door and said, meekly, 'Won't you come in?'

On the drive down from Baltimore, Mary Pat had asked her bodyguard if he had a problem with her spending a few minutes alone with one of her employees in her apartment.

This was just a tiny sliver of the truth, but it served its purpose. The burly security officer did a quick walk around the tiny apartment and then went back outside to stand underneath the umbrella.

While he did this, Mary Pat stood in the living room and looked around. It did not take the head of the American intelligence community long to derive the situation. It was easily discernible that the occupant of this apartment was moving out. Two suitcases were open against the wall. They were half filled with clothes. Several cardboard boxes were already sealed with tape, and several more were still unfolded, lying flat against the wall.

'Have a seat,' Melanie said, and Mary Pat sat on the tiny love seat. Melanie herself sat on a metal bistro chair.

'I wasn't going to just leave,' Melanie said by way of explanation. 'I was going to call you tonight and ask if I could come by.'

'What are you doing?'

'I am resigning.'

'I see,' Foley said. Then, 'Why?'

'Because I lied on my background investigation. I lied so damn well I beat the polygraph. I thought it did not matter, the thing I was lying about, but I see now that any lie can be used to compromise someone, someone who knows America's most closely kept secrets.

'I was vulnerable, and I was duped. I was used. All because of a stupid lie that I never thought would come back to haunt me.'

'I see,' said Mary Pat.

'Maybe you do, maybe you don't. I am not sure what you know, but don't tell me. I don't want to do anything to compromise you.'

'So you just fall on your sword?'

Melanie chuckled a little. She reached down to one of several stacks of books on the floor along the wall and, while she talked, began packing them in a plastic milk crate. 'I didn't think of it like that. I'll be fine. I'll go back to school, find something else that interests me.' She smiled a little more broadly now. 'And be damn good at it.'

Mary Pat said, 'I feel sure that you will.'

'I'll miss the job. I'll miss working for you.' She sighed a little. 'And I'll miss Jack.' After a pause she added, 'But I won't miss this fucking town.'

'Where will you go?'

She slid the full milk crate to the side, and then pulled over a cardboard box. This she began filling with more books. 'I am going home. To Texas. To my dad.'

'Your dad?'

She said, 'Yes. I turned my back on him a long time ago for a mistake he made. Now I see that what I did was not so very different, and I don't think I'm a bad person. I've got to get home to him and let him know that despite everything that happened, we're still a family.'

Mary Pat Foley could tell Melanie was resolute but still pained by her decision.

She said, 'Whatever may have happened in the past, you are doing the right thing now.'

'Thanks, Mary Pat.'

'And I want you to know that your time in this town was worth it. The work you did made a difference. Don't ever forget that.'

Melanie smiled, finished filling the box of books, slid it to the side, and then reached for another.

After the funeral, Jack returned to the Ryan family home in Baltimore.

President Jack Ryan and his wife, Cathy, were there for the weekend, as well as the children. Jack made his way through his dad's Secret Service detail to see his father in his study. Ryan Senior embraced his son, fought off the tears of relief to see him in the flesh and in one piece, and then held him tightly by the shoulders, just looking him over, up and down.

Jack smiled. 'I'm fine, Dad. I promise.'

The elder Ryan said, 'What the hell were you thinking?'

'Had to be done. I was the only one available, so I went and did it.'

Senior's jaw flexed as though he wanted to argue with this, but instead he said nothing at all.

Junior was the next to speak. 'I need to talk to you about something else.'

'Is this just a way to change the subject?'

Jack Junior half smiled and said, 'Not this time.'

The two men sat on a sofa. 'What's up?'

'It's Melanie.'

Ryan Senior's eyes seemed to sparkle. He'd not hidden the fact he was smitten with the young intelligence analyst. But the President quickly picked up on the dark tone from his son. 'What is it?'

Jack told him almost everything. How Charles Alden had her looking into Ryan's relationship with Clark, and then how Darren Lipton, working for the Chinese, duped her to bug his phone.

He did not tell his father about the Russians in Miami, or any of the details of Istanbul or Hong Kong or Guangzhou, or about the shoot-out with Divine Sword commandos in Georgetown. The younger Ryan had reached the level of maturity that he no longer felt the need to tell war stories that would only upset those who worried about him and his safety.

For his part, President Jack Ryan did not ask for details. It was not that he did not want to know. He was a man finely tuned to seek out information. It was, rather, that he did not want to put his son in the position of feeling like he had to tell him.

Ryan Senior realized he was dealing with Jack's dangerous exploits much in the same way Cathy had with his own. He knew there was more to the story that he wasn't getting, a hell of a lot more, as a matter of fact. But if Jack Junior wasn't going to offer it, Jack Senior was not going to ask.

When he'd listened to everything, Senior's first response was, 'Have you told anyone about this guy Lipton?'

Jack said, 'He's being dealt with. Mary Pat will eat him for lunch.'

'I suspect you're right about that.'

The President thought for a moment more and said, 'Miss Kraft was in the West Sitting Hall and the dining room at the White House. Do I need to have the detail concentrate their next sweep for listening devices on those areas?'

'I believe she told me everything. I was Lipton's target, not you, nor the White House. Also, I'm sure they would have already found anything if she'd planted something – but go ahead, you can't be too careful.'

Senior then took a moment to compose his thoughts. Finally he said, 'Jack, each and every day I thank God that your mother has stuck with me. It's a million-to-one shot that I found someone willing to put up with the life of an intelligence operative. The secrets we have to keep, the associations we are forced to have, the lies we have to tell as a matter of course. It's not conducive to a good relationship.'

Jack had been thinking the same thing.

'You made the decision to work at The Campus. That decision might bring you some fulfillment and excitement, but along with that comes a lot of sacrifice.'

'I understand.'

'Melanie Kraft won't be the only time your job interferes with your personal life. If you can walk away, right now, while you're young, you should do just that.'

'I'm not walking away, Dad.'

Senior nodded. 'I know you're not. Just know that broken relationships, violated trusts, and a constant rift between you and the ones you love come with the territory. Everyone you ever care about will be in danger of becoming a target against you.'

'I know.'

'Don't ever lose sight of how important the work you are doing is to this country, but also don't give up on being happy. You deserve that.'

Jack smiled. 'I won't.'

Cathy Ryan leaned into the study. 'Dinner's ready, boys.'

The President and his son joined the others for a family-style meal in the dining room.

Jack Junior was feeling somber with the death of his friends, and his breakup with Melanie, but being here, home, around his family, brightened him in a way he did not expect. He smiled more, relaxed more, allowed his operational mind to wind down for the first time in months, unafraid of compromise by the mysterious forces that had been targeting him and his organization.

Life was good, and it was fleeting. Why not enjoy it when given the opportunity?

The afternoon turned to evening, Cathy turned in early, the kids opted for video games in the den, and the two Jack Ryans returned to the study, this time to talk about baseball, women, and family – the important things in the world.

He just wanted a decent book to read ...

Not too much to ask, is it? It was in 1935 when Allen Lane, Managing Director of Bodley Head Publishers, stood on a platform at Exeter railway station looking for something good to read on his journey back to London. His choice was limited to popular magazines and poor-quality paperbacks – the same choice faced every day by the vast majority of readers, few of whom could afford hardbacks. Lane's disappointment and subsequent anger at the range of books generally available led him to found a company – and change the world.

'We believed in the existence in this country of a vast reading public for intelligent books at a low price, and staked everything on it'
Sir Allen Lane, 1902–1970, founder of Penguin Books

The quality paperback had arrived – and not just in bookshops. Lane was adamant that his Penguins should appear in chain stores and tobacconists, and should cost no more than a packet of cigarettes.

Reading habits (and cigarette prices) have changed since 1935, but Penguin still believes in publishing the best books for everybody to enjoy. We still believe that good design costs no more than bad design, and we still believe that quality books published passionately and responsibly make the world a better place.

So wherever you see the little bird – whether it's on a piece of prize-winning literary fiction or a celebrity autobiography, political tour de force or historical masterpiece, a serial-killer thriller, reference book, world classic or a piece of pure escapism – you can bet that it represents the very best that the genre has to offer.

Whatever you like to read – trust Penguin.